ICED

___

GOLD HOCKEY BOOKS 1-3

ELISE FABER

Elise Faber

SNARKY BOOKS FOR SNARKY MINDS

ICED
BY ELISE FABER

ICED
Copyright © 2020 Elise Faber
Print ISBN-13: 978-1-946140-78-4
Ebook ISBN-13: 978-1-946140-77-7
Cover Art by Jena Brignola

GOLD HOCKEY SERIES

BLOCKED

GOLD HOCKEY #1

ONE

Brit

THE FIRST QUESTION Brit always got when people found out she played ice hockey was *"Do you have all of your teeth?"*

The second was *"Do you, you know, look at the guys in the locker room?"*

The first she could deal with easily—flash a smile of her full set of chompers, no gaps in sight. The second was more problematic. Especially since it was typically accompanied by a smug smile or a coy wink.

Of course she looked. *Everybody* looked once. Everyone snuck a glance, made a judgment that was quickly filed away and shoved deep down into the recesses of their mind.

And she meant *way* down.

Because, dammit, she was there to play hockey, not assess her teammates' six packs. If she wanted to get her man candy fix, she could just go on social media. There were shirtless guys for days filling her feed.

But that wasn't the answer the media wanted.

Who cared about locker room dynamics? Who gave a damn whether or not she, as a typical heterosexual woman, found her fellow players attractive?

Yet for some inane reason, it *did* matter to people.

Brit wasn't stupid. The press wanted a story. A scandal. They were desperate for her to fall for one of her teammates—or better yet the captain from their rival team—and have an affair that was worthy of a romantic comedy.

She'd just gotten very good at keeping her love life—as nonexistent as it was—to herself, gotten very good at not reacting in any perceptible way to the insinuations.

So when the reporter asked her the same set of questions for the thousandth time in her twenty-six years, she grinned—showing off those teeth—and commented with a sweetly innocent "Could've sworn you were going to ask me about the coed showers." She waited for the room-at-large to laugh then said, "Next question, please."

TWO

THIS WAS IT, the call up of her life.

And Brit was sitting in the parking lot of the arena, unable to force her fingers off the steering wheel.

"Get it together," she muttered. "Or you will suck on the ice."

Harsh, probably. But the truth.

Still, the words were enough. Enough to get her body in motion, to pop her door, and walk around to the trunk of her ten-year-old Corolla.

Her gear was shoved inside the small space like a sausage threatening to burst from its casing. Brit grabbed the strap and hauled out her bag before slinging it across her shoulder.

"You know they have guys for that."

The voice made her jump, and her gaze shot up, then up some more until she stared directly into the eyes of the captain of the San Francisco Gold, Stefan Barie.

The slight tinge of a Minnesotan accent made her shiver.

Uh-oh.

And seriously, only a hockey fan would find a Minnesotan accent sexy.

He smiled. "It's the coldest-winter-is-summer-in-San-Francisco thing." When she frowned, he cocked his head. "The wind chill."

What?

"You know? Mark Twain?"

Her brows pulled together. "I know who Mark Twain is, and I'm familiar with the quote. Though it's a common misnomer, and Twain didn't actually say it. Still, it is windy in the city . . . I just don't know why you think I'm cold, and it's not—" She shook herself. What was the point in her rambling? "Never mind."

This was what her mind did.

Every single time.

It drifted, focused on mundane details she then couldn't prevent from bursting free.

No surprise that once they *were* free, her conversations were punctuated with awkward pauses.

Like the one happening now.

Brit sighed. Give her an interview any time. Let her spout off sound bites to the camera and no problem. It was the real life human interactions that were terrible.

"No," Stefan said. "Tell me. What is it?"

It was only because he seemed genuinely interested that she answered.

"It's not summer."

"What?"

Another sigh. *Yep. Way to go, genius.* "It's technically fall. Summer has been over for six-and-a-half days."

There was a moment of quiet, a long, uncomfortable pause during which neither of them spoke.

Then surprisingly—*shockingly*—Stefan laughed. Her heart gave a little squeeze, her brain said, *Uh-oh*, but then before she could really panic, he spoke, "You're absolutely right. Now come on." Snagging her sticks, he nodded toward the arena. "I'll show you the ropes."

THREE

OH NO, this wouldn't do.

This. Would. Not. Do.

Brit stared up at the obviously hastily created sign—black squiggles of Sharpie and crumpled computer paper tended to highlight that fact.

This would not do.

"Okay then. See you on the ice," Stefan said, handing over her sticks and walking down the hall.

Brit dropped her bag to the black skate mat laid across the concrete floor, pushed open the door, and peered inside the room, just to make sure it wasn't full of her teammates, that this wasn't a lame joke for the new girl.

It wasn't.

Hot rage slid through her that she tried to swallow. She needed to be on her A-game. Needed to focus.

And this wasn't the players' fault. Apparently, management had decided to go for this little endeavor on their own. Likely, they were trying to keep things PC in order to avoid a potential lawsuit.

But this was Brit's future.

She fumbled for the switch and flipped on the light. Her heart sank further as a wave of disappointment welled up.

It was exactly as she'd feared.

A single bench. One equipment rack.

Yup. Getting dressed by herself was sure going to help her integrate into the team.

The locker room was the heart of any hockey team, where joking and ribbing and plenty of cursing took place. It was where she'd always felt most comfortable, and where she'd been able to find at least a few allies.

How was she supposed to receive coaching sequestered by herself? Should she just watch the team bond and draw up plays without her? Miss the talk about D-pairs or changes in the system?

She wasn't the first woman to sign a contract with a professional men's hockey team, but she was damn sure the first to have earned a chance at the backup goaltending spot.

Which might someday lead to a starting position.

A major step of which was connecting with her teammates.

Brit let the door slam closed, shouldered her bag, and walked down the hall.

She heard them before she saw them.

"Chin up," she murmured and pushed into the room.

It took a few moments for the guys to notice her. Silence fell, stifling, hot, embarrassing.

Not that a little embarrassment would stop her.

Spotting an empty bench and rack, she walked across the room. Her bag hit the floor with a thud; her sticks clacked together as she set them against the wall.

She could have heard a pin drop, could practically smell the smoke coming out of her teammates' ears.

Not about to let them get the drop on her and having been through this more than her fair share of times, Brit knew it was best to get the awkwardness over.

She unzipped her bag, hung up her gear, then toed off her shoes and stripped down.

All the way down.

"Everyone get that good look," she said into the quiet locker room.

Her gaze slid around, meeting each of the guys' in turn. Some were obviously confused or shocked, a couple were irritated by her or her interruption, and some were typical men—if their eyes glued to her breasts were any indication.

Others—like Blane, her teammate now three times over—were familiar with her methods. He didn't even blink at her nakedness, just kept his eyes on hers and nodded in greeting.

"Get it out of your system," she told the interested ones, "and get over it," she said to the irritated section. She was here to stay, and if they had a problem . . . well, they could suck it.

To the rest, she said, "Now let's play some fucking hockey."

With that, she snagged her sports bra and underwear and started getting dressed.

"Style points, sweet— I mean, Brit."

She grinned up at Blane, who was half-dressed and standing in front of her, and feigned indifference, even though her heart was pumping with jitters. This may not be her first professional hockey rodeo, but it was still the NHL, where the best came to play.

No way she wanted to screw that up.

"You know how it is," she told him. Her anxiety eased when he stepped closer and gave her a quick hug. It was nice to have him there, especially since the two of them went *way* back, having played together in juniors.

"Ten points out of ten." His voice dropped. "You okay?"

"*Now* I'm fine." She was. And as soon as she got onto the ice, she'd be even better.

"Good."

Her lips twitched. "Good for *you* to catch that *sweetheart.*"

Blane grimaced, tapped his nose. "Hasn't been the same since the first time I made the mistake of using it."

She'd been young with a chip on her shoulder the size of a redwood. Blane had made the mistake of trying to prove to his friends he could get in her pants.

The result had been a broken nose for him and a month-long grounding for her.

But they'd gotten that nonsense out of the way, had settled into a warm and easy friendship.

"I'd say sorry—" she began.

"But I wouldn't believe you anyway." He grinned. "Glad you're here," he said and crossed back to his spot to finish getting dressed.

Brit grabbed her pelvis protector, pulled it on, then snagged the black and gold striped socks that had been in the other dressing room. Just as she was about to slip one over her foot, a soft voice interrupted her.

"Well done," Stefan said.

She turned to look at him, not having noticed he was in the stall next to hers, and her heart gave a little tremble.

Which she ignored. Obviously.

He raised two fingers in silent salute before continuing to get dressed.

Slowly, noise filtered back in through the room, lewd jokes punctuated by awkward pauses as the guys glanced toward her for her reaction.

"You'll have to do better than that," she called after a particularly bad one. "I've heard that lame excuse for a joke before."

Stefan snorted, and her eyes flashed to his. Was it pride in his gaze? Annoyance? She couldn't tell a damned thing.

She'd just knelt atop her pads and begun strapping them on when Coach Bernard came in. He hesitated for the briefest moment, as though surprised to see her, then plugged an iPad into a cord in the corner of the room.

The image on the tablet's screen was projected onto the far wall, and he ran through each of the drills in turn.

"Move it," he told them. "Ten minutes."

On the way out, he paused near Brit, glared, then inclined his head to an open door just off the main part of the locker room. "When you're finished."

She nodded, tied the last couple of straps, and stood. Leaving her chest protector and helmet on the shelf above the bench, she walked to Bernard's office. Her pulse raced, and her palms were sweaty.

His expression had said this chat wouldn't be concerning her welcome party.

The buckles on her leg pads clinked when she hesitated on the threshold. Bernard glanced up from a stack of papers on his desk and waved at her. "Come in."

Brit shuffled her way inside, waited.

Bernard studied her, his face completely impassive, and yet there was something under the surface. It wasn't dislike exactly, but she got the feeling he hadn't been one hundred percent on board with her being there.

Well, tough. She'd prove herself to him as well.

Just as soon as she figured out a way to end this god-awful silence.

A minute went by. He stared at her as she stood there, half-dressed and awkwardly taciturn.

Eventually, she cleared her throat and asked, "You wanted to see me?"

"Yes, Brittany—"

"Brit," she interrupted automatically.

Bernard didn't say anything for another long moment, only regarded at her with a raised brow.

Her gut went tight as she stared back. Last thing she wanted to do was get on the wrong foot with management and, between her locker room striptease and interrupting the coach, she had the feeling she was off to a very bad start.

"Brit," he finally said, "I think you're a good player, don't doubt that. But I'm not sure you being here is the best thing for the Gold."

Ouch.

The Gold were the NHL's newest expansion team, a controversial addition—and an unnecessary one at that, some thought—in the already professionally crowded, but hockey-hungry Bay Area.

As with most expansion teams, they weren't very good, which wasn't unusual, but the owners were running out of patience, and the team had gotten some bad press last season: carousing, the odd DUI, then a scandal involving one of their top players and a rape allegation. Couple that with losing the majority of games . . .

Rumor had it, if the team didn't improve this season, the owners might sell.

"You think I'm a publicity stunt." A way to clean up the Gold's image rather than a valuable addition to the team.

It wasn't something she hadn't already thought of.

Bottom line, though, was it didn't matter what management's motivations were. This was her chance to play at the highest level possible. To be the first woman to do so.

It was a really big deal, no matter the pushback she would have to withstand.

God knew, she'd already endured plenty of it from the media, from other players in the league, from her own mother, who worried she might be in over her head.

Outwardly, she held onto a shield of confidence, pretended all of the naysayers had no freaking clue.

But inside? She *did* wonder if she was good enough.

Only time would tell.

Still, Brit knew one thing. And it was a big one.

She knew she could deal with pretty much anything if it meant she could play hockey.

The sport was in her heart, in every single nerve ending and cell. She *never* felt more at home than when she was on the ice.

"Maybe you're a publicity stunt. And maybe it'll work out." He shrugged, like it wasn't her future he was so casually dismissing. "But my experience tells me not."

"Well, thanks for the vote of confidence." She didn't bother trying to keep the sarcasm from her voice. Any bridges she might have worried about conserving had been burned long before she'd even set foot in the locker room.

Bernard sighed. "You're talented. I'll give you that much. Your glove hand is one of the fastest I've ever seen. But you're shorter than the male goalies and weak on your upper blocker side. That will need improvement if you want a chance at a start."

"Noted," she said. "I'll work on it." And she would.

"Good." A beat of quiet. "See you on the ice."

With a nod, she left the office, knowing that despite Bernard's lack of confidence in her abilities, he had spoken the truth.

She *was* shorter. Her blocker side—the hand that held her goalie stick and was protected by a large rectangular pad—*was* her biggest weakness.

It wasn't as if she could grow six inches on the spot, but . . . she could work on her technique, bust her ass, and practice hard.

Harder than she ever had before.

FOUR

A MAN STOOD next to Brit's stall when she came out of Bernard's office. Mid-fifties with close-cropped white hair, he wore a black tracksuit with the Gold's logo and skates. A pair of gloves and a stick were propped next to her gear.

"Brit," he said, putting out his hand for her to shake. "I'm Frank, but the boys call me Frankie, so feel free."

Call him Frankie?

Words literally would not form on her tongue.

Because she already knew who the man was. Had researched each member of the Gold's coaching staff before she'd signed her contract.

But that didn't stop her from being starstruck.

Frank wasn't just Frankie. He was Franklin Todd, renowned goalie coach and former professional player, and just about as close as she got to a hockey orgasm.

Meeting him, *talking* to him was better than shutting down a cocky forward on a breakaway, better than stacking the pads and stealing an almost-guaranteed goal.

He was her idol.

Except . . .

Her heart sank because he probably felt the same way as Bernard. She was an annoyance, a not-quite-good-enough player.

Worse. She was a girl.

Well, fuck that.

Straightening her shoulders, Brit glanced up and forced herself to witness the derision in Frankie's eyes firsthand.

Except it wasn't there.

She stumbled for a moment before settling on "H-hi, Frankie."

He grinned, grabbed up his stick and gloves. "Hi, yourself. Don't let Bernard get to you. He's a hardass to every new player, and he especially doesn't like rookies."

She shrugged into her chest protector and began securing it in place. It was strange to be considered a rookie at her ripe old age. In hockey, rookies tended to be in their teens, or sometimes their early twenties. Definitely not well on their way to their third decade.

But that aside, she decided to ask the bigger question. "Why'd he agree to have me on the team?"

If she'd been expecting a platitude about Bernard really liking her on the inside or some crap, she'd have been wrong.

"He had no choice."

Okay then.

"I wanted you and threatened to walk if management didn't give you a contract."

Brit was dumbfounded for a long moment before she found her voice. "But . . . why?"

She'd had her fair share of supporters through the years, her brother, some coaches and players, a small—*very small*—segment of fans who knew who she was.

But why would someone she'd never met—someone she didn't know—put his neck out for her?

"I saw you in Buffalo."

She frowned, thought back to all the times she'd played in

Buffalo. Only one game stood out. And not because they'd domi-nated. "But we got creamed."

Her team had lost 8-1, and she remembered each of the four goals that she'd let in with crystal-clear accuracy. The two periods she'd played had been some of her worst hockey ever.

"I know."

Confused, she just stared at him.

"You let in some soft ones."

Was that supposed to make her feel better?

"But after you were pulled"—after the coach had taken her out of the game and let the other goalie play—"you stayed on the bench instead of going to the locker room."

Brit remembered sitting there, at first because she hadn't wanted to make the walk of shame past her teammates, and then in sympathy when the score continued to rise.

"Yeah, I did."

Frankie watched her for a long moment, his eyes fixed on hers, as though willing her to understand.

She didn't.

Big deal. She sat on the bench. It isn't like she'd done it for unselfish reasons.

Frankie sighed, clapped her on the shoulder, and turned toward the hall that led to the ice.

"Five minutes."

FIVE

THERE WAS nothing like those first few moments of stepping on the ice.

The crisp, dry air coating her lungs, the slight tingle as the cold hit her cheeks. The smell—part sweat, part residual gas fumes from the Zamboni, part the cool, clean scent that had been present in every, single rink Brit had ever been in.

She bobbed her head toward her chest, sliding her helmet from where it rested at her hairline down over her face without using her hands. It wasn't repainted yet and still had flames of red and gold interspersed with the Kansas City Panthers' logo—the AHL, or minor league, team she'd been playing with only four days before.

Her contract had been freshly modified to allow her to play with the Gold, but it did possess a clause that enabled management to bump her back down to the Panthers if she didn't perform well enough. The clause sucked, but her position as a *rookie* meant they hadn't been able to negotiate much better than a standard, entry-level NHL agreement.

Though, if she performed well enough during training camp and the preseason games, her agent had managed a section that would enable her to secure a one-way contract—meaning she couldn't be demoted back to the AHL without being paid at the NHL rate.

The boost in pay was both a perk to her and a deterrent for management to get rid of her. It wouldn't guarantee Brit's position with the Gold, but it was the best she or any other new player could hope to get.

For now, Brit's goal was to prove herself good enough to stay in the big leagues.

She hoped—

No, dammit. She would do it.

Shrugging her shoulders, she tugged at her jersey. It was black, her pads white . . . and none of that mattered because . . .

She was delaying.

Enough already. One tap of her stick against her leg pads, one against the right side of the open door—she was nothing if not superstitious, just like every other goalie she'd ever known—then out onto the ice.

Normal people had bad dreams of being late or giving a speech naked.

Brit wasn't normal, not by a long shot.

Her worst nightmare was eating shit on that first step. But today, just like 99.99 percent of other days, she was fine.

Still, skating into a new rink, for a new team, in a new city meant Brit was stripped bare and vulnerable.

Which really, *really* sucked.

She despised vulnerable. Hated weakness—

A puck glanced off the glass less than six inches from her head.

It may have been an accident, but she doubted it. These guys had too much control to miss the net by a good ten feet.

No doubt, the shot had originated from the irritated section of the locker room.

Awesome. She stifled a curse and continued warming up.

Brit had spent way too much time having pucks shot at her to flinch. In fact, she was much too desensitized to the high-pitched clang to react in any noticeable sort of way. But inside she noted the action for what it was.

A warning.

SIX

Stefan

HOCKEY WAS IN HIS BLOOD, in his gut. His soul.

Vulcanized rubber smelled like ambrosia. Hockey tape could fix anything. And there was no better feeling than skating every, *single* day.

Stefan wasn't the best player in the league, not by a long shot. But he worked hard, maybe harder than anyone else.

He also wasn't an asshole.

Which was how he'd ended up as captain midway through last season.

After Devon Carter—the General Manager or GM for the Gold —had made the disastrous decision of choosing Peter Gordaine at the beginning of the previous year, management had decided to let the team vote.

For some reason, they had chosen him.

Of course, it was probably because Gordaine had very nearly destroyed the team—a team of professionals, who were paid to do a job, and typically didn't bring bullshit to the table.

He'd done it with a streak of meanness that burned everyone in his path—player or employee alike. It had been Stefan's most miserable season of hockey ever, which was saying something, because he'd had his fair share of jerky coaches and prima donna teammates.

But, at least, Gordaine was gone, with Stefan in his place.

Being captain was both a blessing and curse.

It was a pretty special thing to have the team look up to him, the notion humbling and a little daunting, especially with the added pressure to both perform and set a good example.

The curse part came from dealing with the fallout from last season's scandal and now with Brit rocking the boat—

He heard the distinctive *pop* of puck meets glass and turned, watching as one collided with the boards less than a foot from Brit's head.

"Son of a bitch," he muttered and started to skate over.

Brit met his eyes, and he stopped mid-stride when she shook her head.

"Ignore it," that shake seemed to say, before she adjusted the grip on her stick and skated to the empty net.

Stefan bit back a curse. Had he just been thinking the team was special? Nope. Special was definitely not the right word.

Idiotic was more like it.

He was dealing with a bunch of *idiotic*, teenaged-boys.

SEVEN

THIS WAS GOING to end badly.

It was less than ten minutes into practice, and Stefan was stretching along the boards.

Which wasn't the problem, though the fact that he felt a little stiff and sore from his early-morning workout was concerning. Namely, because it showed that he was getting old.

Thirty years on the planet, and he was on the downward side of his career. Not that he wasn't going to be hanging around for the next five or six seasons—hopefully—but hockey was truly a young man's sport.

Stefan had already been in the NHL for nine seasons: six with the Calgary Flames, one with the Ducks, and the last two with the Gold.

He was lucky in that he hadn't had to fight his way up from the AHL.

It had been *dumb* luck, really, paired with a couple of unfortunate injuries for some teammates that Stefan's opportunity to play in the NHL had come at the beginning of his first professional season.

But after that, it had been his work ethic that had secured the position.

He'd taken the opening and worked like hell to fit right into the Flames' lineup. Then the Ducks'.

He'd been happy in Anaheim. Secure. Figured he'd hang around there until his retirement. But the Gold were located in San Francisco—a place his mother had always wanted to live—so he'd requested a trade.

Ducks' management had understood, obliging his request and allowing him to be traded to the Gold. He'd moved his mother out from Minnesota, jumped into forging a new place on a new team . . . upon which he'd been thrust into a shit-show of epic proportions.

Backstabbing. Laziness. Poor coaching.

The switch had become instant regret.

But that wasn't the current problem, or at least not the one that was troubling him at the moment. The Gold were on a better track this season and had a real chance at redeeming themselves to the general public. What was making tension shoot down his spine was the fact that the guys were taking it easy on Brit, and that with every soft wrist shot slung her way, Stefan could see her frustration level rising.

He was surprised there wasn't smoke coming out of the ear holes in her helmet.

It was his duty as captain to make sure everyone came together, worked as a unit. To that effect, he couldn't help but wonder if he should go over there and rip a shot, just to set the tone, to let the guys know it was okay.

But would that cross the line with her? Step on her toes? Or—

He agreed with Brit's decision to come into the locker room. Female or not, she was a teammate and deserved a space with the team. Further than that, the team wouldn't take it easy on a male goalie in practice, so they shouldn't do any different by her.

But . . . what if he hurt her?

Which was probably a stupid thought, because it wasn't like Stefan's shot was that hard, not by NHL standards.

Still, it went against his vein to even chance hurting a woman, and he knew that most of the guys—with the sole exceptions being Stewart and a few other idiots—felt the same.

There might as well have been a tightrope strung across the ice.

On one side was how they would normally react. The other was what they were doing now. How were they supposed to navigate it?

Turned out he—*they*—didn't need to.

Another shot fluttered toward the net, barely making a sound as it hit Brit's leg pads.

She chucked her glove, blocker, and stick on top of the net then yanked back her helmet.

Her strides were rapid but quiet as she skated toward the top of the circles. Her words, when she got there, were not.

"What the fuck do you think you're doing?" Brit shoved the player hard in the chest. Chad was one of their forwards, a second line right-winger, and the push meant he had to scramble to stay on his feet, barely escaping a fall straight back onto his ass. "I can shoot harder than that in my sleep. How the fuck am I supposed to get some fucking practice if you won't shoot the fucking puck with any-fucking-power? Are we in peewee fucking hockey or the fucking NHL?"

The string of f-bombs unleashed impressed Stefan—and a few others on the team, judging by the bemused expressions emerging on their faces. She was well-versed in using hockey's favorite curse word as both adjective and verb.

Chad, for his part, appeared equally shocked and awestruck.

When Brit paused for breath, he nodded, said, "Okay."

Man of few words . . . that was Chad.

Brit narrowed her eyes at him, and he nodded again. She whipped her glare to a few of the others before skating back to her crease—the blue half circle directly in front of each goal.

Helmet down. Blocker and glove on. Stick in hand as she reached for the water bottle on top of the net.

Stefan saw what was going to happen before anyone else did. He burst to his feet and—

"Watch—"

Too late.

Crack. A stick collided with the ice. The puck flew through the air and collided . . . with Brit's back. It hit with a sick *thunk*—the noise akin to a pumpkin cracking in half—and she went down to one knee.

Here was the thing about goalies. All their padding was in the front. Their backs had basically no protection. Players knew that, which was why rule number one in hockey was never shoot the puck when the goalie wasn't looking.

Fucking five-year-olds knew it. Dumbass, twelve-year-old boys knew it. And certainly professional NHL players knew it.

Mike Stewart knew it.

He was also a giant bastard.

Stefan was just about to launch himself at the no good son of a bitch who was wearing a smirk the size of Mona Lisa's, when there was the sharp *trill* of a whistle.

"Take five!" Frankie hollered as he skated toward Brit.

Before Frankie reached her, Brit shoved to her skates and picked up her stick. She pointed it at Stefan and nodded.

He hesitated midstride. Did she want him to—?

She banged her stick on the ice, a sharp tap that caught his attention. Nodded again.

Okay then, Brit wanted him to shoot. And . . . *what?* He shouldn't? He should?

After a moment, he figured he'd at least better make it count.

Stefan wound up and ripped a shot at the net. Not a simple one either. A far side, lower-corner slap shot that . . . she stopped easily.

He grinned.

"I'll be damned," Max, his defense partner and one of his best friends muttered. "She's good."

"Of course she's good, you moron," Frankie said, with a whack of his stick to back of Max's calves. "Now show the rest of the team that."

Max took a slap shot. His was one of the fastest on the team, and it bounced off Brit's pads with a *thud* that reverberated through Stefan's stomach and the empty arena.

One of the guys whistled in surprise, and then they were off, the break forgotten, more shots, more surprise . . . more respect gained for Brit's ability.

By the time Bernard called them all into a mid-ice huddle before dispersing them into their individual groups, Brit looked to have earned more than half of his teammates' approval.

Including his.

He watched her out of the corner of his eye: her helmet propped back onto her head, her cheeks slightly rosy from exertion, one tendril of blond hair having escaped her ponytail to curl around one cheek.

She looked like an angel.

Stefan almost snorted. Okay, no angel. She looked tough and serious and fierce and . . . like every single one of his hockey wet dreams come to life.

She was also his teammate. And he was captain.

So he needed to forget that she had smelled like roses when he'd walked into the arena next to her, forget the way her pale brown eyes had flashed with hurt when she'd seen the room management had wanted to stick her in.

He also really needed to forget the sight of her naked breasts. Forget they were just the right size to fit in his palms—

Bernard gave a puff on his whistle, and the team stood, skating to their assigned locations.

Stefan hadn't heard a single word his coach had said.

Good thing he always studied the drills for the next day's practice the night before.

He joined Max and sent a small but fervent prayer to the hockey gods that Coach hadn't changed anything up on him.

EIGHT

STEFAN LUCKED out with respect to the drills.

Everything else was a clusterfuck.

The team wasn't coming together. At all.

Their former captain, Gordaine, had been a great hockey player, despite his complete failure at possessing any of the morals a normal human being might have. But Mike Stewart was a cancer to the team, eating away at every single bond Stefan had managed to erect.

It would have been annoying, or maybe just a little sad—the way Stewart so effectively tore people apart—if not for the impact it was having on Stefan's, and every other person on the Gold's payroll, livelihood.

If the Gold were sold, chances were the team and staff would be dismantled, parceled off to other teams or maybe just let go altogether.

Which was the nature of hockey, he supposed. Players were traded all the time. Families were moved or separated. But ninety-five percent of the team and coaching staff were good, hardworking people.

He didn't want the Gold reduced to pieces under his watch.

Yet Mike was almost certainly ensuring that would happen.

He'd been bumped to third-line defense when Bernard had joined the coaching staff this season and seemed to think it was his personal duty to show everyone how unhappy he was with the decision.

If the drill called for no contact, Mike used his stick, elbows, and fists instead of his shoulders and body. If it called for light contact . . . you'd better watch it. Your ass was getting laid out.

After the third time Mike drilled their rookie, Blue Robertson, into the boards, Stefan had had enough.

It was unnecessary, and someone was going to get hurt.

He skated over and got into Mike's face, yelling at him to back off. Surprisingly, Mike nodded, muttered an apology, and got back into line.

Alternate universe. Clearly Stefan had just stumbled into one.

He turned to Blue. "You okay?"

"I'm fine," the nineteen-year-old snapped. "I can handle myself. I don't—" He broke off, peeled himself up from the ice. "Mind your own fucking business."

Stefan watched Blue skate away and tried to figure out where in the hell that conversation had gone wrong.

When he turned and saw Mike with a smirk on his ugly mug, Stefan knew.

The cancer was spreading.

USUALLY STEFAN STAYED LATE and did off-ice conditioning—stairs, squats, wind sprints, that sort of thing.

It was comfort and training all in one short forty-five-minute workout, doing the exercises he'd learned as a kid when he and his mom hadn't had any extra money for a professional off-ice coach. And it probably said strange things about him that one of his happiest childhood memories was running through the routine with his mom.

But then again his mother had always been his rock. Add in hockey? No question why it had become so important.

Typically a few of the guys joined Stefan for the workout, but today he undressed, hung his gear, and showered as quickly as possible.

"Stairs?" Max asked, mid-sock removal.

Stefan shook his head. "Not today."

"Everything okay?"

That was the proverbial question, wasn't it? Part of the reason he was so concerned about the Gold disbanding.

His mom's doctors were in San Francisco.

"Everything's good," he forced himself to answer in a neutral voice. "Just have a meeting."

"This about the restaurant?"

Stefan's lips twitched. "You know there's no way I'm investing in your restaurant, right?"

"The food will be incredible."

"Half of restaurants fail in the first year."

"*Pff*. Minor detail," Max said as he straightened and stripped out of his jock. He stood there for a long moment, dick flopping, completely naked, then his eyes flashed over Stefan's shoulder.

To where Brit sat, unbuckling her pads.

Max's eyes widened, and he sank to the bench, covering his groin with a black-and-gold hockey sock.

"Nothing I haven't seen before," Brit said, in a voice slightly louder than stage whisper. Her gaze was focused on her pads as she fussed with one of the straps. "Don't let your balls smell on my account."

Max's cheeks went a little pink, but he pushed off the bench, dropped the sock, and hit the showers. He snagged a towel along the way—probably the first time in history he'd done so. Max was one of those guys who didn't mind being naked.

"*Air drying*," he always said, "*is the way to go*."

Stefan thought it more likely that Max's mouth was moving so fast his brain didn't have a chance to remember pesky things like public nudity.

Still, he glanced toward Brit. "Shh-wetty balls?"

Her lips twitched. "You quoting SNL on me?"

"Those were the better days."

Stefan had meant the show, but a wave of nostalgia rolled over him, softened his words until they had taken on a completely different meaning.

One he really didn't want to discuss with anyone.

Son of a bitch.

He bent, tied his shoe. He just wanted to get out of there as quickly as—

"Everything okay?"

Brit's question was gentle, way more so than anything he'd heard come out of her mouth in the last couple of hours.

Dammit.

"I'm good."

"You su—"

"I'm sure." He shouldered his small workout bag, pushed his wallet into his pocket. The equipment guys would take care of the rest. "You've got enough to deal with. Why don't you worry about yourself?"

Stefan hadn't meant to sound like a dick.

He had anyway.

Brit's expression locked shut, all the softness disappearing as her face went completely smooth. She held his eyes for another second, scalding russet depths that seemed to pierce right through him.

Then she turned back to her equipment without another word.

It was a dismissal, plain and simple. One he'd facilitated, but damned if he didn't hate it.

Not the time, Barie. Not. The. Time.

"See you tomorrow," he told her.

Brit nodded.

With a sigh, and feeling like he'd just blown a *Golden*—no pun intended—opportunity to bond with Brit, Stefan turned and left the room.

He couldn't worry about hurt feelings, about dickwad defensemen, or investing in a Gold-themed restaurant that was probably going to sink and sink fast.

His mom needed him.

NINE

Brit

HER SHOULDER HURT LIKE A MOTHERFUCKER.

Every motion as she pulled off her gear was a knife-prick of pain that had Brit gritting her teeth. It wasn't as bad as when she'd dislocated the joint there, but it wasn't comfortable by any means, and she'd have a hell of a hard time lifting her arm in the morning.

Just what she needed when Bernard had basically told her she needed to improve a hell of a lot if she wanted a chance at playing. Dammit. But this wasn't helping so she allowed one more moment of fury before forcing herself to get it together. It wasn't like she hadn't dealt with this her whole life.

With the men it was always the same, always making her jump through a hundred hoops to feel welcome.

And, she remembered with a shudder, sometimes those hoops left scars.

Every women's team she'd ever played on had been different. Still competitive as hell, but supportive . . . at least in terms of her teammates not peppering her with slap shots when her back was turned.

If she found out who'd taken that shot—

No. It didn't matter.

"How's the shoulder?" Frankie asked.

Brit hadn't heard him come up, but that wasn't exactly a surprise, considering how deep she'd been in her thoughts.

She needed to pull free of the anger and the past and focus.

"Fine," she said. She was. Really. And her shoulder would be too —after a gallon of ibuprofen and a bottle of wine.

Frankie snorted. "Sure you are. PT after you shower. Then we're going to talk." When she opened her mouth to protest, he narrowed his eyes. "Hustle up, I don't want to be here all day."

Well, then.

She nodded and went back to work on her gear. Less than a minute later, she pulled the remaining pad off and set it down before crossing to the showers. It was tempting to stay and fuss with the buckles, straightening, checking her clasps.

But that was her version of a security blanket, and she knew she needed to respect the equipment staff's ability to do their job.

So Brit shoved the nervous habit to the back of her mind and snagged a towel.

She peered inside, checked the showers. They were mostly clear. Or at least most of the guys were on one side—whether that was in deference to her or just chance, she didn't know.

Or care.

Okay, care *much*. Her heart pounded, and a fine sheen of sweat coated her skin as she made herself step inside.

This part had become okay: the stepping inside and getting clean. So long as there were others showering, too. So long as she wasn't alone.

And Blane was in the other room. Brit knew he'd have her back.

Suck it up.

With a few quick movements, she stripped down and dunked her face under the water.

A long slow whistle made her roll her eyes. *"Damn,* girl.*"*

Seriously?

She'd thought her not-so-sexy striptease would have done the job. She flicked a gaze over her shoulder, ready to loose a retort, and saw Max staring at her.

Or *not?*

Because his eyes were locked on her back, not her butt, not trying to sneak a peek at her breasts.

"What?" she asked.

Max flicked his gaze up to hers as he tucked the edges of a towel around his waist. When it was secure, he took a few steps closer, just near enough to make those old feelings inside of her well up. For the fear she normally kept locked tight to slither free.

This was why she changed with the team. Why she *didn't* shower alone anymore.

Because there was strength in numbers.

Max stopped immediately, freezing a couple of feet away, and Brit felt a wave of shame wash over her. How much had shown on her face?

The honest truth was that she really should be over this by now, over the fear, over glancing around every corner for the monster to come out again.

But she wasn't. No matter how much she tried to convince herself differently, she wasn't.

"You okay?" Max asked, all teasing lost from his expression.

So he was sweet in addition to really good-looking.

Which really wasn't what she should be thinking about. But it was a relief to grasp onto the inane thought, to get lost in something stupid and superficial.

Her heart slowed enough that she was able to shove the fear down.

So deep she could almost fake normal.

Max was tall, strong, and built, a steam engine on two legs. Yet that wasn't what called to her. There was something soft about him, a kindness in his eyes, a teddy-bear-like quality that made her want to confide in him.

Brit wondered if she'd ever be able to open up to a man, especially one like Max.

He'd be protective, tough, and—

Crap. She didn't have time for this, for imaginings that would get her nothing but trouble.

Plus, she didn't need a man to protect her.

"That's one hell of a bruise," Max said when she didn't respond, and if his voice was carefully light, Brit was ignoring it.

No need to come across as a total basket case. At least not on her first day.

"I'm fine," she said, forcing her eyes away and stepping into the water. "It's just swelling and blood under the surface of the skin. You know, capillaries were ruptured with the impact of the puck and the blood pools under the skin. It looks bad, purple and. . ."

She was rambling again, introducing all sorts of unnecessary details to the conversation.

"Well . . . I'm glad you're okay," Max said when she managed to clamp her mouth shut.

"I bruise easily," she blurted. Or not. Word vomiting was her specialty.

Max paused. "Good to know. Hurt?"

He was throwing her a lifeline. Brit glanced back over her shoulder and grimaced as she poured shampoo into her hand. "Like hell."

His eyes crinkled at the corners, his lips curved. "How about a beer tonight? Couple of the guys like to go to a place around the corner, Alberto's."

Her heart gave a little squeeze at the invitation, at the offer of inclusion. It felt good, but . . .

"Can't. Frankie wants me to hit up PT," she said, turning slightly so she didn't have to crane her neck to look at him. "Thanks for the invite, though. I'd rather that than spend an hour with some kooky sports therapist."

Max laughed. "I wouldn't let Mandy hear you say that."

A frown pulled down her brows. "Why?"

"You'll see." He started to walk out of the showers, paused, and called, "See you tomorrow."

Social skills. She still had a long way to go.

With a stifled sigh, she quickly finished her shower and dried. Unfortunately, her thoughts weren't so easy to stifle. Not about physical therapy, but about her inability to have a relationship. About walls and barriers and barbed wire strung tight around a person's heart in order to keep it safe.

Maybe Brit didn't *need* a man to protect her, but . . . sometimes she longed for one.

TEN

ICE BATHS WEREN'T ALL they were cracked up to be.

"Quite whining," Amanda—or Mandy, as the boys called her—said. She was the head of PT and took absolutely zero shit. "I swear, you're worse than the boys."

"It's really cold."

"That's kind of the point." The other woman, petite and brunette, vivacious with curves for days—basically everything Brit wasn't—glanced at the clock. "Two more minutes."

Brit wasn't sitting in a tub of ice, a la *Major League*, but with the combination of the cold stuff and some botanical version of IcyHot on her shoulder, she might as well have been.

Despite her discomfort, she had to admit the physical therapy suite was . . . well, sweet.

Pale grey walls were emblazoned with the Gold logo. White built-in cabinets held a variety of Mandy's torture instruments. There was a stim—or TENS machine—in one corner, an ultrasound unit in another, and all varieties of tape, bandages, and braces.

She sat on one of the three exam tables and thought her dad would have loved it.

But then again, he had loved anything that involved putting bodies back together. If it wasn't broken or bruised or sprained, he hadn't been interested.

Wow. Really?

Maybe all the pucks to her head over the years were finally catching up with her.

She'd been in the suite an hour, first filling out her medical background forms, even though Mandy appeared to know everything about her, from her distaste of mushrooms—they'd ordered in for dinner—to the three fractured fingers her senior year of high school. Then she'd undergone Mandy's prescribed treatment.

Which wasn't bad or anything Brit hadn't had experienced a hundred times over, but with all the memories cropping up and making her feel vulnerable, she was ready to get the heck out of there.

A couple-mile run would push the crap from her mind, and tomorrow she'd be able to function.

"I'd say you should probably take a day off—"

That cleared Brit's mind right up. She shot her gaze toward Mandy, who appeared amused.

"I didn't say you *had* to take the day off. Just that you *could.*"

Brit snorted.

"Yeah. Didn't think that was likely." Mandy snagged a roll of KT tape—a special type of kinesiology bandage that reduced swelling and bruising. "I won't tell Bernard that you need a day off so long as you promise to tell me if the pain gets worse."

"Of course."

Mandy shot her a glare. "Seriously. Promise."

Irritation and humor coursed through Brit, and she put her hands up in surrender, not for the first time since she'd walked in.

In the sixty-plus minutes she had come to know Mandy, she'd learned it was easier to accept defeat than argue with the therapist.

Clearly Max hadn't been exaggerating in the shower.

"I promise," Brit said.

"*Promise,*" Mandy pressed. "For real."

"What are we, in second grade?" Brit rolled her eyes. "*I promise. Or maybe I should say I solemnly swear* to not overdo it?" She reached up with her good arm to hold her hair out of the way when Mandy bent to tape her shoulder.

"Yeah. Sure. You and every other professional athlete I know who pushes through injuries they shouldn't." The other woman huffed, finished the tape job, then leaned back and met Brit's eyes. "You know what this means, right?"

"Um. No?"

Had Mandy not realized she was joking? Was she really going to tell Bernard—

"You've just locked yourself into a *Harry Potter* marathon with me."

Relief coursed through Brit. She let out a breath, her heart settling. "*That* I can do. *Harry Potter* is everything."

Mandy laughed, a delicate tinkling sound that counteracted her tough-as-nails demeanor in the PT suite. "Agreed."

"Good. I'll bring the popcorn." Brit stood. "We done here?"

"Yup. Do those stretches, and we'll reevaluate after tomorrow's practice."

Argh. But it was better than being benched over a stupid bruise. "Okay."

She hightailed it for the door.

"Brit?" Mandy called.

Hand still on the knob, she turned. "Yeah?"

"Watch out for Mike Stewart," Mandy said. "He *always* goes for the cheap shot."

It didn't surprise Brit that Stewart had taken the shot. Or at least that was what she assumed Mandy had meant with her cryptic statement.

The professional hockey community was fairly small considering the amount of teams in its various leagues. But over time, rosters tended to overlap as players moved up the ranks.

Brit had played on her fair share of teams. Owing to that, she knew a lot of people.

And hardly anyone liked Mike Stewart. He was crass. He was arrogant. He'd gotten popped for two DUIs in the last few years and had even spent the night in jail for a bar fight the previous season.

If there was one person she needed to watch out for, it was Stewart.

Except there was nothing she could do but keep her guard up. With a sigh, she walked to her stall in the locker room to finish packing up her backpack.

Keys, dirty clothes, wallet, phone. Her gear would stay, now in the hands of the equipment guys.

The room was quiet, and half of the lights were off, bathing the room in shadow.

Something moved on the far side.

It was so similar to that night that Brit had to bite back a gasp. But it was early, she told herself. There were still plenty of people around.

This wasn't *that* night, and she was a lot more experienced now than three years before.

Multiple courses in self-defense, a can of pepper spray, and way too much money at a therapist would do that.

The shadow moved again, and speaking of spray, Brit reached into her backpack to grab the smooth metal can.

Frankie's voice both soothed and startled her. "How'd PT go?"

Brit had completely forgotten they were supposed to talk after her session with Mandy. "Good—"

Her eyes flicked to the corner again when the shadow rotated.

Frankie's gaze followed hers. "Eunice, could you come here?"

A woman in her mid-forties rose out of the darkness, walked toward them, and all the fear that had stiffened Brit's spine dissipated. She realized that the older woman must have been cleaning something, given the towel and spray bottle in her hands.

"Brit, meet Eunice," Frankie said.

"Pleasure to meet you, Ms. Plantain." Eunice extended her hand as though to shake before biting her lip and drawing it back.

Brit didn't know if it was because the other woman wore gloves or just didn't make a regular habit of shaking players' hands.

She didn't care about either.

Reaching across the space between them, she smiled and grasped Eunice's palm.

"Nice to meet you too," she said. "And Brit, please."

The other woman's smile lit up her face, settled the last of Brit's nerves.

"Eunice helps with cleaning on practice days. She never misses a shift." Frankie cocked his head, winked. "Unless her son is playing."

God, Brit loved this sport. Loved the way it put a look of pride on parents' faces, loved the way it lit up kids' lives.

Of course, there were assholes, and people who got hurt or had negative experiences.

But all in all, she'd never been part of anything better.

The three of them chatted for a few minutes more, Brit learning that Eunice's son was getting a shot at Junior As—a decent prospect for a California kid—and that he played center.

"She works in exchange for equipment," Frankie said quietly once Eunice had gone back to her cleaning. "Couldn't afford it otherwise. Bernard brought her on with the stipulation that she never work on a day her son plays."

"You're trying to soften me up to him."

"No need," Frankie said. "He's a good man. You'll see that soon enough. He's hard as hell but . . ."

Brit sighed, even though in her heart she already knew the truth —having seen him interact with the team at practice.

She'd had bad coaches. Bernard wasn't one of them.

"He's good," she said in agreement. Which really shouldn't be annoying, but somehow still was.

Frankie grinned. "Now, you're getting it." He nodded toward Eunice. "And her son is the best-outfitted kid on his team with his NHL *rejects*."

"Well, damn," she mock-griped, thoroughly charmed despite herself. "Why'd you have to go and tell me that?"

"Can't have you laboring under a misapprehension."

She blew out a breath and slung her backpack over her good shoulder. "I could have labored for a few more days."

"Better that you don't. Come on." Frankie gestured toward the hall. "I'll walk you to your car."

Brit felt relief at his words, which tempered some of her amusement. "I'm fine."

Frankie didn't reply, just started walking, and she had the feeling that even if she refused his offer, Frankie would still walk her to her car.

As Mandy had demonstrated, some battles weren't worth fighting.

Especially when the outcome was what she needed deep down anyway.

ELEVEN

Stefan

STEFAN PULLED up to his house, a decent-size older bungalow in a small suburb just south of the city. The lights were on, and he knew his mom was still awake.

She always waited up for him.

He pulled into the drive and got out, wondering how, at thirty years of age, he'd come full circle and was back living with his mother.

The move to San Francisco had been for her, to make her dream of living in the famous city come true. After she'd battled and beat cancer, Stefan had wanted to make that happen for her.

And somehow living with his mom had become okay.

She wasn't obtrusive. They got along. It had been just the two of them when he was growing up, and it hadn't taken much for them to get back in the groove.

Still, his intention had been to buy her a condo or house—whatever she'd wanted.

Then she'd gotten sick again, and everything had shifted.

Stefan hadn't been around for her first battle with cancer—no amount of begging would move his mom to Canada—and though he'd flown to Minnesota as often as possible, he'd still been in the middle of the season. His visits had been limited, and her care had been mostly regulated to health care professionals and the few friends she'd let help.

But things were different now. Even though the season was gearing up, she was close, and he would damn well be by her side.

Where she'd been for him countless times.

His road to playing professional hockey meant that he'd had to move a fair amount growing up. Some players stayed with host families, others boarding schools. *His* mom had always managed to find a new job in the new city and had moved with him, so they'd lived together. More than that, she'd always had an uncanny ability to make every place they'd ever lived feel like home.

Which was something his sixteen-year-old self had resented. His adult-self? Well, he understood how much of a sacrifice it must have been for her.

The garage door rumbled open, and he walked in, right past his mom's battered 1999 Honda Civic.

He shook his head as he walked past the old rust bucket, its license plate askew and the headlights stained yellow from age.

How many times had he offered to get her a new car?

With a sigh, he pushed into the kitchen. It was quiet, which was unusual, and there were no cooking smells, which was even stranger.

He frowned, glanced around, almost feeling like this was some sort of joke, like a cameraman would pop out and yell, *"Gotcha!"*

But of course, nobody did.

"Mom! I'm home."

There was no response. No hurried footsteps down the hall, no hum of the TV.

Stefan's heart stuttered. He slung his bag and keys onto the counter and took off running.

If something had happened to her while he was at work . . .

He didn't take note of the small framed photos she'd filled every corner of his house with or the bright purple throw pillows he'd given her such a hard time about buying.

No, he just sprinted down the hall toward her bedroom, his feet pounding against the hardwood floor.

Her bedroom door was ajar, and he pushed in without hesitation—

She was asleep.

Soft breaths punctuated the silence, soothed the frantic beating of his heart.

Carefully, he backed out of the room, shutting the door behind him. But he'd barely made it two steps before he had to sit down, his spine right there against the pale green wall his mom had repainted just after her diagnosis.

Stefan could do three-hundred-pound squats until his trainers were blue in the face. But the thought of something happening to his mom made his knees buckle.

Cancer.

Recurrent Stage 2 breast cancer.

When he'd heard the news six weeks before, Stefan had immediately flown back to Minnesota and packed his mom's belongings. She'd refused to come the previous year, not wanting to "cramp his style" in a new city, but he'd finally worn her down and she'd been planning on coming later in the season, after she'd found and trained her replacement at her job.

He hadn't cared about any of that.

No way could she manage her appointments through a Minnesotan winter—not to mention clearing the driveway of snow, brushing off her car, and the million other things that crept up when someone lived in a place with a shit-ton of the white fluffy stuff.

Stefan could have hired someone to take care of those things for her, like he'd done before, but that wasn't what the Baries did. That wasn't what was right.

His mother had taken care of him. So he would take care of her.

Even if he had to personally pound every cancer cell into submission.

After a few minutes, the adrenaline let down, leaving him shakier than a playoff game. He pushed to his feet and walked to the kitchen.

It only took a minute to throw together a turkey sandwich for himself then set out crackers and dish up some chicken noodle soup. He'd heat it for his mom when she woke.

Stefan wished she would eat more, gain back some of the weight she'd lost. But his mom had just finished her second round of chemo on Friday. And though she had this week off, residual nausea still made it tough for her to keep anything heavy down.

He ate his sandwich in a few bites, made another, and grabbed a beer and bottle of water—no one could say he didn't take hydration seriously—before sitting down in front of the TV and trying to push all of his fear for his mom to the side.

For once, it worked.

He watched random stories on ESPN, reveling in the way his mind went numb, not absorbing anything. For the first time in weeks, he actually relaxed.

Gradually, the sunlight coming in through the windows dwindled as day turned to night. His mom still slept, but that wasn't a bad thing. She needed her rest.

It was almost dark when he heard something that snapped his mind to razor-sharp focus.

" . . .trouble with the Gold already?" the female announcer said. "Notorious womanizer Barie is seen flirting with the first female slated to play for an NHL team, Brit Plantain."

A picture of him talking to Brit in the parking lot flashed on the TV. They were both leaning over the trunk of her car. It was a cozy shot. He and Brit close enough to touch and him smiling down at her.

If Stefan didn't know better—if he hadn't actually *lived* the scene —he might have believed the story the announcer was spinning.

But he *did* know better, and despite the rumors, he didn't actually sleep with every member of the opposite sex.

Not any longer anyway.

Hitting the bar, staying out too late, and screwing everything in sight had lost its appeal after just a few seasons.

Unfortunately for him and Brit, his reputation hadn't gone away quite as easily, and the press loved to regurgitate his so-called *conquests*.

One—*one!*—fucking date with a very popular celebrity had ensured that. They'd decided they weren't right for each other, and Stefan had been photographed out with someone else the next night. There was no bad blood between him and Kelsey, but that picture had cemented his place as a playboy.

Ah. The stupidity of youth. Especially since the second date hadn't been any better than the first.

The camera cut back to the anchor, who gave a coy smirk. "Is Brit going to fall just like every other female in Barie's path? Or will she be able to hold her own against those baby blues, and be the one to knock Stefan to his knees?"

"Christ," he muttered and switched off the TV, blinking against the sudden lack of light. "This is why I watch *SportsFocus* and not *Entertainment This Evening.*"

Knock him to his knees? *Hell no.* But Stefan couldn't deny his surprise at how sweet Brit seemed. He'd expected there to be nothing feminine about her, and though she was fierce as a wildcat—as she'd demonstrated so clearly on the ice—she was also eager, a little anxious, and almost . . . soft.

Like there was a vulnerable core under that tough exterior.

Not to mention gorgeous—

"Brit, huh?" his mother asked. "Is she pretty?"

TWELVE

STEFAN NARROWED HIS EYES. "You promised not to pull out those ninja skills, Mom."

His mom's lips twitched as she sat onto the couch next to him. "I wasn't quiet. You were engrossed."

In Brit. In memories of her smile, her cute but awkward social skills, and . . . an ass he wanted to grab with both hands.

"Stevie?" she asked, making him jump like a guilty toddler.

"I'm not engrossed. Just have a lot on my mind." Yeah, like Brit. When he should really be worried about his mom. Plus, if he was thinking about the team at all, he should be coming up with ways to corral Mike Stewart before his presence did any more damage.

The man was a black hole. Stewart sucked a team down, and they were never seen or heard from again.

"I didn't know you'd gotten up." Stefan pushed to his feet, trying to not notice how fragile his mom looked. "How are you feeling?"

"Fine."

He bit back a groan. It was always *fine* with his mom, even when she was puking from the chemo or being jabbed with ten different needles. But instead of arguing with her, which would get him absolutely nowhere, he turned for the kitchen.

"Good. I'll heat you up some food. You've missed dinner."

"I'm not hungry," she said, even as she stood and followed him into the kitchen.

His eyes flicked to hers, and he glared. "You need to eat. And it's just soup and crackers."

"But—"

"Please, Mom." Realistically, he knew he couldn't fight the fucking cancer for her, but at the very least, he could make sure she ate and was well-rested.

She sighed, sinking into the kitchen chair like it was a torture rack.

"Want to cross your arms too?"

That earned him a smile. "I can't believe I raised such a stubborn son."

"Where do you think I got it?"

Her snort was familiar . . . and welcome. Any sign of his BS-spotting, tough-as-hell mother eased the vice around his heart.

The microwave dinged, and he put the bowl, a spoon, and crackers in front of her, not breathing until she actually began to eat.

Relief spread through him, loosened the muscles of his neck and shoulders. She would be okay.

She had to be.

"You going to tell me about Brit?" she asked between bites. "Or am I going to have to pull it out of you?"

Here we go. "Mom."

She tilted her head to the side, studied him intently. "Do you want to date her? I know inter-office relationships are frowned upon, but I think this situation could work with a little creativity . . ."

"Diane," he warned and shot her a look that would have made a rookie piss himself.

Did his mom have a similar reaction? No, of course not. She smiled beatifically and kept on talking. " . . .and you know you're getting older. Now's the time to start a family, when you're young. And virile."

He gagged. "Seriously. That word is never allowed to come out of your mouth again."

"What? Family? Or *virile?*" Her eyes glittered with amusement, and even though it was at his expense, Stefan laughed along with her.

Then he lied.

"I'm not interested in her, Mom," he said. "She's a teammate. That's all."

His mother glanced up at him, lips twitching. "That's not what *SportsFocus* said."

He sighed. "When have you begun believing anything the media says?"

"Since you haven't given me anything else."

"Today was her first day, and you were sleeping when I got home."

His mother took another bite, her appetite apparently restored by the fervor of her curiosity.

"So is she pretty?"

He groaned.

This was absolute agony, being questioned by his mother about Brit—who he absolutely couldn't be interested in, no matter how good she looked naked.

Stefan had more than appreciated the view, even if it had been in the middle of the locker room.

Grudging respect had joined with the attraction at that point. But then add in her attitude on the ice?

Well, that had cemented it for him.

In his book, tough as hell also happened to be sexy as hell.

But it didn't matter that his body had reacted to Brit's strip-down like a Mack truck hitting a brick wall, that it had been a fucking exercise in control just attempting to tamp those feelings down.

What was important was that he view Brit solely as a teammate, both for himself, as captain of the team, and for her.

This was her shot at the show, and she needed to grasp it with both hands.

Still he couldn't help but think his mom would like Brit's balls-out attitude.

"Yup, she's pretty," his mom said and took another bite.

For the first time, Stefan considered that this line of questioning might be worth it if his mother continued to eat.

"Pretty has nothing to do with it."

"It does where the media is concerned." She set her spoon down. "Pretty gets more ratings. So what were you doing talking to her in the parking lot?"

Son of a bitch. Just how much of that story had his mom seen?

"I got in at the same time as Brit, wanted to show her the locker room."

"She's changing with you boys?" she asked, wrinkling his nose. "Isn't it stinky?"

His mom still remembered the days when his gear would smell up whatever one-bedroom apartment they'd been staying in.

Not that his shit hadn't stunk something fierce, but these days the equipment staff for the Gold kept the team's gear smelling fresher than his laundry.

"Yes," Stefan said. "Brit was quite adamant about it." He shrugged when his mom's mouth dropped open. "Makes sense to me. She needs to bond with the team, not miss any system or lineup changes."

"But the showers? And changing? Doesn't she want privacy?"

He smiled. "I'm guessing she's used to changing with a bunch of dudes. Plus, the nudity thing is pretty much ignored. She's not going to be looking at anyone, and no one will look at her."

"Really?"

Maybe. "Really."

"Hmm. I wonder if she's gay."

Irritation filled him, and he had to work to keep his tone light. He'd already caught this question being posed about Brit more than was comfortable . . . which meant he'd heard it exactly more than zero times. What did it matter who she was attracted to, anyway? Plus, that wasn't the vibe he got from her. "She's not gay."

"How do you know?" his mom asked.

"*I know*," he said.

He hoped. *No.* It didn't matter.

"I guess you'd know . . ." His mom hesitated. "So is she good enough to play with you guys? Or is this a publicity stunt?"

Stefan's head shot up in surprise, and that surprise deepened when his irritation tightened into a thread of anger.

It was a fair question. Maybe. But it still pissed him off that anyone was questioning Brit's skills.

He'd seen her on the ice. He'd watched tapes of her games. She'd earned her spot the old-fashioned way.

The problem was that the focus of his anger was his mother. His *cancer-stricken* mother.

Fuck.

Guess he'd bonded with Brit more today than he'd realized. Or . . . he was feeling a little caveman for another reason.

Like possessiveness. Like desire.

Nope. No way. He was defensive of his teammate. Just like any other captain would be.

"She's good enough."

But as he told his mom about practice, about the cheap shot Stewart had taken and the way Brit had handled it like a boss, his mind wasn't quite convinced.

Especially as it conjured up a replay of Brit stepping from the showers, her skin glistening, her towel wrapped snugly above those fabulous breasts.

The season had just gotten a hell of a lot more complicated.

THIRTEEN

Brit

THE BLARING of the alarm on her phone was both unwelcome and unsurprising.

With a groan, Brit turned it off then shoved the covers back and pushed to her feet. Her body was still on East Coast time, but five a.m. came early, no matter where she was.

Plus, blackout shades weren't exactly conducive for waking up, especially when she hadn't gotten much sleep the night before.

Her shoulder had bothered her a fair amount, but that ache—bruised skin, irritated nerves and muscles—was familiar. The anxiety plaguing her had been much worse.

Usually, after her first practice with a new team, all of her nerves disappeared.

The Gold were different.

Bernard was against her being there. Stewart was going to try to stir the pot.

And for the first time in her life, it was hard for Brit to shake off the notion that she *was* nothing more than a stunt, a cute little story about a girl who liked to dabble in a man's sport.

That she would never be good enough in Bernard's eyes to earn a start—

Wow. That was way too much self-pity for five a.m.

Grabbing her workout clothes from where she'd laid them out the night before, Brit surveyed the room that would be her home for the next little while.

The team had put her up in a decent hotel just three miles from the rink. She'd be able to run to the arena most days. Though on game nights, she expected that she'd need to drive so as to not encounter post-game rowdy fans.

If she was even around that long—

Stop it.

Shoving the annoying little pity party to the back of her brain, Brit pulled on her clothes, tied her shoes, and slung her backpack over her shoulders.

The city was surprisingly quiet as she pushed through the lobby doors and turned in the direction of the arena. She'd memorized the route the night before and immediately took off at a slow jog, just fast enough to warm her tight muscles. When everything began to loosen, she picked up the pace.

San Francisco was different than any place she'd ever lived. Though summer was barely over, a thick blanket of fog shrouded the lightening sky. It made everything feel quiet and otherworldly, almost as if that layer of gas and water in the sky was actually a buffer between reality and fantasy.

Brit's footsteps echoed on the pavement as she ran, a quickening pace that chased her rising pulse.

By the time she arrived at the arena and had pulled out her identification badge, she was breathing hard, sweaty, but feeling about a million-and-a-half times better.

"Morning," she told the guard at the gate and held up her badge.

He blinked at her, glanced at the ID then back at her. "Ms. Plantain?"

"Call me Brit," she said. "And you are?"

"Richie."

She smiled at the man, skinny as a pole with bright red hair. "Nice to meet you." They stared at each other until she finally took a step forward. "Not too many of the guys run in, huh?"

"Um, nope."

Brit shrugged. "Different is good, sometimes."

Richie's lips twitched, and he nodded, his eyes sweeping down and up appreciatively. "That it is."

She couldn't help it. She laughed.

Richie flushed. "That came out really bad, didn't it?"

"Yup."

"Well, damn." He shook his head. "Way too early for this. I'll write you on the list so you don't have to check in every day, Ms. Plantain. Will this be your typical time?"

She nodded. "It's Brit. And thanks."

"You're welcome." He gestured to the gate. "Go on with you."

Brit nodded and ran forward.

The locker room was quiet but not empty. A few of the players, including Blane and Max were already there. They looked up as she walked through the door and murmured quiet hellos.

"Morning," she said and walked to her stall, which she was pleased to see actually held a nameplate with her name.

Her equipment was laid out, exactly as she preferred, pads to the left, chest protector hung up.

But it wasn't time to get her gear on.

She walked down the hall that led to the ice, waving at Mandy through the window of the PT suite as she went. Mandy gestured at her to come in, but Brit mouthed "later" and kept moving.

Past the therapy room, past the gym. All the way into the arena.

It was impossible to hold back the awe that washed over her.

This was her dream.

Brit could picture the stadium full to the brim, filled with 17,000-plus fans, screaming and shouting. The *crash* of players into the boards, the *crack* of sticks against the ice, the sting of the puck hitting her glove.

She shook herself, dislodged the image.

That wouldn't happen unless she worked as hard as she could.

Starting now. Continuing for the indefinite future.

After sliding in her headphones, she cranked the volume and turned for the stairs.

Not that she'd tell anyone, but her kryptonite was boy bands. In any form, shape, or number. If they sang catchy pop music, she was sold.

Backstreet Boys, N'Sync, One Direction, 5 Seconds of Summer. Heck, even BTS. It didn't matter. Brit loved them all.

She grinned as one of her favorite songs blared to life in her headphones, snorting as the guys sang about being one of a kind. *Yup.* That she was. But maybe according to Bernard, not in a good way.

"Move it," she muttered, blinking away the previous day and focusing on the present.

And so she ran.

Up one section, over, and down the next. She kept it strictly to the lower bowl for today, not wanting to overwork her legs before practice.

Left. Right. Left. Right.

The rhythm was so ingrained within her that she could have almost run blindfolded.

Except she wasn't.

A fact which Brit was abruptly glad for when the *pat pat* of footsteps very close behind her permeated the music blaring through her ears.

FOURTEEN

IT WAS DARK, only a few of the lights on inside the arena.

Brit was on the far side of the ice, as physically distanced from the locker room as she could possibly be.

Glancing behind her, she saw a tall, shadowed masculine form. He seemed to fill the space, to loom over her as he worked his way up and down the stairs.

Following her.

Her.

Some logical part of her mind recognized that the man must be a Gold player, that he was probably doing the same thing she was.

The rest of her—the piece that had been damaged three years before—was stronger.

It took over her mind.

She picked up the pace, cutting across rows as quickly as she could.

If she could just get back to the locker room, she would be safe.

The footsteps behind her sped up.

Brit's heart pounded, breath whistled in and out of her mouth.

Her feet were a blur as she watched them carry her body through the sections.

Only two more to go.

But the man was gaining. Closing the distance as effectively as a great white to a seal.

She put every last bit of energy into her feet. So close. Her eyes flicked behind her, desperate now to get away.

What she saw didn't help. The man wore a grey sweatshirt, its hood pulled up and over his head. It was just like—

She stumbled. Saw a row of steps coming straight for her face. One arm came up, an attempt to shield the inevitable fall.

Which didn't come.

Instead warm hands caught her and pulled her back. She collided with a strong, hard chest, and they went down in a heap.

The man grunted as she landed hard on his stomach, but her mind had shut down. She struggled, her only thought to get as far away as humanly possible.

Next they'd grab her ankles, shackle her wrists. Fear was an icy blade down her spine. It spurred her to fight, even as part of her registered the chest beneath her rumbling as the man spoke.

The words didn't penetrate.

"No," she said, thrusting her elbow back, fighting to get free with everything she had.

The man held tight.

Then her earbuds were plucked out—not that she'd really heard the song over the *whoosh* of blood in her ears, the rapid pounding of her heart. But with the music not blaring, she was finally able to comprehend the voice.

"Hey. *Hey*! It's okay."

Stefan.

One beat of her heart to understand. Another for her panic to fade. One last one for embarrassment course through her.

Except it wasn't the typical hot, scalding version. This was frigid, a blanket of frost settling over her skin, burning, but only because it was so cold.

It was heavy. Stifling.

And full of shame.

"Are you all right?" Stefan asked.

A single jerky nod was as much answer as she could muster.

Silence stretched. It was awkward and filled with the expectation. He was anticipating, *waiting* for an explanation she couldn't provide.

She'd just been intimidated, cornered . . . scared.

Really scared.

And the fear leftover from the assault—that something *could* have happened, that she could have been so easily overpowered—had fractured something inside of her.

It was a lot harder to regain confidence than to possess it in the first place.

"Let—let me go," she managed.

"Okay." Stefan slid to the side, depositing her on the step next to him.

For a moment, she actually missed the warmth of his chest, the security of his arms—which was absolutely insane because Brit hadn't found comfort in a man's embrace in so long that she'd actually begun to believe she no longer possessed the capability to do so.

Which wasn't the point, but the stray thought helped the last dredges of panic fade from her system.

Stefan hadn't said anything further, just sat next to her in silence as she focused on getting her breaths to slow to a more reasonable rhythm.

"I'm sorry," she murmured, not willing to talk about it and totally unable to put into words the abrupt terror that had gripped her when he'd approached her from behind.

"I—" He thrust a hand through his hair, and unconsciously Brit flinched back. Stefan froze, looked at her, a wealth of emotions in his expression. "What . . . what happened to you? Did—"

Brit swallowed hard, was ready to laugh off the whole scenario as staying up too late the previous night, watching scary movies or some other such nonsense.

Except . . . there was a flash of something in those baby blues—not quite pity, not quite remorse—and it pissed her off.

She *shouldn't* be mad, not when he'd stopped her from breaking her ass on the row of stairs, not when he was trying to be kind now.

But he was looking at her like she might be broken.

"I'm not weak," she spat. "I just—"

Just *what?*

Freaked the heck out.

Because she *was* a little broken.

But she didn't show that side to the world, and definitely not to Stefan Barie, who never went out with a girl more than once, who'd dated half the city's available—and not so available—females between the ages of eighteen and eighty, according to the tabloids.

For *him*, she needed walls of steel, coated in barbed wire. Hell, she could use a couple of those pots of boiling oil at the top, ready to pour down and burn the tendrils of whatever she was feeling—attraction? gratitude?—to ashes.

For the love of pucks, she was a freaking wreck.

With a shove at his chest, Brit struggled to her feet, her legs like Jell-O.

Stefan didn't say anything, just studied her with an intensity that made her heart beat faster—and not from nerves this time . . . or at least not entirely. He stared as though he could see inside of her, view the very depths of her soul.

The arena was quiet, the crisp coolness of the ice creeping up to coat her sweat-laden skin. She shivered. Stefan stood, took off his hoodie, and slung it around her shoulders.

And just like that, her anger dissipated, was wrapped in a layer of cotton, traded for the scent of sandalwood and spice that crept into her nostrils and loosened the iron grip on her emotions.

Her eyes burned.

Hell no. Just no. She didn't cry. Not ever.

"It's okay if you don't want to talk about it."

Stefan's voice was gentle, not demanding in any way. But that almost made it worse.

She could deal with someone barking at her, cursing at her to move faster, to stop the fucking puck.

What she couldn't deal with was sympathy.

"It's nothing."

"Okay," he said after a moment and when he reached for her hand it took everything inside of her to not flinch back.

If the expression on Stefan's face said anything, it was that he knew exactly how much of a struggle it had been for her not to move.

Still, his touch was light, a careful brush of calloused fingers against calloused fingers. He tilted his head in the direction of the aisle. "How about we finish these stairs then?"

Disbelief he wasn't going to press or demand an explanation coursed through her. The relief that chased it was a powerful thing, one that loosened the stranglehold of the past and allowed her to extract herself from its oppressive force.

"Yup," she said. "Last one done buys the beer tonight."

As Brit stood, she thought she saw a flicker of something—of *blond*—out of the corner of her eye. But when she turned to look fully, nothing was there.

Stefan started to get up, and, not wanting to lose, she took off, smiling at the shock on his face, at the surprise *she* felt for having made the invitation at all.

It was better than the past.

And that was all she could ask.

FIFTEEN

Stefan

STEFAN HANDED a twenty to the bartender, thinking he was a sucker, through and through. They hadn't been able to go out for drinks that night a week ago. Brit had gotten sucked into an extended physical therapy session with Mandy, but he'd challenged her to a rematch on the stairs just before practice that morning.

The result being that he'd somehow ended up buying beer for four.

"Only two pitchers?" Max asked when he returned to the table.

Brit laughed.

"Do I need to remind you that we have practice tomorrow?" Stefan set the pitchers down then went back to the bar to retrieve glasses for him, Max, Blane, and Brit. When he returned, he sat in the only open spot, which was in the booth next to Max, and tried to push aside the bizarre sensation that he was on an episode of *The Bachelor*.

Max huffed. "The day I couldn't handle two pitchers—"

"Would be like every other time we come here," Stefan said dryly.

Brit snorted, and his eyes flashed up, studying hers. There was no trace of fear, not like the terror that had dominated her expression the other morning on the stairs.

Max continued to act like his usual annoying self. "That's not true—"

"Shut up, and drink your two and-a-half beers," Stefan said as he poured the first round.

They all picked up their cups and took a drink. Their gazes met over the rims of the frosted glasses, and awkward silence fell.

Surprisingly, Brit was the one to break it.

"So . . . you guys come here often?" she asked.

Though—since their responding laughter made her eyes widen in shock—Stefan didn't think the attempt was intentional.

"You're just the same as you were five years ago, Brit. Promise me you won't change." Blane punched her in the arm.

Stefan wondered if he was the only one who saw her wince.

Was it because of the punch or Blane's words?

Blane wouldn't hurt Brit intentionally. He was a good guy and Stefan hadn't missed the longing glances coming from the first-line forward when Brit wasn't looking.

Blane watched Brit like she was *a woman*.

Not a teammate.

Which was a familiar feeling, Stefan knew. There was something about her—fragility mixed with strength, drive, and confidence. It was impossible to not want some of that essence.

His thoughts drifted to her shoulder, to the monster bruise she'd been sporting in the locker room. He hadn't *wanted* to notice it . . . or the creamy white skin dotted with a pattern of freckles he wanted to trace with his tongue. Or the ass he could bounce a dime off—

It took Stefan's groin tightening for him to cut off the image. For fuck's sake. He needed to get his shit together.

Brit had been solid in practice, so a casual observer might think her shoulder was fully recovered. But they were professional athletes.

Playing through the pain was nothing new.

"Let's hope I'm a little bit better," she said, soft enough that Stefan thought he might have been the only one who heard it. Especially since Max and Blane had moved on to laughing about some video on YouTube.

The words, laced with a hint of sadness, made his heart squeeze tight.

"You've gotta see this," Max said, leaning diagonally across the table to thrust his phone in Blane's face.

"I can't—" Blane got out of the booth, came around the table, and shoved Stefan's shoulder. "Move."

Normally, Stefan would have snapped at his teammate—ever heard of the word *please?*—but since the end result was him sitting next to Brit, he got up and crossed to the other side.

"You good?" he asked softly. Her eyes flew to his, questioning. "After that—" He shrugged, searching for the right words and failing miserably. "The fall didn't hurt you, right?" It was the first time he'd brought anything to do with that morning up, but Stefan found that he needed to reassure himself. Brit had been beyond frightened—*of him*—and though he knew it wasn't his fault she'd been so scared, being the cause of someone's fear wasn't a normal occurrence for him.

"Fine," she said, her tone a little tart. His words clearly hadn't found the right mark and he almost let it go. Probably *would have* if not for her hand. The one nearest him was clenched into a fist and trembled where she rested it on her thigh.

Stefan couldn't stop himself. He reached across the six inches of space separating them, took that shaking hand into his, and carefully separated her fingers. The skin wasn't smooth like most of the girls he'd been with. There were callouses, scars.

They were capable fingers, strong, and yet somehow still feminine.

Perhaps just a different version than many would expect.

Brit had jumped almost a foot at the contact, her lips parting in surprise. But when he gave her hand a light squeeze, she relaxed.

Words weren't necessary in that moment. It was simple. Comfort freely given then received.

The action was instinctive in the way he consoled a teammate after a bad shift or tapped Julian's—the Gold's starting goaltender—pads with his stick after a goal. Small gestures that taken alone meant nothing, but could be pieced together into a larger expression of camaraderie.

But unlike the others, *this* comfort was laced with something else. Heat licking up his arm, coiling in his stomach . . . and lower.

Which was why he forced himself to pull back.

Even though what he really wanted to do was lace his fingers with hers and tug her close.

He knew the thought was wrong but it didn't stop him from wanting. And while normally he might have been able to shrug off his desire as a stupid male thing, this need tempered with tenderness made the situation extra complicated.

He couldn't cross the line between teammate and woman and him getting in her space was probably the last thing she needed after what had happened in the arena.

So he returned his fingers back to his own lap, even laughed when Blane turned the phone to them and played the video of some idiot attempting to use a roof as a diving board.

Still, when Brit glanced at him, a small smile on her lips, her eyes soft, Stefan couldn't suppress the notion that he'd just . . . somehow become tied to the woman next to him.

SIXTEEN

STEFAN CALLED his mom the moment he was in his car.

"Hi." It was perfunctory because the more important thing was "How are you feeling?"

Diane sighed. "I told you to stay out and have a good time. You don't need to worry about me."

Impossible. But he couldn't tell her that. Didn't want to add to her stress.

"We have practice tomorrow. A late night isn't in the cards."

"Stefan, really?" she said. "You're worried. I understand that. But you need to live your life."

Not surprising that his mom would see through him. She always had. But the excuse had worked with the guys, a finite end to the evening, allowing him to get home without anyone knowing the one person who'd been his steady throughout his life might not survive her battle.

It was too soon to talk to anyone about what his mom was going through. Too soon to know her prognosis and be able to confide his fears to his friends.

Besides that, his mom had asked that he not let Max know, the one person he might have actually told. Their mothers were friends, and she'd said, *"I don't want Betty fussing over me for nothing."*

Nothing being recurrent Stage 2 cancer. Surgery and chemo. Bloodwork and fatigue.

"Have you heard anything from the lab?" he asked, setting the phone in the cup holder as the Bluetooth kicked on. He put the car into gear and pulled out of the parking lot.

"No." She paused. "But you know the initial report came back okay. It's smaller this time and less aggressive. I'm going to be fine."

"So why don't you want Betty to know?"

"Stefan." His mom was rolling her eyes; he could practically hear it through the airwaves. "You know she would fly out, and Max's sister just had her baby. They need Betty's help more than I do. You're not going to ruin her first experience as a grandmother, are you?"

Stefan wasn't sure he believed that, but he also wasn't about to verbalize any of his fears. His mom was going through enough without him needing to dump those on her—no matter how much he would have liked to have steady, capable Betty at his mom's side.

"Fine." He sighed, though having his mom manipulate him was much better than the pallid, civilized version of herself she'd been since the surgery. "I won't destroy the sacred bond between grandchild and grandmother. But you're going to have to tell her eventually."

"I know."

There was a moment of quiet, a pause where it seemed as though they were both thinking of the possibilities of what *could* happen but were unwilling to say them aloud. Then he shoved that garbage away.

"Milkshake?"

His mom laughed. "When have I ever said no to milkshakes?"

"Never." Which was why he'd asked. Empty calories at this stage weren't a bad thing. "And done. I'll be home in twenty."

Stefan drove to the all-night dairy, got out, and ordered his mom's milkshake—a vanilla malt with chocolate sandwich cookies mixed in.

A few fans came up to him as he waited for the shake, but no one got out of hand.

That was the thing about the Bay Area.

People were huge sports fans and, though hockey's popularity was on the rise, Stefan wasn't so recognizable that he couldn't just go hang out somewhere.

For the most part.

Just as the worker handed over his mom's milkshake, Jessica approached him.

He mentally groaned.

She was a puck bunny—which was a not-so-nice term for hockey groupies—who also happened to be a local reporter who'd been around the locker room so many times that he actually remembered her name. He'd yet to ride her particular bicycle and had no foreseeable plans too. His taste had evolved past easy lays.

Hell, that was when he'd even *had* a sexual appetite—which hadn't been often over the last season and a half. He'd poured every last bit of his energy into the team and helping the Gold recover from last season's scandal.

Not to mention, since Brit's appearance, his fantasies had been less about buxom brunettes with a pound of makeup on their face and more about lithe, unmarred femininity.

Which was very, very dangerous for the team he'd been working so hard to rebuild.

"A picture with my favorite hockey star?" Jessica all but purred.

Fake breasts pushed into his side, and lips, obviously injected with something that made them look as though they would explode, pursed in the idiotic fishy pout that was so popular nowadays.

Stefan figured the best course was to take the stupid picture and get the hell out.

"Sure." He grabbed the phone, used his long arms to his advantage, and took the photograph. It a quick move he'd learned over the last couple of seasons: ignore the advances, mitigate any potential unhappiness, then get as far away as possible.

"Gotta go," he said and started toward his car.

She followed him.

Shit.

Unlocking the driver's door—and only the driver's door, a lesson learned after another fan had jumped into the passenger's seat when he'd been trying to make a quick getaway very similar to this one—Stefan stowed the shake inside and started to fold his body into the very narrow frame of his Mercedes.

The hand on his arm stopped him, at least for a moment. Then he brushed it off and started to close the door.

"I can—" she began.

"Thank you, but I'm not interested." Had never been. Would never be.

Jessica's beady blue eyes narrowed . . . or maybe it was just the result of all the black crap outlining them. "You don't even know what I'm offering."

He actually *did* know what she was offering, had heard about it five times over.

She gives the best head, dude. And then when you actually hit it . .

Yeah. Sloppy ninths or tenths didn't appeal to him.

"Goodnight, Jessica."

"Who's the milkshake for?" she asked, a hardness coating her expression. It gave Stefan a moment of pause. She *was* a reporter after all. "I know you wouldn't drink that crap during the season."

The lie was easy. "Doesn't everyone deserve a cheat day?"

With that, he shut the door and drove away, a sick feeling in the pit of his stomach. It was common knowledge that, aside from Jessica's bedroom antics, she could spin a story into a tangle of half-truths and sensationalism like no one's business.

Damn. He was probably screwed. They'd have him paired off with some visiting actress just because she'd been in the city.

But he also couldn't worry about that now. There was a milkshake to be delivered, tapes to be studied, and drills to memorize.

His mom practically snatched the shake from his hand the moment he walked through the door then oohed and moaned about how good it tasted. So far, the treat was the single guaranteed thing she could keep down.

Hopefully that lasted.

It wasn't until he'd finished his prep for tomorrow's practice and lay down to go to sleep several hours later that he remembered Jessica's cold look.

Stefan had clearly overreacted, his worry was unfounded. He'd been getting a damn milkshake after all. There was nothing there. Nothing to spin.

What could she possibly say?

It wasn't until he woke early the next morning and turned on the news that he realized Jessica could say a whole, whole lot.

SEVENTEEN

Brit

SHOES TIED. Phone tucked in her pocket. Earbuds in. Or one this time. After her freak-out with Stefan, Brit wasn't about to make the same mistake of not being totally aware of her surroundings.

Therapy had helped after the *incident.*

But it hadn't cured all. She still hadn't been able to tell anyone else what happened. Not her brother, not her parents.

Of course, one had to actually *talk* to their parents in order for that to occur.

And that wasn't her reality.

The best that someone could have said was that her parents were detached.

Her father had been so wrapped up in his career as an orthopedic surgeon, until he'd died eighteen months before, that, as an adult, she had only spoken to him on Father's Day, his birthday, and Christmas.

He'd never taken time off when she went home to visit, never turned down a surgery.

Brit's mother wasn't a bad person, but she'd made an art out of creating excuses for Brit's dad not being, well . . . a dad. Worse was that she had never supported Brit playing a *man's sport* like hockey.

Needless to say, it made things tense at home.

Luckily, she had her brother. And when he was in the country, however infrequently that ended up being, they always got together.

He didn't know about the incident either. There was nothing Dan could have done, and it would have only made him feel guilty.

Brit hadn't wanted that, so she'd talked to a therapist who'd agreed with her assessment. What had happened to her was sexual assault, no matter that the team had tried to play it off as good-natured team building, or at worst hazing because *all* the rookies got the same treatment.

Hazing was a word she had barely known before the incident, and something she'd never spent more than ten seconds thinking about until after she'd seen a random news story about it occurring at a college fraternity and realized *that* was what the guys had tried to claim happened to her.

The news story had been her catalyst for therapy.

Because it *hadn't* been hazing. It was assault.

Brit hadn't gone to college, had always felt safe with men. She'd grown up in locker rooms with them, had never had an issue until then, and while she knew that it wasn't her fault, that her lingering fear and anxiety were a normal part of the healing process, it still really fucking sucked.

She didn't like feeling weak or broken.

But she did.

And so she continued to deal with the normal part of recovering

A totally shitty part, but not abnormal.

Which didn't necessarily make it easy to get over.

Especially when she was by herself in a strange city or quiet arena.

Being in a new place wasn't a unique experience for her; she was used to the moving and upheaval. Especially early on, it had been exciting to see so much of the world, to be in a different place every night.

It was unfortunate that one of those nights had managed to cast so large a shadow on her life.

THREE YEARS ago

THE HAND on her shoulder made her jump.

She turned and saw it was Sergei, her captain. He wore his trademark grey sweatshirt, the hood pulled up over his head like some idiotic version of Rocky.

"Hey," she said, gripping her towel tight to her breasts. She'd been about to jump in the shower. "What's up?"

"Strip."

Brit blinked. "What? No," she said, not liking the gleam in Sergei's eyes. Two of the biggest players on the team stood behind him. The rest of the guys looked on. "Back off. Now, Sergei."

The room went suddenly and utterly quiet. Brit could have heard a pin drop, let alone the collective sucking in a breath.

"You don't get to make that call."

The air frosted with malice, and shivering, Brit took a step back.

Sergei and the two players behind him moved as a unit.

Fingers manacled her wrists, strong arms immobilized her kicking legs. And faster than she would have thought possible, the towel was torn away.

She fought. Struggled.

It was only when Sergei bent over her that real fear settled in.

"I knew your body would be fucking hot," he said once she was pinned. He trailed a finger down her throat, between her breasts. Then he gripped her nipple, twisted it hard enough to make her cry out in pain.

Bile burned her throat when his hand slid lower.

This was actually going to happen. She was going to be a statistic, one of the twenty-five percent of woman who were sexually assaulted in their lifetimes.

But just as the hand reached the apex of her thighs and her eyes slid closed, her mind desperately attempting to grasp onto some sort of numbness, to find a dark, empty place in her mind, Brit was tossed through the air.

She collided with a slick, tiled surface. Hit her face hard against the floor. Blood exploded in her mouth, and icy cold water hit like bullets against her back.

There was laughter. The sound of skin against skin as palms met for high fives all around.

Then the locker room went silent.

Brit didn't know how long she stayed in the shower, the cold water pounding against her back before she managed to shove to her feet and stumble into the adjoining locker room.

Her clothes were nowhere to be found. But her equipment was in its normal spot. She grabbed the shorts she always wore under her gear, wrestled them on, and threw her jersey over her head.

Shivers wracked her body. She had never been colder in her entire life.

Somehow, she made it to her apartment without wrecking her car and stumbled into her bedroom. She didn't bother to change, just huddled under a mass of blankets until morning light had begun filtering in through her windows.

It took everything she possessed to get up and walk into the locker room the next morning.

"Sorry about the fat lip," was the first thing Sergei said when she walked through the door. "You were fighting us so hard that you slipped from my hands."

One of the defensemen who'd held her in place laughed. "You're fucking strong, Brit. I almost got dunked."

"Dude," someone called, whose face Brit was way too shocked to register, "the water is the worst part."

"At least you got cold," another player had chimed in. "My ass got roasted."

BRIT STRUGGLED to grasp the invasive memories, wanting to shove them back into the recesses of her mind, but it didn't matter she was three years in the future and playing for a different team in a different city. The dark thoughts didn't want to be shut away.

She rested her head against the smooth wood of her hotel room's door and, run temporarily forgotten, she breathed. Just breathed.

Her teammates had been so cavalier about the violation. They'd done it to others. They would do it to more.

If she didn't do something stop them.

So Brit had reported the incident to her head coach . . . and found herself cut from the team a matter of days later.

It was all history now, part of a past that was painful and usually buried deep in her mind.

But the assault was also another reason she'd done her little stripper stunt on day one of joining the Gold. Let the guys see whatever they wanted to see. Remove the notion of forbidden fruit for some, and, at the same time, diffuse the awkwardness of having a member of the opposite sex in the room.

Because there was strength in numbers. Usually.

For the rest of it, she would be aware of her surroundings, and she'd had a shit ton of self-defense training since then.

She just needed to remember to use it.

With that thought, Brit opened the door to the hotel room, jogged down the stairs, and was out the front door in less than a minute.

She would be fine. She was *always* fine.

Except, when she arrived at the arena twenty minutes later, *nothing* was fine.

Insanity had been unleashed on the front gate.

EIGHTEEN

REPORTERS WERE LINED up along both sides of the road like some sort of loud and very obnoxious receiving line at a wedding.

When they spotted her, it instantly felt much more like a gauntlet. The questions were loud, vicious blows to her senses.

"Is it true?"

"Did the Gold pick you up because you're sleeping with Barie?"

"What does Bernard think of your relationship?"

Her feet slowed, the single earbud she had in place falling from her ear, the music blaring in short staccato bursts of vibration against her chest.

That single moment of surprise—of hesitation—cost her. The reporters closed in, encroaching on her personal space. Pushing. Yelling.

It was too much. Her heart pounded and cold sweat took the place of the exercise-related version.

"Back up! Make a path, people!"

A few seconds later, Richie was by her side, his cheerful, smiling façade she'd come to know over the last week closed down and dark.

He slung an arm around her shoulder, tucked her against his side, and started to pull her through the crowd.

"Stay close," he said directly into her ear.

She nodded and lifted her chin. Despite the nerves and assault on her senses, she wasn't going to let anyone see her as weak.

He pushed them forward, and when they neared the gate, another security guard she'd never seen before let them pass.

Richie dropped his arm but stayed close.

"What the hell was that?" she asked.

"*That* is the media on a scandal." He rolled his eyes.

"What kind of scandal warrants that?" She waved a hand over her shoulder, encompassing the myriad of news trucks, of shouting men and women with microphones and black handheld news cameras.

"A good old-fashion Gold scandal. Not that I believe anything that reporter says, Ms.—"

"Brit," she interrupted. "Is this because of the whole first female thing?"

Richie laughed then sobered rapidly when he glanced down and found her frowning. "No. Not that."

"Then what—"

The side door he was leading her to opened abruptly.

"Bye, Ms. Plantain." Richie stepped back and gestured her inside.

"Brit," she reminded him again, stepping through.

He just waved as the door swung shut.

Bernard stood on the other side of the plank of metal, and he wasn't happy.

The man wasn't appealing even on a good day, but the frown pulling his bushy grey brows together at the moment—hello, unibrow—was ferocious.

He didn't say a word, just pointed down the hall.

Which was when Brit's stomach sank pretty much to her toes.

She followed Bernard past his office, past the locker room, and into a conference room she hadn't known existed.

Inside were a bunch of suits—five men, one woman—and all looking very serious. They sat around a large mahogany conference table, which was empty, save a pitcher of water and a handful of glasses.

"Sit," Bernard told her, pointing toward an empty chair.

Brit sat even as Bernard remained standing, taking up a position behind her left shoulder. She would rather be facing a breakaway in sudden-death overtime than the six people in front of her.

The addition of Bernard at her back made her feel as though she had two enemies, one coming at her from the front and one from the rear.

"Would you care to explain this?" Devon Carter, the general manager, asked. He was dressed in an expensive-looking suit, and his face was handsome, though, like most former hockey players, he hadn't escaped his career completely unscathed. A scar bisected one brow, and his nose sported a few bumps from the times it had been broken over the years.

Devon slid an honest-to-God manila folder across the table, and Brit had a flash of one of those interrogation scenes from a cable police show.

Good cop. Bad cop.

She almost snorted to herself. Then she saw the picture inside the folder.

Her gasp was loud in the silent room.

"What is that?"

"Why don't you tell us?"

The photo was clear, despite the limited light, and it showed . . . oh God. Her eyes slid closed in embarrassment. In the shot, she was sprawled on top of Stefan, their faces very close, their bodies pressed together.

It was from the arena. From the week before, when Stefan had accidentally scared her and—

And what? She felt violated? Exposed? Vulnerable?

Yes to all of those things.

She swallowed against the rise of tears in her throat, struggled to put her face back into an expression of calm.

Because she also looked to be very close to losing her job.

"I don't know what that is—" she started.

The woman, mid-sixties, with a severe bun of grey hair and more diamonds around her neck than the crown jewels, snorted.

"I was running stairs, didn't hear him come up behind me because I had my headphones on." She shrugged, tried to push away the fear that had crept back into her at the memory of being chased, the sick heaviness that had sunk into her limbs. "I startled, and we both went down."

"Then didn't get back up?" the grey-haired woman asked with a sneer.

"A photograph only takes a second."

Bernard's voice surprised her. Especially since it sounded as though he were standing up for her.

"Why are you asking me this?" Bernard's support—as trivial as it might turn out to be—gave her the strength to set aside the memory and focus on the present. "I've done nothing wrong."

"You're here because of these pictures. Because of the news stories," the older woman said. "And because the sheer volume of attention this picture has wrought presents us with a particularly unique opportunity."

"Susan is right," Devon said. "We know there is nothing going on with Barie. He told us as much just a half an hour ago. But that doesn't mean we can't turn the rumor to our advantage."

The nerves Brit had managed to bank were suddenly back and battering her insides like hell. She had an inkling of where this might be going.

Devon and the others were waiting for her to speak, waiting for her to ask the obvious question. Her mind recoiled . . . and yet she plunged ahead anyway. "What kind of opportunity?"

Susan's lips curved slightly, not quite a smile, but enough to make the older woman look more than a little possessed.

Perhaps she was. Because Susan's words turned Brit's inkling into her worst nightmare.

"You're going to seduce Barie, and then you're going to take your relationship public. Dates. Hand-holding. PDA," Susan stated, her voice calm, as though she hadn't just asked Brit to prostitute herself for the team. "You'll give the press what they want."

"I—" Brit scrambled for a moment, trying to figure out what the hell she wanted to say. The fury and disgust she felt were obvious reactions, but ultimately, she ended up blurting the most persistent question that was bouncing around her skull. "Why?"

"Public opinion," Susan said. "After the unfortunate situation with Peter Gordaine and Rhonda Campbell, we need good press. The team barely got the necessary tax breaks from the city to return this season, and unless we make a significant dent in our public image, they've told us we won't receive them next year."

Devon nodded. "And we need money. Filled seats. Merchandise sales. Think of the marketing opportunities from a relationship like this."

Brit dropped her gaze to the table, her mind spinning as she tried to find a way to talk them out of this. It couldn't be real. *This* couldn't be her reality.

"You never wanted me on the team to play did you?" she asked softly.

Devon snorted. "Women don't belong in the NHL. Still, when Frankie wanted you, we agreed because your presence presented us with an opportunity." He paused and she glanced up, saw the cold calculation there. "Feminism sells. You'll make sure of it."

Fuck. She hadn't expected her run with the Gold to be rainbows and puppy dogs. She'd expected reactions like Bernard's, expected some pushback from the other players.

But this?

Playing for a team with a board that wanted to openly manipulate their players and lie to their fans?

It was tempting—so damned tempting—to turn and walk out. Except . . .

This was her shot at the NHL.

Her gaze swiveled around the room, attempted to find an ally. But Devon and Susan were the only two who would make eye contact; the rest kept their gazes on the table, their expressions vaguely uncomfortable.

"This is bullshit." Bernard's voice was gruff.

Her jaw wanted to fall open in surprise at the show of support, but she clenched her teeth together, unwilling to let it drop. She turned, saw her coach's expression had gone thunderous, and was relieved the depth of anger wasn't directed at her.

"This is *fucking* bullshit," he said. "Come on, Brit. Leave these morons to their own devices. You're not doing this."

"Clear your office."

The three words from Susan were quiet, but crystal clear and laced with steel.

"What?" he asked.

"You're fired," she said. "You're still on probation, and we can let you go at will."

"I know what my contract says," Bernard snapped. "And it doesn't matter. If this gets out—"

"It won't." Susan's expression was shrewd. "Because you know what will happen if it does."

Bernard's face paled. "You can't make that decision. The board—"

Devon chose that moment to speak up. "Well, I can speak for the board. We're all in agreement, correct?" The nods were small, but they were there. The rest of the board wouldn't interfere. "Bernard, you block this in any way, and your job is forfeit."

There was a moment of terse silence then Bernard spoke, "Do what you will, but I won't go along with it." He touched Brit's shoulder, startled her into motion. "Let's go. You're not doing this."

She stood, started following her coach to the door.

Susan's voice caused her feet to hesitate at the threshold.

"Do you really want that man's job on your conscience? Did you know his wife is sick? Apparently she has very rare form of blood disease." A twist of an old wrinkled mouth shrouded in pink lipstick. "Tragic, really."

Bernard cursed. "That's enough."

Brit turned. She would have thought Susan to be a sweet, older woman if not for the calculation in those cold blue eyes.

"Do you really want her to lose her health insurance?" Susan pressed.

Brit's eyes flicked to Bernard's hoping, wanting . . . to *what*? See Susan was lying? That it was all just a ploy to get her to go along with the truth?

Except when she looked at Bernard, the truth was there.

His wife *was* ill, and if the tortured expression on her coach's face was any indication, the illness was a serious one.

Fuck. Her gut clenched. Her heart squeezed hard. She couldn't do this . . . but dammit, how could she *not*?

Bernard blinked, and his face went blank, a calm, clear slate that was an epic sort of mask. One she didn't buy for a moment. His words, when they came, were laced with such tension that he might as well have just agreed with Susan.

"Don't listen to her," he said. "My wife is fine."

She wanted to believe him. Desperately. But—

"His wife is *sick*. And he's up to his eyeballs in debt." She clucked. "Gambling is such a hard habit to kick."

"You're a conniving bitch," Bernard gritted out.

"At. Will," Susan countered.

The room fell silent for one long, slow breath before the scheming resumed.

"We also received a very interesting delivery the other day." Susan's gaze locked with Brit's. "Some pictures from three years ago that were quite . . . *revealing*."

Panic swelled.

Hands grabbing. Laughter. Cold water. Biting back tears until her heart bled.

Bernard slammed his hand against the doorframe, a sharp *crack* the made everyone in the room jump, except for Susan and Devon. "Shut your goddamned mouth—"

"I'll do it," Brit interrupted, forcing her gaze from Bernard and meeting Susan's frosty indigo depths. "But once the press is on the Gold's side, I'm done. We'll break up, and everything will go back to normal." She was quiet for a beat. "And I won't fuck him."

She could do this, could manipulate and save in equal terms. But only if she didn't feel, only if she could convince herself that Stefan wouldn't get hurt. She'd keep things innocent and light, protect them both.

Otherwise . . . it would be too difficult to bear the person she'd become by agreeing to such an act in the first place.

"The relationship will be in name only," she told the plethora of blank faces surrounding the large conference table. "And you'll take the 'at will' clause out of Bernard's contract, plus provide health insurance for him and his wife for the remainder of their lives."

Susan hesitated only the barest of a second. "Fine."

"I want my lawyer to look at and approve Bernard's contract before I do anything."

"Fine," Susan repeated. "But you breathe a word of this to Barie, and the deal's off the table. Your contract as well as Bernard's will both be void. Stefan is too moral for his own good and—"

Brit interrupted with a wave of her hand, having had enough of the other woman. "I agree. Send me the contract, and let's get this over with."

"Stop." Fingers gripped her arm tight, halting Brit when she would have swept from the room.

Her stomach sank. What more could the woman possibly want? Wasn't it already bad enough?

Susan's words were a hiss. "Don't think you're dictating anything else. I've abided by your terms because they're easy to allow and you're going to give me what I want. But if you sabotage this opportunity in any way, understand that those pictures will be splashed over every market within the hour." A squeeze of those bony fingers. "I know what they're worth. Right now, you and Barie are a bigger cash cow. Don't make me changed my mind. Understood?"

"You—"

Another squeeze. "I asked if you understood. Is that too much for your puck-addled brain to comprehend?"

She saw red but . . . Bernard, his sick wife, and her throat tightened, *the pictures*. Brit needed to keep a calm head and remember why she'd agreed to this.

"I understand," she said from between clenched teeth.

"Good," Susan said. "Now run along and give the press a good show."

Anger raged inside her as she left the room. This wasn't Hollywood. There wasn't a freaking casting couch to sleep her way across.

Which apparently didn't matter because, regardless of how violently her body and mind protested, she was still going along with it.

What kind of person did that make her?

Her eyes slid shut on one slow, controlled exhale.

A person who didn't want to examine herself too closely, that was what.

She slid past Bernard—whose expression was one of utter shock—then went into the locker room to gear up.

It was time to play some goddamned hockey.

NINETEEN

Stefan

STEFAN KNEW something was wrong the moment Brit stepped onto the ice.

Her fury was a tangible thing, a heavy fog that spread across the rink, inundated the team with tension.

Practice was typically a noisy affair with pucks colliding against the boards, ringing off the glass, curse words and ribbing mixed liberally amongst the sounds of good ole hockey.

Today, twenty-four skaters went quiet. Even Julian Beausoleil, the starting goalie who was usually completely oblivious to any and all social cues, stopped fussing with his crease and stared at Brit.

Crunch. Scrape. Crunch. Scrape.

Brit rasped her skates across the front of the net she'd claimed, scuffing the ice so that when she dropped into butterfly—the best position for a goalie to make a save when the puck was on the ice— and scrambled from post to post, she wouldn't slide too far out of the crease.

Max skated up to Stefan and murmured quietly in his ear. "Is this about the news story?"

"No." Stefan sighed. "Well, partly, I guess. I'm assuming management pulled her in too. They tore into me, and I imagine they weren't any nicer to her." He shrugged. "I told them nothing happened, but you know how they get when it comes to the media."

Max raised a brow. "That didn't exactly look like nothing. I mean, come on, man. She's one of us now. You need to leave her be."

Stefan fixed his friend with a look, hostility boiling his blood at the implication, even as his brain mercilessly reminded him that Max was right. He *was* attracted to Brit in a very inappropriate way.

But that was the physical only.

The rest of it—the respect, the confidence in her abilities—was acceptable. He was good at compartmentalizing, and he'd shoved her very firmly into the teammate zone of his mind.

Plus, this was nothing more than instant chemistry. Or at least nothing more than insta-*lust,* and lust he could deal with.

No problem.

So he glared at Max and said, "You of all people should know that pictures don't always tell the full truth."

It was a low blow. Max had felt the brunt of a particularly brutal and untruthful media campaign over the summer. It had cost him everything—his wife, his kid—all because of some falsified pictures and a forged paternity test. The truth had come out. Eventually. But the damage had been done.

They locked eyes for a long moment, Max's past a corporal and uncomfortable presence.

The tension broke when Max grimaced. "You're right. I'm sorry."

Stefan nodded, acknowledging the apology even while trying to communicate his own. He shouldn't have brought it up . . . but then again, he shouldn't have done a lot of things.

"There's nothing between us," he told Max. "She had her headphones in, I startled her, we got tangled up and fell."

"Gotcha." A pause. "You both okay?"

"Besides the bruise on my ass the size of a fucking elephant?"

Max laughed but went abruptly silent when Brit's gaze whipped toward them. "Fuck. She's scary."

"Naw. She's just like us."

"What do you mean?"

Stefan grasped onto the sudden bit of clarity with two fists. "She's pissed, maybe a little hurt. And she's needs a way to work off some of that frustration."

"How?"

"Dude. She's a *hockey* player."

"Oh."

He waited. Wasn't disappointed. Max could be seriously dense sometimes.

"I don't get it."

"Come on, man! Go take some fucking shots on her. That's how she gets rid of her frustration. *She plays hockey.*"

"Oh." Max glanced at him. "Are you sure?" But his friend's lips were twitching.

"Oh my God," Stefan said. "You're an idiot. Go."

Max grabbed a puck, skated to the top of the circles, and waited for Brit's attention.

When she nodded, he ripped a slap shot that collided with Brit's pads in a resounding *thud*.

More of the guys joined in. More shots. More saves. And the tension in the rink began to dissipate.

Frankie came out and began running the drills about five minutes later. Stefan joined in, skated his ass off. Sweated. Rushed. Shot. Defended.

It was a typical practice.

Except for the fact that Bernard never appeared.

And Brit didn't smile. Not once.

In the small amount of time he'd known Brit, one of his favorite things about her was the giant grin adorning her face every time she stepped on the ice, made a save, or hell, took a sip of water. He'd even seen it in the scouting videos and in her interviews.

Her enjoyment in the game was palpable and inspiring . . . and somehow in the last twelve hours, that joy had disappeared.

WHAT DID an idiotic male say to the fuming female next to him?

Stefan sucked in a breath, reminded himself to man up. "Are you—?"

"No," Brit said. "I'm not okay or fine or on my fucking period. *Okay?*"

His fingers froze on the laces of his skates. Was that a rhetorical question, or did she want an answer?

"Jesus Christ," she muttered, tossing her chest protector to the floor and kneeling to remove her leg pads. "I'm fine."

"I just thought—"

"That's your problem," she snapped. "Thinking."

Well, fuck that. He might respect Brit a whole lot, might think she was hot as hell, and a damn good goalie, but fuck her pushing him around. He wasn't a weak-ass rookie. He was the captain. And more than that, he was a man who wouldn't tolerate someone giving him bullshit.

Didn't matter if the mouth the crap came from was male or female.

Carefully, *oh so carefully*, so he didn't step on her fingers, didn't slice through any of that gorgeous porcelain skin with the sharp blades still strapped to his feet, Stefan knelt beside her.

He brushed her fingers aside, said, "Let me get that."

Then he pretended to help her untangle a particularly bad knot on the lace holding her pad to the underside of one skate.

"Let's get one thing straight," he told her, gripping her ankle tight, his tone mild, but his words no less fierce. "I will not be pushed. I will not be snapped at. I'm the captain of this team—"

She shoved his hand away. "Get the hell away from me. You don't know shit, Barie."

He caught her wrist when she would have shoved him again. "I know enough." A squeeze. A warning. "I know more than enough." His tone was laced with steel.

Brit's eyes widened, but she let him reach forward to untie the bottom lace on her pad.

When it was loose, he stood then sank back down onto the bench in front of his cubby. His skates were off seconds later, the rest of his equipment and sweaty clothes following suit.

The locker room had quieted during the exchange with Brit, but Stefan was beyond giving a shit.

He strode naked into the showers.

Living the dream. He was living the fucking dream.

TWENTY

STEFAN HAD a moment of fuck-the-record-breaking-California-drought and stayed in the shower long past the recommended three minutes.

Unfortunately, the lukewarm water did nothing to temper his . . . temper. Frustration rode him hard and mixed with confusion to create a lethal combination.

He wanted to punch something. He wanted to fuck someone.

In one abrupt moment that made the pipes groan in protest, Stefan cranked the water off, wrapped a towel around his waist, and walked back into the locker room.

The lights were partially off, but the space wasn't empty.

Or at least not entirely.

Brit was still at her station, still half-dressed in her gear.

Her face was so forlorn that all the anger twisting him up inside faded.

"What's up?" he asked, kneeling next to her.

She jumped and big brown eyes flashed to his. "Nothing." Fingers pushed her blond hair back from her forehead, but several short wispy pieces didn't cooperate. They slid forward, curled around her temples, her ears. She gave an irritated sigh. "We already went over this."

Hands up, Stefan rose and began getting dressed. "Whatever, Brit. Keep it to yourself or don't. But cut the bitch act. It doesn't suit you."

She sucked in a breath, and he tried not to feel guilty. He really tried.

Dammit. He would not apologize.

Underwear on. Then slacks and his button down. He was bending to put on his shoes when the fucking guilt got to him anyway.

But just as he opened his mouth to apologize, Brit spoke. "I'm sorry."

Stefan shook his head. "No. That was a shitty thing to say. I shouldn't—"

"It's not you," she said and peeled down the black and gold hockey socks she wore. Her legs were bare underneath, and he worked really hard to not notice how sexy they were.

They were muscular, maybe a little hard—not unlike Brit—but her skin held a soft glow to that made him want to press a kiss to her ankle . . . then lick all the way up.

His hands clenched, and he shoved the image away.

Teammate. She was his teammate.

Shit. That wasn't working.

"I've got some stuff going on in my life. Complications, I guess," she said. "Then with the pictures." She shook her head, but met his gaze straight on. "I took it out on you, and I'm sorry."

Those eyes—he suddenly had a craving for milk chocolate—left his and focused on removing the rest of her equipment.

"What's going on?" he asked. "Maybe I can help?"

It was an offer born of the man in him, the piece of him that wanted to fix, to do something to remove the sadness in her.

He had no business making such a proposal, not with his own life in shambles—the team, his mother's illness, the goddamned media—but he found himself unable to take it back.

Her hockey pants and girdle dropped to the floor with a soft *thunk*. She released a breath. "Thanks for the offer, but I'm the one who needs to sort this out."

Somehow, he doubted that was the truth. But he figured he'd pushed her far enough.

For now.

"You want me to turn on the lights or get out of here so you can shower?"

"No, thanks." She shook her head, the gesture casual, except there was something in her tone—too abrupt, too quick to answer—that made his hackles rise.

Questions. This woman filled him with so many damned questions.

"I'll just shower back at the hotel."

He frowned. "You haven't found a place to stay yet?"

She rolled her eyes, turned her back, and stripped off her sports bra.

Creamy skin. Delicate muscles on her back. Stefan's mouth watered. His fingers tingled with the urge to touch, to stroke. To kiss the giant bruise that still marred her skin and make it all better.

He almost groaned. He was so fucking screwed.

Gripping his thighs hard enough to cut off circulation north of the border, he forced himself to appreciate the workmanship of the large Gold logo on the far side of the room.

"No," Brit said, her tone just acerbic enough to make him grin. "I haven't found a place to stay here. I've been in San Francisco for less than two weeks. Between training camp and practices, I've been too tired to look." She paused. "Plus, I don't know that I'll still be here in a month. Makes no sense to look until I'm sure."

Stefan's position on the team had been so safe over the last few years that he'd forgotten what it was like to be a rookie . . . or at least a rookie on an NHL team.

First was the call up. Then the hurdles of training camp and preseason games. Brit had showed well at the first, but that didn't necessarily mean her place on the team was cemented. The preseason games would be her next biggest obstacle.

He'd assumed management bringing her in meant her spot was locked, but now he realized that had been ridiculous. *Everyone* had to earn a place on the first go-around. Hell, if he hadn't had excellent seasons the last few years, he would have been just as stressed about earning his own position.

But Stefan didn't give voice to any of that. "I know a good real estate agent for when you officially make the team."

A moment passed where neither of them said anything, and Stefan wondered if he'd overstepped his bounds.

"Thanks."

There was something strained in Brit's tone, so he flicked his eyes over, was surprised to find her in the same position, back to him and topless.

Except, her hands were wrapped behind her back in an impersonation of a pretzel as they scrabbled up toward her shoulders.

"You okay?"

"No." She sighed and dropped her arms then leaned forward to rest her head against the wall.

"What is it?" he asked.

"Mm shmpf," she said, her voice muffled and completely indecipherable.

"Was that English?"

Her head tipped back, and she stared up at the ceiling. Half the recessed lights were off, bathing the usually stark white and black room in soft golden light. It gilded her skin, and the beauty of it took his breath away.

"I said I'm stuck."

"Stuck?"

Brit was standing, free and clear, a few feet away from her locker. A little shriek of frustration escaped her. "Oh my God. This seriously isn't happening." She turned, arms crossed over her breasts.

He tried to not notice the way the action pressed them together, the way his mouth watered with the urge to bury his face there.

"I'm stuck," she said. "I'm sweaty, and my shoulder hurts, and this fucking bra is all twisted, and I'm stuck!"

Her chin wobbled, and for one awful second, Stefan thought she was going to cry.

Then her eyes slid closed, and she sucked in a breath. "Can you help me?"

"Um—"

"Never mind," she snapped and turned again.

Reaching up—for the first time, he noticed the strip of black fabric twisted over her neck and shoulders—to grab at the back of her bra. But though her fingers could touch the bunched-up band, they couldn't get enough purchase to untangle it.

His brain finally began working again. "Here." He closed the distance between them, tried to ignore the way she smelled—floral, like roses, with a slight tinge of salt from the exertion of practice—as he slipped his fingers under the edge of her bra and pulled down.

It came. Partway.

The sides were still twisted, and he couldn't stop himself from running his fingers around to the front, under her arms, unwinding the bra and brushing the sides of her breasts in the process.

She sucked in a breath. So did he.

Forward. His fingers moved forward, tugging the bra down.

Stefan's chest pressed close to her back, and he looked over her shoulder as he carefully worked the Lycra over her breasts.

He totally looked. He shouldn't have.

But, damn, was he glad he'd done so.

He tugged the soft black material down, covering the rosy tips, even though all he wanted was to see how well her breasts fit in his palms.

Instead, he forced his hands to slide down her ribs. They came to a stop on her waist, unable to completely break the contact.

Especially when she sighed, and her head tilted, exposing her neck. It was screaming for a kiss, a lick, a *nip*.

He leaned down, inhaled the soft scent of her, and she shuddered. His groin went impossibly hard.

"Thanks," she murmured, her posture tensing just the slightest bit. Brit didn't pull away, but she wasn't fully in the moment any longer.

Stefan stepped back, dropped his hands. "Anytime." His voice sounded like he'd spent some quality time with a flamethrower. He swallowed, tried to clear away the desire.

Lush lips quirked. Chocolate eyes twinkled. "Somehow I knew you were going to say that." She was laughing at him, and he found he didn't give a damn. He'd take the brunt of any humor if it meant she smiled at him like that.

"Yeah?" His amusement surged to match hers.

She shrugged. "It's the Y chromosome."

Laughter burst out of him, and he slipped on his suit jacket. "Are we that easy to read?"

Brit pulled on her t-shirt and sweats. "Yup." Sneakers in hand, she sank onto the bench and stepped into them. "What's with the monkey suit? Bernard only requires them on game days, I thought."

"That's true. Just got used to wearing them, I guess."

"Suits you. No pun intended." She stood. "See you tomorrow."

Her footsteps were quiet, her stride determined, as she crossed the industrial carpeting—except Stefan was watching her so intently that he saw her slight hesitation at the door.

"Barie?" She turned.

"Yeah?"

"Thanks"—she waved a hand at her breasts—"for this. And . . . I'll get my shit together by tomorrow."

He nodded, but when she would have walked out, he hurried to close the distance between them and put a staying hand on her arm. "There's nothing to get together. You're doing fine."

Brit seemed as though she would protest. Then she shook her head and forced a smile. "Thanks."

He released her. "See you later."

"Bye." The word was chipper, but it didn't hide the undertone in her expression. Brit didn't think she was doing fine at all.

Both the man and the captain in him were aligned for the first time in recent history.

He wouldn't let Brit self-destruct.

No matter what it took.

TWENTY-ONE

Brit

FINE.

Brit was doing fine.

She snorted. Yeah, sure. Ordered to all-but-screw the captain of her team in front of the entire populace of the United States and Canada, and she was fine.

Son of a puckhole.

With a sigh, she picked up the pace until she was practically sprinting through the city streets. Security had offered her a ride from the arena back to the hotel, and she'd taken it . . . for a couple of blocks.

Until her frustration had boiled over, and she'd had them pull over so she could run the rest of the way.

Thankfully, there were no news vans, no shouting reporters or smartphones pointed in her direction.

Brit could run.

Though, she couldn't quite escape the fact that she and her

teenage-boy-esque-hormonal body weren't going to be able to keep their distance from Stefan.

She wanted him. Which she could have endured, if not for—

"Stupid," she muttered with sigh.

The problem—or *problems*, rather—were her brain and her heart. Those traitorous organs liked Stefan's wit, appreciated his concern and sensitivity.

Unfortunately, management had taken her chance away of actually pursuing something with him along natural channels. They'd ruined the might-have-been.

Which sucked. But she had to put on her big girl skates and deal.

She'd agreed. That was that. She would wait for the contract to be approved by her lawyer, and then she would jump headfirst into a relationship with Stefan. Get the shots and coverage and get the hell out.

There wouldn't be anything real. There was no potential for a future.

Hell, they were teammates, a future wasn't realistic anyway.

The trick was keeping Stefan interested for more than a date or two. Although, she only had to frame it to the public as though they were dating, so perhaps that would help.

Despite all of the plans bouncing around her skull, Brit still had the notion that she was in way over her head.

She thought of how Stefan had behaved in the locker room. He'd been sweet, understanding . . . at least until she'd pissed him off.

Then he'd been fierce and hot as hell.

If management hadn't ordered her to pursue him, if he wasn't her teammate, Brit thought that Stefan might be the man to help her put all of her anxieties aside. He might be a man she could just be *herself* with.

Which didn't exactly help the *in over her head* feeling.

Warm, calloused fingers on her back, her breasts . . . the spice of masculine aftershave teasing her nose . . . a muscled chest right against her spine—

The door came out of nowhere.

Well, not *nowhere,* since Brit had noticed the SUV parked on the sidewalk. She just hadn't expected the door to slam open six inches from her nose.

She jumped out of the way.

Nice to see her reflexes were intact, in spite of the crap swirling around in her head.

"Oh! I'm so sorry!" The voice was feminine and apologetic but didn't quite ring true. "I didn't see you there. Wait! You're Brit Plantain!" The woman—dressed in a skin-tight red suit—turned her head. "OMG, honey! It's Brit Plantain!"

Forcing a smile while trying not to step back, Brit nodded. "Hi," she said. "Nice to meet you."

"I'm Jessica," she said and stepped even closer, encroaching uncomfortably into Brit's space. "I almost hit you with my door! What if I'd injured you?" Heavily lined eyes narrowed. "Do you really think it's safe to be running by yourself after all the money the Gold spent on your contract?"

If Brit's smile had been forced two seconds before, now it was tortured. And *all* the money? Since when was the league minimum a lot? By the time her agent took her cut, it wasn't much more than the dot-commers populating this part of the city made.

"I'm fine, thank you," she said. "But it's been a long day. I'm going to—"

Brit started to move off, and the woman stopped her, long talons —okay, long red varnished *nails*—gripping her arm.

"Wait! Could you sign something for my niece?" She fumbled in her jacket pocket and produced a notepad. "She's only nine and just started playing."

Brit relaxed. Now that she could get behind. Supporting girls in sports, fostering their confidence, improving their discipline, their teamwork?

Hell yeah.

"Sure. What's her name?"

"Umm . . . Sophie."

Again that weird intonation in the woman's voice. But at this point, all Brit wanted to do was get the hell back to her hotel room and soak in the tub. She scrawled a quick note of encouragement then signed her name and handed over the paper.

"Here you go. Nice to meet you, Jessica."

"Likewise!" A toothy grin. "Hope to see you again, Brit!"

The words made the hairs on her nape stand up, especially when she glanced over at the car and noticed the driver's seat was empty.

Who had the woman been talking to?

Shaking herself—she'd probably just been on Bluetooth—Brit forced herself to give another smile before waving and jogging away.

Tomorrow she was driving.

THE NEXT DAY dawned cloudy and cold, but Brit didn't care.

Because it was game day.

She sat in the back of a car—after having to call security for a ride because her hotel was absolutely inundated with press. It had been scary enough running through the gauntlet the previous day, let alone trying to navigate through a mess of news vans and cameras in her little beater.

Nope. This was better. The car had swept up to a side door, and they were zipping right over to the arena.

Her life had gotten really freaking weird.

She wished she could run to the arena because nerves were making her antsy as a mother. Her foot tapped against the grey carpet lining the floor of the black sedan, a rapid *tap-tap* that annoyed the crap out of her. And if it was bothering her, the poor driver had to be—

"Nervous?" he asked, his eyes meeting hers in the mirror. There was amusement in their depths.

"Nope," she lied with a rueful smile.

Josh had also driven her the previous night—at least before she'd jumped ship—and couldn't be older than twenty-two. He seemed nice enough, despite the terrible indie grunge music trickling through the speakers.

"Just ready to be on the ice." That part was true at least.

"There's nothing like it," he agreed.

"You play?" she asked, surprised. He was maybe a buck-forty soaking wet. *She* outweighed him and had a good six inches on his five-feet-nothing frame.

"Yup."

"Grow up on the East Coast?"

Another look in the mirror. More amusement. "Nope. Grew up here, but I like the sport. Started as an adult." He focused on the road. "I suck, and there's *still* nothing better than those first couple of strides on the ice." He paused. "Well, when you manage to stay on your feet, that is."

Brit always forgot that Northern California had such a large contingent of hockey players. In fact, they had some of the largest recreational leagues in the states. It was great for the sport . . . but still weird to think of beach babes and surfer dudes strapping on skates and picking up sticks.

Total misconception, of course. Especially in the Bay Area.

For her, growing up in Maine meant winters outdoors, skating on frozen lakes, white puffs of condensed breaths, and trying to not bust her ass on divots the size of the Grand Canyon.

Winter in California was more like occasional rain and a light jacket.

But there were some things that were true for all players. "I agree."

"Is it true you're getting the start?" he asked. "I heard it on the radio." His eyes flicked to hers then back to the road. "That's big."

It *was* big. Hence the anxious foot tapping. "As far as I know, I'm starting. Julian's knee is bothering him a bit." Which meant this was her shot to show her stuff.

The nerves were eating at her. They always did. Right up until she strapped her pads on.

Then the nerves disappeared, were replaced with calm, laser focus.

"That sucks." The car stopped at a red light, and Josh tossed a grin over his shoulder. "But I just know you're going to stone the Ducks."

She grinned back, felt the first twinges of excitement rather than nausea. "Damn right."

The light turned green, and Josh navigated the sedan through the crowd of journalists at the front gate of the arena. Security waved them on, and a moment later, they were safely ensconced in the lot.

Josh parked as close to the side door of the arena as possible. "Let me get that door."

"I got it," she said, popping the handle. "Thanks for the ride."

He nodded. "I'll meet you right here after the game. And Brit?"

She paused, halfway out of the car.

"Kick some avian ass."

TWENTY-TWO

TWO MINUTES LEFT in the game and the Gold were up three to one.

A two-goal advantage was considered to be the most dangerous lead in hockey. And the Gold were demonstrating perfectly why that was true.

Her team was getting complacent.

Sure it was preseason, but that didn't mean they should be letting up on the boards or giving the Ducks' players so much space as they carried the puck into the zone.

It also meant she was taking more shots than she should have this late in the game when she was already tired, and her team was slow to clear any rebounds.

She sighed, bolstered her strength, and crouched into ready position just as the ref dropped the puck for a face-off in their own zone.

Winning this game was going to have to come from her.

Her center lost the draw, and a Ducks' defenseman shot from up high. Hard.

Brit watched it come, saw the slight deflection off her own player, and had to move quickly. But instinct guided her, and she had made the necessary adjustment before her next heartbeat.

The crowd gasped before cheering loud enough to make her ears ring when she caught the puck in her glove. She held tight until the ref blew his whistle.

Her eyes flashed to the scoreboard.

A minute fifteen left.

The next faceoff was to her right, her strong side. Stefan lined up at the hash marks in front of her—the short red lines at 3 and 9 o'clock on each of the circles—and Max took the space directly on her blocker side.

At the whistle, she raised her glove, and the ref dropped the puck. Brit heard nothing but the beat of her own pulse as the Ducks' center won the draw back to his player for the second time. She was ready for the shot when it came screaming through Stefan's legs.

Except it didn't go straight through.

The puck hit his shin pad, and this time she wasn't prepared for the deflection. The shot went from being six inches off the ice to rising rapidly and screaming toward the far side.

She lunged.

There wouldn't be anything graceful about this save. It was desperation, brute strength. And she might not make it.

Stretching. Reaching out. Then her glove was . . . *there!*

Clenching the puck so hard her hand was cramping, Brit collapsed to the ice in a heap. The stick that made contact with her head then stomach wasn't a surprise—the opposing team had free reign until the whistle was blown.

That was the reason she was closing her glove so tightly.

But that also didn't mean it hadn't hurt.

What *did* surprise her was Stefan's reaction.

"Don't fucking touch her!" he yelled.

A runaway train had nothing on him. He launched himself at the Ducks' player, taking them both to the ice. His gloves and stick went flying, and then his fists were colliding with the opposing player's face.

The refs pulled him off, hauled him to his feet, and shoved him in the direction of the box.

"Four minutes for roughing, Barie," the head referee said before skating toward the scorekeeper and reporting the necessary information. The normal penalty length had been doubled because Stefan had drawn blood on the Duck with the punches he'd landed.

Brit's frustration was a boiling, writhing mass under her skin. Why had he done that?

The contact had been normal, easily discouraged by Stefan giving the other guy a shove or warning tap with his stick.

What he'd done instead had crossed the line from being protective of his goalie to bat-shit crazy.

And now she had a minute to kill, one player down, with a team that was lethargic at best.

Mike Stewart blew her a kiss as he skated by to take up position in Stefan's former spot. "Don't screw up now," he said with a smirk.

So that was how it was going to be.

Down not one, but two players.

The ref blew his whistle. Brit took note of the angle of the players, got herself set in her net.

She raised her glove, shored up her spine.

The puck dropped.

BRIT CAME out of the showers to find a package on her bench. There was a Post-it on the outside.

AS REQUESTED. Impressive results so far. Keep it up.
—Susan

. . .

SHE UNFOLDED the brad and opened the flap on the manila envelope. Inside was the revised contract for Bernard.

"Yeah. Not until my lawyer looks at it," she muttered under her breath as she shoved it in her messenger bag.

"You showered," Barie said from his spot next to her.

Brit stifled a sigh, still pissed he'd lost his cool during the game and still wholly unable to understand what the hell he'd been thinking.

That frustration loosened her lips. "Strength in numbers."

Stefan got very quiet, so much so that she heard the rustle of his pants against the wooden bench of his locker space.

He was going to ask her to explain and, damn, she had to come up with something innocuous, an excuse that had nothing to do with years-old scars about an assault she should really be over.

Her eyes locked on the Gold logo in the center of the room. The miner—pick ax over one shoulder—looked almost demonic as it clutched a large gold nugget in his palm.

Someone really should do something about that. Make it look less creepy.

"Sorry about losing my cool."

"What?" Her mouth dropped open.

That was pretty much the last thing she would have expected Stefan to say. Apologizing didn't come naturally for men in general, and definitely not in this sport.

She glanced over, saw his face appeared genuinely contrite.

"I'm pissed at you," she told him.

"You should be." His gaze connected with hers. "I took it too far."

Five words, and her anger drained. "Don't let it happen again."

Stefan nodded before his expression darkened. "But I won't apologize for protecting you in the crease. It's my job."

She felt her brows pull together. "I can handle my—"

"*It's my job,*" he repeated, and her face went hot. She opened her mouth to snap back, but he went on, "Look, I get it. This isn't some alpha bullshit—"

She snorted.

"It isn't," he insisted. "Okay fine. Maybe it was. But it won't be anymore. I went a little nuts, but I won't take it too far again."

Tucking her towel tighter around her, she fixed him with a look. "You do realize they're going to poke at me more now to try and get a reaction from you."

He grimaced. "I know. But"—his lips twitched—"what you did to Stewart with ten seconds left will have anyone second guessing that course."

A shrug. "He was in my way."

"Stewart was being an asshole."

"True."

He'd hung in front of the goal, blocking her view, not going after the puck even when it was clearly his to take. At one point he'd fumbled *accidentally,* and Brit had needed to scramble forward and launch herself on top of the puck.

It was in that scramble she had committed an *accident* of her own.

Seeing a six-foot-six, two-hundred-and-twenty pound piece of shit flying ass-over-teakettle into the net had been pretty amusing.

Plus, she'd managed to hold onto the lead, so Stewart and his shenanigans could suck it.

"So . . . are we cool?"

Brit rolled her eyes. "We're cool." They were going to be a lot more than cool if this contract checked out, at least according to media.

"Just keep it on the level next time, 'kay?" she said.

"Noted."

She finished dressing, packed up her gear, and left, the manila envelope burning a hole in her bag.

TWENTY-THREE

Stefan

STEFAN WALKED into the arena the next day, feeling as though the weight of the world was resting on his shoulders.

Between his mom and her treatment and the media camped on his doorstep, the cheap shot on Brit had been bad timing. A coincidence that had pushed him past his breaking point. But Stefan had meant it when he'd told Brit he wouldn't go crazy again. He was a professional, and that meant keeping it locked up.

No matter that the press was insinuating they were in a relationship—pictures of them having beers had surfaced . . . without the inclusion of Max and Blane, of course.

No matter that his mom was exhausted from the chemo, had another week to go, and still wouldn't let him call any of her friends.

He understood his mother's health was her secret to keep. But it was eating at him, being so helpless. He wanted to have someone with her. A nurse, her friends. *Someone.*

But she'd refused, and unless he wanted to go against her wishes, his hands were tied.

Hence the frustration and going off on Dimitri Petrokov the night before. The Ducks' forward had left with a swollen lip and black eye, but no hard feelings, especially after Stefan had taken him out for a beer.

They'd played together before Stefan had been traded to the Gold.

"You're going to have to let her handle it herself," Petrokov had said as they shared that pitcher.

Stefan knew Dimitri had been talking about Brit—and his former teammate was right—but it also applied to the situation with his mother.

The trouble was, he didn't want either of the women to have to handle things on her own.

Which made him a total chauvinistic asshole.

He found he didn't care.

Crease versus cancer—remarkably different and yet similar all the same.

At least Brit's position gave him an outlet. He could punch someone . . . so long as he didn't take it too far and jeopardize the game.

Like he'd done the previous night.

Like a fucking rookie. *Jesus.*

He walked down the hallway leading to the locker room, its walls bare-white with black trim and bright fluorescent lighting shining down from the ceiling.

Stefan had come in early, just like every other morning. It didn't matter that by the time he'd finished his post-game cool-down routine —thirty minutes on the bike, stretching, then the beer with Petrokov, it had been almost one.

Now it was barely eight, and the arena was empty.

But Stefan got antsy when he wasn't here, didn't do his normal routine. Especially since they had another game tonight.

Brit wouldn't be starting this one. Not because of her performance. She'd played like a champ, had held the team together when they looked flat.

But because Julian was still the starting goalie. He had maybe one more year of professional hockey in him, and he wouldn't give it up.

Stefan didn't blame him.

Hockey was all he'd known, and to not have it was unthinkable. And yet . . . a human body could only endure so much. Julian had a history of injuries—to his shoulder, his knee, his groin. It made this season precarious, but it also meant that Brit might get more of a chance to play at the Gold than she would have gotten on another team.

She'd made a very smart career decision coming here.

As he neared the locker room, he heard voices. Bernard's office light was on, the door cracked open.

He would have walked by . . . if he hadn't heard his name.

"I'll talk to Barie," Bernard said. "Make sure he doesn't do it again."

"He won't." Brit's voice made Stefan's feet skitter to a stop.

"What makes you so sure?"

She chuckled. "Because he apologized to me in the locker room. And it was a genuine one."

"Bet it sounded like he'd swallowed glass."

Stefan smiled—it was true, after all—but he did believe in owning up to his mistakes. He started to move past the office.

"My lawyer is going to look at this." There was a *crinkle* of paper, and Stefan's feet stalled again.

"Brit, I told you," Bernard said, "you don't need—"

"I *do* need to do this . . ."

Do what?

A few seconds later, Bernard's rumbling voice drifted into the hall. "I still don't feel right about it."

"It doesn't matter if you do or not. This is what management wants, and . . . your wife—" Her voice went firm. "It's important."

Tense silence filled the office, slid into the hall.

"Plus, Susan sent a note last night," Brit said. "Said she was happy with my progress with Barie."

Stefan's heart gave a jerk. Her *progress?*

"It's bullshit." Bernard sounded both fierce and contrite. Stefan had never heard that particular combination from his coach before. Tough as nails? Yes. But remorseful? No. Definitely not.

"Look," Brit said. "They've got your balls in a vice. My metaphorical ones as well. We just need to ride this out. Let me handle Stefan."

Handle? Fuck that.

"I—" Bernard began.

The sound of a chair scraping against concrete echoed into the hall. "I need to get on the ice."

"Brit."

"Yeah?" Her voice was very close to the open door, but Stefan didn't move. He didn't care if she knew he'd overheard. He was going to find out what the hell was going on. How it involved him and management and *handling* things.

"You played good last night."

Stefan wondered if Bernard heard Brit's soft inhale, or if she was too far away. He'd have bet his right arm that her eyes had gone wide, her expression surprised for one long moment.

Outright compliments didn't come often from professional coaches.

"Thanks," she said, a little hesitant.

He imagined her dutifully wiping the expression away, nodding, and walking out.

Which was exactly what she did.

Straight into his chest.

TWENTY-FOUR

STEFAN GRABBED Brit's arm to steady her then quickly stepped back, remembering how she'd reacted to his being in her space on the arena stairs.

Though she hadn't seemed to mind when he'd helped her with her bra, which he really shouldn't be thinking about—not if he wanted to discover what was going on with her and management and Bernard.

A phone rang, Bernard's "Hello?" as he picked up clearly audible.

"Keeping secrets?" Stefan asked, rough—*too rough*—but the best he could manage, considering the frustration coursing through him. "Or maybe you're going to *handle* me some more?"

"I—uh—"

Her eyes flicked to the slightly ajar door, Bernard's voice pouring out the opening.

"What?" Stefan snapped. "Afraid he'll hear?" Anger won out, and his voice rose. "What kind of game are you playing?"

"Shh."

"I—"

She slapped a palm over his mouth and grabbed his arm before tugging him away from Bernard's office. "Just wait a second."

Stefan let her pull him down the hall, both because he didn't want Bernard interrupting and . . . also because he had the sinking sensation it would be nearly impossible for him to deny this woman anything.

He ignored his inner voice telling him to man up.

Brit opened the first door they reached—which happened to be the temporary locker room management had wanted to stash her in—and flicked on the lights.

It was still nearly empty, just the single locker space taking up a third of one wall, and a trail of black skate mats placed on the concrete floor leading from the bench to the hall.

"It's not like you think," she said once they were inside, and Stefan had closed the door.

His rage was a potent thing. He crowded into her, forgetting his promise to give her space, to not exacerbate the fear she'd shown in the arena.

Stefan liked to think that if she had freaked, he would have backed up, but truthfully he *wasn't* sure. His draw to her, as both teammate *and* woman was already strong.

Add in a touch of secrets?

He fucking *hated* when people kept things from him, and hearing her discuss him like he was a problem child with Bernard . . .

Well, something inside him had snapped.

Rationality was toast and so he crowded her.

Brit didn't back down. In fact, something hot and dark flashed across her eyes that made his nerves alight.

"I think you're playing with me," he said.

"I'm not."

Another step toward her. Inches separated their chests, the clean scent of her inundated his senses.

"Then what?"

Brit must have recognized something in his tone—probably how the far fuck-gone he was—because now she stepped away from him.

He didn't care. He closed the distance, reveled in her sharp inhalation.

"What is it?" he demanded.

One more step backward. Stefan let her retreat, knew she had nowhere to go. The wall was just inches behind her.

"Tell me."

The order did something to Brit, shored up her spine, made sparks fill her eyes. Her chin lifted. "Don't pull that captain bullshit with me. This doesn't involve the team."

"Like hell it doesn't," he snapped. "It involves me and Bernard. The Gold is firmly entrenched in this."

"Fuck off."

"Fuck *this*." He stepped close, backed her against the wall until his chest was against hers, until the softness of her breasts pressed against him. He lowered his head, felt her breath against his lips. "Tell me."

Stefan searched her eyes. No fear there. Only heat . . . and regret.

She shook her head. "I can't."

"*Tell me*." His hands dropped to her shoulders.

"No."

The anger boiled over. He released her, turned away, and slammed his fist against the wall.

Sheetrock gave way with a small puff of white powder, but he barely felt the sting of the impact.

"Why is every single goddamned woman out to fuck with my head?" he asked, slamming his fist into the wall a second time.

Twin fist-sized holes stared back at him, accusing.

Stefan hadn't punched an inanimate object—Ducks' forwards aside—since his teenager days, and no other action could have made him feel more like an idiot.

Rationality intruded like a bucket of ice-cold water. He was out of control.

Again.

Shame swept through him as he pushed away from the wall and brushed off his hands.

"Whatever." His voice shook, but instead of anger, it was with disgust. "Keep your goddamn secrets."

Stefan pushed out the door, and went straight down the hall to his locker. It took thirty seconds to change and hit the stationary bike. Stairs would have been better, but he didn't want to risk running into Brit.

It was an unfounded worry because she kept her distance. But it was only after the game that evening—a game he'd fucking dominated—that he realized everyone else had kept their distance too.

For once, that didn't feel like a bad thing.

Numbness had inundated him.

And honestly? It was a relief to finally not feel *anything*.

TWENTY-FIVE

Brit

BRIT HAD SERIOUSLY SCREWED UP.

She should have just invented an excuse. But when Stefan had gone all caveman, demanding answers and getting in her space, she couldn't help it. She'd dug her feet in and pushed back.

Still, that wasn't what had stopped her from telling him the truth, threats from management aside.

No. There was another reason. A deeper one.

Shame.

The elevator opened with a *ding*, and Brit sighed as she stepped into the subdued quiet of the hall. The blue paisley print of the carpet was familiar now, a little slice of home until she established her own.

Which she really needed to get on. Especially if she was going to do this relationship-thing with Stefan. They would need some place more private than a hotel surrounded by paparazzi.

The sharp, all-encompassing shame reared its ugly head again, threatened to burn a hole her throat.

It would have been so easy to confide in him, to come up with a plan. Except, Stefan wasn't the type of man to take something like that lying down . . . not like she had.

How could Brit look him in the eye and acknowledge that she hadn't possessed the strength to act differently?

Ostensibly, she'd made a stand for Bernard.

But Bernard's sick wife hadn't been the only reason she'd capitulated.

Brit wanted to play in the NHL. It was what she'd dreamed of even as a five-year-old strapping on the pads for the first time.

Apparently, she would sell her morals to do so.

"Jesus," she muttered. "Stop bitching and suck it up, Plantain."

"Talking to yourself again?"

The voice made her jump, and her fear was a palpable force, freezing her veins, raising goosebumps on her arms.

It wasn't in Brit's nature to shriek, and she didn't this time. But it was a close thing. At least until her ears and brain took a moment and actually processed the voice.

"Dan!"

She closed the distance between them in a leap, launched herself into her brother's arms.

"Missed you," he murmured, holding her tight.

"Me too."

So, *so* much.

Dan released her, and she bent to retrieve her bag from where it had fallen to the floor.

"Nice digs." He nodded to the wood-paneled walls and lush carpeting that filled the hotel. "A little nicer than where I've been staying."

"Well, it isn't a motel, that's for sure."

He grinned, trailed her to her door. "That would be a step up."

"Afghanistan again?"

Dan shook his head. "You know I can't tell you that."

And *that* was what worry for someone other than herself felt like.

She was dealing with a fake relationship because she wanted to play hockey, and her brother was protecting the country.

Nothing like putting things in perspective.

"You okay?" he asked as she tapped the plastic key card against the reader.

His hand on her shoulder made her stiffen for a moment before she made herself relax. "Just peachy."

It was just her brother, for God's sake.

The familiar scent of Dan's cologne—spicy and masculine and . . . *home*—wafted up over her shoulder. "How'd you find out where I'm staying?"

"I'm your older brother," he said and she felt rather than saw him roll his eyes. "It's pretty much my job to know your business." A pause. "Plus, I tracked your phone."

Brit snorted. "Illegal *much*? What would your boss say?"

"She'd probably tell me to keep a closer eye on you." He laughed. "You know Allison worries."

"True." Allison was Blane's mom and also happened to be a bigwig at the FBI. Dan was one of her agents.

But it was true. For some reason, she worried about Brit.

It still boggled Brit's mind that Allison and Sean—Blane's dad—had been willing to take her in, to make such a big commitment so that a girl they barely knew could play on their son's team.

Of course, Brit's *own* parents hadn't hesitated to agree when she had approached them about moving a state away.

But Allison and Sean hadn't hesitated either. They'd welcomed Brit into their home, committed to getting her to practices and games, feeding and clothing her, making sure she did her schoolwork.

Not to mention that bringing a teenaged girl into a household filled with four boys between the ages of nine and seventeen couldn't have been easy. But they'd done it. And more.

For the three years she'd lived with them, they'd made sure Brit never lost touch with Dan, allowing him to stay when he managed to come up for a game. They'd encouraged, cheered her on, even when she'd spent half a season warming the bench.

More than that, Allison had become a surrogate mother, had stitched together the gaping wound within Brit that had been the result of her parents' indifference.

It would probably never permanently heal, but Allison had helped stop the pain from shading every happy memory with sadness.

A hand waved in front of her face before a saliva-wet finger poked at her ear. "Earth to Brit."

"Ugh. Seriously!"

She shoved Dan's chest hard, had the satisfaction of making him fall back a step. All the drama with management was making her maudlin.

No. *She* was making it that way, with her moping around and growling at everyone. With that thought, Brit shook herself and made a mental note to give Allison and Sean a call. Talking with them always made her feel better.

She had tap the key again before turning the handle and pushing the door open to her room. Dan followed her in. "You this charming with your dates?"

He grinned. "Always."

"Yeah, sure. 'Cuz stalking is sexy."

"Hey"—he turned and threw the deadbolt—"it's sexy when *I* do it."

"Sure." She snorted before going serious. "How's work treating you? Have you been safe?"

"You know me," Dan said. "I'm always safe."

"Except when you're not."

Dan had been shot last year, and any comfort or casualness Brit might have felt for his job had disappeared.

"Hey, come on now," he said. "I was never in any real danger." He took a couple of steps, closed the distance between them, and wrapped her in his arms.

"Yeah, except for the fact that if the bullet had been six inches to the right, you would have been dead."

His face pulled into a masculine grimace, but he didn't deny her statement. "You can't worry about me. I'm always prepared, always careful."

"But—"

He waved her off. "We've had this conversation before, sis."

Brit had a choice. Get into another argument with Dan over something she was particularly sensitive to because of their past—one that wouldn't change a damn thing, no matter how much she nagged —or she could enjoy the fact that her brother was in town for the next little while and shut her mouth.

Which was so. Freaking. Hard.

Dan raised a brow, probably at the screwed-up expression she could feel dragging her lips into a pout.

Dammit. All right. She gave. The breath she blew out was a long hiss. "Okay."

His eyes sparkled. "Just okay?"

"That's all you're getting, so shut it." Her glare should have eviscerated him. Instead, he laughed.

Brothers. For real.

She walked across the room and turned on the bedside lamp then pulled the curtains closed.

Dan sank back on one of the two queen beds, not bothering to take off his shoes. "You wound me."

"Shut up." Bending, she scooped up the room service binder and tossed it on his chest. "I'm too tired to go out. Call and order us some food."

"Bossy."

"You know it."

TWENTY-SIX

BY THE TIME room service knocked on the door, Dan had Pay-per-viewed some terrible action flick, and she'd glanced over the contract for Bernard.

It looked right, but until her lawyer gave her the okay, Brit wasn't going any further with Stefan.

She flipped the contract closed and stuffed it into the manila envelope when Dan didn't move from the bed. "Don't get up or anything."

Her brother just grabbed the remote and turned up the television, until the sound of machine gunfire and shattering glass filled the room.

"I'm so eating your burger," she muttered.

It would totally be worth ruining her in-season diet of rice, greens, and chicken, just to see his face.

"I can take you, squirt," he said. "Any day of the week."

Brit rolled her eyes, but she was laughing as she pulled back the deadbolt and opened the door.

Her lips parted, about to say she could take the tray from the staff member.

Except it wasn't a hotel worker.

Stefan was outside the door. He was in sweats and a t-shirt, more casual than she'd ever seen him.

"Hey," he said softly.

The world went quiet. Still. Everything inside of her froze the moment she saw Stefan's blue eyes, smelled his familiar scent.

"Hey," she returned.

Scintillating conversation from the two of them.

But Brit didn't know what to say or why he was there.

All she knew was that he affected her.

Safe and risky at the same time.

Stefan was a man who wouldn't hurt her physically, wouldn't cage her or throw her naked into a shower. But he was also a man who threatened to unfreeze her heart, to implant a bunch of barbed strands in the organ then grip tight the fibers.

The cool distance, her normal eminent focus was impossible to hold on to when he was nearby.

And if the contract currently sitting on her desk checked out, that pull wasn't going to get any easier to deny.

Ding.

They turned as one at the sound of the elevator arriving, its doors sliding open with a *whoosh*.

Room service.

The worker was a young Hispanic man who'd delivered to Brit before. Mario wore his standard, a black polo and khakis, but this time his typically wide smile disappeared, and he stuttered to a stop in front of them. "I-is everything okay?"

Brit didn't blame him for faltering. Stefan's presence alone filled the entire space with tense expectation.

The tray rattled, and Stefan reached out to snag it. "Here. I've got it."

Mario glanced at Brit, curiosity in his gaze. "It's fine," she said and put out her hand for the receipt to sign.

She scrawled her name then placed her usual cash tip into Mario's outstretched hand. "Thanks."

They watched in silence as Mario stepped back onto the elevator. When Stefan turned to face her, his hands held the tray rock steady, and the penetrating gaze he gave her threatened to turn her knees to jelly.

She wanted to close the distance between them, to feel the stubble adorning his cheeks on her palm, her temple, her inner thigh—

No.

Brit locked her knees. He was hot, no doubt. Even a little sweet. But she was tough. She was the first woman to play in a professional NHL preseason game, could out-squat half her teammates . . . and that was saying something.

So no, she couldn't allow her legs to turn to jelly. She couldn't soften toward Stefan, especially not with the truth of what she had to do.

Their interactions needed to be fake, distant, a facsimile of reality.

Because, otherwise, her heart was going to be shattered.

"What?" It was a defensive question. "I live in a hotel," she said. "It's not like I can get my Betty Crocker on."

He laughed. "We need to get you out more."

"Good luck with that." The voice wasn't hers.

Dan had come up behind her without her noticing. She jumped when he whispered in her ear, "Everything okay?"

She nodded.

"Dan," her brother said, reaching past her to offer Stefan his hand.

Stefan glanced at the tray and back at her. His eyes had turned into flecks of ice, the dark black of his pupils standing out in sharp relief against the pale blue of his irises.

She would have chalked it up to jealousy, except Stefan didn't seem like the type to get jealous. Plus, no man had ever bothered to exhibit such an emotion over her before.

It just didn't compute.

So this must be coming from a captain-like place, protecting a teammate, looking after the team's resources. It was the only thing that made sense. Except Stefan was glaring at Dan, and if looks could kill—

Pushing aside that thought, Brit reached out and snagged the tray.

"Dan, this is Stefan, captain of the Gold," she said into the silence that had grown taut in less than a minute. "Stefan. Meet Dan, *my brother*."

Holding the tray steady, she slipped back into the room. Enough of the worry and angst. Enough stressing about circumstances that couldn't be changed.

She was going through with the fake relationship.

But . . . it wasn't going to happen until tomorrow.

Until then, she was going to focus on the things that were easy to solve.

Fatigue. Boredom. Hunger.

The bed was cozy, the movie stupid but entertaining, and the food would be filling and tasty enough.

She ignored the voice in her head that said the hunger for the man outside her door wasn't quite so easy a problem to solve.

TWENTY-SEVEN

Stefan

HER BROTHER.

A ball of tension relaxed in Stefan's gut. It was irrational, but he found he didn't care.

Dan fixed him with a look that screamed he knew what Stefan's visceral reaction had been at seeing another man in Brit's room.

Rage. Liquid-hot rage that had demanded he sink his fist into the bastard's face.

He'd resisted, barely. Mainly because he had no rights to Brit whatsoever.

At least that's what he kept telling himself.

But it was getting increasingly more difficult to ignore the piece of him that wanted to claim her as his.

Damn the team. Damn anything that stood in their way.

His body was so in-tune with Brit's that he heard the rustle of cloth as she moved through the room, the soft *rattle* of the tray, the *click* of an interior door closing.

The sound of running water filled the air.

"You like burgers?" Dan asked. He seemed as though he were studying every minute nuance of Stefan's expression.

"What?" He blinked.

Dan rolled his eyes. "Do. You. Like. Burgers?"

Okaaay . . .

"Yeah." Stefan shrugged. "Sure."

"Good. There's hope for you yet." He turned and walked into the room, hitching his thumb at Stefan to follow him.

Brit's brother grabbed the plastic key card sitting on the desk next to the television, turned, and fixed Stefan with a glare that could have peeled muscle from bone. "I'll be back in an hour. You eat. You talk and take care of the pain in her eyes. But you *don't* fucking touch. Got it?"

Stefan nodded. The water still ran in the bathroom as Dan left.

Brit's room was pretty standard-issue for the Gold. Two queens, a wall-mounted air conditioner, a desk that doubled as a TV stand, and a small armchair shoved into one corner.

He sank onto the edge of the bed but immediately stood again.

"The bed? *Really*, Barie?" he muttered.

The toilet flushed, the water turned off, and anxiety gripped his gut. He hadn't felt this nervous since sneaking into Tracey Rickman's bedroom his senior year of high school.

Tracey's dad had been very demonstrative during his whole boy-dating-his-daughter spiel. He'd even included props—a pair of scissors and a shotgun—and had been happy to describe what he'd do to Stefan if he ever hurt his *"darling little girl."*

Just the memory had him shuddering.

The door to the bathroom opened, and Brit walked out.

"Ready to eat?" she asked. "I'm starv—"

Her words cut off as she spotted him standing in the space between the desk and the bed, his arms akimbo.

"What are you doing in here?" The question wasn't snapped out as he'd expected. Brit had proven over and over how tough she was. But in this, she just seemed curious.

Cautious but curious.

"Your brother invited me in."

Her brows pulled down into a frown, and he found that his fingers itched with the urge to smooth it away.

God, she was pretty.

Stefan liked women—all shapes, sizes, and ethnicities. He'd dated across the spectrum, but he had a particular weakness for the girl-next-door look.

Brit was that personified.

A light dusting of freckles across the bridge of her nose. No makeup, slightly flushed cheeks, and delicately pouty lips that he wanted to taste.

Of course, she'd probably sock him if he tried.

His mouth twitched. Brit scowled. "Is there something funny?"

"No." And because he loved the way she looked when she was a little discombobulated, he said, "I actually came to apologize."

His mom had torn into him when he'd returned home after the game . . .

"The fire in your eyes wasn't the good kind, Stefan," she'd said. *"It's not healthy for you or the team."*

"It's fine, Mom," Stefan had replied. *"And it worked. We won."*

Her scoff had come in the form of a loud snort. *"Your team won because they were lucky and the opposing goalie let in two soft goals."* Then she'd hugged him, as if to soften the blow, and whispered in his ear, *"You play better with a clear head. You know that. Bernard knows that. Fight fire with clarity, honey. With a blast of freezing-cold water that snuffs out the other team. Not with a blaze that will flame out quickly and ratchet up everyone's tension."*

Of course, she'd been right.

Definitely about the way he'd played. His mom had a knack for seeing the game in a way that made it impossible for Stefan to ever discount her opinion completely.

What she didn't know, however, was that her advice could also be applied to how he'd handled the situation with Brit.

"Apologize?" Brit asked, that frown back, his fingers burning with the need to stroke it away.

No. He'd promised Dan he wouldn't touch, and he hadn't come here for that anyway, would never take advantage of Brit in that way.

But—and it was a really fucking-big but—Stefan *wanted* to touch her.

"I shouldn't have pushed you," he said and forced himself to meet her eyes. "You don't have to tell me anything you don't want." His throat got a little tight, and he cleared it. "I didn't have the right to demand anything from you. I'm sorry."

The pause as Brit processed his apology was long and uncomfortable. But just as he was about to say something else—to grovel further —she spoke.

"What if I'd said the secret was something you should really know?"

The question was quiet. Hesitant.

"How could it be?" he asked bluntly. "We hardly know each other. You've been with the team less than a month. What kinds of secrets could you possibly have that involve me?"

Her eyes dropped, and she murmured something he couldn't make out.

Two steps brought him within touching distance, but he resisted the urge. Instead, he bent a little, crouched so that he could meet those brown eyes, and asked again gently, "What secrets?"

Time stretched. The frown disappeared, her expression softened, and he thought for sure she'd tell him.

Then her lids fluttered closed, a breath passed through those kissable lips, and when she looked at him again, all of the softness was gone.

In its place was something different entirely.

Heat. And determination.

He retreated a step.

She closed the distance, walking forward until her breasts were pressed firmly against his chest, until he could smell the delicate floral scent of her.

That fragrance was at odds with her career, with her intensity on the ice, but Stefan was beginning to think it might fit perfectly with the woman underneath.

She went up on tiptoe. Pressed her mouth to his.

And suddenly, thinking was the last damned thing on his mind.

TWENTY-EIGHT

HER LIPS WERE SOFT, her mouth slightly tart. She tasted of desire and just . . . sweet.

So damned sweet.

Heat arrowed straight toward Stefan's groin, sensation exploding across his nerves. Liquid heat flooded his veins.

And Brit . . .

Her name was the sole recurring thought that cycled through his brain—*Brit. Brit. Brit*—until even that thought ceased.

He yanked her close, plastering her to his chest, and pressed them so tightly together that even a knife would have a hard time separating them.

Brit was tall, and he didn't have to bend much to keep kissing her. He stroked his tongue across the opening of her lips, swept inside to taste her more fully.

Her hands tugged at the hair on his nape, hard enough that his mind cleared slightly.

Oh shit. He froze. Had she not wanted this? Was he going too fast? Overwhelming her?

Stefan yanked his head back, dropped his arms.

"Brit. God. I'm so— Oof!"

She'd shoved him. It was so unexpected that he stumbled back and went down . . . onto the bed. Not a second later, she was on top of him, straddling his hips and bending to kiss him again.

His body said, *"Hell yeah."* But there was something in *her* body that began to make warning bells go off in his mind.

A stiffness, maybe. As though she were distancing herself from the moment.

Her hand reached between them and gripped the hard length of his erection.

His eyes rolled into the back of his head. *Holy shit.*

Maybe he was reading too much into this. Because Brit's fingers on him, the rough strokes through the thin cotton of his sweats were heaven. He needed—

Stefan scrambled to hold on to his sanity.

But her fingers stroking him, wrapping around him and pumping . . . it was too damned good.

At least until he got a glimpse of her expression.

His arousal disappeared like so much smoke.

Because Brit's eyes were wet.

No tears had actually escaped—the moisture was contained by her thick blond lashes—but the sentiment was there.

She was hurting.

And he had a fucking hard on.

Had. He'd *had* a hard on.

Stefan gripped Brit's shoulders with gentle hands and set her away from him before sitting up on the bed.

Their breathing was rapid, loud puffs almost in unison.

"Why"—he began, but she went rod stiff, her eyes dropping to the garish red, blue, and gold patterned bedspread, and that quickly, Stefan banked the question. He stood—"don't we eat before the food gets cold?"

She was frozen for a long moment, staring at him with wide eyes until he took the cover off one plate of food—the hamburger—and sat down to eat. "I'm assuming the chicken and rice is yours, but I'm happy to trade."

"My brother—"

"Is giving us time to talk."

Her lips pressed down into a firm line. "I don't want to talk," she said, petulance in every syllable.

Stillness invaded him, followed by confusion and frustration and . . . a shit-ton of anger. He had no clue what was going on with her, what strings she was pulling, only knew that he was ridiculously attracted to her, and that she was a damned good hockey player.

Beyond that, he was lost. Which pissed him off.

"And you wanted *that?*" he asked pointedly, tilting his head toward the bed.

Silence.

It stretched, fraught with tension, until finally, finally she whispered, "I did want it."

"Bullshit."

The word was torn from him, almost violent in the delivery. Brit jumped, but he didn't feel guilty.

Not for pressing this. Not for trying to understand. Not for—

"You had tears in your eyes, and your body was stiff as a board," he said. "You may think me a fool you can manipulate, but I damn-sure know when a woman wants to fuck me. And *that*"—he waved a hand—"wasn't it."

"It's not— I—" Her voice was pained. "My past—"

All at once, he wondered why he'd come at all, why he'd bothered to think she needed an apology.

His behavior might have been atrocious, but hers was worse.

They'd been building something—camaraderie, a friendship . . . the potential for more.

Her secrets had shit on that.

"You know what," he said, plunking the cover back onto the plate. "I'm not hungry after all."

He stood and left.

TWENTY-NINE

Brit

TEARS.

The salty, stinging fuckers had been conspicuously absent from Brit's life for a really, *really* long time.

Yet in the last few hours she'd shed too many of them to count.

About fifteen minutes after Stefan had left—the door closing with a firm finality that made her heart ache like hell—Dan had come back.

He'd taken one look at her face before shoving her over on the bed she'd still been sitting on and pulling her into his arms. They'd watched that stupid action movie from start to finish, her pretending not to cry and him pretending not to notice.

Now it was a quarter past four, and Dan was snoring in the bed next to hers. Their food from the previous evening sat untouched on the desk, and Brit was both not tired and beyond ravenous.

Quietly, she slid from the bed, snagged some clothes, and walked into the bathroom.

She felt vulnerable and fragile and completely deserving of

Stefan's frustration. He'd heard her talking to Bernard, knew she was keeping secrets that involved him.

After slipping on her sweats and tank top, she quietly left the room. Maybe she couldn't run to the arena because of the media coverage of the team, but she damn-sure could tear up a treadmill.

Except the hallway wasn't empty.

"What are you doing here?" she hissed, torn between going right back inside the room and sprinting passed the man sitting on the floor.

Stefan's head jerked from where it had been resting, chin on his chest.

Long fingers thrust through his hair, mussing the dirty blond locks. "Waiting for you," he said.

"Waiting—? You can't *wait* in the hall. Why didn't you just knock?" Her voice was slightly shrill, and she made herself modulate the volume. She might not be sleeping, but the rest of the hotel was. "If the media caught wind of you sitting outside my room, they would . . ."

She trailed off, realized she was about to crap on the pink elephant in the room.

"Is that what this is about, then? The bullshit in the press?"

All she could do was shrug. He had no freaking idea. When she carried through with what management wanted her to do, the local reporters who were following them would turn into many, many more.

"I heard you crying."

Quiet words that threatened to melt her.

Brit couldn't let it happened. She'd committed to do this, to help Bernard, to not give up her own career.

Her sigh was both silent and accompanied by an internal bitch slap.

She'd really made a mess of things.

Yet when had that ever stopped her from doing anything?

She was the first female goalie for an NHL team. She could be friends—*more* —with a hunky defensemen.

And, if nothing else, she could endure.

Of course, the problem wasn't exactly enduring. Stefan made her feel too much. Which—

So what?

He made her feel.

Big effing deal.

It was time to woman up, lock down her heart, and just do it.

Stefan was a playboy anyway. He'd get tired of spending time with her in a month or two—hell, maybe a couple of weeks—and they could go their separate ways.

She ignored the little voice inside her mind that was shouting to consider Stefan's feelings.

What happened if *he* felt too much? What if she broke *his* heart?

Hysterical laughter welled up. Like that would ever happen.

Stefan's heart didn't get involved. Ever. She'd seen the pictures, the parade of women through the media, knew his reputation.

There was no way *she* could hurt *him*.

Holding that thought tight, she blew off his concern, tried to minimize his statement about her crying. "I *am* a girl, you know."

His pause was brief.

A beat later, his eyes locked with hers, and the corners of his lips turned up. Just that easily, the tension between them faded.

"That—the girl thing—I think, is most of our problem."

Brit snorted, extended her hand, and helped him to his feet. "Come on."

He followed her onto the elevator and she pushed the button for the gym. "Hope you're ready to run."

Stefan chuckled. "Is this where I say I'm always ready?"

"Wouldn't have it any other way."

He grinned at her, and she smiled back. The strange fluttering in her chest had nothing to do with him. It was heartburn. Or gas.

Definitely gas.

The doors slid open on a *ding,* and Brit started to step off, eager to escape, to gain that perfect distance between them again, but Stefan stopped her with a hand on her arm.

"Hey," he murmured, and when she glanced up into his eyes, she saw they were serious, the easy affability of the moment before completely dissipated. "I'm sorry I made you cry."

"Yeah," she said. "Me too."

Distance.

Ha. That was a joke.

THIRTY

"I KNOW you're keeping secrets from me," Stefan said all of ten minutes later. He'd popped up in front of her treadmill like a freaking whack-a-mole.

Brit froze and immediately almost ate shit. Jumping with a move that showed her impressive reaction time—thank you very much—she landed with her feet on the plastic sides and glared at Stefan.

"Don't do that," she snapped.

"Don't tell the truth?"

Here they went again. He wasn't going to let this go, and she didn't know how to move forward without giving him *something*.

"Look," she said. "I already told you. There are things about me I can't share. Secrets that aren't mine to tell—" She broke off, jabbed at the stop button, the *whir* of the motor as the belt slowed the only noise in the quiet gym. "I—"

Her eyes flicked up, and her frustration faded.

He looked so earnest standing there, like a little boy trying to coax his puppy into rolling over.

And, *damn her*, she wanted to oblige him. Except she couldn't give in for a stale-as-hell biscuit of affection, for the mere potential of what-ifs and maybes. Not if she wanted to come out of this unscathed.

So she went on the offensive. "Why does it matter to you?" she snapped.

Stefan frowned, stepped back and, sensing victory, Brit pushed just a little more, enough to place a barrier between them that would protect her but, hopefully, not alienate him.

It was her job as a goalie, always looking ahead, always planning the next three steps before the players on the ice had even grasped step one.

"Look," she said again. "Everyone has secrets. I'm no exception."

"I'm not asking you to spill every dirty entry from your diary, for God's sake. I just want to know the secret that involves me."

Part of her wanted to tell him. Part of her thought he *deserved* to know, and it would be so much easier to not carry the guilt and shame and worry. But if she told Stefan, and he went to management, Brit had no doubt that Susan would carry out her threat to void both contracts—hers and Bernard's.

She couldn't let that happen.

But she also didn't think Stefan would let it go unless she gave him *something*.

"Okay fine." She released a loud sigh, called on every one of the skills she'd honed in her many interviews, and lied. "Bernard wanted to bench you for the stunt you pulled against the Ducks."

Stefan's eyes narrowed, but there went the corners of his mouth again, twitching upward and looking all-too-kissable as they did so. "*That's* your secret?"

Of course not, but she was already all in.

"Yup. I told him we'd talked and you had promised not to do it again. Don't make me regret standing up for you." And then she released the big guns. "So tell me what it was like to date Kelsey Lake"—the famous movie star he'd dated and dumped—"Is she as pretty in person as in her movies?"

"Oh." He glared. "You're mean."

"I've been told that a time or two." Brit tilted her head. Her heart was pounding, but amusement had crept onto the edges of her emotions, and it steadied her. There was something about Stefan that just made it so damned fun talking with him. "So are we going to be friends?"

He stared at her and several tense moments passed, each ratcheting the turmoil in her gut, because no matter her previous confidence, Brit thought Stefan still might say *"Screw it"* and be done with the whole damn thing.

Finally, he blew out a sigh. "You're asking a lot," he said. "I don't trust easily—"

God, did she know how that went.

"—but I'm going to trust you in this, and hope your other secrets won't come back to bite me in the ass."

"No ass-biting, promise." He smirked and she grinned. "So can we braid each other's hair now?"

"Only if you paint my nails first."

She stepped up onto the treadmill, turned it on. "Fatal flaw, Barie. You paint your nails *after* you do your hair. Don't want to mess up your mani."

He took the machine next to hers. "I can't believe we're having this conversation."

Her heart lightened. "I'm a wealth of information."

Stefan turned up the speed so it matched hers. "I'm impressed."

"Yup," she said and hit her button so the treadmill went just a little faster than his. She might be pursing this relationship for a whole host of complicated reasons, but Brit still liked to win, couldn't step away from a challenge.

And there was definitely challenge in Stefan's eyes.

He sped up, two clicks more than her speed.

Yeah no. That wouldn't do. Three *beeps* on her own machine.

"I can also do a mean smoky eye," she announced.

He glanced at her, jaw agape. "A *smoky* what— Shit!" He slapped at the stop button and jumped clear of the belt when he almost fell.

Brit started laughing so hard she had to hit her own button and step clear.

"You did that on purpose," he said, glaring at her while she tried to catch her breath.

"I regret nothing."

He huffed out a sigh and sat on the end of the machine. She did the same on her own treadmill, enjoying the sensation of just being next to him, of smelling the spicy scent of him, mixed with the salty tang of sweat.

It was probably a sign of insanity that she thought the scent of his sweat was sexy—because, really, what was she going to do next? Sniff his dirty shirts? But Brit found she didn't give a damn.

"You can't really do a smoky eye, can you?" he asked.

Hell no, she couldn't. Even putting her hair into anything more complicated than a ponytail was impossible. "I'm a woman of many talents."

There was a brief silence before they both started laughing again, even harder than before.

Stefan was a good man. Funny, charming, athletic—a trifecta of temptation wrapped into a muscled package of sex appeal. But the draw was more than that.

She liked being with him. Which was the most dangerous part of the entire situation. Standing, she wiped her hands on her sweats, and climbed back on the treadmill. "Let's finish this workout and get to the arena."

An hour after they'd arrived at the rink, her lawyer called to tell her the contract was sound, and she walked it over to Bernard's office so he could sign.

It took her almost that long to convince him to scrawl his chicken-scratch-of-a-signature on the paper, but the relief in his eyes when she finally convinced him it was okay made the whole situation worth it.

She delivered the contract to Devon and watched as he signed his name beneath Bernard's before making two copies.

By the time she'd delivered Bernard his printout and stashed her own in her backpack, she was feeling very much like a law intern.

But it was done.

She was doing this. There was no option of going back.

Especially not after pictures of her and Stefan sitting on the ends of the treadmills, laughing their heads off and smiling at each other exploded all over the Internet before she'd suited up for the mid-morning skate.

Susan approved apparently, if the indiscreet thumbs-up the older woman had given her in the hall was any indication.

Blane—who was walking next to her—frowned. "What was that?"

Brit shrugged. "That's Susan. One of the board members."

They stepped into the locker room. "I know *that*. What's with the thumbs-up?"

"No clue."

"Brit."

She glanced up.

Blane's expression was worried. "You know I'm here for you, right? If you're ever in over your head? This thing with Stefan—"

Her heart swelled, and she couldn't resist giving him a hug.

Blane froze for a heartbeat before hugging her back.

She wasn't surprised. She'd never been a touchy-feely kid, and after the incident, things had gotten worse.

Brit couldn't remember the last time she'd initiated a hug with someone other than her brother.

"Thanks," she said before covering Blane's hesitation with a laugh. "Things with Stefan are complicated. He's a good guy, but the press"—*and management*—"is insane."

"Hey, at least they won't ask if you're gay anymore."

She rolled her eyes heavenward. "That's a positive, I guess. But only a small one, because now they just want to know every detail of my relationship with Stefan." The press were still pushy, relentless, and unfortunately, a necessary evil.

"And do you?" Blane asked.

Brit pulled back and gave him a blank stare even as her heart jumped. What did he know? "What are you asking?" Her tone was controlled, careful.

"Do you have a relationship with Barie?"

"I—" She sighed, the truth and lies all tangled up. "Maybe." Hell, she didn't know where they stood at that moment.

"You like him."

No point in denying it. "Yup."

Blane was quiet for a beat before his lips tugged up. "Barie and Brit, sitting in a tree. K-I-S-S—"

"I can't believe you!" But she was laughing. He made a kissy noise, and she smacked him. "You know you may be my brother in everything but blood"—she glared —"but don't forget I caught you checking out my ass the last time we were together."

"Yeah, no," he said. "You're *definitely* not my sister." He met her gaze full on. "As you well know."

Idiot. Why had she brought that up? She laughed again, this time awkwardly with a dash of old guilt thrown in. Because she *did* know that. Problem was, her mind might see Blane as a strong, attractive male, but her body said, *"Meh."* That hadn't made things easy on their friendship, and she generally wasn't so callous with Blane's feelings, didn't joke about what couldn't be.

Or at least she hoped so.

She sighed. Social skills. Seriously, she needed to improve hers.

"Hey. It's okay." Blane touched her hand. "I know you don't feel the same. We covered that enough times over my teenage years for me to write you off as a total lost cause."

Her smile was small and tinged with misery. She was a lousy friend and an even worse surrogate sister.

"Brit." He squeezed her hand. "I'm fine. It was a joke. Let it go."

"You mean like how I *punched* your crush out of you?"

"Exactly. So abusive." He gave her sad puppy-dog eyes, but at least they held no genuine hurt. "My nose has never been the same."

She gave a mock shudder. "Let's hope your kissing ability has improved, okay? Because that much tongue—"

"You wound me." His hand went over his heart, as though to protect the precious organ, before his tone took on a serious note. "My kissing ability aside, I count you as my friend and I will kill anyone who hurts you. Okay?"

There her heart went again, expanding like a balloon.

"Okay." She bumped her shoulder with his. "Thanks."

"I'm still going to ogle your ass."

Her laughter was loud, accompanied by a shake of her head. "Wouldn't have it any other way."

THIRTY-ONE

Stefan

STEFAN WATCHED Brit walk into the locker room, Blane at her side. It took everything in him to curb the vicious jealousy tearing at his insides.

He wondered if she'd seen the pictures before quickly dismissing the notion. No, she couldn't have. She looked too happy and relaxed for that.

After the first news story, she'd been violently angry, the cloud of her anger perceptible.

Now he wondered how pissed she was going to be when she *did* see them.

Or if she discovered he actually liked the pictures.

The images of the two of them laughing as though they'd just shared the world's funniest joke had filled him with such a sense of rightness that it had been almost painful.

He'd had to breathe through the longing, the desire to claim her as his own.

Brit had set boundaries, and he'd obey them.

Except, after the scene in her hotel room, he didn't really know what those boundaries were.

Was that a red herring? Some sort of self-destructive tendency to self-harm? She certainly had other hang-ups with personal space.

Though—he watched her hug Blane—apparently not with her former teammate.

Maybe it was more. Perhaps she was simply as attracted to him as he was to her.

Did the reasons really matter? They'd be stupid to act on it anyway.

Blane leaned close to her, his expression serious and a twin of Brit's. It made Stefan's gut clench. He wanted to be the one she turned to.

Where in the hell had that come from?

They could be friends—and maybe they were already tentative ones—but he didn't need to be her lover, her partner—

His lace snapped.

Forcing a breath, he pulled off his skate and yanked out the broken lace. Before he could go in search of a new one, Rich, the equipment manager, had brought a replacement.

"One-twenty and waxed, right?" Rich said, confirming the length and texture preference before setting a new lace in Stefan's hand.

"Yup. Thanks, Richie."

Two minutes later, Stefan's skates were on, and he was pulling on his practice jersey. He was on the black team today, which meant, for some God-awful reason, Bernard had decided to pair him with Stewart.

Clearly, he'd pissed someone off in his last life.

But he was captain, and that meant he needed to get along and work with every person on the ice.

Practice was a lesson in perseverance.

Mainly because Stewart was a pain in the ass.

Only when the coaches weren't directly next to them, of course, only when screwing up the play made someone else look bad. Mainly Stefan.

When one of the coaches was watching, Stewart was a lesson in proper play, but when they rotated to another group . . . Mike pulled shenanigans.

He made Stefan skate to pucks he should have taken, threw passes without looking . . . was uncooperative, lazy, and generally uninspired.

Which mostly made Stefan want to punch him in the face.

He didn't, of course. But the fantasy of his fist colliding with Stewart's nose and blood gushing everywhere was what got Stefan through that interminable practice.

Still, Bernard wasn't an idiot, and whatever had kept the coach off ice the previous week hadn't done so during the last few practices.

He saw more than Stefan gave him credit for.

"That's it for today. Hit the showers," Bernard told the team as they gathered at center ice. "Take the morning off tomorrow, but be here for a pre-game meeting at two."

The guys disbanded, headed for the locker room. "Stewart, Barie, wait."

He and Mike both stopped, Stewart with a teenage-sized sigh, and Stefan with a quiet sort of resignation.

Dread tied his intestines in knots. What—

"Ladders. Twenty. Each side. Go."

Stefan's relief was strong. The skating drill sucked, but it was better than being benched, than losing his captaincy. He skated toward the far side of the ice, ready to get it over with.

"Why?" Mike asked.

Stefan gave an inward groan halfway to the goal line. For fuck's sake, that man could not keep his goddamned mouth closed.

A sharp trill of Bernard's whistle. "Thirty."

"But—"

"Forty."

Finally, Mike shut the hell up and skated over to where Stefan waited.

"Together," Bernard said as he stood over the Gold's logo at center ice. "Go." He blew his whistle.

Stewart burst forward from the goal line in a show of speed that was both unnecessary and excessive. They'd need all of their strength to finish, especially post-practice.

The drill was deceptively simple, just skating and stopping at every line from one side of the ice to the other. But there were a lot of lines.

Blue line. Stop. Red line at center ice. Stop. Far blue line. Stop. Far goal line. Stop.

And they only had to do it forty times . . . per side.

Not to mention, Mike had basically set them up to fail with the pace he'd started.

Still, Stefan wasn't the type to back down from a challenge. It had taken everything in him earlier to cease his pushing Brit for her confidence, and then he'd only succeeded because he figured he'd win her over eventually.

But he wasn't going to yield to Stewart. Not when he trained harder and longer than every other damn person on the team. Not when he could still draw breath and move his legs.

No fucking way.

Sprint. Stop. Sprint. Stop. Rinse. Repeat.

By ten, Stewart was sucking wind.

By twenty, Mike's pace had slowed to a snail's pace.

By thirty, even Stefan's legs were burning. But Mike was in worse shape. He was green, looked ready to blow chunks, and they still had ten more to go.

It was on the second half of thirty-three that Stewart stumbled and fell. He scrambled to get up, only to fall again.

Stefan didn't think, just reacted. Closing the ten feet of distance between him and Stewart, he shoved his shoulder under Stewart's arm and pulled him to his feet.

"Keep moving," he gritted.

"Fuck off," Stewart growled.

"I want to get the hell off this ice. So shut the fuck up and skate."

The last seven were torture—with him all but carrying Stewart—but finally they finished.

Bernard had been passively standing at center ice as they struggled. Now he blew his whistle. "Cool down then hit the showers. I expect you both to be on time tomorrow."

He skated off the ice without a backward glance.

The silence was deafening.

Or it was until Stewart unloaded. "Do you want a fucking medal or something? Always got to be the hero?" he screamed, shoving at Stefan's chest. A feather would have had more impact at Stewart's level of fatigue, but that didn't stop him from unleashing a few more choice words.

Stefan had enough. "Dude," he said and shoved Mike back, not bothering to help the other man up when he hit the ice for the second time. "I couldn't give two shits about you as a person. You're lazy, just barely talented enough, and a first-class asshole. I do what I do for the good of the team. Not you. *Not ever.*"

"Who do you think—"

Stefan cut him off. "Let me guess. You're going to give me some version of 'Who do I think I am?' or 'Do I know who you are?'" He rolled his eyes. "I know *exactly* who you are. You're a self-entitled bastard who has no sense of team. Do what you want. Just stay out of my way."

He turned and skated off the ice.

Brit was standing in the hallway leading back toward the locker room, still in her gear, her face serious.

"Hey," she said when he stopped in front of her.

His hands were clenched inside his gloves, and his blood pressure must have been off the charts, but his voice was calm enough. "Hey."

Brilliant conversationalists, they were.

And great, now he sounded like Yoda.

"Are you all right?" she asked.

He nodded.

"Good." She bent and picked up her helmet from where it sat on a chair then turned to walk down the hall.

Stefan followed her in silence. Until he couldn't.

"Why'd you stay?" he asked.

"Why did you help Stewart?" she countered.

He paused, both mentally and physically. They were next to the wall of pictures, game shots of each of the former captains. Just four of them, since the Gold were a new team.

They'd had a similar wall in Calgary when he'd played with the Flames. But as an older team, the Flames had history, rows and rows of history.

His shot was on *this* wall, a picture of him skating in full black and gold.

It was weird seeing himself there, imagining that his photograph would in the beginning of a long line of captains, that he would be part of the history of the team—

If the Gold didn't fold.

The possibility sat like a rock in his gut.

"I helped him because I had to," he said, not looking away from the pictures.

"Exactly," Brit said. "Which is why you're the best person on this team to be captain and"—her voice faded as she slung her helmet on her head—"why I hope we'll manage to stay friends when this is all over."

Her first statement made his mind spin, her confidence in him intoxicating.

She was already pushing into the locker room before the second half of her sentence hit home.

" . . .*stay friends when this is all over?*"

Letting Brit keep her secrets had just gotten a lot harder.

THIRTY-TWO

STEFAN WALKED into the house to the scent of lasagna and . . . the sound of his mom being sick.

He'd dropped his messenger bag on the floor and was hauling ass before the front door slammed shut behind him.

His mom was in the small bathroom, kneeling on the ground, retching into the toilet.

"Mom—" he began.

She waved him off, shoved the door closed in his face.

Her cough was violent, and he tried the knob. Locked. "Mom—"

"Don't make me send you out of the house for another night. *I'm fine*—" She retched again.

Stefan stood for a minute outside the door, listening to her suffer and wishing for the millionth time since he'd found out about her illness that he could shoulder the burden for her.

Anger, violent and intoxicating, rushed through him. He wanted to destroy something, punch the wall, bust through like a tornado—

Which would help absolutely nothing.

Of course, he might feel a hell of a lot better if the object he was busting through was Mike Stewart's face.

With a muttered curse, he turned, walked to the fridge, and pulled out a bottle of water. The freezer held some damp, cold cloths, so he grabbed one for his mom.

By the time he'd set both on the counter, the toilet flushed, and Diane staggered out, her face blanched and her brow sweaty.

"Sit down," Stefan murmured and grabbed her arm to help her do just that. He pressed the cloth to her forehead and put the bottle of water in front of her just as the timer went off.

"The lasagna—"

"I'll get it," he said.

But as he pulled the pan out of the oven, his mom slapped a hand over her mouth and bolted for the bathroom again.

It was barely a decision. He took the pan and was out the back door before the thought had processed.

Pan and all went into the garbage before he went back inside and opened every window in the vicinity. Next, he cranked the vent over the cooktop to high.

Stefan allowed himself one moment to let the anger rage. Then he tucked it away, saved it for motivation for later.

Cancer was a Class-A asshole.

But that wasn't a new fact, and his mom needed him more.

By the time Diane came out from the bathroom a second time, Stefan had opened a can of chicken noodle soup and was heating it up on the stove.

He moved to help her, wanting to make sure she didn't fall, but she glared at him and shook her head, pulling out the chair, before sitting down in the careful movements of someone who felt like shit.

God, she is ridiculously pale.

It took every bit of discipline at his disposal to stay at the stovetop and stir the fucking soup. When it was warm, he poured it into a mug —his mom preferred to sip it rather than use a spoon—and got some saltines out of the pantry.

"So," he said as he brought both over to her, "well done on the whole christening the porcelain-goddess thing."

His mom almost dropped the mug she'd brought to her lips. "Stefan, that so isn't funny."

He'd been intending to force a smile, to push the joke forward, to inject some fucking levity into the situation. But his mom's reaction was so typical, so *mom-like* that he didn't have to force anything.

Lips twitching, he said, "It's pretty funny."

"Stefan Benjamin Barie. Me puking my guts out is *not* funny." But her lips were curving too. Blue eyes so similar to his own narrowed even as amusement clouded their depths.

She sighed, crossed her arms. The smile grew.

"Okay. Fine. It's a little funny. *But . . .* know that next time you're sick or throwing up because you're hungover, I'm laughing in your face."

He laughed. "I thought you were the parent. Aren't you supposed to be all saint-like?"

Her snort was loud. "If you think that about me, then I've failed as a mother."

Happiness filled him, buoyed his mood. His mother had always had enough personality for three people. She was spicy, high-spirited . . . and every other damn adjective he could think of for firecracker.

Cancer had drained that away. To see her like this—even for a moment—gave him hope that things might actually be okay.

"Ha," he said. "As if you could believe that with a son like me."

"A son with an ego the size of a planet?"

"A son who is—" He faltered for a moment. Normally he would have said something about being a successful captain for an NHL team or the leading defensemen. But after that practice he wasn't feeling all that successful at anything hockey-related. *Shit.* Now she was looking at him, and he blurted the first thing he could think of. "—going to sit down with you and watch *Dancing with the Stars.*"

The strangled gasp of air that followed came from his mouth, not his mother's. Had he really just locked himself into watching a crappy show? Into several hours of hell interspersed with interrogations during the commercial breaks?

On the smooth meter, it was about a minus five.

His mom gave a little laugh before picking up her soup. "That expression. Since when have I ever pushed you to talk?" When Stefan snorted, she shook her head. "Okay, when in the *last couple of years* have I pushed you?"

He snorted again. Really, sometimes she was delusional.

"Oh my God. Seriously, kid. You're pissing me off." She fixed him with a glare "I. *Don't*. Push. Now eat some lasagna. I'll give you couple of hours before I start pestering."

He sighed, and any dredges of hope that throwing her favorite show at her would knock her off the scent disappeared.

His mother was nothing if not a lesson in perseverance.

He wouldn't have it any other way.

"I love you, Mom."

"I love you too. But don't think that's going to get you out of *Dancing with the Stars*."

For fuck's sake.

And he still had to tell her—

"About the lasagna . . ."

STEFAN'S MOM had snapped at him about wasting the cooking she'd slaved over, made even worse because he'd thrown away her favorite pan.

Then as abruptly as she'd yelled, she'd stopped, pressed a kiss to his cheek, and murmured, "You're a good boy, Stefan. The best a mother could ask for."

Such a small thing, those words, the affection. His mom was hard to predict sometimes, tough and strong as nails. But he'd never once doubted that she loved him.

Always, she'd been free with her affection, unwavering in her support.

It was because of *her* he'd gotten so far.

Even when things hadn't worked out with his father, when she'd been abandoned and newly pregnant, when his dad copped out on child support, his mom had been there.

Early morning practices. Long drives to tournaments. Skimping money for new equipment—

"I like you with Brit."

"What? How—" He broke off because, really, those pictures had been *everywhere*, and his mother was all over any news story involving him.

He should pay her instead of his publicist.

"She seems like a nice girl."

"She is."

His mom gave him a penetrating look. "Baggage?"

Stefan shrugged, but because his mom would understand, he told her what had happened.

"She's skittish around men. Freaked when I came up behind her. That's why we . . . in the pictures . . ."

Why they had ended up in Classic Bedroom Position #1.

"Do you think she's been sexually harassed?" his mom asked then added, after a pause that said way more than the words, "Or maybe more?"

He started to say no.

How could Brit have possibly been hurt? She was tough, strong, and vibrant. Could kick ass with the best of them.

That couldn't be ignored.

But it also couldn't be ignored that she was still smaller than every member of the team, that if she was taken by surprise—from behind—or outnumbered . . .

Something could have happened.

He could imagine how *easily* it might have happened.

"I—"

Good God. A memory swept over him. He'd cornered her in the locker room, pushed into her space, trapped her against the wall.

It was scary to think how easy it would have been for him—*for anyone*—to take advantage.

But there hadn't been fear in Brit's eyes. Not that time. When he'd pressed his body to hers, her russet irises had been on fire, had scorched him with fury and desire.

She wasn't scared of him. That much he was sure.

Still, she'd all but admitted to having a multitude of secrets and if his mom's inkling about the nature of Brit's secret was correct, if she'd been hurt or violated, she would need to the chance to tell him on her own terms.

It wasn't something she should be ashamed of—not that feelings often followed logic and reason.

Shit. He didn't like this—

"Okay, seriously, how is he still here?" his mom said, pulling Stefan from his thoughts and pointing to the celebrity chef that was fumbling his way through a terrible rendition of a tango. "He's the worst."

"He *is* pretty bad," Stefan agreed. And the costume—glittery and with more fake feathers than a peacock—was horrendous.

"Ba-ad?" Her question was punctuated by a yawn. "He's absolutely terrible."

"Here." Stefan tucked a blanket around her shoulders then winced as he stretched his aching legs in front of him. All he wanted to do was lie down. "How long is this show anyway?"

He'd spent a full hour cooling down after the practice from hell. Thirty minutes on the stationary bike, followed by stretching, and then hitting the PT suite for some targeted massage. Not that any of that had helped.

His quads were on fire, and the burn would only be worse in the morning.

"Two"—his mom yawned again—"hours."

There was no way he'd make it. After staying up the previous night with Brit and now the sleep-inducing, so-called entertainment of the show . . . well, he'd be lucky to make it through another dance.

Turned out he didn't have to.

His mom was snoring even before the chef got his scores.

He waited a few minutes, made sure the DVR was recording, then gently lifted her in his arms and carried her to her bedroom.

As Stefan tucked his mom in, he couldn't help but remember all of the times he'd woken up in his bed after falling asleep on the couch, couldn't help but wonder how many times she must have done the same thing when he'd been little enough to carry.

It made his heart ache.

Because the fragility in her expression, her innocence as she slept, raised a wave of fierce protectiveness in him, stronger than he ever thought possible.

He would do *anything* to protect her.

Even fish her favorite pan out of the trashcan.

THIRTY-THREE

Brit

GAME DAY.

Two words that incited excitement and anxiety in most hockey players. There was always the odd athlete who managed to stay calm, or worse, who was good enough to play professionally but hated the sport itself.

That wasn't Brit.

Even if she wasn't starting in tonight's game, she would be on the bench with the rest of the team, ready to step in at a moment's notice.

There was absolutely nothing like being in an arena filled with screaming fans, listening to chants encouraging the team, chased soundly by the slightly tipsy segment of the crowd yelling that opposing players sucked.

It was familiar. It was an epi pen to her heart without the assistance of drugs.

"Ready?" Frankie stood next Richie, who had opened the door of the car for her. They appeared to just have arrived at the arena, their coats still on and bags slung over one shoulder.

"Heck yeah." She thanked Josh for driving her and stepped out. "Is the extra security necessary?" She pointed to the fenced lot, the gate now patrolled by a half-dozen guards. And that wasn't counting Richie and two others closer to the entrance. "There are hardly any journalists out today."

Despite Stefan's night at the hotel and the resultant pictures of them on their respective treadmills, most of the media had moved on to far more exciting things—a scandal in the governor's office and a celebrity having her baby.

Susan would be disappointed, not that Brit cared.

She was doing this her way, one that wouldn't sacrifice herself or Stefan or the team.

And regardless of the idiotic attempt in the hotel room, she wasn't ready to go further with Stefan. If things happened between them, it wouldn't be driven by the fake relationship.

It needed to be pushed by real feelings.

The assault hadn't broken her, exactly. Brit had even had sex since then.

Okay, not much. But enough that she knew she wasn't going to turn back into a virgin.

But it was different with Stefan. The other times had been filled with distance, and that was okay. That was what she'd needed. Release without emotion.

They'd felt good. She'd had orgasms, had gone home with a sense of satisfaction.

Yet, she'd frozen in that bed because Stefan *was* different. She couldn't keep a part of herself back, couldn't frost over the threads of emotion—of respect, caring, *affection.*

Stefan had felt it, had demanded more.

And she'd wanted to give it.

Her body didn't want distance, not when he was melting every last one of her defenses.

" . . .journalists," Frankie said, and Brit blinked, trying to remember what she'd asked before her mind had gone straight down its favorite daydream.

Stefan.

And his glorious mouth. And hands. And abs.

And—*shit*—arms and . . .

"Management seemed to think they would be back in force," Richie said and hurried to open the door to the arena. "More security isn't bad. The reporters were ravenous just a few days ago. They want everyone to be safe."

The equipment manager smiled at her, and her heart melted a little bit. He was so sweet.

"Thank you, Richie," she told him, sincerity in her tone. "Thanks for keeping us safe."

His cheeks creased even as they went a little pink. "It's nothing," he said. "Just my job, after all."

"Still." She squeezed his hand as she passed through the door. "Thank you."

So management thought that the press might return. Because of the game? It was against one of their biggest rivals, the Sharks. But that wasn't unusual. They would play the other local team eight times that season. It—

Her heart sank.

Management wasn't guessing the press would be back because of a tough game.

Nope. It was a message.

They wanted something to happen. Something that would guarantee press coverage.

And the envelope in her locker—filled with only a single paper that read, *MORE*—confirmed her instincts.

Funny how the truth of what she was doing hadn't really hit home till then.

Funny how she felt more violated by those four letters, by something that was really only her own fault—for agreeing in the first place—than she'd felt at any point in her life.

The crinkle of paper was only vaguely satisfying as she balled the note and chucked it in the trash.

This crap could wait.

She had to push her feelings aside and focus on getting ready for the game.

Her team needed her.

———

TURNED OUT, that wasn't exactly true.

Julian had the net, and the team won easily. Brit cheered them on, wincing whenever the guys took a bad hit—because seriously, even though they were big, tough hockey players, getting checked still hurt—and shouting encouragements as they battled it out on the boards.

She'd lost her head for a second when Blane and Stefan collaborated for a gorgeous 2-on-1 goal, screaming like a banshee when it went in.

By the time the final buzzer sounded, her throat was slightly sore, and she was hopped-up on adrenaline.

Such was the life of the backup goalie. So often the bridesmaid and rarely the bride.

Though with Beausoleil in potentially his last season, more ice time should be coming her way soon.

She hoped.

Because seeing her team out there and not playing was almost unbearable.

Patience, Brit reminded herself. *Keep working hard, and it will come.*

She followed the team back into the locker room, waited through the post-game interviews, gave a couple of sound bites when the media asked her opinion.

By the time she'd finished, most of the guys were gone or were in the shower. Frankie caught her eye from across the room, and she nodded. Far as she was concerned, their post-game ritual should continue.

When they played on home ice, whether she was in net or not, they worked through a couple of buckets of pucks.

She needed to improve her blocker side, and Frankie had a knack for placing shots.

He crossed over to her. "Same thing?"

Brit nodded. "It's not good enough yet."

Frankie grinned. "It's getting pretty damn close, though."

"Then we'll have to make it harder."

He clapped her on the shoulder. "Like the attitude, Brit."

She did too. It was easy with Frankie. He had an inbred optimism and positivity that made her want to work harder than she'd ever done before.

It wasn't like she'd been a slacker on her previous teams, but having Franklin Todd at her back gave her confidence.

Plus, it was nice to not have a coach yell after every play, to actually hear some positive—*gasp!*—things, instead of everything she did wrong.

"Let's do this," she said and led the way back to the ice. It was freshly cut, all the maintenance done, a pristine sheet of white and red and blue. "Sure Ken doesn't mind if we mess up his ice?"

"Not at all. He always does a cut"—referring to the Zamboni clearing off the excess snow and laying down a thin layer of water to fill in the divots and scratches in the ice—"first thing in the morning."

Brit skated to the goal that had been set up for her, scuffing up the crease in her usual manner, as Frankie pulled on his skates and grabbed the bright orange bucket.

He poured the pucks onto the ice—at least fifty of them—and used his stick to spread them haphazardly around.

"Ready?" he asked once he was done and took up a position just inside the blue line.

She tapped the ice with her stick, gave a nod.

Crack! came the first shot. It was low and to the outside, and it was a scramble to cover the angle, especially when she'd expected a high-glove side. But at this point, it was almost cheating if she knew where the shot was going.

She wouldn't know in a game, after all.

No one was going to tell her where they shot, and though she could study up on a shooter's preferences, there were simply too many players, and they were too good at shooting *anywhere* for her to keep track.

She dropped to her knees, pushed hard, and slid to the far side of the net. The puck hit her pads, rebounded wide.

Brit didn't worry about exactly where. Instead, she was scrambling to her skates.

Because Frankie had moved and was already lining up the next shot.

It continued like that for a long while, Frankie occasionally calling out a pointer or adjustment before peppering her with more shots.

By the time he finished shooting—she'd lost count after sixty-two —her legs were shaking, and her hip flexors were on fire.

At least the bruise on her shoulder finally felt better, its only reminder an occasional twinge.

She'd just stretched her arm out, testing the joint when she caught a flash of movement.

They weren't alone.

The slight blast of fear was as normal as it was annoying. A breath slid out from between her clenched teeth, and she forced herself to calm.

Calm.

She wasn't alone. Frankie was there. And no one was coming up behind her.

Plus, even if they were, Brit needed to get the hell over that particular trigger. Three years was long enough.

Only once her heart had settled from a sprint into a jog did she allow her gaze to swivel.

Bernard, Blane, and Stefan were sitting on their bench. Apparently deep in conversation, though their eyes were on Frankie and Brit.

"You're there," Frankie said, skating over. As she stretched, he went over a few more points. They were small tweaks, but she knew they'd make a huge difference.

"Thanks for staying," she said. "I know it makes for a late night."

"Not at all, Brit. Anytime."

"I'll help you with the pucks—"

"I've got it."

Bernard's voice surprised Brit. She hadn't realized he'd put on skates. They looked ridiculous with his slacks, button-down, and tie. He'd shed his suit jacket, at least, but the beat-up boots with shiny silver blades were still incongruous with his professional attire.

"I can—"

"I've got a few things to talk with Frankie about," Bernard said before a twinkle entered his eyes, "and I'm fully capable of picking up some pucks." A twitch of his lips. "I may have done it a time or two."

"But—"

He gave her an even look, one that was determined and intense and very . . . well, coach-like. At least the amusement in his eyes hadn't faded. He made a shooing motion. "Go."

It was an order, and Brit had too many seasons of coaching under her belt to not obey.

"All right." She hesitated. "Thanks."

"Go on," Frankie said. "It looks like the boys are waiting for you."

Brit glanced over, saw he was right.

"But don't forget to stretch properly. You don't want to tighten up."

She nodded then skated over to the bench and stepped up to

Blane and Stefan. They had been in a pretty intense discussion, one that stopped when she approached.

Blane had that look, the big brother, protective stare, but Brit couldn't find it in her to be annoyed.

Yes, she already had a brother, but it was nice for another person to have her back.

"Did Dan make it in okay?" she asked Blane as their awkward trio walked down the hall to the locker room. Her brother had attended the game, but Brit wasn't sure he'd be able to find his way to the family waiting area, even though she'd given him the proper clearance. The tunnels were decidedly maze-like, even for an FBI agent.

She probably shouldn't have kept him waiting by practicing with Frankie, but Dan had never given her crap for following her dreams and wouldn't hold it against her now.

He nodded. "Yup. He's waiting in the PT suite."

Brit frowned. That was weird. But then she remembered Mandy and knew the petite brunette was very much Dan's type.

That's to say . . . she's a woman. Who's single.

"Seriously?"

Blane nodded. "I'll see if I can peel Dan out of there and meet you in the locker room."

"Thanks." She turned to Stefan. "We're going to dinner. Want to come along?"

It was an invitation she would have made to anyone. Brit was inclusive by nature, knew what it was like to be on the outside, and didn't like feeling as though she'd left anyone out.

But with the tangle of emotions in her mind, with the task management had given her—the job she'd *agreed* to—knotting with the things she *wanted* to do . . . well, it felt wrong.

Stop whining. Stop seeing an ulterior motive in everything.

Except, she *did* have an ulterior motive.

Brit sighed inwardly. This was the way things were. She either followed through—

Or she didn't.

But she couldn't keep beating herself up for it.

Maybe she could get her and Stefan out of this unscathed. If she played things carefully, maybe they could remain friends.

Because she felt too much to casually dismiss Stefan.

How could she risk hurting him?

THIRTY-FOUR

HIS HAND on her cheek startled her.

Brit glanced up, saw Stefan was very close, blue eyes staring down at her full of concern, his suit-clad body only inches from hers. The rich spice of his aftershave filled the air, and they were near enough that Brit could see the scars on his face—a thin slash above his brow, a small, jagged dash across his chin.

"What is it?" he asked, brushing his fingers down her cheek again. *God,* how she wanted to lean into the touch, to lose herself in the feel of the slightly calloused roughness against her skin.

The truth.

It would be so damned easy to tell him the truth. To lay it out there and let the chips fall where they may.

"Have you ever been in the middle of doing something that you're already regretting but you can't stop?" she blurted.

He stiffened and leaned back slightly. The distance wasn't much, given the narrow hallway they were in, but it still hurt. Especially when those blue eyes went a little cold. Stefan stared at her, studying her as though he could see right through every protective layer she'd ever erected.

She looked away. "So dinner? Yes?"

There was a long moment of quiet, then Stefan tugged her pony-tail. Cautiously, she flicked her gaze back to his and saw the chill in his expression had been replaced by something Brit really hoped was understanding.

"Yes," he said. "And also"—quieter now—"yes, I have."

She smiled broadly, and the happiness she felt at the small acceptance in his eyes made her tongue loose. "Good. I like spending time with you." She mentally groaned but couldn't stop more words from coming. "You're funny and sweet and a good hockey player—"

Shut. Up.

Good God, her social skills needed an overhaul. As in a little more smooth and a little less verbal diarrhea.

Girls didn't just tell guys they *liked* them. Not so explicitly, anyway.

For fuck's sake, she was terrible at this. At life in general.

"I like spending time with you too," he murmured.

Oh.

Funny how one sentence from Stefan, and things were all right.

"Are we going to do this, Brit?" He took a step toward her. There was less than a foot between them, and good Lord, how she wanted there to be none.

"D-do what?" For a second she thought he knew about her plan with management and the media. Then she got a good glance at his eyes.

They were molten, burning as he watched her.

Her breath caught. Because—*holy shit*—never, *ever* had a man looked at her in such a way.

Not when she'd been fully dolled up. And especially not when she was sweaty and wearing hockey gear, the slight funk of wet equipment permeating the space between them.

"Explore this thing between us." He leaned in, pressed a kiss to the corner of her mouth.

"Th-thing?"

Lips on her jaw. Her throat.

"This attraction. The chemistry threatening to ignite the room." Teeth on her neck, a sharp bite soothed by a smooth flick of his tongue.

Her sucked-in breath was loud . . . and shaky.

"I don't think we should." The words were out before she'd had time to calculate how it would affect her plan, the feel of his lips—soft and hot and wet—against her skin better than a truth serum.

Stefan pulled back slightly, one side of his mouth quirked in humor. "No?"

This was her chance to tell him everything.

She shook her head. To herself. To him. Not yet. She couldn't tell him yet.

After he knew the truth he might not look at her in the same way, full of laughter and heat and temptation.

"No." Brit couldn't. She needed more time, had to shore up more barriers against Stefan's charm. The allure was too much. It led to too much vulnerability and too damn much of her heart being involved.

He smiled fully then, a flash of bright, white teeth against pale pink lips. "Why not?"

"What about the honor clause in our contracts?" she asked, mind scrambling even as she felt her head tilting on its own volition, as if merely exposing the skin of her neck would draw his mouth back to the spot.

It worked. He kissed just beneath her jaw before stretching to whisper in her ear, "That only extends to dating Gold employees. Not players."

"One could make the case that we *are* employees," she said, humor crawling into her, sweeping aside the anxiety. He was just so . . . Stefan.

He unlocked something inside of her, made it so damned easy to be with him. Comfortable. Warm. Okay—blazing hot and filled with so much desire that she was almost desperate for his mouth on hers.

"One would be wrong," he murmured.

God, she wanted him.

He kissed her then, his fingers sliding into her sweaty ponytail, lacing through the locks without revulsion or hesitation. A little sweat didn't bother Stefan, and it made Brit like him even more.

No other man she'd dated had wanted to be near her post-game. She'd had to shower first, slap on something girlie to hide the scent of her exertion before they'd go out.

It wasn't like she wanted to walk around smelling gross and stinky. She considered herself a decent human being, and with that came well-rounded hygiene skills.

But Brit had always wished the man she was with would want— no, *need*—every part of her, whether or not it was pretty or polished or smelled like freaking petunias.

Stefan being that kind of man wasn't surprising.

He was good, sweet and charming, and—

All thoughts fled as he deepened the kiss.

His fingers trailed down her back, moved forward to brush the sides of her breasts, and a firm stroke of his tongue across her lips had her opening her mouth, completely forgetting they were in a public place where anyone might see.

She couldn't think, couldn't do more than process the electrifying sensations that Stefan invoked.

"I don't know why— Ugh! *Come on!*" Dan's voice was disgusted and loud enough to snap her out of the haze of desire.

Her eyes flew open on a gasp. She started to pull back, but Stefan caught her head and pressed one more soft kiss to her lips.

"I think that went better than our last kiss," he said with a wink before dropping his hand and turning to face her brother.

Blane stood behind Dan, arms crossed, eyes narrowed at Stefan.

"Go shower, if you want," Stefan murmured. "I'll take care of Dumb and Dumber."

Her brothers—because, really, Blane was as good as one—glared fiercely, but she'd seen Stefan on the ice, knew he could take care of himself.

"Thanks." In her skates and with Stefan in shoes, she didn't have to stretch to kiss his cheek.

Leaving the men to tend to themselves, Brit pushed into the locker room and found it crowded with equipment staff and a few players. There were enough people to make her feel comfortable, so she hit the showers and dressed.

For the first time since management had thrown down the gauntlet, Brit felt confident in scooping it up.

She could do this.

Perhaps even make something real of this thing between her and Stefan.

THIRTY-FIVE

Stefan

"I DON'T REMEMBER GIVING you permission to touch her," Dan said the moment his sister was out of earshot.

Stefan resisted the urge to roll his eyes even as he did his best to hold on to the post-kiss glow. Brit was fucking incredible and her mouth—

"It's not yours to give," he told Dan, shifting discretely to hide any evidence of how much he'd enjoyed the kiss.

"I'm her brother."

"And Brit is her own woman," he countered.

Blane stepped forward then, going shoulder to shoulder with Brit's brother and forming a barrier of angry men between him and the exit.

"What are you doing?" Blane asked. "Don't you think that she's going to have a hard enough time without fucking a member of the team? How do you think that will make her look in the media?" He thrust a hand through his short brown hair. "It's already bad enough with the pictures."

"It's not like that," Stefan began.

"Then what *is* it like?" Sharp words from Dan this time. "From what I've seen, you don't stick around. After our parents, *our dad—*" He shook his head. "Brit doesn't need another flakey asshole in her life."

The implication that he was taking advantage of Brit stung, mostly because it was a thought he'd had more than a few times. But he couldn't seem to stay away from her.

He didn't *want* to.

"You don't know anything about me. This thing with Brit, it's more. It's—" God. How could he even begin to categorize what was happening between them? Yes, it was new and intense and he really liked her.

But it was also way more than just a desire to get in her pants.

And still . . . they had hardly even begun.

Stefan blew out a breath. "I don't want to hurt her."

"You've hurt her already," Dan said. "She spent half the night crying after you left her room."

Fuck. He'd known that, of course, had heard how upset she'd been through the hotel room door and guilt sat heavily on his heart.

"You're a fucking asshole," Blane spat.

Yes. Yes, he was. But it was also—

"All we did was talk." Or close enough because he definitely wasn't going to tell Blane and Dan about the kiss or the way Brit had sprawled on top of him, pressing every sweet curve and lithe muscle against him.

Stefan shook his head, shoved the image to the side.

"I needed to know—" He broke off, not wanting to divulge what little he knew of Brit's secrets. "She was upset about something else, and tap dancing around the draw between us was only making things worse," he said, ignoring the glowering expressions on the men's faces. "I can't guarantee Brit and I are going to end up with a white picket fence and two-point-four kids, but I do know she's the first woman to ever make me want that."

Blane snorted. "It'd be better if you just left her alone."

"Be real. I've seen the way you stare at her," Stefan snapped. "If Brit had chosen *you*"—he glared at Blane, the idea of Brit in the other man's arms, of kissing the tall, good-looking forward made Stefan angry on a bone-deep level—"you wouldn't turn her away. You'd grasp the chance and hold on until your fucking fingers fell off. Don't piss on me because I feel the same damn way."

"I—"

Dan put his hand on Blane's shoulder and squeezed, cutting off the other man's words.

They stared at each other, a standoff in which none of them were willing to budge.

Stefan had decided to go for it with Brit, regardless of the secrets and complications, and he just didn't have it in him to kowtow to anyone. Brother or old friend aside.

Brit was different. He wanted her, would do whatever it took to keep her.

"It goes without saying," Dan began before pausing and shaking his head. "Fuck it, I'm going to say it anyway."

He stepped into Stefan's space, crowding him, not stopping until they were nose to nose. "You've hurt her once already, so there goes your free pass. Know that if you do *anything* to hurt her again—or to hurt her chances of playing in this league—I will break every bone in your body and then dump your ass in a military prison so secret you will never, *ever* see the light of day again."

Stefan felt the blood drain out of his face but didn't look away.

He was sincere in his intentions, didn't want to cause Brit pain. He liked her—probably way too much, given the circumstances.

"Noted. I won't hurt her. And"—he hesitated, wanting to choose his words carefully—"if there is any sign that my presence would do something to jeopardize what she's worked for, I will walk away, immediately and without a fight."

Stefan would. He knew that in the very fiber of his being. It would be hard as hell, considering how strongly he felt for her in just the short time they'd been dancing around each other. If and when he felt more, it would be agonizing.

But it would be a hell of a lot worse if *he* were the reason she didn't achieve her goals.

That was completely unacceptable.

Dan stuck out his hand, and they shook. The cool approval in the other man's eyes made Stefan relax slightly, until he turned to Blane, whose expression could have sliced clear down to the bone.

Well, tough. He was just going to have to deal.

Stefan stuck his hand out. "We cool?"

Blane was silent for so long that Stefan didn't know if he was thinking of punching him in the face or considering putting the tension between them aside.

Probably punching.

"We're cool," Blane finally said and took Stefan's hand, "as long as you stick to your word."

Stefan fixed the other man with a look. "When have I ever not stuck to my word?"

A grudging nod. "Fine."

Brit breezed out of the locker room just then, her hair wet and slicked back into a ponytail. She wore a fitted blazer and slacks with a white button-down, her messenger bag over one shoulder.

He crossed over to her, took the bag, and slung it over his own shoulder. "You stretch?"

"Yup." She nodded. "I'll do some more after dinner. But for now, I'm too hungry to do anything else. Let's get some food."

He glanced at Dan, who was watching them with silent, assessing eyes, waiting for him to step out of line, probably, then Blane, whose expression had softened when Brit came out. When he saw Stefan looking, it turned to granite.

This was going to be a blast.

"Come on," Stefan told them. "I know just the place."

THIRTY-SIX

AFTER STEFAN STEPPED out to make a quick call to check on his mom, he joined the others, and they took Blane's SUV to the restaurant. It was south of San Francisco, a small hole-in-the-wall burger joint in the town of Belmont.

The decorations were the weirdest, campiest around. Blood-red velvet curtains ran floor to ceiling, and the light ranged from dim to sketchy.

Headshots of celebrities, politicians, athletes, and gangsters flitted across the flat screen mounted on one wall in an odd slideshow of young and old, popular and infamous.

Thirty people at most could fit inside, but this was closing time and the chef had never failed to make room for him.

Tonight was no exception.

They crammed themselves into a booth in the corner, three athletes, plus Brit's brother, imitating sardines in a can.

Maybe the booth would have been fine for normal people, but he, Blane, Brit, and Dan weren't normal.

Well, Dan was, he supposed. But Brit's brother was still huge, an inch taller than even Blane and broader across the shoulders and chest. And at six-four and two-hundred-twenty pounds, Blane was no slouch himself.

Stefan was slightly more *petite*, as the boys liked to tease him—only six-one and two-hundred-and-five pounds.

Brit was—

Hell. He didn't know. A couple inches shorter than he was. Maybe about the size of Blue Robertson, the Gold's rookie this season. So probably, five-ten or eleven and a hundred-seventy-five, maybe even a hundred-eighty pounds. She was toned and well-muscled, but goalies got away without the bulk a skater needed to make a presence on the ice.

As they squeezed in together—he and Brit on one side, Blane and Dan on the other—Stefan was thankful that Brit was next to him, not just because her thigh pressed against his felt really fucking good or because the delicate floral scent of her shampoo was teasing his nose . . . but also because Blane and Dan looked like two adults sitting at the kids' table.

He had to bite back a grin when Dan shoved Blane over. "My ass is halfway in the aisle."

Brit snorted. "Dramatic much?"

Blane joined Dan in glaring at them. "Why did we let you pick this place again?" he asked Stefan.

"Because this place has the best bacon-and-bleu-cheese burger on the planet," he said. "And because milkshakes. 'Kay? Enough said?"

"We shouldn't be drinking milkshakes," Blane grumbled.

"Seriously," Brit said. "We've got two days off. I, for one, am having a burger and a milkshake. Mint chocolate-chip. Or maybe cookie dough. Or maybe—"

Laughter swept through Stefan. "Like ice cream, do you?"

She shifted in the booth, turned to smile at him. "Maybe just a little."

"Are you kidding?" Dan asked. "Ice cream is your crack."

"For real," Blane said. "Once she stole my skates and wouldn't tell anyone where they were for a week because I ate her Cherry

Garcia." A martyred expression crossed his face. "I had to wear *rental* skates."

"It was Chubby Hubby," Brit said with a chuckle. "And that was the third time you'd eaten the entire pint. After *I'd* bought it."

"We lived as a family. We shared everything."

Stefan's brows pulled down. He'd known Brit and Blane were close, that they'd played on the same team in juniors. But living together? *That* he hadn't known, and as much as he tried to ignore the pang of jealousy in his gut, it was still there, caustic and burning.

"Now children," Dan began, "I know you had your differences—"

"Oh geez, Blane," Brit cut in. "We lived together for three years, and you ate more of my food than Dan did during my entire childhood."

"I was a growing boy."

Brit threw her head back and laughed. Hard.

The sound was electric, and Stefan felt every nerve in his body stand up and take notice. He wasn't the only one.

Though the restaurant was almost cleared out, there were a few patrons still nursing beers . . . or the occasional milkshake. At Brit's laugh, their eyes turned her way. The dim lights made her hair shine like spun gold and her skin look like a bowl of peaches and cream he wanted to lick up.

Or maybe that was just him.

Because the sound of Brit's joy unknotted something within Stefan, made him hope.

Made him want.

God, how he wanted.

The server came over then and took their order. It was nearly impossible to take his eyes off Brit, to focus on the words.

Thankfully, he only had to nod when asked if he would be ordering his usual.

"I love you, you know that, right?"

For a second, Stefan thought that Brit was talking to him. Then he realized that she was looking at Blane.

Christ.

The feeling that swept through him wasn't jealousy.

It wasn't.

Nor was it liquid rage as he studied Blane's face and saw the intense longing there.

Because he *should* be feeling relief—relief it wasn't him that Brit was in love with, relief she was referring to the brotherly, platonic love she felt for Blane.

It made no sense for him to want to hear those same words. They'd barely stumbled into the start of something, and there damn-well shouldn't be any desire on his part to plant his flag—rhetorically speaking—and claim Brit as his.

Good God. It hadn't even been a month since he'd first seen her in the arena's parking lot, struggling to pull her bag from the trunk of her crappy car.

There would be no flag planting, at least not in the whole put-a-ring-on-it, cave-man-style claiming.

Things were tentative, new. Light and easy.

For now.

Blane blinked, and the longing was gone, replaced with a mock-frown. "I still won't ever forgive you for the rental skates."

"Good Lord," Brit said, exasperated, but her lips were twitching. "A woman does one thing—"

"It was a *huge* thing."

"Not Ben-and-Jerry's huge."

Dan caught Stefan's gaze and rolled his eyes, throwing a sigh of frustration in for good measure. "Children, can we forget about something that happened almost ten years ago?"

Brit put up her hands. "I can. Don't know about Hulk over there, though."

Blane's lips twitched. "I seem to remember buying you a fresh carton of ice cream."

"Oh! That's right." She released a little breath and smiled

broadly at Blane. "You did! That was really sweet." Her eyes narrowed. "Still not going to apologize."

Stefan snorted. He couldn't help it. This side of Brit was new. Relaxed and . . . just really, really cute.

"What?" She turned, brushing against him in the tight confines of the booth.

Not that he minded.

Nope. In fact, he wanted her closer and, figuring she wouldn't make a big deal about it since they were in a public place, he stretched out an arm across the back of the booth and closed the few inches between their upper bodies.

She fit perfectly. Having her against him was right.

Utterly right.

"What?" she asked again.

"Nothing," he replied. "I just didn't know you were so . . ."

"Weird? Is that what you were going to say?" She frowned, tried to put some distance between them. Stefan didn't let her. Instead, he wove his fingers through the ends of her ponytail and tugged the slightly damp tresses gently.

"No." He glanced across the table, saw that Blane and Dan had moved on and were talking about something else, then bent so he could whisper in her ear. "So damned cute. So sweet I want to lick you up and see if you taste as good as you sound."

"I'm not—" Her cheeks heated. "That doesn't even make sense."

He shrugged. "Doesn't make it any less true."

"Oh—"

The server returned with their drinks then. An Oreo milkshake for Brit and beer for him, Blane, and Dan.

Brit took a sip of hers, and a look of such pleasure suffused her face that Stefan's cock twitched.

Shit. Between the flag planting, the talk of licking, and now the soft moan of pleasure as Brit took another sip . . . he'd be lucky if his brain had any blood left in it.

Fortunately for him, he didn't need to speak. Blane, Brit, and Dan dominated the conversation.

Stefan was happy to listen as they teased each other about things that had happened during their respective childhoods.

It was nice to know they'd had so many good times together, that laughter and memories had come easily.

His own childhood had been good, of course.

But it had also been a little lonely.

Without a father, without siblings and his mother working so damned hard, the house had been quiet far too often.

The guys on the team had been his family. But it was a fluid one.

Rosters shifted continuously as players aged out, moved, or were cut from the team.

There hadn't been too many constants.

Funny how he'd never recognized that before.

Their food arrived, and the four of them dug in, polishing off the half-pounders with ease. It was always amazing to him how much food hockey players could put away.

Even Brit finished her burger, though she took off all the produce before she ate it.

"No veggies?"

She grimaced. "Not by choice. I eat the damn things because Rebecca requires it, but on a cheat day? Hell no, I'm not choking down some lettuce."

"I can throw some quinoa on there for you."

Rebecca was the team's dietician, and she was notorious for her nutritious, but not-very-tasty food plans. Not that the diet didn't work.

Stefan had never been more in shape, never felt so strong on the ice, and that wasn't just the extra workouts. It was Rebecca's food and Mandy's physical therapy.

And Brit.

He felt his lips curve. A trifecta of women making his life better. He'd better not let that thought slip out.

Brit would give him no end of crap just for having had it.

Still, as he sat next to her, reveling in her scent, in the way her body had relaxed and gradually softened against his, Stefan thought he might get a kick out of telling her.

Just to see those brown eyes spark at him.

"Thanks for inviting me," he murmured into her ear as Blane related a funny story about a Gold defensemen *losing*—with the help of the team—his jock, not wearing it to practice, and then unsurprisingly—and with an *accidentally* misdirected shot by his D partner—getting hit right in the unprotected area.

He'd only heard it about a hundred times since it had happened.

Sometimes hockey players were more like children than well . . . children.

"It's nice to get out."

Brit turned her face up to his, a slight frown pulling her brows together. "Why would you have a problem getting out?" She cocked her head, and her tone was light, but her eyes held a note of seriousness that he couldn't ignore. "Do you have a secret love child? A wife?"

Brit didn't know it, but the explanation was simple. He didn't go out because his mom was sick, and he was on the road enough that he didn't like leaving her when he was in town.

"Just a dozen or so," he joked, instead of telling her what was really going on. "You don't know it, but I'm making a run to star on the show *Sister Wives*."

She snorted. "You're an idiot, just so you know. And also, how do you even know about that show?"

"My mom," he said. "She's all I've got, and we spend a lot of time together." He hesitated before telling her part of the truth. "Actually, she's living with me for a while. It's nice."

Brit stared at him, and he waited for it. For her to make fun of him because his mom was living with him, to make a comment about him being a mama's boy or the like.

She didn't.

Instead, she just smiled and said, "That's really nice for you both." Then she settled back against him and joined the conversation again, adding her side to a childhood story Dan was sharing about some mishap while skiing.

Easy acceptance. How strange.

How wonderful.

They stayed at the restaurant way past closing, the four of them each having such a good time that apparently no one wanted to leave.

There was a lot of teasing and laughter, and when Stefan finally peeled himself out of Blane's SUV and got into his own car, he realized he couldn't remember a time when he'd had more fun.

Sharing it with Brit, with her dash of cuteness and gentle smiles, made it simply the best night of his life.

THIRTY-SEVEN

Brit

FOR ONCE, Brit didn't pull herself out of bed before the sun was up. Her brother had left for the airport a couple of hours before, bussing a kiss on her cheek before telling her he'd see her soon.

There would be no early morning run, no stairs. The Gold had a player's meeting and light practice the following day before they left on their extended road-trip. But, for now, she was going to be lazy in bed.

So the knock at the door was completely unwelcomed.

With a groan, she slid out from between the sheets and walked over to peer through the peephole.

Then wanted to bang her head on the door.

She'd forgotten to put on the *Do Not Disturb* sign. The knock came again, along with the sound of a keycard being pushed into the lock. Brit glanced down, made sure she was decent, and threw back the deadbolt.

"Hi," she told the surprised maid. "Sorry. I don't need cleaning service today."

"Oh! I'm sorry, Ms. Plantain. I didn't realize you were in today."

"It's my fault," she told the woman. "I should have put the sign on."

"Do you need fresh towels?"

What she needed was to crawl her butt back into bed and turn on some crappy morning television show, to veg like a mofo, so that by the time she emerged, all of this guilt she was feeling over deceiving Stefan would have disappeared.

Instead of saying any of that, Brit shook her head. "No, thanks." She reached down and hung the sign on the outer doorknob.

Thirty seconds later, she was in bed and watching a celebrity answer interview questions about his latest film release.

Part of her admired the suave way with which he deflected the less-than-flattering inquiries about an anger scandal in the not-so-distant-past, but the rest of her was disheartened.

This was what it would be like with Stefan, a relationship that was all veneer and a smooth finish, but zero substance underneath.

Truth hit her like a slap shot to the gut.

The reason she was so torn up about this fake relationship was because it was the first time in her life she'd spent time with a man who *could* be more.

So much more.

The door to the next room slammed shut, echoing through the walls of Brit's suite, and she sighed.

Gold management had offered her a new contract a few days before.

And she'd signed it.

But whether they'd presented it because of her game play or solely because of the stuff with Stefan, she didn't know. The contract itself didn't have the biggest payday or the longest terms—just two years—but her agent had managed to eliminate the two-way part of her clause, so she'd be staying in the NHL for at least that long.

Which was more than Brit could have expected, and though she wasn't stupid enough to believe the agreement with Stefan didn't factor in, she was relieved to be in one place for a while.

Unless, of course, management traded her.

And that was a lovely thought for so early in the morning.

Signing the revised contract also meant the Gold were no longer paying her for her lodgings. She'd been planning on keeping the room at the hotel until the team got back from their nine-game road-trip, but with the morning free, maybe she should begin looking for an apartment.

The vacuum turned on next-door, making the decision for her.

Le sigh.

She shoved out of bed and took a shower where she spent a fair amount of time shaving her legs and underarms before washing and conditioning her hair.

Just because she was a professional athlete didn't mean she couldn't feel like a woman.

After de-Wookie-fying herself, she toweled off and dressed. Then instead of slapping her hair into its normal ponytail, Brit dried it carefully. She even put on mascara and blush.

Being in an ice rink for most of the year wasn't exactly conducive for a nice summer glow.

Her fingers hesitated over the lip-gloss before setting the tube aside. She couldn't abide the sticky slimy stuff. No matter that it made her lips look *"lush enough to kiss"*—which was an exact quote from the sales person who'd convinced her to buy it.

Brit had worn the damn stuff once—and it had worked as promised—but the tacky residue it left on cups, not to mention her teeth, hadn't been sexy.

Her blond hair framed her face in even layers. It shined, even in the fluorescent lighting and was the single physical thing where she took the most pride.

Obviously she was in shape, but her shoulders were broad, her thighs muscular, her breasts barely existed.

Whoever said that more than a handful was wasted hadn't met her.

Stefan would be lucky to get a finger-full.

Brit caught that thought and shoved it away then scowled at her reflection.

"Seriously," she muttered. "No more thinking yourself in circles."

But it was hard.

She had never felt this way before. Even as a teenager she'd been more focused on hockey than boys, and the few crushes she'd had later hadn't gone anywhere . . . even more so after the assault.

At this point, she wasn't exactly over what had happened, but she *had* come to terms with the fact that it didn't define her.

She wasn't delusional, didn't think she was magically better, especially because having someone at her back still made her uncomfortable as hell.

But she'd push past it.

Just like she pushed past everything else that had stood in her way.

She was living her dream. Everything she had hoped for was finally within her grasp.

So maybe—just maybe—she could grab on to some dreams in the other parts of her life as well.

And maybe Stefan could be part of that dream.

She walked out of the bathroom, picked up her phone, and called the real estate agent Stefan had recommended to set up an appointment in an hour.

Then Brit sucked in a breath, bolstered her courage, and called him to come with her.

As she spoke to him, his sleep-drenched voice like roughened velvet against her skin, she wasn't thinking about the fake relationship. Wasn't calculating the next move that would get them media attention, wasn't worried about management.

This moment was about her.

For one damned moment, it could be about her. About what she wanted.

Which was Stefan.

For however long she could have him.

THIRTY-EIGHT

"TOO SMALL," Stefan said as he glanced around the unit's single bedroom. A queen bed took up almost all of the available space, but there was a small walk-in closet that was plenty big enough to store her collection of jeans, t-shirts, workout gear, and odd pair of game day slacks and button-downs.

Brit was wearing one of her a *nice* t-shirts today, meaning it was new and lacking in stains and holes. Between that and the makeup and her blown-out hair, she'd surprised Stefan.

His eyes had gone wide when they'd met up in the hotel's lobby, and his hand had come up, as though he wanted to touch the strands.

Brit had wanted that too, had wanted his fingers tangled there, pressed against her scalp as he took her mouth in a searing kiss—

It had not really been the time.

But with the bed right there in front of her and the real estate agent having stepped out to take a call, Brit was once again reminded of how tempting Stefan was.

Really, really tempting.

"You okay?" he asked, walking out of the closet and stopping in front of her. He was close enough that she could feel the heat from his body, see the slight scruff of his stubble.

Hear the grumble of his stomach.

Her lips twitched. "I'm sorry," she told him. "I monopolized your morning. I'll buy you lunch."

He gave her a mournful look. "I'm withering away. I'll be skin and bones soon."

"Ha." She snorted, but couldn't—didn't *want* to resist reaching out and stroking the firm muscles of his chest.

They were granite beneath her palms. If granite was scorching hot . . . and lickable.

She brought her other hand up, squeezed his pecs.

What had she been thinking about handfuls earlier? Because this was a really nice one.

Stefan sucked in a breath and stepped closer. Her teeth found her lip, bit firmly, attempted to find control, when all she really wanted to do was ask him to take off his shirt or, better yet, to slip her hands under the soft cotton and take matters into her own hands.

She'd slid them down the rock-hard planes of his abdomen to do just that when he spoke.

"Brit?" The question was soft, husky, and laced with enough desire that her thighs trembled.

"I like spending time with you, remember?" she said, staring up at him as her fingers trailed along the hot, *hot* skin just under the hem of his shirt.

One corner of his mouth turned up. "I know. Me too." But he took her hands in his and carefully pulled them from his skin.

She stuck out a lip. "I thought we were going to explore this thing between us."

His smile grew. "We are."

"Then—" She tried to free herself.

He held firm.

"—why won't you let me—"

The door to the apartment opened and the agent, Lisa, called to them. "What do you think?"

"Because we're not alone," he murmured, the light blue of his eyes darkened with what she hoped was desire and not annoyance. Her eyes darted down, saw the erection straining against the front of his jeans.

Oh yeah, desire. For damn sure.

Not that she was in any better shape.

If he'd touched her, stroked those fingers down and between her thighs, he'd have found her soaked—

"Just give us a moment to finish our discussion," Stefan called.

"Sure thing!" Lisa called back.

They listened to the agent's heels *clack* across the floor, until the noise stopped in what Brit thought was the kitchen.

"You," Stefan said, squeezing her fingers, "are dangerous as hell."

She smiled.

"That wasn't a compliment."

Humor tempered the desire eating at her. Slightly. "I'll still take it as one."

Sex goddess wasn't a role she typically undertook. Hell, normally she was a little shy in the bedroom. But Stefan brought out another side of her . . . and she liked it.

In fact, the attraction between them was so crazy, so *huge*, it might have been frightening had he not been right there with her. She knew she wasn't alone.

She laughed.

Who would have thought?

Stefan's brows pulled together. "Now you're playing with me? Teasing?" A flash of temper, which sent a little shiver down her spine, crossed Stefan's face.

"Isn't that kind of the point of foreplay?" she asked.

His mouth dropped open in shock and his breath hitched.

A little bubble of hope expanded in her chest, competing with the tangle of desire and guilt, pushing them both to the side until all she felt was happiness because she was in this man's presence. Stretching up on her toes, she pressed her mouth to his.

The kiss was short and hot. But just as Stefan put his arms around her to pull her even closer, she stepped back.

"You're sexy," she told him.

"Brit—"

For some reason, spending time with Stefan gave her confidence in her own skin, made her feel gorgeous, wanted. Competent.

She had no clue why.

Or if it was him at all.

Maybe he'd unlocked something. Or maybe she was finally growing into her own.

Whatever it was, Brit decided she liked it. She headed for the door only to stop a couple of inches from the threshold and glance back at him over her shoulder.

"I want you," she said.

In bed and out of it . . . and then right back in it.

Stefan muttered a curse that made even her ears—and she'd long thought herself beyond the effect of swear words—turn pink.

He prowled toward her, and Brit found that somehow her feet had become glued to the ground. Still watching him over her shoulder, she couldn't move.

Or maybe it was that she didn't *want* to move.

"Turnabout is fair play," he said. "You know that, right?" His hand came up to her nape and squeezed. His chest pressed against her back, hard and unforgiving.

A slight pang of nervousness unfurled in her abdomen, but before she'd even had a chance to register the sensation, Stefan whipped her around and slammed his lips down onto hers.

Anxiety withered. Desire roared.

A heartbeat later, he was gone, pushing through the door, a whispered "Oh, there will be foreplay" trailing in his wake.

Brit stood there, her fingers pressed against her swollen lips, heat raging in her skin, her nerves zinging like the needy bitches they were, and tried to figure out how Stefan had turned the tables on her so easily.

Then she decided she didn't really care.

Because if he kissed her like that . . . as if the world would end without one more stroke of her tongue, as though her mouth was the sweetest temptation he'd ever experienced then he could turn the tables any damn time he wanted.

Lisa's voice chimed in from the kitchen and jump-started her into motion.

Brit smoothed her hair from where Stefan's fingers had mussed it, sucked in a breath, and stepped from the bedroom.

As she walked, she forced herself to focus on the apartment. Built-ins lined one wall, and the kitchen was tiny but held stainless appliances, white countertops, and cabinets. Gauzy shades covered the wall of windows.

It *was* small.

But it was perfect. Airy and cozy and just a couple of blocks from the Gold's arena.

The single bathroom wasn't luxurious, but it would do, especially paired with the decent-size living space, and cute kitchen. She loved it.

Of course she had to consider that it would be tight when Dan came to stay. But he was used to sleeping in all sorts of crazy places. He could sleep on the floor or a blow-up mattress.

Or she'd get a sleeper sofa. There was room enough.

"What do you think, Brit?" Lisa asked.

"I'll take it."

THIRTY-NINE

Stefan

HE HATED FLYING.

Seriously hated it.

So much so that if there were a boat, a bus—hell, a covered wagon to get him to the away games, he would have signed up in a heartbeat.

But, of course, he hadn't.

Not only did the team's insurance require them to travel only on approved vehicles, he was the *captain*.

His place was with the team.

Brit laughed a couple rows up from where he was seated, liquid warmth and lightning wrapped in one. It fired his nerves, made every cell perk up in rigid attention.

Blane said something that made her laugh again, and a sharp slice of jealousy cut him deep. *He* wanted to be the one who made Brit happy, wanted to sit next to her, absorb her smiles, her sweetness.

But it wasn't Stefan's place to monopolize her time, and if she didn't want to sit with him, didn't want to give unspoken confirmation that the rumors circling in the media, being whispered in the locker room were true . . .

He wasn't going to stand in her way.

They might be pursuing the chemistry that threatened to flay him to the core, but he hadn't laid claim to her.

Which sounded positively barbaric, stupidly alpha male.

Brit would certainly kick his ass for even having had the thought. And yet, he almost didn't care, would take the verbal chewing with enthusiasm . . . if it meant she could be his.

But—

What?

It was complicated? Hell, yes it was. It was a risk? Definitely. He felt more with Brit since—well—ever.

It was new.

That was the notion that gave Stefan the most pause.

And the reason he was sitting five rows behind her, admiring the golden tint of her hair, the slender slope of her neck, the confidence in her hands as she gestured wildly.

She'd been strong when she'd first come to the Gold—it would have been impossible to get there any other way—but in the almost six weeks since she'd first walked into the Gold's arena, he'd witnessed her strength grow, mature into granite laced with . . . caring, maybe?

But instead of weakening the stone, the undertone of affection for her teammates tempered its core, made it even more solid.

She didn't just care for *him*, though he was egotistical enough to think that was part of her transformation.

It was more than that.

Brit was committed to the team with her whole heart. Even her staunchest critic could see that, and they were only five games into the regular season.

A season in which she'd played maybe ten minutes total, but a season during which she'd been to every practice—optional or otherwise—had been engaged and cheering for their team even while on the bench.

Hence, the so-painful-his-spine-itched distance between them.

But because the draw between them was so new, he wouldn't do anything to risk her career.

Not even when his heart ached to be beside her.

"That bad?" Max asked from his seat next to him. His D-partner always took the window seat, leaving Stefan and his nervous energy free to get up and move around.

Or Max had every time after their first flight together, after Stefan had crawled over him a half-dozen times to pace the aisle.

Further that, Stefan didn't pretend to misunderstand what Max was saying. They'd known each other far too long to play those kinds of games.

And last year's horrible season had created bonds too deep to sever.

"Bad," he agreed. "Really fucking bad. I've never felt like this before."

Max sighed, leaned back in his seat, and took out his ear buds. "It's a really bad time . . ." He hesitated then said, " . . .for both of you."

"I know."

"Might be better if you let her go."

Fury made his fists tighten. He banged one on his thigh. "It's not that easy."

"Why?"

Only three letters, but enough to give Stefan pause.

"I don't know," he said. "I've tried to ignore this thing—whatever it is—between us, but I can't. She's in every thought, every fucking heartbeat."

He bit off the rest of the words before they came. Part of it was because he wanted to save them for Brit. The other part was that *if* he said it—gave voice to the feelings that threatened to unnerve him—he would be even more vulnerable.

"So then what? You continue with this relationship? What has management said?" Max fixed him with a look. "You know, after Gordaine and Rhonda," he said, referring to the rape scandal and resulting investigation that had ended up with the Gold's former captain being banned from the NHL altogether, "management enacted strict rules against fraternizing with staff."

"Brit's not staff."

"She's close enough, and sooner or later someone is going to mention something. Hell, I'm surprised the media hasn't pounced on it already."

That was true enough. The media *hadn't* zoned in on the similarities between him and Brit and Gordaine and Rhonda, and for the first time he wondered why that was.

"My name's cleaner than Gordaine's ever was."

"It's not pristine, though."

"No one's ever accused me of rape."

"No one's ever accused you of getting close enough to try."

"It hasn't been *that* long. My playboy past is still out there."

Max rolled his eyes. "Playboy? Dude. You've hardly even gone out. In the last two seasons we've played together, I can count on one hand the number of times you've been out past midnight, and two of those times have been with Brit in the last month."

"You and I go out," he said, trying not to focus on the fact that he sounded like a defensive teenager. "We've *gone* out."

His friend snorted. "Yeah. For one beer, and then you're safely abed by eleven."

"It's not that simple." Part of it had been his fatigue with the party scene.

The rest of it . . . he sighed. It was hard to be in a partying mood when someone he cared about was sick. And his mom hadn't been well for a long time—two bouts with cancer in four years would do that to someone.

To that end, it was just as easy to settle the ragged edges with a beer or two at his own house.

No media. No women. Just quiet solitude and distance to keep his emotions safely boxed away.

Until Brit had broken the seal, and all sorts of feels had inundated him.

Feels?

Yup. He was losing it, and most of him didn't even give a damn.

"Yeah," Max said. "That's what I figured."

His friend was quiet for a moment, as though waiting for Stefan to spill his guts. But the thing was, Stefan just didn't have it in him.

After a minute, Max sighed. "Okay then."

Stefan nodded. "Okay."

"What are you going to do about Brit?"

"I'm going to win the girl." He shot Max a solemn look. "Just carefully. Very, very carefully."

Max grinned. "That's my boy. Smart wins over—"

"Stupid every day of the week," Stefan finished.

They bumped fists. "Hope it works out for you, buddy."

Brit laughed again, and they both looked forward.

"Me too. Me too."

FORTY

THEY PLAYED in Vancouver the next night and the game went horribly.

It wasn't anyone's fault in particular, just that everyone seemed flat, and nothing was clicking on the ice. In a rare show of temper, Bernard chewed their asses in the locker room between the second and third periods—a misguided but fairly common attempt at motivating professional players to do better.

Stefan never understood that.

Yelling didn't make him play better. It made him worse. Suddenly his hands were a little shaky, and he was jumpy with the puck.

Calm and relaxed was when he played the best.

Some guys played well angry. That just wasn't him, for any sustained length anyway, and it wasn't most of the guys on the team.

Thankfully, Bernard didn't lose his shit too often. Further that, it was hard to argue his sentiments of lazy play and uninspired offense.

Especially after they let in a fourth goal all of twenty-three seconds into the third—making Stefan a minus three for the night.

Two seconds later, Bernard pulled Julian, and Brit took over. It wasn't even that Julian was playing poorly. The move was typical for NHL teams, a way to stall their opponent's momentum and shake their own team into action.

The swap worked.

Not only did Brit play magnificently, practically standing on her head as she was peppered with shots from her first seconds in the game, but her presence actually changed the tenor of the game.

So much so that the Gold finally started playing.

Unfortunately, not soon enough.

The forwards managed to sneak three goals in on the Canucks' goalie but couldn't quite snag the tie.

The locker room was silent after they'd filed in to get undressed. Nineteen men and one woman, sitting on wooden benches as they peeled off their sweaty gear.

Bernard hadn't let the media in yet, and he wasn't in the room proper.

Stefan knew it was a sign for him to step up, to say something.

Trouble was, he didn't know what.

Brit did, though, and her simple words a few minutes into the silence made him fall for her even more.

"We can do better."

That was it. One sentence that was both truth and motivation.

It was also enough to loosen Stefan's tongue.

He tossed his jersey into the dirty pile in the center of the room. "No more," he said. "No more flat performances. Brit played her ass off—"

"Julian too," Brit interrupted, with a serious expression. "Jules gave it everything he had."

At her words, most of the guys glanced up, and many nodded in agreement. They knew the game was on them, knew they had to do better.

"Yes, Jules played well too," Stefan said, making sure he met Julian's eyes, that the goaltender understood he meant the words. "But we can't rely on our goalies to save us. We need to do more."

"Barie's right," Blane chimed in. "I know we're better than this."

"Agreed," said Max.

A lot of the guys gave their support, some with words, some without. But everyone was positive.

Except Stewart.

"Everyone has an off night," he said.

Excuses. The man was full-to-the-brim of lame-ass excuses.

"We're professional athletes," Stefan told him. "We don't have the luxury of an *off* night. We get our shit together, or we won't be around for another season."

Stefan let the room absorb that for a moment. Those that were on the team last year understood how precarious their position was. Half of the team had been cut, most of them—the son of a bitch Gordaine, notwithstanding—without real reason.

It was easy to blame losses on poor coaching, on a lack of support from management, or a young roster.

That wasn't this year.

Management had given them every perk imaginable. They had a good coach who rarely—mid-game verbal assault aside—made mistakes. Their team was beyond talented.

They had plenty of ice time, a decent schedule, state-of-the-art training equipment.

So this sad attempt at hockey wasn't on the higher ups, wasn't on Bernard.

Nope.

It was all on them.

"Stefan's right," Brit eventually said, breaking the terse silence. "There are so many waiting in the wings, ready to pounce on every opportunity. I know. Blue knows."

She nodded at the rookie, who softly replied, "Yeah."

"If they want it more, we're already screwed." The emotion in her tone was fierce, then her lips quirked, and it was pushed aside by the amusement dancing across her blue eyes. "Now this may be my second X chromosome talking, but I'm happy to be here with you guys. I believe we have the talent to do well this season. I believe in us." A beat of quiet. "So do you think you all can get your shit together?"

The guys laughed and continued undressing.

"That your idea of a motivational speech?" Henry, one of the fourth-line wingers called.

"What, Henry? You want me to get my pom-poms out?" Brit called back, before blowing on her fingernails and rubbing them on the strap of her plain black sports bra, in a job-well-done sort of way. Her chest protector and jersey had already been discarded, and she knelt to begin taking off her pads. "I just call 'em as I see 'em."

Henry wolf-whistled in response, and Brit laughed, that wonderful, full-bodied mirth that lightened a room of testosterone-laden jocks.

"You can put it in your spank bank," she said, "but I don't want to hear about it."

"Burn, Plantain," one of the guys called.

The team laughed and began exchanging a series of increasingly bad jokes and innuendos . . . which grew even louder when Henry blushed.

They ribbed the forward then each other until Bernard came in and announced, "Players meeting, eight-thirty tomorrow morning. Plane leaves at ten, and afternoon practice right after we land."

Normally this would have made the team groan—an extra meeting and practice on a game day, interspersed with the team's scheduled flight to Chicago.

But not one person, not even Stewart—who appeared unusually subdued—made a face.

In that moment, Stefan felt like he finally understood his role as captain.

It wasn't that he needed to be the best on the ice or come up with the most original motivational speech, a la Herb Brooks in *Miracle on Ice.*

He just needed to support those who were the best at the

moment, who could capture the essence of the room with a well-timed insight.

Sometimes, he thought it might be the best player both on and off the ice, as Brit had been today with her impressive goaltending and no-fluff words.

Sometimes, it might be those that could loosen a room full of stressed-out players, like Henry had done.

Sometimes, it would have to be him.

But that was okay.

Just knowing he could sometimes share the burden made the task that much less daunting.

FORTY-ONE

Brit

STEFAN'S EYES MET HERS. "Thank you," he said and took off for the showers.

Brit shook her head.

Sometimes the man really didn't get it. A thank you wasn't necessary.

In fact, when someone thanked her for doing something she should be doing anyway, Brit almost felt *less* responsible for her actions.

Especially when she got gratitude for something that *really* should be expected. Some things were optional, and those deserved a thanks. Some—like pushing her teammates and herself to do their honest best—did not.

Maybe it was totally screwed up, but that was the way her mind worked.

If the expectation was there that the team would support each other, would encourage, would deliver a much-needed kick to the ass when necessary, then the road to the playoffs was already half-paved.

"His heart is in the right place," a masculine voice to her right said.

She glanced over at Julian, something inside her settling at the even tone.

There was always a moment of awkward when she relieved a starting goalie. Yes, of course, she wanted to eventually be in Jules' position, but having to actually see him when she'd basically taken the position—even for a limited time—from him was uncomfortable.

He sighed when she looked back down at her pads and continued undoing the straps. "You're not going to make this weird, are you?"

She wanted to say *"Who me?"* but she'd already made things strange enough with her awkward staring. Instead, she shrugged.

"Hey," he said and waited until she looked up. Another sigh. "Yup. You're going to make things weird."

"I'm—" Brit blew out a breath. "Fine. Okay. I *am* making it weird. It's just . . . I've always been a backup, and now to have this chance to maybe work my way into starting. And with an NHL team . . ."

Jules was quiet for a moment, his hair only slightly damp from the early crack he'd got at the showers, but when he spoke, the words surprised her. "I was a backup too."

"You were?"

"Yup. Never thought I'd be more." He shrugged. "Then the starting goalie got injured two weeks after the trade deadline, and it was on me."

She set her pads to one side then turned to face him fully. "What happened?"

"That year we won the whole damn thing."

The mix of pride and reverence in his voice made her ache. She wanted *that*, so badly. Wanted her name immortalized on that silver cup.

"What did it feel like?"

"Everything and nothing." That made her jaw drop open, and he grinned. "Don't look so shocked. It's like any big event. Tons of buildup, so much pressure and working, working, working. Then you've done it, and . . . it's just over." Jules gestured at her equipment, stacked next to the bench. "You get undressed. You celebrate. You move onto the next season. Only it seems even further from reach, because you've already tasted it and know how hard it is to grasp."

Brit was still digesting that long after Julian had gone, and when Mandy came over to pull her into the modified therapy room, she was more than ready for a distraction.

"Shoulder?" Mandy asked, all but shoving her onto the padded table.

"It's fine."

Mandy glared. "You said it was fine when the damn thing was swollen and you had reduced range of motion." She narrowed her eyes. "Tell me the truth."

"It's a little sore. But in a tired way, not injured way."

"You'll tell me if that changes." Her gaze bored into Brit, fierce and intense as hell.

Brit raised her hands in surrender. "Promise."

In a blink, the sternness in Mandy's expression faded away, and the other woman smiled brightly. "Good." A nod toward Brit's raised arms. "And good range of motion. Keep up those exercises."

She nudged Brit to lie face down on the table and began massaging the tight muscles in her shoulders. "So tell me about Stefan," she said. "He is, without a doubt, the hottest guy on the team. That chest . . . those arms . . ." Mandy sighed. "Damn, girl. I'm jealous. Half the time, I want to pull him in for treatment he doesn't need, just so I can touch him."

A wave of cold fear had swept over Brit at Mandy's initial words —the fear of discovery, fear of someone finding out the truth about her and Stefan—but all that quickly, the fear was replaced with jealousy, surging hot and unhindered.

She turned her head and glanced back over her shoulder at Mandy. Okay, glared. Because, dammit, she'd been pressed against those muscles of Stefan's and didn't want anyone else touching . . . or fantasizing about touching.

Mandy grinned. "Guess that look says it all." She dug her fingers into a sore spot, and Brit grunted in discomfort. "Come on, just dish already. A little girl talk makes the world go round. Plus, who else am I supposed to talk to. Rebecca? You know she's about as fun as watching paint dry."

With a snort, Brit plunked her head down on the pads. Rebecca *was* pretty serious and not a whole lot of fun.

"Point made," she said. "But I'm not really good at the whole girl-talk thing."

Especially with non-hockey-playing girls. At least she could connect with the guys on the team about the sport, but chatting with Mandy about hair or men made her downright uncomfortable.

"We'll practice."

Which sounded about as fun as talking with Rebecca, but Brit sighed and didn't protest as she endured the alternating pain, pleasure, and icy cold that was the storm of Mandy's fingers mixed with the therapist's patented muscle cream.

Good God, the woman had strong hands. If she weren't all of five-feet-and-change, Brit would have told her to get her ass in gear and start playing. "You're not funny," she muttered.

"If it makes you feel any better, I'd admire Stefan all day, but when it gets down to it, I like my men a little burlier."

"You're so little, they'd smother you— Fuck!" The therapist had dug firmly into a particularly sore spot.

"Sorry." Mandy chuckled. "Okay. No, I'm not. You've got a smart mouth on you." She popped Brit on the shoulder then dropped down onto the table next to her. "We can't all be tall and willowy like you, Brittany Plantain. Some of us girls have a little meat on us . . . and like our men with the same."

"Meat?" Brit stopped and glanced over at Mandy, lips twitching. Sometimes her mind went really dirty, she couldn't help it. Okay, she *could* help it, but being around guys and their plethora of sexual innuendos and bad jokes has turned her into a twelve-year-old boy. "Really?"

Twin spots of pink appeared on Mandy's cheeks, clashing with her pale skin and red-hued hair. "I didn't mean—"

"Uh-huh. I think there's a dirty mind in there. Hiding under two tons of cuteness."

"Two tons?" A grin. "Jeez, girl, I just told you I was insecure about my size, and you bring up my weight."

Panic seized Brit for one long moment. Until she saw the humor in Mandy's eyes. The other woman was devious.

Biting back a smile, she said, "Okay. Maybe three."

"Bitch."

They looked at each other and cracked up.

When they'd finally gotten themselves back under control, Mandy bumped her shoulder against Brit's. "Did we just become friends?"

Brit nodded solemnly. "I think so." For once, she might have actually met another woman she could be herself with, another woman where things weren't her trademark awkward.

"Good. I'm tired of hanging out with cavemen all the time," Mandy said.

"Other women besides Rebecca work for the Gold."

"Yeah." Mandy shrugged. "There are a group of us, but I'm the only one that travels with the team."

"Well then, we'll need to stick together."

The other woman snorted. "Heck no. Any spare time you've got will be spent with Stefan."

"It's not like that," Brit protested, even as she wondered why she bothered. Management wanted it to be more. She and Stefan wanted it to be more. So why put the qualifier on it now?

"Then what's it like?" Mandy asked. "Because the pictures of you two are smoldering."

"It's attraction."

And possibility. The delicate hope for more.

But it was also a fragile future that could be easily torn apart if Stefan found out the real reason for her initial interest, for her moving forward into something she wouldn't have normally touched with a ten-foot pole, chemistry or not. Probably, the same was true for him. They both understood that any relationship between them would be complicated.

Inter-office dating on steroids.

With an inner sigh at the mess that was her life, Brit rose from the table and tested her shoulder. No matter what they said about Mandy, the woman knew what she was doing when it came to muscles.

Just hopefully not Stefan's.

"If that's attraction, then sign me up," Mandy said.

Brit chuckled, but it wasn't filled with humor. Or at least not entirely. "Attraction complicates things."

Mandy stopped cleaning the table with a disinfecting wipe and raised a brow.

Way to go. Draw even more attention to the convoluted mess between her and Stefan.

"I'd say be careful," the other woman murmured, "but it seems like you already know that."

"Yeah."

Mandy tossed the wipe then walked over. "Okay, then I'll say this. Stefan might seem like an open book, calm and with his shit together, but he feels as much as the rest of us. He's just really good at keeping it bottled up, making it seem as though everything is superficial and doesn't matter."

"How do—?" Brit bit back the question then shook her head at herself. She *wanted* to know—despite feeling jealous that Mandy might understand Stefan better than she did—and asked anyway. "Did you and he—?"

"*God no*. I don't shit where I eat, no matter how much fun it is to look. Plus, remember? Burly men." She shrugged, her expression going a little serious and a whole lot wicked. "But I work closely with you all on a daily basis. It's hard not to get to know each of your nuances." She raised one brow, chasing it with a penetrating look. "All of them."

"So what you're saying—"

Mandy's lips tipped up into a smirk. "Is that I know all."

Now damn, that was a frightening thought.

FORTY-TWO

"COME OUT WITH ME?"

Brit jumped at the sound of Stefan's voice ambushing her the moment she stepped outside the room.

"Jeez, ninja. Don't sneak up on me." Her hand pressed against her chest, tried to soothe the racing tattoo of her heart within. "And it's late. I want to shower and sleep."

"I can help with that."

She snorted. "It's a simple matter of you wash my back . . ."

"Exactly."

Walking into the locker room, Brit noticed that the pile of jerseys and undergarments in the center of the room had disappeared. Her gear was stacked and waiting for the equipment manager to store for their next plane ride.

Never let it be said the Gold staff weren't efficient.

The guys had already finished with their showers, and the room was hushed. Which meant she was showering back in the hotel room.

Maybe it was crazy to feel like a crowd would save her if any of the guys tried to grab her again. A group hadn't stopped the men in the past, but she'd also been the only one showering when it happened.

And so somehow, the notion had become hard for her to shake.

She felt safe when she wasn't showering by herself. She felt exposed when she was.

In the twisted logic of her mind, it made sense.

Maybe someday, she'd get past it.

Today wasn't that day.

Because seriously, she had enough crap on her plate.

"I'm exceedingly skilled with a loofa."

Her mouth dropped open at the soft words, their cheese factor nearly infinity. She was just about to give Stefan a boatload of crap about it when she turned and saw the expression on his face.

It appeared superficial. It seemed light.

Until she looked closer and realized the offer was much more significant than that. He was trying to make her laugh, to relieve some of her stress . . . because Stefan knew there was something about the empty locker room that made her nervous.

That was when Brit knew.

She *had* to tell him. Needed to be honest in this way, since she couldn't in so many others.

"I was . . . well, I want to say attacked, because that's what it felt like." She cleared her throat, pushed past the lump in it. "But it wasn't so much that as some sort of sick ritual the guys had for new players."

His nostrils flared, and his eyes darkened, the light blue going almost navy. "What do you mean?"

She shrugged. "A few years ago . . . the team I was playing on . . . well, they have a tradition." She swallowed hard. "I wasn't immune."

"What. Do. You. Mean?" he asked, somehow managing to inject intensity into the question without actually raising the volume of his voice.

"I mean"—she sucked in a breath and told him the truth—"they waited until I was alone in the shower then came up behind me, held me down, touched me . . . then doused me with icy cold water. They tried to say it was their way at making me feel like part of the team because every single player endured it. I-I just thought it was going a different way."

"You thought they were going to rape you."

The air in her lungs shuddered out on a long, shaky exhale. The floor became blurry through the lens of her tears, but her voice was rock steady. "The way"—her eyes closed—"Their hands. I—" Finally, she breathed out and lifted her chin. "Yes."

And that was the truth. The piece that had shaken her to her very core. Those men had taken something from her—stolen her safety net, ripped away a place where she'd felt protected.

Hockey had been her happy place. Until then.

It had taken her years to find her way back.

Stefan's voice shook with fury. "That's assault. It's wrong."

"Yes."

"But why—"

Brit knew what was coming. It was the inevitable course of questioning. Why had she let it happen? Why—

"Didn't I do something?" She laughed without mirth, the words coming fast now, almost frenzied in their effort to escape. "Except I did. I reported the incident to the head coach. I thought it was a matter of misunderstanding, that they needed to know it was wrong to do it to anyone, male or female. And they . . ." Brit blew out a breath. " . . .they said all the right things, even made a show of pulling the guys into meetings. But at the end of the day, *I* was the one they let go. It was *me* who scrambled to find another team, another contract, and position. That's why this thing with Bernard—"

Shut up!

The thought burst through to the forefront of her mind, silencing the flow of words.

Stefan watched her for a long moment. When he finally spoke, it wasn't to question her further, to pounce on the slip. No, his words, when they came, were supportive.

"You did the right thing."

She shook her head. "I'm not so sure."

"You did."

"My career suffered." It had been rough trying to find another team, and even though she'd eventually managed to secure another contract, Brit had thought her dream finished.

"Maybe," Stefan said. "But you're here now."

He took a step toward her, raised a cautious hand. That tentative action undid her, and she closed the distance between them, nestled into the expanse of his chest. His arms wrapping tight around her were better than making a tough-as-hell save.

Those arms soothed, managed to make the past feel like it was very much in the past.

"Did you ever think about going to the media?" His question was gentle in a way that might have pissed her off, if it were anyone else, but coming from Stefan, it was okay.

Brit didn't allow herself to think about why that might be.

"Yes," she told him. "But there were pictures, and I thought if it all came out, the pictures would too. My career couldn't recover from that."

The old saying that pictures were forever was true. They shaded a person's image, always crept back in when someone was in the news. And a story about a hot button issue?

That would have been regurgitated time and again.

Every time a similar story surfaced, the media would have said, *"Remember that time when the professional hockey team got caught assaulting Brit Plantain?"*

She could have never just been a goalie striving to make it like other players.

She would never have been just the first female goalie on an NHL team.

No.

She would have been a victim.

And Brit couldn't abide that.

"Come on," Stefan said a few minutes later. He dropped his arms, and the sensation of their loss was intense. She wanted to stay curled against him forever, to stay safe and warm. Protected.

Then his fingers laced with hers, and the warmth returned, melting the frosty numbness making popsicles of her insides.

"We'll go to the hotel," he said. "You'll shower. I'll order room service, and we can eat."

Her eyes flashed to his, suspicious. "Are you trying to finagle an invitation to my room?"

"Who me?" he asked, anything but innocent.

She felt her lips twitch. Stefan was charming for all his deviousness, and delight replaced the hooked tendrils of the past.

"And what will *you* be doing while I'm showering?" she teased.

"Watching TV."

Uh-huh. "So this is all about using my TV?" she asked.

"Yup." Stefan shook his head. "I've heard your room is nice than mine."

Brit rolled her eyes, but just as she was about to call him on that bit of BS, he leaned close and whispered in her ear, "I'll also be imagining you naked and wet. My mouth on those perfect breasts, my hands on your ass. Picturing pulling you close as I dropped to my knees and . . ."

The rest of the image he painted in her mind was hot and dirty and . . . sexy as hell.

She wanted—

But he didn't let her catch her breath, just continued painting the scene, his husky voice sweeping over her like calloused fingers drifting down her spine. "I'll be imagining all of that, planning, knowing that when we actually get to be in a shower together—one that's not filled with a bunch of our teammates"—he added with a rough chuckle—"it'll be even hotter than I can imagine."

Holy hell.

Her thighs trembled, the ache between them intense.

And that was only with words.

Still, Brit had never been one to let someone else win, not in sports and not in life.

It wasn't in her nature.

So she found her voice, rose on tiptoe, and whispered in his ear, "But what if I wanted there to be a bunch of other dudes?"

He shivered, his fingers clenching on hers. But then her words must have penetrated because he reared back in comical outrage and glared at her.

She smirked. That would do.

"Come on, Romeo," she told him. For once, she was in the moment, and the tenterhooks of the past were very far away. "I like your plan."

FORTY-THREE

Stefan

STEFAN HADN'T BEEN KIDDING when he'd told Brit he would
be imagining her naked and wet, droplets of water skating down her
skin . . . all that creamy skin exposed for his mouth, his fingers,
his co—

He cursed, grabbed the room-service menu off the desk in her
hotel room, and tried to push the images from his mind.

It wasn't that he didn't want Brit—the raging boner tenting his
pants was more than enough evidence to the contrary—but it was too
soon.

She was vulnerable . . . and they were on date three.

Of course, his dick would like to remind him that the countless
hours they'd spent together in the company of their teammates and
the dinners with Blane and Max and Dan added to that.

They did.

But it was still too soon.

Stefan had slept with enough women in his lifetime to understand that sex was just sex.

And he wanted more than sex with Brit.

But that wasn't the only reason for his hesitation. Although she'd opened up to him, he couldn't help but feel there were more secrets she was hiding, more he needed to know before they took that final step.

Not to mention they had practice and a game tomorrow. If they were going to sleep together, he wanted to take his time, to keep her up for hours into the night.

This wasn't the right moment.

Which he was going to remember, even if ninety percent of his blood was currently in the southern half of his body.

The shower turned off.

"Christ," he muttered and quickly phoned in the order before sinking down onto the edge of the bed. He turned on the TV and cranked the volume, not wanting to engage his imagination further by listening for any faint clue of movement as Brit dressed.

His phone buzzed, but he ignored it because the door to the bathroom opened, and he nearly swallowed his tongue.

He'd seen Brit naked, but this was somehow even sexier.

Her face was washed clean, her blond hair pulled back into a scattered ponytail—which was all he registered before his eyes were drawn back down to her body.

A pale pink silk tank top encased those breasts he'd been fantasizing about, her nipples beaded beneath the thin material, clearly illustrating the fact she wasn't wearing a bra.

He bit back a curse, struggled for a semblance of control. She was the personification of temptation.

Her legs were bare except for the smallest pair of flannel shorts he'd ever seen, miles and miles of bare skin flushed slightly pink from the heat of the shower.

Stefan's fingers actually ached with the need to touch.

Brit tugged her ponytail, a nervous gesture that made her appear all of fifteen-years-old for a moment, but when she smiled and gave a rueful shrug, any thoughts of youth disappeared.

She was all woman.

He wanted her.

"I don't really do the matching lingerie thing," she said.

"Wh-what?"

With a sigh and an eye roll, she walked over to him. "I'm not super girlie."

"Like fuck you're not." He was practically sitting on his hands, so he didn't grab her.

Her lips curved up, and she stopped less than six inches from him. Close enough that her delicate feminine scent coated the air between them.

"You know, I've never felt so powerfully sexy before," she said, stroking a single finger down his shirt, pressing the column of buttons lightly into his skin and setting him on fire, "but hearing your voice go all growly . . . Damn, I kind of like the way you make me feel, Barie."

Sweet baby Jesus, she was a menace.

"Me too," he agreed, even though Brit was making his balls turn permanently blue.

And apparently, she had no plans to stop because she plunked herself down in his lap, leaned close, and pressed her mouth to his.

No preamble. Just hunger, plain and simple.

She wrapped her arms tight around his neck, mouth opening, their tongues tangled in intimate embrace.

Stefan's control snapped.

He grabbed her hips, pulled her flush against him, and twisted one hand into her ponytail, angling her head so he could plunder it even more deeply.

Brit moaned. The sound was sexy as fuck.

He needed more. More skin. Her pinned beneath him. He needed to be inside her.

His fingers found the hem of her tank top and swept it up and over her head.

"I need to get my mouth on these," he said, placing one hand at the base of her spine to coax her closer as he bent to take one pink bud in his mouth.

"What—*Oh!*"

She arched and her soft moan of pleasure echoed through him, ratcheting his arousal to even higher levels. *God.* The woman was hot. Twisting, he tossed her to the mattress and followed her down. She spread her legs, effectively positioning himself in the place he most wanted to be.

Of course, it would be a lot better minus his pants, but he'd promised himself—

Her thighs wrapped tight around his hips, and she moved, undulating against him in a rhythm that literally made Stefan see stars.

He gripped the comforter fiercely, trying desperately to not blow his load in his pants. "Stop," he ground out.

"I can't," she said, panting. "I need—" She rubbed against him again, and he couldn't stop his hips from pressing forward, the layers of fabric between them creating both delicious friction and intense frustration.

He wanted—

"Stefan," Brit panted, "please."

It was in that moment he realized he'd never be able to deny her anything.

Good intentions gone, he reached between them and slipped his fingers beneath the waistband of her shorts, pressing firmly against her clit. She was wet and hot, the dampness of her arousal soaking through the fabric and onto his slacks.

"Please," she said, as he stroked her. "Please. Please. *Please.*"

He circled the bud, stroked until she was writhing beneath him. White intruded on the edges of his vision, blurring all reason, shrinking this moment until he didn't think, until his sole reason for existing was to bring Brit pleasure.

"Oh fuck!" she cried, and her thighs clenched hard around his hips, trapping his hand between them, grinding against his erection. She bucked wildly as her orgasm made her break apart.

That was it for him.

Pleasure exploded in his brain, tore down his spine, and into his groin.

He came in a rush and collapsed on top of her.

Holy shit. "Holy fucking shit," he said aloud when he could breathe again.

Brit looked up at him, wide-eyed and flushed. She brought her fingers to her lips and he noticed that her hand was shaking. "What the hell was that?"

Stefan hadn't come in his pants since he was a teenager. Five minutes with Brit, and he'd regressed fifteen years. But for some reason he was grinning, probably because even though his dick hadn't been where it wanted to be, the orgasm had still been the best of his life.

"That, I think," he said, "was chemistry. A shit ton of it." He flopped to the side and stared up at the ceiling.

They glanced at each other then burst out laughing, so loudly they barely heard the knock at the door.

Stefan reached down, picked up Brit's tank top, and tossed it to her. He gestured at the wet spot on his slacks. "I think you'd better answer the door."

FORTY-FOUR

STEFAN GRIMACED and adjusted his pants as Brit set the tray on the desk. It was a lot more uncomfortable than when he was a teenager.

She turned to face him, pointed at his slacks. "Take 'em off."

And immediately he was hard again.

"Not for that." She yawned. "As sexy as this *chemistry* between us is, it's getting late." Raising her hand up, she twitched her fingers. "Take off your pants, I'll wash 'em in the sink."

"You don't—"

"You're on your own with your underwear, though." Brit was talking a big game, but her cheeks were pink.

He raised a brow. "What makes you think I'm wearing any?"

Her mouth dropped open, and he smirked. How she was such a mix of sweet and sexy, confident, and innocent he would never know. But he loved all of those things about her . . .

Loved.

Holy shit.

That may be the first time Stefan had ever thought the L word with respect to a woman who wasn't his mother.

He went very still, studied the emotions coursing through him. Somehow the notion of loving Brit didn't actually scare him.

Now wasn't that something?

"Stefan?"

He looked up; saw Brit studying him with concern. "You okay?"

"I'm better than okay." In one smooth movement, he rose from the bed and pulled her close. The kiss he laid on her was sweet and gentle, and it *still* filled him with raging desire . . . even more so when she responded without hesitation.

Kissing her until his control threatened to erode for the second time, Stefan forced himself to drop his arms and step back.

"Start eating," he told her and brushed his thumb across her reddened lips. God, he wanted to kiss her again. "I'll take care of the pants . . . and underwear."

He set his phone and wallet on the desk before going into the bathroom and stripping down. After rinsing both his pants and boxer briefs with soap and water, he hung them up to dry before hopping in and taking a quick and frosty shower.

Brit had used every towel in the bathroom for some reason or another, so he scooped one off the floor before drying and wrapping it around his waist.

When he emerged, it was to find Brit curled up against the headboard, a plate balanced precariously in her lap.

She had the determined look of someone who was finishing a plate of food simply because it was good for them.

Not that he blamed her. The regimented diet Rebecca recommended got really old *really* quick.

"That good, huh?"

Brit grimaced but determinedly shoveled in another bite and swallowed. "It's good for us."

"Yes," he said and picked up his plate. "It is. But that doesn't mean it doesn't get boring."

"True." She chewed and swallowed another bite before glancing up and smiling. "But don't think I didn't see what was hiding under the other cover. How'd you know?"

Stefan sat next to her, tucked a stray blond strand behind her ear. "That you don't like chocolate but love mint chocolate-chip ice cream?" He shrugged. "I have my sources. And that makes no sense by the way."

"It makes total sense. You don't taste the chocolate! And besides, ice cream is in a different realm than other desserts. In ice cream, having some chocolate is totally acceptable."

Stefan grinned even as he heard his phone buzz again. He needed to check that, but he didn't want to leave Brit's side. Not yet.

"Your very random dislike of various types of chocolate aside, I want to know everything about you, Brit." Wanted to know all the little things that made her tick. His heart gave a hard squeeze as he realized he meant those words with every piece of his soul. The depth of feeling he had for this girl . . .

He cleared his throat, concentrated on his plate, feeling both at peace and a whole lot vulnerable. "So anyway, choke down that rice and chicken so you can have some ice cream."

When Brit didn't answer, he looked up.

Her face was sheet white, and her fork was almost vibrating, her hands were trembling so badly.

"Brit? What's the matter?" he asked. Had he revealed too much too soon? He'd thought she was right there with him.

"Stefan," she said. "I need to tell you something. I"—she broke off, shook her head—"I . . ."

"What?" he asked when she stopped again. "What is it?"

"I don't really know where to start."

"It doesn't matter," he told her. "Just start *somewhere*."

"Management—"

His phone began ringing, and normally he would have ignored it. But it was his mom's ringtone.

"Hang on," he told Brit. "I need to answer that."

"Of course, but I need—"

He wasn't listening closely. His phone was already on his ear. "Hello?"

No response.

"Mom? Are you there?"

"Stefan?" Her voice sounded weak and fragile.

"Mom?" His gut twisted. "What is it? Talk to me."

"Stefan?" She sounded disoriented. "I . . ."

"Mom!" he said sharply. "Focus. What's going on?"

There was some crackling, the sound of heavy breathing. Until, "Fell."

"Where are you?"

"Kitchen. Blood."

He whipped toward Brit. "Call 911."

FORTY-FIVE

Brit

THE PICTURES of Stefan exiting her hotel room clad in only a towel made the media circuit the next day.

Management was thrilled.

Brit didn't give a shit.

Stefan's mom had cancer, and she was manipulating him into a relationship.

Enough was enough. The contract didn't matter. She was going to tell Susan she was done and damn the consequences.

Being on the phone with 911, relaying Stefan's instructions as he frantically tried to keep his mom alert and reach someone who could get over to his house, had been both heart-wrenching and terrifying.

The moment the dispatcher told her that the paramedics were with Stefan's mother, that Diane was alive and responsive, Brit had shoved Stefan out of the room and told him to pack.

"I'll call Bernard," she'd said, "and arrange the flight. You go and pack."

"I don't—"

Brit had put his wallet and phone in his hand, gestured at the towel. "You'll need clean clothes at least," she'd said. "Go. I'll take care of it."

A car was waiting fifteen minutes later, the flight booked, and Stefan had been home before the sun rose in California.

Brit hadn't slept a wink, not until Stefan had texted midmorning after she and the team had landed in Chicago, telling her that his mom was alive and in the ICU.

Bernard hadn't canceled the meeting or the afternoon skate, and she'd been grateful for the distractions. The mood on the ice had been subdued but determined, and the Gold had handily beaten the Blackhawks with Jules in net.

Later, alone in her room, she texted Stefan and asked how his mom was doing.

No response. But fifteen minutes later, her phone rang with an unfamiliar number.

"Hello?" she asked after picking up.

"It's me."

"Stefan. Thank God. How's your mom?" Nervous energy bunched in her legs, and she began pacing the hideous-green-floral carpet.

"She's okay." Brit released a breath as he continued talking. "Out of the ICU now that her blood pressure has stabilized. But she's still dehydrated, and her blood sugar was very low . . . No surprise, that, since she can't keep anything down."

God, Stefan had to be so frustrated, helpless as he was in the situation.

"I'm so sorry," she told him. "Is there anything I can do?"

"No," he replied. "You've been great, Brit. Thank you. But . . ." A beat of quiet. ". . .did you see the photos?"

Had she ever. "I did. I'm sorry," she said. "I didn't think—"

"Not your fault." His voice dropped. "Any pushback from management?"

"None."

His breath rattled across the speaker of her phone. "Good. I thought maybe Bernard—"

"He didn't say anything." In that moment, she wanted to tell Stefan everything, to lay it out there and take the brunt of his anger.

She didn't.

Because Brit didn't want to heap one more thing on him, not then, not when he was already dealing with so much.

"Hey," he said, "the game went well, huh? I saw the score. Hang on—" But Stefan broke off, and she heard murmured words in the background. He came back on the line. "I've got to go. My mom's awake."

"Okay, let me know if I can help in any way."

"You've already done enough, Brit." He said goodbye and hung up.

She *had* already done enough. Just not in the way he thought.

Because Brit knew that, whatever the consequences to her or Bernard, she couldn't do *this*—the lies and deceit and regret —anymore.

She threw on a jacket, packed her bag, and went down to Bernard's room. He deserved a warning, time to get things in line, because she didn't doubt for a moment Susan would make good on her threats.

The door flew open before she could knock, and her coach seemed to know what she was going to say before she spoke.

"It's all right, Brit," he said, when she stumbled through the words. "Don't worry about me. These months have let me get things in order. Even if management cancels the contract, we'll be okay."

Brit found she had to take him at his word, because if she didn't, if this course led to someone else—Bernard's wife—getting hurt . . .

She already had way too much guilt on her plate.

Swallowing that down, she said, "I've got to go back to San Francisco. Help Stefan."

Bernard nodded. "Take a cab to the airport. I'll arrange a flight.

It'll have to be commercial, though. The team is flying out in a couple of hours, and the plane wouldn't make it back in time."

It was better that way, better she didn't use team resources for personal use. Better that she didn't give Susan any more ammunition.

Once Brit was in the cab, she pulled out her phone and sent a text. Her show of spine, of damn-the-consequences-and-move-forward was long overdue.

But at least it was there.

No more, Susan. I'm done.

BRIT MADE it into SFO on the last flight of the day. It was just after midnight, but her body had been in so many times zones over the last few days it didn't know which way was up.

All she knew was that her place was by Stefan's side.

When things were calmer, when his mom was in the clear, she'd confess everything and deal with the consequences. Even if it meant losing him.

But for now, she was going to be there for him, reciprocate the support he'd shown her.

She shouldered her duffle and walked through the airport. It was deserted enough that her presence only garnered the occasional second look.

There were a few cabs parked outside the terminal, so Brit hopped in one at random and directed the driver to the hospital. It was only when she was a few minutes out that she realized Stefan hadn't told her what room number his mom was in, or even the floor.

Surely, he would have hired security with all of the press. Devon, the Gold's GM, had released a general statement saying that Stefan would miss a few games because of a family emergency, so it wasn't common knowledge his mom was in the hospital.

But that didn't mean the media wouldn't find out, or that Stefan wouldn't take precautions.

And he didn't know she was coming.

Brit could picture it, a hulking security guard standing outside his mother's door, turning her away and, at just the sight of her slightest hesitation, hauling her out the front door of the hospital.

That would give the press something, wouldn't it?

"Not well planned," she muttered to herself and wondered if she should just go back to the hotel. Her apartment wouldn't be ready for another week. Maybe she should just try to catch up with Stefan in the morning.

She started to tell the cabbie, "Can I—"

"Here you are," he told her as they turned into the hospital drive, and, just at the same moment, his radio clicked with a call for another pickup. His impatience was a tangible thing when she hesitated, and he barely waited a heartbeat after she closed the door before speeding away.

Maybe she should call another cab.

It was a silly thought. Ridiculous.

Except now that she was at the hospital, Brit was second-guessing herself.

She'd done a crazy thing, leaving the team. Bernard would pull in a goalie from their minor league team, so at least Jules would have backup, but her leaving was risking her position and any momentum she'd made in the games she'd played.

Bernard understood why she'd left. Still, this was professional hockey. If she wouldn't step in, someone else would be happy to take her spot, and she really didn't like the feeling that she'd put her career in jeopardy.

She'd acted on pure instinct that morning.

The team had been in Chicago and the Gold's AHL team was located in nearby Evanston. It had been an easy fix in her mind. The team would be fine, and Stefan needed her support more.

Except, did he?

He and his mom had been on their own for a long time, Brit knew that.

And he hasn't asked her for help.

Yet she couldn't shake the feeling that he didn't ask for help because no one had ever been there for him, because he and his mom had always needed to do it on their own.

So she shouldered her bag and walked inside. She was staring at the directory, trying to form a brilliant plan of attack when the elevator dinged, and Stefan walked out. His reaction was almost comical—feet skittering to a stop and eyes widening, his mouth opening and closing his mouth a few times.

She didn't hesitate, didn't think, just strode across the distance between them and threw her arms around his neck.

"What are you doing here?" he asked. "What about the team?"

"I needed to be here more," she said and had never felt a stronger truth.

He straightened with a jolt. "Brit," he began, "that's incredible, but you can't—"

She *tsked* and dropped her arms, even though the same thoughts had crossed her own mind only a few minutes before. She'd just realized something incredible.

Stefan was important. More important than so many other things.

Maybe even more important than hockey.

"I talked with Bernard," she said, tucking away that thought to ponder later. "It's fine."

"I—"

"Where were you going?" she said, interrupting what was probably going to be an argument for her to get on the next damn plane and get back to the team. "I'll go so you can stay with your mom."

Stefan was quiet for a beat. Then he smiled, and the impact of it was a nuke to her senses.

Damn, she liked him. Hell, that was a lie.

She loved him. Good God. She *loved* him.

Which was a notion that pretty much rocked her to the core and rendered her deaf, dumb, and stupid.

Thankfully, Stefan was still talking and she had a minute to get her crap together.

"My mom kicked me out," he said. "I was going home to sleep for the night."

Oh. Well, that made her cross-country flight seem awfully pointless.

"Come with me."

Her eyes shot up. "Wh-what?"

"Come home with me," he said. "Let me hold you, to know that, without a doubt, one of the two most important women in my life is safe and whole."

Every bit of air in Brit's lungs *whooshed* out of her on a rapid exhale. "I'm important?"

He touched her cheek, eyes shining brightly. "Yes, sweetheart, you are."

Her heart clenched because some part of her had understood that, but to hear him say the words, especially with the guilt tearing her up inside . . .

It made her want to grasp every damn second she could possibly spend with him and hang on as tight as she could.

To savor. To remember. Because when she told him the truth—

"So? Will you come?"

She didn't even hesitate. "Yes."

Stefan didn't reply with words, but something in his expression released. Relaxed and opened. He nodded, scooped up her bag, and led her to his car.

She followed without reluctance.

He was an incredible man, and Brit was determined to do something good, something *right* by him.

So that if this thing between them went down in flames and carved out a chunk of her heart, crushed it into oblivion, it could at least be said that she'd tried to do something solely for Stefan and his well-being.

In the meantime, she was going to wring out and hold tight to every happy moment she could.

Especially if that meant another moment in Stefan's arms.

FORTY-SIX

THE DRIVE to Stefan's house was short and mostly silent. It wasn't uncomfortable, exactly, but Brit had experienced more relaxed car rides.

They talked about his mom for the first few minutes. She was staying one more night in the hospital as a precaution but would probably be released by the following afternoon.

"I called the home-care agency we've been using, and a nurse is going to stay with her twenty-four hours a day for a while." He slanted a glance toward her as the car slid to a halt at a red light. "Mom's not thrilled, but she's also decided not to argue."

Brit figured it would be hard having help around all the time, especially for someone who appreciated her independence, but it was clear Diane couldn't be left alone.

"Maybe you can eventually arrange it so they just stay when the team is on a road trip?" she asked.

Blue eyes warmed before they returned to the road.

The sensation enveloped her, comforted way more than they should have as an independent woman herself.

But she was hopeless when it came to him, grasping up every crumb of approval, of desire, and caring.

What was it about Stefan that made her crawl? She wasn't broken any longer, wasn't a desperate person. But with him—

Perhaps it was because he'd do the same for me.

They were experiencing this crazy rollercoaster of a desire together and Brit thought that if it had been *her* mother who'd taken ill, Stefan wouldn't have hesitated to drop everything too.

It was at the very center of this draw between them. A deep-seated . . . *trust.*

Fuck. Except nothing was based on trust. Her heart stuttered before she shoved the sensation away. Regardless of management forcing her hand with Stefan, they hadn't poisoned every piece of what was between them.

They couldn't force her to feel, dammit.

And she felt so, *so* much.

So much it threatened to well up and swallow her whole, threatened to make her run the other direction and distance herself from the potential of future hurts. The potential they might not be able to overcome an obstacle Stefan didn't even know existed.

But an inner voice reminded her he was in this too, that he seemed to feel as deeply as her, and that was enough for her anxiety to lessen, for her emotions to settle back down.

It was easier to be vulnerable when she wasn't alone.

Stefan's fingers found hers in that moment, lacing their hands together and giving hers a gentle squeeze.

"That's a good idea," he said, about the in-home nurse. "My mom would probably agree to that."

There were lines of strain around his mouth and eyes—fatigue, stress—and Brit's emotions revved again. But this time they weren't centered on her. They were focused on Stefan and how she so desperately wanted to take away his pain and worry.

"Probably?" she asked, keeping her tone light. "You seem to have a knack for hanging out with women who give you a hard time."

His gaze didn't leave the road, but the side of his mouth she could see turned up. "Pushovers are no fun."

Her laughter filled the car. "So, I'm seeing the man cave. I expect posters of swimsuit models and a boatload of black leather."

He snorted. "Then you're going to be surprised."

"*Naked* posters?" she asked, affecting a scandalized expression. "No, you probably keep the naughty stuff where your mom can't find it. Oh! I just realized!"

"What?" His question was amused.

"I'm dating a man who lives at home with his mother." She shook her head in mock-reproof. "I really need to make better life choices."

Stefan's eyes shot to hers, his smile soft, his expression warm.

"You're both ridiculously cute and completely transparent. But I appreciate the moment of lightness. And"—his smile transformed, went a little wicked—"don't think I didn't see those magazines with shirtless male celebrities in your hotel room."

"*That* is a completely different situation."

"Oh? How so?"

Well, shit. "It's . . ."

"I'll save you," he said, turning into the driveway of a neatly kept bungalow.

It was a bit modern for her taste, with a flat roof and wide windows, but there was no doubt it was well cared for.

"Naked men and naked women are not all that different and also . . . we're here."

They got out of the car—Stefan snagging her duffle from her before she could toss it over her shoulder—and walked up the driveway.

"You don't park in the garage?"

He had what she thought of as the typical athlete's car, a sleek Mercedes with a big engine, butter-soft leather seats, and enough gadgets to make her dizzy.

It put her crappy, little Toyota to shame.

"My mom parks in the garage."

If she hadn't already fallen for him, that matter-of-fact statement would have done it.

"Come on," he said, and she trailed him up the two steps to the small porch. Someone had left on an exterior light, and Brit could just make out a set of chairs and a small table on one side of the structure.

What would it be like to sit outside on a lazy Sunday morning and drink coffee, do the Sudoku?

The Sudoku?

It was strange it hadn't hit her before that moment, maybe not exactly surprising, considering everything else that had led to her and Stefan's relationship and the whirlwind of emotions since.

But Brit had been so wrapped up in the guilt and then in her reaction to him—the flaming desire—that she hadn't really digested the fact that she liked Stefan.

No. That she'd fallen *in love* with him.

So deeply that her daydreams had shifted. Instead of fantasizing about playing in front of a crowded arena, of hoisting a silver cup, she was thinking about lazy mornings in Domestica.

Part of her said those feelings were okay, a normal course of human nature and that she could afford to focus on *something* besides hockey.

The bigger piece was panicked.

She couldn't afford to let off the gas now, couldn't risk losing her dream. Not now. Not so close to completion.

Plenty of people had relationships as professional athletes. It was a job, after all.

But this wasn't just a relationship. This was a tangled mess of deceit and intense sexual attraction.

And somewhere along the way her heart had gotten involved.

Shit.

Shit!

She should leave, fly back to the team, and—

Slightly roughened hands cupped her cheeks.

Brit started to pull away, needing the distance. But Stefan didn't let her.

Those fingers slid into her hair, threaded through the blond locks, and pulled her against his chest.

"Thank you," he murmured after a moment, "for being here."

The panic began to ebb, the racing beat of her heart slowing, matching the steady pace of his.

A moment later, he'd shut the front door to the house and snagged her hand. "You need to get back to the team."

Brit let him tug her down the porch steps and back toward the car before his words processed. That was what she wanted.

Right?

Except what was she going to do now? Fly back across the country, back up for a game when she would be too exhausted to perform well. Knock down the kid called up for a chance at an NHL game.

She'd been that kid too many times, didn't want to take that opportunity away. Not even if she had to pay dearly for it later.

"No," she said. "I'm here—"

"I promised myself . . ." Stefan said, towing her forward. " . . .that I wouldn't do this. Wouldn't do anything to screw up your dreams. It's amazing you came . . . so *damned amazing* . . . but I can't let you take the chance."

His words—his actions—calmed her.

She reached up to slide her arms around his neck and kissed him.

She poured all she had into that kiss. Every fear, every feeling, every bit of the blazing heat that boiled just beneath the surface anytime she was near him.

No more panic attacks. What she had with Stefan was important, valuable, and she was going to grab onto it.

Maybe it would be her happy ending. Maybe it would bring nothing more than a broken heart.

But at least she would know.

Looking back, she would know that she had explored the potential of what might be.

Only when her brain screamed for oxygen did she drop her arms. Grasping his hand, she picked up her duffle from where he'd dropped it to the ground then walked back to the front door.

"It's enough," she said, "that you were willing—" She broke off, shook her head. "The promise is enough. Later, we can argue, but for now, let's eat and recover."

FORTY-SEVEN

Stefan

VULNERABLE.

Stefan was feeling remarkably vulnerable with Brit in his home, which made him a total baby. But if there was ever a day for a free pass . . .

Even now, the fear still gripped him, still made his insides feel like shards of ice.

The flight home had been interminable, the longest of his life. Every worry, every shoulda-woulda-coulda cycling in his mind like Sisyphus and his perpetual boulder pushing.

Finally making it to the hospital and finding his mother exhausted but coherent had made his eyes burn in relief.

He'd stayed with her until she'd kicked him out for some *real* rest, not wanting to go even then, but knowing that arguing with her not only didn't do any good, but also only tired her further.

Stefan glanced over at the sound of Brit coming into the kitchen. They'd slapped together some PB&Js and scarfed them down before she'd gone off to change for bed.

"Everything okay?" he asked.

She nodded, and he couldn't get over how young she looked with her hair pulled back, her skin slightly pink and makeup free. The first word that came to mind was *angelic*.

The second was *his*.

A woman who would soon be in *his* bed.

Except . . . that wasn't what this was about. Brit had come back to help him, to show support, and, fact was, they weren't ready for that step yet.

No matter the wood he was sporting at just the thought of her in his bed, naked between his sheets. He bit back a curse—

"I'll sleep on the couch." His house had only three bedrooms: his, his mother's, and a third that had been converted into his office.

Brit frowned, walked across the room, and glared up at him. "Do you *want* to sleep on the couch?"

Fuck no. He didn't. "It's fine."

"Uh. No," she said, "it's not fine. It's stupid."

"I don't want to take advant—"

"Oh for Christ's sake, stop playing the staid and moral hero of the romance novel that is our lives. If I didn't want to be in your arms tonight, I would have let you put me on a plane back to the team." She hesitated and a hint of indecision slid across her face. "But if you'd rather have your space . . ."

This woman was seriously going to be the death of him.

She'd always drawn him in. He'd always thought her beautiful. But it was so much more than just attraction. It was fire. Kindness. A good heart and a spine of steel. A dash of innocent.

So, *hell yes,* he wanted to have her in his arms. Stefan wanted that and so much more.

He wanted to kiss every inch of her skin, to lick and suck and bite, to taste her . . . everywhere.

"No," he said. "I don't want space."

With a single step, he pulled her against his chest and slanted his mouth across hers, suckling her bottom lip before sweeping his tongue into her mouth and plundering it with a kiss that expressed how he felt very much the opposite.

Space? No.

He wanted nothing between them. Not now. *Not ever.*

After releasing her mouth and pressing a line of kisses across her jaw, down her throat, he tucked an arm around her waist and led Brit to his bed.

Where they stared at each other awkwardly.

Her gaze flicked to the bed, and she bit her lip. Paired with her cloud-patterned fleece pajamas, she looked sweet enough to lick.

"What side do you—"

In a swift move, he closed the space between them and swept her into his arms.

She squealed, a shockingly feminine sound that made him smile, and began to protest. Except he'd already pulled back the bedspread and tossed her atop the sheets.

His shoes were off a moment later, followed by his pants and socks. Barely a heartbeat passed before she was back in his arms.

"Wait," she murmured before squirming from his embrace and sliding off her pajama bottoms. "These are too hot to sleep in."

His brain short-circuited.

If before he'd merely been turned on, now he was starving for her. Seeing her ass barely contained by pale pink silk, witnessing a peekaboo of flesh as her tank top rose an inch, feeling the soft skin of her thighs against his shredded Stefan's control to the finest filament.

She'd accused him of being a hero earlier, but with her in his arms, lithe muscles and delicate curves pressed against him, he was feeling decidedly wicked.

As if she heard every thought in his mind—or probably more likely felt the raging boner tenting his boxers—Brit rotated to face him and stroked a hand gently across his jaw.

"Tomorrow, hotshot," she said. "Tomorrow you can prove to me that you know how to use that . . . rifle?" Her mouth turned up before she yawned. "I'm looking for a suitably dirty euphemism, but I'm just too tired."

Her head snuggled against his chest, blond hair that smelled of roses and apples catching on the stubble of his jaw.

If he had been the only one tired, Stefan probably would have pressed on.

But Brit had called upon his every protective instinct from the very beginning. She was tired, and even if he hadn't been bone-wearingly exhausted, he would have still done the same thing . . .

Wrap her in his arms, tug her close, and hold her as she slept.

He dreamt of a blond angel who made him feel so, so much.

IT WAS AMAZING, he thought, when he woke hours later, that there was never any question of where he was, of who was in his bed.

Brit was in his arms where she belonged, and everything was right in the world.

He savored the moment, for just a few heartbeats, before carefully reaching one arm over to his nightstand.

Somehow he'd ended up on his back, Brit sprawled across him blanket-style, one of his hands cupping his favorite ass in the entire world.

Yeah. Definitely not a hardship.

Resisting the urge to massage, he snagged his phone and checked his messages.

It was just after seven, which meant they'd barely slept five hours, but he needed to make sure all was fine with his mom.

He scrolled through his notifications, saw a text sent not fifteen minutes before.

Discharging this afternoon. I don't want to see you before noon.

The order made him smile.

I'll come in whenever I want, Mom. I'm an adult and therefore order-proof.

The " . . ." signifying her typing a response popped up on his screen.

You'll always be my baby.

A pause before another message came through.

Therefore I'm forever allowed to give you orders.

He snorted then replied.

Love you. See you at noon.

"Your mom seems great," the sleep-rumpled voice came from just below his chin.

"Did I wake you?"

Brit shook her head then tilted it back so she could meet his gaze. "I was just dozing. I didn't mean to . . . eavesdrop, if that's even possible with text messages." She nodded at his phone. "Sorry. I should have let you know I was awake."

His lips twitched, along with his fingers . . . and not the ones on his phone. "You mean, take away my fun of holding onto *this*?"

Her breath hitched. "You make a good point."

"I know," he said and bent to kiss her.

"Wait!" She threw up a hand and thrust it between their mouths.

"What?"

Her eyes darted to his and away. "Don't you need to go to the hospital?"

"You didn't see that part?"

"No." She shook her head. "I mean, yes I did. But—"

"But my mom is a force," he told her. "I've learned to pick my battles, and this isn't one I want to fight. I'm not waiting until noon, but we don't need to rush over."

"Oh."

He set his phone down on the nightstand and used his free hand to grip her thigh where it was slung across his hips.

Her skin was like velvet, and the heat of her teased him, even through the layers of their underwear.

"Any other questions?"

"No."

"Good," he said, pulling her fully on top of him. "So come here."

She didn't hesitate, and it felt almost as good as the sensation of her body against his. Soft against hard, and so goddamned gorgeous she took his breath away.

Her hands grasped the top of his shoulders, her pelvis covered his—

That was pretty much when he stopped thinking, when his reservations of the night before disappeared.

There was only taste and sensation, desire and heat.

"Stefan," Brit moaned as he swept his hand under her tank top to cup one perfect, apple-sized breast. Her thighs clenched his hips, and she ground against him in the same heart-stopping, perfect rhythm that had made him come like a schoolboy two nights before.

Using his other hand, he gripped her waist, stilled her motion in a futile effort to gain control.

He was ready. She was ready. But he *needed* to make this good for her.

"Please," Brit said, squirming against his hold.

"Hold on, baby." He flipped them, pinned her to the bed. In a flash her tank top was shoved up and his mouth was on her breast.

Her fingers slid into his hair and she gripped the locks hard, almost painfully tight. But Stefan didn't care. The feeling grounded him, made him want her even more, until the burn of desire was coursing through his blood like a swollen river rushing down and escaping its shores.

He switched breasts, reveled in her moan of pleasure.

The buzzing began at the furthest reaches of his mind, a barely perceptible annoyance . . .

. . .that got louder.

And louder.

Until the fact that his phone was ringing finally penetrated his consciousness.

Brit seemed to come down to earth at the same time. "Your mom?" she gasped.

Stefan was already moving. He pushed up and picked up his phone without looking at the caller ID.

The masculine voice hit him right in the gut.

"Heard about your mother," his father said. "How much money do you need?"

FORTY-EIGHT

"WE DON'T NEED anything from you," Stefan spat into the receiver. He started to hang up, but his father's next words gave him pause.

"It's not your place—"

The man had the gall to try and reprimand him.

His absentee father, the sperm donor who hadn't made a single goddamn appearance for the first half of Stefan's life wanted to tell him what was *right?*

Stefan laughed harshly. "You gave up your place to talk to me like that about thirty years ago, *dad,*" he said. "What gives you the right to interfere now?"

Silence met his eardrums. Maybe the bastard had hang up.

A soft hand touched his arm, startling him, and he stared down into Brit's concerned eyes. His anger, if not faded, then at least banked.

He cupped her cheek for a second, shook his head when she pointed at the door, a brow raised in question. "Stay," he murmured. As painful as this was—ripping open one of his oldest childhood wounds—he still wanted her next to him.

His father finally found his tongue. "You don't understand—"

"Look," Stefan said. Brit's presence enabled him to calm his tone, to be an adult when his father never had. "This isn't up for discussion. You left. You decided you had better things to do than be a father. There's no place for you in my life or Diane's." He sucked in a breath. "Just move on. You're good at that."

"I can't—"

"I *can't* have this conversation. Stay away, *Dad*," he said and hung up.

Tossing the phone onto the nightstand, Stefan struggled for calm. He wanted to punch a dozen holes in the wall, wanted to scream and yell like a child.

But it had always been like that, hadn't it?

His father could gut him faster than any other person on the planet.

Arms wrapped around his waist, and Brit pressed her cheek to his back. It was amazing how such a small thing could bring comfort.

A hug. Only a hug, and yet the torrent inside him calmed.

He waited for her to ask him questions, to push for an explanation.

She didn't.

Which was what gave him enough strength to open up.

No judgments. No matter what, he'd receive no judgments from Brit.

"My dad left my mom before I was born. He couldn't handle being a father. They married young, barely out of high school. I came along a few years later." He swallowed. "I get it was tough to have that much responsibility, but still."

Brit's breath hitched, a soft puff of heat across the bare skin of his back. "Still," she agreed then hesitated before saying, "I'm sorry."

"I'm not," he said and gently removed her arms, turning so he could look her in the eyes. "My mom was everything. She"—he got a little choked up, had to breathe, to push down the emotion—"gave me so damned much."

Delicate feminine fingers traced the light plaid pattern of his bedspread. Stefan longed to lace his hand with hers then realized she had already given him that right.

So he did.

Instantly, the jagged tears in his heart weren't quite so painful.

"When did your dad come back?" His head jerked in surprise and she gave him a soft smile. "Seemed the likely consequence, given that phone call."

"I was thirteen. He showed up at a game." The memory was imprinted on his consciousness, the day his father had tried to shred the family he and his mother had struggled so hard to create. "I looked up in the stands, saw my mom, her face pale, talking to a man."

Fear had swept through him at seeing his mother so diminished. Strong, tough, feisty as hell were the most frequent adjectives used to describe her. But in that moment, she'd been a poor impersonation of herself.

Anger had followed directly after, and he'd started to get up, ready to leave the bench to go help her.

"Luckily my coach had noticed too, and he stepped in." It still made Stefan furious, the sheer arrogance his father consistently displayed. "Turned out there was nothing to get in the middle of. My dad had decided to sue for primary custody, and since the rink was conveniently close to his house, he'd come to deliver the papers."

"Oh my God." Brit's voice shook. "Did he win?"

"No." So many people had testified, written letters and donated money. They'd even shown up in court. "A teammate's dad was a lawyer. He took mom's case for free, and he won. And, luckily, I was old enough that the judge took my desires into account."

A blond head on his shoulder, a firm squeeze of his hand . . . small acts of comfort, but ones that sewed Brit into his heart.

"I'm glad."

"Me too," he said. "My father didn't even ask to see me before he loosed his lawyers on my mom." Stefan gave a brittle laugh. "And the thing is, my mom would have let him visit, because, ultimately, she wanted me to have the chance at a father. But he decided that just because he'd made a couple of million, he'd steamroll her into it."

"What a prick."

That made a slightly more natural laugh burst out of him. "Agreed."

They sat on the bed for a few moments, Brit curled up into him, their hands laced together.

"Thanks," she eventually said.

"For what?"

"For sharing your story with me." She pushed back a stray strand of blond hair. "I know it wasn't easy."

He bent, pressed his lips to hers. "Isn't that what being in a relationship is about?"

Her teeth found her lip, bit down. "Is that what this is?"

"Is that a stupid question? Yes." He smiled when her expression turned affronted. "But I have the feeling you want me to say the words. Brit, you and me, we're together. You're different. You're *special*."

"But—"

He waved a hand. "Let me say this. I don't do connection easy. I spent so long pouring everything into the sport, trying to make up for all the sacrifices my mom made, not wanting any distractions"—he cupped her cheek—"and regardless of the multitude of supposed women the media likes to pretend are parading through my door, I don't date."

Brit leaned into his hand and closed her eyes. "Everyone told me you were a playboy," she murmured.

He snorted, and her eyes flashed open. "Ask Max if you don't believe me. I'm more of a homebody than a partier. But the media did get *something* right. I didn't do relationships . . . until *you*, I never wanted to."

"Oh." Her gaze stayed focused on him, light brown and gentle, but there was also something almost dark lingering beneath the surface. He waited for her to say more, to respond.

"Oh?" Stefan finally asked. "Just *oh*?"

He'd poured his heart out and *that* was her reaction?

"I'm processing," she said after another tense moment. "It's just . . . I've never felt like this with anyone else either. It's"—her voice dropped to a whisper, vulnerability evident in her next words—"it's actually kind of scary."

His heart squeezed tight. God. The things she did to him. "Then we'll be scared together."

"Yeah?" she asked.

"Yeah," he agreed before wrapping her in his arms and pulling her close.

They sat in peaceable silence for a few minutes, Stefan stroking one hand through her hair and just absorbing the moment. Never had it felt so right to just . . . be.

So," she said eventually, shifting so that her legs lay across his lap. His hand slid from her hair as she tilted her head back to look up at him. "Anymore skeletons in your closet?"

"None." His fingers found the bare skin of her thigh and stroked. "Well, none, unless you count the love child."

She sucked in a breath even as she smacked him across the chest. "That isn't funny."

"It's a little funny." He slid his fingers higher and longing slammed him right in the gut. "Come down here." Bend down and kiss him.

"What—"

"Never mind," he said. "I'll come to you."

Tumbling her back onto the mattress, Stefan took her mouth. He plundered, poured every bit of want and need, of affection and love into that kiss.

Brit took it all and gave back more.

She was open to him. Willing. And he was more than ready to take.

FORTY-NINE

Brit

HOLY SHIT, the man could kiss.

Brit was surrounded, her mouth inundated, her body almost on the brink of overstimulation. Stefan was on top of her and the heat of his skin seared her, even as the hard planes of his body pressed against hers.

Frankly, she was always aroused just from being in Stefan's presence. But *this?* In his bed with just two layers of cotton separating them?

Her desire had been launched straight into the atmosphere.

"Now," she said, tearing her mouth from his to gulp in a huge breath. Her heart tap-danced in her chest, her thighs quivered in anticipation. "Hurry."

She literally couldn't wait another second, didn't want to take the chance to be interrupted again. She wanted to seize the moment and . . . well, quite simply, Brit wanted to screw the man's brains out.

"I don't want to rush this," he murmured. "Not now. Not that I've finally got you here in my bed."

"We've been circling this for—*ah!*—months now . . ." She gasped when his lips found a particularly sensitive spot behind her ear, moaned when his tongue followed suit.

"We've barely known each other for *two* months." A kiss to her throat, her collarbone . . . lower . . . to her breast.

"Long enough." Teeth found her nipple through the fabric of her shirt, tugged. "God! Stefan!"

"Not for me." He sat back slightly, smirked down at her, all smooth skin and muscular lines. "I'm the man with the playboy reputation, remember? I'm the one who needs to demonstrate my *skills*." His expression was pure male—aroused, intoxicating, swelteringly, sexy male.

Her mouth watered for a taste. "Skills . . ." Callous fingers trailed up her abdomen. " . . . I don't give a damn about skills." When she reached for him, he batted her hands away, and she released a frustrated breath. "For God's sake, Barie! Fine, you've got *skills*. Now hurry up and show them off already."

Stefan grinned before his hands found the hem of her tank top and pulled it off. "I fully intend to."

Then those hands were on her breasts, and his mouth joined the party, and Brit decided, really, who was she to stop him?

Especially since he was playing her body as if it was his very own personal instrument.

Mouth trailing south, he kissed her ribcage then her stomach, each hipbone, and finally in between.

His hot breath soaked through the cotton, almost scalding against the damp heat of her. He pressed his palm there, just firm enough that a bolt of pleasure made stars flash behind her eyes.

One tug, and her underwear were off. One shift, and his shoulders pushed her thighs wide.

Good God, the man's mouth should be sainted.

And his tongue. *Definitely* his tongue.

It took her less than a minute to explode around him. She was still gasping when Stefan reached across her, into the nightstand, for a condom.

"Last chance," he murmured when it was on and he was poised above her.

In response, she grabbed his hips, pulled him down. "Now."

He slid into her on a smooth stroke, filled her to completion, and never had she felt more right, more whole.

His groan of pleasure undid her. "God, Brit, you feel . . ."

This wasn't the time for more words. Movement. She *needed* him to move.

"Shh," she ordered, twisting her hips. Her breaths came in short bursts. "More. Now."

Stefan bent to take her mouth in a heated kiss, and then he was pounding into her.

It was hard and rough—and just exactly what she needed.

And when he reached between them to stroke her, to give her the pressure necessary to push her over the edge, she disintegrated emotionally, literally broke into pieces that he deftly caught, one by one, and somehow managed to put back together, making her more instead of less.

A heartbeat later, he shattered, and she returned the favor.

IT FELT like hours before they managed to pull themselves from the bed. After a quick shower—together, because really, what was better than hot water and an even hotter man beside her?—they dressed.

"You don't have to come, you know," Stefan said. "You can stay here, enjoy the free day."

Brit slanted a glare at him, apparently fierce enough that he raised his hands in surrender and drove them to the hospital.

Diane obviously wasn't happy to see her son.

"What are you doing here?" she snapped. "You need more rest— Oh!" Her eyes landed on Brit, hovering cautiously in the doorway.

Despite her resolve to accompany Stefan, Brit was feeling as though she'd made a mistake in coming. Who wanted visitors when they were in their sick bed?

"Come in," Diane said, gesturing Brit forward. "Oh Lord, I'm a mess." She patted her hair. "But never mind that. You're Brit, and you're even prettier in person!"

Brit, not completely comfortable with such compliments, gave an awkward shrug. "Um . . ."

Diane raised her hand, and Brit found herself taking it . . . then being tugged down into a hug. "You're supposed to say thank you when someone pays you a compliment."

"Mom," Stefan warned.

"I'm only stating the truth."

Brit snorted, and Diane glanced at her, gave a wink. "Now go get your woman a coffee. And don't come back for at least twenty minutes. We need to chat."

Stefan shook his head. "I don't think—"

"It's okay," Brit said.

He hesitated.

"Go on," she told him. "But water, not coffee, please." She couldn't stand the disgusting stuff.

Diane patted her hand. "Oh, we're going to get on just fine. I know it."

The glee in Diane's voice made Brit smile. It widened when Stefan gave a groan. "I'm in trouble, aren't I?" he asked.

"Loads." Brit retracted her hand from Diane's surprisingly strong grip, stood, and pecked him on the cheek. Her voice dropped to a whisper. "Now leave me to endure the third degree."

"You don't have—"

"Shh," she said. "I'm kidding." Well, not about the interrogation—there was no way out of it, that much was obvious—but about his mother. Brit had expected a quiet, reserved, middle-aged woman.

Diane was anything but.

Her presence filled the room, though it wasn't overbearing.

Instead, she lit up the space, warmed it in that special charismatic way usually reserved for politicians and celebrity royalty.

It both calmed and unnerved. But Brit was determined to get along with Diane, if only for Stefan's sake.

And, considering the affection in her eyes when Diane looked at her son, that wasn't going to be difficult.

They had at least one huge thing in common.

They both loved Stefan.

When the man himself had left, Brit turned to Diane and raised a brow. "You have questions?"

The other woman's reply was solemn. "Only about a million or two."

They were quiet for half a second then burst into laughter.

"You're the first girl Stefan's ever brought . . . well, not *home* exactly," Diane said, once they'd gotten ahold of themselves. She rolled her eyes at the hospital room and its equipment crammed in along the walls. "You're the first woman I've met that he's dated." A pause. "Ever."

"Ever?"

Brit didn't know whether to be freaked the hell out by the statement—the pressure!—or touched.

"Ever," Diane repeated. "I only knew he wasn't a complete recluse because of the pictures on TMZ. But half of that site is utter crap, so really I only knew that he isn't *half* a recluse." She frowned at Brit. "Why do you look so perplexed?"

Brit tugged a chair over and sat down before answering. "I guess I'm wondering what your point is." She mentally groaned and clapped a hand over her mouth only peeling back her fingers slightly to say, "I'm sorry. I didn't mean it like that—"

"Shh, honey. I know what you mean." Diane smiled, even as she laid her head back onto the pillow. Her face softened, the confident mask slipping slightly to reveal someone who was tired and perhaps a little scared. "My point is my son started living when you came into his life."

The impact of that statement took Brit's breath away.

"He's had a hard time since—" Diane sighed. "Well, he just hasn't had the easiest time, and now with this damn cancer coming back, I could just feel him slipping farther and farther away. Not feeling. Putting all of his energy into hockey and me."

Her eyes whipped up to meet Brit's, slightly glassy in the fluorescent lighting. "I don't want him to live like that, to be a robot who doesn't feel. I want him to be happy, and you seem to be able to break through the ice better than most."

Brit turned Diane's words over in her mind. They confirmed what Mandy had told her before, what she'd already sensed.

"Stefan's dad called this morning," she said. Brit didn't exactly mean it as a test, but it kind of felt like one.

Diane's breath hitched. "Oh?"

"Stefan told me what happened."

The lines of tension eased from Diane's body. Passed. "So you understand."

Brit nodded. "I understand."

She did.

Stefan's life had been rocked as a teenager. He'd almost been torn from his mom, from everything that was familiar in an act of betrayal by someone who was supposed to love him unconditionally.

"And what about your health?" she asked.

Stefan's mom gave a tired smile. "Surprisingly, despite my current surroundings, they think I'll be fine. I was diagnosed at an earlier stage but, since it's the second time, my treatment is much more aggressive than before." She sighed. "My doctors back in Minnesota weren't bad at all—they saved my life—but they didn't have access to the same type of medical advances as here in the Bay Area. My prognosis is very good."

"I'm glad," Brit said.

"Me too," Diane replied before giving her an arch look. "I want to be around for my grandchildren."

FIFTY

THAT NIGHT, Brit took the red eye to join the Gold in Philadelphia. She went straight from the airport to morning skate, more than happy to be back on the ice.

Julian had the start, but since they were playing back-to-back again, Brit would get to play the next night in Boston.

He sat down next to her in the locker room after the skate. "Barie?"

"His mom will be okay," she said, hoping it was the truth, that Diane's determination to beat the cancer would make that outcome a reality. "Just threw him, I think."

"Yeah. It's a tough one." Sighing, Julian stood and put on his suit jacket. "Gotta go. My kids are here for the game. Let me know if you need anything."

"Will do," she said. "Have fun."

After he left, Brit sat in the emptying locker room for a few more minutes before forcing herself to finish dressing. There had been nothing from Susan or the rest of management since she'd sent the text saying she was done.

Sooner or later, there would be consequences for her defiance.

But maybe because she was still seeing Stefan, they wouldn't care. It was what they wanted, after all.

Somehow that didn't make Brit feel better.

The entire situation could implode in a hundred different ways— so many more than she'd worried about before she'd originally agreed to the mess.

Brit had a contract, but the higher ups could still trade her.

Or . . . they could release the pictures.

That was probably the worst of it, at least from her perspective.

Those photographs represented a part of her she never wanted to face again, and yet they could be all over the world in a matter of minutes.

Unfortunately, Brit knew that Susan wouldn't hesitate to use them to get what she wanted.

For now Brit was still giving her what she wanted. Kind of. Her relationship with Stefan was in the local news, had been picked up by a national market or two, and attendance at Gold games was higher than ever.

But—and here was the piece that nagged at Brit—what would Susan do now that Brit had tried to yank the reins back?

Susan wasn't the type to take a power struggle lying down, and, not for the first time, Brit wondered if she'd made a mistake.

She snorted, bent to zip up her boots. *Of course* she'd made a mistake. A fucking huge one, agreeing to the deception in the first place.

Yet a part of her couldn't ignore the fact that she probably wouldn't have made the leap with Stefan, if not for Susan's inter-ference.

She stood and picked up her bag. The tap on her shoulder made her jump, but though her heart skipped a beat, and her tongue went dry, Brit didn't freak out by the man coming up behind her. If nothing else, if—no—probably *when* this situation blew up in her face, she could at least say that she'd bettered herself in that slight way.

"Brit?"

Mike Stewart's tentative question made her brows rise.

She turned, glanced up at him. His usual smirk wasn't in place.

"What's up, Mike?"

"I—" He'd never looked so unsure, so insecure. "Can we walk?"

"Walk?"

"Yes," he said. "You and me, go for a walk."

Her recalcitrance must have been obvious because Mike blew out a breath.

"Look, I'm trying to apologize here, okay?" he snapped.

"You are?"

"Yes." The words were ground out.

Brit gave him a beatific smile. Okay, it was tinged with a little mischievousness. "For what?"

"Oh my God," Stewart said. "Please, just walk with me for five minutes."

She paused to make him sweat it a little bit. Her shoulder had hurt like a bitch, and though she'd seen improvement in his attitude since he and Stefan had skated together in the ladder-drill-from-hell a few weeks back, it wasn't like he was Little Ms. Sunshine.

"Please," he said again.

She sighed. "Fine."

He held the door open then walked out behind her. "You heading to the hotel?"

She nodded. "Gonna catch some rest before the game."

"Good," he said. Then nothing.

They walked out of the arena and to the hotel, since it was only a few blocks away.

"You're wasting your five minutes," she told him about a block in, the wind gusting around them, the sound of traffic a distinct roar in the background.

Stewart sighed. "I find now that I'm here, it's harder than I thought."

"Apologies are never easy," she agreed.

"I was a dick." Eyes on the concrete, he kicked at a pile of leaves in their path. "A really big one."

"Yup," she said.

But it was easier knowing that Mike felt some remorse, instead of thinking he was some sort of sadistic bastard who liked to prey on woman and start shit on hockey teams.

And for all the silent-male routine he was pulling now, his eyes were alight with contriteness.

"You really were," she added when no more words came.

His lips twitched, and he shoved his hands in his pockets. "Agreed."

"So . . . you gonna tell me why?"

"Why I'm a dick to everyone, or was one to you in particular?"

Brit tilted her head to look up at him. "Both, I guess."

A breeze kicked up, cold enough that she pulled her jacket tighter around her. California had thinned her blood, made her a wimp about the temperature.

"Well, I'm a dick to everyone because that's who I am." He ran a hand over his stubbled cheek. "But I was a particular dick to you because . . ."

"I'm a girl?" she supplied. It wasn't that much of a stretch.

"God!" Mike laughed, a sharp, harsh sound. "That makes me sound even more like a dick."

"If the shoe fits," she muttered.

He glanced down at her. His expression was mostly amused, but there was something underneath—a chink in his supposed armor?—that undermined the tough exterior of his words.

"I'm going to do better," he said, and his voice took on an earnest tone. "When I'd realized what I'd done, how far I'd sunk . . ."

Mike stopped, snagged her hand, and tugged her to a halt next to him. "Hell, I could have really hurt you. Then Barie stepped in and dragged my ass across the fucking ice during that damn ladder drill because I'd been punished like a twelve-year-old boy." He frowned. "He didn't have to do that. He's too . . ."

"Too good?" Brit tried to bite back her smile. Stefan *was* a good captain and an even better man. She'd never seen him do the wrong thing.

He especially didn't do the wrong thing just because it was *easier*.

"Exactly." Stewart dropped her hand and starting walking again. She trailed next to him. "He always used to rub me the wrong way, like he was trying too hard to be everyone's friend, to ingratiate himself. Now, I realize he's just like that."

Brit chuckled as she approached to the hotel door and pulled it open. "He is," she said, stepping through. "I don't think you'll ever meet a more genuine guy."

"I'd say you haven't known him long enough to make that judgment," Stewart grumbled, "but it's the damn truth."

They walked to the elevators then hit the buttons for their rooms. Typically, the team took over a floor or two. This time, they were split onto two, Brit on the sixth and Stewart on the fifth.

As they went up, she said, "So that was your apology? You break a cardinal rule in hockey, and I don't even get an out-and-out *sorry*?"

She had the pleasure of seeing him stammer before deciding to let him off the hook. "We're good," she said.

His head swiveled toward her, and she raised both hands in surrender. "I *swear*. We're fine, but take it easy on Stefan, okay? He's had a rough go of it."

"I will." The door slid open with a *ding*, and Stewart made to step off before hesitating. "His mom?"

"Should be okay."

Stewart nodded, pushed back the elevator doors when they tried to close. "I'm going to be better," he said. "For the first time in my life, I refuse to fuck up a good thing."

Brit smiled at him, feeling another piece settle into its rightful place inside her heart. Stewart was notorious for his poor attitude. He was good, more skilled on the ice than most, but he'd never been a team player.

Maybe that was about to change.

"As cheesy as it sounds, Stewart," she said, "I believe in you."

His eyes warmed, and the smile he returned was surprising—laced with emotion and almost gentle. "Thanks, Brit. See you later."

She nodded, let the doors close, and rode up to her floor. Less than five minutes later, she'd texted Stefan and changed into her jammies.

His response made her heart feel as though it were filled to bursting with helium.

Miss you. Are you all right with how things went?

He wasn't referring to the red eye or the morning skate.

Feeling pretty fantabulous myself. You?

Not even a question. Can't wait to see you. I find that my life feels so much more complete when you're near.

Aw. Those words ensnared her heart further. The man was lethal. In a good way.

In the best way.

Her phone buzzed again.

Rest up for the game. I'll be watching.

BRIT'S PHONE rang early the next morning, and, hardly awake, she picked up.

"Do I need to ask Mr. Barie his intentions?" Allison's voice was chipper, way too much so for Brit, who hadn't gone to bed until after midnight.

She grunted and rolled over, trying to clear the sleep from her brain. "How are you, Allison?"

"Good," Blane's mother replied. "I'm just worried about my favorite daughter is all."

"You don't have any daughters," Brit said, sitting up.

"*Pish.* I've got one very special one—if not in blood then in heart." Allison's tone took on a serious edge. "And one who I'm slightly worried is going to get *her* heart broken."

"Stefan's a good man," Brit said. "The best kind."

"Then I'm happy for you, sweetheart. You deserve it." A beat then, "Okay, enough sappy stuff. For now, give me all of the locker room gossip. All of the dirt I can't get from my sources at the Bureau."

Brit obliged and listened when Allison returned the favor with family gossip. Blane was the only one of the brothers to make it into the NHL. Two of the others had been successful in the AHL, and one was a college professor.

"I'm glad the boys are doing well," she said before they hung up. "I'll try to squeeze in a visit the next time Dan is home."

"You don't worry about us, honey. Concentrate on playing well. We'll catch up once you're not so busy."

Allison had always been just like that, Brit thought later as she readied herself to take the ice. She understood the game and its demands, and not once had she faulted Brit for going after her dreams.

FIFTY-ONE

Stefan

THREE DAYS LATER, Stefan exited his room and headed for the elevator.

Brit was waiting for him.

Well, *that* particular part was a surprise, since she didn't actually know he was back.

He'd only just arrived in New York and dropped his bags in his hotel room. His mom was home from the hospital and settled, a nurse staying with her for the foreseeable future.

Management had been more than lenient with him—letting him miss four games at a critical part of the season, when the team was just starting to gel. But Stefan was the captain and knew he'd needed to get back to the team.

As hard as it had been to leave his mom, he'd gotten on the plane. Their lives needed to get back to normal, for both his mother's and his sanity, which meant he'd had to trust in the care they'd put in place.

So he was back with the team and, since tomorrow was an off day, he was going to kidnap Brit for the night then try and talk his way into her room.

It was way better sleeping with her wrapped in his arms than sitting in a dark room all alone.

Stefan smiled as he rode the elevator up a floor and thought of what her face would look like when he'd sweet-talk her.

It wasn't even the sex—though God knew that had been fan-fuck-ing-tastic—but because Brit had a huge heart. He'd seen it. His mom had seen it. The entire team knew it.

For the first time in his life, the thought of holding a woman's heart in his hands didn't frighten him. Stefan wanted to protect the delicate organ. To shelter it.

So he would.

The first step of that was taking care of Brit right back.

His stomach growled, reminding him of his hunger and calling an end to the sappiness that seemed to afflict him of late. He wondered what her reaction to the hole-in-the-wall restaurant would be. It wasn't fancy, but it had the best thin-crust pizza around.

He stepped off onto the floor, and a whiff of roses and apples had his body coming to full attention. Brit was just down the hall, he knew, having managed to wrestle the information from the front desk clerk earlier, and that scent—

It was hers alone.

Stefan was just about to knock on Brit's door when he heard voices. One he knew almost better than his own.

He turned from the room and started toward the sound, anticipation in every cell.

Even as he closed the distance between them, he tried not to listen, not sure if the conversation was private.

But who would have a private conversation in the hallway of a hotel?

Still, he tried not to listen. He really did.

Then he heard his name from Brit's lips.

FIFTY-TWO

"I CANNOT ALLOW you to do this," a female voice said in response. The cadence and tone was familiar, but Stefan couldn't place the sound with a face.

"I'm done," Brit said. "It's wrong. I need to tell him."

The woman's scoffed disbelief was loud.

"It's true," Brit said, and it sounded like she was chewing on glass. "I *care* about him. I can't keep doing this to him—"

"As if I give a shit about your feelings. We had a deal. Bernard—"

"I told you before, I *cannot* do this anymore. Bernard is willing to take the chance."

The other woman made a noise of disgust. "Then Bernard suffers. His *wife* suffers."

"Bernard will be fine," Brit replied. "God knows, he didn't want me to do this in the first place."

Stefan took another few steps, inched toward the voices.

"Bernard will gamble this salary like he's done with the previous six," the woman snapped. "His wife won't receive proper care, and that will be on you."

Brit went quiet, but Stefan could sense her tension, even from the hall. "You're a monster, you know that?" she said, soft enough that he had to strain to hear.

"I may be a monster, but I'm creating a dynasty," the woman said. Her voice was clear as a bell and confident to a fault. "When people think about hockey, the first team they will think of will be the Gold."

"And if this gets out . . ." Brit said. " . . .if this thing between Stefan and me goes bad, it'll be in infamy."

His gut clenched. If *what* went bad?

"Who cares?" the woman said. "Plenty of other sports teams are infamous. We'll never become a powerhouse without blurring a few lines."

"I won't. Not anymore."

Stefan stopped outside the alcove that held a few vending machines and one icemaker. The rumble of the motor was barely enough to disguise his presence and definitely not their words.

Both women were frustrated and getting louder by the second.

"You can't—" the woman said.

"I can, and I will," Brit all but spat. "Fire me if you want. But I can't do this to Stefan." Her words were laced with so much pain that he felt the slice in his own heart. "The Gold has gotten their press. It's enough. He's dealt with *enough*."

"I'll be the one to say when it's enough," the other woman began.

"No." He stepped into the alcove.

Stefan couldn't focus on how this conversation would impact what he and Brit had been building, not at that moment. This was deeper than that, *more* than the betrayal freezing his insides.

Brit was hurting, and, no matter the truth of what was between them, he cared about her too much to allow that to happen.

He leaned back against a vending machine. "No," he said again. "*I'll* be the one to say when it's enough."

The other woman was Susan Depratt, he realized, once he saw the perfectly coiffed grey hair and hideous pantsuit. Her eyes were furious, her lips pressed into an unflattering line.

Susan was one of the oldest board members, but also the ex-wife of Donald Depratt, the man who'd funded the Gold's journey to San Francisco.

Which meant she was powerful, connected, and not someone he would normally want to fuck with.

A disagreement with Susan usually led to a few games down in the minors or a multiple-game benching. Sometimes even a trade.

"This isn't any of your business, Barie," she said.

Despite the inherit threat in the words, Stefan bristled. It sure as fuck was.

It involved *him*. It involved Brit.

"Does Devon know?" He asked the question of Brit, completely ignoring Susan for the moment.

Her eyes were wide, and perhaps there was the slightest glimmer of tears. But Stefan couldn't focus on that.

Not right now.

He stepped toward her. "Does Devon know?"

A nod.

Dear God. How far up did this go? The GM was involved. A high-ranking board member was involved.

And Brit.

Who'd been new to the team.

Probably threatened. Or at least cajoled into . . . what?

He realized he didn't know yet.

"What exactly did they have you do?"

"It"—she shook her head—"it doesn't matter. It was wrong. I knew that from the beginning. I shouldn't have done it."

"Done *what?*" he asked.

His gut was sinking fast now, a heavy anchor pulling it down, filling the cavity with dread.

"It wasn't *all* about them," Brit said, her words coming rapid and jumbled. "I-I liked you. I didn't— I wanted to spend time—"

"Might as well tell him, girl," Susan said and there was something gleeful about her tone. "Ms. Plantain was to seduce you into a relationship so the team could get more press. But now that you know, you can help with that . . ."

His eyes slid closed on one long, slow blink.

Susan kept talking.

He ignored her, opened, and turned to Brit. "Is it true?"

Her eyes met his, fell away, clear brown pools of despair, and any hope he'd held onto until that moment disappeared like so much smoke.

But he had to hear the truth from her lips.

"It wasn't like that—" she began.

"Is. It. *True?*"

She crumpled. Her shoulders folded in. Her chin dropped to her chest.

But her voice was clear, firm even.

"Yes."

Three letters that were a knife to his heart. But the pain, the absolute eviscerating quality of that word wasn't something he could deal with. Not right then.

Sucking in a breath and burying the hurt and anger deep down, burying it deeper than he'd ever hidden his emotions before, he merely said, "Okay."

Brit's head shot up, probably surprised by the even tone of his voice.

But he was barely holding it together, barely able to hold onto the calm front he was projecting for Susan.

It *hurt*. God, it hurt. He'd opened up to Brit and—

Stefan rotated to lock glares with Susan. "This"—he gestured between himself and Brit—"is done."

She opened her mouth, probably ready to protest or threaten him.

Stefan didn't give a shit. An icy numbness was soaking into him, sweeping away the anger, partitioning it away, and, blessedly, taking the pain alongside it.

"It's over," he said, "or I'm gone from the Gold."

Brit gasped.

That was the thing. The single bargaining chip that gave him the power in this situation.

Stefan had a clause in his contract, one that would allow him to demand a trade. Before this, he never would have enacted it, because of his mother. He wanted to be close to her, wanted her with the doctors she was comfortable.

He'd also been wholly committed to the team.

But now? With this?

He sure as hell wouldn't hesitate to pull the trigger.

Susan stammered for a moment, shaking her head, pressing her lips together, then finally sighing. "Fine."

"Go."

If Susan said anything further before she left, Stefan didn't hear it.

It was just he and Brit. In the entire universe, it was only the two of them. His battered heart gave a hard squeeze at the sight of her before he shoved the traitorous emotion back down where it belonged.

Normally, she was so bright, strong, and invulnerable. But in this moment, she was diminished. Small.

Or maybe that was just his opinion of her.

The betrayal from management was one thing. The betrayal from Brit was another issue entirely.

Stefan stared at her, felt his gut twist at the agony on her face, and the emotions he'd shoved down battered at the iron door in his mind, threatened to break through and surface. He wanted—

No.

He *couldn't* look at her, couldn't be in her presence. Not after this. Not after—

It took everything in him to keep his tone light.

"Well, that was fun," he told her. "See you at practice tomorrow."

"Stefan—"

He whirled away from the entreaty in her eyes, from the small part of his soul that refused to be caged, that wanted him to talk to her, to figure it out together.

To fight for them.

No.

Hurrying, he strode past the elevator, pushed into the corridor for the stairs, and walked.

He walked the streets of New York until the city got quiet. He walked until the shredded organ that had been his heart iced over.

It was only then that he went to the arena.

And he ran the stairs.

Up. Down. Up. Down.

Up.

Down.

FIFTY-THREE

Brit

IT WAS hell having Stefan in front of her. He wouldn't look at her, or at least not more than playing hockey together required.

But she needed to tuck her emotions away, shove them deep down and lock them the fuck up.

The puck didn't stay out of the net just because she was heartsick.

Using the flat of her stick, she pushed the extra buildup of snow into her goal, took a sip of water, then turned to ready for the faceoff.

The ref gave a sharp trill of his whistle, dropped the puck, and the game was on.

Brit watched them play through narrowed focus, shifting from side to side in her net as the players moved across the ice.

It was a tough game, with lots of shots, and she saw the breakaway forming even before her team did.

Stefan pinched—cutting hard to the net to intercept the Islanders' attempt at clearing their end of the ice. But in a rare moment of miscommunication, Max didn't slide back to cover for him.

Thunk. Stefan's shot was blocked, and it deflected out of the zone, one of the Islanders' forwards racing toward it, with her team chasing hard behind.

They wouldn't catch up.

Barely a second later, the Islanders' player was bearing down on her.

He deked—shifted the puck on his stick to try and fake her out . . . so much so that Brit had to restrain herself from rolling her eyes. The extra and unnecessary movements of that vulcanized disc of rubber as he carried it to the net were both showy and stupid.

No way would he get off a good shot now.

The player cut hard to the left, but she knew his game by then.

With a sharp thrust of her stick, she poked the puck away. It bounced into the corner where Max corralled it then passed it up to Blue. And just that quickly, play was tearing the other direction.

During intermission, Stefan glanced at her and said, "Good save." There was no warmth, no fluff or affection.

It was the most neutral praise she'd ever received.

"Thanks. I—"

Except Stefan had already turned away, and then Bernard came in to the room to discuss things the team needed to improve. Ten minutes later they were back on the ice.

They won, but victory had never tasted so empty.

———

Six weeks later, Julian broke his ankle, shattering the bones and tearing ligaments. It was a huge injury, probably career-ending.

Brit stepped in and carried the shaken team to a hard-fought victory.

And then seven straight more.

The wins put the Gold at the top of their division and second in the conference. For a team that had been the bottom of the barrel only the season before, it was huge progress.

The stands were full. The team was happy.

Brit was not.

She'd gotten everything she'd ever wanted, and yet . . . it felt empty.

A bunch of the team was going out tonight, and while she'd dutifully carted her butt out to all of the team events, even though she felt like sitting at home in her cozy, little apartment, watching *Pride and Prejudice* on repeat and gorging on mint chocolate-chip ice cream, this one she couldn't face.

Stefan was coming.

Things had been smooth between them. Polite. Cool and distant.

The night after he'd overheard her and Susan arguing, Brit had tried to apologize.

He'd replied, a charming smile on his lips, his eyes utterly aloof, *"Totally understandable, Brit. We all get pulled into things sometimes. No hard feelings."*

Then he turned his back on her and engaged Max in conversation.

She'd let that go, not wanting to draw him into a confrontation just before the game, but every single time she tried to talk to him, he'd had the same reaction.

Casual dismissal.

It would have been so much easier if he'd gotten angry, if he'd yelled and screamed. This fucking polite conversation was going to be the death of her.

But she didn't know what to say, didn't think she had the right to be pissed off—not when she created the mess, not when she was the one in the wrong.

So she kept trying, attempting to glimpse any sign of the kind, caring man she'd known intimately for the best weeks of her life.

"Coming, Brit?" Blane called from across the locker room.

"Not tonight," she called back as she slipped into her sweats and a t-shirt.

"No?" Stewart asked as he undressed next to her.

Stefan had moved lockers, taking the space adjacent to Max's and bumping Stewart over near her. It would have been a logical move for Stefan—he and Max were D-partners, after all—except for the fact that he'd done it directly after New York.

The team wasn't blind. They'd seen the tension between her and Stefan before the game against the Islanders, and switching spots was like waving a very juvenile red flag.

Brit had gotten several sideways, sympathetic looks, a few *"Are you okays?"* but, other than that, her teammates had done very much the same thing as they had when she'd first started dating Stefan.

They'd ignored it.

Which she could kiss them all for. Because, even though they had to be gossiping about her and Stefan's obvious breakup, she hadn't heard a whisper.

To do so would've have been salt in an already open wound.

Stewart cleared his throat, and Brit blinked. "Sorry," she said. "No, I'm not going. Mandy wants to work on me, and then I need a little girl time."

He frowned, and she could almost see the wheels turning as he processed her words. "Is that code for crying?"

She laughed, and it sounded a little rusty. When was the last time she'd genuinely laughed? "Normally, no." She twisted her lips, shrugged. "Tonight? Maybe."

"It pains me to ask this," Mike said with a grimace, "but do you need to talk about it?"

"Hell no." Brit didn't need to hash out her mistakes for the thousandth time. She'd done that plenty on her own. "Sorry," she hurried to say when she saw his face cloud slightly. Could she have hurt his feelings? Mike was usually so secular that she would have thought it impossible. But he'd turned over a new leaf too, was probably feeling as fragile as she was. "I just want to forget for a little while, you know? I'm tired of thinking about it every waking minute."

"I get that." He bent to tie his shoe.

"Mike," she said.

His eyes found hers.

"Thanks."

A grunt paired with a shrug was her only response before he packed up and left, but it was enough to quiet the pain inside her.

At least for a few minutes.

She shoved her stuff into her bag then left it in her locker and went down the hall to PT.

Mandy waved her in. "You look miserable."

"Thanks." Brit snorted and lay on the table. "You're a good friend."

"The best," Mandy said, heavy on the sarcasm. "And if *you* were a good friend, you'd let me come over and binge on ice cream and bad reality TV."

"My place is small, and going out to dinner is easier," Brit said. "Plus, no clean up."

"That part is true, at least. But it's not the real reason you don't want me to come over."

She and Mandy had been out a few times. They'd laughed a lot and bonded over cooking shows and love for all things *Doctor Who*, but she hadn't realized Mandy had seen how much she'd been hurting.

Firm hands began working over the muscles of her shoulder, hard enough to make Brit grit her teeth. "Good friends don't let friends eat extra calories just for solidarity," she said, trying a different tack.

"Bullshit," Mandy said and hit a spot that made Brit hiss in pain. "That's half the reason to be friends with someone. Guiltless extra calories."

Brit sighed. She'd had weeks to shore up her defenses against the pain inside of her, to try and bury it deep. Not that it had worked, since both Mandy and Mike had seen right through her.

But apparently, no one was going to let her denial slide today.

She could only be thankful Dan was on assignment, that she and her brother had exchanged just a few emails because of that.

For once, the distance was a good thing, because Dan didn't know anything was wrong and hadn't come storming home to beat up Stefan.

The Gold needed their captain healthy and uninjured at this point in the season.

"I'm not ready to talk about it."

"That might be the first honest thing you've said tonight," Mandy muttered. "But seriously," she said, "when you're ready . . ."

"Noted." There was a moment of quiet. "Thanks."

"Anytime," Mandy said before chatting her up about all of the latest team and television gossip.

An hour later, her muscles sore, but much the better for it, Brit returned to the locker room.

Her phone buzzed, and she glanced down to see a number on the screen she would have never expected to see. Worry tore through her, and she scrambled to answer, her fingers trembling.

"Hello? Diane?"

"Could you come over?" Stefan's mother asked. "I tried Stefan, but he's not picking up, and it's my nurse's night off."

It wasn't even a question. "I'll be there as soon as I can." She started to say goodbye then hesitated. "Do I need to call an ambulance?"

"No, I'm just feeling a little shaky," Diane said. "And I don't think it's safe for me to be alone. There's a spare key under the bear statue on the porch."

"Okay, don't move. I'll be there soon."

Brit hung up, canceled on Mandy with a promise to explain later, and raced to her car. The plus with moving was that the media had backed off enough for her to drive again.

Two minutes later, she was out of the lot and en route to Stefan's house.

Fifteen minutes beyond that, she was at Stefan's front door, reaching under the statue for the spare key.

It wasn't two minutes after, she smelled a rat.

Diane was sitting at the kitchen table, two plates of delicious-smelling pasta in front of her.

"Hi, dear," she said when Brit hesitated in the doorway. "Come in. Sit down."

"You're not sick," Brit blurted, her heart in her throat. She shouldn't be here. Not like this. If Stefan came home . . .

Diane smoothed down the scarf tied over her hair. "Not sick," she said. "Sorry about the deception, but I didn't know how else to talk to you."

Brit took a step into the kitchen. Stopped. "If you're all right, then I really should go."

"I am all right," Diane said, "or at least physically. My treatment is finished. No more ER visits, and all the tests are clear so far. Only time will tell on that front, of course, but I feel better than I have in years." She shrugged. "That's something."

"Yes, it is." Brit bit her lip. "I'm so glad."

"Me too," Diane said, then chuckled when Brit's stomach growled loud enough to shake the house. "But enough about me. You've already come this far, why don't you at least eat?"

"I shouldn't."

But she walked to the table anyway and sat down, drawn by the wonderful smell of the pasta and maybe also a desire to alleviate some of the deeply rooted loneliness that had filled her since Stefan had found out about her deception.

The first bite of the pasta was heaven on her tongue, tangy and spicy and loaded with glorious carb after carb. "Oh, my God, this is incredible." She moaned between bites.

"Baked ziti," Diane said. "My specialty." She let Brit eat for a few minutes before saying, "You know, Stefan's never been good with sticking through the hard times, me and hockey aside. I love my son, and God knows, he's been so darned good to me, but the first sign of a bump in the road, and he cuts ties."

What had driven them apart was way more than a bump.

Try the freaking Grand Canyon.

But—

"What happened between us wasn't Stefan's fault," she said. "It's totally on me."

Diane smiled gently. "Nothing is one-hundred percent, sweetheart."

"Trust me when I say this one was."

Diane frowned, opened, and closed her mouth a few times before sighing. "I won't ask you to tell me, because that is something between the two of you," she said. "But I worry about him. He's unhappy."

"I know." Brit voice's cracked. "It's my fault. I'm sorry."

"Oh, honey." Smooth fingers grasped hers, squeezed gently. "I'm not trying to make you feel bad. It's just that Stefan . . . he's always been able to hide his emotions well. Even when his dad tried to take him, Stefan was calm and confident. Just said he wouldn't go, no matter what. But I've never seen him like this."

A knot of dread curled in Brit's gut.

"He put his fist through the wall in the study. Has been beating the punching bag in the garage to death." Diane shook her head. "*This* is different."

Brit dropped her forehead to her free hand and sighed, her heart hurting so much more than she would have ever thought possible. "Stefan's so cold anytime I talk to him. I don't know how to get through, how to make him understand that I'm so incredibly sorry."

"The thing about Stefan is that you just have to keep at it, keep battering at his walls. You have to almost force him to feel—"

The front door slammed open, and Brit's head shot up.

"Mom? Are you okay?"

"Tell me you didn't call him," Brit said.

"I didn't call him," Diane murmured. "I *texted* him."

Oh, for fuck's sake.

"Mom?"

Brit tried to pull her hand free. To stand and flee . . . somewhere. But Diane was surprisingly strong for a cancer patient.

"You're seriously devious."

"Sometimes." Diane smiled broadly. Then called, "In here."

"I got your message—"

Stefan stuttered to a stop in the doorway.

FIFTY-FOUR

"WHAT ARE YOU DOING HERE?" he bit out.

Well, there was the anger Brit had wanted.

"I called her," Diane said, standing and taking the empty plates to the sink. They made a soft *clink* against the cast iron, but Brit found that she couldn't keep her attention on the other woman.

Rather, it kept drifting back to Stefan, standing so stiffly in the doorway.

A soft hand on her shoulder made Brit jump, her heart in her throat. But just as quickly as it had come on, she pushed the tendrils of fear aside.

She wasn't that person any longer. And despite her cowardice of the last weeks, she wasn't the type to not fight for something she wanted.

Yeah, she had plenty of *she's-not-worthy* vibes bouncing around in her mind, but not fighting for Stefan, just giving up—

Now she saw that wasn't an option.

"Take a chance, sweetheart," Diane whispered as she moved toward the other room. "Batter at those walls."

Brit nodded.

"Stefan," she said, once they were alone, "we need to talk."

He sighed, walked across to the fridge, and pulled out a beer. His demeanor was still distant, but there was a softer edge to his words, as though the ice surrounding him had melted slightly. It gave her strength to push on when he asked, "What's there to talk about?"

"A whole fucking lot."

Pop. He removed the bottle top and threw it in the trash before taking a long swig of the beer. "Yeah, I guess there is."

"Look," she said. "What I did was all kinds of screwed up. I should have refused, and, barring that I should have at the very least told you what management—what *I* was doing. It's just—" She blew out a breath and swallowed down the tightness in her throat. "They had the pictures, Stefan. And then they threatened Bernard—"

"I know," Stefan interrupted. "Bernard told me."

"He t-told you?"

"Yup." He sat down across from her. "Why are you here, Brit?"

"Your mom—"

"I get that. But why stay?"

Her soul itched to round the table, to crawl into his lap and revel in the feel of his arms around her. Never had she felt safer, more whole, than just being held by him.

"I wanted to—"

Damn. Now her freaking eyes were getting all misty. She didn't cry. She was a badass hockey player. Tears weren't on the freaking menu.

"I wanted to make things right. I did wrong, I know that." She bit her lip. "I guess I was hoping . . . I just want another chance at us."

Stefan didn't look at her, just stared at the floor for a long, quiet moment. But when he did finally meet her eyes, her heart sank down to the floor.

"I don't think we can, baby." The endearment tore her insides to shreds. "What we had was something special, but now there's this thing, this *betrayal* between us, and I don't know how to get past it."

It was killing her to not touch him, so Brit stretched across the table, laid her hand atop his.

He pulled back.

Crack. She actually felt the fissure form right in the center of her heart.

"We just do it," she said, pressing her rejected hand to her chest in a feeble attempt at holding the broken pieces together. "One day at a time. It's not like I cheated. I made a bad mistake, but it was for all the right reasons."

"And what happens the next time someone threatens you with the pictures? Will you sleep with *them?* How far will you go to hide what happened?" He shook his head. "I can't be with someone who's got skeletons. Not like the ones you have. Not when they affect our life together."

She stood, paced the floor. "*Fuck,* Stefan," she said, finally finding her mad. "*Everyone* has skeletons. That's part of being in a relationship with someone. You accept their faults. But even *you* aren't perfect. The crap with your dad, that's a pretty big skeleton."

Brit knew she'd said the wrong thing the moment the words rolled off her tongue. It wasn't that they weren't the truth, but rather that this was an absurdly wrong time to say them.

The doorbell rang just as Stefan opened his mouth to reply, and she watched as the noise made drew him back into reality, erasing any warmth she might have gained with a deliberate, icy cold.

"I've got it," Diane called.

"You need to go."

Brit shivered at the frost in Stefan's tone, knew she'd pushed him too far.

Resigned, she nodded and started to leave the room. The door slamming shut with an abrupt cry from Diane made Brit hurry into the hall.

"Are you okay?" She rushed to the woman's side. Her face was pale, and, when she swayed, Brit led her to the couch before sitting beside her.

"Stef—" she began.

But he was already there, kneeling in front of his mother. "What is it?"

The doorbell rang again. Followed by a loud banging.

Stefan stood, and Diane grabbed at his hand. "Don't."

His face hardened. He pulled away, walked to the door, and flung it open.

An older man with salt-and-pepper hair and an expensive-looking business suit stood there. When he saw Stefan, a self-satisfied smirk curved his features.

"Your father wanted you to hear the good news first." The man thrust an envelope into Stefan's hand, turned, and left.

Stefan closed the door.

"Who was that?" Brit asked into the silent room.

"My ex-husband's right-hand man." Diane's voice was a little steadier. She pulled her hand free and stood. "I'm sorry. It just took me by surprise, seeing him after all these years."

Stefan tossed the envelope into a nearby trashcan.

"Aren't you going to"—Brit gestured toward the wastebasket —"you know . . ."

"No," he ground out. "I don't give two shits about what my father wants." He fixed Brit with a fierce gaze. "You need to go."

"I know." She rose and walked to the front door.

Diane cleared her throat when Brit reached the trashcan.

She glanced back over her shoulder.

Diane nodded at the envelope. "Read it."

Brit hesitated.

"Please."

She picked up the envelope.

"Mom—"

"Shh," Diane told Stefan. To Brit, "Open it."

With trembling fingers, Brit obliged her and tore back the flap. Inside was a legal document saying—

Holy shit.

"What is it?" Diane asked.

"Stefan's father bought the team."

FIFTY-FIVE

Stefan

STEFAN CROSSED the room and snatched the paper out of Brit's hands. He rapidly scanned the document, his gut sinking more and more with each word.

His father *had* bought the team.

Somehow his paternal sperm donor had managed to skirt all of the media outlets, to not let a single trace of a rumor out and . . . he'd bought the Gold.

"*Fuck!*" Stefan turned and slammed his fist into the wall. "Why the fuck can't he just leave us alone?"

Gentle fingers on his shoulder made him stiffen. His gaze snapped to Brit's. "Why are you still here?"

Those brown eyes widened with hurt, but the resultant slice of guilt didn't stop him. He pressed on. "Why, Brit? So you can get off on manipulating me some more? Why don't you fuck Blane instead? At least he's in love with you."

"*Stefan!*" His mother's voice held a tone he hadn't heard since he was a sixteen-year-old boy.

It made him see reason.

"Hey, I'm sorry—" No matter what she'd done, Brit didn't deserve to be treated like shit. He took a step in her direction.

She backed away.

Her bottom lip wobbled, but her chin was high, her shoulders squared. She looked over at his mother. "Call me anytime, Diane."

His mom rose from the couch, pulled Brit into a hug, and whispered something in her ear.

Red-hot envy inundated his nerves, and the ice around his emotions cracked and gave way. Regardless of everything, *he* wanted to be the one holding Brit, murmuring in her ear . . .

Well, now he'd gone and thoroughly blown any chance of that, wounding her time and again, rejecting her when she wanted to move forward.

Brit stepped out of his mother's arms and slid past him, obviously careful in her efforts to not touch him.

Stefan stopped her with a hand on her arm anyway. She stiffened but didn't pull back.

That was something, right?

When she flicked her eyes downward, he couldn't help but follow suit. Her arm looked so small encased in his fingers, so delicate and fragile.

Kind of like her expression.

"Brit," he said. "Please. Just—"

That spurred her into motion. With a tug, she extricated herself. "I've had enough for tonight, thank you." Cool, calm words that did nothing to hide the wealth of pain inside her heart.

Pain he'd caused.

He'd never even considered how guilty Brit must have felt through the whole relationship debacle, but if it was one iota of what he experienced in that moment, Stefan realized he might finally understand.

There had been occasional flashes of agony, of a deep, dark secret she was hiding from him, sometimes even during their happiest moments.

Feeling as he did then . . . well, it gave him clarity to what she'd gone through.

"Brit, I—" he said.

"That's enough." His mother's tone brokered no argument, but he might have still pushed the issue if not for the relief in Brit's expression at the interjection.

"Okay," he said and blew out a breath. "Just *okay*."

Stefan couldn't bear to watch as she left. Instead he went to the kitchen, grabbed another beer, and drank.

Then another. And another.

And another.

Sometime in the night, he made it to his bedroom and collapsed onto the mattress without bothering to strip.

It felt like ten whole minutes had passed when voices penetrated his consciousness.

"I don't care if he's sleeping—"

His door slammed into the wall with a bang. Stefan's eyes snapped open, and he groaned as a million stabbing knives jabbed at his brain.

"Wh—?"

A splash of water had him sputtering, but it also had him fully awake.

If he'd thought he couldn't feel any worse . . .

His father, Pierre Barie, was standing two feet away, an empty glass in his hand.

"You bastard," his mom spat. She rushed toward him and tripped on the rug.

Stefan lurched forward, but his father caught Diane before she fell.

"Let me go," she said and wriggled out of his grip. She shoved at Pierre's shoulder. "How could you? After everything?" A rasping breath. "You barge in here and—" Her sob sounded as though it were torn from her.

Stefan was already moving. His mother hadn't cried when the doctors told her she had cancer. Not the first time. Nor the second. She hadn't even cried during the entire drawn-out court process of his teenaged years.

In fact, he'd never seen his mom cry, except while reading her trademark romance novels or watching sappy romantic movies.

But in less than two minutes, Pierre had achieved the feat.

Stefan's hands clenched into fists as he held his mother. She was crying hard, wrenching, tearing sobs that hurt his soul.

The pain. There was *so much pain* in them.

"Shh, mom," he said, holding her tighter, releasing his fists to stroke her back. "It's okay. We'll be all right. I'll just ask for a trade—"

She gasped in a breath, sobbed louder.

And he was getting frantic. Tears were one thing, but this hysterical crying was something else. She was going to make herself sick.

Stefan's father—no, *Pierre*—knelt next to them.

"Let me," he said.

Stefan snorted. "Just go. You've already done enough."

His mom cried harder.

"Shh . . . Mom. Come on, it'll be okay."

A firm hand on his shoulder had him glaring up at Pierre.

"You smell like you took a bath in a keg," his father said harshly. "Go shower and leave your mother to me—"

Stefan shifted, pulled his mom closer. "I'm not—"

"I've only seen her like this once before, son," Pierre said, "but I know what she needs."

The sound of Pierre's voice seemed to soothe his mom. She quieted a little, slumped against Stefan, even as tears still continued to pour.

That slight calming was enough to make Stefan waver.

"Come on, son," Pierre coaxed. "Let me do this for her."

He was about to refuse, just on principal. But then Pierre put his hand on his mother's back, and she reached for him, turned to crawl into his embrace.

A jagged pulse of pain—of jealousy—lanced Stefan's heart before he managed to tuck it away. If his father was what his mother needed . . . he could suck it up.

Pierre ignored Stefan when he crossed to the dresser to grab some clothes and went into the bathroom to shower.

By the time he came back out, less than ten minutes later, his mother was sitting on the floor, her back against the mattress, her face red and splotchy.

But she wasn't crying.

She glanced up when Stefan came into the room, her eyes flicking between him and Pierre, who was holding up the far wall. His father looked totally together and distinguished, despite the wrinkled and tear-stained suit jacket.

"We need to talk," his mother said without preamble. "It's time you had the whole truth."

And that was when the bottom fell out of Stefan's world.

FIFTY-SIX

"YOUR SISTER DIED when she was two years old," his mother said.

Stefan staggered, barely made it to the mattress before his legs collapsed.

"I was newly pregnant with you, not even eight weeks along. I was so tired." His mother shook her head. "Pierre was traveling for business. I hadn't even told him the good news, wanted to do it in person."

Agony was stitched into every syllable of the words, and his subsequent pain was a punch to the gut. He wanted to take it from his mother, to help her—

She pressed on.

"Between Sophia's teething and the hormones, I was barely making it through the days. I was nauseous all the time, exhausted."

Stefan scrambled to comprehend, to understand. Because . . . he knew the other shoe was about to fall.

"Then I fell asleep one day while Sophia was napping—"

He sucked in a breath. Dear God, what had happened?

"She woke before I did and I guess I didn't hear her. Or maybe she didn't call out for me that day." Diane swallowed, her voice barely a whisper. "I don't know. I only remember hearing the crash and seeing her fall down the stairs." Her breathing hitched, but there were no more tears. "Sophia died in the hospital not even a week later. She'd hit her head, and the doctors couldn't get the swelling down."

Stefan sat very still, trying and failing to keep the images from his brain.

Of a child falling, his mother devastated, and his father—

"Where were you?" He turned, wished he could shoot fire from his eyes at Pierre. "During all of this—"

"Your father came back," Diane said. "As soon as I called him, he was on the next flight home. But the moment Sophia was gone, so was he." She paused. "I hadn't even told him about you."

Stefan flinched back, the words almost a physical blow to his senses.

His father hadn't known?

He hadn't abandoned Stefan—

No. Just his mother, who'd been ravaged by the death of her daughter.

The information didn't change his view of his father. Pierre was still a selfish, unfeeling bastard. "It doesn't matter. *He left.*"

His mom rose and sat next to Stefan on the bed. "Yes, your father left," she said, "I didn't know where he'd gone. There were no cell phones then, no Internet to track or emails. I tried leaving messages at the hotels I saw on our joint credit card statement, but then he stopped using the card." A pause. "And then I had you."

He stared into his mom's eyes, the hurt welling inside him, threatening to overtake everything.

"But why didn't you tell me?"

Diane stared down at her hands for a long moment. "There is really no good excuse except that it was so much easier for me to pack it all away. To box up the pain and never feel it again." His mother pressed a hand to her stomach. "It hurt so much to lose Sophia, but then you were there. My bright, sweet boy. And it was just the two of us."

She touched his cheek, and Stefan knew that he could never fault her for not telling him.

His mother had sacrificed so much for him, so to be hurt because she'd kept such a thing to herself? A private, shattering pain she'd been forced to endure on her own?

He could allow her that secret without a shred of anger or resentment.

"When your father didn't come back, I moved into a smaller place. I'd given the big stuff away—Sophia's furniture, clothes, the car seat and stroller," she said. "The rest I packed up . . . and I just never found the strength to open it again. It was so much easier when I didn't have to look at the reminders of how I'd failed her—"

Her voice broke, and Stefan bent to wrap her in his arms. "I'm so sorry, Mom."

She sniffed. "I'm the one who should be apologizing. I kept it from you."

He pulled back and put both hands on her shoulders, holding her in place until she met his eyes. "I understand why."

Her chin dipped down to her chest, and a long slow breath escaped her lips. "Thank you," she murmured.

"It's not your fault, Diane," Pierre said. Stefan stiffened. He hadn't heard his father come over, had forgotten he was in the room at all. "And I should be the one apologizing."

Stefan opened his mouth, ready to retort, but his father beat him to it.

"I'm sorry," Pierre said, a guileless expression on his face. "I failed as a parent . . . as a husband." He reached out, touched Diane's shoulder. "I have so many regrets when it comes to us. Yes, I was crazy with grief, but that's no excuse. What I did was unbelievably weak—both with S-Sophia and then later with Stefan."

Diane turned to face him, her eyes dry but the sorrow evident. "It's not your—"

Pierre shook his head. "I'm not looking for absolution or forgiveness."

"Then what?" Stefan said.

His anger toward his father wasn't red-hot any longer—more like a cool burn—but he sure as hell wasn't willing to just let this go. Putting aside that fact that Pierre had left his mother during her darkest moments, what he'd done when Stefan was a teenager—

For Christ's sake, it had almost ripped both of their lives to shreds.

"You can't go back," he told Pierre. "Not after all this. Too much time has gone by."

They all fell quiet, and Stefan could hear every damn breath, every freaking rustle of clothing. There was a tension swirling within him, tighter and tighter, until it threatened to burst.

"I don't want to go back," Pierre finally said. "I understand that we can't, that we may never have the kind of relationship we *might* have had. But . . . I would very much like to move forward."

Brit had said much the same thing, so much so that it was impossible for Stefan to ignore the similarities.

Except, he didn't want to move forward, dammit. He wanted to stay in his own peaceful world, to not have every buried memory uncovered and exposed to the world.

Yet when his mother said, "I'd like that, too," Stefan found he didn't have the strength to disagree with her.

THE NEXT MORNING, Stefan walked into the arena. They still had a few hours before their scheduled practice, but he'd seen Brit's car in the lot and hadn't been able to resist pulling in.

A few members of the media called at him for a picture, but Stefan ignored them. No doubt, he and Brit would make the news.

Their relationship was still going strong, at least if one believed the media.

Which clearly proved the press didn't know a damned thing.

There hadn't been any fallout, any reports of their breakup, partly because the team had been travelling a lot, and partly because Julian's injury had made it so the press was much more focused on Brit's skills and the Gold winning—actually *winning* games—than following them around and documenting *Brifan*—the honest-to-God term the media had dubbed for their coupledom.

Of course, if they found out the dirty details of their so-called relationship's inception . . .

Thankfully, that hadn't happened.

Instead, Susan had gotten her press. Brit had gotten her dream. And he—

He shook his head. He didn't know what he'd gotten.

His inner conscience called bullshit on that one.

Which was why he was at the arena in the first place. Because Brit was there.

He walked down the hall, barely noting the pictures and closed office doors as he passed by. There was nothing like the smell,—disinfectant, *IcyHot*, eau de Hockey. Nothing like the almost-revenant quiet.

It was as close to a religious experience as he got.

People had accused him many times of being distant. But Stefan wasn't that. He felt. He sympathized, raged, *hurt*.

But what he didn't do was punish himself, the last six weeks aside.

When things went to crap, he typically cut ties first. It made things easier, kept his heart more intact. Usually, it was less painful.

Not with Brit.

He'd said goodbye so many times in his life—to teammates, to coaches—left them behind while he'd gone ahead, enduring the cool slices of jealousy, of things changing in an agonizing, irrevocable way he couldn't control.

Keeping relationships superficial eased that transition.

But it was impossible to cut ties with Brit. He couldn't. She was a teammate and . . . the truth was he didn't want to.

Forget the deception. Fuck the lies. Brit had said she'd cared about him, and Stefan knew it was the truth. She'd trusted, showed him her weak spots, her soft, feminine side. He knew her well enough to recognize that those shared times hadn't been fake.

No matter what she'd told herself. No matter who had forced her hand.

Finally, he understood that their relationship had been real. *Special*.

And, idiot that he was, Stefan thought what he'd said the night before might have ruined that.

He had accused her of putting obstacles between them.

Well now, he'd thoroughly succeeded in topping that, both by insulting her and her relationship with Blane, and then by jabbing his fingers into the open wound that was all that remained of their relationship.

He sighed as he slipped past the locker room and into the arena.

The *crack* of sticks, plural, surprised him. Brit and Frankie were there, which he'd expected—she and the goalie coach usually did an extra practice together on non-game days.

So, no, that wasn't the surprise. What made his jaw drop open was that Stewart was on the ice.

He loosed a slap shot that Brit stopped handily then laughed when she ribbed him, "Next time put something on that, will you?"

Stewart laughing? Stewart spending extra time on the ice?

Since when?

Except . . . now that he thought of it, Stefan couldn't ignore the fact that Mike Stewart *had* been working hard to become part of the team. He hadn't missed a practice, had gone to more outside events than even Stefan.

He'd even seen Mike at a charity function, which the defenseman typically avoided like the plague.

Had he changed? Really, *actually* changed?

Frankie called, "That's good for now, Brit. Cool down and see Mandy so you're ready for this afternoon."

She skated off the ice, Frankie following suit. They both nodded at Stefan as they walked by, but there was a distance in Brit's eyes that made his gut sink . . .

Then twist into knots as Stewart stopped in front of him. "Hey," Mike said.

"Hey," Stefan responded.

And silence.

Stefan started to move away.

"I—uh, wanted to talk to you," Stewart blurted.

Stefan looked at him in surprise. "Talk?"

Stewart shrugged. "Yeah, I know," he said. "I'd joke about it being a girl thing, but I don't want Brit to kick my ass."

Stefan chuckled, and it felt rough, underused. But it also felt good. Really, *really* good to laugh after the last twenty-four hours of his life. "She probably would," he agreed. He waited a beat then asked, "What do you want to talk about?"

"I had some shit happening in my life," Stewart said. "Things that were really screwing with my head. They're better now, and my goal is do right by the team, but I wanted to say"—he hesitated—"I'm sorry. For all of it. The snark. The not trying. The general asshole-ness."

Tension Stefan hadn't even realized he was holding onto loosened, made it so he could breathe a little easier. If Stewart was saying that, making that big of a change . . . maybe he could too.

Mike glanced up, a slightly guilty look in his eyes. "And also, thanks for helping me with the ladder-drill-from-hell."

Stefan shrugged, feeling a little uncomfortable with the absence of Mike's snark. "I'd say it was my pleasure . . ."

"Yeah. No," Stewart said. "The words *my pleasure* should never come out of your mouth when referring to me."

Stefan snorted. "Yeah. Okay." He tilted his head in the direction of the hall. An idea had come to him suddenly, a way to make things right. "We good?"

"We're good," Stewart said. "Well, almost. There's one more thing."

"What's that?"

"I know where the pictures are." He fussed with the finger of his glove. "I want to get them for Brit."

Hope and respect swept to life inside of Stefan. He didn't ask how Stewart knew about the pictures when not another soul seemed to. That piece didn't matter. Brit's happiness was more important.

He nodded in agreement. "Yes. Along those lines, I've been thinking, and I have an idea."

Stefan had a number programmed into his phone that he hadn't used yet. He scrolled through his contacts, selected the name, and dialed.

It rang once before the man on the other side picked up.

"Dan," he told Brit's brother. "I need your help."

FIFTY-SEVEN

Brit

BRIT DROVE HOME from the afternoon practice wanting nothing more than a bath. Hours in Stefan's presence had grated, and his words from the previous evening were on repeat in her brain.

"Why don't you fuck him too?"

She stepped out of the stairwell and into the hall then promptly cursed under her breath.

Apparently, a bath wasn't in her immediate future.

Susan and a gorgeous blond woman—who looked vaguely familiar—were waiting outside her apartment door.

"Hello," she said, stopping in the hall and not bothering to unlock the door. She sure as hell didn't want Susan inside, and the bitchy pout on the other woman's face didn't particularly strike Brit as friendly.

"We need to talk. Now," Susan said without any of the usual pesky formalities, like *"Hello"* or *"Good to see you."*

"I think we've had all of the conversations we need to have," Brit said and tried to move past her.

"Not quite." Susan glanced around the hallway, gaze stopping pointedly on the five other doors dotting the walls. "And this isn't exactly one you want to have here."

"Fine," Brit snapped. "You can come in. But you'll say your piece and leave. I meant what I said before. I'm done." The blond woman snorted, and Brit glared at her. "Why are *you* here?"

"I'm here," the woman said, "because I'm critically important to your career. So invite me in and offer me a glass of wine."

For the love of all that was holy.

Brit unlocked the door and pushed it open. "Sit," she told them, gesturing to the cute little sofa she'd picked up at a used furniture store.

"This is . . . *cozy*," Susan said. "Jessica? Isn't it just darling?"

Brit ignored the jab. Her apartment had made her happy from the first moment she'd walked in. She'd painted the walls a cheerful blue, filled the space with mementos she'd gathered over the years.

It was delicate. It was feminine.

There wasn't a single detail of hockey.

Well, there were a few drawers crammed with awards she'd won over the years, but the rest of the space was hers alone. Just a woman carving out her own niche, reveling in a space that was hers alone.

Alone.

The word sent a wave of pain through her, but Brit dutifully shoved it away and walked into the kitchen.

She snagged three beers—because, if nothing else, her mom had engrained it in her to be polite to guests—and went back into the family room.

"Here," she said, handing them two of the beers. Susan gave the bottle a disgusted look and promptly set it on the coffee table then elbowed Blondie, who begrudgingly followed suit.

"You wanted to talk," Brit said, taking out her cell phone and setting it on the table, "so talk."

Susan and the woman glanced at each other then back to Brit. "I believe some introductions are in order. This is Jessica, my niece."

"I'd say it's nice to meet you . . ." Except Brit had no idea what this was about aside from it involving Susan. And that meant, it couldn't be good.

"Jessica is the reason that the Gold have gotten so much good press lately. She's a reporter for *The Herald*."

Brit didn't say anything. Didn't know *what* to say. Congrats? Thank you?

"But because of some . . . *conflicts* with her employer, she finds herself without a position."

"What kind of *conflicts?*"

Jessica rolled her eyes. "The kind where my boss is an asshole who accused me of sleeping with another reporter's source to steal the article from her."

Brit plunked down onto her pale-blue armchair, sinking into the comfy cushions. "Did you?"

"Of course I did," Jessica said without rancor. "That's how women get ahead in our fields. It's a necessary evil."

"No, it's not."

Or at least, it *shouldn't* be. No one should have to endure the secret shame, the guilt, the not-being-good-enough, just because they didn't own a pair.

Jessica sat up a little straighter, thrusting her chin and boobs into the stratosphere. "I'm going to write an exposé on the Gold and what they forced you to do—"

"Your aunt was the one who forced me to do it," Brit interrupted, her voice shrill with incredulity. "It was *her* idea."

Jessica smirked. "Mine, actually. My auntie here just supports my career. I needed a really good way to get back at Stefan. What's better than painting him as the blackmailing bad guy?"

Brit's mind was spinning as it scrambled to keep up. *Jessica and Stefan? Stefan as a bad guy?*

"Blackmail?"

"Yes." Jessica smirked. "Some of the pictures I took of the two of you weren't *PG* enough for the traditional media, but I know of some websites that might like them—"

"Stefan is the best man I know," Brit said. "You can't do this to him."

"I can do what I want," Jessica sneered. "He refused—" She sniffed. "Never mind. I'm too good for him anyway."

Brit glanced around the room.

"What are you doing?" Susan snapped.

"Looking for the cameras, because I'm clearly on some scripted reality show. People don't act like this in real life." Her eyes flashed back to the pair. "You two cannot seriously be interested in ruining a man's life just because he turned you down for a date."

"This is not about a date," Susan said. "That's not important—"

Jessica opened her mouth. "It *is* impor—"

"Shut. Up." Susan shot her niece a dirty look. "This isn't about a date and it's not just about Stefan. We're going after what matters." The older woman's frown lines increased ten-fold. "Men are scum. They take what they want and then throw you away when they're done."

"That's not true," Brit protested.

"Yeah?" Susan asked, cold cruelty filling her words. "So where is Stefan then?"

"That's not the—"

"Point?" Susan interrupted. "Brit. That's *exactly* the point. We're going after the Gold. The board. Devon Carter. We're going to show we're not disposable. That they have to respect—"

"Auntie," Jessica interjected, probably wanting Susan to shut up just as much as Brit did.

"This is the time to fight." Susan said, waving her off. "For *all* women."

"Yes. Yes. Women's rights, blah, blah, blah." Jessica rolled her eyes. "But further that, this could be the story of the century. If we work together . . ."

It could be a huge story.

If Brit were going to be a part of it.

If she believed a word Susan was spouting.

Which she wasn't. Which she didn't.

"No one is going to believe Stefan acted on his own," she told Jessica. "Not after the scandal last season with Gordaine. Lightning doesn't strike the same place twice, and management—your aunt right alongside them—is going to take the fall."

It was that part Brit found hard to believe—Susan supporting this risk to herself. Then again, the older woman hadn't gotten as far as she had without knowing how to protect her own back.

"Definitely not," Jessica said. "Management is going to fall. But not my aunt. She's a victim, same as you, and has certain items to . . . *ensure* that fact."

Of course she did.

"Well, I'm sorry to tell you this"—no, actually, she wasn't—"but I will not be a part of this story. Write what you will, but I won't cooperate. And I definitely won't confirm anything."

Not like this. Not being forced into a situation where she knew the people on the other side of the lens, so to speak, didn't give a damn about her as a person and certainly didn't give a damn about the wrongs that had been committed.

No, if—*when*—Brit discussed this with the media, it would be on her terms with a person of *her* choosing.

"I don't know what Stefan sees in you," Jessica muttered. "You're not pretty and only mediocre at hockey. He could . . ."

Brit stopped listening. Because yeah, no. The person Brit poured her heart out to definitely wouldn't be the prissy bitch sitting across from her.

Susan stood. "I would encourage you to reconsider. This story is, pardon the pun, pure *gold*. A female player rises above the ranks, finds her way through horrible circumstances, only to gain a staunch supporter in a woman who fought her way up the management side." She paused, tapped her chin. "Devon will have to go, of course, and the rest of the board. But I have enough on them to make that happen."

Brit wondered why Susan hadn't mentioned Pierre's purchase of the team. Surely that would shake up things, management-wise, alter these carefully laid plans. But if Susan *didn't* know, Brit sure as hell wasn't going to tell her. She needed to hold on to as many cards as possible.

"I'm not doing this," Brit said, even though they were basically ignoring her as they discussed their grand plans to take over the world.

"Photographs," Susan and Jessica said in unison without turning to look at her.

For God's sake.

"Fuck the photographs," she told them, slamming her beer down hard enough on the table that some of it frothed over the top and splashed down the sides. Susan and Jessica turned, regarding her with calculating expressions, but Brit wasn't about to back down.

Hell. No.

"Print them or don't," she said. "Put them on a goddamned billboard, for all I care. I'm done with giving them any power over me."

"Little late to get a conscience, don't you think?" Susan asked. "Maybe I need to arrange a trade . . ." It was a musing statement and full-to-the-brim with derision.

Even though Brit's stomach churned at the thought of being forced to leave the team, she knew that it was now or never.

If she didn't find her spine now, she might not. *Ever.*

"It's time for you to leave."

"I thought you told me that Stefan and Stewart both said they would activate their trade clauses if you released Brit?" Jessica asked.

Susan made a noise of disgust even as the terror gripping Brit's heart diminished slightly. She needed to remember she wasn't alone.

"Those clauses are the worst thing management ever allowed," Susan said as she grabbed Jessica's arm and yanked her niece to her feet. "And you need to learn the art of keeping your mouth shut."

At the door, she paused to look back at Brit. "I'll give you twenty-four hours to reconsider. Then Jessica is running the story. With *all* the pictures."

Brit swallowed but stood and squared her shoulders before walking across the room. Her voice was rock-steady. "I don't need twenty-four hours or minutes or seconds," she told the women. "I'm done being manipulated, so take your story and shove it up your—"

She slammed the door.

FIFTY-EIGHT

THEIR GAME the following night was one of the tough ones.

The thing about hockey was that sometimes the other team got the bounces, and there wasn't a damn thing anyone could do about it.

Tonight had been one of those games.

They'd lost 3-5, and only one of those goals had been something Brit should have stopped. Two had gone off defensemen, one had been on a missed offside call by the officials, and the last had been an empty netter when Bernard had pulled her in exchange for a sixth skater during the game's last minutes.

It was only one game, but Brit had a hard time shaking off the goal she should have stopped. She'd let it in just when her team had finally tied the game.

Totally demoralizing. Completely killed the momentum.

Post-game, she'd had her standing appointment with Mandy where she'd spent a few extra minutes chatting—okay, dawdling and avoiding the rest of the team—in the PT suite afterward.

But her delay had paid off, and the locker room was empty when she slipped back in to change.

At least, now she didn't have to make up an excuse to miss the team dinner Stefan had planned for Blane's birthday. No one had been much in the mood for celebrating after the game, but she knew they'd warm up.

Brit didn't *want* to warm up.

She wanted to get her fucking blocker up to snuff.

The thing about professional players was that they could shoot, which meant they could exploit her weaknesses. And if the Gold were going to go all the way, she *couldn't* have a single one.

With a sigh, she grabbed her bag and slung it over her shoulder.

Brit was moping, she knew that. Just as she knew that by morning she would feel better. She'd hit the ice again, schedule some extra sessions with Frankie—though she was monopolizing his time already.

Wrinkling her nose—because she smelled like musty gym socks and B.O.—Brit turned to the door.

First order of business when she got home was a shower.

Except . . . she hesitated . . . did she really want to sit in her stink the entire way? Did she really want to continue to let the unreasonable fear rule the way she lived her life?

Why not just take a freaking shower?

And with that thought, Brit decided. It was time. She would take a damn shower.

Two strides brought her into the tiled space. A *creak,* and the water from one head was on. With a fortifying breath, she walked out, dropped her bag on the bench, and stripped.

By the time Brit had slipped her feet into her flip-flops and snagged a towel from the stack, her heart was pounding and a light sheen of sweat covered her body.

Every part of her, all of the nerves that had been wired to *fear* screamed at her to stop, to get dressed and go home.

She walked into the showers anyway.

Then jumped when the water nearly scalded her.

Some of the tension within her disappeared. She could do this.

After adjusting the temperature, Brit stepped into the spray and began washing.

The scent reached her as she was rinsing conditioner from her hair. Spicy. Masculine.

Stefan.

She was delusional and her longing was acute. So painful that it threatened to take her to her knees. How she wished things were different—

"Hey."

Her eyes flashed open. Stefan was there. Three feet away. Fully dressed and standing just outside the range of the water.

One side of his mouth was curved up, and his eyes were warm, exactly like they'd been two months before.

"You did it," he said.

"I—" She swallowed. She *had* done it. But even as she reveled in that, Brit was very aware of Stefan's eyes traveling down and heating to a molten shade of blue.

Just that quickly her heart was pounding for a completely different reason.

Her nipples tightened, her stomach quivered, and the space between her thighs ached.

"Stefan," she said. It was an invitation. A plea.

No matter what he'd said, how he'd hurt her and she him, her body still wanted his.

But her heart wanted his more.

"I didn't come here for this." He raked a hand through his hair. "Not that I don't want—" He stopped. "It's just that . . . I heard the water, saw your stuff, and I knew what it meant." His eyes locked with hers and glimmered intensely. "I'm so damned proud of you, Brit."

"What?" she asked. The water was dripping into her ears, obscuring her hearing. Because no way could he mean . . .

"I'm proud of you. What you've done with the team, with your-

self. It makes me so damn ashamed that I wasn't as strong. I should
have—"

"No," she said. "I'm the one—"

"It was a fucked up situation, sweetheart. A bad beginning to
something I want more than my next breath." He took a step closer
until the water licked at the toes of his boots.

"Be careful," she said. "You'll ruin your shoes."

Stefan grinned. "Who gives a damn about my shoes, Brit? I know
I don't. Not when I have you in front of me."

Another step. Water splattered on his slacks, soaking them,
encasing them around the wide breadth of muscles there. Then he
came closer, and the water seeped into his shirt.

"I want you," he said.

Good God, did she ever want him back. The need was a fire
within her, a burn only he could extinguish.

He was inches away, and her fingers cramped with the urge to
touch him.

So she did.

It was as if the contact shattered something in him—the distance,
the last wall around his heart. The moment her hands touched his
skin, he was a flurry of activity.

He kissed and stroked, caressed and touched her in all the places
that ached—her throat, her breasts, her stomach and thighs . . .

In between.

It was too much and not enough. The sensations coursed through
her, drove her higher until she was desperate for release—

But that wasn't the part of Stefan she wanted.

"No more," she gasped, yanking up on his hair.

He stood and plastered her against his chest, his mouth on her throat,
then her ear. Warm puffs of air punctuated his words. "No condom."

"Then be thankful I'm on the pill," she said.

Stefan pulled back, the desire in his eyes a physical caress to her
system. "Please tell me you're not joking."

"Serious as a breakaway," she told him.

"God," he said. "I love you so much."

She barely had time to process that before his pants were down, and she was pinned to the wall. The tiles were an ice-cold shock.

A heartbeat later, he was inside her, his body flush against hers, every inch—both inside and out—rock hard.

The cold was forgotten. The past, the fears, the deceit—it all disappeared.

Brit lost herself in the moment, in the hard strokes and hot kisses, and when she tumbled over the edge, her words followed suit. "I love you too."

Stefan held her close and slanted his mouth across hers in the most tender kiss imaginable, and Brit knew she'd never look at those showers in quite the same way again.

And that was totally fine with her.

FIFTY-NINE

Stefan

STEFAN GRABBED Brit's elbow when her legs proved a little unsteady, then cranked the water off, and wrapped her in her towel.

He grimaced as he zipped up his pants. His clothes were soaked, having moved into the uncomfortably tight stage.

"Why am I always ending up with wet pants around you?"

Brit laughed, but the sound wasn't as carefree as he'd expected or had hoped.

He closed the distance between them and cupped her face in his palms. "You okay? Was it too much? Did I—"

"No." She sniffed. "It was perfect."

Then why was she looking as though someone ran over her dog?

"It's just that I almost ruined this." Her eyes dropped to the floor, and her voice was decidedly watery.

Stefan's heart grew a full size. It seemed impossible that Brit made him feel so much, but every moment in her presence, he felt more.

Loved her more.

He snagged her chin, forced her to meet his gaze, dead on. "And that's the last time that I want to hear you say that. We *both* made mistakes, and we won't ever move forward if we keep looking back." His fingers slid to the back of her head, wove into her hair, and he kissed her.

Because he couldn't *not* kiss her, because her mouth was irresistible, and—most important—because the feel of her lips against his was everything. "I want this, Brit. Us. When I'm with you, I feel whole." He blew out a breath. "I don't want to spend another moment not feeling whole."

"But what if we fight?" she asked. "We were together once, and it nearly ruined both of us. What if next time it affects the team? This whole thing could be a recipe for disaster."

"Could be," he said. "But I think we and the team have been playing pretty damned good, fighting or not." He flashed her a smile and stepped back. "I think we'll have more to worry about when we're both limp and satiated."

She snorted. "*Satiated*, really?"

"Yup. I might not have gone to college, but I can pull out a big word every now and then."

Brit bent to pick up one of her flip-flops that had apparently fallen off her foot and slipped it on. "I'm impressed."

"You should be. Now come here. I've got something to give you."

What he'd been planning to give her before he'd been distracted by the sight of her naked in the shower.

His pants got tighter at the memory, more so when Brit walked over and snuggled up to him.

"Is it a present?" she asked. "I like presents."

"Kind of," he said and walked over to his bag. "Just so you know, I didn't do this alone. Dan and Stewart helped."

She paled as he handed her the envelope.

"I didn't look, and neither did Stewart. I think Dan only looked so much as he had to for the investigation."

"Investigation?" Her hands clenched, wrinkled the brown paper. "My brother *looked*?"

"Turns out that a lot of funds have gone missing from the Gold's coffers, enough that the IRS noticed and alerted the FBI."

"Dan?"

Stefan knew what she was asking. Had her brother known when he'd come to visit months before?

"No, Dan didn't know. It wasn't his case." Stefan paused. "But it turned out he knew the FBI team investigating. When I called him a few days ago, he talked to his buddy and found out about it. He was able to cash in a few favors, so the original and digital copies of your pictures were *lost*."

Brit's eyes were suspiciously glossy. "You did all that?"

"I didn't do anything." He touched her check.

"You called." She bit her lip. "Thank you."

"It was nothing."

"Not to me."

They sat in quiet for a moment. "So what about your dad? Why did he decide to buy the Gold?"

"Apparently, he's been wanting to buy an NHL team. He thinks it's a good investment—or at least that's what my mother says. Devon was so panicked to hide the tax mess he caved when my father put in an offer."

"Your mother—"

"I don't know." He clenched his jaw, tried not to put into his voice how much the notion infuriated him. "They've talked some. I think they're trying to put the past aside."

"That's good," Brit said. "Your mom deserves to be happy."

"Be reasonable, why don't you?" he said then, "And yes, she does."

He stifled a sigh and took Brit's hand. The envelope crinkled, and she glanced down as though surprised to still find it in her fingers, then released a shaky breath.

"Oh, God." She sank to the bench, dropped the folder into her lap, and put her head in her hands.

Stefan sat next to her. "It's okay. It's *finally* okay."

Releasing her head, she asked, "How did Stewart know?"

"Overheard Susan and Jessica talking. Apparently, he has some lock-picking skills, and you know your brother is as good as any hacker."

"I didn't even know he'd finished his assignment."

"He was just heading back to the States when I called."

Brit nodded, her eyes back on the envelope. A moment passed before she opened the small metal brads and pulled out the pictures.

Stefan looked away.

"No," she said. "This is it. The thing I was most ashamed of and"—she flipped to the next and the next until she'd looked through the entire stack—"as I'm seeing them now . . . I wonder what I was so afraid of. They're bad. Terrible, even. But they're also not any reflection on *me*." She turned to him. "How could I have ever thought otherwise?"

"Because you're human." He stroked a finger down her cheek, the skin slightly flushed but still as soft as silk. "And something was done to you without your permission. It was unacceptable, and when you went to the people who should have had your back, they didn't. What's the saying? 'You can't cure normal'?"

Brit rolled her eyes. "I'm hardly normal."

"No," he said. "You're so much more. Which is a big part of why I love you."

She smiled and rested her head on his shoulder, pressing the wet cotton of his shirt into his skin. "I don't think I'll ever get tired of hearing that."

Fingers trailed through her now-damp hair to the delicate skin of her shoulder as he joked, "You could say it back, you know."

He felt more than saw her smile. "Yeah, I could. I love you, Stefan."

Brit shoved the pictures back into the envelope and set it on the bench then rotated to face him. "You want to know when I knew we had something different?" Her expression had gentled, those brown eyes melting with affection.

"When?"

"From the beginning."

Stefan laughed, and her cheeks were tinged with the slightest hint of pink.

"The attraction was always there," she continued, "but seeing you react to the team, your tenderness when I freaked out on the stairs . . . well, I"—her lips curved—"I've got a weakness for men who protect my crease."

He chuckled. "Couldn't resist, could you?"

"No." She reached up, cupped his cheek. "Bad hockey puns aside. You get me, Stefan. And if you'll take me, I'm yours."

His arms wrapped around her waist and held her tight. *This is right.* She was right. "Only if you promise to take me in return."

"As if that were ever in question." One side of her mouth slid up. "I feel like I should be promising something like, '*In sickness or injury, in the event of a trade or penalty shot.*'"

Stefan laughed, pressed a kiss to her ear, her throat, her lips. "Proof positive that goalies are weird."

The notion was a common one. Who signed up to have hard cylinders of rubber shot at them at speeds faster than the typical car traveled?

The woman he loved did.

"So biased," she said. "And I'm not weird. I'm quirky. Quirky is cute. Weird is . . . just weird."

"Noted."

"Also, I have something that should help Dan with his investigation." She reached into her bag and pulled out her cell phone.

A few taps on the screen then Susan and Jessica's voices poured out of the speakers. *"What's better than painting him as the blackmailing bad guy. . . Men are scum . . . We're going after the Gold. The board. Devon Carter . . ."*

"How—" Stefan shook his head.

Brit smiled. "Jessica and Susan decided to pay a house call, but apparently they also didn't know cell phones could record their scheming." She shrugged. "Or maybe they just thought me too dumb to think of it."

"God, I *love* you." He pulled her close. So close that the towel slipped, and her breasts pressed against his chest, until her scent wrapped around his very being and soothed all the ragged edges.

He bent and sealed his mouth to hers, fell headlong into the swell of love.

Things wouldn't be easy, wouldn't be perfect.

But they had the sport. Had the team.

And each other. They definitely had each other.

Which was how he knew they would be okay.

EPILOGUE

Six Months Later

"PIERRE WANTS to see you in his office," Max told Stefan as he came out of the shower after the first day of training camp.

His gut got a little tense, but it no longer churned at the mere mention of his father's name.

They were working toward something that might resemble a friendship someday. It wouldn't ever be the father-son relationship he'd dreamed of as a child, but Stefan also no longer possessed a soul deep fury at the man who'd fathered him.

Brit had been a big part of that.

She'd never told him he should forgive his father, but she had facilitated opportunities for them to begin building bridges—weekly dinners when they were in town, the occasional team outing.

Another reason he loved her more every day.

It was getting easier to be around Pierre, and while the past wouldn't just disappear, Stefan found it wasn't quite so hard to shove it back where it belonged.

"Want me to wait for you?" Brit asked when he sat down next to her. He'd promptly shoved Stewart out of *his* spot after he'd patched up things with her last season.

Her face was freshly scrubbed, her blond hair back in its usual ponytail. He wanted to kiss her.

So he did.

Then flipped off the room at large when somebody wolf-whistled.

"No, go on," he told her once they'd broken apart. "I know it's your night for dinner with Mandy. I'll fend for myself."

"Or grab the guys and go out," she teased.

"Or that." He laughed and stole another kiss. "See you tonight."

His eyes trailed her as she grabbed her bag then headed over to the PT suite. She was gorgeous as ever, maybe even more beautiful because the secrets and pain that had once weighed her down were gone.

Last season, she'd led the team to the third round of the playoffs before they'd lost to their conference rival, the Minnesota Wild. She'd been capable and strong, but the team had gotten tired after having gone to seven games in each of the previous two rounds.

Despite the elimination, she still ended up with the second best GAA—goals against average—in the league and had endeared herself to hockey fans for life with her goaltending acrobatics.

Stefan still didn't know how she managed to anticipate the play so well, how she seemed to instinctively *know* where the players would shoot.

It was thoroughly impressive, and her skill at her job was just another thing he loved about her.

"Whipped, dude," Stewart said. But there was no smirk in his tone, only amusement.

Mike had done as promised. He'd checked the attitude at the door, worked hard as hell, and as thus, had become one of the Gold's biggest assets.

Stefan was happy to have him on the team.

He turned to Mike and narrowed his eyes. "Dinner. Text me, and I'll meet you and the guys after I talk to Pierre."

Two minutes later, he was walking into his father's office.

Pierre had dismissed the entire board—well, with the help of Dan, Brit's recording, and the rest of the FBI, they'd *resigned* . . . then promptly been indicted on charges of money laundering and embezzling.

Susan and company would be enjoying all of the comforts of a prison cell for many years.

Once the board was out of the picture, Pierre had hired a new GM, appointed a new board, and things were in much better shape, management-wise.

Stefan had half-expected his father to be at the rink every day, making snide remarks and generally making a mess of things.

He hadn't.

Pierre travelled often for his various businesses, and though he seemed to be in touch with the pulse of the team and checked in often, his father hadn't been a nuisance.

Despite everything, he might even be starting to tolerate—okay, *like*—the guy. With Brit in his life, everything from the past seemed very much in the past, and the anger . . . well, the anger was getting very hard to drum up.

"You wanted to see me?" Stefan asked once he was through the office door.

"Yes. Want to sit?" Pierre indicated an empty chair in front of his desk. "It'll only take a moment."

There was a note of something in Pierre's voice. Nervousness?

"Okay." Stefan sat. "What's up?"

Pierre straightened a stack of papers, opened and closed the drawer.

Definitely nervous.

Was it about the team? A trade? *Brit?*

"I'll just get straight down to it," Pierre said. "I want your blessing to court your mother."

Stefan's fist shot out before he'd even comprehended what had happened. It collided against his father's jaw with a loud *crack*.

Pierre's head whipped back, and Stefan felt a moment of horror at what he'd done.

Then his father grinned, and the pang eased. "I guess that is up for interpretation?"

Stefan didn't reply, only glared. What had he been thinking? *Like* his father? Fuck no. He was going to kill the bastard.

"Look," Pierre said. "I did wrong by your mother and you. So damned wrong." He rubbed his jaw, the red mark from Stefan's fist large and spreading by the moment. "But the thing about getting older, about working hard and getting everything you thought you ever wanted is that it feels empty without someone to share it with."

Unfortunately, Stefan understood that feeling very clearly.

Pierre watched him, eyes serious now, all signs of the previous grin wiped away. "I'd like to have an opportunity to change that."

Stefan thought about what his father was saying, knew how lonely and miserable he'd been without Brit. He couldn't give his blessing. It was too soon for that, but—

"It's really up to Mom," he told Pierre. "If she says yes, I won't stand in your way."

A flicker of emotion crossed his father's face. "Thank you."

"Don't thank me. Just don't hurt her again, and we'll be okay. You so much as make her cry and . . ."

Pierre nodded, was quiet for a moment before he said, "I'd like a chance with you too."

That wasn't so easy. Part of Stefan wanted it, had *always* wanted it. The rest wasn't so willing. "We'll see."

"Tough crowd," Pierre quipped.

"Can you blame me?"

"No," his father said, voice filled to the brim with remorse. "No, I can't."

Stefan wanted to tell his father to fuck off, to leave him and his mother alone. But it had been *six* months since Pierre had reentered their lives. Six months of building tentative bridges and not being a total asshole.

So, with a mental shrug, Stefan gave into the part of him that wanted to see where things went with his father. If nothing else, the last months had taught him that sometimes it didn't hurt to take a risk with his heart. "The guys and I are going to dinner. Want to come with?"

Pierre's eyes were suspiciously shiny. He cleared his throat, looked away. "I'd like that very much."

As they walked out together, Stefan thought that, for the first time in a long time, happily-ever-afters might actually be a reality.

BACKHAND

GOLD HOCKEY #2

ONE

Sara

THE LIGHT WAS PERFECT . . . until it wasn't.

Sara glared up at the large, brick-wall style shadow that was marring her perfect view.

Did the person not understand just how *freaking* long she'd had to wait for the moon to peek out from behind the fog, to gild the rotunda at the Palace of Fine Arts and reflect off the water in perfect symmetry?

She clutched her pencil—the same one that had been sketching furiously just seconds before—and leaned to the left, trying to get one more glimpse of the scene, to commit it to memory before it was . . .

Gone.

Son of a—

"I know you."

The male voice was chocolate ice cream with hot fudge and marshmallow fluff, warm sand sifting between her toes, the perfect ending to a dramatic rom-com all rolled into one.

The hairs on her nape rose, and she shivered, wanting to snuggle into the sound, to pull it close like a cuddly sweatshirt—

At least until alarm flared to life, and she remembered she was totally alone.

Suddenly, skulking around the Marina District in the middle of the night seemed like a horrible idea.

Her sketchbook fell to the ground, the book light that had been clipped to the top making a sickening crack as it hit the concrete and went out. She blinked, trying to get her eyes to adjust, but darkness descended as fog swallowed the moon back up. She gripped her pencil like a knife and held it threateningly . . . or at least as threateningly as a pencil can be held. "Back off."

Her attempt at a growl, a warning.

And not a very scary one at that, if the man's reaction was anything to go by.

A soft chuckle was the only thing she heard before the pencil was plucked from her fingers. Sara opened her mouth to scream, but instead of jumping her like she'd half-expected, he sank into a crouch and handed the pencil back.

"You shouldn't be out here by yourself," he said.

"Noted," Sara muttered and shoved it into her pocket before bending to grab her sketchbook and light. "And you shouldn't ruin a perfect setup."

A flash of white teeth penetrated the darkness. "Noted," he said and put a palm to his knee, as though to push himself to standing.

Her eyes dropped. They'd adjusted enough to see his hands. And those hands were *gorgeous*. Long, lean fingers and neatly trimmed nails with enough character to make them interesting. She flipped to a blank page of her sketchbook, flicked the switch on the light, and spread his fingers on her thigh. The contrast, the shadows, the scars on his knuckles. His hand was the perfect juxtaposition and she *had* to get it on paper.

"Umm—"

"Shh." Her pencil flew across the page. It made a soft scratching sound as she worked, outlining, shading in the image, blending and building until his hand was captured on paper.

She didn't know how long she worked, just that when she'd finished, her neck ached and her legs were stiff and . . . a strange man had his hand on her thigh.

Her breath caught, and she looked up.

He was beautiful. Oddly familiar with his face half-illuminated in the lamplight, eyes as dark as ink, several days of scruff on his cheeks and chin, nose just slightly askew, as though it had been broken a time or two. And was that a bruise just above his right cheekbone?

Sara didn't have a chance to look closer.

His fingers flexed on her thigh, and every one of her thoughts beelined straight for that particular body part. She was in jeans, so it wasn't like he was touching her skin. But he might as well have been.

The warmth of his palm seeped through the thick material, made her quads flex. He was huge, his hand spanning the width of her thigh easily, and just the kind of man she liked. Big and strong, tall and wide-shouldered. Here was a man who could do all the clichés: protect her, shelter her, weather proverbial storms.

"You done?" The soft question held just the slightest hint of amusement, except there was a bite to the humor, as though that piece of his personality hadn't been used in a good long time.

No. She wanted to sketch his face, flip his hand over and draw the lines of his palm, but she'd submitted enough to her artist-crazy for the evening. And her hand was sore.

"Yeah," she said, ignoring the slightly breathless quality to her voice and standing.

Sketchbook into her pack, light off and into her pocket, stiff and aching hip, ribs, and shoulder from sitting too long on the cold, hard ground. Yup. All was as it should be.

The man stood as well. His size on the ground hadn't done his real breadth justice.

He. Was. Ginormous.

Okay, so she was petite, barely five feet three, but this man towered over her.

Yet she didn't feel scared. Embarrassed, maybe, that she'd hijacked his hand for—she pulled out her phone and glanced at the time—an hour and a half. But definitely not scared.

And she'd focus on that at a later time. For now, she should probably make an escape before she looked even more crazy cakes.

"Sorry I messed up your sketch," he rumbled.

She nibbled on the side of her mouth, biting back a smile. "Sorry I stole your hand for so long."

He shrugged. "My mom's an artist. I get it."

Well, there went her battle with the smile. Her lips twitched and her teeth came out of hiding. If there was one thing that Sara had, it was her smile. It had been her trademark in her competition days.

Which were long over.

Her mouth flattened out, the grin slipping away. Time to go, time to forget, to move on, to rebuild. "Thanks," she said and extended a hand.

Then winced and dropped it when her ribs cried out in protest.

"You okay?" he asked, head tilting, eyes studying her.

"Fine." And out popped her new smile. The fake one. Careful of her aching side, she shrugged into her backpack. "I've got to go." She turned, ponytail flapping through the hair to land on her opposite shoulder.

"That—" He touched her arm. "Wait. I *know* I know you."

She froze. That was the second time he'd said that, and now they were getting into dangerous territory. Recognition meant . . . no. She couldn't.

There had been a time when *everyone* had known her. Her face on Wheaties boxes, her smile promoting toothpaste and credit cards alike.

That wasn't her life any longer.

"Thanks again. Bye." She started to hurry away.

"Wait." A hand dropped on to her shoulder, thwarting her escape, and she hissed in pain.

"Sorry," he said, but he didn't release her. Instead, he shifted his grip from her aching shoulder down to her elbow and when she didn't protest, he exerted gentle pressure until Sara was facing him again. "It's just that know I *know* you."

No. This wasn't happening.

"You're Sara Jetty."

Her body went tense.

Oh God. This was *so* happening.

"It's me." He touched his chest like she didn't know he was talking about himself, and even as she was finally recognizing the color of his eyes, the familiar curve of his lips and line of his jaw, he said the worst thing ever, "Mike Stewart."

Oh *shit.*

TWO

Mike

SARA *FUCKING* JETTY.

Mike watched the horror cloud Sara's face, drawing her brows up and her mouth down. Even in the near dark, he watched her skin go ghostly white.

"It's been a long time, Jumping Bean."

Her head jerked up at the old nickname, and that horror turned to anger. He understood why. Didn't mean he liked it, though.

"I need to go." She whirled away.

"Hey. *Wait.*"

She didn't, just took off along the path, not running exactly, but definitely not waiting either.

Which didn't matter. Because he was taller. And faster.

He caught up to her in a couple of strides, snagged her elbow, and, careful to not hurt her again, tugged her to a stop.

He expected to catch up with her, to be able to stop her from escaping. What he didn't expect was the shit fuck of a crocodile-death-roll she pulled on him.

Sara spun, struggling in his hold and probably bruising her arm to hell and back. "Let. Go."

Jesus. "All right. Fine." He released her, raised his hands in surrender. "I was just trying—"

"I know all about men *trying*," she muttered. "Just leave me alone."

"Christ, woman. It's been ten years. I only wanted to find out how you're doing."

"You're kidding me, right?" she asked, brows practically in her hairline.

Why did he suddenly feel like this was a trick question? "Uh. No."

Her arms flopped down to her sides, and Mike was reminded of how small she was. Her backpack straps practically dwarfed her shoulders, and she was still so dang short. Put-her-in-his-pocket, Teacup-Poodle-in-a-world-of-Great-Danes short.

"You have to be kidding," she snapped, "because you cannot possibly be serious about asking me how I've *been*."

Okay, now Mike was starting to get pissed. Here he was, trying to be nice, trying to catch up with an old friend, and she was being a total bitch. He ignored the voice in his head telling him that he should really know what she was talking about.

"Sweetheart, I haven't got a clue what you're spouting off about," he growled. "So either tell me what's up or answer the damn question."

"I've been fucked, Mike. Royally and permanently fucked. *Okay?*" Whipping around, she started stomping away.

What the hell did that mean?

"Sara—"

"Oh. My. God." Her feet skidded to a stop, and she threw him a dark look over her shoulder. "Just leave me alone. This isn't like when we were kids. You can't fix it, you can't fix *me*."

The weight of those words hit him in the gut, stealing his air more effectively than getting checked into the boards on the ice.

And by the time he recovered, she was running, running down the path that led to the street.

Running straight out of his life.

Damn, was that a familiar feeling.

NOTHING WAS BETTER than being on the ice. *Nothing.*

The way his skin went tight when the cold hit it, the crunch beneath his skates, the sounds—laughter, pucks colliding with the glass, pinging off the goalposts, the Zamboni rumbling to life. He even loved the smell.

Akin to wet asphalt after a rain, there was already the slight odor of moisture in the air, not in a bad moldy way, but in the best hours of his childhood.

Escape. Friends. Camaraderie.

Family.

"Looking awfully introspective for a hockey player, Stewie," Blue, the rookie, said, using the new nickname the boys had decided to bestow upon Mike, mostly because they knew it drove him nuts.

"Rookies who tease better watch themselves," Mike responded, his tone falsely threatening.

Blue wasn't exactly a rookie, not any longer anyway. He'd had a phenomenal season the previous year that had him in the upper echelon of NHL stat charts—sixty goals, thirty assists, and a gritty, tough-as-shit work ethic.

"Good thing then that I'm not a rookie." Blue grinned, not intimidated by Mike in the least. The kid had always had way too much confidence, but they were at a better place this year. Namely, Mike had burned his asshole card and started acting like a good teammate.

He bumped his shoulder to Blue's, and Blue, thinking he was returning the friendly gesture, leaned in to do the same. But Mike scooted away, just enough that Blue was off-balance, then dropped his gloves and stick.

In a flash, he had Blue's jersey up and over the kid's head.

"Still a rookie in some ways," he said, patting him on the back, grabbing his gear, and skating away.

"Oh look! A present!" Brit shouted from the net. "For me? *Aw.* Mike, you shouldn't have."

Blue wrestled with the fabric encasing him, pulling it down and knocking his helmet askew in the process.

"Fucker!" he called, but he was grinning, and so were the rest of the guys.

Family.

Mike hadn't thought it possible, but somehow the shit in his life had settled, and he'd found his family again.

Then he thought of Sara, running head down, shoulders bowed through the street, and his grin faded.

THREE

Sara

THE BELL to the shop tinkled as a customer pushed through, but Sara didn't bother to put her pencil down. She'd worked at the gallery long enough to know with a simple glance if a person was buying or not.

And this one wasn't.

Then the bell jingled again. Her eyes flicked up, and her pencil hit the paper. She straightened and tried to look professional when a well-dressed man came in and approached the counter.

He was hot, had a body like Jason Momoa, and he was . . . her boss.

He also, unfortunately for the female population, wasn't straight.

"Sara, honey," Mitch said, leaning over the artfully cut piece of granite to buss her cheek. "I've told you before, I don't care if you draw while you work, honey."

He had. Many times, but Sara couldn't just put the oh-God-her-boss-is-looking-at-her fear aside. She'd never been friends with her teachers or coaches because she had a problem with authority.

Namely with always bending to its will.

"Pathetic," she muttered.

"No, you're not," Mitch said fiercely, and her eyes flew up to meet his. "You're talented and sure as shit shouldn't be working behind the counter of my shop." He bent close, his voice softening. "Hun, your stuff should be all over my walls."

Sara let her gaze slide away, tracing the display of metal sculptures in the store's windows. They were good, way more intricate than anything she could ever come up with.

Then again, her strength wasn't sculpture. It was pencil sketching.

"My stuff is fine. Nothing inspirational, nothing amaz—"

Her words cut off as he snatched the sketchbook from beneath her hands and strode over to the older gentleman, the not-buyer, who was now perusing a set of postcards. Mitch flipped through pages as he walked, stopping on a drawing of the Golden Gate Bridge.

The sketch was her favorite, though probably not her most technically sound, with the swirls of shadow and light, her version of the notorious fog curling around the span, creeping over cars and pedestrians alike.

Done all in shades of gray, it had only the barest hint of the bridge's famous coppery red.

"What do you think of this?" Mitch asked the customer.

Sara's throat closed up, sweat broke out on her forehead, and her heart absolutely galloped in her chest.

The man's eyes went wide, brows climbing almost to the wisps of white hair sparsely covering his shiny scalp. "That's amazing," he said, his voice soft and practically breathy. He raised a hand as though to touch the image, and Sara winced.

Mitch slid it out of reach. "How much would you pay for it?"

"Is it an original?"

"Yup."

"Two grand."

Sara's heart was no longer galloping. It had stopped, frozen in her chest, along with every other part of her body.

Mitch laughed and put on his master negotiator hat. "It's worth three times that."

"I'll give you four." The man pulled out his wallet.

"Fifty-five hundred," Mitch countered.

"Five."

Mitch glanced over at her for the first time and raised a brow. She read the unspoken question in his expression. Did she want to sell?

For five thousand dollars? Hell *yes*, she wanted to sell.

Approval slid across Mitch's face. "Sold," he said, and they began talking about framing and matting options.

And in the span of five minutes, she'd sold her first work.

Holy balls of Satan.

She might actually make a go of this artist thing.

Later when the store had closed, Mitch handed her a check for the drawing. She blinked when she saw that no commission had been taken out.

He tapped her on the nose before she could protest. "First one's on the house, sweetheart. Just make sure to save something for taxes."

Her eyes filled with tears.

"None of that," he said. "I know you've had a shit time of it, but things are going to get better. I promise."

Oddly touched, she pressed a kiss to his cheek. "Thanks, Mitch."

"Give me some more drawings to sell, and that'll be thanks enough."

The thought made her nervous, but she gave a determined nod, shoved her sketchbook into her backpack, and shrugged into her coat.

Sara called her good-bye and left, thinking the world might be just a tad bit friendlier than she'd previously thought.

Of course, she was disabused of that notion exactly ten minutes and three blocks later when the skies opened up.

It was February, smack dab in the typical rainy season of

Northern California, and the downpour shouldn't have come as a surprise.

The weatherman had even predicted it. And gotten things right for a change.

Unfortunately, her umbrella was currently sitting in Mitch's office.

Well, nothing to be done about it.

Tugging her hood up, she moved faster. Her apartment was a good nine blocks away, and since she was already soaked through, she might as well press on.

A car drove by, and she flinched away from the curb. Though it was too soon for puddles to have formed and for the tires to kick them up onto her, the instinct had been honed by five years of San Franciscan living.

She did *not* want whatever was in that water or on the street anywhere near her.

Her obsession with avoiding the nonexistent puddle was probably why she missed the car stopping. At least until the driver's window whirred down, and she heard Mike's voice, trailed by a cacophony of screeching tires and blaring horns.

"Sara," he said, calmly. As though he wasn't just chilling in the middle of the lane, as though cars weren't swerving around him and delivering fingers and curse words alike.

"What are you doing?" she asked.

Water streamed down her face, soaked through her clothes. She pulled her backpack off and clutched it to her chest, thankful it had a waterproof inner layer.

He raised a brow. "Want to get in?"

Mike Stewart, unwelcome blast from the past, professional hockey player, and former Mr. Popular of Nowhere, Minnesota, had parked in the middle of Market Street to have a casual roadside chat.

"Yeah, no," she said. "I'm cool." She started walking again.

The tires of his car made a whooshing sound as he trailed after her.

"What are you doing?" she shouted and waved a hand at the line of angry drivers behind him. "You're blocking traffic."

"Get in, Sara. We need to talk."

Yeah. That wasn't happening.

"No, we don't, Hot Shot."

"Sara," he growled, probably as much at the old nickname he hated as the fact that she wasn't obeying his orders, and kept pace with her. Which meant he was driving all of five miles per hour down the busy San Franciscan street.

The stoplight in front of his car turned red, and he slid to a stop. Not even Mike would blow a red light. He might have the same slice of reckless as every other member of the male populace, but he didn't risk other people.

Or he hadn't used to, anyway.

Which is why she wasn't getting anywhere near him. He didn't need to be mixed up in her garbage.

With a wave, she hurried around the corner, starting down a side street that would actually take her farther from her apartment.

But since it was a one-way street—the wrong way for anyone particularly pesky and exceptionally annoying to follow—she would be safe.

Mike had different ideas.

"Sara." He'd gotten out of the car and was right behind her. And that voice, melted chocolate and velvet all mixed up in one, slid down her skin. It stopped somewhere in the vicinity of her lady parts. Damn. That intensity, the *alpha* inside him making an appearance . .

.

Shut it, haters. She could be a feminist and still like the growly way the man ordered her around.

Liking didn't mean she was going to obey, after all.

Except maybe in the bedroom, or against the building, rain sluicing down their faces, soaking into their clothes, cooling their heated skin as Mike pounded into her—

And holy crap-on-a-stick, where had *that* come from?

The Mike she knew had been gangly with acne on his chin. He'd been sweet and kind and . . . not interested in her in the least.

Her Mike no longer existed. Which tended to happen when more than a decade passed.

Straightening her shoulders, Sara turned around. "What do you want?"

"It's been years, sweetheart. Last I heard, you're on the podium with a gold medal around your neck. Then nothing. No word, no email." His voice dropped, and she shivered, not in a good way this time, since his gaze was pinning her in place. "You just pop up in my city with demons in your eyes."

"I don't have demons," she said, taking a step back.

"Yes." He came closer, bent so his head was near hers. "You do."

She opened her mouth, but he didn't give her a chance to respond, just plucked her backpack from her arms and strode back down the street.

"Hey!" she shouted. "Stop!"

He didn't.

"Mike! Wait!"

He tossed her a look over his shoulder, not stopping, not waiting, just walking away. "Doesn't feel good, does it?" he asked.

No, it damn well didn't feel good.

But then again, she'd had plenty of experience burying the hurt that came along with people walking away from her.

FOUR

Mike

MIKE TOSSED Sara's backpack into the passenger seat, dropped himself and his sopping wet suit into the driver's seat, and waited.

Five. Four. Three. Two—

Sara didn't disappoint. She wrenched open the door and reached for the backpack. "What the hell do you—?"

Yeah, not happening.

Mike snatched it up and gave her a look, waiting for her to sit down and close the door.

Her eyes went heavenward, and she sighed. "Can't I just—"

"No." He tucked the backpack down by his legs.

A horn blared behind them, jolting his mind back to the present, back to the fact that he was in the middle of Market during rush hour and had just casually parked his car in the right lane.

An SUV screeched by, its driver waving a certain finger.

Mike raised a brow. "Gonna get in, sweetheart? Or you planning on playing *Frogger* all night?"

Huffing, Sara collapsed into the seat, slammed the door, and glared at him. "Happy now?" she snapped.

Attitude.

He had to bite back a smile. At least that piece of her hadn't changed.

And neither had the fact that he liked when she gave him sass.

"Not yet." He slanted her a look. "You know the rules of my car."

"No seatbelt, no move," she muttered, snapping the belt. "Yes, I remember your caveman nonsense all too well."

"Good."

Mike turned off his hazards—traffic in this city meant people did way crazier shit than just blocking a lane—and shifted the car into drive, happy that the locks automatically engaged. The look on Sara's face was half-irritation, half-pure-terror, and he wouldn't have been surprised if she'd tried to launch herself from the moving vehicle.

"Where to?"

She was silent and after a moment, he shifted back into park.

Her eyes flashed to his.

"Where. To?"

Her lips moved, but no sound came out, and he could almost picture her mental count to ten.

Right about eight, he said, "I can do this all day, baby. You know I can."

Ice. Frosted spikes hit him in the chest. Directly in the heart. Or at least, that was what her glare said. She crossed her arms, sighed, and then gave her address.

Without another word, he took off.

The car was silent, not uncomfortable exactly, but it also wasn't the easy familiarity of their youth when he'd driven her to their local rink.

They'd both had private lessons before school, Sara for figure skating, Mike for hockey. And since her parents hadn't allowed her to get her license until she was eighteen, and he'd been two years older, they'd had a lot of early mornings together.

"Remember the first time I drove you?"

She was quiet for so long that he thought she'd refuse to take the trip down memory lane with him.

But eventually her lips quirked up, and she smiled.

That smile took his breath away. It always had.

"Yeah," she said. "You weren't much of a morning person."

He stopped at a light, backed up and clogged with cars. People in California really couldn't drive in the rain. It probably also didn't help when assholes from Minnesota blocked traffic for diversions down one-way streets.

"No, I'm still not," he said, grinning at her, wanting to find some of their old camaraderie. "But you were."

For a second, he thought she wouldn't play along. Then her mouth curved. "I was nervous back then. I blab when I'm nervous."

"Nervous?" he asked. "Why?"

She snorted. "Because you were gorgeous and older and popular, and I was—"

He waited for Sara to finish the thought but was met with silence. Eventually, he settled for touching her cheek, shocked at how silky soft it was.

Her breath caught, and he saw something reflected in her eyes. Not desire exactly. Instead, it was more like . . . fear?

What did Sara have to fear? Especially with him?

The thought made him unreasonably angry. *He* was different. They were different together. Always had been and—

Ten years had passed.

He dropped his arm.

"How long have you lived in the city?"

"Why?" she asked, suddenly suspicious.

His eyes rolled heavenward, and he mimed a steering wheel. "Me drive. You small talk."

The wariness dropped off her face, and her eyes sparkled with amusement.

Sara had the best eyes, cat-like and slanted up at the corners, long lashes, and irises that were the clearest, deepest blue . . .

A car honked behind them, and he jumped, glancing forward and seeing the light in front of him turn yellow. He sped through just as it changed to red.

Ah well. His driving karma was certainly taking a beating today.

"So I have to confess I don't know where I'm going," he admitted as they pulled to a stop at the next signal.

Sara sighed. "Turn left ahead."

He did and followed the remainder of her directions until he pulled his car up to the curb in front of an older-looking building. A Chinese restaurant, a laundromat, and a watch repair shop, all with neon lights and peeling paint, took up space on the ground floor.

"*This* is where you live?"

She rolled her eyes. "Not everyone is a millionaire athlete, Mike."

"Last I heard you were on your way to becoming one."

Her shoulders stiffened and her chin came up as she met his stare head-on. Finally, she *looked* at him. Those cat eyes hit him like a fist to the gut, serious and holding a hurt that hadn't been there a decade before.

"You really *don't* know, do you?"

FIVE

Sara

MIKE SHOOK HIS HEAD, and Sara couldn't believe he hadn't heard, that he didn't know how violently her life had imploded.

For a few years, it had seemed like every person in the world knew her pain, that she'd become the poster child for unsportsman-like conduct in professional sports. She'd been banned from the U.S. Figure Skating Association for life. She couldn't compete, couldn't coach.

The sport had been everything to her.

And then it had all been taken away.

Her purpose, her endorsements, her friends, her parents.

She was all alone—

Ugh. That didn't matter. She needed to shove that all down. Get over it. There was no going back to change the past. *This* was her life now.

Reaching over Mike, she snatched her backpack, holding it tight to her chest. "Google it."

"Google *what?*"

Raising a brow, she said, "I think you know what." Then she popped the passenger's side handle and slid from the car.

The downpour hadn't let up, and rain soaked through her shoes, wetting her socks. It dripped from her ponytail, trailed down her spine.

But she hardly noticed any of that, because the passenger side window rolled down, and she heard his voice.

"See you soon, Sara."

Not likely after he Googled her.

She turned and jogged for the stairs on the side of her building.

Later that night, she sat beneath the crappy light of the exposed bulbs in her studio apartment's ceiling and watched the San Francisco Gold play.

For the first time in years, she watched something with an ice rink in it, and while she'd felt a little jab at seeing the pristine sheet of white, hockey was different enough from figure skating that it was okay.

Or maybe it was because Mike was there on the ice.

His face serious, his muscular bulk even larger with the pads.

And he was magnificent.

Fast, strong, crafty, and creative, Mike was a master at defense. Paired with Stefan Barie, captain of the Gold, along with Brit Plantain in net, the first female goalie in the NHL—no big deal there, right?—and the team easily defeated their opponent.

Next would come their postgame routine—cooling down, meeting with the trainer, showering, and getting ready to do the same thing all over again the next day.

Sara couldn't deny that her heart ached for that routine. Not for hockey, as she'd never had the right temperament for the sport, but for competing. For giving every last drop of herself on the ice, skating until her quads threatened to give out, trying a jump—and trying and trying—and ending up covered in bruises only to crawl out of bed before the sun rose the next morning and getting right back out there.

For her, the sport was expensive skates and fleece-lined leggings, rolling bags full to the brim with Band-Aids and wraps and blister pads. The smell of the rink, the moisture in the air, the black skate mats, the left-behind water bottles from a kids' hockey practice the night before.

It was cold air tightening her skin, the crunch of the ice beneath her skates. Fogged-up breath clouding the air in front of her nose and mouth. It was—

—never going to happen for her again.

Not now. She was too old. She'd lost her chance.

"No," she murmured and scrambled for her notebook. Dutifully shoving those memories aside, she took the easiest way to numb her thoughts. The quickest and least dangerous.

She drew.

Except this time, it wasn't the architecture of the city, not the clean lines of skyscrapers mixed with Gothic peaks and curves of Victorian moldings emerging from beneath the point of her pencil.

Instead, she drew a sharp nose, stubble dotting a strong jaw, a scar bisecting one arched brow.

She drew—as she'd done too many times before—Mike.

HER ALARM CAME WAY TOO EARLY, and Sara spent the first half hour of her day muzzy and stumbling.

But same as she'd done since she was ten years old, she pulled on her workout clothes, did a short yoga routine, and went for a run.

The run was her favorite part, even though it was a lesson in pain management nowadays. The yoga she merely tolerated.

It made her bendy and all that jazz.

Not that she needed to be bendy. Not any longer at least.

Still, she ran because she loved it. Getting lost in the city, earbuds in and nothing but the sidewalk in front of her simplified everything else.

People didn't care about her past. Not here. They had jobs to get to, deals to make, tourist sites to see.

Running was easy anonymity.

An hour later, she'd showered and was walking toward the studio. Mitch didn't open the doors for a couple of hours, but Sara always got there early on Fridays.

It was shipment day.

Or basically Christmas and her birthday all rolled into an hour of awesomeness.

She let herself into the studio and made her way to the storeroom. Ryan, the delivery guy, was waiting outside the back door and helped her get the heavy boxes inside. After signing the shipment form, she spent a happy hour digging through the packages like a kid on Christmas morning.

Sara was just dragging a reclaimed metal depiction of Sisyphus pushing his proverbial rock up the hill—and boy, was that ever *the* metaphor for her life—from the storeroom into the studio, when she heard a knock.

She glanced up and was promptly assaulted by a stomach full of butterflies.

None other than Mike Stewart was standing outside the store's glass windows.

He waved when he saw her looking.

It really wasn't fair. No one had a right to look that good in jeans and a leather jacket.

He knocked again, pointed at the door.

For a second, she debated ignoring him.

Except, it was Mike.

If he'd parked his car in the middle of the street to chase her down, he probably wasn't going to let a pesky pane of glass stop him.

Dusting her hands on her pants, she walked to the front of the store.

Mike watched her approach the door and slipped through literally the second she'd unlatched the bolt, like he was afraid she was going to change her mind and lock it right back up.

She gave a mental shrug, thinking he had the right of it. Her impulsivity was almost as widely known as her downfall.

Once inside, he locked the door then swung to face her, his nose an inch from hers, his eyes holding her frozen.

They were furious, dark-brown depths that she half-expected to shoot sparks.

"Why didn't you fight it?"

Shocked by the force of his anger, she stammered out, "H-how did you know where I worked?"

Eyes narrowed. "I saw you come out last night as I drove by." He lifted a hand. "How, Sara? How could you—?"

She flinched, took a half step back. Not from his hand, but because she'd heard those words too many times.

Mike hissed out a breath and, instinctively, she jumped.

Very rarely had she seen him furious and *never* had she seen him like this. A cloud of black anger surrounding him, spilling into the space between them.

His hands came to her shoulders, his grip tight, and he jostled her slightly, made her teeth clink together. Her ribs and hip protested the movement, but she didn't tell him to stop. Some sick part of her felt the pain on the outside should match that within her heart.

Despite her intentions, Mike must have realized he was hurting her because he dropped his hands, though his words didn't soften. "Sara, why in the *hell* didn't you fight?"

It all finally clicked, and she couldn't hold back her wave of disappointment.

He'd obviously taken her advice and Googled her. Knowing Mike had seen her like that—at rock bottom, broken, defeated—was almost worse than her going through it the first time.

The one person in her life whose view of her hadn't been tarnished and she pushed him to go ruin it.

Every emotion from those horrible weeks of her life flashed right back into the forefront of her mind.

Mike had burst the dam with his quiet demand, and it didn't matter to him in the least that she had reasons for wanting to bury that part of her, for trying to shove it all down and forget. He *wanted* to know why.

Icy calm flooded her veins.

It was better this way. Better that he knew now, that he hated her from the get-go. Certainly, it was better that any and all expectations were crushed before they grew too large.

Sara put her hands on his stomach, but it didn't feel good—those hard, flat abs certainly *didn't* feel good beneath her palms. She shoved him hard and took a couple of steps back.

Mike followed her.

"Stop. No," she spat when he took another stride in her direction. "I'm serious. This"—she waved a hand at the shop—"is my life now. Not skating, not the past. If I wanted to talk about that shit, I'd be seeing a therapist. Don't bring it up again."

She turned and snatched up a pair of scissors from the counter, then stomped into the back room.

"Sara."

She didn't respond, just got to work on the next box.

And suddenly he was there, crouching slightly so he could look her straight in the eye. "I just want to understand."

Her hands plunked onto her hips, and she winced when the scissors jabbed at her side. She didn't protest when Mike plucked the pocket-sized metal death trap from her grip and set it on a box.

She did, however, sigh. Everyone wanted to *understand*. Trouble was, no one wanted to believe what had actually happened.

"I don't have anything more to say about it."

"So you cheated? Paid off the judges for higher scores? Is that what you're saying?" He touched her cheek. "Because, Sara, I don't believe it. You wouldn't—"

Good. God. Men. Could. *Not*. Listen.

She pushed past him, strode over to the door, unlocked it, and held it open. "Out."

"No." He leaned against the wall just outside the storeroom, crossed his arms.

She resisted the urge to cross her own in return. "I'm not talking about it."

"You need to talk to someone about what happened."

Ha.

It took every ounce of her restraint to hold back bitter laughter.

When had talking *ever* solved anything for her?

"Been there, done that." She pulled her phone from her pocket. "Now go. Or I'm calling the police."

And there they were, staring each other down like they were on opposite sides of an old Western street, about to draw their guns and duel.

Sara surprised herself by not backing away from the challenge. She'd given in so many times over the years, but she didn't bend today.

That was something.

Lifting her chin, she held the door in one hand, the phone in the other, and waited.

And—surprisingly, shockingly, and a whole slew of other adverbs —Mike caved.

"Fine," he said, walking toward her. "No talk of the last decade. We'll discuss other things. Deal?"

She hesitated. Why was he here now? Why, after all these years, did he want to spend time with her? Why did he seem to care when no one else did?

"Sara."

Her eyes found his, and her heart skipped a beat at the gentleness in them.

"We were friends once." His voice was soft, kind.

"Yeah." They *had* been friends, aside from the fact that she'd had the biggest, most painfully unrequited crush on him.

"I'd like to be friends again."

It was scary, but she *liked* the sound of that. She was so tired of being lonely. Tired of holding everyone at arm's length. "You would?" she asked.

He flashed her that grin, the one that had turned her teenaged heart to mush. "Yeah." In two steps, he'd closed the distance between them and plucked her phone from her hand. "There," he said, pressing some buttons before handing it back to her.

She heard his phone buzz.

"Now you have my number."

All casual-like, he carefully pushed her aside and strode through the door, closing it behind him.

"Lock up," he called through the glass.

Numbly, her fingers obeyed.

"Talk soon."

And, hurricane in her life that he was, Mike was gone.

SIX

Mike

FLYING in a private jet wasn't awful.

Aw, fuck, Mike couldn't pull off humble. Or not very often anyway.

Flying in a private jet was awesome. Lots of leg room, bathrooms someone could actually fit in, direct flights, and no crying kids.

The only annoying people were his teammates, and since he was used to their particular brand of annoying, the flights were usually fun.

They were flying out of SFO, delayed by the fog as per usual, for the first stop on an extended road trip. Management tried to organize games so that the whole renting-a-private-jet thing was kept to a minimum in order to save money.

This leg they'd be playing against teams in Columbus, Chicago, Philadelphia, Boston, and New York. Then they'd have two nights off and play the Capitals down in D.C. before returning home to the West Coast for a stretch.

Playing that many away games in a row—being out of their

normal practice schedule, their typical routines for almost two weeks —was grueling, but it was the life, and it was exciting in a way.

Less exciting now that he was old as fuck.

Or at least old according to hockey standards. Almost thirty, and he was on the leeward side of his career, grizzled and scarred.

Okay, yes to the scarred—it was tough to keep a pretty-boy face in a sport with flying pucks, blades on feet, and sticks in sometimes temperamental hands. But he couldn't agree with the grizzled part. He was in the best shape of his life, playing the best hockey of his career.

He'd gotten past self-sabotaging.

He'd been cured of his very serious, life-threatening asshole condition.

Things were looking up.

Mike couldn't help but think of Sara. She was still tiny as hell, barely coming up to his chest. But something had changed about her . . . well, obviously a lot of things had changed. He was just hung up on the most noticeable one.

She'd become a woman. He felt his face tilt into a smile and knew, *just knew*, that his buddies were going to give him shit for the grin.

But what a *woman* Sara had turned into.

She was petite, yes, her face almost elfin with its small delicate features. But, that wasn't what had made his mouth go dry when he'd spotted her through the window bending over a box that morning at the gallery.

No, his body had perked to complete attention because of the rest of it. Curves for days, pert little breasts he wanted to try out in his hands, a heart-shaped ass that he somehow just knew would be firm enough to bounce a dime off, a flat stomach, and delicate ankles.

He was an ankle guy. Which was weird as fuck, he knew. But something about the little glimpse of skin beneath the cuff of a woman's pants, the hint at what was hiding beneath, turned him on.

Yes, he was a freak. And she wasn't his little Sara any longer.

She'd *never* been his.

Oh, yeah. There was that.

"Whatcha smirking about, Stewie?" Max. Resident funny man—at least *he* liked to think so—of the team and general shit-stirrer.

And commence the shit-*giving*.

"Your mom," Mike countered, bending to snag his earbuds from his backpack. The insult was old and overused, perhaps, but still a good one, given the spots of red appearing on Max's cheeks.

"Ha. Ha." Max slammed down into the seat next to him and began pulling things out of his backpack.

And by things, Mike meant enough toys and books and snacks to keep an entire flight full of toddlers busy for hours.

"Dude," he said when Max started powering up some sort of video game system on his tray table. Little plastic characters towered precariously on the flat surface. "You're an adult."

"Young at heart, old man," Max said, pulling out a controller and headphones. "I'm young at heart."

A piece of plastic—some sort of dragon-horned toy—fell off the tray and landed on his foot.

It stung. The fuckers were heavier than they looked. "God, Max."

"Just God is fine."

"You're not funny."

One side of Max's mouth turned up. Mike had seen entire Reddit posts devoted to that mouth when someone had screenshotted and printed out pages of comments and memes to hang in the locker room. No one had ever claimed responsibility, but his guess for the perpetrator was captain, Stefan Barie, because though the guy came across as clean-cut and nice as hell, he had a wicked sense of humor.

Multiple women had declared Max's lips perfectly pouty, expounded on his mouth being kissable enough to make their ovaries explode, sinful enough to kill them dead.

Regardless of the grand adoration from the opposite sex, at that moment Mike was thinking he might prefer a plane full of screaming kids to Max's mouth.

"I'm hilarious," Max declared.

Yup. Definitely give him the crying babies.

He bent and snatched up the toy, pulling his tray table down and plunking the little devil-horn-dragon thing onto the surface. "You are a *lot* of things. Hilarious not so much . . . unless that is, you're referring to your face. Which is definitely a lesson in comedy."

Max chuckled then nodded at Mike's tray table. "Thanks. I could use the extra space," he said and proceeded to fill the entire surface of Mike's table with more toys.

Good God. They'd just taken off, which meant he had four more hours of this.

He jammed his earbuds in, cranked his music, and hoped that Max would take the hint to just. Stop. Talking.

Max didn't.

Of course not. He prattled on about the game he was playing, going into way too much detail about the characters and gameplay.

Mike also found he didn't really mind it.

Especially since the eager way Max jabbered on reminded him of Sara chatting his ear off during their early morning car rides.

Not that he would admit *that* to Max.

"Why ya smiling, Stewie?"

"Because you're an idiot."

Max grinned. "Why were you late to the game yesterday? Thought Coach was going to scratch you. He was that pissed."

Max had been late to the usual pregame festivities because he'd driven Sara home.

Not that he was sharing *that* particular piece of information with the class.

He'd let Coach know, calling him after dropping Sara and he was back on the way to the arena. Surprisingly, Bernard had been understanding after Mike had explained the situation.

In the past, Mike would have said, *"Fuck it all,"* and shown up late, not caring if he was scratched or not.

Things were different now. He had more at stake. He actually wanted to do well.

But that wasn't any of Max's business.

"How is it you're a grown man playing a game designed for ten-year-olds?"

"Hey! The graphics in this . . ."

And Max was off, easily diverted as he talked about pixels and plot lines. Mike closed his eyes, tuned his teammate out, and wondered if there would be a text waiting for him when he landed.

SEVEN

Sara

SARA GLANCED down at the screen on her phone, trying and failing to ignore the little green box with a bright red circle in the upper right corner.

She'd seen Mike's text that morning, watched it appear on the locked screen of her phone. And she hadn't opened it.

Oh, she'd read it all right.

Read every single word.

Hey, Jumping Bean. How goes it?

Which was really nothing.

Except that it was Mike. All casual-like. All relaxed. As though the fact that he'd texted her hadn't made her heart threaten to pound out of her chest.

As though the last decade hadn't happened.

So his text just sat there, the red notification on her message icon glaring and guilt-inducing.

Because she hadn't responded.

It had been hours, and she had *not* responded.

And the Jerk-of-the-Day Award went to . . . (Cue her award show presenter voice here.)

Except what *could* she say?

What's up?

Too abrupt.

How are you?

So formal.

How 'bout those Niners?

She didn't even watch football.

Hopeless. Sara was utterly hopeless.

"You know just because you stare at it doesn't mean it's going to ring, right?"

She blinked, glanced up at Mitch's smirking face. "Shut up."

Mitch ignored her retort and pointed at a painting she'd unpacked that morning. "What do you think of the Prescott?"

She thought it was brilliant and, accordingly, had hung it dead center on the studio's most prominent wall. The lighting made the texture of the acrylics really pop.

"It's going to sell fast."

He nodded. "Yes, it is." One of his brows came up. "And you'll be taking that spot. So get something ready."

Dread. It poured over her in a tangible wave, prickling the hairs on her arms, twisting her stomach, causing sweat to break out on her palms, the backs of her knees.

"Mitch, I—"

"No excuses this time," he said. "I thought we were past this.

You're talented and the discomfort you have with your work is insane." He bent close, placed his hands on her shoulders. "You're an incredible artist, and you deserve to have the world know that."

The world was what she was afraid of.

"I-I can't."

"You will," he said, his tone somehow both gentle and firm at the same time. "If you want to keep working here."

The slice of betrayal burned.

She stepped back, snatched up her backpack. "I'm a good employee." Her chin lifted. "If you don't want me working here—"

"Ah, honey, that's not it at all." He started toward her, but she put up a palm to stop him. "I love having you here. What I don't love is that it's still holding you back. *I'm* holding you back. You shouldn't be selling paintings to idiots with way too much money and unpacking boxes of other artists' work." He pointed to the Prescott. "You should —you *deserve*—to be right there."

Her heart raced for the second time that day.

Sara couldn't deny that she wanted that too. But the risk—media attention, dredging through her past for the umpteenth time, barbed comments from her family, the people she considered friends—it was too much.

She could not go through that again.

"I know you didn't cheat."

Her breath hitched, and she froze.

Mitch had never mentioned her past. She'd assumed he hadn't known.

"I—" She shook her head.

"Have you met me, honey?" He smirked. "While there are plenty of gay men who don't love sparkles and music and dancing, I'm not one of them. *Of course* I'm familiar with figure skating. I just didn't expect to find out that a disgraced Olympic champion was a fabulous artist as well." He touched her cheek. "Is there anything you can't do?"

So, *so* much.

She'd been great at skating, naturally talented and a skilled show-woman. She'd excelled at giving soundbites, never failed to put together a spunky-yet-sweet answer to even the dumbest of dumbass questions, but *Mitch* had struck her mute. All she could do was shake her head and clutch at the straps of her bag.

"You're too honest to cheat," he said. "It took barely five minutes with you for me to know that." His mouth twisted into a sad smile. "It's just unfortunate the rest of the world couldn't figure that out."

She snorted. Now that was for damn sure.

"Yeah, I know," he said. "So, here's what we're going to do. You bring me something to sell on Monday, and you'll still have a job. You don't, or you decide you've had it with my dictatorial-push-you-out-of-your-comfort-zone days, and we'll just be friends."

He grabbed her coat, shoved it at her, and pushed her toward the door. "Because, honey . . ." He did a cheesy jig and sang, " 'You've got a friend in me.' "

She found her tongue. "Of course you'd quote a Disney song."

"And do it in a bad rendition at that." He smirked. "For now, take off early. Think about it. *Dooo it.*" The last was a whisper that made her lips twitch.

Sara had stepped out the door and was turning in the direction of her apartment, awkwardly shrugging into her jacket, when Mitch's voice stopped her. "And while you're at it, maybe respond to that text you've been staring at."

Her hand came up, starting as a perfect princess wave before transforming into a very particular one-fingered salute.

He just laughed.

"You know I won't let you fire me, right?" she called.

"I know," he called back. "Just like I know you'll bring me some-thing fabulous come Monday."

Her stomach was in knots at the thought because she suspected he was right. Shaking her head, she turned and started walking.

"And Sara?" She paused, middle of the sidewalk, wind blowing, people pushing past her, as Mitch yelled, "Forget texting back. I know it's shocking in this day and age but just *call him!*"

EIGHT

Mike

THERE WASN'T a text waiting for Mike when he turned his phone back on.

Acute disappointment swept through him, even as he tried to convince himself that it was for the best. Sara didn't need his drama in her life.

"All good, Stewie?"

He glanced up into the deep brown eyes of Brit Plantain, star goalie, kickass chick, and general all-around woman-with-a-heart-of-*gold*, no pun intended.

She wore only a black sports bra and the bottom half of her equipment and looked as though she were a reflection in a funhouse mirror. Don't get him wrong, she was gorgeous and strong and super fit, but Brit was also very lean.

Pairing that with blocky leg pads and baggy goalie pants meant the funhouse mirror-effect was in all its glory.

Her blond brows pulled together, and Brit frowned. "Mike? You okay?"

He blinked and forced his eyes away. "Yup. I'm good."

"Then why are you staring at me like I'm a bug?"

Mike bent to tug one skate off. "Not staring so much as thinking."

That made her pause, made her glance at him like *he* was the bug.

He snorted. "I know. It's uncommon for me, but it does occasionally happen."

One toned arm came up to perch on her hip and, good God, did the girl have guns. She'd always hit the weight room just as hard as the guys, but, just saying, Michelle Obama would be jealous.

"It's a girl," she said.

A groan built up in his throat, but he shoved it down. Now wasn't the time to show weakness, to let on how close Brit was to the truth.

Because the amount of razzing he'd take for it—

He almost thought, *it wouldn't be worth it*, but the words couldn't even cross his mind. Not when he knew that he'd endure any amount of teasing for Sara. She'd always been that way, always able to invoke his protective instincts. His wants. Desires.

His phone buzzed at his thigh, and immediately Mike's pulse picked up, heart jumping around his chest like a teenager going crazy at a pop concert.

Heaven help him, that he actually knew who the hot current boy bands were, but between the rookies and Brit having a turn with the weight room stereo, his music knowledge had become a little more . . . diverse.

Which was so *not* the point—

Buzz. Again.

"Idiot," he muttered, and snatched at his phone, almost dropping it in his efforts to both answer it and conceal the caller I.D. as Brit leaned over his shoulder.

He swiped across the screen and put it to his ear.

One-half of Brit's mouth quirked up. "Sara, huh?"

"Shut up," he snapped.

"Um." Sara paused, asked hesitantly, "Is this a bad time?"

"No!" he said, way too loudly, given the way the entire locker room shifted its attention to him. Shit. "No," he said, softer. "This is a perfect time."

Her breath hitched. "Oh, o-kay."

Mike stood and walked out the locker room door. Well, he more tiptoe-stomped, tiptoe-stomped since he still wore one skate and his other foot was bare. Once in the corridor, he leaned back against the wall, careful to keep his skate's blade on the black protective mat.

Not that his edges mattered much considering the game was over, but dull skates were the bane of any professional hockey player, and old habits died hard.

"Hey," he said, shoving all of his extraneous thoughts aside.

"Hey," she replied.

Silence.

"I—"

"I—"

"You go," he said.

"No, you."

And more silence.

He finally got his shit together and broke it. "So, what did you do today?"

"I got fired."

"What?"

Sara gave a little chuckle. "Okay, not fired so much as threatened to be fired, but it's a good thing, I think—"

"Wait. What the heck are you talking about, Jumping Bean?"

She laughed, and it tinkled across the airwaves, slid down his spine like warm rays of sunshine on his back.

What in the *what*?

Now he was writing mental poetry?

But hearing Sara's laugh brought him back. It reminded him of the girl she'd been, the boy he'd thought he would always be.

It pulled him into the past. To a time when things had been so much simpler.

"I'm going to sell my work in Mitch's shop," she said. "Well, at least a couple of pieces and . . ."

"That's amazing," he said after she'd told him about the drawings she was working on.

"Yes." She paused, and he could almost picture her giddy smile, her white teeth biting into the blush pink of her bottom lip. "But that's why I'm calling actually. I wanted—um . . . I wanted to see-if-I-could-use-the-one-of-you," she finished in a hurry.

It took Mike a few moments to decipher what that rush of words meant.

But she continued before he could respond. "The one of your hand. Not the one of your face. I wouldn't do—I mean, I *couldn't* use that—"

For some reason, he was grinning. "You drew me? More than my hand?"

A muffled word that sounded very much like "shit," then Sara sighed.

"Yes."

"Was I clothed?"

"Mike!"

He laughed. He couldn't help it.

"Oh for God's sake," she snapped. "Yes, you were clothed. I— *Grr* . . . never mind."

Billy, one of the equipment managers, came around the corner and started walking down the hall toward him. "Use whatever part of me you want, sweetheart," he murmured, pausing to nod at Billy as he moved past.

Her breath hitched. "Mike."

His voice dropped an octave lower. "I mean that, Sara. Anything of mine is yours. Always has been, always will."

"Mike!" she said, slightly shrill. "You can't say things like that."

"Why not?"

"Because that's not how normal people talk. We haven't seen each other for a decade. You can't just—"

"Sweetheart, I've never cared much for rules."

Sara snorted. "*That* much I remember."

"And I always say what I mean." Or he did with Sara. "You feel me?"

There was only the slightest hesitation before she whispered, "Yeah."

"Good. Now I'm going to finish changing out of my gear and when I get back to the hotel I'll call you, 'kay?"

He could hear her smile through the phone. "Okay."

"Good," he said again. "And Sara?" he asked before hanging up.

"Yeah?"

"I'm glad you called."

"Me too, Hot Shot," she said and for once the nickname didn't make him scowl. "Me too."

NINE

Sara

SARA TOSSED DOWN HER PENCIL, abandoning her sketch of the city's rooflines for the moment.

The work was a lost cause anyway, since instead of the jagged peaks of the Gothic building, she kept drawing the chiseled line of Mike's jaw, the hash marks of scars he had on his knuckles.

Groaning, she flopped back onto the carpet.

She'd been dumped into a parallel universe; that had to be it.

A universe where men actually cared, where old friends had faith.

Where she actually kind of liked the alpha-act that Mike was putting on.

Not that she thought Mike's alpha-ness was an act, per se. He'd always been the type of guy who was confident in his own skin, wholly comfortable with the man he was inside, the kind of person who just lived unapologetically.

The difference was more because she actually liked it when Mike got a little bossy with her.

And now she needed to tear up her feminist card.

Pathetic.

Except—and this was the big one—Sara was so damn tired of doing everything on her own. Of being so locked up inside that she felt nothing. Of having no one able to wield an axe large enough to smash through the ice surrounding her heart and . . .

She was lonely.

Her eyes flicked to her cell. It sat, screen darkened, on the floor next to her sketch.

The sketch of Mike's face, eyes laughing as he stared out from the paper, hand extended, waiting.

Waiting for her to take hold and—

Ugh. *She* was ridiculous.

And yet she couldn't get him out of her head.

With a sigh, she picked up the pencil and gave in. She sketched the lock of hair that fell across Mike's right brow, the tiny scar at the corner of his eye, the scruff he'd been sporting in the game earlier.

Because of course she'd been watching. She'd held her breath each time he'd made contact with another player. Cheered when he'd made a particularly good pass up to the rookie, Blue, who was on a hot streak and had taken it up the ice to score the game-winning goal. Winced when he'd blocked a shot.

Her phone buzzed, pulling her out of her revelry. Groaning, she stretched her aching neck. She was getting way too old to be lying on the hard floor for—her eyes flicked to her clock as she snatched up her cell—over an hour, drawing.

Her phone buzzed again, and she slid her finger across the screen, heart pounding at the sight of Mike's name there, before putting it up to her ear. "Hi," she breathed.

And mentally groaned. Good God, she sounded like a nervous little schoolgirl.

Pathetic.

"What were *you* doing?" Mike asked.

"What?" Her eyes flicked to the sketchbook, to her ridiculous collection—yes, it was now growing into a freaking *collection*—of drawings. "Nothing," she rushed to say and even to her own ears it sounded guilty.

Oh. Em. Gee. She flopped onto the rug, tapping the back of her head to the floor a few times, just for good measure.

Or rather, to knock some sense into her idiotic brain.

"Hmm." His voice had an edge of rasp, as though that scruff she'd seen on his face earlier was scraping against the inside of her thighs, sliding up, up—

Her breath caught.

"Something to share with the class, Sara girl?"

Oh for God's sake. She needed to get it together.

She cleared her throat—and clenched her thighs. *PG, woman. Keep it PG.* "I was just working."

"Oh." His tone went serious. "Did I interrupt? You can just hang up on me—"

And there her heart went filling with helium, floating in her chest, somehow resuscitating the piece of her she'd thought long dead.

"No," she said. "If I'd been engrossed, I wouldn't have answered the phone. I probably wouldn't have even heard it."

"I'm glad you did," he said. "And that you picked up."

She smiled and rolled onto her stomach, stretching out the kinks in her neck. "I've missed you."

For the last few days.

For the last decade.

He'd been her best friend. And then he hadn't.

Sara released a slow, steady breath because it wasn't until he'd come back into her life, started to help her cast off the fog she'd been living in that she realized just how much she'd missed him.

Mike inhaled rapidly. Well, she heard a burst of noise that her brain identified as Mike sucking in a gasp of air. But before she could ask what was the matter, he spoke, and his words froze the breath in her lungs.

"Sure do like you saying that, honey."

Sweetheart. Jumping Bean. Honey.

When was the last time someone had addressed her with an endearment? Besides Mitch, that was, for whom honey and sweetheart and a plethora of other sweet nothings were as common as the F-word was for hockey players.

But the same words out of Mike's mouth . . . *whew*. Those words made goose bumps come to life on her arms, twisted her stomach into knots—in the *best* way—and caused her inner teenage girl to sit up and squeal.

The last was what finally brought her to her senses.

She pushed to sitting and rubbed her forehead. Why was she always so impulsive? Why had she said she'd missed him? "What are we doing?"

Silence. "What do you mean?"

Sara snagged her sketchpad and flipped to a new page. Her pencil was on the paper in nearly the next instant, forming dark and angry squiggles across the blank white space.

"I mean." *Scratch.* "What are we doing?" More lines. "We haven't talked in a decade." Smudge. "Now, we're just casually chatting on a Friday night?" Add shadow. "Running into each other on the streets?" Fill. *Scratch.* Smear. Erase. No. *Darker.*

"Sara." His tone held a note of warning, and the audacity of that pissed her off. He was warning *her*? Really? Yeah, not going to happen. "You've always been important to me," he said.

No. *This* was important. Finding out his ulterior motives for striking up a relationship with her here and now were even more so.

Hell, if she was so *important,* then why hadn't he even tried to keep in touch with her?

After she'd left, she hadn't received a single phone call. Not one email. Not even a friend request on Facebook.

The worst was that *she* had called, *she* had emailed and . . . nothing.

"Yes, Mike," she bit out. "I asked what we're doing."

"We're talking."

Her pencil lead snapped, and she tossed the useless chunk of wood to the side. After reaching up to grab another out of the jar she kept on her desk, she continued drawing, her words almost as furious as the strokes of her pencil.

Some distant part of her mind wondered why she was so angry, but it was easy to push that aside, easy to focus on the rage.

Pissed off was safer than being vulnerable.

"Don't give me that bullshit. Why now? Why not then?"

One more line and she'd finished the drawing. Almost with disgust, she dropped the pad and pencil.

Why hadn't she been good enough then?

Charged silence stretched between them.

Then Mike sighed. "Weren't you the one who wanted to forget the past? Why can't we just focus on the now and move forward with our friendship?"

"No," she said. Sara *had* to understand. If she was going to open herself up to Mike again, then she sure as fuck needed to know what had happened after she left. "If I was so important, why did you find it so easy to let me go?"

His laugh was a horrible thing, brittle and broken, jagged and sharp. "Easy? Fuck, Sara. Nothing about you leaving was easy, but—"

She waited for him to say more, and when he didn't, she asked, "But what?"

"Google goes both ways, sweetheart. I'd suggest you use it." She could hear rustling on his end and just knew he was thrusting a hand through his hair.

He only did that when he was really frustrated.

And that made her anger fade, regret sneak forward to make her heart hurt. Why was she pushing this? Why was she pushing him away?

For once in her life, why couldn't she just leave things alone?

But she didn't get the chance to take the words back, to try and repair their easy rapport from the previous minutes.

"I'll call you when I get home from this road trip, okay?" He didn't give her a chance to respond, just hung up the phone.

That *click*, the sudden loss of Mike's voice in her ear, sliced Sara clean through.

With a pained breath, she put the phone down then picked up her pad again.

"Well, you sure do know how to ruin things," she muttered, putting pencil to paper.

She drew until the sun came up.

She drew until she saw Mike's face on television the next night.

She drew until she passed out from exhaustion and his features were no longer on the paper but tattooed in her mind.

She drew to forget.

Except she didn't.

TEN

Mike

MIKE WAS in a hell of a mood. Three days had passed since he'd fought with Sara. Three days had gone by without her voice and smell and laugh and ... *dammit*, she was right.

How had he managed years without her but now missed her after only a few days?

It made no sense.

Except that it had been easier to forget the last good thing of his childhood after all the upheaval of his late teens, easy to be swept up into the life of a professional hockey player.

And when his past had refused to be shoved away, he hadn't wanted to bring anything good into contact with it.

His family contaminated everything.

They were a scene from a cheesy sci-fi movie, a cloud of black sweeping through the air, engulfing everything in its wake before tearing it all to shreds.

His parents had almost destroyed him. He'd nearly let their bullshit destroy the one thing that made him happy.

Hockey.

So finally, he had his head straight. He'd thought karma had brought him Sara because he actually had his shit together for a change.

Little did he know what she'd been through.

Cheating.

How could anyone believe that of her?

Sara had been the best skater he'd ever seen. Effortless, graceful, beyond gorgeous on the ice. And her level of difficulty had rivaled the male skaters.

But her coach had admitted in a tell-all interview that he'd paid off the judges, that he'd done it on Sara's instruction, had even released video of Sara meeting privately with them.

That had been bad enough, but deniable. There hadn't been audio, the accusations were just that. But then the media had dredged up evidence of large cash deposits into sketchy off-shore accounts.

Yet none of those had done what Sara's own ability had.

Because the killing blow was her scores.

Which were higher than any other skater in history. Clearly, it had been because of the money, not because she was exceptionally talented.

Except, that wasn't true.

He could almost understand how someone who didn't know her might believe that. But her friends and family? The way they'd crucified her on social media and to the press . . .

Sara's fall off her pedestal had been abrupt and from an exceptional height. She was banned from competitive skating, both in the U.S. and internationally. She couldn't coach, wasn't even allowed to teach a four-year-old how to stand up on a pair of skates.

"Fuck," he muttered, shoving his feet into sneakers and popping his earbuds in.

The Gold were still on the road, would be for another four games. Mike had arrived at the arena early. He'd played for the Philadelphia Flyers for a season, knew the ins and outs of their home rink.

Which was good because he needed to blow off some steam.

What he didn't account for was Brit and Stefan standing outside the visitor's locker room. Oh, he knew they came to the games early— initially separately and now that their relationship was out and proud, so to speak, they came together.

They each wore sneakers and had their headphones on. Ready to go. Except that they appeared to be waiting for him.

Mike paused, wondering what the hell to say. He'd been upset since the fight with Sara, but he hadn't gone off the deep end. Had his inner turmoil screwed with the team?

He waited for them to lay into him, but his teammates, hell, his *friends* didn't speak. Instead, Brit raised a brow at his hesitation, pushed past him, and jogged into the arena.

"Oh God, you're going to let her go first?" Stefan moaned, taking after her.

Mike shook his head, confused as he turned his music to blaring and followed.

It took him two-point-two seconds to understand Stefan's complaint.

Brit set a blistering pace, jogging up the stairs of one aisle, down the opposite side, then across a row and into the next section. Up. Down. Across. Over and over.

And, fuck, but she was fast.

Mike was sucking wind by the fifth aisle, almost ready to puke by the last, and Stefan was no better off. When Brit stopped after they'd made the full weaving circle of the lower bowl, both of them collapsed to the ground, chests heaving, breaths coming in rapid gusts.

Brit stood lithe and graceful as a ballerina, one foot calmly bent behind her to stretch her quad.

She wasn't even out of breath.

"How?" he gasped, yanking out his earbuds. They vibrated from the music still blasting in them against his shoulders, the rapid *pound-pound-pound* of the punk band he preferred.

"How what?" Brit switched legs.

"How . . . are . . . you"—he sat up, sucked in a huge breath, tried to steady his racing heartbeat—"not even tired?"

She smirked and sank down next to him, continuing to stretch like a pretzel with what also appeared to be very little effort. "You're listening to the wrong music."

Mike frowned. "What do you mean?"

"I mean"—she dropped her voice and glanced around, as though imparting state secrets—"your music sucks. Makes you run slow."

Stefan groaned and pushed up to sitting next to them. "Don't listen to her, Stewart. Remember that her idea of good music is Miley Cyrus."

He winced. Yeah, if he heard "Party in the U.S.A." in the locker room one more time he might blow chunks.

"Yeah," Stefan said, "knew you'd see it my way."

"Whatever, losers." Brit stood. "Just remember who runs faster," she called, heading back down the hall toward the visitors' room.

"But who can skate faster?" Stefan called back.

"I'm a goalie! I don't need to skate fast." Her voice was almost drowned out by the pop music kicking on in the locker room.

Mike chuckled and reached for his phone, pausing his playlist.

"You know we're here for you, right?" Stefan said.

In the past, Mike might have made some snarky remark about heart-to-hearts, and Stefan not really giving a damn.

But Stefan did.

In Mike's entire playing career, he'd never seen a more devoted captain. Stefan cared about every single person in the Gold organization.

Legitimately cared.

Mike hadn't believed it at first, had thought it was a superficial façade. And if there was one thing he hated it was liars.

Turned out, he'd been wrong about Stefan.

So instead of brushing off his captain, he told the truth. "I'm fucked up over a girl." He thrust a hand through his hair. "It's like high school all over again."

And his feelings, lust and love and frustration, were tangled up inside his gut. Pathetic, really, but there it was.

"This Sara?"

Mike cut his eyes toward Stefan who shrugged unapologetically.

"Brit," they both said simultaneously then grinned.

"Never seen you with a girl," Stefan said after a moment.

"Never been any but this one."

Stefan blew out a breath. "Well, fuck. It's that?"

Mike nodded. "Yeah."

"So why aren't you going after her?" Stefan bumped his shoulder. "Or did you already fuck things up?"

"Not really." He stood. Well, truthfully, he had fucked it up with Sara. Both then *and* now.

"Aw, shit man, that means yes. Well, I'm sure you can fix it. Turn on some of that Stewie charm." Stefan's lips twitched as he pushed to his feet. "It's got to be in there somewhere."

"It's not that easy."

"Why not?" Stefan asked. "You love the girl, you go after her."

Ha. "And it was that simple for you and Brit?"

He rolled his eyes. "Brit and I were different. We had complications because we're on the same team, because she was the first woman in the league."

Mike nodded in agreement. It was the truth. "I know you guys had it tough, but Sara's had a bad run of it too."

Stefan froze, his blue eyes blazing with fury. Their captain was an easygoing guy, but mess with his teammates or someone he considered innocent or vulnerable, and the man did *not* mess around. "Did someone hurt her? Do we need to—?"

A noose Mike hadn't realized was wrapped around his insides loosened.

Stefan hadn't asked, "Did *you* hurt her?" Instead, he was ready to kick the fucker's ass. Or at the very least, hold the jerk down while Mike did the honors.

Unfortunately, Sara's problems weren't on so small a scale—not that he wouldn't give his left nut to break every bone in her former coach's body. But her issues were on an epic, global, very public format.

"I almost wish it were that simple," he said.

"Then what?" Stefan asked. "What can we do?"

There went that loosening again, the bindings on his lungs slackening, feeling as though he could truly breathe for the first time in years.

"I don't know," he said honestly, "because *my* Sara is Sara Jetty."

"Well fuck," Stefan breathed.

"Yeah," Mike said. "Tell me something I don't know."

ELEVEN

Sara

SARA STIFLED a curse when she stubbed her toe on something large and heavy that hadn't been there the night before.

"Oh come on," she muttered when her inner teenager giggled at the unintentional sexual innuendo and then thought, *That's what she said.*

"You're an adult, Sara. Act like one." She fumbled along the wall, turned on the storeroom's lights.

Then winced when they revealed the sight.

The room was packed, absolutely packed, with wooden pallets and crates.

A whining noise escaped her, and she didn't bother to berate herself for the un-adult-like behavior. "Ugh. Why Mitch?"

Today was Wednesday. Friday was shipment day. *Friday* she expected the storeroom to look like this.

This wasn't Friday.

And she was tired.

Really, really tired.

Ten days since her argument with Mike. Ten days since sleep had gone by the wayside.

The plus was that she'd drawn a lot. The minus was that she couldn't sell any of it, since everything was of Mike.

And so it was Wednesday, and she was a real-life version of a walking, talking zombie.

Red eyes, pale skin, shuffling steps.

"Ugh," she said again. Why had Mike come back into her life and peeled back the layer of numb she'd surrounded herself with?

Life had been so much more comfortable when she hadn't really felt anything.

But Mike had traipsed back into her existence and burst through her barriers, and now she was all exposed and uncomfortable and . . . shit.

The bell above the front door dinged, and she straightened, her ribs already aching in anticipation of dealing with all the boxes, before calling out, "This is fucked up, Mitch! You do *not* pay me enough to deal with the amount of shit packed into this room!"

And silence.

And—shit, shit, *double* shit—there was only *silence* in response.

Which meant she must have forgotten to lock the front door of the store, and a customer had snuck in early and—

"Always did have a mouth on you, Jumping Bean."

Every single cell in her body froze then rocketed to full attention, honing in on the voice, whirling her body in a movement so fast that ninjas would have been jealous.

Mike.

She couldn't hold back the breath of relief that slipped through her lips.

If she'd had a cartoon bubble over her head it would have read, *Thank-freaking-God.*

He hadn't left her in the past, hadn't decided she wasn't worth the trouble.

And Sara hadn't even realized that she'd been worried about that until Mike was in front of her, eyes cautious but hopeful.

"Hi," she whispered.

One brow rose. "Hi." He leaned back against the doorframe, crossed his arms. "What did Mitch do?"

A snort, a wave of her hand to the disaster zone that was the storeroom. "Umm. Basically all this wasn't here when I left last night."

Mike's gaze flicked around the space. "All of it?"

Her shoulders sagged, and with a sigh, she bent to open the first box. "Yeah. All of it." She tore the flaps open. "Mitch does nothing halfway."

"*That*, I can see."

"He has this idea for an online art store. Which would be great—" She pulled out a gorgeous glass vase and carefully set it beside her before pushing the paper in the box to the side and retrieving two more nearly identical pieces. "—if he bought reasonable amounts. Or we had the storage space available."

Sara picked her way through the room and managed to place the pieces in a velvet-lined niche of cubbies that was built into one of the walls. Which was already full and, even though they moved merchandise at a pretty good clip, it would take weeks to make room for the pieces that Mitch had ordered.

And they still had their regularly scheduled delivery on Friday.

Which she knew since the delivery company had confirmed the previous day.

Closing her eyes, she let her head flop backward and sighed. How her boss survived the business world was beyond her.

The sound of wood scraping against concrete had her eyes flicking open, her gaze whipping to Mike.

Who was bent over a pallet, shifting it to the side.

"What—?"

He shook his head. "Let me help."

"But—"

"If we shift the bigger pieces to the side and take out the little boxes in between, we can get more space." A grunt as he shoved the entire square of wood against the back wall. "Then we can stack the less-fragile stuff."

"But . . ."

Mike straightened, flexed an arm. And good God, what an arm it was. She wanted to bite into it like a drumstick.

Holy balls, Sara. Get a grip.

"I've got muscles, sweetheart. Put 'em to work."

That he did, but still, Sara hesitated. "Are you—"

Two steps.

That was all it took for him to get in her space, to tower over her, to crowd her back against the stack of boxes.

Except it wasn't aggressive . . . or well, it wasn't disconcerting. Hell, that was a lie. It was both. The really unnerving part was that she liked it. Liked Mike so close, wanted him to come even nearer. She wanted *nothing* between them.

Not inches. Not air. Not clothes.

Her lungs hitched, and desire shot straight between her thighs.

Mike as a teenager had been nearly impossible to resist. Mike as a man—strong, tall, muscles-for-days, not to mention the sexuality and confidence oozing out of every pore—and resistance was useless.

"You have a game tonight. I don't want you to be tired."

"You know my schedule, babe?" His flash of white teeth made her stomach tremble. It also made her lean closer for a better look.

"Which is your fake tooth?" she asked, since she wasn't going to answer his question about the schedule.

Yes, she'd been watching the games. Yes, she knew that he was playing that night at home before heading to Los Angeles for their game against the Kings. Then they would be back at the Gold Mine— the fans' nickname for Reynolds Arena—for an extended home stand.

But come to think of it, knowing Mike had a fake tooth wasn't really much better than knowing when and where his games were.

Obsessed, meet pathetic.

Mike stared at her for a moment before reaching down and gently encircling her wrist. He tugged her hand up, tapped her pointer finger to the tooth one left from the center. "This one."

Sara might have been embarrassed that she was practically performing a dental examination, if not for the fact that his movements had the side effect of bringing her very close to his body.

She sucked in a breath, felt her breasts rub against his chest, and stifled a moan.

Her hand was suddenly on Mike's shoulder, her back firmly pressed against the wall.

And—*God*—he smelled good.

He had mint on his breath, the faintest hint of cologne on his body, spicy and wholly male.

She wanted to burrow into him, to wrap the scent around her like a cat.

She wanted him to press into *her*, to feel that body of his firmly against hers.

And maybe she wanted to climb him like a tree so she could slant her mouth across his.

"Sara."

His voice was gravely, and when she met his eyes, the need within them was enough to take her breath away, enough to finally spur her into motion.

Enough for her to say, *"Screw it."*

She rose on tiptoe, leaned in, and pressed her mouth to his.

Mike froze, but Sara didn't immediately back away. She'd dreamed about this, wished for it, hoped that it might—

Arms banded around her middle, a solid chest pressed tightly against hers, lips opened, and tongues tangled.

And it was . . . glorious.

Heat blossomed in her stomach, spread to her limbs, desire pooled deep and heavy and low.

Her other arm came up, wrapped around Mike's neck, and she tangled her fingers in the soft hairs on his neck. His hands slid, hitching under her butt, and pulling her closer to his mouth.

She was wrapped pretzel-style around his body and not giving a damn when the very loud, totally indiscreet cough came from behind them.

TWELVE

Mike

MIKE GAVE a mental groan and gently released Sara's legs, letting them slide down to the floor. He made sure she was steady before turning to face whatever asshole had interrupted them.

A tall man with shaggy dark hair, tan skin, and green eyes smirked from the doorway. He wore a fitted purple suit with brown shoes and a paisley shirt.

If there was one thing besides hockey that Mike knew, it was suits —because he had to wear so many of them for game days.

This man brought the suit game.

Sara slid out from behind him and crossed her arms, glaring at the man. "What is this, Mitch?"

Ah. So that was Mitch. The boss.

And he should probably be feeling guilty for potentially getting Sara in trouble at work, but the kiss—her lips, her moans, her lithe body in his arms—was everything.

Mitch cocked his head to the side, his gaze flicking between the two of them. "I'm thinking that I should ask you the same question."

"No," Sara warned. "Really, you shouldn't."

"Is this Text Message?"

Mike's brows raised, and he glanced over at Sara, whose cheeks had gone a little pink. "Text Message?" he whispered.

"Shh, you," she muttered before raising her voice. "Who he is doesn't matter."

Ouch, Mike thought. *Tell me how you really feel, Sara.*

"We need to discuss your ordering," she said. "There's not enough room for all this."

"I've secured a warehouse for the online items. They'll be shipped here for photographs, then picked up, and transported there." Mitch waved away Sara's words when she started to respond. "We'll discuss the details later." His eyes cut to Mike. "For now, I think you'd better tell the truth to Text Message here."

"T-truth?"

"Yeah," he said. "You know, like the fact that who he is definitely *does* matter, given that you've been moping around here for the last week and a half."

Mitch turned, paused. "More kissing," he called over his shoulder. "More kissing might soothe the sting of that one, honey."

And he disappeared into the front of the store. The phone rang, and he heard Mitch answer it.

Only after Mitch seemed to have settled into a long conversation did Sara move.

She rotated to face him, teeth nibbling on her bottom lip. Which made him want to kiss her all over again, not exactly the best thing in this moment, all things considered.

Who he is doesn't matter.

Yup. That sounded about right. *That* sentiment had been drilled into him plenty of times over.

"Mike," she said.

"Did you Google me?"

He'd surprised her with the turn in the conversation. "U-um. No," she stammered before lifting her chin, straightening her shoulders. "If you want me to know about your past, I figure you'll tell me."

He snorted. Women were confusing as hell.

"So why did you tell me to Google *you*?"

She sighed, shoulders slumping slightly. "Because it was easier."

"Easier for whom?"

"For me."

He shook his head. "And you don't want to give me the same courtesy?"

White teeth pressed into soft pink lips. "No. It's not that."

"Sara."

"Okay fine. It's stupid. I mean part of it is that I didn't want to hash it all up again. It was easier if you thought the worst and just left me alone." She took a couple of steps, sat on the edge of a pallet. "But I mean, I know it's not common knowledge or anything, but everything you read on the Internet isn't necessarily true . . ." Her words faltered for a second. "I didn't want to read something bad about you and ruin this picture in my head, you know?"

"Ruin something more than the fact that the boy who had been one of your closest friends ignored your emails and calls? That he didn't make an effort to talk to you for a decade?"

That he'd been in his own personal hell and unwilling to bring Sara into it.

She laughed, but it wasn't a lighthearted one. Hers was broken, fractured slightly at the edges. "Yeah. I guess there's that."

He crossed the room and sank down next to her. "I'm sorry I put all that distance between us. I shouldn't have."

"That's true." She sighed. "But I guess what I'm saying is that I kind of understand you needing to."

The tension between them softened, and he finally asked the question he'd come to the store in the first place for. "Come to the game tonight?"

Given her reaction, Mike might have stabbed her with a hot poker. Sara went stiff as a board; her mouth dropped open in horror.

"I can't go to a *game*." After popping to her feet in signature Jumping-Bean style, she began to pace the room. "It's—rather, *I*—"

"You could sit with the WAGs, not be in front of the cameras at all."

She paused, her gaze darting back to him. "WAGs?"

"Wives and girlfriends. They watch the game from a suite. It's very private."

Her laugh was shrill, slightly hysterical. "Yeah, except that I'd be with the *wives and girlfriends*. Are you insane? The press would have a field day with this. *Cheating Figure Skater Dates Bad Boy Hockey Player*. It's like a fucked-up version of *The Cutting Edge*."

"And how do you know I'm a bad boy? High school, I was squeaky clean."

She froze. He pushed to his feet, came directly behind her, the fresh floral scent of her skin drifting up and teasing his senses.

"It's just an expression."

"Try again." He pushed her hair to the side, exposing her nape, and unable to resist, pressed a kiss there.

Sara shuddered, released a shuddering breath. "Fine. I Googled. But just a little."

He chuckled. "God, Sara. You never did make anything easy."

She whirled around. "So?" She poked a finger into his chest. "If I'm so difficult, why are you here?"

Catching her hand, he smiled. "I never said it was a bad thing, Sara girl. Sometimes the best things in life are the hardest."

That he knew from personal experience.

"I understand, Mike, but I still can't—"

He kissed her, unable to resist. He'd had his taste, and now he needed more.

So much more.

Lips melded, tongues tangled, his dick was harder than he thought physically possible.

And when he broke away, saw that her expression was glazed,

that her blue eyes were blurry with passion, he wanted to take her mouth all over again.

Except, Mitch hollered from the front of the store. "Two more minutes, Sara. That's all I'm giving you. God knows I don't want to stumble upon a naked woman in my storeroom!"

Sara blinked, desire starting to clear from her expression.

And Mike didn't want to let it. He ran his thumb across her bottom lip, leaned in to press a kiss to her jaw. "Come to the game, sweetheart," he whispered into her ear, reveling in her shiver, in the hitch of breath slipping from her mouth.

"I-I can't." But the refusal was gentle. He could press this; he could get his way.

Except, he didn't want to manipulate her into accepting. He wanted her to come because *she* wanted to.

"Watch it from my house then," he said, tucking a strand of hair behind her ear.

"I—" Her hands fell slack to her sides. "That's not a good—"

"Please, Sara girl?" He gave her the puppy-dog look. The same one that used to work on her as a teenager.

Okay, so he took his previous thought back—a little manipulation never hurt anyone, especially when she would get the privacy she needed and he would get to have her in his house.

And just like before, his sad puppy expression worked.

"I— Dammit, Mike. Not the *eyes*." She shut hers. "Okay, *fine*."

THIRTEEN

Sara

SARA GOT out of the Uber and stared in shock at the house in front of her. Just outside of the city, it was tucked into a rare patch of green and surrounded by oak and eucalyptus trees.

A long walk led up to the house, a twisting row of stairs crawling toward a front door obscured from view of the street.

And directly in front of her was a large gate.

She swallowed, pulled her phone from her pocket, and approached the intimidating row of iron.

The keypad was easy to spot, and she plugged in the code that Mike had sent her. Silently, the gate opened, and she slipped through, waiting until it was completely closed again before she hiked up the staircase.

Muttering a curse when her body protested as per usual, Sara pushed the pain down and continued up.

Six years since the accident and her bones still ached.

But she was walking, running, jogging, drawing. Things the doctors had never expected her to do, so really life was looking up.

The daily pain was manageable. God knew she'd done it enough in her competing days—pushing through hurts, ignoring injuries, continuing on when it felt as though she couldn't do one more jump.

But that was different than the emotional pain. *That* hadn't been as easy to compartmentalize. It bled into everything, crept back in at the most inopportune moments.

So she focused on the physical. The physical she could deal with. The physical she could do something about.

With a wince, she climbed the twenty or so steps leading up.

Another keypad was by the front door, and she put in the next code from Mike's text message, waiting, listening to the *whir* of the lock as it rotated and clicked open.

The knob was oil-rubbed bronze, dark brown and beautifully crafted, but it was nothing compared to the inside of the house.

"Holy mother of God," she murmured as she stepped inside.

For a minute, she just stared at the huge space in shock. Then the alarm gave an ominous beep, spurring her into action. She closed and locked the front door before locating the panel just to the right and inputting another code.

Mike's house was like Fort Knox.

But she supposed there were perks to not having to carry keys or wrestle with a deadbolt, like her apartment. Half her morning workout was trying to get the damn thing open after she'd returned home from her run.

Mike had told her to make herself comfortable, given her carte blanche to explore . . . except, where to start?

The entry was huge, with vaulted ceilings and a spiral staircase. She could spy a kitchen behind the stairs with a sunken great room and a wall of windows beside it. On her right was the only wall she could see on the first story. A pair of double doors broke up the expanse of white, and when she crept forward to peek inside, Sara saw it was an office.

She meandered forward, slipping off her sneakers and tucking them near a side table, lest she track dirt across the pristine marble floors. Since the upstairs—hello, bedrooms—seemed too intimate, she bypassed the stairs and went into the kitchen.

A vase smack dab in the center of the huge island held flowers.

Her breath hitched, and her eyes filled with tears.

Daisies.

He'd remembered her favorite flower.

Sniffing, she walked forward to touch one of the silky soft petals and spotted the note.

DON'T BE SHY, *Jumping Bean. Snoop away. Eat all the good snacks in the fridge. And when you find a room you're comfortable in, make sure it's got a TV.*

We're on channel 723.

—Hot Shot

A GIANT GRIN. Her cheeks were actually aching from smiling so hard.

She traced a hand over the stone countertop. It didn't look like marble or granite, more man-made, like Corian. But it was a pretty gray and the cabinets were a bright white.

Little dots of color—of bright-yellow and pale-blue—were sprinkled throughout. A cookie jar here, a decorative plate there. The look wasn't masculine or something that she would have associated with Mike's personality. She suspected he'd hired a designer.

But the space was homey, somehow warm despite the white and all the stone, and Sara found that she liked it a lot.

She could almost imagine cooking a meal with him, laughing and jockeying for position around the stove. Or maybe sneaking down for a midnight snack, eating ice cream straight out of the container while perched on that gray countertop.

And . . . yeah. She needed to chill out.

They were friends. Just friends reestablishing an old relationship. That's it.

Friends who kissed with enough passion to out-flame a match to kerosene.

Aw crap.

But so what if she preferred his kitchen to the crappy one in her apartment? *Anyone* would.

"Idiot," she muttered, snatching her hand back from the countertop as though it had possessed the offensive thoughts and not her own brain. "Chocolate. I definitely need chocolate for this."

Glancing around, it took her a minute to find the freezer. A built-in panel disguised the drawer from view.

Thankfully, ice cream was inside.

Unfortunately, or maybe *fortunately*—at this point she was beyond confused—there was a note on one of the lids.

On the pint of Phish Food.

No. *I didn't get lucky with the daisies. I remember all your favorites .. . and how I used to be one.*

—H.S.

Sara blew out a breath, swallowed down the tightness that had appeared from Mike's thoughtfulness. But sweet baby Jesus, the man was *killing* her.

Especially when she saw the P.S. on the back of his note.

Spoons are *in the drawer behind you.*

"Give me a break, Mike," she muttered, not that it stopped her from opening said drawer and pulling out one.

After leaving the ice cream on the counter to get nice and soft, Sara went out the door in the great room and stepped onto a huge deck. Immediately her heart skipped a beat.

The view was absolutely beautiful.

The city was in the background, rooftops undulating over rolling hills, a red snake-light chain of brake lights visible in the waning sunshine. The deep-blue, almost-black of the bay encircled the chaos.

Her fingers itched to sketch the scene. To capture it exactly as she was watching it now.

But she hadn't brought her sketchbook.

Rookie mistake, Jetty.

Staring intently, she tried to commit the sight to memory to draw later. She did it even knowing that she would fail miserably.

She did it because her heart wouldn't let her do anything else.

Finally, Sara forced herself to turn away from the sight, and that's when she spotted it.

The sketchbook.

Her preferred brand.

The cup of pencils.

She crossed to them, took in the little square of paper tucked under one edge.

Do it. But don't forget about the game . . . or the ice cream.

Mike, the boy, had been dangerous to her heart, wrapping it around his finger with easy charm and a plethora of kindness.

Mike, the man, was devastating. He'd cut straight through her armor and transported her back in time.

God. She just liked him so much.

And so, with a smile on her face, she picked up a pencil and drew until the sun went down.

Despite his warning, her ice cream was soup when she finally returned back inside, sketchbook in hand, but Sara didn't mind, just used the spoon to fish out the good bits and then drank the leftovers like milk.

If this was confession time, she might have done that to her ice cream a time or a hundred before, but she'd be the first to tell anyone that it tasted just as good melted.

She rinsed the spoon, dumped the container, and managed to turn on the TV in the great room just as the puck was getting ready to drop.

Sara had never been much of a hockey fan.

The game wasn't in her heart. She'd always appreciated the starkness of a single skater on the sheet of white, the beauty of using the ice to her advantage, circles and zigzags to cover every inch. Hockey had seemed so chaotic in its place. So many skaters, so much noise, so many blades cutting into pristineness.

She'd seen her fair share of games growing up, but none had been like the ones Mike played now.

And she was able to find the beauty in how the players threaded passes through the other teams' skates, landing them directly on their teammate's stick, how they roofed pucks over goalies' shoulders. The scenes were filled with chaos and hits and bursts of color traveling at tremendous speed.

It was a choreographed routine of eighteen players and two goalies—hopping boards, opening doors, jumping into the play even as the action didn't stop.

Sara found that she liked *this* version of hockey very much.

Or maybe it was seeing Mike on the ice.

Maybe he'd changed it for her.

She snorted. *Of course*, he'd changed it for her. She was in his house, watching the game on his TV, flowers and sketchbook on the island, and reliving his kisses from earlier in the day.

He'd changed *everything*. He wanted something she'd never expected to give.

Not again.

Vulnerability was akin to death.

And yet, Mike didn't make her feel vulnerable.

He made her feel cherished.

The first period ended, and the reporter grabbed Mike for an interview before he headed to the locker room.

The Gold were down a goal, and she watched as he deflected the pointed questions about Brit's play and whether or not she should have made the last save. Instead, *he* took responsibility for the play. He didn't pass it on to the defense in general either, but shouldered it himself, saying he needed to improve, needed to read the play better, needed to work harder.

Sara watched in amazement. The respect she felt for this man . . .

He'd handled the tough questions with aplomb, barely sweating —or rather he was sweating only in the physical sense, not the mental.

With a wink to the camera that felt decidedly for *her*, he headed back to the locker room.

She picked up the remote, heart suddenly pounding in her chest.

That old impulsiveness reared its ugly head as she clicked off the TV, stood, and left the room.

FOURTEEN

Mike

MIKE WALKED into his darkened house and felt disappointment course through him.

She'd gone.

Or, hadn't come in the first place.

With a sigh, he closed the door to the garage, locking it before setting his keys on the kitchen island.

Which was when he spotted the sketchbook.

His heart expanded like a balloon being filled with helium. He strode over to the freezer, saw the pint of ice cream he'd bought for Sara was gone.

Like some insane paparazzi, he peeked into the trash, grinning when he found the empty container within.

And though he probably shouldn't—his mother hadn't liked him looking at her drawings—Mike didn't have the strength to resist looking inside the notebook.

Sara must not care too much, right? She'd left it on his counter after all.

Gently, he opened the cover and flipped through the sketches.

His amazement in Sara grew with each turn of the page.

He might not know much about art, but it didn't take a genius to see . . . well, genius.

She'd somehow captured both the realism and whimsy of the city, turning the rooftops into scales of a sleeping dragon, traffic into the beast's tail. Then he turned the sheet over and the next held a perfectly rendered drawing of the Golden Gate Bridge being engulfed by ocean fog.

No wonder her boss wanted to sell her work. They'd both make a fortune.

He closed the book and walked to the fridge to pull out a beer. So Sara had come and gone.

The disappointment for her having gone home was there for sure, though it was tempered by the fact that she *had* come in the first place.

He wanted to play this carefully, to not push Sara too hard, but at the same time, he needed to push her enough that they actually moved forward. They'd both been hurt, but she'd always been it for him.

They were right for each other.

He knew that more now than even when they'd been teenagers, when he'd forced himself to not act on his feelings.

To not hold her back.

God, he wished he'd ignored his chivalrous side. If he'd stayed in touch, been there for her—

No. His drama would have just bled over into her life.

They needed to move forward. Together.

He grinned, taking a swig of beer. Now he just needed to convince Sara of that fact.

And figure out how to deal with the press when the news came out.

Which it would.

With a sigh, he finished his beer, rinsed the bottle, and put it in the recycle bin. He flicked the lights and checked the alarm was functioning before crossing to the stairs.

He was tired, but that was a good thing. It meant he was working hard.

Of course, part of that was probably from allowing Brit to lead him on a wild goose chase through the lower bowl of the Gold Mine. He'd been following her on her workout since Philly and still hadn't gotten any closer to catching her.

He probably never would.

But he'd noticed a difference on the ice.

Hence, the continued hamster wheel of Brit stairs.

Round and round they went, never catching up and not really minding in the least.

His distraction with Brit's locker room music from earlier in the day—*Backstreet Boys,* good God—was probably why he didn't comprehend the light in his bedroom.

He strode through the door and screeched to what was certainly a very comical stop, had anyone been awake to see it.

Anyone being *Sara*.

Who was curled up on his bed, one of his T-shirts dwarfing her, a blanket half-draped over her body and giving him a glimpse of one bare leg.

Holy. Fucking. Shit.

Mike blinked. Glanced away and back.

But no, Sara was still there. In *his* bed. Wearing *his* shirt.

Suddenly, he wasn't the least bit tired. He was hard and aching and—

The Sleeping Beauty—no *Goldilocks*—that was Sara stirred slightly on the bed. Mike whirled away, unsure if he should be looking, and caught sight of her clothes folded neatly on a chair in the corner of the room.

He had to walk by them on the way to his closet, and he couldn't even lie and say he'd accidentally caught a glimpse of her bra and panties.

No, he actually stopped and pushed her jeans aside, nearly groaning when he saw the matching black lace set folded neatly atop her shirt.

Sara was in his bed, in his shirt, without a bra and underwear.

He bit back a curse and walked through the door into his closet.

Unzipping his slacks was the hardest—yes, literally the *hardest*—part. Jacket on the hanger, pants and dress shirt in the dry-clean hamper.

One sock off. The other and—

Cool hands on his back.

"Christ!" Mike jumped and whipped around, almost knocking Sara in the face with his elbow. He'd only just been able to adjust, to shift his weight and not accidentally clock her, but it had still been a close thing.

"Hey," she whispered, sleep in her eyes and an impish smirk on her lips.

His heart had been pounding because she'd startled him and he'd nearly hurt her. Now it threatened to burst from his chest for a whole other reason.

Mussed blond hair, naked breasts barely concealed beneath cotton, long bare legs, pink toenails.

Fuck. Her toenails were *pink*.

The same pink he imagined the hidden parts of her were.

And imagining those hidden parts was not helping his control in the least.

"Hope you don't mind," she murmured. "I got tired waiting for you after the game." A fingertip trailed down his chest, his abs, slipped under the waistband of his boxer briefs—

He caught that naughty hand and pulled it free. Her skin was like silk beneath his palm, warm and sleep-flushed, pale with just the hint of a rosy tone. She was strawberries and cream, and he wanted to lick her up.

"You can be naked in my bed anytime you want, sweetheart."

"I'm not naked."

He brought her wrist up, pressed his mouth to the delicate skin there. "*Nearly* naked then."

"Mmm." She lifted her other hand, gripping his shoulder as she rose on tiptoe to whisper in his ear, "So why did you stop me?"

He kissed her neck. "Who said anything about stopping?" A nip of his teeth. "But we should probably discuss the circumstances."

Sara huffed out a sigh. "I don't want to discuss anything. You're sweet and hot, and we're together. No talking." She dropped back onto the balls of her feet, met his eyes, and the mix of need and confidence in her stare made his blood pulse under his skin. This woman. She was hot as hell.

Especially when she tugged the T-shirt over her head and said, "I want you inside me. I want you to give me multiple orgasms and then wake me up in a few hours to do it all over again. I want—"

Her words were hot, but his mind stalled on her breasts, all perky and bouncy as she tossed the shirt aside.

In one quick movement, he swept her into his arms and strode back into the bedroom. "I meant more like I'm clean, and I have condoms."

"Oh—*oh!*" She gasped when he tossed her on the bed and pinned her to the mattress.

He was moving too fast, taking advantage, but this girl had been inside Mike's head for more than a decade. He didn't have patience when it came to Sara. He wanted her, *needed* her almost more than his next breath. If not breathing meant that he could have still brought her pleasure, found his own when he was inside her, then he'd have gladly given up the ability.

"I'm on the pill," she said and bit her lip. "I was clean the last time I got tested. Admittedly, it was a while ago, but I haven't been with anyone since . . ."

"Good." He reached for the nightstand drawer, extracted a condom, and set it on the pillow next to her head. Birth control pills or not, he wouldn't risk Sara.

"Good?"

"Yup." A smirk as he leaned back on his heels and picked up her foot. In reality, she was tiny, significantly shorter and smaller than him, especially since she always seemed so much larger in his mind.

But it was hard to deny the evidence of her size when her foot was in his hand. He massaged the sole, her toes with that delectable pink polish, and could easily feel the delicate bones beneath the surface of her skin.

Fragile. She was beyond—

Her other foot stroked up the side of his calf, his thigh, his groin, coming to rest just a hairsbreadth away from his cock.

Hot.

She was so fucking hot.

One toe stroked along his length, base to tip, before she allowed her leg to drop to the side, knee bent and effectively exposing—

Fuuuck. The pinks matched.

Mike felt his control slip another notch and forced his eyes up to the ceiling. He thought about tsunamis and short-handed goals, about stick length—

So. Not. Helping.

"Hey, Hot Shot. Getting lonely here." His gaze snapped down, and he saw Sara's hand trailing lower, drifting south. And . . . *hell no.* He dropped her foot and dove for her.

His mouth plundered on its way to her center, nipping, licking, kissing, until he reached the apex of her thighs. He gripped her hips, spread her legs with his shoulders, and went to work.

She tasted like cotton candy, sweet and soft.

"Mike!"

"Mmm." His tongue traced an intricate pattern that had her gripping his hair like a steering wheel.

He guessed she liked that. And so he did it again. And again. And again.

She bucked, twisting on his sheets, squeezing his head in the vice-like grip of her thighs.

And he wanted more.

One finger inside. Two.

"*Fuck,* I'm going to—"

She exploded around him, drenching his mouth, holding him tight both inside and out for a long moment before collapsing back to the bed.

Mike rode out the wave with her, gentling her descent back to reality. Only when she had stopped convulsing around him did he remove his fingers and sit up.

A kiss to that pretty mouth of hers, sipping in her rapid exhales as she tried to get her breath back. A touch of his lips to the space between her breasts, to one nipple, the other.

"Mike," she breathed.

He tucked a strand of hair behind her ear. "Like you saying my name like that."

Her eyes slid closed and a smile smoothed her features. Her breathing went slow and even.

Sleep. She'd fallen asleep.

Mike almost didn't care. Yes, he was hard and aching, covered in a layer of sweat, and his balls were probably indigo, but this was Sara.

His Sara.

He tugged a blanket from the bottom of the bed, covered them, and pulled her into his arms.

As she nestled against his chest, her hair got all up in his face. He was so hard that his dick could hammer a fucking nail and she immediately hogged the blanket.

But he didn't give a damn because she was next to him.

FIFTEEN

Sara

SARA WOKE UP WONDERFULLY WARM. She stretched, frowning at the soreness of her muscles, the stiffness of her right hip and ribs.

Had she overdone her run the day before?

But then she registered the heavy arm across her middle, the rough hair of legs pressing against the back of hers, the erection prodding her butt.

And—*shit!* She'd fallen asleep.

She'd had one orgasm and then *fallen asleep.*

Before Mike had gotten his.

Guilt poured over her. She'd basically assaulted him in his closet, begged that he have sex with her, gotten hers . . . and fallen asleep.

Good Lord, she was the *guy.*

That thought made a giggle bubble up in her throat.

But *dang*, she was a jerk. Once he woke up, she needed to find a way to—

"What's so funny?" Mike's voice was raspy from sleep.

She rolled over and stared into his brown eyes. They were soft, not irritated, but there was an underlying heat in them reminding her quite blatantly that she'd left her man hard and unsatisfied the previous night.

Her man?

Had she honestly just thought that?

Except what else was Mike if he wasn't hers?

She'd belonged to him in some way—they'd had this unbreakable, silent connection—since she was sixteen and he was eighteen. Wasn't that the definition of *hers*?

Whatever. She wasn't going to spend time worrying about it. Instead, she was going to embrace it, enjoy it. It had been ages since she'd felt this alive.

Mike made her feel whole.

And since she was embracing this whole *her man* thing, then she was going to take very good care of him.

"Sara?" He touched her cheek. "You okay?"

Her lips curved, and she turned her head so that she could kiss his palm. "I'm better than okay."

One brown brow lifted. "Yeah?"

Sunlight poured through the windows, turning Mike into the equivalent of a Roman god. His skin was golden-hued, his chest squeezable, his abs clearly defined.

She pushed him back against the gray comforter, letting the blanket he must have covered them with slide down her back as she straddled him.

"Six yummy squares," she murmured, running a finger around the defined muscles. "I hear they're hard to get."

Mike hissed out a breath when she moved up and brushed his nipple. "Well, when you don't have anything else to do besides working out . . ."

Mmm. Pecs. They overflowed her hands when she gave them a squeeze. "Really?" she asked and bent down to press a kiss to his chest, then to each of those six squares. "Not anything to *do*?"

She traced her tongue along that little trail of hair that disappeared beneath his boxer briefs, that led to his decidedly *not* little erection, and pushed the waistband down, her mouth actually watering—

And found herself on her back, Mike above her, eyes hot, hard body pressing into her . . . everywhere.

"I believe I promised you multiple orgasms."

"I—"

She didn't get more than that one syllable out before his mouth was on her breasts. The sound that came from her was almost inhuman, but Mike didn't seem to mind, just switched to the neglected side.

He ran a hand down her torso, tracing his fingers straight down and in . . . *in.*

"Mike!" she cried.

"Like it when you call out my name, sweetheart."

Her vision was blurry, her every nerve was on edge, and she was rapidly approaching—

No.

But she was already over the brink, cruising over the peak, cascading down the other side. Pleasure made her limbs lax and her legs—which had been squeezing his arm like a vise—flop open to the mattress.

"What did you put in that ice cream?" she asked, suddenly way too relaxed to move.

He laughed and she joined in, loving the light in his eyes. It felt like those mornings from before. Just the two of them sharing a private joke, her and Mike against the rest of the world. Only *this* time, there weren't barriers—age, parents, responsibilities, *clothes*—between them.

With difficulty, she lifted her arm, which may as well have been a limp noodle at this point, and touched his cheek.

"I've missed you."

The brown of his eyes intensified as he propped himself up, his elbows on either side of her head. "That's almost better than hearing my name, Jumping Bean."

She stroked the bristles on his jaw, loved the feel of him over her, pressing down, all hard and hot. "We need to talk."

A pained expression crossed his face, but Mike nodded and sat back.

Huh? *Oh!*

"Not now," Sara said, lurching upward to latch onto his shoulder. She flopped down, pulling him along with her. "I meant that as a sometime-later discussion."

"Thank fuck," he said, cupping her face in his palms and leaning down to kiss her.

Hot lips, a searching tongue, teeth nipping at her jaw, her neck. He was a flurry of motion, transforming her languid pleasure of the minute before into a frenzy of need.

His mouth moved to her breasts and, *yes,* she liked that a whole hell of a lot, but when he slid lower, obviously on the trail to south of the border, Sara'd had enough. Look, obviously, she liked oral sex, and Mike was *really* freaking good at it, but she needed him inside her already.

So she used her yoga moves—which made her actually appreciate the torturous exercise for a change—and stopped him by wrapping her legs around his hips.

"S-Sara," he hissed out.

In fairness, she was hissing too. Because her move had brought his cock right *there.*

She could feel the heat of him against her, so close and yet not *in,* and started to shift her pelvis to close that final bit of distance between them.

Mike stopped her, one big hand spanning her waist. "Hold on, sweetheart."

She couldn't hold on, couldn't wait another second, not after waiting ten years.

Her body was on fire, the need coursing through her almost painful.

And so she tilted her hips and brushed against the hard length of him.

"Fuck!" He thrust forward, the tip of him brushing her heat, but just as quickly he was gone.

"Mike, I—"

"Almost, Sara girl, just—"

The crinkle of a wrapper drew her gaze, and she watched as he rolled a condom on. He was back between her thighs, poised at her entrance a second later.

"Yes?" he asked.

"Yes," she replied before he'd even finished the word.

And *thank* God she had because then he was there, filling her, stretching her from the inside out. But it wasn't just physical. Somehow, he was stretching her heart, filling her soul with more than just—

A swivel of his hips pulled her right out of any semi-rational thoughts she had remaining.

She wrapped her legs tight around his waist, clawed at his arms, and held on tight as Mike rode her like a prized stallion.

In and out, in and out, grinding forward, pressing tightly, retreating . . . basically turning her into a writhing, begging puddle of desire.

But the hottest thing was the way he talked to her. The dirty little sentiments whispered in her ear, naughty enough to make her wetter even as her cheeks flushed.

Her moans were loud, her breathing uneven, and when Mike ordered her to "Come for me. Now," she didn't consider disobeying.

She exploded.

One, two more thrusts, and he was following suit.

Sara had never heard anything hotter than the long, low groan of Mike's orgasm. It drew hers out, pleasure sliding outward from her center to the rest of her limbs, sparks of sensation exploding along her skin.

Holy shit.

Holy fucking shit.

What in the hell was that?

That was soul-shattering, incredible sex, and it meant—

Fuck. What did it mean?

She should—

She needed—

Good God. What *did* she need to do? Run? Jump on top of him for round two? Pretend the whole sexual escapade had been mediocre? That it didn't actually mean anything?

Except he'd heard her verbal orchestra of orgasm—scratch that —*orgasms*. He knew it had been good for her.

Mike must have sensed her panic, because although he had his head buried in her shoulder, rapid exhales puffing against his neck, forearms propping him up and preventing his body from crushing hers, he said, "Later, sweetheart. That talking part doesn't have to come now."

The knot twisting her insides loosened, and he rolled them to the side, shifting to cradle her back against his chest.

"It will all be okay."

She nodded, felt her hair slide against his chest. But it was mostly an empty gesture.

There was no way that things would be okay.

Her life didn't work that way.

SIXTEEN

Mike

MIKE REELED as he held Sara.

He'd just had the most incredible sex of his life, and yet he'd lied to his partner in the process.

This thing between them had the potential to destroy them both.

"Did you feel it?"

Her whispered question undid him.

"Fuck yeah, I felt it, sweetheart." He released her, tugging her shoulder until she faced him. When scared blue eyes met his, he leaned forward and kissed her. He forced his panic to the side, forced that fear of getting burned away, and let himself get lost in the embrace.

This is what he needed to focus on.

Not the what-ifs.

Sara's expression was slightly less petrified when he pulled back. Or at least there was heat and desire tempering her concern.

"We'll figure it out, yeah?"

A nod.

"Together this time." He rested his forehead on hers. "*This* time we're not alone."

She released a breath, and the sweet burst of air caressed his lips. God, he wanted to kiss her again.

He wanted to make love to her again.

But before they could, he needed to know that she was with him. "Yeah?"

She rolled her eyes. "I've always loved when you don't give me a second to think and push me for an answer."

"I've always loved your sarcasm."

"Yeah?"

He chuckled.

Her shoulders lifted and dropped on a breath. "Okay."

"So we're doing this?"

Sara smiled and sat up. "I thought we were going to talk later."

Mike's breath caught when she slipped from the bed then turned in the direction of the bathroom.

He'd appreciated the up-close view of Sara's body, but seeing her like this: sunshine dappling her skin, her ass jiggling slightly as she strode unabashedly across the bedroom, the little peek-a-boo of side boob as she paused at the door to the bathroom and crooked a finger at him, the red scar along her spine, an angry line leading to her hip—

What?

He was up and out of bed before his eyes had finished processing, standing in the doorway of the bathroom, staring at the mark in horror.

"Shouldn't you deal with that?" Sara pointed at the condom he still wore, bending over to peek in a cabinet, then another, as she searched for something.

On her third try—and he wasn't even in the right frame of mind to appreciate the sight—she pulled out three towels. He still stood on the threshold, but when she tossed a box of tissues at him, he mechanically caught it and took care of the condom.

Sara hung the towels over the side of the shower then opened the glass door and cranked on the water.

Only after she'd adjusted the temperature and turned back around did she seem to realize he hadn't moved.

"What's the matter?"

Fury boiled under his skin, blood actually pounded in his ears. *Thump-thump. Thump-thump. Thump-thump.*

Because he knew what that scar was shaped like.

A skate blade.

Sara's eyes closed, her chest lifted on a long inhale. She let that breath out slowly before speaking. "It's not what you think."

"My mind is not in a good place, Sara. So you'd better explain. Quickly."

She crossed her arms. "Don't be an asshole. I don't *have* to tell you anything. You're not my father or my boss or—"

"I'm the man who was inside you less than five minutes ago."

Twin spots of pink appeared on her cheeks. "That's not the point."

He was across the bathroom in two strides, his chest against hers, pressing her back against the shower wall. Water sluiced over their skin, heated trails dripping down his face, soaking into her hair. He reached an arm behind him and closed the door.

"The point is that I thought we were doing this together."

Her expression was as furious as he felt. "The future. Building something together doesn't mean we need to rehash every fucking thing from our past." She lifted her chin, fixed him with a glare. "Especially shit that doesn't matter."

Except, if it really didn't matter, then she would just tell him.

"Spill it, Sara girl."

"There's nothing to *spill*," she ground out, trying to slip to the side.

Mike pinned her in place with his hips and grabbed her cheeks, forcing her eyes to his when she might have turned her stare away. "Yes. There is."

"No." Her lips pressed flat. "There isn't."

This couldn't work. He didn't have a chance at out-stubborning Sara. Never could.

So Mike changed tactics. He kissed her, hard and hot and enticing, and when he broke away, they were both panting. Sara was no longer trying to escape him; rather, she was leaning into him and rubbing her breasts across his chest.

He liked that. Probably too much since he was trying to be lucid enough to figure out why in the fuck his girl had a ten-inch scar along her back.

Just the thought of that jagged, angry line infuriated him enough to pull blood from his dick and funnel it north to get his brain to work.

"How'd you get the scar?"

Her head plunked back against the tile, slipping her cheeks free of his grasp. "Can't you just let it go?"

He pushed a strand of sodden hair off her face. "No, honey. I'm sorry. I can't."

His tone was gentle, the words soft.

And finally, they seemed to get through her armor.

She swallowed hard. "I'll tell you. But let's shower first. I—I can't do this here."

Mike started to open his mouth, to ask why location made a difference, but Sara raised a hand to his jaw.

"It'll make sense later." Her smile was sad. "Just know I need to be warm and dry to tell it, okay?"

He nodded and stepped back, letting her have most of the water. When she'd wet her hair, he handed her shampoo then soap.

"Sorry," he murmured. "I don't have that conditioner stuff girls use."

Another smile that didn't reach her eyes. "I'll survive."

Unfortunately, Mike thought the sentiment was all too true.

SEVENTEEN

Sara

SARA CLENCHED the towel tightly to her breasts, watching Mike rub the cotton along his chest and legs before tying it around his waist.

Unfortunately, she was completely unable to appreciate the sight.

Why hadn't she realized that he would see the scar?

Of course he would notice.

Impulsivity.

Always her downfall.

"Here."

She blinked. Mike had slipped out of the bathroom and dressed without her noticing. He wore sweats and was holding a shirt out for her.

"Oh," she murmured, fumbling to hold the towel and grab the slip of cotton. Both fell from her fingers, puddled on the floor. "Crap."

"Don't move." He bent, slung the t-shirt over his shoulder, then picked up the towel. But when he brought the terrycloth around to her back, she flinched away.

Not the scar. Don't touch me there.

"I said don't move." And gently, oh . . . so . . . gently, Mike brushed the towel along her back, up her spine, between her shoulders, mopping up the water she'd missed.

He slipped the shirt over her head and lifted her into his arms. A moment later, she was back in bed, under the covers and cradled against Mike's chest.

The position hurt her hip, and she shifted, feeling her mind clear slightly when his arms came up to hold her in place.

It almost made her smile, almost, when the hard limbs gripped her tighter.

"It happened six years ago," she said, picking up his hand so she could adjust her position, to allow her aching hip some relief. "I really should be more fully recovered. I mean, I can run again, within reason, but yoga is still a pain. Not that I really work at it. It's still Satan's idea of exercise. I'm fine. It's just that things get stiff if I'm in one spot for too long or if I do some new activity—"

She broke off. One, because she was rambling, and, two, because she realized what *new* activity she'd participated in the previous evening. Her cheeks felt red-hot, and her eyes shot to Mike's.

"I like that, sweetheart," he murmured. "That this isn't common for you, that I'm one of the few men who get to touch you—"

"The one man."

He frowned. "What?"

"You're the one man I've been with," she said then hurried to add when his face paled, "Not ever. Just since the accident." Sara shrugged. "It's why I forgot about the scar."

His silence was followed by a long, slow breath. "That's good."

She frowned at the relief in his words. "Would it have mattered if I *was* a virgin?"

Now was his turn to frown. "Is this a trick question?"

"No." Sara tugged at the comforter. The man was like a furnace wrapped around her, an electric blanket on steroids. "But why would you care if I had been one?"

"Why would I care if you'd been a virgin?" he asked, lifting his arm and pulling down the blanket so it was at their waists rather than their shoulders.

She huffed out a breath, stilled his hand when it went to crawl under the hem of her t-shirt. "Yes. Why that?"

"Because I would have wanted to do a better job."

Oh. *Oh.*

And somehow sprawled in bed, bickering with Mike about something completely unimportant was right.

The story, the truth about the accident slipped from her almost as easily as breathing . . . or maybe it was like getting her breath back after the wind had been knocked from her lungs.

Painful but necessary.

"I'd gone on several dates with Leo Tomskoi after the I'd won the gold, but it never went anywhere. We were both too busy—he was on the professional ski circuit, and I had the skating tour, interviews, endorsements, visits to schools. You name it. My agent and publicist had me signed up for it."

"Sounds exhausting."

She smiled. "Yeah. But exhilarating too. You know I always loved that side of it." Her lips twisted. "Especially since the press had been nothing but kind to me."

"You were good at being the media darling." A brush of his fingers across her cheek. "Too charismatic by half."

"Except with you."

"If you only knew." His words were so tortured that Sara started to ask what was wrong, but he waved her off. "Then what happened?"

"He called me a few years after everything came out, said he knew I wouldn't cheat, that he didn't believe a word of the press's nonsense." The parallels between him and Mike were obvious.

Except, of course, for the fact that Mike actually believed her. And Leo . . . well, Leo had wanted to get back at her.

A hand slid down her spine, and she shuddered out a breath. "He took me out on one date, then another, then he kidnapped me—"

Sara felt him stiffen beneath her. "Not like that. I mean it was supposed to be romantic, and it was. In a way." She shook her head. Rambling again. "Leo blindfolded me, took me to a frozen pond. He had blankets and food, ice skates and candles."

The moon had been bright on that clear night, the stars cheerfully visible. It had been cold as hell, of course, but the most romantic gesture ever.

Or so she'd thought.

And those skates. *Her* skates. They were her kryptonite.

"Turned out his stepsister was Rebecca Julian. She'd finished third at Nationals." Her words caught in her throat. "I—I didn't even know they were related."

"What happened?" Two words, deadly soft.

Sara remembered the surprise push from behind as Leo had leaned down to kiss her, the crack of her face against the ice when he'd moved back to let her fall, the burn as the cold made contact with her exposed skin. She remembered the blood from her nose dripping down her face as she'd looked up to see Leo skating away.

And then the agony of sharp steel piercing skin.

Rebecca Julian had never made it to the highest level of competition.

Because of Sara.

Because of the cheating.

Because Sara had taken *her* spot.

"I got cut." Rebecca had stepped on her, trampled Sara beneath a skate blade like a toddler crunching a fallen leaf. "They left me out there."

"Sara, honey." Gritted out words, false calm from Mike in the wake of furious brown eyes. "That's not an answer."

"She shoved me down. I was cut by an errant blade, and they

left." Sara shuddered, remembering the blood—hot at first, then cold, *so cold*—spreading over her skin.

"They found me the next morning. I had frostbite on my fingers, my nose, but the worst was obviously the injury on my back."

"They left you?" If Mike had been furious before, now that fury looked like mild irritation. "They sliced you with a fucking skate blade and left you to die?"

"I didn't say—"

"You didn't have to!"

He erupted out of bed and paced the room in rage-filled strides. Curse words spewed through the air, many of which she'd thought plenty of times over the years.

"I didn't learn until later that an anonymous male caller had phoned the police that morning. Made sure I didn't die out there."

Leo had an episode of conscience. Or so she presumed.

By the time she'd reached the point of asking, months later in her recovery, he hadn't taken her calls.

Not her finest moment, letting that pass, putting off the doctors and police when they pointed out that her very illogical cutting-herself-on-her-back-with-her-own-skate-blade   explanation   was impossible.

But she also couldn't completely regret the act and her passivity.

Her cowardice was why she'd come to San Francisco in the first place. Running.

Sara had wanted to get as far away from her old life as possible. Somewhere warm, somewhere large with a community for artists. She'd wanted to get lost in a big city, but not one rampant with paparazzi.

L.A. had been out.

San Francisco in.

"Fuck!" Mike. She'd been viscerally aware of his agitation, of his pacing and muttered curses, but the outburst still made her jump.

"It's—"

Furious brown eyes whipped toward her. "If you're going to

finish that sentence with *okay* then don't bother." He was at the bed in an instant. "You're not close to okay, Sara. You're so far fucked that I don't know how to fix you."

Wow.

She'd always been surprised that words could hurt so badly when they didn't create a mark.

Or a physical one, anyway.

Because that slice across her heart . . .

Her breath whooshed out in a rush. "I've never asked you to fix me."

Sara *should* have said she didn't need fixing, that she was perfect the way she was. But she wasn't delusional.

She had problems.

"Christ." He thrust a hand through his hair. "You never do, Sara. You never do."

"What is that supposed to mean?" She clutched the blankets to her chest, a cotton barrier against whatever he was going to say next.

"It means—" Mike blew out a breath, shook his head.

His phone buzzed.

"It means I've got to get to the airport for the team's flight." He crossed to the closet, words suddenly rushed and brusque. "We're flying to Los Angeles for our game against the Kings. I'll be home late tonight. We'll have to table this until tomorrow."

Table this?

This being the discussion about the story he'd all but forced out of her?

The story that had made him furious . . . at her. Logically, she could understand anger as a reaction to what had happened to her. She'd been angry plenty of times over the last six years, at herself for not going to the police, at Leo and Rebecca for wanting to hurt her. But that didn't make Mike's reaction any more palatable.

She wanted him to be mad for her, not mad *at* her.

"Mike," she said.

He popped his head out. "Do we really have to do this now? I've got stuff to do."

"For the game," she said, expressionless.

"Yes, of course for the game."

And she might have believed him, if not for the look in his eyes.

He wanted her gone.

Well, that problem, at least, she could solve.

After tossing the covers aside, Sara stood and snagged her clothes. She was glad she'd had the foresight to fold and stash them on the armchair in the corner of the room.

It made getting dressed quick work.

Mike was talking again, something about pregame routines and puck drop, flights home and potential delays. She ignored him, slipping into her shoes then opening the app on her phone to call an Uber.

One staircase down with stiff legs, one alarm-code input, one door shut behind her.

The Uber pulled up as she was approaching the gate. She was inside, and it was driving away before the metal barrier had begun to close.

Silence reigned on the way to her apartment.

The driver didn't speak, her phone didn't ring, didn't buzz, and her heart . . . that fragile organ, a delicate papier-mâché project still forming—attempting to dry even as its wet weight tried to collapse in on itself—cracked and crumbled.

It dissolved to ash.

But ash sometimes made the strongest type of armor.

EIGHTEEN

Mike

MIKE SHOULD HAVE FELT like the biggest jackass on the planet when he walked, fully dressed, out of the closet and found his bedroom empty.

But he didn't.

Hence, the Biggest Jackass Award.

Instead, the emotion that poured through him was relief.

Relief that he didn't need to hash out the feelings inside him, that he didn't need to face the guilt.

Yes. Guilt.

Why had he let Sara go?

Everything was his fault.

"Fuck," he muttered and swiped a hand down his face.

The martyr complex was stupid, he understood that. He knew it was impossible to control the rest of the world, that he wouldn't have been able to stop her coaches from cheating her, couldn't have hoped to prevent the betrayal.

But he would have been there for her.

She wouldn't have been alone.

"Fuck," he said again and strode from the room. It still smelled like Sara, soft and floral and with just the barest hint of pencil lead. The scent may as well have been embedded into his pores.

He pounded down the stairs, twisted the knob for the door leading to the garage, and stopped.

Had that been there the night before? Or had Sara dropped—

Shaking his head, Mike picked up the folded piece of paper. Of course it hadn't been in the middle of the floor last night. It was obviously one of Sara's drawings, the material the thick white paper from her sketchbooks.

He opened it.

Then almost wished he hadn't.

The drawing was of him and Sara, their faces young, their expressions carefree. The background was the part that gutted him. Slashes and swirls, pencil strokes that were harsh and painful.

Hidden in those writhing lines were older versions of him and Sara. Her face was long and gaunt, tears pouring like blood from her eyes, and he stood, brows pulled tight into a frown, eyes dark and disapproving.

Her tears swirled between the two of them, dripped down to surround their younger selves. It didn't quite reach them, those youthful masks untouched.

But it was what was beneath it all that caused the greatest pain.

She'd done the whole piece in shades of gray, and Mike couldn't help but think that was how she viewed the world.

Lacking in color.

Pain locked beneath cheerful facades.

And suddenly the guilt that had been harping on him a bare half hour before felt like peaches and rainbows. Because *this* guilt—the turning on her when she'd trusted him enough to open up—was a thousand times worse.

He'd hurt her.

Mike cursed for what felt like the hundredth time that hour.

He slammed into the garage, whipping his phone from his pocket and pressing the opener. It rattled up as he dialed and shoved himself into his car.

Stefan answered, sounding suitably distracted.

Mike was sure Brit had something to do with that, especially when he heard a feminine giggle in the background.

Gross.

But the nauseous feeling that was making his gut churn wasn't the thought of his teammates doing a horizontal line change.

He'd hurt Sara. Again.

Jackass of the year. Fuck. The century.

He waited impatiently for the gate to open and sped down the road, back into the city, and away from the airport.

Hence the phone call.

Stefan's voice sharpened, the giggle cut off. "Mike? You okay?"

"No." He swerved around the corner, zipped onto 101 and went north. "I fucked up. Big time."

"Was it the charm? I really thought you could pull some out of—"

"Not the charm," he ground out, pushing his speed. He'd done well with the charm. Scavenger hunt with all her favorite things. Check. Flowers. Check. Multiple orgasms. Check, check, check.

The problem was his stunted little man-child emotions.

"Then what, buddy? 'Cause I thought you'd decided to go for it. I talked to the team's publicist—"

"What?" Mike almost rear-ended the car in front of him.

"Not in specifics," Stefan rushed to say. "I never mentioned her name or even alluded to Sara's troubles. I just asked her to think of some ways to spin a relationship with a player and a person who might be considered infamous—wrongly, of course," he added when Mike spat out a curse.

He didn't like the idea of airing Sara's dirty laundry but hated more that *he* hadn't thought of working with the powers that be preemptively.

If he wanted to protect Sara, then he needed to think of these things first, not rely on his teammates to bail them out.

But that wasn't important because—

"Her story got worse."

"How could it possibly be worse?"

Mike cut over two lanes and took the exit that would lead to Sara's apartment. "Trust me. It did."

"Fuck," Stefan said. "I'm assuming you can't tell me the specifics."

Mike paused at a signal. "Not my story to tell."

"Yeah. Figured." A sigh that slid through the airwaves. "So what now? It's not your fault that her life got worse."

"It is when you're so pissed and angry at the people that hurt her that you don't realize she needed a freaking hug."

Or kind words. Or reaffirmation that it hadn't been her fault.

The light turned green, and he smashed down the accelerator.

"You need to grovel."

"That much is clear," he snapped. "But I have to find her first."

"She left? Fuck, man. You really did screw up."

"Yeah. Sara's got a habit of running when things go bad, and I—"

He hadn't helped matters. He'd freaked, and now she thought he was blaming her and—

"So what do you need me to do?"

The signal turned red, and Mike screeched the car to a stop. Right ahead. Then another left, and he'd be at her apartment.

"Just cover for me with Bernard if I'm late. I should be good but . . ." He trailed off, not really knowing if he'd be good at all. Not if he didn't find Sara and convince her to forgive him.

But his mind was in a fucked-up air space. If he didn't at least try . . .

"Will do." Stefan paused. "It'll be okay."

"How do you know that?" Mike screeched to a halt on the street in front of Sara's apartment.

"Because I'm guessing that Sara already knows you're an idiot."

"I'm hanging up now, asshole."

"I got one more tidbit bit of advice for you, buddy."

"You can take your advice and stick it straight up—"

Stefan didn't let him finish. "In all seriousness, know that I'm—"

A muffled female voice said something.

"—correction, *we're* here for you."

"Thanks. I think."

"Oh, and Mike?"

He popped the door, hesitated before opening it to get out. "Yeah."

"Groveling works better when you get down on both knees."

NINETEEN

Sara

WHY DID SHE *ALWAYS* RUN?

It was pathetic, really, how quickly she cut her losses and took off. What was even more pathetic was the fact that she was tying her sneakers and getting ready to take an actual run, rather than the Uber one from Mike's place.

Her hip didn't need the extra pounding—

And, great, now she was blushing because her mind couldn't think of the word *pounding* without conjuring images of Mike and how good it had felt when he'd pounded into her.

Hot skin, hard muscles—

Sharp words.

Cowardice.

"Goddammit," she muttered and wrestled her hair into a ponytail.

She'd run. Left without standing up for herself.

Maybe she and Mike wouldn't work out. Maybe they couldn't get over all the shared and individual baggage they carried.

But she hadn't fought. For any of it.

Instead, she'd rolled over and died. Again.

Pathetic. And yup, her picture was going in that proverbial dictionary. Sara Jetty: cheating ice princess and connoisseur of avoiding any and all conflict.

Shoving in her earbuds with one hand, she twisted the knob with the other.

The door pushed open, almost smacking her in the face.

In fact, it *would* have smacked her had a large, strong hand not caught the plank of wood and stopped it a half inch from her nose.

She knew those hands. Knew that scar across the ring finger, knew the light dusting of hair on the knuckles.

Slowly, the door was drawn back, and Mike slipped inside her apartment.

He raised a brow at her, no doubt taking in her sweats, sneakers, and firmly contained ponytail. "Going somewhere?"

She lifted her chin, tried to pretend that her heart wasn't racing.

Why was he here? Why did she care so damn much?

"Yeah. For a run."

"Seems to be a lot of that happening."

Her arms crossed on their own, she'd swear it. Either that or Mike had the uncanny ability to piss her off faster than any other person on the planet. "Not really."

"Yeah?" He closed the door behind him, leaned back against it. "So you're going to tell me you didn't run from my house?"

Sara ripped her earbuds out and walked over to her small sitting area. The armchair was a soft blue velvet and beyond worn, but it was the perfect height for her little round table that played double duty as both work space and kitchen counter.

She slammed her phone down onto the table, not caring when the cord to her headphones tangled and the little plastic speakers collided with her cup of pencils, almost knocking it over.

Her mad was on and raring now, and it felt *so* much better than the hurt from before.

Leaving the phone, she whirled around and marched over to Mike. Poked him in the chest. "Don't try and tell me for one second that you didn't want me gone. You all but ripped the truth from me then wanted me to GTFO."

He propped one foot behind him on the door.

It should have irritated her, that action. He was getting street scum on her walls, probably marking up the paint. And yet her mind literally would not let her focus on anything aside from the fact that he could fill out those slacks.

Really fill them out.

As in, she knew now from personal experience how well he could fill out a pair of pants.

Whew.

Was it getting hot in her apartment?

She pulled at the collar of her shirt, needing some cool air on her heated skin.

"I don't know what that means."

"What *what* means?"

Mike snagged her wrist, pressed her palm to his chest. He wore a suit jacket and button-down, so there were at least two layers between her hand and his skin, but her body didn't know the difference.

Or hell, maybe it did.

Because her lady parts were demanding that she slip those buttons loose, part the shirt, and lick his pecs like a popsicle.

"I don't know what G T F O means."

"Get the fuck out."

He blinked, dropped his fingers from her wrist.

The action was abrupt enough for her undressing fantasy to waver, enough for her to realize it was just that. A fantasy.

She and Mike were only a fantasy.

"I—" He cocked his head, eyes flashing to the ceiling as he worked something out in his brain. "Oh. *Oh.*"

"What?"

"GTFO means to get the fuck out."

Well, yeah.

"Not that you want me to leave now."

Except, now that he mentioned it . . .

He flashed her a grin. "Tell me how you really feel, Sara girl."

She huffed. "I *thought* I just did." Turning, she sighed again. "Mike. You wanted me gone. You don't like what happened to me. I get that. But—" Her chair creaked as she sank down into it and dropped her head into her hands. "Truth is, you wanted me to leave."

"Yes."

All traces of heat vanished, her body iced over. "Why don't *you* tell me how you really feel?"

That had come out on a steady voice. If nothing else, there was that. Her hurt was hidden so deep that no one would ever know.

Except for Mike.

Because the jerkwad always saw beneath her armor.

This time was no exception.

He cursed and was in front of her in a second, hands on her knees, face between her arms, forcing her to look at him.

"Sweetheart."

Sara leaned back, crossed her arms. "Don't call me that."

Mike's lips twitched. "Fine. Sara girl, I'm not mad at you. I'm mad at myself."

"Well, I'm pissed as hell at *you*."

The twitch transformed into a full-blown grin. "God, I like you." Her heart stuttered, her words caught in her throat. He stroked a finger down her cheek. "Nothing to say about that one?"

How could she?

He'd taken her armor—the one made from the ashes of her heart —and crumbled it effortlessly under the slightest show of charm.

At her silence, he sobered. "I should have been there to protect you."

She found her voice . . . or at least her scoff. "Protect me from whom?"

"I—"

"My coaches? The media? No one could have protected me from that circus."

His phone buzzed, and he pulled it from his pocket with a curse.

"None of this is your fault." She shook her head. "I should have realized what was going on long before it all came out. I knew—"

Eyes flashed up to hers. "Knew what?"

"That something was off during the competition." She sighed. "I thought it was nerves—"

"Except you never got nervous."

No. She hadn't.

"Born and bred for skating competitions" was what her coaches had always said.

"Clutch," her brother had called it.

Her mother had referred to it as *"grace under pressure."*

But that time it had been different. She'd thought it the large scale, the high stakes, the pressure.

How wrong she'd been.

"Anyway, you need to go," she said, standing and forcing him to back up. "The team's got to be leaving soon."

"I—"

She turned and walked toward the door. "Your team needs you."

"You need me."

Armor was a joke. She had none when it came to Mike. "Come here," she said.

"What?"

"Just come here."

He rose to his feet and crossed to her. When he was within arm's reach, she launched herself at him. He caught her—as she'd known he would—and pulled her tight against his chest.

"Thank you for coming after me."

"I may have been an idiot back then, but I'm not one now."

She snorted.

"Okay, I'm still an idiot, just slightly smaller in magnitude. How's that?"

"Reasonable."

His breath ruffled her ponytail as he chuckled. Sara rubbed her cheek against the crisp cotton of his button down. He smelled . . . like him. "I'll always come for you," he said, "so no more running, okay?"

"Again reasonable."

Arms loosening, he smiled down at her. "We're both going to give this our best chance, yes?" he asked, and when she nodded, pressed his lips to hers softly.

Before the pleasant fire, the stoked flames could turn into a full-raging inferno, Sara stepped back.

She raised a fist. "Do our best."

Mike's eyes went wide at the gesture. They'd said it each time before going their separate ways in the rink. A fist bump and—

"Do our best," he murmured, tapping his much larger hand against hers.

TWENTY

Mike

MIKE MADE it to the plane with literally minutes to spare.

Which meant that the only open seat was next to Max and his collection of plastic toys—sorry, *figurines*.

"It's a short flight," he muttered under his breath as he walked down the aisle and stowed his bag.

One hour. He could make it through one hour.

"How's it?" Max asked, pulling out a *Walking Dead* graphic novel instead of a bucket of toys.

Thank fuck.

"Fine." He plugged in his headphones and . . . waited.

"What did you think of last week's episode?"

Mike knew he had two choices: either answer the question and hope Max got on a monologue about some minuscule detail of the show, or draw out the torture and ignore him.

In which case, Max's questions would just continue until he wore Mike down and he answered anyway.

So Mike asked, "What show?"

"*Walking Dead*, of course."

"I don't watch zombie shows."

"What about zombie movies?"

He shrugged. "Nope. I'm not into the whole post-apocalyptic thing."

"*What?* How can you not like Mila Jochavick in the *Resident Evil* franchise? She's hot and kickass and . . ."

And there he went. Mike turned on his music, Max's droning about zombies becoming pleasant background noise.

"Do you have a minute?" Mike asked Bernard.

Their head coach paused the video he was watching on his iPad before glancing up. "Come in."

Mike stepped to the side, letting Stefan walk into the office Coach had commandeered first. Then he shut the door and sat down.

Bushy white brows were drawn together. "Want to tell me what this is about?"

"Stefan knows some of the story, but I thought as captain, he should know the rest." Mike shrugged. "And I didn't want you to be out of the loop when this all comes out."

Bernard set his iPad aside. He didn't ask the question, that wasn't his way, but instead waited for Mike to give him the remainder of the story.

"I grew up with Sara Jetty."

Stefan's breath hissed out, Coach didn't react so obviously. Instead, he leaned back in his chair and pressed his palms to his desk.

"We skated at the same rink for years, I drove us both to practices before school, ate dinner at her family's house more often than my own." Mike paused as those memories ran wild in his mind.

Sara sweet and soft and shy.

Sara on the cusp of being a woman.

Sara strong and competitive and hardworking.

"And?" Coach prompted.

"I was in love with her then, but she left for the to win herself a gold medal, and I left for juniors and—" He stopped, not wanting to share his reasons for staying away. Not when Stefan and Coach didn't need to know.

"You grew apart?" Stefan asked.

A nod. "We were young, busy with our own stuff, but then I ran into her in the city a few weeks ago. She's working as an artist, and things are . . . well, like they were before." He straightened his shoulders. "We've decided to give us as a couple a try. I wanted you to know only because of the potential blowback on the team."

Coach pressed his lips together.

"I know no one gives a shit about me, but Sara's past—" A shrug. "I don't want to screw with the team, not when we're playing so well, but at the same time . . ."

Sara was important.

More important than anything else.

"I'll discuss with upper management. Stefan, you'll deal with anything that comes up on the team side. Come to me only if you have to. I don't want to be the host of a fucking dating show."

Nice.

"But that being said"—Bernard leaned forward in his chair—"I'm proud of you, son. Proud that you got your shit together last season and proud that you're thinking of the team enough to come to me with this."

The words hit him straight in the gut.

Or hell, if he was getting sappy, right in the heart.

Which was an organ he'd thought totally decimated. But between Sara and Coach going all Hallmark-moment and his girl-talk with Stefan, the little blood-pumper was making a comeback.

Bernard picked up his iPad, dismissing them as effectively as his words. "Why are you still here?"

They bolted, closing the door behind them.

"So you worked things out?" Stefan asked as they walked to the visitors' locker room.

"Yeah." Mike sighed. "Or as much as I could before I had to go. She's at least willing to give me a shot."

"That's something." Stefan stopped outside the locker room entrance. "I hesitate to suggest this, given what happened after I told you to use your charm, but you've got to woo her, bud. Show her how good it could be between you two. Help her understand that the notoriety she's risking dating you will be worth it, 'cuz you're so awesome."

"Woo her? What is this, 1840?"

"No. If it was, you'd have compromised her and already be married." He put his hands up when Mike just stared at him, mouth agape. "Look, I may have read a few of Brit's historical romance books."

Mike chortled then didn't—couldn't—hold back. He burst out laughing. "Whipped, man. You're so fucking whipped."

"Hey, I'm also the one getting sex every night, so suck on that."

"No, thanks. You're not my type."

Stefan huffed. "I liked it better when you were a surly S.O.B. who didn't talk."

"No, you didn't."

"Fine," Stefan said. "Forget about the wooing, just don't fuck it up. How about that?"

Mike sobered, straightened, and tapped his captain on the shoulder. "*That* is pretty much the best advice I've ever gotten."

Shaking his head, Stefan turned and walked into the locker room. "You're insane, Stewart. Totally certifiable."

Mike followed him, and later, after the game was over and he was slipping back into his suit, he noticed something poking out of the corner of his messenger bag.

Fucking Max. Probably one of those goddamned graphic novels he was spouting about on the plane. It wouldn't have been the first time that he'd tried to convert Mike over to the fine religion of nerdom.

Except it wasn't a graphic novel.

Or, at least, not the type that Max read.

On this book's cover were a man and woman. The man was shirtless, and he held the woman, who was wearing a huge, bright-purple dress—that conveniently appeared to be falling off—close to his chest.

The title talked about seducing a viscount, whatever that was.

A foot nudged his shoe. A feminine foot.

"For inspiration," Brit murmured. "Make sure you read Chapter Twenty."

And with that gem of advice, she walked away.

TWENTY-ONE

Sara

MOONLIGHT AND CLEAR SKIES. The lake called to her, and Sara sketched furiously to capture the image in front of her, to order it with the snapshots in her mind and create art on the paper.

Her hand cramped, the one damaged by frostbite all those years before, and she set her pencil down for a second to stretch it.

Then her hip, which was apparently aching too. And now that her body was on full revolt, her back joined the party.

The muscle spasms took her breath away.

Her bubble—the one that had ensconced her in just the paper and pencil and scene before her eyes—burst. She descended back into reality.

From the outside, it surely looked as though she'd been merely taking a break, stretching those stiff limbs. But on the inside, her mind came down to Earth kicking and screaming.

It wanted to stay lost in her drawing, to be swept along with the softly moving water, to understand its place in a strictly black and white world.

She snorted at her inner idiocy and lay carefully back, trying to get those contracting muscles to relax.

Sara wasn't one of those eccentric artist types; she understood the real world.

She sometimes just didn't want to interact with it.

Her phone buzzed, pulling her fully out of her artist's fog—mental, not literal. It took a moment—those stiff fingers again—to tug it out of her pocket.

Mike.

She smiled and her stomach went all gooey. She swiped. "Hey there, Hot Shot."

"Where the fuck have you been?"

The angry words shocked her and as such, it took her a moment to gather her words.

In the meantime, Mike was having a conversation with himself. "Shit. I didn't mean to sound like that. I've just been worried. I called when we landed, and you didn't answer. And then I went to your apartment, and you didn't respond to the knock. I uh . . . *went* in, and you weren't there—"

"You broke into my apartment?"

"I didn't *break* anything."

"Oh. So you just entered my apartment without a key?"

"You need a better lock." He sounded like such a little petulant child that Sara had to smile.

"Mike."

His sigh rattled through the speaker of her phone. "I was worried."

"I'm sorry," she said, feeling a little bad that she'd scared him, but also touched that he so obviously cared.

It had been a long time since anyone had bothered to worry about her whereabouts.

"Where are you?"

She sat up and tucked her things into her backpack. "Drawing."

"Where?"

"At the Palace of Fine Arts. I'm done now though. Want me to come over?"

"I'll be there in five minutes." A clicking sound, the beep of a horn, and she had to wonder if he was single-handedly screwing with the traffic patterns of San Francisco again.

"Want me to let you drive?"

A pause, then, "I love your voice, Sara."

The L-word made her breath catch. "Oh?"

"Talk to me, sweetheart. What are you working on?"

She slipped her arms into the straps of her backpack. "The lake again. Except this time, no one interrupted my light."

One more glance at the space she'd been working in. Other than a few pencil shavings, which she pushed into the planter bed with her foot, there wasn't any sign of her having been there at all.

Just the way she liked it.

Mike's chuckle drew her focus back to the phone.

"Have I apologized for that?"

"No."

Another chuckle.

Another flutter in her stomach.

"Well, I'm sorry I ruined your light." She heard the clicking sound again, and he said, "I'm turning into the lot now."

"I'm almost there too."

And then she was on the sidewalk, and his car was pulling up next to her. She reached for the handle to let herself in . . . and heard it lock.

Her fingers tried it anyway. No. He'd really locked the door.

The car turned off. Mike slid from the driver's seat with a sexy smile. "Hey."

Three letters and she was mush.

He crossed in front of the hood, paused facing her. "I missed you."

She *pished*. "You just saw me."

"Too long," he said and tugged her into his arms.

Being there was perfect. The embrace, her chest pressed against his, Mike's warmth wrapped around her. "I missed you too."

His laughter puffed by her ear. "Come on. Let's get you home."

Releasing her, he stepped back and pressed the key fob. The passenger door unlocked with a beep.

He pulled the handle, helped her into the seat, and then took her breath away when he reached across her body to turn on the seat warmer.

"Missed you," he murmured again, cupping her jaw for the slightest moment. His eyes were hot and liquid beneath the interior lights. His mouth was right . . . there.

Sara wanted him to kiss her. No. She *needed* his lips across hers, his tongue in her mouth, his cock—

But then he was closing her door and walking around the front of the car. Her heart raced, the space between her thighs ached, and she shifted uncomfortably in her seat.

Especially when Mike rested his hand on her leg, just inches from where she was desperate for it.

Sweat beaded on the back her neck.

She definitely did not need the seat warmer. Reaching forward to turn off the little dial, her eyes happened to flick over to Mike.

Or more specifically, Mike's lap.

He didn't need to be warmed up either, apparently.

A giggle snuck out of her.

Brown eyes flashed over. "What?"

"Nothing."

He'd put the car into drive, but at her rebuff, he clicked it into park again and turned to face her.

In the smallest movement, he'd managed to surround her, one hand on the dash, the other on the back of her seat. "What?" he asked again.

"You're frustrating. You know that?"

He smirked, raised a brow.

"Fine. I was just thinking that I didn't need the seat warmer because you've gotten me so hot."

"Fuck, Sara girl. You can't say things like that here." He nodded at the street in the distance, where even though it was the middle of the night, cars still regularly drove by. "Not when I can't do anything about it."

"Not my fault." She put her hand on his thigh, brushed her fingers against the tip of his erection. He cursed again, and now it was her turn to smirk. "You did ask."

"Sweet Christ, woman. I think you're going to be the death of me."

She started to laugh, but then his mouth was against hers, his tongue slipping in between her parted lips to intertwine with hers. He moved, there was a *click*, and suddenly she was in his lap, pressed between the hardness of his body and the unyielding steering wheel.

His hands were on her breasts, her hips, between her thighs, ramping her up and turning that need from before into frenzied desire.

He pressed his palm firmly against her clit. "Mike!" She bucked—

Honk!

They both jumped and . . .

"Ow!" she moaned as their heads clonked together.

"Sorry," he muttered, one hand on his temple, the other steadying her on his lap.

"You did warn me"—her mouth twitched—"that this wasn't the place."

"Exactly." He set her back in her seat then reached across and re-buckled her seatbelt. "But dang, sweetheart, do we have some chemistry."

She couldn't hold back her grin. "That we do. Now take me home so we can explore it."

TWENTY-TWO

Mike

MIKE DROVE Sara back to her apartment, and despite all of the talk of exploring their *chemistry*, he walked her to her door, waited until she'd opened the lock, and then pulled her into his arms.

The kiss he gave her wasn't the one he wanted, but it was the one she deserved.

Sweet and soft, tender lips and slow strokes, and when, finally, he managed to wrestle himself away, he cupped her cheek.

"Good night, Jumping Bean."

Her brows pulled together into a frown that was both comical and wonderfully cute.

"Night?"

He tugged her bag from her shoulders—the cursed woman had insisted on carrying it herself—and pushed her gently across the threshold into her apartment.

"I have two days off," he said. "Lunch tomorrow?" He glanced out the little window in her living room. The sky was already lightening, and it was nearly dawn. "Or rather, today?"

He'd landed after midnight then spent two of the longest hours of his life worried as hell for Sara.

"But—"

"Oh. Let me see your phone." He plucked it from her back pocket. "What's the code to unlock it?"

Her head was moving from side-to-side, a partial shake, confusion marring her brow.

"What's the code, Sara girl?"

"11-14"

His breath hitched and a long, slow grin curved his mouth. "Really?"

"So what?" she snapped, abruptly defensive. "It doesn't mean anything."

Except it did.

"Yeah?" He pulled his phone from his pocket. "Guess what my code is?"

Blue eyes flew up, collided with his. "Really?"

Mike put the code in on his phone, showed her when it unlocked. "Really."

"Oh."

The numbers were their respective birthdays. "You were on my mind a lot."

Sara swallowed then wrapped her arms around his waist. "You too."

"Okay," he said, when she pulled back. "I'm not going to comment on the late-night exploits and you being too distracted to take your own safety seriously." He stopped, fixed her with a glare. "At some point, we will discuss that."

Her chin lifted for a moment, but then she sighed. "I want to argue with you when you're being all dictatorial. Unfortunately, in this, you're probably right."

"No *probably* about it."

Her mouth opened, and he touched his thumb to her lower lip.

"Let's argue about it later. For now, I want to download the *Find*

My Friends app to your phone. So I can see where you are if you're distracted, not to keep tabs," he rushed to add. "You can put it on my phone too. It's not some crazy abusive boyfriend thing, just the easiest solution—"

Soft fingers grabbed her phone from his hand. In a moment, she had the app store open, and it was downloading. "Now you."

He did the same, and they each took a few minutes to get their accounts set up and synced. Seeing their dots next to each other on the home screen felt right.

"Until later, Jumping Bean." Mike pressed a soft kiss to her lips, restrained himself like a grown-ass man so it didn't turn into something way more heated, then started for the stairs.

"I need more nicknames for you, Hot Shot," she said. "The single one I've got can't compete."

He laughed and paused on the top step. "You can call me anything you want." A raised brow. "Or God. That works too."

Her reply was tart, and he loved her all the more for it. "Or Jackass, yeah? That always works well."

"True." He pointed to her apartment. "Now close and lock that door, honey."

She sighed, probably at the endearment. But he couldn't help it. Every sentence that came out of his mouth seemed to need to show her exactly how much she meant to him. Especially since it was way too soon to say the three most important words in his vocabulary.

And contrary to popular belief, those three words were *not* shit, mother, and fucker.

Though those were definitely his second favorite set.

"Night, Mike." He watched the door shut, the deadbolt slide home.

"Night, Sara girl."

WHOEVER HAD COME up with the concept of wooing was a giant asshole.

Mike had Sara exactly where he wanted her. They'd both slept late, and he'd called her mid-afternoon to take her to a late lunch on the waterfront.

Since it was crab season, they'd had their choice of the freshly cooked crustacean before picking up a loaf of sourdough from Boudin's and walking down the backside of Pier 39.

The sea lions were in full force, barking and flopping around on the floating platforms as kids looked on laughing.

They'd found a relatively quiet corner to eat their lunch before heading back to his place to sack out and binge on *Game of Thrones*.

She'd never seen it, and he was tired of Max bugging him about the *"best-show-in-the-history-of-all-shows,"* so they took the plunge together.

Three episodes and they were still going strong.

What was also going strong was his erection.

That particular part of his anatomy could rival those granite statues in Italy.

Sara was curled up against his chest in the media room, cuddled close even though his couch was huge. Not that he minded, except that he'd read the book from Brit on the flight back to the city, finished it after he'd returned home the previous night.

And falling into bed too soon had been the theme of Chapter Twenty.

The main scene in which Brit had underlined repeatedly, writing a giant *No!* in the margin of one page and *Romance!* in the other.

Both of which he'd screwed the pooch on.

Game of Thrones wasn't particularly romantic, now was it? And the sex part . . . Shit, he'd fucked—literally—that up as well.

Though the sea lions had been a nice touch, he thought.

"What's wrong with you?"

Mike blinked. "What?"

"You're all stiff and formal." She popped him on the chest. "When a girl is lying here, she likes to be held. Yes?"

He hadn't even realized that his hands were at his sides instead of around her. He quickly remedied that. "I'm sorry, I just—"

And he shut up because what was he going to say? He'd read a *romance* novel to try and win her over?

Yeah, not happening.

Sara shifted so she was straddling his lap. The television backlit her body, highlighting the blond of her hair, the pale ivory of her skin.

She was so fucking beautiful.

"What's going through that head of yours?" she asked, soft, but there was a layer of steel beneath the words.

No way would she let this go without a straight answer.

And didn't she deserve that much?

"You are the most beautiful thing I have ever seen." Her lips parted, breath hiccupping as it slid through. "I want to do this right, and I'm fucking it all up."

"Okay, overthinker," she said, "I thought we agreed to give this our best shot. So tell me how you're fucking it up. The romantic walk by the bay? The ice cream and sketchpad? The way you've held my hand, touched my back, stroked my cheek?" She smiled and pressed a kiss to his mouth. "You've been romancing me, and I appreciate it. I *love* it." Her brows pulled down. "What I don't appreciate, however, is you being more in your mind than with me."

She held his gaze, and in that moment, he was speechless. Frozen. Because of what was in her eyes.

Warmth. Affection. Desire. Fire.

God, he loved this woman.

Her hands dropped to his shoulders and she leaned in. "I'm not letting you off the hook in the romance department." Her giggle teased his lips. "I want more ice cream, please. But let's just enjoy this moment when it's only us."

Before the outside world intruded.

Because it would, Mike knew that.

"Okay," he murmured and closed the last inch between their mouths.

Heat . . . but more. Love fueled the desire, made it flame with an intensity that should have scared him.

Instead, like a pyromaniac, he embraced the inferno, let it carry him under, and not until he felt the last vestiges of his self-control slipping did he pull back.

He turned Sara on his lap, pulled her back tight against his chest, and looped his arms around her middle.

"But—I—" Her protest was more moan than words. She turned her head toward his, mouth seeking—

"Doing this right, Sara girl." He put a finger to her cheek and gently pressed her face toward the TV screen.

"How about you do *me* instead?"

She squirmed on his lap and, *fuck*, did the motion of her hips against his cock feel incredible.

His hands clamped down on her waist to stay her motion. "Soon, sweetheart. But we're going to take our time."

He didn't want to rush. Not again.

"I don't want time." She rolled her ass against his erection, made stars flash behind his eyes. "I want you inside me."

And every bit of blood left his brain.

It headed south, directly to the part of his body thinking it was an exceptional idea to fuck Sara right there on the couch.

His cell ringing saved him.

That was, until he answered it and realized who was on the other end.

TWENTY-THREE

Sara

MIKE'S entire body changed the moment he heard the person on the other end of the call.

He stiffened, and it wasn't like the formal distance from earlier. His mind wasn't holding him back from connecting with her. *This* reaction was rock-hard, instant fury.

But his hands were gentle.

Head tilting to press the phone between his ear and shoulder, he clasped her waist and carefully slid her to the side.

The couch had been incredibly comfortable, a soft micro-velvet in a cool shade of gray, but now she might as well have been sitting on concrete.

Because something was wrong.

Very, very wrong.

Mike stood and paced the room. Not saying anything as he listened to whoever was speaking, and the longer the call went on, the tenser he became. Rage radiated off his body, spreading into the space around them.

"If you do this—"

Ice cold. His words were a dagger, a frosty sword that should have wounded.

"*No*," he snapped. "It's my turn to talk now. If you do this, if you continue along this path, know we are done." A pause. "Everything. The house. The cars. The art. All gone—"

He stopped for a second as the person he was talking to seemed to cut him off, but only for a second.

"I'm hanging up now. No. I'm. Hanging. Up. Make your choice, and I hope to fucking God that it's the right one."

Sara jumped when the phone clattered down onto the table by her feet.

"What's wrong?"

Mike sat next to her, picked up her hand, and said, "We're out of time, Sara girl. You've got to decide now if we're really doing this."

Her brows pulled down. "I thought we already made that choice."

"Between us, yes." He sighed, shoved his free hand through his hair. "But the rest of the world is about to know. You good with that?"

Flashes.

Burly men screaming her name.

Crowds on the sidewalk yelling obscenities.

Not being able to leave her house, to turn on the TV, to go online.

The images collided with her mind, fear swelled up in her throat, choked off any reply she might have hoped to make.

"I'm sorry, sweetheart." He shook his head. "This isn't how I wanted—"

"Who?"

"What?"

"No. *Who* was on the phone?"

He closed his eyes for a beat before opening them. Regret was clear in their depths. "My mother."

Sara struggled to align the call with what she knew of Mike's mother. But she hardly *knew* anything. Mrs. Stewart had never come to Mike's games, and he'd always hung out at Sara's house, never the other way around.

"She apparently had come into the city to surprise me. Read that as code for hitting me up for money. Again." He stood, fingers slipping from hers as he began to pace the room. "Ostensibly, she saw you come out of my house and decided to follow you. She has pictures of us in my car."

Her brain hurt. Putting aside that his mother had followed her, why the pictures? What had she hoped to accomplish? "I—I guess I don't really understand."

"My mom considers herself an artist." His head dropped back, eyes on the ceiling as he rubbed the back of his neck. "Fuck me. She used to be a pretty damned good one. When she could actually complete a project, that is."

Sara rose to her feet, crossed over to him, and grasped his forearms. "You've got to start at the beginning. I'm . . . well, I'm confused."

"Shit. I'm sorry." He tilted his chin down, met her gaze. "You remember my dad was in that accident and went on permanent disability?"

She nodded. His dad had worked at the local paper mill until a piece of machinery had fallen on his leg and shattered the bones so horribly it had to be amputated below the knee.

"I remember."

"Well, everyone was great about it, getting me to practices, donating money, supporting us until we got back on our feet," he said. "It even gave my mom the opportunity to sell some of her photos. Started her on her career—or what should have been one."

Her fingers tightened unconsciously. "What happened?"

"She hurt her knee pretty bad when she was out shooting one day. Slipped on some ice and just went down hard. There was no way we could afford another doctor's visit, not since we were just getting by."

His hands were fists, his forearms steel beneath her palms. "It's okay—"

"No, it's really not." He laughed, harsh and bitter. "But I know what you're trying to say. Thing is, Jumping Bean, you need to know all of it."

Sara inhaled, released it slowly. "Okay."

"My mom took her first pill that day. My dad was in pain all the time, had a permanent prescription for them, in fact. He wouldn't miss one."

"Or more."

Mike nodded. "A lot more. One turned into a half dozen, which morphed into more than my dad was taking per day. And like a true addict, she hid her addiction until the problem was too large to keep under wraps."

"But how'd she get the pills? Didn't your dad need them?"

"Yup. Except, when you're a patient with as many health problems as my dad, turns out it's easier to up your dosage, to even get another prescription for a different opioid." His shoulders slumped. "My mom learned every trick. Different doctors. Different pharmacies. She had power of attorney for my father, and since part of the settlement with the mill was covering his medical bills, it didn't cost anything. It was almost too easy."

"Why am I sensing the *but* coming?"

He snorted. "Because there is one. While my mom was out on her nature hikes, high out of her mind and definitely not taking pictures, the bills piled up. She wasn't working, wasn't selling her art. We were sinking, only no one knew it."

Pieces began aligning in Sara's mind. Her heart pounded, her knees trembled. "When, Mike?" she asked, voice shaking. "When did you find out?"

"Two days before you left for Europe." He cursed. "So there it is. My whole sordid tale."

"That's why you—"

Another curse. "I couldn't put that on you. Not then."

"Mike." She cupped his cheek. "I mean this with the utmost kindness but you are a fucking idiot."

TWENTY-FOUR

Mike

REBECCA STRAVOKRAUS WAS A SHARK, a shark who was paid very well by the Gold to handle the media surrounding the team and, more specifically, the extra scrutiny that they received because of Brit.

Pierre Barie, Stefan's father and a powerful businessman in his own right, had snagged ownership of the team just over a year ago. Rebecca had been one of his first additions.

As a former publicist for a Hollywood starlet, media shit-shows were her specialty.

Mike just hoped she'd be up for this one.

It was after ten when she pulled through the gate and parked next to Stefan's car. He and Brit had arrived at the house first but hadn't made it past the foyer.

Now Rebecca *click-clicked* up the stairs and breezed past the four of them.

"Close the door," she chirped.

Mike shut the heavy panel and turned to escort everyone to the kitchen, but Sara had beaten him to it.

She'd gotten everyone seated on stools around the island. "What do you want to drink?"

"Nothing for me," Stefan said.

"I'll take a water if you have one," Brit said.

"Same for me," Rebecca said.

"Mike?" Sara asked.

He shook his head and watched as *his* woman opened a cabinet and grabbed three glasses, before filling them with ice and retrieving the pitcher of water from the fridge.

"I'm sorry to drag you guys out so late—"

Mike dropped his hand to Sara's waist and gave it a warning squeeze. "This isn't your fault—"

"Well, I guess that depends on how you determine fault," Rebecca said.

She spoke in such honey-sweet tones that it took Mike a second to process the words.

"Excuse me?" he snapped.

Cherry-red lips pursed before Rebecca brought her glass to her lips. "It depends on whether or not she cheated."

The air in the room froze.

"I don't think—" Brit began.

"I believe the public has already convicted and tried me on that fact," Sara said.

"But not this room," Mike said.

Rebecca set her glass on the counter. "Let's be frank here. This room doesn't mean a damn thing when it comes to the public's opinion."

Sara snorted but placed her hand on Mike's chest, quieting him when he would have spoken. "That's not exactly news, Ms. Stravokraus. I've lived through *public opinion*."

"The question isn't whether you've already navigated a media circus, but rather, whether or not you committed the crimes you've been accused of." Rebecca slipped her heels off her feet, sighing as they fell to the floor beneath her stool. "The truth may not matter to them, but it matters to me."

"I wish it were that easy."

"It *is* that easy."

"And if I cheated?"

Ruby-red lips curved. "I'd be hard-pressed to believe it." Rebecca bent and retrieved her iPad from her briefcase and swiped her finger across the screen.

A graph appeared, colored lines zigzagging across a white background.

"Your scores are in gold, Ms. Jetty." A fingernail painted the same shade of red as Rebecca's lips followed the metallic path. "I've traced these back to your first competitions and find it difficult to believe that you'd bribe the judges for the Westin Rink Winter Performance of 2002 or the 2003 Ms. Dairy Open or—"

"I know my scores, Ms. Stravokraus," Sara cut in. "What I don't understand is your reasoning for bringing them up."

"My reasoning is this. One." She ticked off her fingers as she spoke, little flashes of cherry in the soft lighting of the kitchen. "You could have been cheating since you were a child. Two. There's no payoff in that. Three. Your scores were consistently on a higher level than your age would seem to dictate. Four. You had no motivation to cheat because, five, you were infinitely more skilled than any other woman in that competition."

"Strange things happen in competitions all the time," Sara countered.

"You would have had to fall twice and shortened three of your jumps to match the difficulty level of the next closest girl."

Stefan whistled. "Is that true?"

Even Mike was taken aback. He'd known Sara was good but had his teenaged mind ever grasped *how* good?

"She was doing quads before most of the men were," Rebecca said and swiped her finger across the screen.

A video of Sara as she'd been, graceful legs and arms, but minimal womanly curves, appeared on the screen. She skated across the ice, quickly gaining speed before launching into the air.

One. Two. Three. Four—

Holy shit. It *was* true.

A crunch as she landed on one foot and jumped immediately again. Not another quad, but a double that she also stuck.

"This was practice the morning before the long program," Sara murmured.

"Yes."

Her waist lifted and fell under Mike's hand as she took a deep breath. "How do you know—"

"So much about you?" Rebecca made the iPad sleep and then folded her hands together. "I'm good at my job." A shrug that was paired with the slightest hint of pink on her elegantly made-up cheeks. "Also, I was a big fan."

Sara gave a self-deprecating smirk. "*Was*, I think, is the key word here." She waved away any response Rebecca might have made. "None of this is the point, however. I don't want my past to cloud the Gold's future. I know there was trouble with the press last season, and that the team is playing great right now. I—as Sara Jetty, disgraced figure skater—don't want to impact your chances."

Brit spoke up for the first time. "One thing I've learned is that hockey isn't more important than your happiness."

If Mike hadn't been so close to Sara, he might have missed her little hitch of breath.

"She's right, you know," he said. "At some point, hockey will be over for me, and I'll be left with—"

"Someone who might have taken that from you? Shit, Mike. How can I ask you to risk your career for me? For us?" She pulled away from him. "This is your dream. I should step back and let you live it."

"Sara." Brit slid from her stool and crossed around the island. "I know I'm just this strange chick who has no right to offer advice, but I'm pushy and bossy, and I'm going to offer it anyway, 'kay?"

Stefan choked back a laugh, and even Sara's lips twitched as she nodded.

"Hockey used to be my dream—my *only* dream—and the only thing I lived for. Same as, I suspect, skating was your life. But do you know what I found out once I was playing for the Gold?" She paused, and Sara shook her head. "That I wasn't sharing my life with anyone."

Brit glanced over at Stefan, and emotion was a heavy rope that connected them. "I discovered that going it alone was really lonely, and then I found Stefan, and things suddenly made sense." She blew out a breath, the sincerity in her tone making even Mike feel a little choked up.

Fucking feelings.

"Stefan was a risk. Hell," she said with a chuckle, "I was probably a bigger risk for him. But worse than the risk was the possibility of living a life without him."

"Shit, sweetheart," Stefan muttered, his eyes looking suspiciously glassy, "you're killing me."

Brit ran a finger under one eye as Stefan came around the island and pulled her into his arms. "Sorry, not sorry," she said, cupping his cheek. "There's no getting rid of me now."

"Not even a possibility," he said.

Sara sniffed, blinked rapidly.

"You two," Mike warned softly as he stepped close to his girl and wrapped an arm around her waist. "You make her cry and—"

"Tears aren't bad, Stewie," Brit said, turning in Stefan's embrace and leaning her head back against his shoulder. "They remind us of what's important." A pause as her gaze connected with Sara's. "You understand?"

Sara sighed. "I do. But what about the team?"

Rebecca shoved her feet back into her heels and stood. "That's why I'm here."

TWENTY-FIVE

Sara

SARA WOKE UP SWEATING.

Which, she figured, was mainly due to Mike having curled around her like she was his favorite teddy bear.

Which wasn't a bad place to be, all things considered. Except for the sweating. And the need to pee.

Mornings after were new for her.

This being her second, both of which had featured Mike.

Men weren't regular fixtures in her life, and while she liked sex, she had always kept the sex part of her life and the sleeping part completely separate.

No walks of shame for her.

Carefully, she lifted Mike's arm from around her waist and wrestled herself free of the blankets.

His leg slung over the top of hers.

"Mike," she said, squirming. "I have to pee."

"Mmm." He rolled over, tucked her beneath him. She might have thought the stink was awake if not for his even breathing and clumsy sleep-stunted movements.

But it was like fighting an octopus, trying to get out of that bed.

She'd get one leg loose, and he'd toss his arm over her waist again. Then she'd wriggle free of that, and his leg would be back, shoving between hers and pinning her in place.

She was huffing and puffing and still sweaty by the time she managed to get out of the bed . . . or rather by the time she slipped off the edge of the mattress and fell to the floor in an ungraceful heap.

At which point—because this was her life—Mike decided to wake fully up.

"Problem?" he asked, rubbing his bare chest and yawning.

"Nope." Sara blew a strand of hair out of her face and hello, morning breath.

Toilet then toothbrush. STAT.

She flipped over, stood, and would have been in the bathroom if a hand on the back of her shirt hadn't caught and held her in place.

"Not running?"

"Nope." She crossed her legs, almost dancing in place.

"What happened to the girl who liked mornings?"

"She needs to pee." A pause, a huffed-out breath. "And to brush her teeth." The blankets rustled, and she felt herself being reeled back toward the bed. "I really need—"

"Shh." He turned her around, sitting up and positioning her between his thighs.

Brown eyes met hers. "You good?"

Her head dropped back, she sighed. "Mike—"

"You're good." His hands slid down and spanned her waist. Then they slid lower, beneath the hem of his t-shirt she'd commandeered in an effort to not have a repeat of their last morning after, and gripped her ass.

"Stop." She slapped his hands away. "Unless you're into something a lot more X-rated."

He smirked.

"And I don't mean bondage. I'm thinking more along the lines of golden showers—"

"Go." A tap to her bottom sent her on her way.

She hightailed it to the bathroom and closed the door. After using the facilities, she flushed and started to search the drawers for a spare toothbrush.

They'd crashed after Rebecca and company had left the night before, though not before bingeing a couple more episodes of *Game of Thrones*.

She might not completely understand the appeal of a fantasy world, but Khal Drogo, yeah. That was a man she could stare at all day.

Not finding a toothbrush in any of the vanity drawers, Sara turned to the linen closet set along the opposite wall.

"Crazy girlfriend antics already?"

Sara jumped, almost banging her head on the shelf she was bending over to peer at. "Do you not have a single spare toothbrush in here?" she asked, not taking the bait.

"Here." He opened a cabinet—which she'd skipped, because who kept spare toothbrushes beneath a sink?—and pulled out a pack. "Pink or green?"

"Green."

His breath caught as she snagged the brush and topped it with the toothpaste she'd found earlier.

"What?" she asked, though it sounded a lot more like "Shmut?"

He finished brushing his own teeth before straightening and leaning back against the vanity. "I just remembered that emeralds were your favorite."

She spit and rinsed in the sink then smiled at him. "Yes. They still are, in fact. I can't believe you remember that." Her brows pulled down when he didn't smile back. "What is it?"

He was frozen, every muscle locked.

"Hey, Hot Shot." She touched his chest, and that ice around him melted. He moved abruptly, opening a drawer and tearing open a box of condoms then slipping away to turn on the shower. He pulled a stack of towels out from the linen closet. "Are—"

His boxer briefs dropped to the floor.

Her tongue stopped working.

"Come here."

An order. All male and tempting, kind of like the especially hard part of his anatomy bobbing her way.

But it wasn't his body that made her feet move.

His eyes.

Heat and desire and *need*. For her. If he'd looked at her like that earlier, she would never have been able to get out of bed, risk of golden shower or not.

Melted dark chocolate, his gaze dripped over her, warming her limbs, sticking to her insides, sliding down her inner thighs and making her knees tremble.

But she didn't need to worry about falling.

The moment she wavered, Mike was there, pulling her flush against his body and slamming his mouth down onto hers.

Sparks flew along her spine, spurred her into motion.

She kissed him back with everything she had, lips parting and tongue diving into his mouth.

The man made her insane.

He hitched her body up, grabbing her legs and wrapping them around his waist. His cock was hard between her thighs, making her desperate to shift her hips, to guide him deep inside.

But he wouldn't let her move.

His hands clamped on to her ass, and he turned them both.

Hot water cascaded down her back. It soaked into her hair, rolled down her arms, pooled between her breasts.

Moaning, she arched back, letting the drops drip lower.

"God, you're so fucking beautiful." Mike tucked one hand between her shoulders and adjusted her position so he could reach her nipple.

And fuck, that was good.

She hissed out a breath, then a groan, then a curse.

He switched to the other breast, repeated the circling of his tongue, the tease of his teeth. His scruff abraded her skin, but it was a good hurt, and she was so . . . very . . . close . . .

He tilted his hips, rubbed his cock up, against her clit and—

"Mike!"

She plummeted over the edge, stars exploding behind her eyes, pleasure spreading outward from her center.

And he rode her orgasm out with her, rubbing against her wetness, eliciting little aftershocks of pleasure with each up and down movement.

Sara could barely stand when he gently lowered her legs to the shower floor.

"Christ, I have to have you." She watched through lidded eyes as he reached for the condom he'd grabbed earlier and tore the wrapper open with his teeth.

Watching Mike fist his erection and stroke it from base to tip was just about the sexiest thing she'd ever seen. The laxness that had invaded her limbs evaporated, and she wanted it to be her hands there, *needed* his hard cock inside her.

"Hurry," she chanted. "Hurry. Hurry."

His fingers fumbled, and he dropped the condom. "Fuck, Sara. You're not helping. I've imagined you in my shower about a million times, and now you're in my life, and we're—"

And then it wasn't just about pleasure. It was about this man and how much he meant to her, about her past and present colliding and moving forward.

Her eyes burned, but she blinked the tears back, not wanting to ruin what was supposed to be a happy moment. "I'm here, Mike. Finally, I'm here."

"Beautiful." He leaned in and kissed her. "Amazing." Pulled back and cupped her cheek. "The only woman I've ever wanted."

His words stole her breath, and he didn't give her time to get it back.

"The only woman," he said again then bent and retrieved the condom, sliding it on with suddenly sure fingers.

"Mike—"

He kissed the words from her lips. Hands hauled her up, spreading her thighs, and guiding her down . . . and, good God. Yes, she needed him *right there*.

Deep. Hard. Stretching her to capacity.

And pausing, her back pressed against the cold tile wall.

Why was he pausing?

"Look at me," he ordered.

She groaned, flexed her hips. He had to move. Right then or—

"Sara girl, *look* at me."

Her eyes opened, and the intensity in his gaze took her breath away. Or what little of it was left.

"You're mine." He pulled out. Slammed back in. Swiveled his hips and made her cry out. This was so much more than simple sensation. He made her ache with need and feel completely whole all in the same vein.

And she wanted more.

Out. In. Out. In. More—

"Say it."

She didn't need to ask what. She knew. It was the same truth she'd held close for more than a decade. She would always be his.

"I'm yours."

His eyes slid closed. "Mine," he said.

"Yours." She grabbed his shoulders, yanked herself upright to growl in his ear. "And you're mine."

He chuckled, hot breath mixing with the water to raise goose bumps on her skin.

"Never been anyone else's."

The words spread through her, heightening the pleasure he was raising to a frantic peak.

"I'm going to—"

"Come for me, sweetheart."

As if her body would betray him. She exploded again, inner muscles clenching tightly against his cock and decimating his self-control.

He was a frenzy of movement, mouth on her breasts, her throat, her jaw, hips pounding into her. And then he was groaning against her neck as he climaxed, and she was wrapping her arms around him.

They stayed pressed together, not a molecule of air separating their bodies, as their breathing slowed, their pulses steadied.

He remained close as she washed her hair, rubbed a loofah gently across her back when it was time to soap up.

As the water began to cool, Mike turned if off and wrapped her in a towel.

They didn't speak. Words weren't necessary when their movements spoke volumes. A brush of his towel across her back, dabbing the scar there gently and soaking up the drops of water dotting her skin.

Her fingers combed through his hair, settling it just the way he liked it.

A thumb swiped beneath her eye to catch an errant tear.

Laced hands moved downstairs together. Two sets of lungs not breathing as they turned on the news. A stroke of his palm across her cheek when their pictures were the lead story.

"You're coming to the game tonight," he said after the anchor cut to commercial.

Sara nodded. "Okay."

"You're not alone anymore."

She forced her eyes from the screen when a picture of her on that podium, gold medal around her neck, came on. "I know."

"Jumping Bean." His tone was a warning.

"You know you only really use that nickname when you're getting all growly with me."

His face relaxed. "You like growly."

"Sometimes." She bumped her shoulder with his. "I'm also okay. You're here. That makes everything so much better."

He grinned. "Of course it does."

Her stomach growled, and she flicked off the TV. "What's for breakfast?" she asked before she caught the clock. "Or, I guess, lunch at this point."

Mike's nose wrinkled. "Chicken, rice, and greens with protein powder." He shuddered. "The team's nutritionist is strict as hell."

"She'd have to be to keep you boys in check."

"Hey!" he said, going to the freezer and opening the drawer. "Brit's the worst of the bunch."

"I've seen her body in real life. There's no way that's true."

He grinned. "Okay, it's a lie." He plunked a container of Phish Food on the counter. "But I also have this for you."

"An appetizer," she said, snatching the carton and opening a drawer to grab a spoon. "Perfect size for one."

He made to steal it from her, and she squeaked, but then he nodded at her sketchpad. "Want to go on the patio and draw for a bit?" He pulled a Tupperware from the fridge. "I'll heat some of this up for us."

This man.

Her vision went slightly blurry around the edges, and her heart went all Grinch-like, feeling as though it had expanded by three sizes. "I like you, Mike Stewart."

"It's because I'm so likeable." He grinned then caught a glimpse of her eyes and sobered. "Together, remember?"

Blinking, she nodded. "Believe me, I remember." This time would be different. She'd wouldn't cave, and no way would she let it get as bad as it had been before. With a sigh, she straightened her shoulders and lifted her chin.

"Get to work, Hot Shot. I'm hungry."

TWENTY-SIX

Mike

MIKE SLIPPED OUT onto the patio, two plates of suitably healthy food in hand. Sunlight peeked through the clouds, creating pockets of gold around the deck. Sara's hair, the metal of the screws holding the boards in place, a reflection off—

A camera lens?

His neck crawled.

"Sara," he said.

"Mmm?" she asked, head still bent over the page.

He set the plates on the table and crossed the deck to kneel by her side, careful to keep his back to the place he'd seen the glare. "Jumping Bean."

She blinked, gaze sliding up to focus on his for a brief moment. He saw the urge in their depths, the desire to flick right back down to the sketch she was working on. "What's the matter?"

"I think I saw a camera."

Though her shoulders went ramrod stiff, Sara didn't lose her composure. "Where?"

"To the east, behind that big oak toward the back of the property."

Blue eyes searched the space behind him before returning back to his. "I think you're right."

God, she was amazing. Given her history, she should be a blubbering mess right now. Instead she sat there, regal as a queen, face calm, words calmer still.

"So, the question is," she said, her tone surprisingly light, "do we give them their shot? Or keep the masses frenzied and waiting?"

He leaned close and pressed a kiss to her forehead. "We only give what we're willing."

Standing, he reached for her hand, tugged her to her feet. "Now, let's go inside and have lunch away from the prying eyes."

He was also going to make some calls and see about getting security for his property. A gate had always been enough of a deterrent for anyone before. That had obviously changed.

"Eating from inside a fishbowl isn't relaxing before your game?" she teased.

"Not exactly." Mike smiled, but it wasn't completely genuine. And his tone was off. Because . . . *goddammit*, he hated this. Despised that Sara even had to go through it at all.

But she misread his frustration.

Blue eyes clouded with sorrow, her shoulders fell a fraction of an inch. "I'm sorry you're dealing with this."

He wanted to pull her close, but he didn't want an audience for that.

So instead, he dropped her hand, picked up their plates, and opened the French door to the kitchen, nodding at her to enter. Following after her, he bumped his elbow against a switch on the wall on his way in.

Immediately, the windows darkened as the remote-controlled shades slid down.

The plates were on the countertop in the next instant. "Come here," he said, but didn't give her the chance to respond. He crossed to her, hauled her into his chest, and wrapped his arms tight. "No apologies. Not ever. This is not your fault."

She snorted. "Kind of is."

"Yeah no. That's bullshit, and you know it." Mike slid one hand up and cupped her cheek, forced her to focus on him. "It's bullshit."

Sara sighed. "I'm trying to feel sorry for myself here."

Lips twitching, he tucked her hair behind her ear. "Not happening. Not in my house."

"In your—" A huff. "You're such a caveman."

"Aw," he teased, tugging that strand of hair. "You're so cute when you try to be tough."

"Try?" She crossed her arms and glared. "I don't have to—"

God, he loved her.

It was nearly impossible to smother the urge to make the declaration, but he knew it wasn't the right time, didn't want the moment he finally confessed how he'd felt for the last ten years to be marred by the outside world.

Instead, he kissed her, and when her body melted, he took advantage of having known the girl for so long.

Fingers slipping up, he trailed them along the sides of her breasts. She moaned, and he went in for the kill.

Her armpits.

Digging into the spot, her *only* ticklish spot, Mike had no mercy.

She squealed, mouth breaking away, body squirming so violently that he almost lost his grip.

But he was a professional athlete, and his reaction time was on point.

"You"—she gasped—"are—so dead!"

Her hands lurched up and gripped his hips. He turned, but not in time, and her fingers found the spot on his waist.

"Shit!"

"Payback," she said, smirking as she broke free.

One brow came up. "Payback, really?"

Sprinting around the side of the island, she positioned herself so that it was between them.

But the barrier was nothing.

Still, he let her think that she was safe . . . for the moment.

"You know I hate being tickled."

A step forward. A slide of one barstool slightly to the right.

There. Now he had a clear shot.

Sara leaned forward, plucked a piece of broccoli from the plate, and stuck it in her mouth.

He waited while she chewed, not wanting her to choke, but when she reached for another bite and said, "So, yes, payback and—" She shrieked when he launched himself over the island, and he loved the sound, loved surprising her, loved . . .

Her.

His mouth crashed down on hers, his hands slid under the hem of her shirt, and the chicken was very cold by the time they settled down to eat it.

"Remind me why I let you talk me into this again?" Sara grumbled.

"You'll be fine. Remember, you're charming, and the WAGs are nice."

That wasn't a lie, thankfully, because he'd played on a few teams where the opposite was true.

"Charming," she muttered, slinging her purse on her shoulder. "I still can't believe that Mitch won't let me work."

"He said the store is a shit-show, and he was keeping it closed for the rest of the week because he was tired of people coming in and not buying anything except your stuff." The three pieces she'd given to her boss had apparently sold out within an hour of opening.

"I'm sure people are just going to burn them. Or amplify every single imperfection." She reached for the door leading out to the garage.

He snagged her arm. She huffed. He smiled. It was kind of their thing.

"We need to go, Mike. Traffic—"

"What's going on, cranky pants?"

"I tolerate a lot of your nicknames, but—"

He kissed her, felt her body relax for a half second. At least until she seemed to remember they were bickering and pulled away.

Damn, he'd have to work on that.

"Don't change the subject," he said when she opened her mouth, probably to bitch him out. While he didn't want to fight with her, he wanted her to be able to confide in him, not bottle it up. "What's got you as ornery as a pissed-off cat?"

"What in hell are you talking about?"

"Sara." He pressed her back against the door, not stopping until she had to tilt her head back to look—or rather, *glare*—at him.

"It's nothing."

"It's something."

She sighed. He smiled because, even though he'd rather be having naked fun time with her, every moment with Sara was a good one.

Two hands came up, shoved at his chest. Not that the action budged him an inch.

"Mike." Another sigh.

"I can stay here all day."

Sara shook her head, but her lips were finally curving, and the irritation in her expression slipped away. "I bet you could."

"Did I not give you enough orgasms today?"

Her mouth dropped open, and he had to resist the urge to kiss it, to thrust his tongue inside and—

"I don't think there's such a thing." She gave him the smile, the trademark Sara Jetty grin, except this one reached her eyes.

She was smiling from the inside out.

He puffed up, couldn't help it. Especially when she said, "And no, that's not the problem, Hot Shot. You gave me plenty."

Nuzzling into her neck, he asked, "Then what?"

"I'm nervous."

"This is you nervous?" One of her legs had come up, wrapped around his knee.

Shit. He wanted to hitch it higher, to push her pants down and his fingers inside her wet heat. He—

—stepped back.

"You get horny when you're nervous?"

A wry smirk. "Apparently."

"Come on, Trouble," he said, lacing his hand with hers, the other adjusting his situation south of the border. At this rate, they could hire him to hammer nails into that wall the president wanted to build. "I'll give you the gossip on the drive, make you feel like you're part of the crowd before you even get there and have to hear it all over again."

"Again with the nicknames." She shook her head but followed him to her car. "You're incorrigible."

"That's why you love me," he teased as he opened the passenger side door.

Fuck. He realized what he'd said when she froze halfway into the car.

"Shit, sweetheart. I'm sorry. I was joking. Don't worry about it." He was rambling, couldn't seem to stop. "I—"

She straightened. "Here's the thing." A deep breath. "I think I do love you. That's part of what makes this so hard. The last time I cared about something as much as you, I screwed it up." Her voice broke. "I don't want to ruin us, Mike."

His heart swelled so big it could have been a balloon, a ball of helium right on the precipice of too much air, just about to burst.

"Sit down, Sara girl. There's something I want to show you."

When she didn't move, he gently pushed her shoulder down and lifted her legs into the car. He closed the door then walked around the hood and slid into the driver's seat.

Silence. Complete and utter silence greeted him, but he knew that before he said anything else that he had to show her.

Had to make her understand.

The glove compartment opened with a soft *click,* and he reached inside, shifting the registration and proof of insurance to the side. Because beneath that was a box.

A box he'd had for a really long time.

"I don't know if you know this, but I came to your house two nights before you were supposed to leave."

Sara turned her head, eyes wide and damp with tears. "You did?"

Her voice, steady, calm, laced with hurt, gave him the courage to go on. She was strong, but she also needed to know. And just as important, he needed her to grasp exactly how deep his feelings went.

"Yes. At that point we'd spent two years in a car together, five mornings a week. More than five-hundred hours by ourselves, and I was ridiculously in love with you."

"Was?"

He nodded, hating the way she curled in on herself when he spoke. "Was. But at the same time, I didn't want to interrupt your training, I'd convinced myself to wait until you came back from Italy. Then I got the call."

"Juniors."

"Yeah. I went to the store. It was ridiculously stupid, I see that now, but I—" He gritted his teeth, pressed on. "I picked this out. Had this notion that I'd give it to you as a promise. Your parents were there and they made me understand just how stupid of an idea it was."

"My parents?"

"They were right. You didn't need any more distractions, least of all from me and my family." Mike yanked at his tie. "Hell, I was all ready to argue with them, and then I got another call."

Her hand rested on his thigh for a second. "What call?"

"The police had busted my mom. She got caught trying to buy OxyContin from an undercover cop." He laughed, and it was bitter. His family had cost him so much. "She needed detox and rehab, and I didn't need to bring that shit into your life."

"I would have been there for you."

"I know you would have." Turning, he stared at her, beautiful even in the pale light of the garage. "I wouldn't have let you, and your parents were right. You didn't need my family messing up your chances. It didn't matter anyway. You were gone, and by the time I got everything sorted so I could leave town too, I was ready to leave it all behind." He tapped the box against his leg. "Thing is, I was convinced then that you were better off without me. Hell, all this current bullshit is because of *my* mom, so the logic is there—"

"That's not—"

"Shh. I'm too selfish to live without you again. You make me feel whole, Sara girl. I've loved you since that first morning in my car, and nothing is going to change the way I feel." He opened the box and held it out. "And the thing is, I think you could use an ally at your back."

She glanced down at the ring, and he winced. He should have had it cleaned, or added a giant diamond or something. Instead, it was just the same as it had always been.

A simple silver band, a trio of small emeralds.

"I . . . uh . . . I—don't—"

Fuck. He was fucking this up. Quickly, he closed the lid. "I'll get you something different."

"It's not that. I"—she blew out a breath—"I'm confused."

He was proposing, and the woman in front of him was confused.

"It's okay," he said, the words rushed as he shoved the box into the glove compartment and slammed it closed. "We can talk about it later."

He started the car and began backing out of the garage, had to slam on the brakes when he realized he hadn't hit the opener.

"Mike."

"Later." The door rattled up, and he zipped down the driveway.

Fuck, but he wanted to hit someone.

Luckily he could do that on the ice.

TWENTY-SEVEN

Sara

HOLY SHIT, had that been a proposal?

Dumbstruck, Sara stared out the window as Mike navigated his car down the driveway and through the gate.

It couldn't have been a proposal.

That didn't make any sense, not yet—

Flashes blinded her as they pulled into the street.

"Fuck," Mike muttered, swinging wide to avoid the paparazzi on the sidewalk. The group of men in dumpy sweatshirts and torn jeans crowded near the car, shoving those black lenses up to the windows, clicks echoing through the glass.

"Make sure the gate closes," she murmured, when he started to drive away before it had shut the last few feet.

A nod, though he didn't respond with words. Then the gate was barred, and they were speeding down the road. They'd hit the freeway and the typical 101 slowdown, silence reigning in the car before Sara wrapped her mind around the fact—

"You proposed?"

Male shoulders hunched. Big, strong hands that could touch so gently clenched so tightly on the steering wheel that it creaked in protest.

"Not exactly."

"Then want to tell me what that was?"

A car cut in front of them, and Mike muttered a curse. "Stupidity?"

She sighed. "Want to try again?"

"Not really."

Well, clearly this was getting her nowhere. She reached for the glove compartment and pushed the button to open it.

"Don't."

Too late.

Her fingers found the soft velvet box and extracted it. The brass hinges made a little squeak when she opened the lid. "This is an engagement ring."

Eyes flicked to hers then back to the road. "It wasn't intended as one. Not then." She opened her mouth, but he spoke before she could ask what the hell *that* meant. "I wanted to give you a promise ring. I wasn't stupid enough to think we were old enough to marry."

Her heart pounded. Mike had wanted to give her a promise for more.

Holy flipping shit-on-a-stick.

In the two years he'd driven her to practice, she had never thought he'd noticed her as anything more than an obligation. He'd been borrowing her parents' car, after all. Oh, they'd had some good times together, shared many a laugh about his teammates and her coaches, once they'd gotten past his early morning grouchiness, but he'd never touched her.

Like not ever.

Except, her mind didn't let that lie stick.

She remembered him hugging her when she'd had a terrible practice and ended up bruised and bloodied, having landed hard enough on her knee to tear through fleece legging and skin alike.

He'd rolled her bag to the car for her when her hands ached from the frigid cold rink.

He'd helped her into the passenger seat when she'd twisted her ankle.

A hundred examples of his caring flew through her mind. She remembered what she'd blocked away, what she hadn't understood as a young and inexperienced teenager.

Her love had come in the form of a Minnesota Wild sweatshirt, in homemade cookies, a quick sketch of his team's logo—and not a very good one at that.

She stared at the emeralds, watched them twinkle in the late afternoon sunlight. They were small by today's standards, but that didn't mean any less to her heart. "Why did you give me the ring today?"

Mike jumped, and Sara realized that she'd been inside her head for a while, long enough that they were turning into the parking lot for the rink.

The car slowed; the window whirred down a crack. Which was enough to hear a cacophony of shouts and yells, shutters clicking, and faintly, a male voice, "Go straight through, Mr. Stewart. Security has you covered."

With a *snick*, the sound was gone, and they moved forward again.

Another gate. More reporters.

And then quiet.

Was it possible for a parking lot to give her nostalgia?

Because this one was. The slightly worse-for-wear metal door, the mix of SUVs and sedans, albeit of a nicer breed than those from her childhood rink.

"I haven't been to an ice rink since—"

Mike parked the car, shut off the engine, and faced her. The frustration seemed to bleed out of him, replaced with understanding and compassion.

"Well, this one is a little bigger than ours at home."

"I bet that's what all the boys say." Her smile was tremulous.

He reached out an arm, pressed his thumb to her bottom lip. "I want you in my life, Sara girl." A brush of his mouth against hers. "Know I'll take you any way I can get you."

Leaning back, he unbuckled her seatbelt.

"And the ring?" she asked, for some reason slightly breathless.

"It means whatever you want it to," he said, opening his door and stepping out.

"Whatever I—?"

Mike popped her door and gestured toward the rink. She shoved the ring into her pocket and trailed after him, absolutely bewildered.

Whatever she wanted it to mean.

Fuck, and men said *women* were complicated.

"Hey!"

This time it wasn't a mob of men shouting at Sara, but a single female voice, and a familiar one at that.

"Brit," she said and slowed.

The Gold's starting goalie strode confidently across the parking lot in a silk blouse, blazer, and jacket. She wore heeled pumps and looked like a model's take on a powerful attorney.

Mike whistled. "Looking good, Plantain."

"Shut it, Stewie." She punched his arm.

"It's true," he said, opening the door and holding it for them. "I've never seen you look so—"

"I'd be very careful about how you finish that sentence, Hot Shot," Sara chimed in.

Brit cackled. There was no other word for it, just exploded into evil laughter.

"You breathe one—"

"Don't bother with threats, *Hot Shot*." Blue eyes cut to Sara's. "You have more embarrassing material to provide me with, right?"

"Loads."

More laughter, this time from both of them.

Mike groaned. "I was trying to give you a compliment."

Brit got herself together. She reached up—because even though she was tall for a woman, Mike was still taller—and patted his cheek. "I know. I'm touchy because Stefan got me a personal shopper."

"He *what?*"

Her eyes rolled up. "It's not entirely his fault. I complained about not knowing what to wear, since I didn't really do the suit thing, and he's a man."

Seeing that Mike didn't follow the sentiment, Sara explained. "She had a problem. Stefan went all caveman and wanted to fix it." She touched his arm and softened her tone. "It's kind of what you guys do."

"Exactly!" Brit said. "So I couldn't be mad at him and anyway"—she patted her hips—"I think it works."

"Plus, those shoes," Sara said.

"These shoes." Brit sighed happily.

Mike frowned as he glanced down at her feet. "What about the shoes?"

They were pointed, a polished metallic black with specks of gold. They were also totally killer, with a burnished metal heel and bright red soles.

Sara sighed too. "You'd never understand."

"Apparently not," he said and captured her hand. "Now come on. I'll show you where you can hang out until after the game."

They called their good-byes to Brit, and Mike led Sara to an elevator.

As the doors slid closed, a thought occurred to her. "Don't NHL teams usually have a separate practice rink?"

"Left field, much?"

"Not exactly," she said. "But I remember skating at Nationals. It was on the Blues' home ice, and I feel like all of their practice stuff wasn't at the arena, but at a smaller rink nearby."

"It's true. Sometimes the team will have a pregame skate on the big ice, but the rest of the practices are held elsewhere. The Gold are different. Or at least for the rest of this season." He pushed a button to select the floor. "Barie's father is building a rink, but it took some time to secure the land and permits, I guess."

"Why not just continue to practice here?"

"Bad business," he said. "Our former owners were real fuck-ups, to be honest. They embezzled money, made questionable financial decisions, negotiated with players using underhanded techniques. Arenas make money from concerts and other events."

Oh. That made sense.

"If there are no events, then use the facility, but the Gold Mine is in a prime spot of San Francisco." A shrug. "The owners don't make money from our practices. They'd be much better off filling the stands with Beyoncé fans."

"The Beyhive in the Gold Mine."

He snorted. "Something like that."

"So a practice rink?"

"They're doing a huge multi-sheet skating center. It's good press, and the Bay Area is in desperate need of ice."

The elevator doors dinged open, and Sara let Mike lead her down the hallway. "Why so big? It's California, not Minnesota, after all."

A nudge of his elbow. "Wouldn't let the powers that be hear you say that, sweetheart. Hockey is up and coming in California, and San Jose actually has the largest adult hockey program in the States."

She tried to correlate that in her mind. Ocean waves, redwoods, flip-flops and cargo shorts and tree huggers.

"I can hear your mind working from here." His hand slid up her back to tug her ponytail. "Trust me on the need and want."

Wasn't Kristi Yamaguchi from San Francisco? Or nearby? She'd never really put two and two together before, but really, she'd lived in the city for five years. She should know better.

Northern California was *not* Southern California.

It kind of had seasons, if summer in San Francisco could be considered a season. And it even rained and stuff.

She snorted, and Mike's fingers slipped to the back of her neck. He kneaded the muscles there as he turned them down a hallway.

"Care to share with the class?" he asked, eyes twinkling. He'd obviously put the earlier ring debacle away for the present and—

Dear God, she didn't need to be thinking about *that* right now.

Later. Rings and maybe proposals she would put off to think about until later.

"Just that you'd better come get me after the game. I'm thoroughly turned around."

"Bwahaha!" he mock-evil-laughed. "My plan is working."

A smack to his chest. "You're a dork."

"And you're here."

They stopped in front of a nondescript door. A panel was on the wall outside it, one of those placards that gave the name and number. Mike didn't give her a chance to read it.

He turned the knob, and they walked straight into chaos.

TWENTY-EIGHT

Mike

MIKE WAS USED to the sight and sound of a dozen women talking and laughing in the Family Suite—their voices echoing off the walls, mingling with the sound of several blaring televisions as well as the clinking of silverware against plates, music playing in the background, toy cars being run across countertops, but Sara flinched as he tugged her across the threshold.

A blip of silence trailed their entrance as twenty-something eyes flicked in their direction then away before the conversation started back up.

The sound of the Matchbox cars rolling along the granite abruptly cut off, and little feet pounded in their direction.

"What did you bring me, Mr. Mike?" a little girl who barely came up to his waist asked.

Mirabel was the daughter of their backup goalie, Spence, and as gorgeous as her model mother. Black corkscrew curls, coffee skin, chocolate eyes, bright white teeth and a brilliant smile.

"Nothing today, pipsqueak," he told her.

Her bottom lip came out, and he grinned, well familiar with the young girl's tactics.

"Mirabel," her mother, Monique, warned.

"How about I have Brit make some good saves?"

Rosebud lips pressed together, considering.

"And," he whispered as he crouched down, "this." He slid a chocolate kiss into her hand.

"Mike," Monique said, now warning him. "You'll spoil her."

He tugged one of Mira's springy curls. She unwrapped the chocolate and shoved it in her mouth before her mother could confiscate it.

Smart girl.

"She's the only kid around," he said. "She needs spoiling."

The Gold were a young team, and Mira was the only kid amongst the WAGs. Their players were either single, or those who were in committed relationships didn't have kids yet.

"More will be coming soon and then—"

"She'll lead the shenanigans." Mike winked, teasing a smile out of Monique. "I wanted to introduce you to someone. This is—"

"Sara Jetty, as I live and breathe."

Sara's face paled, and Mike didn't blame her. Monique's tone was completely unreadable. Still, he had to give his girl credit. She didn't flinch or shy away, just extended a hand.

"Nice to meet you . . ."

"Monique LeBrat," she said. "Spence's wife."

Sara flicked her gaze in his direction. "Backup goalie," he said.

"Sorry," Sara murmured. "I haven't been watching the team for long, and I'm not totally familiar with the players." She gave a self-deprecating laugh. "I've kind of avoided everything to do with the ice since . . . well, you know."

Monique tilted her head. "Since the *you know*."

"Yup. *You knows* are painful, if you would believe it."

"You know?" Monique tapped one black painted fingernail against her mouth. "I think I would."

Sara giggled.

"All right," Monique said and slid an arm around Sara's shoulders, tugging her away from Mike. "Come on, and let me introduce you around. I'll even tell you where they store the really good chocolate."

"You good, Sara girl?" He didn't like leaving her, but he also didn't want to mess up her chances of making a friend or two up here. The WAGs were super protective of the team, and once they accepted someone into their fold, it was for life.

Sara had made a good start already and didn't need him hanging around cramping her style.

"She's good," Monique said, pulling her into the other room and making a shooing motion. "Go do your hockey thing. We're going to get to know each other."

But Mike didn't move, not until Sara's eyes connected with his, and she nodded.

He probably wouldn't have gone even then, except her expression was anticipatory, as though she wanted the chance to know the girls.

"I'll meet you up here after the game."

"Good luck," she said softly and let Monique lead her into the next room of the suite.

THEY WERE DOWN two goals in the bottom of the third with seventeen seconds to go.

The crowd was pouring out of the arena, the fair-weather fans leaving to beat the rush while the diehards stayed on.

Hockey was a game of seconds, but they were quickly running out of them.

At the sound of the ref's whistle, Mike skated to the blue line and readied himself for the faceoff. They were in the offensive zone, with an extra attacker—Coach had just pulled Brit—

but they needed to act fast if they were going to make a game of it.

The Gold needed a goal *now*.

And then another.

Music from the arena's speakers cut off, the ref stood between the players, telling them to adjust their sticks, their feet, and—

The puck dropped.

It was a clean win—meaning their center was able to send the puck exactly where he wanted it, in this case to Mike, before the other center even touched it. Mike flicked it to Barie, who in a set play, passed it right back to him for a one-timer.

Blue crashed the net and . . . deflected the puck just enough that it squeaked between the goalie's pads.

Goal!

But he and the boys hardly celebrated. They had more work to do. The season was winding down, and every single point counted.

Line back up at center ice. Ten seconds left on the clock. Setup for the faceoff and . . . go!

This time the puck landed on Barie's stick. He carried it forward, Mike sliding back and middle to cover his position. Blue streaked up the boards, and Stefan spotted him, sending a lofting pass cross-ice to land right on his tape. A deke, a rapid change in direction paired with an acceleration, and it was just the rookie and their opponent's goalie.

Seconds ticked down. Four. Three. Two—

Score!

The remaining fans were louder than the entire arena had been all night, jumping to their feet and screaming as he and the guys mobbed Blue.

Two goals, fifteen seconds. That had to be a record.

They skated to the bench as Brit returned to her net. Another puck drop, and the buzzer sounded.

The game would be decided in overtime . . . or a shootout.

Coach said a few things, but not many. His words of wisdom

mostly came in practice rather than the games, which he believed were the time for execution. Tweaks would be made, but primary system changes were to be cultivated during practice.

Overtime was three on three, and Mike would be on the ice with Blue and Blane, following Stefan's trio.

In close games, the bench was shortened—meaning, Coach gave the hot and more experienced players more ice time.

Luckily, that included him.

Winners wanted the puck. And he was definitely a winner—

And great, now he sounded like Keanu from the bad football movie, *The Replacements*. But his lips twitched when he wondered if Sara had seen it—

Tweet!

He pushed all extraneous thoughts away and focused on the game.

Players streaked across the ice, now with so much more space since each team was down two players. Six instead of ten skaters made for more room, more excitement, more goals.

Stefan peeled off and came hard to the bench. Mike jumped over the boards when he got close and rushed forward to join the play. He picked up a pass, got a shot on goal that deflected into the corner. Seeing that the forwards were tired, he hustled over and snagged the puck.

That gave the rest of Stefan's group time to change . . . and Blue the chance to get back on the ice.

The kid was on a run right now, and Mike wanted to get him the puck.

He turned, skated toward the front of the net, but instead of going for the shot like everyone no doubt expected, he made a quick move and dropped the biscuit to Blue.

Who wound up, shot, and—*fuck*—hit him right in the ass.

There was a reason players weren't supposed to have their backs to the net.

But what made his aching cheek feel better was the offending disk landing right between his feet. He reacted, flicking the puck up and over the goalie's shoulder.

The red light came on. The buzzer sounded.

And hell yeah, *that* felt good.

TWENTY-NINE

Sara

SARA WAS COMFORTABLY TUCKED into one of the ridiculously plush armchairs of the Family Suite reading on her phone and waiting for Mike to finish his post-game routine.

Monique had left a few minutes earlier to take Mirabel home—it was a school night after all—and the others had gone after the game, since they'd brought their own cars.

Sara had been surprisingly relaxed with the women in the suite that night. A couple had given her a curious look when they'd recognized her name and face, but none had been cruel or asked her any questions about her past.

What was going on between her and Mike was a different story.

Apparently, relationships were a hot topic.

Still, she kept things light; telling them how she and Mike had run into each other after so long apart and just hit it off. They'd laughed hysterically at the rain-car-blocking-traffic story, which she had to admit was kind of funny now.

Kind of.

Monique was definitely the most welcoming, and Sara hoped that they would continue to get along.

It would be nice to have some female friends.

The row of televisions on the wall were black, the lights dimmed. Three separate spaces made up the suite: the large open area with TVs to watch the game, another that held a kitchen and a play zone for the kids, er, *kid,* since Mirabel was the only munchkin around, and a bathroom.

The suite was beautifully decorated in pale gold with accents of black and white, and she found herself drifting off under the logo-emblazoned fleece blanket that was pulled up to her chin.

She let her eyes slide closed after reading the same paragraph three times over.

"Hey."

"Mmm." She shifted, almost found herself on the floor.

"Careful." Mike placed his hands on her arms and gently nudged her back. "Sorry I took so long."

Sara glanced at the phone in her hand, saw that it was not quite midnight. "I thought you'd be later." The blanket fell as she stretched and sat up. His eyes flicked down to her breasts, and those little hussies perked to immediate attention. "Nice goal."

A flash of white teeth. "You saw?"

"Of course." She stood. "That's what I was here for."

"I thought maybe it was the wine."

Her cheeks felt a little pink. So, there'd been a little wine to go with the girl talk, but the gossip had mostly stopped when the game came on.

Hockey was serious business in these parts, and the wives and girlfriends fiercely cheered on the entire team.

"Shh." She walked into his arms, stood on tiptoe, and kissed the hell out of him.

Though she'd wanted to knock his socks off and knew they had no shortage of chemistry, the heat that swept through her was almost shocking. It began in her middle, radiating outward to her limbs.

She was on fire—

"You're dangerous, sweetheart," Mike murmured, pulling back to cup her face. He pressed his mouth to hers in a chaste kiss. "Dangerous for my sanity." His smile softened the words. "Ready?"

"Take me home, Hot Shot."

He slung an arm over her shoulder. "Now *that's* a sentiment I can get behind."

THE FRONT GATE of Mike's house was still crowded with paparazzi, but they slid through the barrier barely stopping.

"Wait for—"

"I hired some security. They'll make sure it's closed."

Her head twisted toward him. "When could you have possibly found the time to hire security?"

He shrugged. "A former teammate runs a management firm. He has connections and hooked me up."

"What management firm?"

"Prestige Media Group."

"*Prestige?*" She tried to control her shock, really she did. It still sounded like a shriek though.

"Um, yes?"

Why did Mike sound so confused? How could he be so calm when—

"Devon Scott is your former teammate?"

The garage door rolled open, and Mike pulled the car inside. "Yes." He was amused now.

"*The* Devon Scott."

"I don't know about *the*"—he did air quotes with his fingers —"Devon Scott. Dev used to play for the Gold, but that was before I came to the team. We overlapped for a season on the Kings."

"That's when he dated . . ."

"Emily Perkins. Yup." He rolled his eyes. "And if we're comparing media circuses. . ."

"I love her movies. I wonder—"

"He's married now. Not to a movie star."

Her shoulders dropped. "Oh." A pause. "I'd still like to meet him."

"What, am I second best?" He turned off the car, pushed the remote for the garage door.

"He has dreamy chocolate eyes."

"Dream—" Mike shook his head, expression irritated. *"He's married."*

She couldn't resist pushing his buttons. "And he was still voted 2009's Sexiest Man Alive."

"I think his wife might have something to say about that," Mike muttered, reaching for the handle.

"I also think you're adorable when you're jealous."

He froze, brows pulling down.

"And when you frown."

The corner of his mouth twitched.

"And I think your eyes are way more dreamy."

A full smile. "And I think you are way more trouble than I gave you credit for."

"People underestimate me."

Those dreamy eyes went a little serious. "Yes. Yes, they do."

"No sappy," she warned, holding her hands up, palms out. "I've had enough serious for a while. Let's stick with fun."

"Fun as in you teasing me?"

She shrugged and got out. "Yes, that works."

"Or fun as in sexy naked time?" he asked, getting out and looking over the top of the car at her. The garage was dark, except for the faint light coming from the opener above their heads.

He was gorgeous, as in he *literally* took her breath away, all planes of hard lines softened by his five o'clock shadow and plump lips.

She wanted to sketch him.

She wanted to fuck him more.

"I do like sexy naked time." Sara tugged at the hoodie she'd borrowed from him. It was huge and baggy, but she hadn't exactly packed a bunch of clothes when she'd left her apartment.

She'd need to go over, get a few things if they were going to stay here, and with the group camped outside of the gate, that seemed to be the only reasonable possibility.

"I know you do." Mike grinned, and it was predatory.

Thoughts of the paparazzi faded because *God*, did she love the way he looked at her, eyes smoldering, focus intense. Every inch of the huge, muscular body was tuned into her.

And she wanted every inch inside her.

Her mouth quirked.

He raised a brow.

"Just making up bad innuendos to myself." She gave a self-deprecating chuckle. "Inches. And—" Two steps back, and she was next to the workbench. She picked up a random piece of pipe. What it was doing there, she had no idea. But it served her purpose. "Shaft." The tape measure she held up next. "Length."

Mike snorted, but those dreamy eyes were on fire, and those flames shot straight between her thighs.

Her lips parted, her exhale was shaky—

Then he was there, lifting her on top of the workbench, stepping between her thighs. "And let me guess—" A thrust of his hips, grinding that hard erection against her. "You need to use my *tool?*"

She burst out into giggles, the whole scenario almost too ridiculous for words. "I love you."

His face went soft. "Me too, sweetheart. So much." Then he grinned, wicked and promising. "But no more sap, remember?" He unzipped her hoodie, tossed it to the side.

She ripped his shirt from his slacks, slid her hands over the exposed flesh. "How about hard and fast instead?"

"Hard, I can do," he said, mouth dropping to her neck, hands finding the button of her jeans and tugging down the zipper. "Fast, not so much."

Sara undid the waistband of his pants, gripped him tight. "I think you can do fast, Hot Shot."

"Fuck," he groaned.

A stroke. Another and . . . Mike showed her he could do fast.

THIRTY

Mike

IF HIS AND Sara's first night together after the press got hold of their story had been nearly perfect (and it had been, since Mike was pretending the proposal debacle hadn't happened), then the next two weeks became progressively less so.

The media attention was frenzied.

Twice more, photographers had hopped the back fence to his property and had to be escorted off with threats of criminal trespassing charges if they returned.

The circus outside his gate grew, as did the complaints from his neighbors.

Not that he blamed them. The fucking paparazzi were imposing and annoying as hell, but what was Mike supposed to do? The team was in the middle of the season, and he *had* to be in the area.

And he wasn't about to be separated from Sara, at least not any sooner than the team's schedule pulled him away.

Plus, it was safer.

He had employed three full-time security guards, and enough cameras had been installed to keep an eye on big brother himself.

But now the press was affecting the team.

Sara paced back and forth in front of the television tuned into the gossip show. Blue had been out with a few of the guys, and several belligerent photographers had tried to get a reaction by calling Sara unkind names.

They'd gotten one.

In the form of Blue throwing a punch.

Not that Mike hadn't felt like doing the same when he'd heard the C-word in reference to *his* woman, but it wasn't Blue's battle to fight.

"He shouldn't put his career at risk," Sara said, stopping to stare at the TV. Her shoulders slumped. "Not for me."

"It wasn't for you." Mike crossed to her, placing his hands on those slumped shoulders and forcing her to look at him. "Or at least not you specifically. Blue is a good kid. The team is full of good guys. Not one of us would tolerate that about a teammate's spouse."

"But—"

"Not one." He pressed a soft kiss to her lips. "We just need to ride this out."

Sara opened her mouth to respond but was interrupted by the doorbell.

Since the security team hadn't called up to the house, it had to be either Brit, Stefan, or Rebecca.

Given the video running on repeat, he suspected the later.

His suspicion was confirmed at the second chime of the bell as he strode to the door. Rebecca then. She was nothing if not impatient.

And lived on her phone.

"Yes, Devon. I know," she snapped as she strode through the door, cell to her ear. "We've been behind this thing from the beginning. It's *all* fucking damage control."

All righty then. Mike closed the front door, followed Rebecca into the kitchen.

Sara was perched on a stool, her pencil in hand as she sketched rapidly. He might as well order an entire a box of notebooks at the rate she was filling them.

She didn't appear to notice or hear Rebecca's cellular ranting. Either that, or she was way better at ignoring the publicist than he was. He closed the distance between them and peeked over her shoulder.

Circles on top of circles filled the page. They were intersected with harsh, radiating lines, amorphous figures hidden in the shadows.

He knew immediately what she'd drawn.

They were huddled in his front yard.

Rebecca tossed her phone on the counter, making Sara jump. The pencil hit the ground, but Rebecca didn't seem to notice.

"Dang, girl," she said. "Rumor had it that you could actually draw, but this"—she snagged the sketchpad—"*these* are good. Like really good." Her red nails were in stark contrast to the gray scale drawings as she flipped through the pages. "Oh, this is perfect. I can see it. Instagram. These. Drawings of the team."

Rebecca grabbed her phone and took a bunch of pictures of Sara's sketches before typing frantically into her phone. Then it was back at her ear.

"Do you see those, Devon?" Her voice was positively gleeful now. "Think of how well they'll translate to Instagram. Yes. *Yes.* Exactly. Okay, I'll set it up. Bye."

The phone landed back on the island.

Holy tornado.

"What's going on Rebecca?"

"The usual shit-show, but I think we finally have a way out."

"Through Instagram," Sara muttered dryly.

"Yes." Rebecca turned and began pacing. "It's perfect because you're not on any form of social media—" Her head whipped around and fixed Sara with a glare. "You're not, right? Not even under a fake name?"

"No."

Mike slipped behind her, putting his hands on her shoulders and kneading the tight muscles there.

"Perfect!"

"What's perfect?" he asked.

"Social media personas are easy to craft but hard to undo. We can use these"—she held up the book—"to our advantage."

Sara stiffened. "I'm not sure—"

"Be sure. Look, it's like this." Rebecca sat on the stool next to Sara's. "We need a distraction. The *team* needs a break from the media. So, we give them what they want. Access, carefully crafted, completely controlled on your terms, but access nonetheless."

"And they'll just suddenly leave us alone?" Sara asked. "I find that hard to believe."

Mike did as well.

"Look, the issue is exposure. We don't have enough of the right kind. We haven't given a statement. Everyone is clamoring for the first shot at one. This gives you the chance to control the way it comes out."

Sara glanced back over her shoulder at him, raised her brows.

"This is your decision, Sara girl. They're your drawings, your life you'd share—"

"Well, technically, it's *our* life we'd share," she said, ice creeping into the edges of her tone.

He sighed. "You know what I mean. The exposure is going to be worse for you. The Internet is way harder on women than men."

A roll of blue eyes. "That is true."

Rebecca began humming the *Jeopardy* theme. "Three hundred dollars an hour."

"What?" he asked.

"Three hundred dollars an hour is my going rate, but feel free to take your time."

"That's outrageous," Sara said.

"I'm good at my job."

Mike raised a brow. "I'd hope so."

"Don't talk to me, you overpaid rink rat."

Her insult was delivered with a smile and a wink, and he couldn't help but chuckle, especially when Sara giggled. "She does have a point."

"Of course I do." Rebecca stood and tapped her toe impatiently against the hardwood floor. "So, are you in?"

"Yes." Rebecca fist-pumped at Sara's answer. "Just tell me what you want me to do."

"I'll take care of everything," she said, already heading to the door, heels clicking, fingers typing on her cell. "You won't have to worry about a thing."

Why didn't Mike find her words reassuring?

THIRTY-ONE

Sara

THE GOLD WERE on their worst losing streak of the season. They dropped another game to Vancouver, making it six games in a row.

A few more losses, and their playoff hopes would be in jeopardy.

Sara knew this because it was on every sports news show.

Sara knew this because her poor influence was the lead story on every entertainment talk show.

She also knew this because of the fan in front of her.

She'd ventured out of Mike's house for the first time in ten days, wanting to see Mitch and needing to get out of her gilded prison.

The gallery was doing well, and Mitch had liked several of her drawings enough to display them. Which she considered the least she could do after creating the chaos at his store. Though, thankfully, not showing up for work meant the press had pretty much left.

She'd snuck through the back door, picked through the crowded and disorganized storeroom, cringing all the while, and spent ten minutes in normality.

Then a customer had come in.

One who was also a Gold fan. Who'd recognized her.

And . . . cue awesomeness.

"You're fucking with the team, a goddamned distraction. Leave those boys alone." The man was middle-aged with a huge potbelly, but there was nothing soft about his expression. He stared at her, fury in his eyes, spittle spraying from his mouth as he raged.

Stepping back or cowering wasn't her first instinct. She'd been through this particular rodeo before. In fact, this was actually almost *calm*, based on some of the vitriol she'd dealt with after her medal had been taken away.

Usually ignoring was best, so she didn't know why she attempted to answer. Reasoning with people like this was pointless. But nevertheless, Sara opened her big, fat mouth and got an entire two words out before the man cut her off. "I'm not—"

"I'll tell you what you are. Worthless. A fucking cheater who likes to whore herself—"

"Stop. Right. There."

Mitch.

"Get out of my store."

She'd never heard that tone come from her boss's mouth. It was scary.

"Who the fuck are you?" The man spat—yes, literally spat—at Mitch.

"You have three seconds to leave or—"

"What?" The man gestured to Mitch's plum suit, the pristine striped tie. "You'll make me?" he sneered.

"In fact, I will."

"You fucking fa—" The homophobic slur didn't make it into the air.

"And that's enough, thank you." A huge man in a suit that was not nearly as nice as her boss's stepped from the back room, grabbed the man's arm, and escorted him to the door, which Mitch helpfully held open.

A second later, the pane of metal and glass was locked, and the man turned to face her.

"Supposed to be with you today," he said by way of explanation.

Mitch raised a brow in her direction.

She shrugged. "Apparently, I have a bodyguard."

"I'd say you need one."

She guessed she did.

Her sigh was loud, and he bumped her shoulder, smiling coaxingly at her. "Let's take a look at a few more of these, okay?"

They flipped through her book, and Mitch carefully cut a few drawings out in order to try different matting and frame options.

"This will do for now," he said after they'd spent another hour on the process. "I know this whole situation is screwed up, but it has done wonders for your production."

She laughed. "If there's a positive in the media tracking me like a dog, then it's that."

"Be safe, okay?" He raised a brow in the direction of the security guard standing in the corner, trying to be unobtrusive while being completely the opposite.

Six feet tall and wide as a Mack truck tended to be out of place in a gallery.

"Thanks, Mitch," she said, giving him a hug before crossing over to the man. "I'm Sara."

He glanced down at her outstretched hand and shook it as carefully as he might handle a fragile glass sculpture. "Pascal." A beat. "Perhaps you shouldn't sneak out next time?"

Remorse swept through her because she *had* snuck out. As in, she had slipped through a gate in the back fence and called an Uber from two streets over. But she hadn't done it to avoid the security. She'd done it to evade the press.

"I'm an adult," she said, feeling guilty despite herself. "I don't exactly need a chaperone."

Mitch coughed, and she glared at him.

"Mr. Stewart asked that I keep you safe."

Nice of him to tell her that, she mentally complained, even though in the next heartbeat she knew she was being unfair.

Mike was out of town with the team, would continue to be so at regular intervals. He was trying to protect her from exactly the kind of asshole who'd confronted her in the store.

Holding on to that feeling, she wriggled her phone from her pocket and texted Mike.

I love you, Hot Shot.

He wouldn't get the message for a couple of hours since it was a practice day, but it was vitally important she send it anyway. Second chances didn't come around too often, and she needed, *needed* to not screw theirs up.

"Wake up, sleepyhead," Mike said the next morning.

Early the next morning.

Really, freaking, insanely, crazily early.

Sara rolled over and shoved her head under the pillow. "No."

She'd stayed up late the night before, waiting for Mike to get home, sketching into oblivion after watching the man from the gallery recite his encounter with her phrase-by-bitchy-phrase on the evening news. Never mind that she'd barely gotten two words out.

A story was a story, and hers at the moment was a front-page one. And so, Mr. Potbelly would be enjoying his fifteen minutes, and the local news station had an exclusive.

"Time to get up, sweetheart."

"It's too—" She screeched when the blanket was ripped from her body, and the freezing air hit her skin. "Mike!"

She was naked, of course. The pajamas they'd retrieved from her apartment had lasted all of five minutes.

"Up," he said and smacked her butt. Hard.

"You're an asshole!"

"And you're awake." A kiss to the base of her spine, big hands cupping her butt, kneading, rubbing what was no doubt a red-*ass* handprint on her right cheek.

Her hips canted up, and her temper waned. She sighed, thoroughly out of sleep's clutches now.

"Yes, I am—oh God!"

He'd slipped his fingers between her thighs then bent and flicked his tongue against her—

"Put these on."

A pair of sweats landed on the bed next to her, followed by a shirt. "I need fresh—" she said, starting to sit up.

Underwear smacked her in the face. A sports bra landed in her lap.

With a glare, she got dressed. "I'm afraid to mention socks."

Mike smirked and held up a hand. "I've got you covered." He knelt at her feet and tugged on a pair of patterned cotton crew socks then slipped on her sneakers.

"Anything else?"

"Yup." His fingers wrapped around her wrist, and he pulled her up from the bed.

"Good grief, what else could you possibly—?"

The rest of her words were muffled when he hauled a sweatshirt over her head. "That."

"Mike," she warned.

"You're supposed to be the morning person," he teased.

"Remind me of that when it's a reasonable time."

He chuckled, pushed her into the bathroom. "Brush your teeth."

"I should make you deal with my dragon breath," she muttered, snatching up her brush and putting her hair into a loose ponytail.

"Except you can't stand when your teeth are fuzzy."

She stilled, one hand on her toothbrush, the other on the toothpaste. Little details. He *always* remembered the little details. What type of pencil she liked to draw with. Her favorite ice cream. The way she took her coffee. That she hated kale but loved broccoli.

That she couldn't function without scrubbed teeth.

Why hadn't she accepted that damn ring? That perfect, wonderful promise of a future.

A future he hadn't brought up again over the last weeks. A future she desperately wanted. Because he was being patient. For *her*—a crazy, emotionally frazzled chick with a checkered past.

"You really don't care, do you?"

"About what?"

"My past."

He rolled his eyes, leaned back against the wall. "Now *that* question doesn't even deserve an answer."

This man.

Love spilling over the edges of her heart, she brushed and rinsed, and then with minty fresh breath, she walked over to Mike and kissed him.

Sara put everything she had into that kiss, every drop of love, every bit of pain from the past, every ounce of guilt for refusing to do the right thing and step aside for the good of the team.

She gave it everything she had until her brain screamed for oxygen, and she had to pull back.

"Thank you," she murmured, eyes misty.

"For what?"

"For finding me again."

"Oh, Sara girl," he said, sounding a little choked up. "I shouldn't have let you go in the first place."

"It's not—"

He waved her off. "I shouldn't have brought that up. No more past talk, okay?" When she nodded, he snagged her hand. "Now, come on. I've got your coffee downstairs, and we don't want to be late for your surprise."

THIRTY-TWO

Mike

MIKE GAVE Pascal a fist-bump as he led a blindfolded Sara out the back gate. A car was parked on the street, not his, but a rental the security company had arranged for him.

He buckled Sara into the passenger seat and was driving away from the house just as the sky began to lighten.

It might be insanely early and way before the hour that he normally wanted to get up, but he was practically giddy with excitement.

He'd woken, showered, dressed, double-checked that every detail was in place, all before Sara had moved a muscle.

Though, in fairness to her, he had kept them both up very late into the night. He knew the attention was weighing on her, and though Rebecca was working on shifting the public image of Sara, it wasn't a fast process, especially when the team wasn't playing well.

When Pascal told him what had happened at the gallery—

Suffice it to say, he was glad he hadn't been there.

At least the bodyguard had handled things calmly. If *he'd* seen some asshole come at Sara like that . . . Mike shook his head, knowing there was no way he would have been able to stop himself from punching the fucker.

"Not that I'm opposed to a blindfold in some cases," Sara said, finally speaking and sounding a lot more like her normally chipper early-morning self, "but are you going to tell me where we're going?"

He filed that bit of information—blindfolds could be used in a variety of manners—away for later use. "Nope."

"Umm. You remember that I don't like surprises, right?"

"From me, you do, remember?" When she sighed, he laughed. "And that's still a nope." He grinned at her, not that she could see it.

Before she could question him further, he turned on the radio or rather queued up his playlist.

If he was going full-out for a romantic sunrise surprise, he needed appropriately sappy music.

James Blunt's "You're Beautiful" filtered through the car's speakers.

Heaven help him if the guys ever got a hold of his phone.

But Sara's reaction was worth it.

She stilled, sniffed, and fumbled around until her hand was on his thigh. "Oh, Mike."

"Not too cheesy?" he teased.

"Perfect amount of Swiss," she said, lips twitching.

"Good," he said, taking one hand off the steering wheel and placing it over hers where it rested on the top of his thigh, danger-ously close to his cock . . . which was supposed to be behaving.

Since it wasn't, he casually inched her hand a little lower.

Not slyly enough, apparently. Fingers slipped from his, crept up. "What's in your pants, Hot Shot?"

He snorted. "Pretty sure, you and he are on a first-name basis, sweetheart. Now"—he slid her palm back down—"we're almost there. Behave."

"Where's *there*?"

"Nice try."

Mike waved at the guard and pulled through into the deserted parking lot. Or, *nearly* deserted since there was one other car.

Brit winked at him when he led Sara inside the arena and gave him a thumbs-up as they walked by.

"Why does it smell like disinfectant?"

"Because the crew is thorough."

"Did you bring me to a gym?" she asked.

"Not exactly." He pushed open the door to the arena, felt the rush of cool air hit his skin. "Though there is a gym here."

He slid the blindfold from her eyes.

Two pairs of skates rested on a black pad near the Zamboni door. Two folding chairs were beside them. The lights were dim, just enough to see the ice, but since the arena was technically closed, it was just the two of them out here.

Music, faint at first then growing louder, came over the speakers, and Mike smiled.

Brit was playing her role to a T and he realized he'd have to buy her and Stefan dinner, especially when he saw his captain slipping in behind Sara to set a basket and thermos near the chairs.

Sara didn't notice. Hell, *he* barely noticed because he was looking at Sara.

Watching the play of emotions over her face: fear, longing, pleasure, need, hesitation. Hers was a rolling reel of feelings, and he wondered which one she'd settle on.

Anger, perhaps, that he'd brought her in the first place. Relief that she might feel the ice beneath her feet.

Her eyes slid closed, and she inhaled.

"Mike," she said. "You're killing me."

"You're not mad?"

"Mad?" She shook her head. "I— Can I touch it?"

He didn't answer, just tugged her close to the edge of the open door, up to the strip of plastic that led onto the rink.

She bent, reached down, and touched the ice. Then promptly drew back. "It's cold!"

He laughed. "First time in an ice rink, is it?"

"Shut up." She flicked her fingers at him, spraying flecks of water in his direction. "I'd forgotten how it felt. How it can numb and burn all at once. The freeze permeating your layers of clothes, making you shiver, but that same cold then feeling so good at the end of a routine."

She stood and seemed to truly *see* the space around them for the first time.

Mike knew what she saw. Concrete stairs. Hints of gold fabric peeking out from the black-plastic bottoms of the folded seats. Blank screens around the edges and on the Jumbotron. Advertisements on the boards. A sheet of white broken up by red and blue in front of them.

"So this is your view, huh?"

"One of them," he said, touching her cheek. "Kind of prefer this one, though."

"Can I go on?"

"Well, *I'm* not wearing those pretty white skates."

She laughed. "No *The Cutting Edge* moment for us?"

"Not happening." He crossed to one of the chairs and patted the cushion next to him. "Come over here."

Together they slipped on their skates. Mike was faster only because Sara was having a moment with hers. She stroked the leather like it was the finest silk, touched the laces like they were made of woven gold, and checked the edge on the blade with keen eyes.

"They're sharp," he told her. "Billie—" the team's equipment manager "—took care of it for me."

"Does he even know how to sharpen figure skates?" she teased before consenting that the edges looked perfect and pushing her feet into the boots.

The laces were tightened and threaded around their grommets a few seconds later, and then she was on her feet, or rather, her skates.

"Ready?" he asked.

She nodded. "I can't believe you did this for me."

Her hand fit perfectly in his, two halves coming together to form a whole. It had always been that way. "I would do anything for you."

For a second, her eyes dimmed, but then she visibly shook herself. Straight shoulders, raised chin, smiling lips. "Ready for me to teach you a thing or two, Hot Shot?"

THIRTY-THREE

Sara

SARA PAUSED at the edge of the ice. She was being ridiculous, drawing the experience out when she could already be *doing* it.

But it had been ten years since she'd set foot on the ice—not counting that horrendous night with Leo.

And she wanted to savor the experience.

Breathing in that intrinsic rink scent . . . feeling the damp air in her lungs, the first crunch of ice beneath her feet . . .

"Please tell me that you're not having an orgasm over there without me."

Mike swept his thumb beneath her eyes, wiping away tears she hadn't realized were falling.

"Is it too much?" he asked.

"Honestly?" Her teeth found her lip. "Yes," hurrying to add when his face fell, "but in a good way. In the *best* way. I never thought I'd get this again, and you gave it to me."

"Well, it's not screaming crowds, but it *is* regulation size."

For the first time since her competing days, Sara stepped onto the ice, and just as always, her smile locked into place. Not the fake one that hid pain, but the one that came from deep inside.

From doing something she loved.

From being with *someone* she loved.

"These are so light," she said, lifting a foot and gliding forward. She wasn't as steady as she'd once been, but, like riding a bike, it was coming back. "They must have cost a fortune."

"Skate technology has come a long way," he said. "You'll have to feel how light mine are."

Laughing, she glided away, turning at center ice and skating backward around the encircled Gold logo there.

Cross over. Cross over. Cross—

Whoa.

Throwing on the brakes, she looked sheepishly up at Mike who nodded encouragingly. "Slowly, honey. Take a few laps."

Nodding, she began running through what used to be her warm-up routine. Edge-work, balancing, crossovers, and then, without really thinking about it, she set up for a jump.

The move was a simple one, relatively speaking. A double-Salchow that was sloppy and totally under-rotated, but it felt fucking fantastic.

Applause echoed across the rink, and she glanced over at Mike.

He skated toward her, grabbed her hand, and tugged her against his chest. "Really? A double on your first time out?"

She snorted. "If you could call that ugly thing a double." But she was grinning, and it was almost as though her skates weren't even touching the ice.

"Gonna make it pretty?"

"Hell, yes, I am."

He tapped her butt. "Good, go on and show me what you've got."

Nodding, she skated over and set up the jump. Cool air slid along her scalp, ruffled her ponytail. She bent her leg, tensed every muscle in her body, brought her arms in, and . . .

Midway through the air, her back protested.

Sara compensated, instincts honed by years of competition, and managed to land the jump. The landing was definitely not the prettiest one she'd ever completed, but it was leaps and bounds better than that first attempt.

And she was done.

At least with the tricky stuff.

"You okay?" Mike was at her side in an instant.

"I'm good." In truth, she hadn't felt this exhilarated in years.

"Your back? I should have thought of—"

She jumped.

But this time instead of launching herself into the air, she hurled herself at Mike.

Who managed to catch her . . . or well, steady her, before falling to the ice himself.

Giggles burst out of her. "I'm so—sorry."

He was watching her with such an expression of outrage that she couldn't catch her breath because she was laughing too hard. "I-I would . . . have thought—big hockey guy like you—steadier on your skates."

"'Toepick,'" he said and grabbed her foot.

Instead of cracking her skull on the ice, Mike managed to manipulate her body midair so she landed on top of him, then wrapped his arms tight around her waist. "While you're down here," he murmured.

"Wh—?"

He kissed her.

There were almost too many sensations to process. The cold radiating up from the ice, the heat of Mike's body, his lips soft against hers. Her clothes felt too tight and she wanted them off, wanted him on her, *in* her.

"I can't believe you *toepicked* me," she said, heart pounding, when they finally broke away for air. The line was from *The Cutting Edge*, the scene when the hockey player was trying to learn how to use figure skates . . . and not succeeding because he kept tripping over the set of spikes at the front of the blades that hockey skates didn't have.

"Too tempting to resist," he told her. "Especially with you smirking after checking me to the ice."

"It wasn't a check!"

One brown brow rose.

"I wanted to kiss you, okay?" Her tone was begrudging. "For being so nice."

He chuckled, amusement all over his expression. "Nice? No." He pushed his elbows under him and helped her up to her skates then waggled his eyebrows. "Don't you know that I'm a bad boy?"

"I know that you're ridiculous."

"You love me."

Her heart clenched. "I do," she murmured. "I do love you."

"So," he said, and she noticed that he shifted, one knee on the ice, as though he was ready to stand up.

But instead of rising, he continued to kneel in front of her.

And then he reached into his pocket.

Her breath caught when he pulled out a box.

Covered in blue velvet, it fit easily into the palm of his hand. She inanely noticed that and a dozen other details: the maniacal eyes of the Gold logo behind him as he knelt at center ice, Brit standing at the Zamboni door, phone held up in the air, spotlights shining down on them, the random car dealership advertisement on the boards . . . and the look in Mike's eyes.

"I love you, Sara. Always have, always will. I know I'm not the greatest with romantic gestures—"

She snorted. Which was so *not* her fault, the big liar.

Laughter came from Brit's end of the ice. Mike flicked a gaze over his shoulder and shook his head. "The women in my life—"

"Make it so much better," she finished.

Now a male thread joined Brit's giggles.

"True," Mike said, grinning. "Okay, so maybe I've got the

BACKHAND 515

romance bit down, but without you, my life doesn't mean a damn thing, Jumping Bean."

"Aw . . ." Brit again.

He rolled his eyes. "I'm sorry for the crowd. Brit said you might want a video of this, but really, she's just nosy."

"You're just realizing that?" Stefan called. "Pull the trigger already, Stewie! We know she's going to say yes!"

Mike glanced at her nervously. "You are going to say yes, aren't you?"

Stefan and Brit were joined by more of the team, who catcalled.

God, she loved this man . . . and his friends.

"Mike," she murmured

"Oh, fuck," he said, opening the box and displaying a gorgeous princess-cut diamond in a platinum setting. "Please say you'll marry me, Sara girl."

Sara paused just long enough to make him sweat, but not long enough to be cruel. She did love him, after all.

"I was just going to say your original choice for a ring was perfect."

He burst to his feet and yanked her close. "I love you so fucking much."

Then he was kissing her, and the team was cheering, and he was slipping the ring on her finger.

"I'll put the other one on later," he promised. "For now, I just need to see you with a ring."

She touched her lips to his. "That I can live with."

Someone whooped, and she inclined her head toward the team. "Should we go face the crowd?"

"If we have to."

"You have to!" Brit yelled. "I need to see that diamond!"

THIRTY-FOUR

Mike

EMERALDS AGAINST PALE SKIN.

Mike nuzzled Sara's neck and played with the ring sitting on her finger. It glittered in the sunlight.

She was dead asleep, something he was responsible for. But he was playing eight games in ten days, both at home and on the road, and wouldn't be seeing much of her, so he'd needed to make the most of their time.

Between travel and pre-game routines, plus normal practices and training, he would be living and breathing hockey for the next while.

Not that he minded. Or not normally anyway.

He did worry about leaving her alone so much.

Though Spence had delivered a message from Monique—basically a promise to watch out for Sara while he and the team were otherwise occupied.

And Rebecca had scheduled time with Sara the next day. A progress update on the social media stuff and more *plans*.

But it had been several weeks since the story of their relationship broke, and the press still sat outside his gate. Frankly, it was making him a little crazy. He couldn't go on his patio, have his blinds open without feeling as though eyes were on him.

He guessed they were . . . but knowing that still made his skin crawl.

If only the team could link a few wins together, get the focus back on hockey and away from drama—

"Why are you staring at me?" Sara asked, voice and hair sleep-mussed.

"Because you're beautiful," he said, pushing back the strands to kiss her jaw.

She grunted.

"You used to be a morning person."

"You used to not keep me up to the wee hours of the night."

That was true. But by the time he'd gotten home from the previous night's game, it had been after midnight.

Pascal had already driven Sara home from the arena—they'd found it tended to create less commotion if they drove separately— and she had been asleep before he walked into the bedroom.

"You were naked."

Her face was in the mattress, slightly muffling her words, but he saw her smile, or at least the crease in her cheeks as her lips turned up.

"When do you leave?"

"Couple hours." He kissed one shoulder, then the other, loved that her breathing hitched. "What do you have planned?"

"Monique invited me over for dinner and to watch the game." She rolled onto her back. "Do you think it's safe? I mean, I don't want to stir up anything, not with Mirabel in the crosshairs."

"Pascal will keep you all safe. I have no doubt about that." He twined a piece of her hair around his finger, reveled in how soft it was. "But it would probably be best if you don't go out too much."

"Yeah," she said before making a visible effort to lighten her tone. "Plus is, I've got more money than I know what to do with. Mitch has sold everything I gave him, and he needs more already. Pretty soon, I'll be flush enough to get my own place." Her hands spread, framing an imaginary house. "My own little castle on the hill. I think I'll put in a moat, with alligators . . . except they'll only eat paparazzi."

"Except, you'll stay here," Mike said, bristling, though he knew she was joking.

He wanted Sara to be happy, and if that meant art, then certainly to be successful at that, but he also wanted her in his home, his room, his bed.

She giggled. "Sorry. When Mitch said you'd get all growly and caveman, I should have believed him." A soft palm cupped his cheek. "Thought I made it clear that there was no place I'd rather be."

The security company had moved everything out of Sara's apartment, not that she had much, and she'd prepaid with her art earnings for the penalty to get out of her lease.

Last night she'd offered to pay him rent.

Rent! The other half of his soul wanted to pay for the privilege of staying with him. He should be paying her, for fuck's sake, not the other way around.

Sara was everything . . . and frustratingly independent.

The woman hadn't even let him help with closing down her apartment or getting the drawings to Mitch. She wouldn't let him cook for her on meal days or pick up anything heavier than the TV remote.

Hell, he was surprised he was allowed to have sex.

That would probably go next. Couldn't risk overtaxing his muscles, now could he?

"What are you thinking?" she asked. "Your face went all scowly."

"Rent." One word, a shake of his head, and Sara understood the context exactly.

She rolled her eyes. "What kind of person would I be if I didn't offer?"

"Normal."

A huff as she clambered into his lap. The sheets pooled around their hips, and his cock hardened at the sight of her breasts just inches from his face.

"Really?" Her tone was droll, but her body gave her away. She arched against him, rubbing her wetness along his erection. "Again?"

"You're naked." He nipped at her neck. "And wet."

"There is that."

In one swift movement, he flipped them and pinned her hips to the bed. "I'm leaving in a couple of hours."

A flash of white teeth. "There is that too."

"I'm hard."

Fingers wrapped around his length as she guided him home. "That you are. Now"—she leaned up, whispered in his ear—"show me what you can do with that."

He grinned then proceeded to demonstrate his abilities.

Twice.

LATER, seated next to Blane on the team's jet, he stared at the text from Sara.

Fewer camera goons today. Maybe we're finally old news.

That was the best thing he'd heard, aside from her moans that morning.

He sent a heart emoji, not thinking twice until Blane glanced over Mike's shoulder and shook his head.

"Whipped, dude," his teammate muttered. "Fucking emojis. Might as well turn in your man card."

"Don't even care, B. I've got Sara, so I'll take as much flack as you can dish out about being pussy-whipped." He shook his head, knowing he was grinning like an idiot and not giving a damn.

Max, who was in the row in front of them, turned around and said, "Let's talk about your playlist—"

"Not today, boys," Brit called from a few seats back. She was cozied up to Stefan. Must be nice. "Mike knows his romance. You should be taking notes, not giving him shit."

"But I like giving it to Mi—"

"Finish that fucking sentence, and you die," Mike gritted out.

Max chuckled but turned around and flopped back down into his seat, iPad already at the ready, figurines spilling into the space next to him.

Mike glanced at Blane, who was almost preternaturally still. "You good?"

A flash of pain crossed his face, the same hurt that always seemed on the periphery of his expression whenever he saw Brit with Stefan. The man held a flame for Brit, and while she loved him—they'd grown up playing together—it had never been more than a sister's love.

Fuck, he sounded like Oprah.

Blane's face cleared. "Yup. Just thinking about the next game. We've got to get more traffic in front of the net if we're going to score. Their goaltending is too strong otherwise."

They chatted for a few minutes about the upcoming games and the adjustments Coach wanted them to make, both defensively and offensively, then each plugged in their headphones and tuned out for the rest of the hour-long flight.

When they landed, Blane slipped off the plane ahead of the rest of them.

THIRTY-FIVE

Sara

SARA AND PASCAL pulled up to Monique's house about thirty minutes before puck drop. It had taken forever to shake their tail, but she hadn't wanted to lead the paparazzi to Spence and Monique's home.

None of them needed *that* chaos.

The house was quaint, in an older part of the city, but nicely kept up. It had Victorian details—ornate trim, a pitched roof, was painted in a deep green with bright white accents, and was boxed in by a neat, flower-filled yard.

The sight was homey, and with the sun drifting toward the horizon, she pulled out her phone and snapped a few pictures. She'd have to ask Monique if she could draw it.

"I'll be around," Pascal said after she'd stowed her cell. "Text if you need anything." And then he disappeared into the shadows.

Literally walked into the darkness and vanished from view.

"That's super creepy."

His soft laugh trailed her up to the door.

She hesitated before pressing the bell, suddenly nervous. Like she was a teenager on a date for the first time and—

The knob turned, the panel swung open, and Mirabel wrapped her arms tight around her waist.

"Wow," the girl said. "I forgot how little you are." Small hands measured their heights, passing from the top of her head to Sara's shoulder. Yes, pathetically, the seven-year-old was almost as big as she.

"You're tall for your age," Monique said. "Comes from having a giraffe of a mother and a hockey-player dad."

Mirabel nodded vigorously. "My dad is sixty-six."

Sara grinned. "Wow, he looks good for his age."

"Come in. Come in," Monique said. "Six feet six isn't anything too special amongst athletes, but add in my crazy genes—" She patted her hips, gesturing to the ridiculously long legs holding her up.

"You're beautiful," Sara said, following them into the house. "I always wanted to be taller."

"We're all beautiful in our own ways," Mirabel said.

"That's right," Monique replied, ruffling her hair. "Why don't you go wash up? Dinner's almost ready."

"Can I show Sara my room first?"

Monique's eyes flicked over to Sara's. She shrugged. Looking at little girls' rooms wasn't something she was in the habit of, but if Mirabel wanted to show her . . .

"Okay."

"Yay! Come on!" She grabbed Sara's hand and started dragging her down the hall.

"Slowly!" Monique called. "Show her *slowly*."

Mirabel's feet decreased their speed. Slightly.

Sara was led past two closed doors and through an open one into a . . . pink-splosion.

Pink carpet. Pink walls. Pink curtains and bed coverings. The only thing that wasn't pink was the sparkling silver rhinestones bedazzling the edge of *everything*.

"Do you like it?"

She blinked, eyes trying to adjust to the visual onslaught. "It's very pretty."

"I love pink!" Mirabel yelled, jumping in a circle and doing a little dance in the middle of her fuchsia area rug.

"I can tell," Sara deadpanned, walking toward a collection of stuffed animals. The only non-pink toy in the whole place was a plush Gold skater. It wore a face-mask, goalie pads, and a jersey with . . . Brit's number?

"Don't tell Dad," Mirabel whispered. "But Brit's my favorite Gold player."

Sara laughed loudly. "You're the best, kiddo."

"I know." Mirabel bent to pull a book off her shelf. It had—no surprise—a pink cover.

"Oh yeah?" Sara took the book when Mirabel pressed it into her hand.

"That's what my dad says." A pause. "You can call me Mira," she said. "All my friends do."

She tugged one of Mirabel's—Mira's—curls. "Thanks, Mira. You can call me . . . Sara." When the little girl giggled, she shrugged. "My name is pretty short already."

"True." Mira opened the book, turning pages until she stopped on a chapter. "Can you read this to me?"

Sara smiled. "Just so happens that I love to read."

"Me too!"

She read aloud to Mira until someone cleared her throat from the doorway. Turning her head, she saw Monique watching them, a relaxed smile on her face. "Dinner's ready, and the boys are almost on TV. Wash up, sweetheart."

"Okay!" Mira jumped to her feet and grabbed the Gold plush then sprinted out the door and into the bathroom across the hall. Sara blinked as the door slammed closed, followed seconds later by the toilet flushing, bottles clattering, water splashing, and finally the door was wrenched back open as Mira skidded out and ran down the hall.

The girl appeared to only have one speed.

"Did I keep her too long?" Sara asked.

Monique was studying her, expression unfathomable.

It cleared at her question. "No. She would have gladly kept you here reading to her until she, or you, passed out from exhaustion." A hesitation. "I'm just trying to figure you out."

Sara laughed uncomfortably. "I'm not too complicated."

Monique shook her head. "Exceptionally talented. Nice. Gorgeous. How did you get mixed up in that scandal? No," she added when Sara sucked in a breath. "Don't answer that. It was more rhetorical than anything. You just seem *so* nice."

"Nice people do bad things," Sara said softly, slipping a bookmark into Mira's book and setting it on the bed.

"That is one version of the truth." Monique's eyes narrowed. "But not yours, is it?"

"No."

"You know, in my modeling days, I met quite a few interesting people."

"Yeah?" Sara fussed with the hem of her shirt, pulling it down, smoothing out a few non-existent wrinkles.

"Yeah. One of those is an expert at private investigation. I can make a call, get you in touch—"

The knot in Sara's stomach loosened. "Thank you," she said. "But I think I'd like to try and keep the past where it belongs."

A beat of quiet passed, then Monique murmured a soft, "I understand." She tilted her head toward the hall, voice raising and growing decidedly chipper. "Now let's go eat. Spence has the start tonight, and I want to watch my man skate."

"Brit's not playing?" Mira asked as she ran back toward them. "Aw, man!"

"Don't tell her father she said that, okay?" Monique said, though her eyes were filled with laughter.

"Deal." She took a breath, wanting to force out the tension that had invaded from the seriousness of the last few moments. "Does

Spence know that Brit is her favorite?" She nodded at the plush toy that Mira held.

"Oh yeah."

Sara and Monique both burst into giggles. They were still laughing when they sat down with bowls of rice, chicken, and veggies at the coffee table in front of the TV.

"It's not fancy," Monique said, passing her a fork and napkin, "but it's kind of a tradition."

"I think it's perfect."

As was the rest of the night. Mira cheered for the team between bites of food, coaxed Sara to read a few more chapters during intermission—a clear ploy to get out of doing the dishes that both she and her mom knew and ignored—and conked out halfway through the second period.

At intermission, Monique carried her daughter to her room while Sara washed up the rest of the plates and stacked them in the dishwasher.

"You're not driving, right?"

"No, Pascal is." She frowned. Out of sight, out of mind. She'd forgotten about the bodyguard hiding in the shadows. "He's around . . . somewhere."

"The security guy?"

Sara nodded. "He's really good at his job." Her lips twitched. "Almost too—"

"Good," Monique finished with her. "Yeah, I'm friends with the wife of his normal client."

"You're friends with *Devon Scott's* wife?" she asked then winced, because the question had almost been a shriek.

Monique smirked. "Yes. Becca is super cool."

Sara's cheeks went scorching hot. "Sorry, I'm a little star-struck. Mike mentioned that he used to play for the team, but he's just . . ." She rolled her eyes at herself. "I know I'm being ridiculous and yet those abs—"

"Gorgeous," Monique agreed. "One perk of being a hockey wife is the hot scenery."

They both broke down into giggles again.

When they finally got themselves under control, Monique asked, "How about a glass of wine?"

"Wine is everything," Sara said.

"Dork." Monique pulled out a corkscrew and a bottle of chardonnay.

A shrug. "That's a true story."

Laughing, she nodded at the screen. "Go on and sit. Your guy is on TV. Better enjoy him."

"You too," Sara teased. "*Your* guy is playing his ass off."

"Brit needed the break with so many games on the schedule. She'll be back on it tomorrow." Monique shrugged and poured two glasses. "Such is the life of a backup. Always the bridesmaid."

"Is it really bad?" Sara took the wine over to the coffee table.

"No. I mean, he wants to play, but he also knows his role for the team. His is as important as anyone's."

Sara nodded. Sometimes it wasn't the most well-known player who made the biggest difference.

"Just like I know where to hide my brownie stash so that little— and big—fingers won't find them." Monique held up a plate filled with gooey black squares.

Sara lifted her wine glass in a toast. "You're a genius."

"Hell yeah, I am," Monique said, shoving a brownie in her mouth and setting the plate on the table.

There might have only been eight minutes left in the period, but she and Monique still managed to pack away that plate of chocolate as well as the entire bottle of wine. And when the game ended—in an overtime win, yes!—they were pleasantly tipsy.

"Let's do this again, sometime," Monique said, hugging Sara. Her caramel cheeks held the slightest flush, and her breath smelled like wine.

Not that Sara was in any better state. Her face was hot, probably red as a tomato, and her head was pleasantly muddled. Wine was good for her stress. Look at that.

"Definitely," she said, squeezing back and turning toward the car.

Oh, crap. She should have called Pascal.

Except that he materialized out of thin air, making the two of them squeak with shock. "Stop doing that," she said.

His lips twitched as he stepped into the light of the porch. "'I'm very, very sneaky.'"

Sara tilted her head to the side, studying him. "Did you really just quote an Adam Sandler movie to me?"

He didn't answer, just turned to Monique and said, "Lock up. I'll escort Ms. Jetty home."

Monique dipped to lock eyes with Sara and said, mock whisper, "He did quote Adam Sandler."

"I knew it! The line was from—"

"*Mr. Deeds.*"

"Terrible movie," Sara said.

"Horrible," agreed Monique. "But I still loved it."

"Me too!"

And cue more giggles. With a sigh, Pascal gently pushed Monique back across the threshold and closed the front door. "Lock up," he said loudly.

The deadbolt slid into place. "Movie marathon. Your house. Thursday." Her voice was muffled.

"Deal," Sara said, talking with enough volume to be heard through the wood. "But what about Mira?"

She could always bring her.

"She gave you the go-ahead for the nickname? Dang girl. I don't even have that right."

They both snickered, and Pascal cleared his throat. With emphasis.

"Mirabel is at her grandma's that night."

"Then it's a date."

"Great," muttered Pascal.

"Night, Sara!"

"Night," she called and turned for the car.

Pascal beat her there, opening the door and making sure she was buckled in before he closed it. They were almost home before she came out of her pleasant, muddled, wine-chocolate fog to say, "Thank you. For bringing me."

He shrugged. "It's nothing."

"Except it's something to me."

His eyes flicked to hers for a second then back to the road. "I understand." A pause. "And I'm happy you have a friend."

They drove the rest of the way home in silence. They slid through the gate almost unobstructed—definitely less paparazzi—and he walked her to the door, making her wait in the entry while he did a sweep of the house.

Once he'd gone, she changed into her pajamas and fell into bed.

It felt like only seconds had passed before hands were shaking her awake. "Mike?" she asked, bleary-eyed.

"No," a female voice said. "I'm not Mike."

THIRTY-SIX

Mike

FINALLY, the Gold had won two games in a row. Mike and the rest of the team breathed a sigh of relief. They'd been ahead by a goal early in the game, but had given up the lead late in the second.

That second period had been a clusterfuck of epic proportions. The only good part had been the team rebounding.

First Blue had tied the game, and then Blane had gotten the overtime winner.

And finally, they were back on track again.

He sent a text to Sara, an ooey, gooey message that the guys would give him crap for. She wouldn't get it until the morning, but he wanted the first thing she saw when she woke up to be him. Or, well, his thoughts of her.

Whipped, and he didn't give a damn.

Slipping on his suit jacket, he followed Brit and Stefan out of the locker room and through the maze-like hallways beneath the arena. They stepped out into the parking lot and boarded the bus, the drone from the paparazzi basically nonexistent here in Southern California.

The celebrities watching the game had been way more interesting than mere athletes.

Plus, Sara was at home and not the arena, so the buzz around the team had dropped significantly.

Which was the singular good thing about being away from her.

Maybe the lack of a photo op would make for more peace when he got back.

The drive to the hotel in Anaheim was just over an hour, where their next game was, and he all but collapsed into his bed. He almost preferred the old days of roommates, compared to the empty hotel room without Sara.

Then he remembered how loudly Blane snored.

Empty was definitely better.

He tossed his suit over a chair to deal with in the morning and collapsed into the king-size bed.

And even though he missed Sara with a palpable ache, exhaustion dragged him under almost the moment his head hit the pillow.

MIKE WAS SO DEEPLY asleep that it took him a bit to realize the pounding was someone knocking at his door.

He rolled out of bed, wincing at the bright red numbers on the clock.

Five past five.

The knocking started again, and he hurried to the peephole. Coach was on the other side.

And Mike was in his underwear. Great.

Well, nothing to be done about it. He opened the door.

Coach Bernard's eyes were wild. "Coach, what's wrong?"

"Pants and shirt on. Grab your stuff. You need to go."

Mike moved, grabbing his slacks and undershirt off the chair, stuffing the rest of his suit into his bag. Fuck wrinkles.

"What is it?"

"A plane is waiting," Coach said, pulling open the door. "Normal circumstances don't apply to this."

It had to be Sara. Mike knew that. The knot in his gut knew, the ice pouring through his veins knew.

"Is she—?"

Devon Scott came around the corner then. "Come on, Stewart. Let's move. I'll explain on the way."

His former teammate didn't lead Mike to the elevator, instead pushed through the stairwell and pounded down the stairs. The lobby was quiet as they sped through to a waiting car. Once inside, he whipped toward Devon.

"What the fuck is going on?"

"Sara is . . ."

THIRTY-SEVEN

Sara

SO MUCH FOR her gilded prison.

Turned out all the security in the world didn't mean much when a person disregarded the law.

"You're trespassing," Sara murmured.

The woman who stood at the end of the bed looked crazy. Her ratty blond hair was yanked into a haphazard ponytail, thick black liner was smudged around her eyes, her clothes were stained and torn.

"Get up."

Not happening. Sara reached for her phone. Pascal had put his number on speed dial. She just needed to—

"Stop." The order was accompanied by a gun pointed in her direction.

Sara froze.

The woman smiled, revealing as many missing teeth as some of the guys on the Gold. "Ah, so you aren't *entirely* stupid. Now get up."

Sara slipped from the bed.

"Put on shoes."

She put on her shoes.

"Walk downstairs."

It wasn't like Sara could disobey, not with a gun pointed at her back.

"What do you want from me?" she asked as they descended. Could she delay long enough to get help? There was supposed to be a guard on duty at all times.

"I don't want anything from *you*," the woman snapped. "Freeze," she ordered when Sara headed for the front door. "Not there. Do I look stupid? Go out the back, away from the cameras."

"Where is Pascal?" she asked, stepping onto the back deck.

"You mean the Rico Suave wannabe? He served his purpose." The gun poked into Sara's spine, nudging her toward the stairs leading down to the yard.

Oh shit. Her throat went tight. If Pascal been hurt because of her . . .

Eyes burning, she turned to face the woman. "Why are you doing this?"

"Boo-hoo-hoo," the woman sneered. "Move it. This isn't about you or your tears. I got what I needed from you years ago. Now I need the same from Mike."

Sara hesitated at the top of the stairs then screamed when the gun went off.

Glass exploded around her as the window near her head shattered. "I said move!"

"O-okay." She hurried down the wooden stairs, stumbling when the woman shoved the barrel of the gun into her back again. The metal was hot, burning her skin through the thin cotton of her tank top.

"You always were a stupid bitch. Too dumb to see the connection back then, too dumb to understand it now." Another shove, another moment of just catching her balance.

"To the back," the woman ordered when Sara hesitated at the bottom of the deck.

She turned for the garden gate. "Where are we going?"

"Somewhere to get Mike's attention."

"What?" Sara paused then winced when the gun shoved into her spine again. "B-but why do you need Mike's attention?"

"Because my son won't give me any *money*, you dumb whore!"

Sara gaped then whispered, "Your *son*?"

"My deadbeat of a son has cut me off!" Mike's mother, Patricia screamed. "Now you're going to—"

"You're not taking her anywhere."

The sun was still tucked behind the horizon, orange and red streaks just starting to lighten up the sky.

But she would recognize that voice even in the pitch black.

Pascal.

He stepped toward them, a gun in his hand. Sara had never thought that guns were a big deal. But having one prodding into her back, being sandwiched between two, either of which could easily end her life. . . and her cavalier attitude disappeared.

Patricia spat in Pascal's direction. "Didn't I already rough you up enough? Or maybe I need to hurt little Sara girl." With her free hand, she yanked Sara's hair hard, wrenching her neck and back and making her cry out. "Step the fuck away and let us by."

"Okay." Pascal moved back, tucking the gun away, and putting his palms up. "You don't need to hurt her."

"*Move.*" This order was to Sara and she stumbled forward, her spine on fire, her hip and scalp burning. When, she slipped past Pascal, she saw he had a huge dripping gash above one eye and was favoring one leg. *Oh God.* He was hurt, because of her. "She's got a gu—"

Pascal's eyes met hers for a brief moment before he lunged.

Sara would have been free if Mike's mother hadn't held tight to her ponytail. But her hair was still in Patricia's grip and so Pascal's leap knocked all three of them to the ground.

Pain lit up through her body. Every inch was on fire. The muscles in her back spasmed and lights flashed behind her eyes when her skull cracked against the ground. But Pascal was hurt, and they were scuffling and—

The gun went off again.

She almost didn't feel it. Then a burn bloomed up from the left side of her body.

"Sara?" Pascal's voice was near. And frantic.

"Here," she said inanely. "You good?"

"Hold on." Rustling was accompanied by pressure on her side. It was agony.

She screamed, apologized for the loud noise, knowing distantly that she shouldn't create a scene and draw in the paparazzi.

Pascal's voice rattled around the air, multiplying, overwhelming her senses. Ten Pascals were talking. Maybe more.

Lights. Noise. Pain.

Then black.

The black was welcome.

THIRTY-EIGHT

Mike

". . .Breaking news. Former skating champion, Sara Jetty, has been rushed to the hospital with a possible gunshot wound. The incident occurred on the property belonging to Mike Stewart, her boyfriend and current Gold player, in full view of several camera crews," the anchor said. "We've edited some of the footage about to play, but be warned this may be disturbing to some."

The television cut away from the newscaster in a prim suit jacket to the footage.

Mike wanted to look away from the iPad Devon held in front of them, but he couldn't, not when it was about Sara.

He watched a light turn on in the house then two figures come out onto his back deck—the crew must have positioned themselves near the garden gate. The video was slightly grainy then the film went into full focus.

"Fuck."

Sara was being prodded in the back with a gun . . . held by his mother.

Devon clicked up the volume. The words the women exchanged were faint but audible.

"... too dumb to see the connection back then ..."

His gaze collided with Devon's, who said, "I'll find out."

A gunshot rang out, then a scream and shattering glass. Sara was shuffled forward, his *fucking* mother the assailant.

And the world got another layer of why-in-the-ever-loving-fuck. *This* is why he'd left Sara alone a decade ago. Because his mother was insane, because his mother was so fucking far gone that she might have hurt the woman he loved.

And apparently Mike had been right to worry.

Pascal appeared in the frame, and there was a scuffle, another shot, and then the camera was bobbing, its shot frenzied as it ran toward the trio. Someone off camera was calling 9-1-1, another helped Pascal restrain his mother so he could move to Sara and begin working on her.

"We'll stop the footage there," the anchorwoman said. "Ms. Jetty is currently in critical condition at UCSF Medical Center."

Mike's phone buzzed. None of the flight attendants on the private jet had bothered to tell him or Devon to turn them off. Not with everything that was happening. He glanced at the screen and saw it was Brit wanting to know if Sara was okay.

He wished he knew.

Clicking it off, he glanced at the row of TVs mounted on the plane's wall. Several channels broadcasted the morning news, each breaking down what had happened to Sara overnight.

"Fuck," he said again, standing and shoving his hands into his hair. He gripped the back of his neck and paced the aisle, panic in every single cell.

A plane ride was the fastest way home. He got that. He just needed to be there already.

"She's alive, man," Devon said. "And Monique is by her side. Rebecca too."

"I shouldn't have left her."

"You couldn't—"

"Did you not see that the woman who shot her was my *mother?* Fuck, I can't even begin to describe the levels of how fucked up my life is. The person who delivered me into this world tried to kill the person I love the most."

"It's not your mother. It's the drugs."

Mike froze then dropped his head.

Devon knew all about a parent battling addiction. His father had been hooked on OxyContin, but *his* father also hadn't tried to kill anyone.

"That's not a fucking excuse!" he yelled at the floor, wrenching a hand through his hair, practically yanking it from his scalp. "My *mother* did it. *She* released the pictures, hurt Sara, and—"

Fuck. His voice broke. His knees gave out.

He buried his face in his hands, totally not giving a shit that tears were leaking between his fingers.

Devon placed a hand on his shoulder, squeezed hard. "You're right. The only person my dad hurt was himself, physically anyway. I'm sorry." A pause. "I thought Pascal would be— Well, I don't know how your mother got the jump on him."

Mike blew out a shuddering breath, lifted his head. "He was bleeding."

"Yeah, he was."

"It wasn't Pascal's fault." He stood with shaking legs, walked to the couch, and sank down.

Devon didn't respond. Rather, he was looking at his phone. "Update from Rebecca. They're taking Sara into surgery."

The flight attendant who had been standing—hiding—in the galley came out. "If you could buckle in, the captain has just informed me that we'll be landing soon."

He nodded and clicked his seatbelt, but his mind was on Devon's words.

Surgery.

What if he didn't get the chance to say good-bye?

THIRTY-NINE

Sara

SARA'S EYES were glued shut. That was the only explanation. She couldn't lift her lids a millimeter, let alone open them completely.

Her side burned with a throbbing pain. Her nose was crusted. Her throat dry as a desert.

And there was a warm hand in hers.

The faintest hint of aftershave.

The scent permeated through the air, filled her nostrils, steadied her heart, and the pain dimmed.

Mike was there.

Drawing on her reserve of strength, she wrenched back her eyelids.

He was crammed into a wooden chair, half curled in on himself as he leaned over the bed, his head resting near her uninjured side, his hand gripping hers.

The door squeaked, and a woman in maroon scrubs poked her head in. When she saw Sara awake, she smiled and murmured that she would get the doctor.

Bits and pieces of what had happened began lining up in Sara's mind.

The woman, with a face that was sort of familiar. Mike's mother. The gun. Pascal.

Was Pascal okay?

She looked around as though the hospital room would somehow give her a clue to his well-being. There was nothing except a few food containers and paper coffee cups.

Her eyes drifted to the TV. It was on, showing the Gold were playing against the Ducks.

Why was Mike here when his team was on the ice?

Though—she squinted to read the score in the upper left corner of the screen—they were destroying the Ducks, eight to nothing. She watched the game wind down, the guys kicking butt and Brit making a number of good saves to lock in that shut-out.

When the buzzer rang, the team skated off the ice. Brit was given a pair of headphones, and the announcers began congratulating her on the win. Then they asked a question that wiped the smile off her face.

"How difficult was it to focus with what happened to Sara Jetty today?"

Brit shoved a piece of hair out of her face. "I'll be frank, Jim. It was rough. The team loves Sara. She's part of our family, and it was hard to focus on playing, knowing my friend was in surgery."

Sara's eyes clouded with tears.

"We got an update that she was out of the operating room and in recovery just before puck drop."

"That's the best news I've heard all year." Brit looked into the camera and said, "Sara, if you're watching, know we're thinking about you. Love you, girl."

They asked a few more questions about the game, but Sara barely heard them.

The difference between her previous injury and this one, between her former and current lives, was almost laughable.

"I am so lucky," she murmured.

Mike started, blinking as he lifted his head. But before he could say anything, another voice chimed in. "Yes, you are."

Sara glanced at the door, where the doctor had apparently slipped into her room. He wore blue scrubs and still had booties over his shoes. "I'm Dr. Clark. I did your surgery. Sorry for the delay, I was assisting with a colleague's procedure, but I wanted to see you right away." He crossed over to her and slid the blankets down then lifted her gown enough to see her side. She was bandaged so the incision wasn't visible—a fact Sara was grateful for—but he gently palpated her abdomen. "Good," he eventually said, fixing her gown and the blankets.

"What happened?"

"You were shot."

Her snort hurt. "That much I surmised. I had surgery?"

Dr. Clarks' lips twitched. "They don't call me a surgeon for nothing. But in all seriousness, the bullet was nearly a through and through. The ER thought you were in the clear. Then they realized your spleen had been nicked."

Her spleen? That sounded serious. She didn't even know what the organ did, but it sounded important.

"I was able to repair the nick, but we'll need to watch it. Make sure it takes."

"Why doesn't that make me feel any better?"

He laughed. "Because it's a serious injury. You also had a blood transfusion and will be on IV antibiotics for a few days." Dr. Clark squeezed her hand before picking up an iPad and updating something on it. "The nurse will check in soon. But if the pain gets to be too much, you're attached to a morphine pump. Just push that red button."

A minute later, he was gone, and she and Mike—who hadn't said a word—were alone.

She turned to him, opened her mouth—

"I need to go," he said, pushing to his feet and striding out the door.

"Mi—"

He left, and she couldn't chase after him.

———

MIKE WAS a ghost over the next few days, disappearing when she showed any sign of being awake.

Sara knew because she'd tested her theory.

She'd watched him through slit lids sit next to her on the bed, but the moment she moved or opened her eyes, he was up and out of the room. Ostensibly, he was off to get her a glass of ice or another blanket, but she was onto him.

He didn't want to be with her.

If she was another woman, she might have thought he wanted to dump her. But she was Sara, and he was Mike, and they were like peanut butter and jelly, bananas and chocolate, French fries and ketchup.

They were meant to be together, and she wasn't going to let them fall apart.

Mike came back into the room, blanket in hand, and glanced around like he'd expected to have been gone long enough that she'd fallen back asleep.

That tactic might have worked the previous few days, but she was recovering nicely. Dr. Clark said he would discharge her the following afternoon if everything continued to look good.

So today she was awake more than asleep. And Mike wasn't going to avoid her.

Fate, apparently, had other plans.

The moment he'd sat down in the chair, Rebecca knocked on the door.

"Hey, Sara. You feel up to chatting?"

"I—"

Mike whack-a-moled out of his seat. "I'll leave you two alone to talk."

Slippery little sucker.

Rebecca frowned. "He okay?"

Sara shook her head. "No. I think he feels guilty. Not that he'll talk to me about it."

"Men." Rebecca sighed.

She agreed with every undertone in that puff of air.

"I'll have Pascal bring him back in a few minutes. There's something we need to discuss with both of you." And that little statement screamed of reporting to the principal's office or a *duh-duh-duh* from a movie. Rebecca's red nails tapped on her phone screen. "There. He'll bring him up in ten minutes. Okay, so we never really got to have our social-media talk." She sank into the chair and pulled up something on her phone.

When she turned it around, Sara saw that it was a Twitter page. "I have a million followers on Twitter?"

She'd never made a post.

"Well, you had fifty thousand when we were supposed to meet, then the"—she coughed—"gunshot incident happened, and things sort of grew from there. I've only posted pictures of your artwork here and on Instagram and status updates of your recovery. Nothing specific," she added when Sara started to speak. "Just general things like 'she is okay and healing.'"

Rebecca stopped as Sara scrolled down the feed, half-expecting it to look like her accounts after she'd had the gold medal taken from her.

Oh, the troll comments were there. It *was* the Internet, after all. But, surprisingly, the nastiness was few and far between.

Though one particular trend caught her attention.

"Why do they keep mentioning Mike's mother?" The comments didn't bring up the gun or the attempted abduction. Instead, they kept mentioning collusion and unearthed files.

What was going on?

Rebecca took the phone back and opened Instagram, showing her a profile filled with super cool shots of her artwork interspersed with photos of the city and the team.

"I took a little creative license with this one, reposting some of the official Gold photos—with credit, of course. You've got nearly a million on here too." Rebecca licked her lips. "Now as for Mike's mother—"

The door pushed open, Mike and Pascal stepping through.

"Ah. Perfect timing," Rebecca said. "I was just filling Sara in."

Her gaze flew to Mike's. She could feel the frown pulling her brows together. Mike was paler than she'd ever seen him.

Pascal nudged Mike toward a chair. "Sit. You've had a shock."

"Shock?" Sara asked. Her heart twisted. "What's going on? Why—"

"My mother did it all," Mike said. "Every last bit of it."

He sounded broken, literally shredded inside.

"I—um . . ." She shook her head. "We already knew she released the pictures."

"She did a little more than that," Rebecca said, gently now.

Sara tried to understand. "Well, of course she shot me, but—"

"My mother was responsible for the cheating allegations."

"But—" Her breath left her body as the pieces in her mind began shifting into place. The Twitter comments. And what had Patricia said? That Sara had never realized the connection. Not then. Not now.

"This is a copy of the report from Monique's private investigator. She wanted to apologize for going over your head and hiring him, but I think you'll be glad she did." Rebecca pulled out a file, setting it gently in Sara's lap. "This"—she held up another—"is from Devon's company."

They were each easily a hundred pages long.

"The gist of them is that Mike's mother, Patricia Stewart, met a reporter after you'd won the gold. He wanted the scoop on you, and she was fresh out of rehab, desperate for money and

Hydrocodone. They made a deal and fabricated the evidence for the story."

Sara rubbed her head. Fake. She'd known that, but the proof back then—bank statements, the video of her meeting with the judges, her scores—

"My coach told—"

"Unfortunately, your coach had something to hide," Rebecca said. "A criminal record stemming from a rape charge. He technically wasn't allowed to be coaching at all and the reporter took advantage of that."

Sara's eyes closed. It was even more twisted than she could have possibly imagined. She opened, met Rebecca's solid gaze. "So when those first stories broke while I was on tour—the accusations of me paying off the judges—"

"The reporter and his so-called sources."

"And the video?"

"Not you, but you already knew that."

"No. I didn't." Which had been part of the problem. She'd met with so many people during the lead-up and following the competition that Sara *hadn't* been sure if she'd met with the judges or not.

"Well, it's not." Rebecca tapped the report in Sara's lap. "There's a copy of a check in here to an actress who looks remarkably like you, one who admitted that it was her in that video." The publicist made a disgusted sound. "The idiots didn't even use cash."

"I—" Sara shook her head, trying to comprehend everything.

"And that's not even considering the bank accounts. Easy to trace today, much harder to do so years ago."

"My mother." Mike voice was almost toneless, except for the current of regret threading through his words. "The accounts went back to my *mother*."

"It wasn't just the accounts," Rebecca said gently, taking the files back. "None of the sources could hold up today, not with how pervasive technology is. But a decade ago, they were just strong enough to fool anyone who bothered to look."

"And not many people bothered to," Sara said.

Rebecca shook her head. "No, unfortunately, they didn't. Even the IOC only did a slip-shod job of investigating."

Sara had the feeling it wouldn't have mattered if the powers that be at the IOC had found her not guilty of wrong-doing back then. The public—including her parents and friends—had already lost faith in her.

The media might have loved her as a champion, but a fallen cheater was a much better story.

Rebecca slipped the files into her briefcase. "These will be released once you've been discharged, if that's okay with you?"

"No." Sara shook her head. Her redemption wouldn't come from dragging Mike through the mud.

"Yes." Mike's voice was rough, but his eyes were on fire.

"No," she snapped. "It's not me at the expense of you. You need to think about you—"

"My mother *shot* you! She nearly killed you and ruined your life—"

"But *you* didn't." Sara felt tears well in her eyes. "*You didn't.* Now please come here. I can't"—her words hitched—I can't do this without you."

Finally, he came to her, sitting on the edge of the bed. "I'm sorry. I—"

"It hurts," she murmured. "So much."

"What hurts, sweetheart?" Fingers stroked down her cheeks, wiping away the moisture.

"The distance you put between us."

Regret clouded his face. "Shit. I'm fucking this up again, aren't I?"

She sniffed, but the tension that had been invading her body dissipated. "That seems to be your specialty."

Rebecca's phone buzzed, drawing both of their gazes. "Sorry," she muttered. "And apparently, my specialty is ruining romantic moments." Her eyes flicked down to her phone. "And you may not have a choice about those files." She nodded at Pascal. "Turn the TV to Channel Five."

"Why?" Mike asked.

"You're the lead story."

FORTY

Mike

MIKE HELPED Sara maneuver herself from the car. She didn't complain, but her face was gray.

"Put on that suit of armor, Stewart!" one of the paparazzi yelled, "And carry your girl inside."

"Don't you dare," Sara gritted out. "I'm walking into this house on my own two feet."

He waved, ignoring them as he carefully wove his arm around her waist and helped Sara up the front stairs. Here there were only two, compared to the three in the garage, and this door would bring her closer to the bedroom.

"Shit," she muttered taking a halting step. "This fucking hurts."

"More or less than ice burn?"

She paused, considering. "Less, surprisingly." Then she started slowly forward again.

Fuck it.

Moving before she could stop him, Mike wove his arms around

her legs and shoulders and lifted her up against his chest. The paparazzi cheered and catcalled.

"Let me at least get the do—"

The front door opened before she finished her sentence.

Sara sighed and Mike laughed as he carried her inside, kicking the heavy wooden panel closed behind them.

Brit and Monique squealed from the entryway. "You're home!"

"Yup," Sara said dryly. "And so is everyone else." A curly head popped out from behind Monique's legs. Mira was crying. "What is it, honey?" Sara asked.

"You're hurt."

"Not so hurt anymore."

"Then why is Mr. Mike carrying you?" A lip slid out, pouting.

Sara smiled. "Because he's stubborn."

Mira tilted her head, thinking that over. "My mom says that about my dad a lot." Brit stifled a giggle. "Dad says he learned from the best."

They all laughed . . . until Sara groaned and said, "Don't do that. Doesn't hurt except for laughing."

"And walking," Mike muttered.

"And talking," Monique said.

"And breathing," Brit added.

"And . . . playing Legos!" Mira chirped.

They stopped and looked at her, confused. The little girl shrugged. "When I tried to go into my mom's room last night, she said I couldn't because she and dad were playing Legos." There that lip went again. "*I* wanted to play Legos."

"When you're older," Sara deadpanned after they had all unsuccessfully hidden their laughter. "Now, not to ruin the party, but I'm sure Mr. Mike's arms are tired, and I'm done with the damsel-in-distress act."

Monique and Mira shepherded them upstairs, Brit trailing behind. They got her settled in the bed, covered in blankets and Netflix-cued-up with *The Crown*.

Gentle hugs followed, and Mike walked the girls down. Brit hesitated in the threshold of the front door after Monique had walked off with Mira.

"Pascal gave this to Rebecca to give to—" She shook her head and set Sara's engagement ring into the palm of his hand. "They took it off for surgery and wanted to keep it safe, I guess."

Mike held up the ring, watching the emeralds glitter in the afternoon light. "If I was a better man, I'd leave her to her life. Let her start over."

"If you were a coward, maybe," Brit said. "You guys have history . . . some really shitty pieces of it. But there are also the good times, and I think that if you can get past the guilt, you'll realize those outweigh all the bad."

He thought of those mornings with Sara years ago, punctuated with laughter and private jokes. He thought of her in his bed, feeling the soft, warm weight of her body against his. Her smile. Her scent. Her kind soul and kick-ass attitude.

There just wasn't any way that he could live without her.

She made his life complete.

Brit clapped him on the shoulder. "And know that she's thinking of those good times too. That she doesn't blame you for your mom. That she's more worried about how *you* were hurt from it all."

"That's fucked up."

A shrug. "That's love. You put the other person's feelings first," Brit said. "So don't bother martyring yourself when it will only piss off your woman."

He snorted.

"You know it's true."

Shaking his head, he waved at Brit as she headed for her car, then turned to close the door.

"Play Miley for her," she called. "Girls dig Miley."

"You have terrible taste in music!" he yelled.

"I'm still faster."

Mike closed the door and bounded up the stairs. Sara was in his bed, color returning to her cheeks as she sipped from a water bottle.

"Don't play me Brit's music, okay?"

He blinked. She pointed . . . at the open window.

"You heard?"

"Yup." She patted the bed next to her. "Brit gives pretty solid advice, music excluded."

Mike crossed the room and carefully slid onto the mattress next to her. "I don't know what's going to happen with my mom."

"Me neither."

"I want her to go to jail." He tucked the blankets more securely around her. "She needs to pay somehow."

One-half of Sara's mouth curved. "I'm not opposed to the jail scenario. But I'm not going to worry about it. We've got good lawyers. I'm going to let them fight that battle for me."

She sighed when he nodded.

"What?"

"You haven't kissed me." His face scrunched up, she elaborated. "Since the . . . incident, you haven't kissed me."

He thought, and well . . . damn, he *hadn't* kissed her. Not more than a peck on the forehead at least. He waggled his brows. "Think I should remedy that?"

A smirk. "Maybe."

"Maybe means yes."

"In this case"—one of her hands slid to the back of his head and tugged—"maybe means yes."

Then his lips were on hers, and nothing else mattered. Not his mom. Not the press. Not the team.

Just him and her.

"I love you," he said and held up the ring. "Will you marry me . . . again I guess?"

"I will marry you so hard you won't know what hit you."

He grinned and slipped the band on her finger. "Bring it. I can take whatever you dish out, Sara girl."

EPILOGUE

Sara, Six Months Later

"AGAIN," Sara said, "but this time bend your knee more on the landing."

She watched as Mira skated away and then back toward her, launching herself into a Salchow. The girl wobbled but stayed on her feet.

"Yes! Way to go!"

Mira hugged her around the waist. "Can I can play with my friends now?"

"Heck yeah."

With a laugh, Sara moved to the boards. Mira had talent but perhaps not the interest or drive for competitive skating. In the meantime, Sara was just teaching her a bit here and there.

She reached for a tissue, but a hand—a very familiar one—grabbed the box before she got there.

"You aren't going to wipe it for me too?" she teased when Mike held it out for her.

"Shush, you." He leaned over the boards and kissed her. "Want company?"

She glanced down, saw he had his skates on. "Isn't this a little too tame for you?" It was just public skating, no pucks or sticks in sight.

"You're about all I can handle."

One leg then the other slid over the dasher and onto the ice. Mike laced her fingers with his. "You okay with the verdict?"

His mom had taken a plea deal—twenty years to life for attempted murder and a variety of other charges the lawyers had filed. Sara would be lying if she said that she was unhappy.

After all his mother had done to Mike and then hurting Pascal, not to mention the whole *shooting* her and ruining her life thing, forever would be too soon to see Patricia Stewart again.

"Yup, I'm good with it."

"Good." He grinned. "So you going to set a date for our wedding any time soon?"

The running joke between them made her smile. Mike was ready to make things official. She thought since they'd gotten betrothed so quickly that a long engagement wouldn't hurt.

"Nope."

"I'd like our honeymoon to not be interrupted by training camp," he grumbled.

Mira flew past them, laughing like the little lunatic she was.

"Or we can just start our honeymoon tonight," she said, seeing Mitch walk into the rink. He nodded at her.

It was time.

Mike frowned. "What are you talking about?"

"Funny thing is"—she paused when Coach Bernard skated up to them—"I always thought I'd get married at center ice."

Mike's headed flipped back and forth between her and Coach. "No dress?"

She grinned, ran her free hand down her sweatshirt and leggings. "No dress." She pointed at a white swirl on her thigh. "This is enough white, don't you think?"

Mike nodded, his face grave. "Are you serious right now?"

Stefan and Brit skated over. Stefan had the rings, Brit a small bouquet of flowers.

Spence and Monique slowly made their way toward them, Monique wobbling like a baby deer as Spence basically held her up.

"You owe me a really freaking great party after all this," Monique grumbled. "I'm made for heels, not skates."

Sara laughed. "Deal." She nodded at Bernard, who she was only just starting to know. Brit, apparently, had goaded him into getting his officiate paperwork.

Then she turned to the love of her life, grabbed his hand, and tugged him toward center ice. "Ready to start that happily ever after, Hot Shot?"

BOARDING

GOLD HOCKEY #3

ONE

Mandy

"LESS MUGGLES, MORE MAGIC," Mandy murmured as she scrolled through her *Harry Potter* Pinterest board, trying to find the perfect themed appetizers for the movie marathon she was hosting that weekend. She knew she was unreasonably excited about having a party at her new apartment, but this was big.

As in the apartment was the biggest purchase she had ever made.

Smiling, she leaned back in her chair and continued scrolling through her phone. A hockey game was playing in the background, the volume low enough that the announcers' voices were a muted hum. But that didn't matter, she would hear if anything exciting happened, the crowd's cheers would radiate through the concrete layers of the arena to where her office was situated.

Mandy always joked that her office was Harry's equivalent of his closet bedroom—a tiny cubbyhole in the bowels of the Gold Mine, the home rink for the NHL's newest team, the San Francisco Gold.

Her office might be small, but the physical therapy space certainly wasn't.

A half dozen treatment tables were set up in the large room outside her door, each complete with their own built-in cabinets filled to the brim with the best supplies money could buy.

The PT suite tended to be one of the hubs—players always coming in and out, lots of activity, voices, laughter—for her team, second only to the space where they relaxed, ate, played video games, or binged the latest hit on Netflix.

But for the most part, Mandy loved all the activity. She enjoyed the players crossing through to access the weight room, or take a dip in the pool, or soak their aching muscles in the hot and cold tubs. And with the team's doctor, masseuse, and other support therapy staff's own small offices surrounding hers, it was hardly ever quiet.

Except now.

While the doctor and his assistant were rink side—near the team in case anyone got injured—the rest of the training staff had gone to grab a bite. She'd stayed behind this time, nibbling on a salad and taking advantage of the mental break by blissfully scrolling through wand-shaped appetizers on her phone.

After the final buzzer, the activity would ramp up again. The players each had their own post-game routines—maybe a massage or a soak in the icy, cold tub, usually some time spent on the exercise bike, slowly cooling their muscles after the strenuous sixty-minute game.

As for her?

Her phone and those magical treats would lay forgotten because she'd be running around like a chicken without its head.

Multiple players would need different treatments, and it was her job to coordinate with the masseuse and the doctor to assess injuries old and new, advise beneficial exercises and stretches, and . . .

She spent most of her time trying to pretend that Blane was just another player.

"Idiot," she muttered as just his name conjured up all sorts of very unprofessional images into her mind.

Muscles.

The kind that made the spot just below her belly button clench with need.

Strong legs and, good gravy, but his ass.

Hockey players had the *best* asses.

No pancake bottoms, these men—and *women*—could fill out a pair of jeans. She wanted to squeeze it, to nibble it, bounce a dime—

Mandy dropped her chin to her chest, losing sight of the Sorting Hat cupcakes she'd been pondering.

Blane with his yummy ass had a unique way of distracting her.

No, it wasn't even distraction, per se. He had *always* been able to get under her skin.

And that was very, very bad for her.

"Ugh," she said, tossing her phone onto her desk and standing, knowing that she wouldn't be able to sit still now.

Nope, she needed about forty laps in the pool and a good hard fu—

Run, her mind blurted, almost yelling at the mental voice of her inner devil. *A good hard run.*

Unfortunately, the cajoling tone wasn't completely drowned out. *Some sexy horizontal time with Blane would be more fun—*

But the rest of the enticing words were lost as the roar of the crowd suddenly penetrated through the layers of concrete. Her stomach twisted. Mandy could tell, even before her eyes made it to the television, that it wasn't in celebration of a goal or a good hit either.

This was fury, a collective of outrage.

She was on her feet the moment she saw the prone form lying so still face down on the ice.

Her gut twisted when she spotted the curving line of a numeral two on the back of the player's jersey.

"Not him," she said and the words were familiar, a sentiment she had whispered, had *prayed* a thousand times before. She needed the camera angle to shift, for her to be able to see more clearly *who* was hurt. "Not him."

Then Dr. Carter was on the ice and the player moved slightly, rolling away from the camera, giving a full shot of his back and the matching twos adorning his jersey.

Fuck. Not him. Not Blane.

And that was when she saw the pool of blood.

TWO

Blane

COLD.

The ice was cold.

Some part of his brain knew that was an inane thought, even as the rest of him recoiled from the biting freeze. It burned, but not hotly.

Cold. So cold.

And quiet.

Nothing except for the whooshing sound of his breath behind his ears.

Groaning, he tried to push away from the frost, to get onto his back and away, but hands held him in place.

"Let—"

And with that one word, his mind began working fully again. The lights came into focus, the spotted mix of colors of the crowd— mostly black and gold since they were playing at home—as they stared down at him. The arena had gone remarkably quiet, seventeen thousand plus people somehow not making a sound.

A towel pressed to his forehead, and he realized for the first time that he was bleeding.

He winced.

"Blane," Dr. Carter said, and he knew his injuries must be serious if more than just Brian—the on-bench trainer—had come onto the ice.

"I'm fine," he said. "Just had my bell rung."

Dr. Carter ignored him. "We're going to roll you. Hold still while I put the collar on."

"What?"

"*Hold still.*"

Blane froze, finally understanding. He'd figured that he might have a concussion at worst, but he'd had one before, and this wasn't that. Or at least, he didn't think so. He wasn't nauseous, his ears weren't ringing, but the stern order in the doctor's voice made him realize that this could be a lot more serious than he'd first thought.

Fuck.

"Steady," Dr. Carter said, but he wasn't talking to Blane.

A collar was secured around his neck, and he was carefully rolled to his back and strapped onto a board. Then he was hoisted on top of the stretcher and further strapped in.

"Sorry I'm so heavy, boys," he joked and was relieved when the group surrounding him all smiled, albeit small ones, but they were still there. Meanwhile, Blane was trying to play it cool, trying not to panic as he attempted to move his toes.

Shit, could he?

Yes. Thank fuck.

His fingers?

A heartbeat that lasted for an eternity before he realized that yes, he could also move his fingers on both hands.

Relief poured through him.

"Let's go," Dr. Carter said after a few moments, and they began wheeling him from the ice. It was the strangest thing seeing the arena from this angle, hearing the taps of the players' sticks, the roar from the crowd, as he was being pushed out on a stretcher, unable to do anything more than give a thumbs-up.

Up off the ice and through the door leading down into the depths of the arena, focusing on the squeaking wheels of the gurney rather than the curt, whispered orders of CTs and MRIs.

He would be fine.

He was *always* fine.

And plus, he could feel his fingers, feel his toes.

He was fine.

Until he saw her.

Pale, the light brown of her eyes shimmering with moisture. She *wasn't* fine. Though she held in her tears, though her chin was lifted and her shoulders straight, Blane knew this all had to remind her of another time, another player.

She thought he didn't know, that he couldn't begin to understand.

But of course, he did.

"Stop," he snapped, half-surprised when the stretcher actually did slide to a halt. "Mandy needs to come with."

Dr. Carter hesitated for a brief second then began pushing him forward again. "Let's go, Shallows."

"But—"

"Now."

Nodding, she raced ahead of them and pushed open the arena door. An ambulance was parked outside, back panels already open. Mandy waited until they passed through then helped the stretcher into the vehicle, but when she would have hopped back out, Blane gripped her wrist with his only free body part, his fingers.

"Stay."

A long, slow breath. Her shoulders dropping just the tiniest amount.

The doors closed.

Mandy sat down next to him.

THE MRI WAS loud and Blane had a fucking headache. He'd been in the CT already and frankly felt another scan was unnecessary. But Dr. Carter had ignored him and ordered the test anyway.

"You've got a headache and neck pain, Blane," he'd said. "Yes, the CT is clear, but you still have symptoms. You know I can't leave it at that."

So Blane had shut up and acquiesced, knowing that the sooner he did, the sooner he could get the fuck out. But come on, he'd been blindsided by a six-foot-six-inch, two-hundred-and-thirty-pound player skating at full speed. *Of course* he had pain.

Hell, he'd had pain for the last decade of his career.

Something *always* hurt. That was the life—a strained muscle, a blocked shot, a stray punch to the face caught during a scuffle in front of the net.

So yeah, he was used to things hurting.

And now the magnets whooshing by his skull over and over again were making his head pound even more.

Funny how that worked.

Finally, the machine shut off and he was spit out, still wearing that damned collar. He was done, so *fucking* done that he was only a few heartbeats away from tearing that shit off.

Then Mandy stepped into the room.

And suddenly, he was as well-behaved as a schoolboy.

She had that effect on the whole team.

No nonsense but sweet as hell. Willing to always go the extra mile, to stay late, to research an obscure type of treatment in case it might help with whatever injury they were dealing with.

But recently—fine, pretty much since forever—he'd hidden something else beneath his well-behaved exterior.

Because the moment she'd walked into the room his body had exploded into awareness. His skin went sensitive, his dick—thank God *that* seemed to be working fine—twitched, and every smart, funny, brilliant thing—*ha*, perhaps not brilliant, but maybe he could have at least conjured a semi-reasonable sentence—slipped from his brain.

She was gorgeous. Incredible. Amazing.

He wanted her.

Fuck how he wanted her.

But she didn't want him.

THREE

Mandy

MANDY'S HEART skipped a beat at seeing Blane so still on that stretcher. It was just like—

No.

And look how that ended.

No.

"I won't bite," Blane said softly. "Couldn't even if I wanted to. They've got me trussed up like a fucking turkey."

She snorted, the terror that had frozen her in place loosening its grip. "You need to be tied up."

"Didn't think you were into kink."

The deadpan words froze her tongue instead of her brain because the images Blane conjured up with a single sentence were dangerous, oh so fucking dangerous. Trailing her hands down his body for pleasure rather than treatment, savoring the feel of him beneath her palms—hot and hard and rougher than her own skin. Forearms bulging as her fingers trailed lower, wrists straining against her bonds until . . . *snap* and it became *his* hands on her.

Sweet baby Jesus, how she *wanted* that.

And sweet baby Jesus, how disgusting was she?

The man might have a spinal injury and she was undressing him with her eyes, imagining him in bed, not focusing when she should be helping him get better.

Nothing but a disgusting little whore—

"You okay?"

Blane's question pulled her out of the words, out of another place and time, and guilt swamped her anew.

She was supposed to be taking care of him and instead she was a fucking wreck.

But she also knew how to pull herself out of that particular mindset.

God knew, she'd done it plenty of times.

So she straightened her shoulders and released a long slow breath, letting the tension, the memories, the hurts retreat back into the darker recesses of her mind.

"Sorry," Blane said just as she opened her mouth to get back on track. "I shouldn't have gone there." A hesitation. "Even as a joke."

A joke.

Here she was fantasizing about his body, about spending time in his bed.

And she was a joke.

Fucking perfect.

Mandy bent and faked tying her shoe, knowing that she was being too sensitive, knowing that she was off her game because of the hit and the potential for a spinal injury and the fact that it had been Blane bleeding out on the ice in that moment. She needed to tuck the shit away, to get her head on straight and focus.

"You don't have to apologize, Hartie," she said, gaining some distance by referring to Blane by his most recent nickname, a not very original play on his last name, Hart. "I've heard it all before."

"It was still inappropriate," he said. "I wasn't thinking."

Which made it worse. Because even instinctually he wasn't attracted to her.

So. Much. *Ugh.*

"It's fine," she said, hurrying on when he started to speak again and would have no doubt issued another flipping apology. "Should I wheel you out of here? The docs were gathered over your results a few minutes ago. No doubt they'll have some answers soon."

"Yeah." His eyes flicked over to meet hers as she grabbed on to the gurney and started pushing him out of the MRI suite. "What do they think?" he asked.

She almost made an offhand joke. The MRI was a simple precaution at this point. The concussion protocol had been administered, and Blane had passed. The CT was clear, as were the X-rays. Dr. Carter was just crossing every T and dotting every I.

But it occurred to her that Blane might not know that.

He'd been so calm and . . . himself—agreeable, steady, clear-headed—that Mandy hadn't recognized that he was holding on to some fear.

Rightfully so, of course.

The collision had been a big one, and any loss of consciousness was serious. Plus, he had a two-inch gash on his cheek that had required both internal and external sutures.

So he might seem fine, and his body might *be* fine, but that didn't mean he'd come out of this completely unscathed.

"Gabe thinks you're clear, last I heard," she said and brushed a finger over his uncut cheekbone. It wasn't unmarred, however. A huge bruise was forming, all swathes of blue and black and purple. Not pretty, but standard hockey fare. "Minus the shiner you'll be sporting for the next while."

The little wrinkle that had pulled his brows down and together smoothed out. "Yeah?" he asked, lips twitching. "So how tough does it make me look?"

She rolled her eyes. "*So* tough."

He chuckled. "That's what I thought."

The gurney squeaked as she steered it around the final corner and tucked it into the private room they'd commandeered for him.

And so now what?

They were alone—the nurses with other patients, the doctors analyzing test results. The lights were dim, only half having been switched on in deference to Blane's headache, and there was little foot traffic thanks to the Gold's security having locked down this end of the hall.

No rogue photographers would find their way in and snap a pic of him like this—immobile and helpless and incapacitated. They'd learned from before. From—

Dammit. No.

This wasn't like—

"How are the toes?" she asked and if it sounded mostly desperate, that's because she *was* desperate.

To excise the memories, to forget it had happened at all.

Blane frowned, studying her for a moment. He tried to catch her gaze, to get her eyes to meet his, but she couldn't let that happen. Mandy had a terrible poker face and her emotions always read like subtitles across her expression. There wasn't a chance she'd let them tangle with his. Not when he read too much.

"Toes are fine," he finally said after she'd spent far too long examining his stitches and the bruising on his cheek.

She nodded, all business, before smoothing several wrinkles out of the sheet covering the gurney. "And the fingers?"

Blane wiggled the digits in question. "Cooperating."

"No weakness?" she asked, checking his pulse.

"No." A pause. "Mandy."

"And the headache—?"

"*Mandy.*"

His tone made her jump, made her eyes flash to his, despite her best efforts. *Dammit.*

Her questions came rapid-fire, attempting to distract. "No headache, then? How's your pain level otherwise? Is it manageable?"

Somehow his fingers found hers. He was strapped to a stretcher, still in a collar, and his fingers managed to lace with hers.

"I'm fine, sweetheart," he said gently. "This isn't like—"

He broke off, squeezed her hand.

Tears flooded her eyes, and her throat went tight. But she couldn't cry. *She couldn't.*

"I'm fine," she said and though it sounded wobbly, at least she held back the waterworks. "*You're* fi—"

The door opened with a screech and she straightened, tugging at her fingers.

Blane didn't let them go.

Shit. Shit. *Sh*—She dropped her shoulders and left her hand in his, letting herself take this moment of comfort. She could give herself, give *him* this and still stay safe.

"Good news," Dr. Carter said as he strode into the room, the collective of other doctors on his heels. "The CT is clear. We'll take the collar off, run a few more tests, and I'll need to reevaluate you in the morning."

"Tomorrow's game?" Blane asked. "I'll be able to play, right?"

Mandy's fingers tightened. "No."

Dr. Carter walked around the gurney and gestured for her to help him with the collar. "Mandy is right. No activity for twenty-four hours minimum. You'll miss at least one game, more if you're still symptomatic."

"But I don't have a concussion—"

"At this moment, things are pointing to that," she said, removing the brace from around his neck. "Brains are tricky, yes? And you only have one, so listen to Dr. Carter and don't screw around with it."

A few coughs from the peanut gallery reminded her that she wasn't at the arena, safely ensconced in her half dozen treatment beds.

She winced. This wasn't her domain, and she shouldn't be taking over.

"Sorry," she murmured.

"No," Gabe said and he moved around the foot of the bed to give her arm a squeeze. "You're right." Together they helped Blane sit up. "Tomorrow we'll do another evaluation and go from there. That was a big collision. Minimally, you'll miss a game or two."

Mandy knew what Blane was thinking. On one hand, it was early in the season so this type of injury wouldn't necessarily be a setback to playoff hopes.

But on the other, the Gold was a young team and any time one of their veterans missed games, the whole roster suffered.

He was a critical part of their offense *and* the current leading scorer.

It wouldn't be easy to replace him.

"No negotiations," she said, stuffing a pillow behind his back. "But know you'll be of far better use to the team when you're healthy."

He sighed, frustration evident in the lines of his face. "Yeah."

"Great." Gabe snapped up the railing on the bed and stepped back. "Let me get a few things in order on the hospital side and we'll get you out of here."

Mandy followed him out of the room, eager to escape both her memories and her body's reaction to Blane. He'd been cut out of his equipment—jersey sliced, shoulder pads in pieces, hockey pants and socks shredded. The only things that had escaped unscathed were his shin guards and his gloves. But because he *had* been stripped down, he had far too much skin showing for her comfort.

What was it about Blane that made it so she couldn't distance herself? Why couldn't he just be another player?

"I'll Uber to my car at the arena," she said once they were in the hall and the rest of the doctors had gone off to take care of other patients. "Make sure everything is good there and come back to pick you up. I'm guessing you'll be done by then?"

He was glancing down at his phone, a frown on his face.

"What is it?" she asked. "Dr. Carter?"

He looked up, made a face. "Gabe," he said. "There's too much of this *Dr. Carter* nonsense going around already."

One half of her mouth tipped up. "Well, you *are* a doctor."

"Why did I hire you again?"

The familiar rapport brought her back into herself.

"Because I'm the best?"

He snorted. "True. But you should still call me Gabe."

She bumped her shoulder with his. "I *could,* except I have this thing with authority, and calling my boss by his first name is just too weird."

"*You're* weird. And a liar."

"Nailed it," she joked, tapping her nose. "Now, what's up with *that,* Gabe?" She nodded at his phone.

"Blue's down in X-ray. Possible broken hand."

"Shit."

"Yeah."

When it rained in professional sports, it tended to pour. "I'll get my car, check on the crew, and make sure Blane gets home." She pulled out her own phone and glanced at the time. "An hour to discharge him? I'll get security to send him a car."

"Thanks." He turned for the elevators then paused. "So you can't use my first name, but cursing in front of your boss is okay?"

"I'm weird." A shrug. "And it annoys you. Plus, this is hockey."

He laughed as he left, calling over his shoulder, "Make sure you sleep at some point tonight, Mandy."

"You, too, *Dr. Carter.*"

Smirking at the one-fingered salute he gave her, she headed back toward Blane's room and pushed the door open—then promptly cursed and let it slam closed.

Shit. Shit. *Shit.*

Dammit. *Fuck.*

Why hadn't she knocked?

Because now she had the image of Blane—naked, yummy, *naked* Blane burned into her brain.

And it was a fucking amazing image.

She'd already seen a lot of him, but this was . . . all of it. She had seen *everything*. And fuck, what right did he have to look so good hours after a potential career-ending collision? Mandy dropped her head against the door, fingers coming up to press against her mouth, trying to contain the mental stream of cursing to just her brain.

If one word, hell, one *sound* escaped, she was going to lose it.

She'd been pushed and pushed and *pushed*. By the memories, by her attraction. She wasn't levelheaded, wasn't remotely calm in that moment.

Nope. She was a woman on the edge and—

The door swung open.

Her arms flailed, her fingers lost their battle at containing the streak of curse words, and she toppled into Blane's room, her face on a breakaway with the hard tile floor.

But she didn't even come close to hitting.

Because Blane pulled her against his chest, steadying her against the wide expanse of smooth, hot skin and hard muscles.

And then it wasn't just with curse words that she lost her battle.

Instead, she lost her head, her body, her . . . heart.

She kissed him.

FOUR

Blane

CLEARLY HE'D HIT his head harder than he realized.

That was the only rational reason for why he was hallucinating, for why Mandy was in his arms *now* after he'd been dreaming about her for months.

But fuck it all, dream or hallucination or real life, he wasn't going to let this opportunity slip from his grip.

She was small, so much smaller than his bulky ass and so he lifted her, pinning her against the door so that her mouth could reach his more easily. Her legs wrapped around his waist and her hands came to his shoulders, pulling them even more tightly together.

Her lips were soft, her body lush, her moans—

Fuck. She was everything.

Until the hands on his shoulders began to push away instead of pull closer, until her legs dropped from his hips and scrambled for purchase on the floor, until her mouth was torn from his.

"*Blane.* Fuck. Shit. Dammit. I—"

He was hard and aching, and his headache had transformed into a dizziness he knew was less from the hit and more from the tornado that was Mandy, but when she got all flustered and started running through her repertoire of curse words, he couldn't help but want to make her feel better.

"It's okay," he said, lowering her to the ground and holding her steady as she got her feet under her. "Let's just blame the brain injury."

"I—" Her head plunked onto his chest and he took the opportunity to run his fingers through her ponytail.

Silk. Just as he'd suspected. Chocolate brown and silky and *soft*.

"I could have hurt you."

Blane scoffed. "You? Hurt me? Sweetheart, you're what, a buck ten? It's more likely my clumsy ass will crush you."

"Mandy," she muttered, talking to herself instead of answering him. "You are unbelievable." She shoved out of his arms and turned to face the door.

He stared at her rigid spine, the tense set of her shoulders.

Yes, she was. So fucking unbelievable it took his breath away.

But he'd also been around her for three seasons now, and he knew that when she was like this—stiff, tense, stubbornness radiating from every pore—that there would be nothing he could do to get through her shell.

She'd lock her armor down tight and it was strong enough to resist a nuclear blast.

Nothing would get through.

Except maybe—

"Do you think you could find me some pants?"

And there it was. She whipped around to face him. "What?"

He pointed down. "Pants."

He felt like cheering when her cheeks went pink, when her eyes drifted down to . . . well, his cup had gotten uncomfortable, so he'd taken it off. And it wasn't like there had been a towel or a hospital gown or even a suit nearby. All his gear had been cut off him except the fucking cup.

Which had been a cruelty in and of itself with Mandy popping in and out of eyeshot and making his jock go uncomfortably tight.

His fault, he knew, for making sure she'd come.

But whatever. He'd finally been untrussed, and lying there like a lump after everyone had gone wasn't going to make anything better.

So he'd gotten up in search of clothes or a gown and to get rid of the fucking cup already.

Unfortunately, he'd also given Mandy an unintentional eyeful.

After spending a lot of his life in locker rooms, nudity was just what it was. He wasn't embarrassed or shy in the least.

But when Mandy looked at him like he was a gallon of Ben and Jerry's and she was the spoon . . . yeah, he liked *that* a lot.

She coughed, eyes flicking back down and up again. He'd covered himself with his hands because he was a fucking gentleman. *Ha.* Fine. But at least he was trying, right?

"P-pants?" she asked.

He grinned.

"Yes, please. I'd like to walk out of here without creating the next Gold scandal."

"I"—she licked her lips, and his grin faded because *fuck* did he want this woman—"can find you . . . um . . . something."

He sent a mental prayer up that the *something* in question might be a bed with her naked and willing in it.

"Yeah. Uh—pants. You definitely need pants." She bit the corner of her mouth and nodded sharply before turning back for the door and struggling with the handle.

"Hey, Mandy?"

Her chin dropped. "Yeah?"

"You kiss real good."

Not even close to proper English or even a reasonably sensible statement, but when his mind was spinning with all the dirty things he wanted to do to her at that moment, public space be damned, it was enough.

She kissed like a fucking goddess and the taste he'd had wasn't nearly enough.

"I shouldn't have done that," she said softly.

He ran a few strands of her ponytail between his fingers. "I'm really glad you did."

"It was a mistake." She pulled open the door.

"I understand."

Her eyes flew to his.

He nodded. "I won't bring it up again."

Emotions flew across her face, too fast for him to process. Gratitude maybe? And relief. But also something else. Disappointment?

Fuck. He didn't know and frankly, he was too tired and dizzy to figure it out now that the adrenaline from having Mandy in his arms was fading.

The pain was back.

He wanted to be home, relaxing on his couch with a beer.

"Bring what up?" Her lips curved just slightly and she turned back to face him, brushing her fingers across his cheek. "Sit down before you fall down. I'll be back as soon as I can and then we'll get you home."

Blane wanted to tug her close for another hit of that pure Mandy energy, but she pushed through the door and was gone before his ass hit the mattress.

FIVE

Mandy

"OH GOD," she murmured, stopping to thunk her head against the wall the moment she was around the corner from Blane's room. "*Oh my fucking God.*"

She had not just done that.

She had not just opened up the can of worms that was her sexual attraction to Blane.

He had not just kissed her back.

Why had he kissed her back?

Adrenaline. Worry. A man's reaction to a highly charged situation.

That had to be it.

So why didn't it feel like that?

Why did she feel like she'd just stood on the edge of a cliff, thought *Why the fuck not?* and jumped?

She was a woman in a man's profession. She didn't fraternize with players or the team's staff, couldn't afford to fraternize, not when her contract had a clause that forbade it. And frankly, she also didn't date within the organization because it was so cliché. Oh, girl falls for hot guy on the sports team, gives everything up for him, and lives happily ever after.

Except it didn't work out that way.

She'd lived in the product of such a happily ever after and believe her, life had not been a fucking fairy tale.

A simpering mother.

An abusive father.

Being told to be sweeter, prettier, *better* so that her dad wouldn't find fault in her, and therefore find fault in her mother. Being called ugly, stupid, useless by both parents when he inevitably *did* find fault in her.

Because he always found something that needed to be improved upon.

Except it wasn't encouraging a kid who'd missed one word on the spelling test to practice it a few times so they got it. No. Instead, it was making that kid sit down and write the word out a *hundred* times.

He hadn't scheduled some extra time on the tennis court when she lost the championship match.

He'd taken every evening, every weekend and filled them with private lessons and camps and thousands of serves and volleys and backhands.

Thank *God* she hadn't played hockey.

She had that thought every single day of her life. Thank God her dad had played in the NHL, thank God he'd been away half the year, and thank God *she* was a girl and had *no business* playing a man's sport.

And yet, she'd loved him, had wanted him to love her.

Unfortunately, sometimes people were only able to love themselves.

She'd figured that it was fate's cruel joke, her getting the job with the Gold, and she probably would have turned it down flat if it hadn't been for Gabe.

They'd met in med school, staying in touch after they'd both graduated. He'd gone on for his residency program and she'd left the field for physical therapy, completing a certification program while he'd slogged through ninety-hour weeks.

She'd quit medicine, disappointing her father one final time before he'd died.

It had been the single bravest thing she'd done, and also the stupidest . . . according to him.

But she'd never wanted to be a doctor, not in the way Gabe had. She was more interested in the body as a whole, in treating it to remove pain, to help it accomplish more.

Mandy *could* have gone into orthopedics, but she hadn't wanted to be in a hospital setting broken bones. She'd wanted to stop them from getting to that point in the first place, to get someone who had been injured back to normal, to help with chronic pain.

She wanted to fix all those things that had been unfixable in her father.

A pipe dream.

That was all it had been.

Her phone pinged, and she glanced down at the screen, saw it was her assistant. "Fuck," she said and took a breath. "Enough." After swiping a finger to answer the call, she put it up to her ear. "Hey, Callie. You guys okay?"

She listened to the rundown and was proud at how much the rest of her team had stepped up. Callie listed a few new injuries, including Blue's hand, and the treatments they'd issued. They'd done great, perfectly executing the post-game routines, and she told her assistant that before passing on the information about Blane.

"He's being discharged, actually. CT and MRI are negative, but he'll be out a game or two, depending on how he feels over the next few days."

"That's great news," Callie said. "We were all worried after a hit like that." A beat. "They've said Player Safety will review the head contact."

"Good." She'd now watched the collision on replay several dozen times—initially attempting to distract herself from the potential for a spinal by coming up with a treatment plan for exactly how to alleviate the inevitable whiplash and muscle pain, and then afterward because some sick part of her just couldn't let it go.

As if watching again might somehow change the outcome.

Foolish.

But that aside, Blane was still waiting for some freaking pants and she had the feeling that if she didn't come back with some soon, he would start trolling the hospital halls for a pair.

At which point, Rebecca Stravokraus, the publicist for the Gold, would not be happy with Mandy, and then she wouldn't be getting her delicious recipe for brownies.

And Rebecca's brownies were the shit.

If there was one thing the women of the Gold didn't fuck around with, it was chocolate.

So no naked scandals on Mandy's watch, thank her very much.

"Look, can you send a car over for us and make sure to include some clothes for Blane—comfortable stuff, sweats and a T-shirt. Everything was cut off him, and I can't have him walking out of here bare-assed."

Callie giggled. "I mean, *you could.*"

"You, madam, are evil," Mandy said, "And a bad influence. Car. Clothes. STAT."

"Yes, Dr. Shallows."

Mandy huffed. "I'm *not* a doctor."

"You graduated," Callie said. "That's close enough."

"I'm hanging up now."

Callie giggled again. "I'll send a car."

"And clothes."

"Bye!"

"Callie," Mandy warned as the phone clicked off.

She sighed and slipped the cell into her pocket. The car had better have a pair of pants in it or so help her, she would put Callie on towel washing duty for the foreseeable future.

Her phone buzzed. She pulled it out and saw a text from her assistant.

And clothes, I promise. I don't do laundry.

Car's ETA is twenty minutes.

Mandy sighed and headed for the elevator. She might be evil, but the woman was efficient.

SIX

Blane

BLANE HAD MANAGED to bow out of the wheelchair.

Mainly because he'd walked right by it and had taken Mandy's hand, tugging her toward the elevators.

She'd brought him pants and news of the car's arrival just as he'd been dozing off.

Good thing, too.

Who knew what his dreams would be like?

A replay of the collision? Or maybe, and probably more likely, a replay of the kiss Mandy had laid on him?

Option one would have been disturbing, but option two would have been more problematic, considering his unclothed state and the thin cotton blankets. Not that the pants she'd brought were much better. He was threatening to pitch a tent from her mere proximity.

Think of unsexy things. Global warming. The exchange rate of the British pound. How the rubber of hockey pucks was vulcanized to form a precise disk that weighed exactly six ounces.

What the fuck did vulcanized mean, anyway?

He played with pucks, knew when they felt right, knew when they didn't, but he couldn't explain what vulcanized rubber was.

But he was, apparently, good at getting rid of his burgeoning boners. Look at him go, just one year past thirty and he could finally control himself.

He snorted.

Mandy glanced up. "What is it?"

"You don't want to know," he said and then pressed on before she could question him further. "How mad at me are you?"

Pale brown eyes rolled heavenward. "What would be the point?" A shrug as the doors dinged and opened and they stepped from the elevator. "I'm sure Rebecca would say it didn't look good if someone caught sight of you in the wheelchair anyway. You need to appear strong and uninjured, despite being stretchered off the ice a few hours ago."

The tone of her words—equal parts begrudging and annoyed—had him biting back a smile. "Oh yeah?"

She huffed. "Yeah."

"Rebecca's holding her brownie recipe hostage again, isn't she?"

Mandy's mouth dropped open, and she missed a step before recovering. "What the heck do you know about Rebecca's brownies?"

They stepped through the back door of the hospital. A car idled near the curb. Blane waved away the driver when he started to get out to help them.

"I know that those brownies are delicious. And that you've been trying to get the recipe for months." He grabbed at the door handle before she could, tugging it open and gesturing her inside. If his mother had taught him one thing, it was how to be a gentleman.

Even when—like now—he really didn't feel like being one.

Mandy hesitated. "You should go—"

"Sweetheart," he said, knowing he shouldn't be using the endearment, knowing it might be misconstrued as sexist or condescending, but unable to stop himself. She meant too much—

So not the time, Hart.

Not when she was scared and anxious, and he had her partway off balance.

Not when her shell had finally cracked the slightest bit.

Not when he might somehow worm his way in.

So he continued talking, knowing it was stupid and risky, but pushing on anyway. "Sweetheart," he said again, "I'm exhausted and I know you are, too. I want to be at home in my bed, passed out with late-night TV blaring in the background, and I want you to get into that car because I'm two seconds away from lifting you in myself, and I think we both know where things might end up if I get you in my arms again."

She froze for a long moment, eyes wide and staring, before she released a breath on a long, slow exhale. "*Oh.*"

"Yeah, *oh*," he muttered, giving her a little nudge. "Now, into the car before you start regretting selling my safety for Rebecca's brownie recipe."

Mandy slid into the car and he followed. "That's not exactly fair," she protested as he closed the door.

"The truth isn't always fair."

"Where to?" the driver asked. "Back to the rink or your house?"

"We'll take Blane home first," Mandy said as he opened his mouth to tell the driver to take her home first. She was tired and needed to rest.

"You should go fir—"

She leveled him with a glare. "Buckle up and don't argue with me, Blane. You've been through the wringer tonight. You're going home first."

His eyes met the driver's in the rearview as he buckled his seat belt. They seemed to say, "Don't look at me. I'm following her orders."

And Blane knew there wasn't any point in arguing. When Mandy got like this, she just dug in her heels and budged about as much as a mountain resisting the elements. That's to say, not much and any fractional movement had earth-shattering consequences.

The car's destination was *not* earth-shattering.

"Those brownies had better be good," he grumbled.

"What brownies?"

"The ones you're going to make me."

"WAIT HERE," Mandy told the driver and hopped out after Blane.

They'd pulled into his driveway, a small cottage not far from where Brit and Stefan lived.

"I'm fine," he told her, pressing a few buttons on the keypad so the gate swung open. Luckily, he had another pad on his front door, since his keys were still at the rink.

"You're not—"

"I'm fine," he grumbled. "And I'm getting really fucking tired of you telling me I'm not."

"You're grumpy," she said, trailing him to the front door. "That means you're decidedly *not* fine. You only get grumpy when you're hurt."

He input the code on the keypad, pushed the door open, and stepped inside.

"Or horny."

Her eyes went wide. "Wh-what?"

"Nothing."

So maybe she was right, maybe he was tired and hurting, but dammit, he was also horny as fuck. Which meant she needed to leave before he did something stupid.

Like haul her against his chest and kiss her senseless.

Blane plunked himself on the couch, feeling grumpier by the moment. "I'm safely ensconced like the damsel in distress you think I am, 'kay? Night, night." He closed his eyes, felt her not move from her position behind the couch.

"What?" he asked after a few moments of silence.

"Are you okay?" Her voice was hesitant, wobbling just slightly at the end.

And Blane's heart went to Jell-O.

He sighed and patted the couch cushion at his side. "I'm really okay," he said when she sat next to him. "But I don't think you are."

SEVEN

Mandy

MANDY SANK down onto the couch next to Blane. She was exhausted and vulnerable and knew it was a shit idea.

She sat down anyway.

"You scared me."

He rested his head back against the couch. "*I* scared me."

"But you were so calm."

His hand came up and tugged her ponytail lightly. "It's easy to pretend sometimes."

She dropped her head back to match his position on the couch, thinking of all the times she had pretended in her own life. "Yeah, it is."

"So you want to tell me why I scared you?"

"I care about all the guys on the team."

He moved so that his jaw rested against the fabric of the couch, his brown eyes looking almost black in the dim light. "I mean why did *I*, in particular, scare you?"

Men.

She huffed. "Blane. It was one kiss. Don't start thinking that I'm hard up for you. It was adrenaline, fearing for your life, whatever."

"I didn't mean the kiss. Though it was pretty fucking incredible, if you ask me. And"—he shrugged—"I'm definitely hard up for you. I've wanted you for months, Mandy. You're hot and capable and don't take any shit."

"I—"

His mouth curved. "Just so we're clear. But we're not talking about the kiss, remember?" He sat up enough to tap her temple. "I was referring—clumsily, I realize—to what happened with your dad."

What was the expression? All of the air had been sucked out of the room?

Yeah. That.

She turned away, swallowing hard against the memories. But it was already all so fresh in her mind, had been from the moment she'd seen Blane on the ice. "Your house is nice, *really* nice actually."

"Brit decorated it for me."

When she stood up, he followed. "Mandy—"

"I'd forgotten she'd told me about that." Her heart pounded as she pointed to the walls and inched toward the front door, the need to escape growing with every beat. "I really like the gray and yellow together. I'll have to tell her. Well"—she smacked her lips together —"I should go. You need to rest."

Blane touched her arm. "Look, obviously you don't want to talk about it and that's fine, but I get why you were so upset. I know what it must have seemed like. I just . . . I *get* it, okay?"

The tone was more insulting than the words. Hell, if she'd been feeling reasonable, both probably would have been sweet and kind.

But that was a big *if*.

Because she wasn't feeling the least bit reasonable.

She was flayed open and a fucking emotional wreck.

And Blane being all calm and all-knowing and sensible made

every single one of those long-buried feelings about her father just burst right to the surface.

She shoved his arm away. "How could you possibly understand? *Hmm?*" She snapped when he stared at her in shock. "How? I've met your parents, they're fucking incredible." A laugh, broken and jagged. "My par—" She sighed and the flare of anger that had burst into flames died out rapidly, leaving only embarrassment and shame in its wake. This wasn't her. She'd vowed to *never* be like them. "Mine," she said, forcefully shoving the unreasonable outburst of emotion down. She wouldn't be like this, wouldn't explode for no reason. Not like they always had. "Mine are not."

"Sweetheart—"

"No." She took another step away from him. "I promised myself I wouldn't do this. I vowed that when I took this job, I wouldn't let them keep tearing me up like this." Her eyes filled with tears. "I *fucking* promised."

Blane took a step toward her and she raised her hands. "Don't."

He glared, closing the distance. "I'm going to hug you because you're my friend and you need a fucking hug. Just shut up and let me."

She shut up.

And he hugged her.

It was everything.

His chest was the perfect amount of firm and he was warmer than the electric blanket she cuddled under every night. But it wasn't just his body. Blane was a good hugger, holding her tightly without suffocating her, somehow knowing that she needed that much pressure in order to not fall apart.

Just like he'd known she'd needed the contact.

Somehow he knew.

How? *Why?*

"You're thinking again," he murmured. "Don't."

She laughed. "Are you a mind reader or something?"

"No." He loosened his grip and leaned back slightly. "I just know you, sweetheart."

Her breath caught.

"I know that what happened to me tonight must have reminded you of your dad, and I'm sorry for that."

Shit.

Her heart rolled over in her chest, exposed its vulnerable underside.

"Oh look, Brit picked out the perfect painting." She pointed to the pencil drawing of the Gold Mine shining brightly, the lights of San Francisco dancing around in the background. "That's one of Sara's, isn't it?"

Sara Jetty was a former professional figure skater and also a supremely talented artist, who happened to be married to Mike Stewart, one of the Gold's defensemen. The thought of Sara actually made Mandy feel a little guilty. Sara's upbringing had been tough—she'd been betrayed by both her coaches and her family—and the media shit storm that had followed was almost unthinkable.

Sara had had it way tougher than Mandy.

Which meant she needed to buck up.

Blane huffed at her obvious avoidance. "We don't have to talk about it. But I do just want to say I'm sorry it happened. I'm sorry you were hurt." He nudged her toward the front door. "Now *and* then."

She dropped her chin to her chest, equal parts won over and annoyed. "Tell me again, why do you have to be so perfect?"

He opened the front door. "It's a skill I've honed over many years."

The sound that came out of her throat was half appreciation, half disgust.

"Now, go home and get some sleep." He leaned down and whispered in her ear. "And maybe dream about that kiss." His lips brushed her skin, made her shiver. "I know I will."

Her jaw dropped open, but he simply nudged her in the direction of the car and closed the door.

She was in a fog the entire way to her apartment.

And Blane was right. She did dream about the kiss.

But she also had nightmares about all the ways that sort of kiss could go wrong.

EIGHT

Blane

BLANE WATCHED the game from a box and tried really hard to keep his expression neutral as he watched his teammates struggle on the ice below.

He knew this was the right call, not playing, but that didn't make it any easier.

He should be down there.

Fuck.

Wincing when a bolt of pain shot down his neck, he forced himself to relax and really study the boys. Maybe he couldn't play, but he could at least be useful by finding a hole in their system or something that could be used against the other team.

He'd been evaluated that morning and while his spine was fine and he wasn't showing any further signs of a concussion, his neck was seriously fucked up.

The muscles were in a permanent state of spasm, and the pain was radiating down to his shoulder. He could barely turn to the right, let alone shoot a puck or take a hit.

And he was wearing a fucking suit.

They were a necessary evil in his profession, but he still hated them. Give him shoulder pads any day of the week over a button-down and a tie moonlighting as a noose.

Okay, fine. They weren't *that* bad. But they also weren't a Gold jersey.

Especially when his team was down on the ice trying to grind out a victory against the number one squad in the league.

Not thinking, he brought a hand up to the collar of his shirt, tugging slightly to loosen his tie and then cursing under his breath when the movement made pain flare down the entire right side of his body.

"Freeze."

Mandy.

He glanced behind him and couldn't hold back his grimace. Shit. *Note to self, don't turn fast and don't move the entire right side of your body.*

"I said freeze, you big lug," she muttered. "Not move."

"Then don't sneak up on people," he grumbled.

"Cranky again." She laughed softly. "Men are such babies when it comes to pain."

"I don't want to hear the spiel about natural childbirth again." He gritted his teeth when her fingers slipped under the collar of his shirt to feel the muscles of his neck.

"It's not a spiel." Her thumb pressed hard enough for him to hiss out a curse. "It's the truth. You're just cranky that you're not playing. Now, hold still or I'll have to pull you down below for treatment and you won't be able to watch the game."

"I would just like to point out that we block one-hundred-mile-per-hour slap shots."

"And women keep having babies."

"With epidurals."

"Because we're not stupid," she countered, gripping his jaw and tilting his head one way and then the other before returning to the massage. "I also would like to think that I'd get out of the way of one of those shots. Or at least wear some of those thick ass pads that Brit has."

They both paused and watched Brit line herself up to block a puck on the ice, holding their breath against the booming sound it made when connecting with her shin guards.

She popped back up and made another save, this time covering the puck for a whistle.

Mandy glanced at him, shook her head. "Goalies."

"Now *they're* the crazy ones."

She grinned. "I'll agree with you on that." Her fingers drifted a little lower. "Your shoulder is hurting, too."

Blane went to shrug and winced.

"That's a yes," she said. "I can't work on it here without giving the fans a show, so make sure you see me after the game."

"I don't want to take time away from the boys."

Her eyes flicked to his, narrowed. "And *I* don't want you to miss any more games than you have to."

The crowd erupted as Mike picked an opposing player, sending him neatly over his shoulder when the young gun didn't keep his head up. The kid took it well, popping back to his feet and joining the play as the Gold took the puck down to the opposite end of the ice.

Stefan snuck in down low, avoiding the player guarding him, and got off a nice shot their goalie stopped and held on to.

The ref blew his whistle and the red light came on, signaling a TV time-out. A replay of Mike's maneuver began streaming on the Jumbotron, and the ice crew came out, running their shovels across the surface to collect the snow that had been created from both teams.

Coach huddled the team close and was drawing something on his whiteboard.

Blane sighed. "I'll come down."

"I know you want to get back out there." Mandy rested her hand on his shoulder. "I want you there, too."

His lips twitched. "You just want to get rid of me."

Her mouth followed suit. "Maybe."

She turned for the door, pausing when he called, "Mandy?"

"Yeah?"

"I thought you were avoiding me."

She'd practically hidden in her office the entire time he'd been down in the PT suite, popping her head out periodically when Dr. Carter called out a question but generally keeping her distance.

He'd known why. He'd pushed her too far the previous evening, after she'd already been shoved clean out of her comfort zone.

But dammit, he'd expected something that morning.

A softening to the distance she kept with everyone, for him to be . . . fuck, was his mind *really* going there?

He wanted to be special.

Barf.

He'd never given two shits about being special before. He wasn't one of the best players in the league, though he worked hard and put up good numbers.

But he wasn't an all-star like Brit and Stefan, and he was fine with that.

He earned his place. He'd had a long career.

That was all he had ever dreamed of.

And he'd spent so much time focusing on hockey, fantasizing about a relationship that would have never, *ever* worked out, pretending it wasn't the right time yet, that he couldn't risk her career—

Yes, he'd been in love with Brit for half his life.

She'd lived in his house for several years when they'd both been teenagers playing junior hockey. Blond, lithe, and beautiful, Brit also had a huge heart and was incredibly down-to-earth, and the entire team had crushes on her. But she'd friend-zoned him from the beginning and with her living in his house, it wasn't like he could hit on his "surrogate sister."

So friends. He'd figured he could live with that until they were older, until things changed.

Except, things hadn't changed and Blane had finally realized that what he'd imaged as true love wasn't that. Of course he *loved* Brit, wanted her to be happy, and he'd also loved the idea of having his best friend as the person who completed his life.

But then she'd found Stefan, and Blane had realized she could have never completed him.

He needed to complete himself.

Look at him being so healthy and shit.

Mandy's chuckle pulled him out of his head, her words further so. "I *was* avoiding you this morning."

He hadn't expected her to admit it so readily.

"Evals come with a ton of paperwork," she said with a dismissive wave of her hand.

Blane pushed out of the chair and crossed over to her. "Really?" he asked. "That's how you're going to play this?"

Her smile stayed fixed in place, but her eyes went sad, and that loss of spark hit him right in the gut. "That's how I've got to play it, Blane. This job is all I have, and I c-can't— I'm sorry. I just can't."

He forced his tone to go light, to curve his mouth up into some semblance of a grin. "Well, the good thing is that I know all about coming in second to a career, so at least there's that." He turned back for the game. "I'll see you later."

"Blane," she whispered, but he didn't face her, just strode over to his chair and determinedly watched the game. "I'm sorry."

"It's fine," he said and felt her hesitate before she left.

Second best. Yeah. That was a familiar feeling.

NINE

Mandy

MANDY WENT BACK to hiding in her office. Which was where she should have stayed in the first place.

Idiot.

She'd seen Blane wince one time on the live broadcast before the camera had cut back to the players on the ice and she'd all but run upstairs to the box he was watching the game from.

He was hurting. She needed to save him.

Ha.

She needed to run. To keep her distance because the dream last night had been too good, because the memories were too real, because his kiss had made her stupid.

Her kiss, she reminded herself. She was the cause of all this trouble. She'd started it and so she was the one who needed to finish it. Which meant she had to force her relationship with Blane back into the strictly professional, if slightly friendly, box from which it had burst.

Her contract forbade fraternizing with the team. She knew that.

He knew that. Some quick sex wasn't worth losing her job or the inevitable tension that would come when their interlude came to an end.

No matter that the kiss had blown every single one of her previous sexual fantasies out of the water.

The man's mouth and tongue were better than any penis—

Okay. She was getting off track.

The point being, this job was important to her and she couldn't risk it. Also, there was the fact that Blane would soon be under contract negotiations because this was the last year of his current deal. He was older, and this was probably his final chance at a really good contract.

How could she possibly risk that for a couple of orgasms?

She couldn't.

Groaning, she dropped her head onto her desk. Then there was the fact that he played hockey. The risk that he might turn out like her father.

Wouldn't that be the real mindfuck in this whole played-out scenario?

If she somehow ended up just like her mother. Unhappily tied, never measuring up, lonely.

Except Blane wasn't like that.

She sighed and lifted her head, rolling out her shoulders before reaching for the salad she'd packed for dinner.

"That green stuff will kill you," Blane said from the open door behind her.

Mandy jumped and the container flew from her hands, landing on the floor. Luckily, the lid stayed on. "So will stalkers who sneak up on people.

"I knocked," he said. "You were too busy groaning to hear it." He grinned. "I'd be groaning, too, if I had to eat that."

She shook her head. "You do *have* to eat it. This is straight from the nutritionist handbook."

Blane wrinkled his nose, and Mandy's heart pulsed. The man was way too cute for his own good. "I like PR-Rebecca better."

"Nutritionist-Rebecca has you all playing better than ever."

A shrug. "PR-Rebecca has brownies."

"I know. Now I've got you thinking about those chocolate squares of deliciousness, too, huh?" Mandy grinned when he gave her a sad look and nodded. "They're like two sides of a very evil coin. One will torture you with veggies and the other will fatten you up with baked goods."

"It's true."

"So?" Mandy asked when he didn't say anything further. "What brings you down to the dungeon earlier than ordered?"

Blane started to shrug then froze and clenched his jaw. "Figured you'd be busy after the game. Thought you might want to get me out of the way now so you don't have to stay late."

Mandy had wanted him to come by after the game because the PT suite was currently empty, the other staff off to grab dinner, Gabe and company on the bench. This was her quiet time, but this was also a dangerous time for Blane to be there because they were alone.

But she couldn't tell *him* that.

Not when she was trying to shove him firmly back into the friend zone.

Friends didn't worry about being alone with each other.

"Never mind," he said when she didn't move. "I don't want to interrupt your dinner."

He turned to leave, and Mandy noticed the stiff set of his shoulders, the tilt of his head. Immediately, guilt filled her. He hadn't come down to get her alone or to disrupt her meal.

He'd come because he was hurting.

Not that one of her stubborn hockey players would ever admit that. They might be babies when it came to shots and deep tissue massage, but they were still "tough" and didn't like to show any sign of weakness.

And she'd been about to leave Blane suffering because she was having difficulty separating her attraction to him.

Nice.

She pushed to her feet. "Are you kidding? I'm looking for any excuse to not eat the damned stuff. Come on." She slipped by him and patted the nearest table. "Shirt off, hop up."

Opening the drawer, she surveyed the contents then began pulling out what she'd need and stacking it on the tray next to her.

She rotated to face him after she'd finished, mentally preparing herself for the visceral shock that always came when seeing Blane without a shirt. What she wasn't prepared for was for him to still be wearing one *or* for him to be struggling with his tie.

"Damn," he muttered before dropping his hands and tilting his head to stretch his neck.

He didn't look at her as he began fumbling with his buttons, biting back a curse every time he lifted his right arm.

"Stop," she ordered, thinking that someone out in the universe must really hate her. "I'll do it."

This would not affect her. He was a patient. Nothing more.

Lies.

Every last one of those was a fucking lie.

Because when she walked around the table and stood before him, it didn't matter that they were currently standing in a huge room blazing with fluorescent lights. The space shrank and darkened, until it was as intimate as if she were undressing him in a candlelit bedroom.

Blane's breath caught when her hands came to his tie. "I'll come back—"

"I've got it." And despite everything, her voice was husky, her pulse thundering.

Slowly, she slipped one end of silk free from its knot and tugged it from the collar of his shirt. It fell, landing soundlessly on the floor. She reached for the buttons—

"Don't." His hand caught hers.

"Ignore it," she murmured. "Please, just ignore it."

A nod, his teeth so tightly clenched that she could hear them grinding in the near soundless room.

Her fingers fumbled with the first button, struggling to push it through the little oval hole in the cotton for a long moment before she managed. They both released breaths when that first inch of skin was exposed. The space behind her navel quivered in need and her thighs trembled, but she ignored her body and reached for the next button.

This one was easier. It slipped free and more of his chest was in her view.

Another shoring breath, another button, another inch of skin.

She could do this. She was a fucking professional.

But then she undid the last fastening and spread his shirt wide.

Her breathing was rapid, her hands shaking but still she pressed on, carefully helping him slip the cotton from his shoulders.

Oh, fuck.

So much skin. Her mouth watered, dying to taste, to run her tongue along the hard plans of his chest, down around the squares of his abdomen.

She sounded like she'd run a fucking marathon, and she might as well have with as much as her body ached to go to him, to rub herself against him, to slip his pants—

"Shit," she hissed and slammed her eyes closed.

He was hard.

And not his chest.

Fingers cramping, palms itching, she forced herself to turn back to the table. "Up you go."

"Sorry," he muttered, sitting down and putting his shirt over his lap.

"Happens," she lied. Because it didn't fucking happen.

Or very rarely anyway. And definitely not from just taking a shirt off. Maybe during a thigh massage, but she usually was able to dissuade any funny business because though a thigh massage might sound like a good idea to a few of the young ones, the older players knew it wasn't comfortable. Frankly, it bordered on painful, and that was typically enough of a mood killer, young or old.

Blane lay down and closed his eyes, his lips moving in a way that looked like counting.

"What are you doing?"

"Thinking about player stats," he gritted out.

She frowned. "Why?"

"Because I have a fucking boner and I'm trying to get it to go away."

Her hands froze, the bottle of topical pain relief lotion six inches from his shoulder. "Oh."

"Yeah," he muttered. "*Oh.*"

Mandy bit her lip, tried to stop the sound from escaping. It didn't work.

Blane's eyes flashed open, darkened to espresso by a combination of irritation and attraction. "Are you seriously laughing right now?"

"Uh-uh." She shook her head, chest still shuddering from stifling her giggles. "Nope."

"Oh, my God," he groaned. "You are. I'm in pain over here and you're cracking up about it."

Her amusement faded and she quickly opened the bottle. "Shit, Blane. I'm so sorry. I shouldn't have—" Moving rapidly, she spread the lotion onto his neck and shoulder. "That was wrong of me."

His left hand came up to stay her wrist. "That's not the pain I was referring to."

Heat flashed across her cheekbones. "Oh."

He rolled his eyes. "You and your *ohs.*"

She snorted.

"You're laughing again."

"It's a ridiculous situation." She began massaging the pain cream into the knotted muscles of his neck and shoulder. "Flip over," she told him. "This will be easier from behind."

One brown brow rose and her cheeks flared hotter.

"Shut up, you."

"I'm not the one who's doing all the sweet-talking."

She motioned for him to turn. "Lips. Zipped. Roll onto your stomach and we'll kill two birds with one stone. Erection gone"—she made a popping sound with her lips—"and I'll be able to get some of the knots out. You have spasms all over."

Blane shifted so that he was facedown. "That's not the only place I have—"

Mandy gently, but persistently forced his face down into the table. "Don't finish that sentence."

His shoulders shook in silent laughter, but thankfully his sentence remained unfinished and finally, she got down to real work. Some basic massage since that wasn't her specialty—they had a full-time masseuse on staff for that—but it loosened the muscles enough for her to help him with some stretches. Then came the TENS machine, followed by ultrasound.

By the time the final buzzer for the game sounded, Blane's muscles were relaxed and he was snoring on the table.

Erection to snoozing. Yeah, she was totally irresistible.

Twenty minutes later most of the players had finished with the press and began filtering into the PT suite.

"You killed him," Brit teased, coming over.

"It's a gift." Mandy shrugged. "But seriously, I doubt he got a good night's sleep with all that muscle pain."

"Yeah." Brit sat on the next table over, her finicky shoulder already on full display. She winced when Mandy set an ice pack onto the offending limb then flicked her gaze toward Blane. "So when's the wedding?"

Mandy's eyes shot over to Blane's snoring form before lobbying a quelling glare at her friend. "Brit," she warned.

"What?" Blue eyes widened innocently. "You guys are perfect for each other. You know I've been telling you that for months."

Mandy sighed. "And I've been telling *you* that I have no interest in a relationship right now. This isn't the time, not with my plans to expand my role here, to focus more on keeping the team healthy."

"It's not that I don't want us healthy," Brit said and wrapped her fingers around Mandy's wrist. "It's just—"

"That you want me to be happy." She pulled free, bopped her friend on her good shoulder. "And I thank you for that, but—"

"You're too scared to take a chance." A piercing look. "Work is a convenient excuse."

"It's not an excuse." Okay. Or not much of one.

Brit's expression said that she saw through that lie.

"Look," Mandy said. "I've dated around some since I've been in San Francisco. The schedule is too much to build something serious. I'm gone more than I'm here for half the year and even when I'm in town, the days are long." She shrugged. "And I'm not one for a casual fling."

"Which is perfect." Brit clapped her hands. "Blane doesn't do casual. You shouldn't worry about him and me, you know. He never looked at me the way he looks at you."

Her breath caught. "How does he look at me?"

Brit grinned. "Like he wants to get you alone in the PT suite and bend you over one of these tables."

"Oh, my God," Mandy said, her eyes shooting to Blane—who thankfully snored on—and then around the room to make sure that no one was in hearing distance. "You did *not* just say that."

An unrepentant shrug. "So what if I did. It's true, and plus Stefan and I—"

"La. La. La." Mandy covered her ears.

Brit pulled one hand off. "Seriously though, if you ever decide that it's the right time, give him a chance okay? He's solid. And attractive, if you like the built, super sexy but sweet athletic type."

"Brit," Mandy sighed.

"Okay, fine," her friend said. "I'll leave it alone. For now."

Considering that Brit had been bringing up Mandy dating Blane like clockwork every few weeks for the last six months, she knew that her friend's *for now* really meant *for now*.

"So he's not hurt too badly, right?" Brit asked as Mandy helped her stretch out her shoulder.

"No. It was a lucky thing that he ended up with just muscle pain."

Brit nodded. "Yeah, lucky for sure. I don't like seeing any of the guys get hurt, but it was especially bad to see him. He's like my brother."

Mandy paused, helped Brit move to another stretch. "I get that."

"He's always just seemed so infallible, you know? Like, he's my best friend, Stefan aside of course, but I mean, I've known Blane practically forever, and I don't think I've ever seen him stay down." She shrugged, dislodging Mandy's hands. "It just reminds you that everyone's place in this game is fleeting, you know? It can be lost"— she snapped her fingers—"like that."

Mandy knew that. Viscerally. Had experienced it in her own family.

"I just . . . it's—"

"Shut up, Brit." Blane turned his head toward them.

Brit grimaced. "Shit. Sorry, Blane. I was talking loudly again, huh?" She bit her lip. "I didn't mean to wake you up."

He slowly rolled to his back and pushed to sitting. Mandy moved to help him, and neither of them clued Brit in to the fact that she had not, in fact, been talking loudly. Rather, Blane had been saving Mandy. Again.

Saving her from rehashing in her mind the fact that her father had been paralyzed on the ice from a hit very similar to Blane's.

That he hadn't been okay.

That he'd been plagued with health problems until his death.

That the paralysis had left him angry and hurtful.

Well, he'd *always* been that way. Being unable to play hockey had just ramped up the volume on each and every one of his horrible characteristics.

But she didn't really want to get into that with Brit, not when mentioning her father always brought around the same lamentable reactions. First, before his injury, her dad had been a great PR perk for the NHL—he'd been good-looking, charming, the perfect exceptionally talented but down-to-earth family man.

Which just basically meant that he'd hid his abuse and affairs really well.

He'd been popular enough to have big advertisers with primetime commercials. He even had a movie cameo or two.

And on the ice, he'd been well on his way to smashing scoring records.

Then the hit came.

He'd put on a good show afterward, broadcasting a bit, keeping himself in the public eye, until health complications had made even that impossible.

Which was the point when it got *really* bad at home.

She'd been fifteen, old enough to understand a bit of what he lost, but still young enough to want his approval and love.

It was not meant to be.

No matter how hard she tried or how many A's she brought home or serves she hit.

Approval from her father was not to be had.

But Blane didn't know any of that. He'd just made the connection that she, Mandy Shallows was the only daughter of Roger Shallows, former NHL great to most, but drunken, abusive asshole of a father to her.

"How's the neck?" she asked softly.

"Better." He squeezed her hand as Stefan came over to talk to Brit, then he leaned close to ask. "You okay?"

She slapped a little more pain-relieving gel on his neck. "You need to stop worrying about me. You've already got enough on your plate."

He shook his head. "I don't think that's possible." A beat. "Have dinner with me tomorrow."

Mandy straightened. "You know I can't."

"It's easy," he said. "You just say three letters."

"A. B. C." She sighed when his face fell. "You know there are a lot more than three reasons for me to say no."

"I *don't* know," he said and stood. "But I get that this is probably not the time or place for this discussion."

Her shoulders relaxed when she realized he wasn't going to push. But there was also a drawback to him being so intuitive and thoughtful, and it wasn't one she wanted to admit, not when some of the armor that she held so tightly around her heart was weakening.

Hell, it might as well be cheesecloth when it came to Blane.

"Hey!" Brit called. "I wanted to ask if Blane could come on Saturday. Stefan can't make it, and Blane is more into HP than Stefan anyway."

Mandy glared at Brit. So much for leaving it alone. Her friend just shrugged as if to say, *"It's later."* Sighing, Mandy turned back to Blane, expecting him to give her another out.

That wasn't to be, however.

His lips curved into a smirk. "What's Saturday?"

"*Harry Potter* marathon!" Brit said, one hand taking the ice pack Mandy shoved back at her, the other waving an imaginary wand. "Come on, do it! Blane might know more random movie and book trivia than I do, and that's saying something."

"Oh." Her eyes flicked to his. "Really?"

He pointed to his chest. "Nerd central. I love the little lightning-scarred dude. I can't help it."

Stefan snorted.

Blane extended his finger—not the pointer one this time—in Stefan's direction. "You, my crazy American, don't know what good literature is."

"Hey," Brit said. "*I'm* American."

"Well, you lived in Canada with me long enough to be an honorary Canadian."

"Also, your mom is American, dude." Stefan pulled his phone from his pocket. "And I think that she needs to know that you think Canada is better."

Since this was a typical argument-slash-chirp-slash-threat between Blane and Stefan, Mandy and Brit ignored them for the time being.

"You going to be up for it?" Mandy asked. "We could reschedule—"

"Are you kidding?" Brit exclaimed. "I'm dying to see how you decorated my old apartment. The pictures of the floors looked incredible. I bet the space looks so much bigger now."

Mandy couldn't stop herself from smiling, even though she felt slightly embarrassed, as though she were bragging, when the only reason she'd been able to afford the apartment at all—student loans were a big ol' bitch—was because Brit had cut her a spectacular deal.

"It looks good. Brit—"

"You're not allowed to thank me again," her friend said. "I needed to get rid of the apartment, and you needed somewhere permanent to stay."

"I guess. But—"

"Wingardium leviosa."

Mandy frowned.

Brit shrugged, dislodging the ice pack. "I panicked," she said. "Couldn't think of the spell to stop someone from talking."

Mandy paused, wracking her brain.

There *had* to be such a spell and further that, it was probably very obvious.

"Damn," she said after a moment. "I can't believe it, but I don't know it either."

Blane broke away from his argument with Stefan long enough to say, "I think the spell you're looking for is *Silencio*."

Her gaze flicked to Brit's, who grinned. "Told you he was good."

"*That* I know," she muttered.

"So?" Brit asked after Mandy had strapped the TENS machine to her shoulder. "Is he in?"

"Yes." Blane had come behind her and his mouth was very close to her ear. "Is he *in?*"

She shuddered, turning to face him . . . or rather to glare at him because the tone of his question had been decidedly wicked, and he knew it. Of course, he knew it. She pressed her fingers to her cheeks, attempting to will away her blush. "You can co—"

Come.

Mandy had been about to say come.

The fucker saw right through her hesitation, too.

Except how could she finish the sentence now?

Thus far, he'd managed to turn way too many of her sentences from something innocuous into something very dirty.

He would definitely do that if she told him he could come. Or in. Or—

Got it.

"You're invited," she said triumphantly.

"Yes!" Brit fist-pumped as Blane merely smiled, his eyes amused.

"Looking forward to it." A wave to Brit and Stefan. "See you all tomorrow." He brushed his fingers across hers before walking out of the PT suite.

Mandy couldn't help but feel like a piece of her heart went with him.

TEN

Blane

THANKS TO MANDY, his neck pain was near to nonexistent the following morning and he practically skipped into his follow-up evaluation with Dr. Carter.

"Much better, Blane," the doctor said. "So long as you stay symptom-free, I'll clear you to play on Friday."

Which meant he would miss another game, but considering the alternative—that arguing with Dr. Carter tended to get players more time off the ice than on it—Blane clamped his jaw closed and accepted the doctor's orders.

He had just sat on a stationary bike when he spotted Mandy walking into the PT suite.

Fuck, but she was beautiful.

There was something about a woman who was comfortable enough to wear T-shirts and sweatpants, her hair pulled back into a ponytail that spoke of a certain confidence.

Don't get him wrong. He'd loved women in all shapes, sizes, and colors, dressed up or down or in between.

But women in athletic wear—and yoga pants in particular —were hot.

Or maybe that was just Mandy.

He had the feeling that she could be wearing a plastic garbage bag and she would still be the most beautiful woman in the world to him.

So yeah, he had it bad.

Now what to do about it?

She was into him, that much seemed obvious, but it wasn't like he could push her. This was where they worked and attraction or not, he couldn't risk making her uncomfortable.

So what?

Wait around for her to make the first move?

It had taken her close to three years to kiss him.

He shook his head and started peddling, acutely aware that while they'd worked together for three years and while he'd thought her pretty and competent from the get-go, he'd been nursing a broken heart for much of that time. It had only really been the last six months that he'd been obsessing over her.

Despite her grumbling from the evening before, she loved salads, though she never put dressing on them, the weirdo.

She was, obviously, super into *Harry Potter*.

Her favorite color was orange and she had a pair of bright orange sun-shaped earrings that she wore when she was feeling really happy.

Her eyes were brown, but they were more—milk chocolate with streaks of dark and gold.

So no, he didn't think he had another six months' worth of patience in him.

And he was right back at square one. How was he going to convince her that—jobs aside—he was worth taking a chance on?

The door swung open, and Brit and Stefan strolled in. Blane quickly tore his eyes from Mandy and focused his gaze on the screen in front of him that was counting miles and calories.

"We missed you at our run this morning," Brit said, claiming the bike next to him.

"I don't think my body can take another beating at this point," he said.

Brit's marathon sprints up and down the arena stairs were as legendary as they were brutal . . . and the woman simply flew. His best hope was just not to be left too far behind.

"True," she said, blowing on her nails and mock-buffing them on her shoulder. "You're slower than a tortoise."

He shook his head. "You need to work on your chirps."

"I know. I'm hopeless." Her nose wrinkled. "So did Doc clear you for tomorrow?"

Blane made a face. "No. But Friday, as long as things are good."

Stefan had stopped for towels, and he reached across Blane to hand one to Brit before taking the bike on the other side of him. "Don't rush it."

"I'm fine." Blane peddled a little faster, feeling a bit like the filling of a very talented sandwich. "I'm getting better every day."

"I agree with Stefan," Brit said, hanging up the towel and starting to move on her own bike. "The season's young. We'll need you more later on."

"Yes." Stefan nodded. "Exactly what she said."

"Right." Brit flashed a smile at her boyfriend. "And those are the words every woman dreams of hearing."

He blew her a kiss. "I love you."

"I know you do." A nod that made Brit's blond ponytail fly forward.

Since Blane was feeling like a seesaw trying to keep up with the couple's banter on either side of him, he kept his eyes forward and satisfied himself by simply rolling his eyes. "You two are disgusting. You know that, right?"

Brit reached over and threatened to press a button on his screen. He batted her hand away and then froze.

The pedal hit him in the back of the leg. "Is that—?"

She bit back a smile and nodded.

A year ago, he would have expected to feel bittersweet, perhaps a little sad. But all Blane felt in this moment was joy. His best friend was happy, and that was all that mattered.

"Congratulations," he said, jumping off his bike to pull her into a hug.

"Careful," Brit warned. "Don't hurt yourself."

"Shut it." He folded her in his arms, smelling the familiar floral scent of her shampoo. "I'm so happy for you, Peanut."

"You realize that I have way more embarrassing material on you than a bad nickname, right?"

"Damn right, you do." He stepped back. "But seriously"—he shook Stefan's hand before punching him on the shoulder—"It's about time that you made an honest woman out of her."

Brit rolled her eyes.

"I'm kidding," he said. "I'm happy for you both." When her expression clouded slightly, he asked, "You okay?"

"I think I should probably ask *you* that. Is this"—she pointed between the three of them—"all right?"

He snorted. "It's about three years too late to be asking that question."

"Blane!"

He tugged on the end of her ponytail. "I'm fine. I promise," he added when it looked as though she would protest. "I'm happy if you're happy."

"Good." She wrapped her arms around him for a quick squeeze. "Now, get your ass back onto that bike so you can be in shape to backcheck for me on Friday."

"So bossy," he joked as he returned to his bike.

"I think you mean, so right," she said.

Mandy popped her head in at that moment. A few of the guys were behind her and they all wore curious expressions. "I saw hugging. What's wrong?"

"This." Brit held up her hand, showing off the giant diamond that had first caught Blane's eye.

Mandy squealed. There was no other word for it. She turned to Stefan. "You did it!"

He gave a little shrug.

"About time." She pushed into the room and hugged Brit. "I'm so happy for you guys."

The rest of the team piled into the weight room, filling the space with congratulations and gentle ribbing.

"Brit will poke her eye out with that," Mike Stewart, Stefan's D partner, joked.

Blue, his hand still wrapped but thankfully not broken, asked innocently, "Do you even have any money from that big contract left? That ring could feed a small nation."

"*Finally* you're going to make an honest man out of him, Brit," Max, another defenseman and a total kid at heart, complete with an obsession with video games and figurines, teased.

Blane slipped to the side, looking on with a smile on his face. Brit and Stefan's happiness was a palpable force in the room.

"All right, all right," Brit finally said after a few more minutes. "Let's get back to work, people."

Blane crossed over to her acting like he was going to give her another hug . . . but instead moved quickly to grab her head and put her in a headlock. He messed up her hair before letting her go. "Yes, boss."

She pointed her finger at him, hair tumbling all over her face. "So. Much Trouble."

He saluted. "Sic Dan"—her brother who was currently working as an FBI agent—"on me if you want. But, somehow, I think he'd approve."

Grumbling, she fixed her hair and got onto her bike. "You're lucky I love you."

"You're lucky *I* love *you*," he countered then called to the room at large. "Dinner at my place tonight to celebrate these two jokers."

She glared. "It had better be your pasta."

"As if I know how to cook anything else."

Her lips twitched. "True," she said, her words halting for a few seconds as she began peddling through a difficult stretch of the program. "But I'll tell you why *you're* the lucky one when it comes to me loving you."

His own pulse was speeding up as he got down to work. "Why?" he puffed.

"Because of this—Mandy!" she shouted before the object of his fascination could slip out the door. "You're coming to Blane's tonight, right? You told me earlier that you didn't have plans, and you're definitely invited." She nudged Blane with her elbow and he nodded.

Mandy's cheeks were bright red. "I should leave you guys to it."

Which was exactly the wrong thing to say in front of a group of players who were in such good shape largely because of her efforts in the training suite.

The room was filled with urgings for her to come from all sides.

After a few seconds, she caved like a cheap suitcase. "Okay, okay. I'll be there," she declared before leaving the room.

Brit flicked her eyes to his. "*That* is why."

"You're an evil genius."

A flash of white teeth. "Don't you forget it."

ELEVEN

Mandy

WHAT IN THE hell was she doing?

Well, technically, she was standing on the front porch of Blane's house, an engagement gift in one hand, a bottle of wine in the other, but the mental chastising wasn't because of her gift choice or her decision of red wine over white.

Nope. She was trying to find some distance from Blane, and here she found herself at his house.

Again.

What makes an idiot for two thousand, if you please, Alex.

Then a picture of her face would flash onto the screen.

She wasn't going to come, had actually planned to beg off with a headache, until Brit had texted with a picture of *her* beautiful face pulled into a hangdog expression.

Don't flake, please.

You're as much a part of this team as I am.

Come. Please.

So Mandy had come.

And now she couldn't reach the doorbell or the handle. But just as she'd almost resorted to knocking with her skull, the panel of wood swung open and she was face-to-face with Blane.

Or rather face-to-*back*, because he wasn't looking forward. "I'll just grab it from my car—"

"Uh—*oof.*"

"Wh—*shit.*" His hands came up to her shoulders, steadying her. "Sorry, sweetheart, didn't see you there."

Warmth radiated from his fingertips down through the light jacket she wore, through the T-shirt underneath, straight into her skin. It swirled below the surface, shooting sparks out her own fingertips, making them itch with the need to touch. That heat slid down her chest, her stomach, *lower.*

So much need from such a simple touch.

"You okay?" he asked. "I didn't hurt you, right?"

She cleared her throat. "Nope. I'm fine." She held up her full hands. "I come bearing gifts."

His smile stole her breath. "I'm glad you're here."

Words wouldn't come. She wanted to reply that she was glad, too, but instead all the desire for Blane was twisted up with fear and a need to keep herself safe.

He seemed to realize that fact.

"Go on in." He nudged her shoulder gently. "The crew is mostly here. I just need to grab my bag from my car."

Mischievousness was rampant in his last sentence.

She plunked her hands, gift and wine bottle and all, onto her hips. "And what's in that bag?"

A grin. "News articles."

Mandy raised a brow. "What about?"

"Stefan's removal from a few of the most eligible bachelor lists."

A *few?* Ha. Not likely. Still, these were hockey players, and they could take a little ribbing as easily as they gave it out.

"How soon until Brit guts you?" she asked, stepping inside.

He strode out onto the porch. "Probably from page one."

She laughed, walking past the couch where she'd sat with Blane only the night before and following the sound of voices. They eventually led her into a stunning kitchen.

Gray cabinets, white countertops, a turquoise backsplash. The space could have been straight out of an HGTV show. And that was all she saw because about ten of the guys were gathered around the huge kitchen island, beers or glasses of wine in their hands. They turned almost as one when she walked in, and then she was surrounded in a sea of greetings and fist bumps.

Brit emerged from behind them, a spoon in her hand. "Try this," she said and practically shoved it in Mandy's mouth. "Isn't it good?"

It *was* delicious, in fact, and probably both the reason the kitchen smelled so good and also why the guys hadn't strayed far.

They were probably desperate for a meal that wasn't approved by Nutritionist-Rebecca.

"It *is* really good," she agreed and handed Brit the gift bag. "Here."

"What is this?" Brit asked.

Mandy set the bottle of wine on the counter. "Just a little something."

She'd bought the pairs of matching cozy socks a few weeks ago, after Stefan had secretly shown her the options for rings he'd been considering, because one, they were cozy socks and no one could go wrong with cozy socks, and two, they'd made her laugh, emblazoned as they were with "Do these socks make me look engaged?" Then, en route to Blane's house, she'd stopped at their favorite restaurant on the Peninsula and bought a gift card to round out the silly gift.

"Stefan!" Brit called, clapping her hands. "Presents!"

The guys dutifully stopped talking and watched as Brit opened the present.

"The pink pair is for Stefan," Mandy quipped.

He snagged them and held the socks up by his ankle, modeling. "Pink is definitely my color." He winked, before setting them carefully next to the gift certificate Brit had pulled out. "Thank you for this"—he hugged her—"and your help with the ring."

Mandy shrugged. "Of course."

"You knew?" Brit gave her squinty eyes.

Mandy brushed them off. "*Of course,* I knew."

"Why didn't you tell me?"

She tapped her chin, pretending to stare up at the ceiling in intense thought. "Because it's *supposed* to be a surprise."

Brit wrinkled her nose. "I *hate* surprises."

"Lies," said Mike as he walked into the kitchen with his wife, Sara, in tow. "Sorry, we're late." The guys turned to greet him.

Stefan tilted Brit's chin up to press a quick kiss to her lips. "He's right. You love surprises."

Brit crossed her arms. "Maybe," she conceded, flashing Mandy a smile before going over to hug Sara and Mike

"You're a good friend."

Mandy didn't jump. She'd felt Blane come into the room a few minutes before, her body intrinsically in tune with his presence.

Danger. Danger.

But in that moment, with her friend so happy, with her little surrogate family around her, she couldn't force the armor back up around herself. These were people she trusted, people who trusted her.

She just wanted to relax and not be on edge.

"She's easy to be friends with," Mandy said, smiling up at Blane. "But then again, you already know that."

"I've got my half of the *Best Friends* necklace already, don't try to steal it."

She laughed. "I wouldn't dare." A pause. "Do you still wear it now that she has Stefan?"

"Every night when I cry myself to sleep."

Mandy snorted. "You're ridiculous."

"And you're beautiful," he said, making the air hitch in her lungs. "Now, go on." He nodded in the direction of Sara and Brit, who had been joined by their friend Monique. "Enjoy yourself tonight."

Blane slipped back to the stove, stirring a massive pot of sauce, and something inside her tightened further, the tension ramping up so tightly that it threatened to break.

She forced herself to head over to Brit, Sara, and Monique.

Instead of letting her last thread of control snap and launching herself into Blane's arms.

Enjoy herself.

Yeah, she had a few ideas about that.

Sighing, she forced the *ideas* out of her brain and joined in on the conversation.

"I can't believe your drawings are going to be at the de Young," Monique was saying to Sara.

"What?" Mandy asked. "Sorry to interrupt, but that's amazing!"

Sara glanced down, biting back a smile. "I know. I mean, I shouldn't say that because it sounds super braggy, but I'm so, *so* excited."

Brit put her arm around Sara's shoulders. "You're allowed to be excited. You've worked hard."

Sara blew out a breath. "You're right. I did."

"Can we all go to the opening together?" Monique asked. "I'll call up some friends"—she was a former model with designer *friends* —"and get us all dresses."

Brit wrinkled her nose.

Monique crossed her arms. "It's either this or wedding dress shopping."

Brit made a fake vomiting sound.

"It'll be both," Mandy said, shooting Brit a glance. "You know Monique is the only one we trust with this sort of thing."

"Is she?" But Brit was smiling. "Look at you, all gleeful over there.

You've been trying to get me into one of your designer dresses for months."

"That's because your body is incredible, girlfriend."

Brit rolled her eyes. "I acquiesce to your dress up skills. For these two events *only*," she hurried to add when Monique's face went from pleading to ecstatic to overjoyed in the span of a microsecond.

"No take-backs!" Monique decreed and they all burst into laughter.

Mandy grinned. "Watch out, Brit, pretty soon you'll have hired yourself a full-time stylist."

Brit stopped laughing. "And now we can't be friends anymore."

"I've worked on you in PT for years—you should know I'm impervious to threats by now."

Sara cackled. "Owned. And anyway, I don't see why you're so against clothes. Like Monique said, your body is incredible, but I'm sure it's hard to buy something off the rack. It might be easier to let someone dress you properly."

"Properly?" Brit huffed. "I have T-shirts and sweats. I'm covered."

Monique rolled her eyes. "You're hopeless sometimes, you know that, right?"

"The last time you tried to get me to wear something it had ruffles!"

Mandy chuckled as the conversation went on, loving the banter between her friends, the inside jokes and funny references. She about died of laughter after they'd all eaten their fill of the delicious pasta and were gathered in small pockets in the living room, and Blane produced the laminated news articles and tweets lamenting the fact that Stefan—and also Brit—were now officially off the market.

"I haven't married him, yet," Brit grumbled, but her expression was amused.

"True," Stefan said, holding up a sheet. "This woman says if I marry her instead, she'll get my face tattooed on her—"

Brit snatched the sheet. "So. Much. Trouble."

Stefan grinned then kissed her softly on her jaw. "I only want you," he whispered, softly enough that he'd meant it just for Brit's ears. Mandy had been sitting on the couch next to them, but now stood and slipped away, wanting to give them their privacy. "It's only ever been you."

Her heart clenched, and if she were being truthful, she was jealous.

She wanted that.

Eyes drifting away from the happy couple, her gaze landed on Blane.

He was watching her, his brown eyes warm. Hopeful.

She wanted *him*.

TWELVE

Blane

HIS HOUSE HAD CLEARED OUT. Only Brit, Stefan, and Mandy were still sitting on his couch. The girls were laughing over some scene from the most recent episode of *Real Housewives* while he and Stefan were discussing the latest from Pierre, Stefan's father and also the current owner of the Gold.

Blane hadn't been joking about becoming the latest Gold scandal. In the four short years of the team's existence, they had first weathered sexual assault allegations—the player in question having been rightfully fired and found guilty after a trial—then they had hired Brit, the first female player in the league. After which, the GM had been fired and the board completely dismantled when they'd attempted to extort Brit. That didn't even include the firestorm of Brit and Stefan's romance or Mike dating Sara Jetty, the former disgraced—but now reinstated—gold medalist and the media furor that had ignited because of it.

Walking pantsless out of hospital probably wouldn't have even made anyone's radar after all that, but Blane figured he should help PR-Rebecca out as much as possible.

Especially if he wanted her to make brownies.

"I don't want to like him," Stefan muttered after telling Blane how his father had taken his mother on a trip that summer. "But he makes my mom happy."

Which was said with about as much enthusiasm as Blane felt when he was eating off Nutritionist-Rebecca's meal plan.

"Well then you have to suck it up," Blane said. "He's good for the team."

"I guess." He stood. "Ready to go, babe? We should let Blane get his house back."

Brit nodded. "Yes, we should. I'm tired and you have that *thing* in the morning"—she shot Blane a look that made it clear there was no *thing*—"oh, but before you go, Mandy," she said when Mandy stood as well. "You should have Blane give you the name of his cabinet guy. I know you were thinking about redoing them in the apartment, and his are really nice."

Mandy's brows drew down and together. "I—"

Brit strode over to the kitchen and yanked open a drawer. "Show her the soft-close slides. They can't slam. *Show her.*"

"This has to be the most pathetic thing I've ever witnessed," Blane muttered under his breath.

Stefan snorted before crossing over to Brit and grabbing her arm. "We'll let you show Mandy your *drawers*. Later, Blane."

Brit gave him a thumbs-up as Stefan hustled her out.

Neither he nor Mandy moved as the front door opened and closed.

Then she shook her head and picked up her purse. "I know she's my friend, but that woman is about as sly as a two-ton bull in a china shop."

"I would agree with you."

She played with the strap of her bag and addressed the elephant

—or bull, rather—in the room. "Brit has apparently decided we'd be good together."

"I don't think she could have made her feelings any more obvious if she tried."

She nodded. "I should go."

"I'll walk you out," he said and began heading toward the front door. "I can bring the name of the cabinet guy in tomorrow if you really do want it. He did a good job."

"Soft-close drawers?"

"You know it."

She touched his shoulder. "I do want to replace them, so I'd appreciate it. Thanks."

"No problem."

They both hesitated by the closed door.

Finally, he released a breath. "God. This conversation is the worst."

Her laugh was relieved. "It is seriously the worst."

"I don't exactly know how to save it," he said and then internally rolled his eyes. *Smooth, Hart. Real Smooth.*

"I—" She broke off with a sigh.

"You what?"

"I can't lose my job, Blane," she said, stepping back, eyes glittering with tears. "It's all I have."

"Why would you lose your job, sweetheart?"

She huffed, turning away for a second before rotating back to face him. "It's in my contract, Blane. It's in yours. Fraternizing between the staff and players results in job loss for me and a fine for you."

"That's not—"

"And furthermore, your contract is up at the end of this year. You can't afford to look bad, not when it's possibly your last chance at a really big deal before you retire—"

Whoa. Retirement? He was, hopefully, years away from considering that.

"And if you get mixed up with me, sooner or later someone will realize who my dad is, and I can't—*I can't* pretend that he was all great and good and expound to the media about him."

Her chest rose and fell in rapid movements.

"Sweetheart," he said, placing his hands carefully on her shoulders. "First, you would never have to talk to the media if you didn't want to—"

"I'm sure PR-Rebecca would say different—"

"Never," he repeated, waiting until her gaze met his, until she saw he meant it. "Second, my contract is *my* worry. I've been doing this for a long time now, and I know how things go. I trust my agent to do his best for me."

"But—"

"No buts." He brought his fingers up to brush her cheek. "And retirement isn't something that is remotely on my plate—"

She frowned. "It needs to be."

"My 401K is in good shape. That's the only thing that really matters."

"What if you don't get another—" She broke off.

"Contract?" he asked. Her nod made him shrug. "If I don't get another offer, I'll figure it out. I always do, but I can't worry about it here and now, or I'd never be able to focus on playing. It'll work out, it always does."

She sighed and stepped away. "Except when it doesn't."

"What's this really about then?" When she didn't answer, Blane braced himself, a sinking sensation gripping his inside. "Are y-you not feeling what I'm feeling?"

Silence. Then . . .

"No."

Well fuck, that didn't feel great at all. He grabbed the door handle.

"I feel more." Mandy's shoulders dropped. "I feel *so* much more. It's crazy and it's not even really anything yet, but I'm drawn to you. More than any other guy. Ever."

He took a breath, releasing the handle. "If that's the case, then why aren't we going for it?"

"Because of our jobs—"

"That's not it," he said. "So let's just retire that excuse here and now."

"It's not an excuse—"

He fixed her with a look. "Brit and Stephan are dating, are *engaged* for fuck's sake. *You know* we could go and talk to Pierre, run it by him and find a way to make this work if there really is a future between us. But you're too scared." He bent, eyes locking onto hers. "And you know it."

"So what?" she said, exasperation in every syllable. "Normal people are scared about this kind of stuff. Normal people don't feel—"

"That's bullshit, and you know it. Normal people fall in love all the time."

Mandy plunked her hands on her hips. "Well then, maybe I'm *not* normal."

"You aren't," he said, brushing his knuckles down her cheek. "You're special, sweetheart, and I want to give this thing between us a chance. I want to find out if we're *it* for each other."

She took a step toward him, close enough that he could feel the heat of her against his clothes, that her breasts brushed his chest when she sucked in a breath. "I—"

One more centimeter.

She only needed to move one more centimeter.

God, it would be so fucking easy to close that last little bit of distance between them, to haul her close and kiss her, to strip off every stitch of clothing and worship her with his mouth.

But he knew deep down that if he pushed her in this moment . . .

He *couldn't* push. He'd break something deep inside their relationship, something that had hardly formed.

And so he waited and hoped.

And then he swallowed his disappointment.

"I can't," she whispered, hands reaching behind her as she scrabbled for the handle.

He closed his eyes and shored himself up then pushed her hands to the side and opened the door for her. "See you around, Mandy."

She didn't spare him a single glance back, just fled for her car.

THIRTEEN

Mandy

SHE WAS A GROWN WOMAN. An adult. She was responsible, even occasionally sensible.

So why did she feel like she'd just made the biggest mistake of her life?

Sighing, Mandy plunked her head down onto her steering wheel while stopped for a red light. It was the right call, the *safe* choice, to end things with Blane before they even got started.

This way neither of them would get hurt.

Except . . . it *already* hurt.

She lifted her head just as the light turned green, and as she drove to her apartment, she tried desperately to hold on to the belief that she'd just saved herself and Blane a lot of heartache.

"Ah, *fuck*," she groaned and before she could second-guess any further, slid her car into the right lane and executed a quick turn.

She had to go back.

She had to jump on this chance with Blane.

She had to risk it.

Except, as soon as she completed the turn, her stomach knotted and all of those second thoughts drifted right back into her brain.

"Dammit!" She punched the steering wheel but stopped herself from completing the loop that would put her back in the direction of Blane's house. Instead, she continued forward and then made a left at the next signal.

No. Home.

It didn't matter that the action made her a weakling who was afraid to take a risk.

At least she would be a safe weakling.

"Ugh!" She stopped at another signal, warring with herself. "You're pathetic, you know that, right?" She asked her reflection in the rearview mirror.

How was she nearly thirty-years-old and this pathetic?

Disgusting.

She made a right turn.

And lasted a block before she went left.

Shit. At this rate, she'd be home next week.

Her phone rang, trilling through the hands-free system on her car. The number was one she didn't recognize—which normally would have gotten the offending caller an immediate ignore and block, but tonight she jumped at the opportunity for distraction. Maybe they'd try to sell her a timeshare in Hawaii.

Maybe she'd buy one.

Hitting the button to accept, she waited for the call to connect then said, "Hello?"

"Is there a reason you're taking the labyrinth tour of the city this evening?" Blane asked.

"What?" Her eyes flicked to the rearview, to the car stopped behind her at the red light. "Are you *following* me?"

"Maybe."

"But *why?*"

She heard more than saw his shrug. "I was worried about you after you left. You were upset."

Understatement of the night, she'd been a wreck and not because of Blane, but because of her own hang-ups and all the shit that went along with them. She'd left home more than a decade before, been on her own for a long time. Why wasn't she over her childhood already?

"I'm fine," she whispered, accelerating when the light turned green.

Blane trailed her. "Yeah. Somehow I knew you'd say that."

Another signal, but this time it didn't change on her, and she cruised through with his car still behind hers.

"I'm a grown woman," she said, half trying to convince herself and half wanting to hear what he'd say in response. "I can take care of myself."

"I know you can." A beat before his voice dropped and went a little husky. "And I know you are. Hell, sweetheart, I can still feel the imprint of your ass on my palms, your tongue against mine. Fuck, I've been dreaming about the way your body felt since that kiss."

She turned left again then stopped right before the entrance to the underground garage for her building. "Uhh . . ." Fuck, why couldn't she admit to him that she was feeling the same way?

He cleared his throat. "Well, I'm glad you're home safe. I'll see you tomorrow."

He signaled, readying to pull around her, and she almost let him go, but then some inner force gripped her tightly and shook her hard.

She could *not* let this moment pass.

Mandy might be able to run from a lot of things, but she couldn't live with running from this.

This was Blane. He'd followed her home, not expecting anything, after they'd argued. He wasn't mad that they didn't agree, wasn't punishing her over and over again. He was understanding, support-ive. He—

"I have a guest spot."

The signal stayed on, but his car didn't move. "Mandy?"

"It's yours if you want it," she said. "For tonight, it can be yours."

"And if I want it for more than just tonight?"

Her throat tightened, fear in every cell. "I don't know if I can give that much."

Silence.

Pulse pounding beneath her skin, tears stinging her eyes, she let off the brake—

"I'll take whatever you're willing to give."

"Oh." Her breath shuddered out.

"Turn, sweetheart," he said gently. "I'm hanging up now."

The phone clicked off, and she was acutely aware of Blane's headlights as he followed her car down. She pressed the button on her remote to let herself in then waited on the other side of the gate to do the same for his car.

Two minutes later, she was in her spot and Blane had parked next to her.

A knock on her window made her jump.

Mandy cracked her door.

"I can go, baby," he said. "Right now. No consequences, no expectations. It's *okay*."

The words were enough.

Because he truly meant them.

Because her situation wasn't the same as her parents'.

Because it was about time that she finally started living her life for *her*.

Not for them. Not for him.

For her.

She grabbed her purse and opened the car door enough to slip out. "Stay," she said. "Stay for me."

His hand came up to cup her cheek. "Always."

Sliding his free hand into hers, he waited for her to close and lock her door then let her lead them to the elevators. She slid her card over the sensor then hit the button for the sixth floor. Less than sixty seconds later, she'd unlocked her apartment.

"You sur—"

Mandy didn't let him finish the question, just rose on tiptoe and pressed her mouth to his.

That was enough.

The door closed, the dead bolt slammed home, and then his hands were under her thighs, urging her higher, coaxing her legs to wrap around his waist.

And his mouth . . . good God, his mouth.

It was against hers, teasing and demanding in equal measures, his tongue slipping between her lips, urging hers to tangle with his. Every bit of banked desire she'd been suppressing over the last months roared to life with the speed of a raging brush fire.

One second all was good. The next she was burning up.

He took a step and stopped and that was all it took for her mind to flare to attention.

She tried to slip from his arms. "Oh God, Blane. Your neck. I've hurt you."

"*No.*"

His sharp tone snapped her out of her panic immediately. "Then what?"

"First—" His lips, slightly reddened and swollen from her mouth, twitched into a self-deprecating smile. "I've wanted you for so long that I'm trying not to blow my load like a teenager."

She relaxed, attempted to suppress her own grin. "Is there a second statement to go with the first?"

"Yes." His mouth dropped to hers again, urgent and hot and dizzying. "But I'm a grown man." His kissed the tip of her nose. "Problem solved."

"Problem solved what?"

"I remembered where the bedroom was."

"*Oh.*"

"God, I can't wait for you to make that sound when I'm inside of you."

Her mouth dropped open.

"Can't resist that," Blane said, and then his lips were against hers and he was carrying her across the room and through the door that led to her bedroom.

Her back hit the mattress a moment later, and he broke the kiss long enough to lean back and say, "If you need to stop at any point, just say the word." His chocolate eyes locked with hers. "At *any* point, sweetheart."

She put her hand on his chest, just above his heart. His pulse pounded against her palm. "Thank you." She gripped at the fabric. "But for now, less talking, more kissing."

He ripped off his shirt, reached for the hem of hers, his expression almost predatory.

"*That* I can do."

FOURTEEN

Blane

BLANE SLID Mandy's shirt up and over her head, stopping only to toss it to the floor and toe off his shoes before reaching down to unzip the hot-as-hell knee-high boots she wore.

He almost told her that next time she needed to wear them and nothing else.

But there might not be a next time.

Fuck.

He couldn't think that. Not this time. Not now when he wanted to savor every single moment.

Her jeans came next and then she was in her bra and underwear before him.

Not lace, not some fancy see-through push-up number.

No, this was cotton and comfort and yet somehow still intrinsically female. In other words, it was purely Mandy.

"You're beautiful," he said when her hands hitched as though she were fighting the urge to cover herself. "Perfect."

She snorted. "Not hardly."

He kissed her cheek. "This is the time to accept all compliments gracefully. You do it for me, sweetheart."

"I—*mmm*."

Her retort transformed into a moan and her fingers slid into his hair as he trailed his tongue along her jaw, stopping in the space just behind her ear. Filing away her reaction, he whispered, "I've dreamed about you for ages."

Her breath hitched and gooseflesh rose on her skin.

"Wait—" she protested as he made his way down her throat, but then he'd pushed her bra aside and sucked one nipple into his mouth. "*Blane*."

A quick movement and he'd unhooked her bra, tossing it to the side somewhere in the vicinity of her shirt. Then both breasts were free. He didn't know where to go first, to her nipples—hard and ready for his mouth—or to her mouth, swollen and calling for more of his kisses.

Or lower.

Mandy made the decision for him, leaning up to slant her lips across his for a hot, drugging kiss before gripping his hair tightly and shoving his head toward her breasts.

His neck twinged slightly at the movement, but then her fingers were on the ache almost before it registered, massaging away the slight pain.

"Sorry," she panted. "I'm sor—"

He flicked his tongue across one nipple, using his free hand to tweak her other, not wanting anything to pull her out of this moment. If he only had this one shot, then he was damned well going to take advantage of it.

"Oh, God," she groaned as he sucked on her nipple, teasing it with his teeth, using his tongue to tease her until she was writhing beneath him.

And then he switched sides.

Her fingers were in his hair, tugging, straining as he brought her higher, until her hips were rubbing against his and he could barely see, so strong was his need to be inside her.

Trailing his mouth lower, he kissed across her abdomen, the outside of each hip, the top of her pelvis. Then he was sliding her underwear down as he made his way toward the hot, wet center of her.

The first touch of his tongue against her pussy made her scream. "Blane. Please!"

His cock went impossibly harder, his fingers clenched into fists, every muscle in his body went ramrod hard. He licked her again, forcing his hands to relax so that he could spread her wide and slip his tongue through her folds.

She was absolutely dripping and the best thing he'd ever tasted.

One thumb teased her entrance then slipped inside as he kissed her clit, learning what she liked, finding the rhythm that had her grinding against his mouth and crying out his name as she exploded.

"Fuck," she said. Her breaths came in rapid exhales. "That was—"

"You're incredible," he said, grabbing his shirt to wipe off his mouth.

"Hey." She cupped his jaw. "You stole my line."

Blane's cock was threatening to crack in half, he was so hard, but somehow she made him smile. He was also probably two pumps away from embarrassing himself, so when Mandy trailed her hand down his chest, heading in the direction of the button of his jeans, he captured her palm and brought it to his mouth.

"I need a minute," he said.

She hitched one leg around his hip. "And I need you inside me."

"I want to make it—"

"No expectations, remember?" She rolled to her side, stretching for the drawer of her nightstand and pulling out a string of condoms from inside. "This is just us. This moment. And we have all night."

While Blane liked the sound of *all night*, he also knew that he wasn't about to come like a schoolboy after two strokes, his woman needing more.

Not going to happen.

So he grabbed the condoms from her hand and stuck them near her head. Then he proceeded to use every single trick in his arsenal in order to make Mandy insane with desire again. He kissed along her jaw to that spot behind her ear, he sucked on her nipples, slipped his hand between her thighs, rubbing her clit until she was moaning his name again.

And then, only then, did he allow himself to tear off his jeans and put on a condom.

She was gorgeous, her creamy skin flushed pink with desire, her eyes hazy with need, her thighs spread, her pussy glistening.

Fuck, did he want her.

But he also wanted to keep her.

"Now," she demanded, grabbing for his cock and positioning it by her entrance.

When he hesitated, trying to find just a little more control, she shattered every last thread of it by thrusting her hips up and taking him inside.

"Fuck," they both hissed.

His forehead dropped to hers, and he concentrated on just breathing, just trying to hold on.

"I need you to move," she said. "*Now.*"

She flexed her hips against his, and he was gone.

He moved deep and fast and she urged him on, meeting him thrust for thrust, her head writhing back and forth on the pillow, her eyes shut tight, her muscles straining for . . .

Then, *thank fuck*, she exploded a heartbeat before his own release rose up and swallowed him whole.

He came to cradling her against his chest, both their hearts still thundering, sweat coating their bodies.

"I knew it was going to be good," she whispered. "I just didn't realize *how* good."

Blane held her close, knowing that this was the type of *good* he would never want to give up.

FIFTEEN

Mandy

MANDY SHOT AWAKE AROUND SIX, heart pounding. She pressed her hand to her chest for a second, trying to figure out why she felt so off.

Oh.

Because she was alone.

Her bed was empty, the side that Blane had slept on cold.

"It's for the best," she murmured. How many times had she told him that it was only for the one night? He'd obviously listened.

That was a good thing.

Sighing, she slid from beneath the covers and stood.

Ouch.

Every single muscle in her body was sore. In a good way. In the *best* way. But . . . she wanted more.

And *this* was why she didn't make rash decisions late at night, while feeling emotional about her past. Blane had given her a string of the best orgasms of her life as they'd worked their way through her stash of condoms, but she'd also opened up a part of herself to him, and she didn't know how that was going to work out.

Would it be awkward at work?

Would he just jump to the next girl?

No. That wasn't fair. Blane wasn't one of the guys on the team who dated anything with a pulse. He was steady and solid. He focused on the game.

But what if he wasn't interested in her any longer? What if he'd gotten his fill and was done?

What if she wanted more?

Because, dammit, she kind of did.

He'd held her tightly the night before, resting his chin on her head, each of their heartbeats slowing, their breathing returning to normal.

The contact had felt . . . nice.

Ugh. No, that wasn't the right word. It was just that her job was filled with contact, with touch. But it was always *her* touching the players and honestly, often times she was putting them through some discomfort in order to get them back into fighting shape.

They didn't touch her.

Which was probably a good thing and spoke of a healthy work environment.

But sometimes days would go by before she realized that she hadn't had a single "normal" touch—a hug, a fist bump, a brush of someone's fingers against her arm.

And it had been years since she'd been held by a man.

Plus, if she was continuing with this honesty thing, she'd never been held like how Blane had held her, never felt safe and important and valuable.

He'd made her feel that way.

So it was just perfect that'd she woken up and found herself alone.

She walked naked to her bathroom and pushed open the door. Then promptly shrieked and whirled around.

Apparently she *wasn't* alone. Steam curled around the room, caressing her skin in hot damp tendrils. The sound of the shower was obvious, now that she was actually paying attention.

She'd walked in on Blane naked. Again.

Heat teased her spine. Fingers brushed down her nape. "You're making this a habit." He kissed the spot behind her ear, the one that never failed to make her shiver. "Though"—he trailed calloused fingertips down her arms then forward to cup her breasts—"I like this version of you bursting in on me better."

Mandy's gaze drifted down and her stomach clenched at the site of Blane's big hands cupping her breasts. "I'm sorry," she breathed as his thumb traced over the hard peaks of her nipples. "I didn't realize . . ."

He tugged her closer, until his chest pressed against her back, until the hardness of his erection nudged at her bottom. "I'm an early riser."

She snorted.

"You're as bad as some of the guys." He chuckled. "I didn't mean it that way," he said, half-scolding, though amusement was ripe in his tone. "I was going to run out and surprise you with breakfast."

Aw.

A blip sounded in her brain, reminding her that this man was dangerous, but she ignored it as she turned in his embrace. "What would you have gotten me?"

"Chocolate croissant and a dirty chai latte."

Her lips curved. One, because that was her exact order and two, because watching his mouth form the word "dirty" was a treat in itself.

"You know my order?"

He shrugged. "I pay attention."

"Mmm." She rubbed her nose against his throat, loving the way he smelled, the way the stubble of his unshaven jaw caught her hair. "Well, how about we get breakfast later?"

"Yeah?" he asked, hand coming up to cup her nape. He hissed out a breath when she nipped his neck. "What could we possibly do now?"

She leaned back, waggled her eyebrows. "I may have a few ideas."

"We should probably get to them before the hot water runs out."

"I have a tankless water heater."

He grinned. "God, I love it when you talk dirty to me."

"Soft-close drawers," she whispered, her own smile impossible to contain. "*Farmhouse* sink."

"Fuck, you're hot."

She burst out laughing. "I like you, Blane Hart."

He scooped her up in his arms. "Good. Because I like you, too, Mandy Shallows." One brow came up. "Now tell me that you have more condoms."

"What will you give me for them?"

"How about an orgasm?"

"Make it a double."

He rolled his eyes. "Greedy."

"I just know my man."

Blane froze and she realized her slipup, but instead of letting her talk herself into a full-on panic, he just kissed her until her brain turned to mush, until she was concentrating so hard on trying to catch her breath that she couldn't have summoned a frantic thought to save her life.

"Condoms?" he asked when he eventually broke away, both of them breathing hard.

She pointed to the cabinet and he used his free hand to open the drawer and pull out a packet.

"Orgasms now," he said, stepping into the shower with her. "Dirty chai's later."

"Why does that sound like the title to a bad porn film?"

He set her on her feet, testing the temperature before nudging her into the hot water. "If you're still able to make snarky comments, then I'm clearly not doing my job right."

"I'm always able to make snarky—"

His lips came down on hers, hard and demanding.

She broke away after a minute, pulse pounding, breath coming in short staccato puffs. "See. It's impossible to stop. Sarcasm is just part of my—*oh*."

His hand slipped between her thighs, and she forgot all about snark and sarcasm and witty one-liners.

"I swear to God," he said, dropping to his knees and tossing one of her legs over his shoulder, "you making that noise is the sexiest sound in the universe."

Her hips tilted toward his mouth, so close that she could feel his hot breath mere centimeters away from where she wanted it.

"See if you can make me make it again."

A smirk as he closed the distance between them and flicked his tongue over her clit.

For the record, Mandy made the sound.

More than once.

SIXTEEN

Blane

IT FELT FUCKING incredible to be back on the ice again.

Blane ran through his usual pregame warm-up—skating two circles around their half of the ice, a brief stretch along the boards, a few shots to help Brit focus and to loosen up his arms.

The buzzer blew, and they cleared off the rink to let the Zambonis come out to clean the ice.

This was the time that some coaches would come in with last minute comments and things to watch out for, but Coach Bernard didn't work that way. He'd said everything he wanted to say earlier in the day and, instead, left them to their own devices, which usually meant Frankie came in to talk to Brit, and Stefan gave some sort of motivational speech that was punctuated by bad jokes from Max.

"We should watch the—"

"Latest episode of *The Bachelor*," Max interjected with a cheeky grin. "You would *not* believe who he gave a rose to. I mean, Celina is just such a bitch."

Stefan was well-used to the interruptions by now and he'd

confided in Blane that he actually thought the casualness in the locker room in these moments relaxed everyone so they played their best hockey.

Not that there wasn't something to be said for being focused and intense.

But there were times that too much tension made them cautious, everyone holding their sticks too tight and afraid to make a mistake.

And Max actually had *some* self-control. He didn't usually make asinine comments when Stefan was really trying to make a point.

"How many women are left?" Stefan asked, proving that he was a good captain. "Six?"

"Four!" Brit chimed in as Frankie left.

Mike shook his head in disgust.

"Shut it, you." Brit pointed at him. "Sara told me that you watch—"

Mike chucked his glove at her. "You're not allowed to talk to my wife anymore."

"Oooh!" Max clapped his hands together. "Dish, Brit. Now."

"Children," Stefan said, interrupting them before they could really get going. "It's fifteen minutes until game time. Can we focus?"

Brit and Max made faces, but they both shut their mouths as Stefan went over a few last points and by the time he'd finished, the guys were dressed in dry gear and ready to play.

Brit led them back to the ice.

The crowd roared as they strode into view, lights flashing, music blaring as the team took a few quick laps and then settled onto their bench, the starting lineup at the blue line and facing the flags.

As always when he played, the anthem was a total blur. A few quick notes and then he was readying himself to take the first face-off of the game.

A short blare of a whistle, jockeying to get his stick in the best position to win the puck back to Stefan, and then . . .

The ref opened his hand.

The introduction of composite sticks—rather than wood—meant

that the sound of his and his opponent's sticks colliding didn't sound like it used to. Instead of a *crack* or a *snap*, they almost made a zipping noise as he battled for the puck.

But neither the fight nor the sound actually lasted more than a fraction of a second.

Wait. Wait. Wait. A breath. Then go, go, *go!*

Blane won the puck back to Stefan, and his team was off.

A pass to Mike, who flicked it up the boards to Blue. Over the line and into the offensive zone. A blocked shot that Blane managed to recover and send over to his other winger, Trent. Another attempted shot that was deflected up and out to the netting for a whistle.

And that fast the first shift was over.

Blane skated to the bench less than thirty seconds after he'd started, feeling winded and exhilarated all at once.

The offensive coach tapped him on the back as he snagged a towel to wipe his visor.

"Nice start."

He nodded in response, handing the towel back to one of the trainers and squirting some water into his mouth before refocusing on the game.

The second line was struggling to get the puck out of their defensive zone, and Brit had to make two really strong saves in a row in order to stop them from being down barely a minute into the first period.

Finally, they got the puck out and hurried for a change. The third line jumped onto the ice and spent half a minute in the other team's end before returning for the fourth line to take their turn.

Then Blane was on again and skating hard with the puck down the right side of the ice.

He saw the skater coming for him and dodged, turning enough that the hit only grazed him and he slipped by, managed to get a pass to Blue's stick, who pulled off some sort of dipsy-do maneuver around the defense Blane could have never hoped to make.

Blue broke toward the net, made another deke, and . . . was picked.

Just that quickly, play moved back into their zone.

Back and forth, sprint up, sprint back, shoot, pass, hustle, work, breathe *hard* in between whistles.

Again. And again. And again.

The period ended in a tie.

A quick chat from Bernard, a few pointers as they tore off wet underclothes, skates, and gloves and swapped them for dry ones.

Then they were back on the ice for the second period and the third.

More hits, more face-offs, more battles along the boards for free space in front of the net—

The puck found its way to his stick and he shoved it home.

Fuck, yeah.

Blue rushed over and hugged him. Stefan, Mike, and Trent following suit as they skated for the bench.

They were now in the lead with two minutes left.

Blue nudged him on the bench, a smirk on his face. "I do all the hard work and you steal my goal?"

Blane grinned. "Better lucky than good sometimes."

"Don't you know it."

Blane squirted him with water, but they were both laughing. The young one wasn't so young anymore, and he'd gotten good with a snarky comment.

They both focused on the game then jumped on the ice when Bernard wanted them out there instead of the fourth line. The opposing team pulled their goalie and added a sixth skater, making it a struggle to get out of their own end.

But eventually they did, Blue managing to scoop the puck up just past the red line and carrying it down for an empty net goal.

They skated back to the bench, relieved to have the cushion of the extra point.

"See," Blane said. "I've left the easy ones for you."

Blue snorted and shook his head.

A few minutes later—Brit having not needed that second goal because she'd secured her shutout—both teams skated off the ice and headed for their locker rooms.

Media first. Then showers and the PT suite for those who needed it, the pools or the weight room for those whose routine demanded it.

Dr. Carter had wanted to give Blane one final check after the game, so freshly showered, he headed that way.

Well, he would have gone there anyway, but Doc had given him a pretty excuse.

Mandy had been avoiding him again. Well, they'd had the best fucking shower sex of his life, followed by a breakfast filled with their usual joking and banter. But then they'd both gone to work and when he'd texted her after practice yesterday, she'd ignored him.

Then had given him a wide berth that morning.

And even now, she wouldn't look at him. She'd glanced up when he'd walked into the room and then quickly looked away, focusing on Blue's hand.

The disappointment that had been festering since the previous evening grew.

Sighing, he submitted to the stretches and exam that Mandy's assistant—even that made him grumpy since usually she would have looked at him herself—put him through and then waited as Doc looked over his paperwork.

"All's good, Blane," Dr. Carter declared not much later.

"Thanks, Doc."

Doc nodded, hesitating for a moment before indicating the table at the end of the row. "You should probably wait for Mandy to check you out though."

"Wh—"

Blane's protest cut off when he saw the look on Doc's face.

"She likes you, Blane." He sighed. "And she never likes anyone. Don't give up now. Go for it."

Blane glanced around, dropped his voice. "I'm not giving up, but it's kind of hard to go for something when it's all one-sided."

"If it were all one-sided, she wouldn't be avoiding you."

"You noticed that?"

Dr. Carter shrugged. "Kind of hard to miss the sexy eyes you two keep throwing at each other."

Sexy eyes? Blane ignored that for the moment. "She has barely looked at me."

Doc pointed to the TV screen and Blane squinted, relief pouring over him when he saw that her gaze was fixed on the two of them.

"She's good at hiding," Doc said. "But not that good. You just need to know when to look."

Blane sighed. "That's not all. She's worried about her job."

Dr. Carter's face went hard. "You going to fuck her over?"

"*No.* Of course not, but I don't want to hurt her either." Blane shoved a hand through his hair. "She's scared, fucking petrified, no matter what I say—" He blew out another breath. "And frankly, I don't know how to get through her walls."

Doc nodded. "I've known Mandy since med school, so I can tell you this: she's never looked at anyone the way she looks at you." He rolled his eyes. "Part of me can't believe that we're even having this conversation. But, we are, and dude, she's into you."

Blane flicked his gaze over his shoulder, watched as she examined Blue's hand. She was beautiful, capable, and a puzzle he'd yet to completely solve. "Maybe," he said, slanting Dr. Carter a rueful look. "But how in the hell am I going to get her to take a risk on us?"

Doc clapped him on the shoulder. "I'm guessing she's going to make that leap herself." A beat, his eyes flicking to the reflection again. "Just be patient. She'll come around." He lowered his voice. "And talk to Pierre for fuck's sake. Take that fear away for her, at least."

"I wi—"

"Blane?" Mandy asked, slipping between them. "Is everything okay with your neck?"

Doc nodded. "Everything looks good on my end, but I'd like you to evaluate his flexibility at C-five and six again. I'm not sure these numbers are right."

"Definitely." She pointed to the table, her eyes meeting Blane's for a fleeting moment. "Have a seat. I'll be over in just a second. Gabe, I need you to check on—"

Blane shot Dr. Carter a grateful look then sat down and waited for Mandy, plotting his next move.

He wasn't going to let this chance slip through his fingers.

Not with Mandy on the line.

Especially not when he had the feeling that she was it for him.

SEVENTEEN

Mandy

MANDY FINISHED CHATTING with Gabe and was then pulled into the pool room to take a look at another player's knee, and then the conditioning coach wanted her advice on a stretching routine.

She kept trying to get back to Blane but was being pulled in a million directions at once.

And he kept waving her off when she popped over to apologize.

"Go," he said. "Finish what you need to. I'll wait."

But she didn't want to wait.

She'd spent the last twenty-four hours stuck in her own head, replaying their night together, going through the memories of their interactions from the last few years.

Searching for a red flag, for an excuse to not jump.

She hadn't found one.

Yes, he was an NHL player like her dad had been, but that was the *only* thing they had in common. Blane was kind and thoughtful, well-liked by his teammates. He wasn't an alcoholic misogynist like her father had been.

Brit—female, shattering barriers left and right—was his best friend, for fuck's sake.

So she either needed to cut this off at its head or to just jump in and go for it.

And since this was the first time in her life Mandy had struggled to keep up her walls with a man, she was taking it as a sign that things with Blane were different, that *he* was different.

By the time the Gold had hit the ice that evening, she'd mentally shored up her spine and decided she was going to do this.

Fingers crossed it didn't blow up in her face.

After a few more words, she sent the strength and conditioning coach on his way and started for Blane, only to be stopped two steps later by Coach Bernard.

Her eyes met Blane's and he shrugged as if to say, "*What can you do?*"

Bernard only kept her for a couple of minutes, but as much as she wanted to break away from the conversation and go jump Blane, she was also thrilled by what she was hearing.

The board had voted to fund her request for new equipment and another trainer.

They were supportive of her plans—to prevent injuries before they even happened—and were backing her.

The pieces of her life were finally falling into place.

And it was because she'd pushed aside her fear and leaped into something new.

There was a lesson there.

But she was too busy making eyes with Blane to focus on it fully.

"Hey," she said, finally at his side.

A brush of his fingers along her cheek. "Hey, sweetheart."

The spot tingled, and she just stared at him for a long moment before clearing her throat and moving to check the flexibility and muscles on his neck.

"Turn to the left. Now the right," she said after he complied. "Okay, reach your ear to each shoulder." Hmm. There wasn't a digression. In fact, the sides had balanced out even more. "Any pain?" she asked, fingers on his spine as she palpated.

Blane's palm came up to cover her hand. "No." He tugged her forward. "Are you okay?"

Her lips flattened. "*I'm* fine. Why did Gabe—?"

One brow lifted.

Oh.

She'd been had.

Mandy crossed her arms and glared at him.

Blane put his hands up in surrender. "Not my idea. Doc was just throwing me a bone since you've been avoiding me."

"What?" Mandy began cleaning up the stations, throwing away the trash and organizing the supplies back into their proper positions. "I haven't been avoiding you."

There that brow went again.

"Stop." She reached up and nudged it back down. "I'm not lying."

He began ticking off fingers. "Okay, but one, I texted you and you didn't reply. We had breakfast and nothing. Two, you weren't here when I came in this morning. Three, you didn't examine me after the game. Four—"

"Because I was worried if I touched you, I wouldn't be able to stop."

Blane's fingers curled into a fist. "What?"

Her lips curved into a rueful smile. "I want you. I want *us*. I was just worried that if I said something with the room full that I might do something stupid and jump your bones."

"Oh."

"Yeah," she said. "*Oh*. Also, I wasn't here this morning because I was giving a presentation to the board and asking for new equipment, which they approved, by the way—"

"That's great." His eyes lit up before going a little mischievous. "Maybe another hot tub?"

She rolled her eyes. "Considering you all refer to the current one as Ball Soup, I don't think we'll be investing in that."

He chuckled and grabbed her hand. "Seriously, though, that's great." A squeeze. "I'm proud of you."

Tears filled her eyes. For absolutely no reason.

Except maybe, that no one had ever said those words to her.

"It's for new equipment and another trainer," she said, dropping his hand and her gaze to the drawer and straightening the already straightened supplies.

Fingers came to her jaw, tilted her face back up. "That's good news. So why are you crying?"

She shook her head. "I'm not crying." Except, she kind of was. She'd lost her battle with the blasted moisture and teardrops were leaking out of the corners of her eyes.

"Did I do something—"

"*No.*" She sniffed. "Fuck. This hasn't been about—this isn't about *you.*"

He dropped his hand, straightened. "I'm—"

Shit. Mandy grabbed it back, holding his palm between both of hers. "I didn't mean it like that."

Here it came. Here came the secret. The shit that had her so knotted up and closed down inside. Here was the shame, even though she logically knew that none of it was her fault.

"It's not—I didn't mean to hurt you. I just . . . I'm really good at keeping my distance from people." Her laugh sounded broken, even to her own ears. "I've never had many friends. Hell, I only tolerated Gabe in medical school because he took really good notes."

And he hadn't left her alone.

"Then I came here and met Brit, and I felt like we were kind of kindred spirits. We hit it off."

"Not a lot of women around here."

Mandy nodded. "Yeah, but also, she's just really fucking cool. And then I realized you two were friends and that you were in love with her"—he opened his mouth, but she dropped his hand and placed her finger over his lips—"It's okay. I understand now. Hell, I'm half in love with her myself. She's Brit."

He kissed her finger then tugged it free. "Yeah. And I do love her, but after she met Stefan, I finally understood that it never would have worked between us."

She smiled. "They are pretty perfect."

"Sickeningly perfect."

They laughed.

"But you being Brit's friend was a good thing. It made you seem 'safe' and somehow you slipped in under my defenses."

"Well, that," he teased, playing with the end of her ponytail, "and the fact that I'm the sexiest man you've ever seen."

"Just call you Chris Evans?" she teased back.

"*Ouch*." He slapped a hand across his heart. "I'm wounded."

A snort. "Not hardly. But six months ago, things shifted for me."

"Probably because that's the time I started having wet dreams about you."

"Blane!"

He tugged her down next to him on the table. "You're beautiful, sweetheart. You breathe and I'm hard. I want to bend you over—"

She stood up again, gaze flicking to his lap and then back up. "You've done it now."

"I don't need to do anything," he murmured. "*That's* all you."

Her breath caught. "*Oh*."

Eyes darkening, he stood. "You know how I feel about that sound."

"I didn't mean to."

"Mmm." He rose to his feet, slipped a hand behind her neck—

The door slammed open. "Post-game workout in five," the conditioning coach, Joe, shouted, before letting it crash back closed.

"Fuck," Blane muttered, lowering his forehead to hers. "Sorry."

"We both need to finish up," she said. "It's the job."

"Will you come to my house when you're done?"

She nodded.

He kissed the top of her head. "Thank you." Halfway to the door, he stopped. "So to be clear, you haven't been avoiding me?"

Mandy rolled her eyes. "No."

"And you want to be my girlfriend?"

Her heart skipped a beat, but she brazened on. "Will you give me your letterman jacket?"

"Don't have one, but if I did, it would be yours." A smoldering grin that had her catching her breath. "I can get you a jersey with my name on it though."

"Sold." She lifted a hand as he slipped out of the PT suite. "See you later."

"I'm counting down the seconds."

Then he was gone and Mandy found herself with a hockey-player boyfriend.

Life was really weird sometimes.

EIGHTEEN

Blane

BLANE MADE it through the post-game workout and shower in record time then popped back into the PT suite afterward. The space was empty and dark, so he hurried out to where Mandy usually parked her car.

Also empty.

He was about to go back into the arena when his phone buzzed.

Sorry I didn't text you back.

I was scared.

Frowning, he replied.

I don't want to scare you.

The ". . ." signaling she was typing something began almost immediately after he'd sent his text.

Was. I WAS scared. But I'm not anymore.

Tension he hadn't even realized he had leached out of him. That was good, really good.

His phone buzzed again.

Also, look up, Super Star.

Blane looked up . . . and saw she was standing next to his driver's side door.

Wanna carpool?

He grinned, shoved his phone into his pocket, and strode over to her. "Save on that toll lane?"

"You know it."

"Hi," he murmured.

One half of her mouth turned up. "Hi, yourself."

While he really wanted to kiss her senseless, Blane hit the button to unlock the car and helped her around and into the passenger seat. Then, because he couldn't have stopped himself if he'd tried, he reached over and buckled her seat belt, brushing all of the parts he'd gotten so familiar with the night before along the way.

"Blane."

He closed her door and walked around to his own.

"Let me get that for you," she said when he went to clip in his restraint.

She grabbed the buckle from him and—

Snapped it in place.

But it was her other hand that was the cause of his trouble.

"I can't find it," she teased, fingers running up his thigh.

He snorted. "It's not *that* small."

She cupped him, squeezing tight. "It's not *small* at all."

"Mandy," he breathed. "You're killing me."

"Mmm." She squeezed him one more time then sat back into her own seat. "I hope you have condoms at your house."

———

THE DRIVE back to his place took an eternity.

Mandy sitting next to him, slanting heated glances in his direction, smelling so fucking incredible, just existing in the same realm as him, and the twenty-five minutes seemed like twenty-five hours.

Finally, he pulled into his garage and shut the door behind them.

Then he shoved his seat all the way back, unbuckled his seat belt and hers, and tugged her onto his lap.

"Bl—"

He kissed her.

Blane slid one hand in her hair and the other down her back to cup his most favorite ass of all time, pulling her hips so she was pressed tightly against him.

She tore her mouth from his on a moan. "Mmm. *Baby*," she panted. "I . . ."

He kissed her again, encouraged her to move against his cock.

Fuck that felt incredible.

Her hands dropped to his seat, gripping the headrest as she rode him. He slipped his fingers under her shirt and up, slipping beneath her bra to her breasts.

"Fuck," she hissed when he pinched one nipple between his thumb and forefinger. "I—that feels—I need—"

He twisted, shoving the material out of the way as he sucked her neglected nipple into his mouth. Her hips bucked, thrusting against him hard enough to make him moan, and he shifted forward wanting—

The horn blared, making them both jump.

Her hazy eyes flashed to his. "What—?"

"Shh," he said. "I got you."

He popped the door open and stepped out with her in his arms.

"Wait—" she began.

"My neck is fine," he said, nipping at her jaw.

"No." She hissed when he sucked hard on the spot. "I need my purse. It has the condoms—"

Blane set her on the hood of the car. "I have one," he said. "Don't worry. I would never *not* use one until we—" He shook his head, cheeks creasing into a smile. "I've got this, okay? Let me take care of you . . . at least for a little while."

She froze, head dropping forward as she sucked in a huge breath. "You don't know what you're asking."

A finger under her chin, deep chocolate eyes locked on hers. "I *know*, sweetheart."

She swallowed hard. "Okay."

"Okay?"

When she nodded again, he kissed her gently, pouring every bit of tenderness he was feeling for this woman into the press of his lips, the stroke of his tongue, the way he held her carefully against him. He scooped her up from the hood, knowing that she needed more than a quick fuck against his car, that she needed him steady and present, that she needed slow and stable and *permanent*.

They'd just revisit the car later.

Because the image of her naked and restless on top of it, him on his knees, between her thighs . . . yeah, that was something he needed to tick off his mental checklist.

Carefully, he made his way to his room and set Mandy on the bed.

His heart skipped a beat, seeing her there, on the mattress, in his home, in his life. He hadn't really recognized how much he'd wanted this, wanted *her*, until this moment.

Last night had been hot, don't get him wrong.

But that moment had felt as though it had an expiration date.

This? *This* felt like the beginning.

He'd played in the finals, had pushed through moments of pressure, had stepped up to sink home a clutch goal in the final seconds of a game. He worked hard and pushed and pushed and *pushed*.

But never with women.

Oh, he'd had his share, especially when he'd been young and on the road and lonely and bored.

Those had been easy, quick expenditures for mutual satisfaction.

Last night had been more than that, but it hadn't been this. The need to make it perfect so that she would see, so that she would stay—

His stomach knotted hard enough for him to lose his breath.

This was important because he loved her.

The feeling had been growing over months, fueling the desperation to batter down her defenses and make her see . . . him.

And now she was there.

She was in his bed, and he had to hope to fuck that he didn't screw this up.

Mandy deserved—

"Hey, Super Star?" she asked quietly, her expression concerned. "Why is there smoke coming out of your ears?"

He froze, realized he'd been staring at her for a good minute. "I'm so—"

"Don't apologize," she said. "Just tell me what's going on."

"This isn't—it's not *easy*."

She grabbed his hand, reclining back on the bed and tugging him along on top of her. "I know."

"It's not simple."

Her palm came up to press above his heart, which was pounding like the beat to one of the rap songs that Max was obsessed with. "I know."

"I'm afraid I'm going to screw it up."

Mandy's hand twitched, fingers digging into his chest before smoothing out. "Why do you think I ran for so long?"

He snorted. "Not *that* long."

"I've wanted you in my bed for an eternity, Blane. I was just too scared to go for it."

"So why now?"

"You know all of those things you just mentioned? All of that . . . this isn't simple or easy, the worrying about fucking it all up stuff?" He nodded. "I realized that I could either stand by and be scared for the rest of my life—pretending to let people in but not actually allowing them to know the real me, not permitting anyone to see who I am deep inside, to give them the chance to judge me and find me lacking. Or—"

"Or?" he asked when she didn't go on.

Her expression softened alongside her voice. "*Or* I could take a chance on the only man who's ever made me want to take off my armor and show him *every single part* of me."

His throat went tight. "Fuck, sweetheart."

She bit her lip. "I know." A pause. "So puck's on your stick, Super Star. What are you going to do about it?"

NINETEEN

Mandy

TO SAY that Blane simply kissed her would have been the understatement of the century. He consumed her, filled her veins with fire, with desire, until she threatened to burn from the inside out.

Okay, she was being dramatic.

But with just the press of his mouth against hers, his body, his chest, his *cock* hard where she was soft, she was more turned on than she'd ever been.

He slipped his hand under her head, not breaking the kiss as he rolled onto his back and took her with him. One second she was flat against the mattress and the next, she was straddling his hips, his erection cradled between her thighs.

"Not bad, Hart," she said when they finally broke for air.

She rested her palms on his chest, squeezed two perfect handles of pecs. Yeah, that feeling right there was probably why guys liked boobs so much.

He smirked, and she realized she'd spoken aloud. "It *is* better when you're topless," he said.

"Mmm, *that* I can get behind." Especially considering what Blane did to her breasts when she was half naked. She straightened, tugging off her T-shirt before reaching for the buttons of Blane's dress shirt.

"Me, too." His eyes hadn't lifted above her neck, and Mandy was glad she'd worn her best bra. Lacy and see-through, it pushed her modest set of breasts up and together, giving her a rare moment of legit cleavage.

"You like?" she asked, leaning down to press a kiss to his chest.

"I"—one hand rose to rest on her back and he unhooked her bra —"do like." Both palms cupped her. "But I like this better."

Her eyes rolled into the back of her head. She liked *that* better, too.

But she wanted him naked. And inside her.

But naked first.

Her fingers shook as she undid the rest of the buttons. He played with her breasts, squeezing them gently, teasing her nipples as he did so, distracting her, making her hands slip more than once.

"You're making this hard," she panted, head spinning, thighs clenching, pussy aching.

He flexed his hips, making her moan. "Isn't that the point?"

She kissed him, hard. "Blane?" she asked when she pulled away.

He did something with his thumb and forefinger that had her seeing stars. "Yes?"

"Normally, I'd be all about foreplay and taking our time, but can we just"—her words broke off on a gasp as he thrust up with his hips again—"forget that?"

His fingers slipped beneath the waistband of her pants. "Forget what?"

"Can you, please, just forget foreplay and fuck me until I can't walk?"

He froze, mouth slightly agape. Then he smiled, a slow, scorching grin that had moisture pooling between her legs.

Until he spoke.

Because confusion treaded along the edges of her desire.

"No."

"What?"

He flipped her, kneeling between her thighs and then, in a movement so fast she could barely track it, her pants were off and her underwear pushed to the side.

Blane dove at her, his mouth meeting wet, hot flesh and he gave her a kiss so sensual that she was ramping up the edge to an orgasm in seconds. He spread her wide, laving his tongue over her clit, pressing one finger of his free hand inside of her.

It was too much and not enough.

Too intense. Too little. So much sensation that she threatened to burst through her skin.

And not Blane. Not inside. Not—

He slid in a second finger.

She came with a scream, chest heaving, covered in sweat, her muscles limp as cooked noodles.

"Holy—" Mandy jumped when he flexed his hand, fingers still inside her and making her nerve endings flare to life.

"See?" he asked, pressing a kiss to her clit that had her shuddering. "Isn't that better than me just sticking it in?"

He nipped at her side, soothing the small hurt with his tongue, before slowly making his way up her body as he licked and kissed and bit every inch of her exposed skin.

"Yes," she gasped, gripping his shoulders as he feasted on her breasts. "But *now* would be a good time to *stick it in*. I want you inside me, Blane."

"Hmm," he murmured against her skin, ignoring her as he kept teasing her.

Which was pretty much the point she'd had enough.

She reached down and grabbed his cock.

"Christ, Mandy." His head dropped to her chest as he pushed into her hand.

"You. Inside. Me." She punctuated each word with a squeeze.

"But—"

Stubborn men. Seriously.

She pushed him onto his back and slid down the mattress, sucking him into her mouth, both hands encircling his erection, taking him deep enough to make him unleash a blistering set of curses.

And she'd pretty much thought her ears were unblisterable.

One stroke. Two—

Next thing she knew, she was back on the pillows, breath whooshing out of her, and Blane was reaching into his nightstand for a condom.

A crinkle as he tore the wrapper open. A moment to roll it on and then he stopped and stared at her.

Her nape prickled, her insides roiled with a combination of desire and fear. She'd succeeded in finally snapping the leash of his control.

He was normally so calm, so together.

But the man staring down at her was neither of those. His eyes were molten, his jaw clenched tight. Every muscle in his body was taut with need. "Last chance, sweetheart," he gritted out. "Last chance for slow and sweet."

Any slice of fear faded. This was her Blane, her hot, sexy, *unhinged* Blane. But he was still there, still hers. She gripped his shoulders, yanked him down.

"Enough slow and sweet," she said, clamping her teeth onto his earlobe. "I need hard and fast."

That was it.

A heartbeat later he was inside of her and, *fuck,* did it feel good.

"Better hang on tight, baby," he said and thrust deep.

Her head spun, but Mandy did as he said, and she certainly didn't regret it. Blane stroked in and out in a rhythm that had her nails digging into his shoulders, her moans bordering on screams. He hurtled her to the edge of another orgasm and then . . . arched her back, lifted her hips to meet his.

And exploded.

Or at least, that was what it felt like. Pleasure flowed through her body, and her mind went fuzzy. She was vaguely aware of crying out, of Blane thrusting once, *twice* more before he shouted her name.

It was a long time before she came back to Earth to find him cradling her against him, his fingers stroking through her hair.

She smiled. "See?" she said, her voice slightly raspy after her verbal accolades of Blane's skills. "Even after hard and fast, you still bring the sweet."

His chest shook with laughter.

Mandy stayed pressed against it and lifted her hand, palm up.

Right on cue, Blane high-fived it.

"Go team," she deadpanned.

He chuckled, lacing his fingers with hers. "Go team."

TWENTY

Blane

BLANE WAS MISSING the third movie and trying not to feel salty about it.

So what if it was his favorite of the series? This was more important.

This being waiting in a fragile-looking armchair in the sitting room of Pierre Barie's office and hoping the owner of the team and current acting GM would be able to see him that evening.

He'd begged off on Mandy's party, knowing that it was more of a girl's night than anything and figuring meeting with Pierre was more important.

Life and all its baggage was hard.

The fewer hurdles their relationship needed to clear, the better.

He'd already spoken to Bernard, and obviously Dr. Carter had given his all clear, but he didn't want any barriers between them.

He wanted Mandy to feel safe in breaking things off with him if necessary.

Not that he planned on letting her go . . . but he also didn't want to do anything to risk the career she'd worked so hard for.

More than that, he didn't want her trapped. He wanted her to . . . *choose* him.

So instead of being *with* the woman who'd managed to infiltrate every part of his brain, he was at the arena, dodging fans from a pop concert and waiting for Pierre.

His phone buzzed.

Stefan.

We're coming up now.

Convenient that Pierre was his captain's father and Stefan had called in a favor from his dad for tickets to the concert for their backup goalie, Spence, and his daughter. It put the very busy Pierre in the arena at the right time.

At this point, Blane would take any advantage he could get.

He shoved his phone back into his pocket and stood, trying not to pace as he waited for Pierre to show up.

The handle turned and the door pushed open. Stefan and Pierre strode into the room.

Show time.

"Blane," Pierre said. "Good to see you're up and feeling better. That was quite a hit you took."

They shook hands.

"Doc and Mandy fixed me right up," he said, following when Pierre indicated his office. "We're lucky to have them on staff."

Stefan hesitated on the threshold, but Blane waved him forward. Anything he was going to tell Pierre, his captain needed to hear as well.

"Hiring Dr. Carter and Amanda is probably the single useful thing the previous owner did," Pierre said, sitting behind his desk. "But you're not here to discuss our staffing."

Blane straightened his shoulders. "Actually, we are."

Pierre frowned. "Is there an issue? I haven't heard from your agent—"

"No," Stefan interrupted. "Hang on, Dad. This isn't like that. Blane's here because he wanted to talk to you about something important, and he wanted to do it in person, not through a proxy."

"Oh yeah?" Pierre's face went blank. "Is there an issue with our sports medicine staff?"

"No. I mean *yes*. It's not—" *Shit*. He was fucking this up. "I—" Finally, he just blurted out the truth. "I'm in love with Mandy Shallows."

Stefan raised his eyebrows. Pierre's expression didn't change.

Blane prattled on. "We've both been avoiding each other for months, trying to ignore it, but I can't any longer. She means too much. She's—" He sighed. "She's everything. I can't imagine seeing her every day and not being able to be with her. This isn't a quick fuck because she's here and convenient. Mandy's special. She talented, whip-smart. She has us all in the best shape of our career."

"And if that's true, why would I risk that for a relationship that might implode any second?" Pierre's brows drew together, his blue eyes swimming with irritation.

"I wouldn't if I were in your shoes." Blane swallowed hard, knowing that this meeting wasn't going as he'd planned, but knowing he had to keep trying anyway. "But I also know that while this is my job and I love it and I feel so lucky to be playing for this team, hockey isn't more important than her. If you had to choose between her or me, I'd want you to choose her. Every single time."

Silence.

Pierre stood and turned to gaze out the window. The bright lights of the city shone through in a mishmash of glittering spots.

Shit.

Because there was no response. Just silence.

Blane opened his mouth, about to continue speaking but Stefan kicked his chair. When he glanced back over his shoulder, Stefan shook his head.

Getting the message, Blane sat silently in the chair and waited.

For several long minutes.

Or an eternity.

That too.

Finally, Pierre sat back down in his chair and folded his fingers together on his desk. "That was the right answer, son."

Blane relaxed. "Yeah?"

Pierre nodded. "I appreciate you coming to me, that speaks both a lot about your character and also how important Amanda is to you." He paused, glancing at Stefan before returning his gaze to Blane. "I'll speak to her, but so long as this is her choice, too, I don't have a problem with it."

"And her contract?" he asked. "I believe there's a clause—"

"My guess is that it's time for Amanda to get a raise. And a new contract."

Blane figured that was his cue—to leave, not fist-pump in joy. He stood, extending a hand. "Thank you, Mr. Barie."

Pierre shook it. "I hope your agent will go easy on *your* contract's terms after this."

"Honestly?" Blane asked. "I don't think Prestige Media Group has ever gone easy on any negotiation." He shrugged. "That's why I hired them."

Pierre's lips twitched. "I wouldn't expect anything less from Devon Scott's crew." He winked. "Keep racking up those points, and you won't have anything to worry about."

"Noted."

Pierre's office line rang and he'd barely waved Blane and Stefan off, before snatching it up.

Stefan waited until they'd entered the hall to comment.

"So you love her, huh?"

Blane nodded then waited for the chirp, the joke.

Instead, Stefan just grinned and punched him on the shoulder. "Welcome to the club, brother."

"I'm screwed, aren't I?" Blane asked as they rode the elevator down.

"Totally and royally and in the completely best way possible."

Blane couldn't do anything but smile . . . and pull out his phone to text Mandy that he missed her.

For once, he didn't even tease as Stefan pulled out his, presumably to send the same sentiment to Brit.

The buzz in return, the message in return of *I can't wait to see you later*, was so much better than the buzz from any goal he had ever scored, no matter how clutch.

He was in love with Mandy.

And it felt fucking fantastic.

TWENTY-ONE

Mandy

OKAY, so the sorting hat cupcakes looked a little . . .

"That's disturbing," Brit said, tilting her head.

Mandy tilted her head as well, trying and failing to find an angle the dessert looked appetizing. Maybe it was the globs of black icing or the way it seemed to be slithering off the tops of the cupcakes, but the treats were definitely *disturbing*.

There was something clearly wrong with the frosting.

As in it was melting.

Why was it melting?

She sighed. "I think the icing was too hot when I added the butter."

Sara joined them. "Why was the icing hot?"

Mandy swiped a finger of the frosting up and plunked it into her mouth. Then almost spit it out. Gross. Her buttercream had somehow ended up greasy.

"It's Swiss Meringue buttercream," she said, making a face. "It's supposed to be foolproof. You whip egg whites to stiff peaks and heat sugar up to one hundred sixty degrees. Then you add it—" She broke off when her friends stared at her incredulously. "It seemed easy on YouTube."

"You're insane," Brit said.

"We still love you, though," Sara added.

Brit frowned. "It looks like you tried to murder the Sorting Hat in a vat of acid."

Mandy swiped the platter of cupcakes from the table and dumped them into the trash. "So what if I did?" she muttered.

Monique, sans Mirabel and Spencer who'd gone to a concert at the Gold Mine, gave Mandy a quick squeeze. "Your broomstick pretzels are super cute, though."

"Unfortunately they taste horrid," she said. While tying sour strips around pretzel sticks had definitely given them a broomstick feel, actually eating the combination was a lesson in . . .

Barf.

"They can't be that bad," Monique said, plunking one into her mouth before wincing then chewing with the determination of someone who wasn't willing to spit out a bite of food, no matter how bad.

"Here." She grabbed the trash can and held it up to Monique's mouth, who daintily disposed of the offending appetizer.

"Okay, so they're not good." She plunked her hands on her hips, gorgeous chocolate curls bobbing with the motion. "Where does that leave us?"

Brit held up her phone. "Movies and DoorDash."

Mandy knew when to admit defeat. She trashed the pretzels and put on the first movie as Brit ordered a boatload of Indian food.

The doorbell rang, and Sara opened it, letting in PR-Rebecca alongside Nutritionist-Rebecca. Greetings were exchanged, wine glasses distributed and filled, and then they'd gorged themselves on PR-Rebecca's brownies as they'd waited for the delivery guy.

"I know I'm supposed to be encouraging you to fuel your body with super greens and low-fat protein," Nutritionist-Rebecca said, taking a giant bite of brownie. "But these might be the best things I've ever tasted."

PR-Rebecca waved a hand. "You've spent too long eating that crap to know mediocre food when you eat it.

"You're insane," Sara said. "I'd swear you put drugs in these brownies."

They all froze when PR-Rebecca didn't immediately deny the fact.

"What?" she asked as they stared at her.

"Are these pot brownies?" Brit demanded.

"What?" PR-Rebecca said. "No. Literally, I got the recipe from the Food Network. No leaves in sight—super green or otherwise."

"I," Monique said, "for one, don't care what you put in them so long as you keep bringing them."

"Agreed," Mandy chimed in and got up to answer the door when the buzzer rang. She returned, her arms laden with bags of food, to five pairs of eyes studying her closely.

PR-Rebecca raised a brow. "Do you have something to tell me?"

"What? No."

Except that she was apparently dating Blane.

That he wanted to be boyfriend-girlfriend.

Good grief, that sounded so juvenile.

Surprisingly, it was Nutritionist-Rebecca who outed her. "She's hiding something. Look at her face."

Again five pairs of eyes locked onto hers.

Brit squealed and they all winced. "Holy shit, you did it, didn't you?"

"Did what?" Sara and Monique asked in unison.

PR-Rebecca narrowed her eyes.

"You finally got it on with Blane."

"Wh—" She shook her head. "I—Why is that any of your business?" Ten brows raised in her direction. "Okay, fine. Blane and I are . . . dating."

Brit fist pumped.

"Holy shit," Sara said. "Really? That's great."

Monique grinned and even Nutritionist-Rebecca smiled. And she was normally so serious that it was hard to get a read on her. Maybe PR-Rebecca really *had* spiked those brownies.

PR-Rebecca was the only one without a happy expression. She crossed her arms, tapping her foot on the new floors Mandy had installed. "When were you going to tell me?"

Mandy winced. "Uhhh."

The other woman's brightly painted red lips pulled down. "So that's never."

"I—uh. It's new?" Mandy tried to spin it.

"Hmph." PR-Rebecca pulled out her phone and made a few notes. "With your dad who he was, this might be a bigger story than you expect."

"I won't talk to the media," she said. "Not now. Not ever."

"You might—"

"*No.*"

PR-Rebecca froze, studying her for a long moment before nodding. "Okay. It blows up, I'll take care of it."

"Thank you." Mandy straightened her shoulders and began passing out food. "So am I crazy? It's—I really like him, guys." She bit her lip. "What if he decides—"

"You're not crazy," Brit said. "He's a good guy. You can trust him."

Monique nodded. "And plus, hockey guys are the best."

"I can second that," Sara said.

PR-Rebecca grinned. "He hurts you . . . no brownies."

"I'll gut him if he hurts you." Eyes wide, they all slanted their gazes to Nutritionist-Rebecca, who'd spoken a line that normally would have been straight out of PR-Rebecca's playbook. She shrugged. "What? I just think we all make a good team."

Mandy smiled, heart threatening to burst, thinking she was so lucky to have these strong, capable, funny women in her life.

"*You guys.*" She sniffed.

Brit grabbed the remote, turned up the volume. "No crying until *Goblet of Fire*. That's an order."

The girls seconded that sentiment, and they all began digging into their meals as Mandy sank down onto the couch. She cuddled close to her friends, her container of chicken marsala in her lap.

"Thanks for the push," she whispered to Brit when she took a momentary break from hoovering the delicious food into her mouth.

Brit shrugged, but her lips were curved into a grin. "You're his Ginny."

Mandy grinned back. "Why do I think he would like that comparison?"

"Because we are all big ol' nerds."

"I can live with that."

Brit bumped her shoulder. "Me too."

MANDY GLANCED down at the contract Pierre Barie's assistant had set in front of her in disbelief.

"But that's *double* what my current—"

Pierre steepled his fingers beneath his chin, waiting as his assistant strode out of the office, shutting the door behind him. "Rule number one in negotiations: don't act shocked when someone wants to pay you money." His lips quirked. "Ask for more."

"But—"

"Both Bernard and Dr. Carter sing your praises. Hell, three-quarters of the team have been up in my office swearing by your treatments and begging me to not let you go."

Mandy frowned. She'd been petrified when she'd arrived at the arena Monday morning and Gabe had said Pierre wanted to talk to her.

He'd found out about Blane.

She was going to be let go. She should have known better. Blane couldn't protect her from this. Stefan was allowed to date Brit only because he was the owner's son.

So basically, she wound herself up into a full-blown tizzy by the time the elevator had dinged open on the top floor.

But now she was in Pierre's office and the conversation wasn't going as planned.

"I still have two years left on my current contract."

Pierre switched tack. "Do you want to be in a relationship with Blane Hart?"

Her breath froze in her lungs.

He leaned back in his chair. "Because if you don't, and you're feeling pressured or—"

"No!" she hurried to say. "It's not like that. I swear, neither of us meant for it to happen. It's—"

What? Different? Not a quick fling? Wouldn't affect her job?

All of those.

But also more.

"He's . . ." Mandy sighed, tried to find a way to encapsulate just what Blane meant to her.

Aside from her friends, she didn't really have anyone.

Her mother was wrapped up in her own life, and while Mandy called on holidays and her birthday, the same courtesy wasn't received in return. Her father was gone. She didn't have any siblings. She had Gabe, of course, and Brit, and the girls—

Okay, she wasn't alone. Not anymore. She'd been steadily building her own family since working for the Gold.

But Blane was different.

Even with Gabe, for all the years she'd know and trusted him, she still kept him at a distance.

Yet Blane managed to penetrate all the layers of steel she held tightly around herself.

And he made it look effortless.

Or maybe, he didn't *have* to barge through.

Maybe he made her want to loosen her grip on those sheets of armor.

"He's . . ." She began again before laying it all on the table. "Blane is more important to me than any other person in my life."

Silence.

Now she'd done it.

She'd just screwed them both—

"Check page eight."

"What?"

Pierre leaned across the desk and flipped through the papers before arriving at the eighth page. He placed his finger on a paragraph about halfway down. "Read."

". . . romantic relationships are discouraged between players and staff," she said aloud, her heart racing, "but can be sanctioned by management should extenuating circumstances apply." Her eyes flew to Pierre's. "I—"

"Blane spoke to me," he said, almost gently. Which was a word she'd never heard associated with the notoriously hard-ass businessman before. "But that will mean absolutely nothing if this isn't what you want, too."

Her eyes prickled with tears, and Mandy swallowed hard. "It's what I want," she said with a sniff. "So, so much."

"Good." Pierre picked up a pen and signed his copy then reached across and signed hers as well, leaving the pen in front of her so she could repeat the process. "That's done, then," he said, almost brusquely now. "I'll pass this copy along to the lawyers. Keep yours for your records."

Mandy stood and nodded, knowing that was her cue to disappear. "Thank you, Mr. Barie. I won't forget it."

His eyes dropped to his phone, as though willing it to ring so he could end the conversation.

It didn't, so she hurried out of his office and out into the hall.

That had been excruciating . . . and amazing.

And so she didn't know whether she wanted to kiss or kill Blane.

Kiss, she decided once she'd entered her office. Definitely kiss.

A beautiful bouquet of flowers sat on her desk, alongside a note.

Practice this morning at RoboTech.

You staying at my place or am I staying at yours?

-B

The few minutes of terror had been worth it, though she really wished he'd warned her that he was going to talk to Pierre. Yes, it was a logical step if they were going to make a go of their relationship, but a little preparation would have been nice.

It had been like being called to the principal's office.

Not cool.

But considering the end result, she couldn't complain too much.

She and Blane could see where their relationship went without any pressure.

And the money wasn't too bad either.

Smiling, she leaned in to smell a pale pink rose and nearly jumped out of her skin when Max shouted from her doorway.

"Flowers? *Oooo,* who from?"

What had she been thinking about no pressure?

She and Blane were in for no little amount of teasing once they all found out. Which was probably going to be in two point two seconds, since Max had managed to snatch up the note from her desk.

"Your place or mine?" he asked, eyes dancing. "Signed just *B?* Oooo, who could that be? Brit?" He smirked, waggling his brows. "No? Fine. Only in my fantasies, I guess."

She fake-vomited and made a grab for the note. Not that it mattered, since he'd already read it.

"Brian?" he asked. "No. I don't think I've seen a Brian around."

Mandy finally managed to snag the letter and shoved it into her back pocket. "Not Brian." She crossed her arms. "You should go or you'll be late for practice. It's at RoboTech"—the company had sponsored the building of a multi-sheet ice rink for both the team and city to use, and it was where most Gold practices were now held—"No one is here today."

"Except the person who brought you flowers," he said. "Not Brit. Not Brian. Not Bob or Billy. It can't be Blue, he's too young. *Oh*"—his gaze locked onto hers, smile almost blinding—"I got it. Byron."

"Oh my God," Mandy muttered. "That was a poet, not a date. I'm with Blane, okay? It's new and good, and you'll just keep your mouth shut about it until we're ready. Got it?"

Okay, so maybe the finger wagging in his face was a little much, she thought as Max paled and took a step back.

"You're scary sometimes, Mandy," he said, trying to slip out the door.

She stopped him. "Just remember who helps make your workout," she warned.

Max raised his hands in surrender. "I don't know who the B is," he said. "Not a clue until you tell us."

Mandy narrowed her eyes. "That's right. Now hurry up before you're late."

He turned, hesitating before rotating back to face her. "For the record, Blane"—she cleared her throat meaningfully and he jumped—"whoever this *B*-person is. Well, he's a good guy, okay? Don't hurt him."

She had to stop herself from making her *Aw*-face and only just managed to hang on to her serious expression because she knew if she gave Max an inch, he'd take a mile. She'd find both herself and Blane teased mercilessly.

So no. No softening up was allowed.

"Go," she ordered.

He went. Stopped again a few feet away.

"Just so we're clear. I'm still allowed to give Blane a hard time, right?"

Mandy lifted her phone so it was in his view and began typing out a text. "Just so we're clear, you want extra reps of abs today?"

Max hot-footed it to the door. "No teasing. Got it."

"Bye, Max."

"Bye, Mandy," he called adding right before the door closed. "He's lucky to have you, by the way."

It slammed shut, nearly rattling the pictures from the walls.

She shook her head.

But she was smiling.

TWENTY-TWO

Blane

ROAD TRIPS WERE a typical and lonely part of a professional athlete's life.

Players were away from their families, isolated in hotel rooms with too much free time on their hands.

Oftentimes this equated to trouble.

But this time, he was traveling with the person he was in love with.

In love with.

He still couldn't believe it.

He was head over heels, completely gone for Mandy.

A smile spread over his face as she boarded the team's private plane, her backpack slung over one shoulder. She wore a long-sleeved T-shirt emblazoned with the Gold logo, and her ever-present ponytail was tucked through the back of a team hat. There wasn't a lick of makeup on her face, and she wore loose-fitting sweats.

She was beautiful.

And she was his.

As she walked down the aisle, she paused to talk with Gabe then continued back toward where Blane sat. Usually this was the unofficial players' zone, but fuck if Blane was going to sit by anyone but her.

Eighty-two regular season games already meant that free time together was hard to come by.

So he was going to steal every single free second he could.

Mandy paused by his row, eyeing the empty seat next to him, and apparently felt the same way because she asked, "Is that seat taken?"

Since bantering with her was pretty much his favorite thing, he pretended to consider that. "I don't know," he said, tapping his finger to his chin. "I really like to spread out on these flights."

"Hmm," she said, a smirk teasing at the corners of her mouth. "I guess that just means I have to go sit with Blue."

Blane snagged her wrist and tugged her down into his lap. "You're not going anywhere." Her lips were right there, so he kissed her. "Now, do you want the window or aisle?"

She went very still, her gaze flicking around the cabin. He followed her stare, saw that the whole team was watching them, no little amount of curiosity on their faces.

"Did you expect me to hide it?" he asked softly, brushing his knuckles along her jaw.

"No," she said. "I mean, I was coming to sit by you. I just"—she shook her head, a tinge of pink on her cheeks—"didn't expect you to declare it so loudly is all."

He tipped up the brim of her hat so he could see her eyes more clearly. "That bother you?" It was a serious question, but one that he didn't know how he'd be able to address if his actions *did* bug her.

Blane didn't want to have to consider every action with her. He wanted to be able to hug or kiss or touch the woman he was in love with and not be scared she might not like—

Mandy slung her arms around his neck. "If it bothered me, would I be doing this?" She leaned close to rub her nose along his. "Or this?" She kissed him, long and slow and deep.

Catcalls filled the plane after she pulled back.

"Your affection doesn't bother me, Super Star," she said gently. "But I'm not used to it. If I freeze up—and I probably will—just smack me around."

Never.

"How about I kiss you instead?"

Her laugh made him feel about ten feet tall. "Cheese ball. But kissing, I can agree to." She shoved his shoulder. "Now scoot over. I want the aisle."

The boys teased him as he gathered his stuff and shifted to the other seat, but Blane didn't give a damn.

He had Mandy.

And he was going to keep her.

———————

BLANE TOWELED OFF and slipped back into his suit, wanting nothing more than to be in a pair of sweats and a T-shirt, vegging out with a very not-meal-plan-approved post-game beer.

The game that evening had been a tough one. Their flight had been diverted to another airport because of weather the previous evening, and then their flight had been delayed that morning.

Routine was important to hockey players, and theirs had been all kinds of fucked up.

The delays meant their guys had struggled to get vehicles to transport their gear, and then a traffic jam just outside the city had delayed the buses further. They'd made it by game time, but it had been a close thing, and there certainly hadn't been time for their normal pregame procedures.

It had shown on the ice.

Oh boy, had it shown.

But the game was over now. Tomorrow was another day and all that shit.

Sighing, he shoved his shoes on his feet, grabbed his bag, and left the locker room.

Get him to the bus and the hotel already.

He weaved his way through the arena's hallways, up the stairs, then pushed out the doors and strode over to the bus.

Brit and Stefan were already seated in the back, cuddled up together, and Blane sighed as he sank into a seat in the row next to them.

Lucky bastards, getting to be together all the time.

Brit's eyes flashed to his, her brows drawing together. She whispered something to Stefan then got up and made her way to him.

"Uhhh," she said. "What the fuck are you doing?"

"Tonight sucked," he muttered. "Can we just get back to the hotel and rehash it all tomorrow?"

"We," she said. "Is the key word."

He shoved a hand through his hair, still wet from the shower. "I'm tired and not following, Brit. Just lay it on me."

She huffed, crossed her arms. "Are you or are you not dating Mandy?"

Blane straightened, stomach clenching. "Oh, fuck."

"Yeah." Brit rolled her eyes. "Most boyfriends don't forget their girlfriends."

"I didn't—" He cut himself off because obviously he *had* forgotten Mandy. "Stefan has it easy. You're already here."

"Get your ass off the bus and go grab your girl before you fuck this all up." Brit stepped closer as a few of the guys slipped into their seats. "And I'm only telling you this because you're my best friend, and when you're not being a pouty, obtuse jackass, you're a great guy, but"—her voice dropped further—"she's got abandonment issues, Blane. I don't know all of the circumstances, but she's told me enough." She poked his chest. "So don't ruin this by assuming that you've crossed the biggest hurdles between you two now that this has gone public. We girls are really good at holding on to hurts, at burying them deep, and letting them fester. And we're *really* fucking great at thinking we're totally fine only to have something from our past spring up and dynamite our present."

He slung his bag over his shoulder. "I didn't have it easy either, you know." There had been asshole kids and one particularly shitty bully, not to mention the fact that his parents had gone through several rough patches—his dad had even moved out for a time before they had reconciled. There was also the entire decade of unrequited love for the woman in front of him.

She patted his cheek. "You're cute. But seriously," Brit added when he opened his mouth to snap at her, "there's normal. *We*"—she pointed between them—"had normal life shit that was thrown at us." Her eyes darkened. "Or maybe a little more than normal at times, but I think Mandy has us beat, you know?"

Guilt swamped him because, *fuck*, he'd seen the shadows in Mandy's eyes. He *knew* Brit was right.

"Yeah." He clenched his hands into fists. "I don't know the whole story yet, but I think she damn well does have us beat."

"Me, too. So"—Brit pointed to the door—"go. Before you really fuck things up."

Blane squeezed by her, thankful for the kick in the pants, though it hadn't felt good. "Thanks, Bestie," he said and tugged her ponytail.

She batted his hand away then punched his shoulder. "I'm still waiting for my half of the heart necklace."

"You're getting better with your chirps," he retorted as she moved to sit beside Stefan again.

"Never let it be said that I don't work on all aspects of my game."

He snorted and hurried off the bus.

Pierre was talking to Coach Bernard. They broke off their conversation as he strode by.

"I'd hurry if I were you, son," Pierre said.

Bernard nodded. "In Dr. Carter's office, last I saw."

Blane started running.

TWENTY-THREE

Mandy

MANDY TOOK the iPad out of Gabe's hands. "I'll finish the reports. Go," she urged when he started protesting. "Your mom is waiting." With his job on the West Coast but his family on the East, Gabe didn't get to see them much, and she knew he worried about his mom, who was recently widowed.

"I don't like leav—"

"*I'm fine*," she said. "Just exhausted after today's craziness." Hours on the plane, followed by hours more on a bus.

But she'd been by Blane's side, so it had been more of an adventure than a trial.

Until now.

Gabe bent to meet her eyes. "You sure that's all it is?"

"Yes."

He crossed his arms. "And it's not the fact that Blane isn't here?"

Yes. *Yes*, of course it damn well was. He'd all but declared himself to the team and then . . . forgot her. "He's busy with the team," she said, hating that he'd made her feel like this.

Like her dad used to.

"I'm good," she said, shoving that feeling deep down and pushing Gabe out the door. "Seriously. I'll just finish with these and then head back to meet Blane."

Nice words, but would that actually happen?

Of course, it would. This was just a weird day with extenuating circumstances. With all the delays and the subsequent rushing around, they hadn't had a chance to talk about what would happen following the game. Plus, they hadn't been on a road trip together as a couple. There were bound to be quirks to work out.

A total misunderstanding.

That was it.

But she couldn't put out of her head that—plans or not—he'd always come before.

Maybe Bernard had pulled him into a last minute meeting?

She bit her lip and started scrolling through the reports on the iPad, archiving some as old, healed injuries, marking others as priority cases, reading through and updating treatments that had been completed that evening.

A knock on the doorframe and Pierre popped his head in. "Sorry to interrupt, but have you seen Dr. Carter?"

Mandy stood. "I sent him on"—she glanced at her watch—"maybe twenty minutes ago now? He had family in the building."

"Okay." A beat. "Will you pass along that I'm heading out of the country for two weeks? Terry will be here in my place." Terrance Freidman was a former player, present assistant GM, and currently being groomed to take over GM duties from Pierre—who while a good owner and GM, had more business than sports experience.

Then there was the complication of him being Stefan's dad.

"Will do," she said. "Thank you again for the . . ." She shook her head. "I just really appreciate the funding for my requests and the new contract. And Blane," she added. "Thank you for understanding."

He nodded. "It's good business. Nothing more. Happy, healthy players, happy staff. That part isn't rocket science."

"Pierre—"

"Sorry," Bernard said when he came equal with the doorway and realized he'd interrupted. "I didn't mean to intrude, but did you need a few minutes? The bus is loaded and the players are ready to go."

Mandy's stomach clenched. "Was—?"

"Blane?" Bernard glanced over, eyes softening. "Last I saw, he was leaving the locker room. I'm sure he'll be over—"

"Of course," she said and held up the iPad. "But don't let me keep you from your meeting. Pierre, I'll be sure to pass on your message to Dr. Carter. Thank you again. For everything."

Pierre's brows drew down, but he nodded and both men said their goodbyes before walking down the hall and disappearing out of sight. Her eyes flicked to the locker room door, currently wide open as the equipment staff hurried in and out.

They had to walk by the office she was in to exit the hall.

Just as the players had needed to.

Just as Blane had to.

So why wasn't he there yet?

Sighing, she sank down into the chair and forced herself to focus. He would come or he wouldn't. God knew she'd spent too much of her childhood waiting for her father to show up.

He rarely had.

The single good thing she'd learned from those experiences was that she *couldn't* sit and wait. She had to do *her*. Had to live her life and not put everything on hold.

Like her mother had. Like *she* had for ages.

Well, not anymore.

Mandy was going to finish these reports, catch a car to the hotel, and then spend an hour in the tub with a book. She might even splurge on room service.

Yes. A twenty-dollar sandwich would make everything just perfect.

She sniffed.

"Dammit." Huffing, she wiped the tears away and tried to keep her focus on the reports. This was her job, a job that she'd just been given a raise for and in that moment, she was bawling like a baby, not even able to finish some fucking reports.

"Ugh." Mandy used her palms to wipe her eyes then inhaled and released it slowly.

It sucked to be forgotten.

She could just leave it at that.

Shove away the hurt and focus on the indignation. She deserved to be remembered, for fuck's sake. She was important. She was valuable.

This wouldn't be like it had been with her dad.

No. She wouldn't let it.

"Okay," she whispered and blew out another breath. "Just—I'll be okay."

The reports came back into focus. She scrolled through them, making adjustments and notes, doing her job like a fucking adult, thank her very much.

She'd just saved the reports to the team's cloud and stashed the iPad into her backpack when her phone buzzed. It took a minute for her to dig it out of the bottom of her bag, but when she saw the lock screen showed a text from Brit, her heart both leapt and dropped.

Because if she was being truthful, Brit was *not* the person she wanted to hear from.

And then the screen flashed with an incoming call from her mother.

Fuck. Her. Life.

"Okay, drama queen," she muttered to herself. "Man up and answer the phone." She gave herself one more second before swiping a finger across the screen. "Hi, Mom."

"You're in town and you don't call?"

The gut punch was real.

Those were the words her mother used to say to her father, before he'd gotten hurt, before every single moment of her mother's day had been dedicated to his care, his appointments, the exact fucking brand of socks or carrots or laundry detergent he preferred.

Her father had been a paraplegic and yet he'd still been able to control the women in his life.

Her mother. *Her.*

And this call felt like a fucking blast from the past, the perfect karmic reminder that she was letting a man determine *her* moods, affect *her* day, put *her* through the emotional wringer.

But Blane was different.

Or was he?

"I'm sorry, Mom. I'd hoped to meet up with you, but there was an issue with the plane and—"

"I'm lonely, Amanda."

She dropped her head to the table, felt like banging it repeatedly. "How's tennis going?"

"The women are mean there."

"Oh, did you—"

"And I don't like sweating. It's too hard."

"What about the quilting class I signed you up for?"

Her mother *pfted.* "Did you know that you have to make sure all of the lines are perfectly straight before you sew? It's impossible."

"Mom, you can draw on eyeliner in a perfectly straight line the first time, every time. That seems like the perfect activity. Plus, no sweating."

"I don't like it."

She imagined her mom sticking out her bottom lip, affecting the little girl persona she'd always taken with her dad.

Because, yes, her dad had been an alcoholic asshole who'd cheated and been his own biggest fan, but her mom wasn't a fucking angel. She was needy, couldn't make a decision before jumping back and forth a dozen times. She liked everything. She liked nothing. She couldn't do a damned thing without a helping hand.

And so every few weeks, Mandy found herself in a conversation such as this.

Except, this time she'd done it to herself

She had thought that if she could only find her mother a hobby, then she would get busy and focus on someone else.

Her mom needed a project and that project needed to be far, far away from Mandy. She'd spent too long trying to be okay without her parents, with never being good enough or smart enough or exacting enough. Just because her father had died didn't mean that she would take his place in micromanaging her mother's life.

And yet, here she was, arranging sewing classes and tennis lessons.

She was seriously screwed up.

No. She didn't want her mother to be unhappy. That made her a good person. But she couldn't also open herself up to be hurt by her all over again. Hell, she'd spent as much time during her childhood chasing her father's approval as her mother's attention.

"How about the makeup classes?"

"You mean doing makeup for those gross old ladies at the home?" her mother asked, obviously affronted.

Fuck it.

Mandy banged her head against the table a couple of times for good measure.

"Mom. I'm tired, and I have a job to do." She sighed. "I'm living my own life, okay? You need to find something to fill yours."

"Baby, I want to—"

"To clarify, *I'm* not the piece to fill yours." Mandy let her head fall back, keeping her eyes shut as she held the phone to her ear. "I can't be your filler for dad, okay? It just hurts too much."

Let her think that it was because she missed the old bastard, rather than the fact that she wasn't willing to open that part of her heart up again.

Too much had happened.

"Well, I—" her mother sputtered.

Mandy had learned, growing up in a dysfunctional, co-dependent, booze-filled, angry, and resentful household meant that she had to embrace every means to protect herself.

Which meant cutting ties at some point.

For her own health and sanity, she needed to keep her mother at a distance.

"Goodbye, Mom."

She hung up then read the text from Brit.

He's an idiot. But not an idiot on purpose.

Mandy snorted, ready to write a reply when she felt it.

Or rather, *him.*

TWENTY-FOUR

Blane

HER EYES WERE sad and rimmed with red.

Fuck.

"Sweetheart, I—" He took a step toward her, gut clenching when she put a palm up to stop him.

"Hold on." Her shoulders rose and dropped on a sigh. "I need to say this."

He stopped, nodded. "Okay."

"You hurt me tonight. A lot," she said then lifted her chin and straightened her shoulders. "But I don't think it's exactly fair for me to be mad and hurt and miserable about it without you knowing why it affected me so much."

Blane reached out a hand. "Can you at least let me hold you while you tell me? I can't stand that look on your face, can't stand knowing I hurt you, unintentionally or not, without trying to at least make you feel better."

Mandy froze.

Then her shoulders crumpled and she began sobbing.

Those tears were like acid to his soul. He strode forward and took her into his arms, knowing she hadn't okayed it but not able to let her cry alone.

"I'm sorry," he murmured over and over again.

She buried her nose in his chest. "It's not you exactly. I—I just—" She sniffed and took a deep breath. "I talked to my mother and then with you not being here, all of the shit from my past is super fresh. I was scared to date you because you're a hockey player and my dad was one, and he was a total asshole." Her words rushed together, and Blane struggled to follow. "He drank so much, but that part wasn't even the worst. It's like he got off on these mindfuck games."

Her hair was in her face, so he brushed it back, cupped one cheek. "Like what?"

"Like he'd promise to come home and then wouldn't"—brown eyes locked on his—"but it wasn't that he forgot to come home or something. He'd get a kick out of making us wait and wait and *wait*. Sometimes he'd call and say he was coming, for my mom to change into a certain outfit, and then he'd turn around and head out to a bar."

He couldn't help the frown that pulled his brows together, but he hesitated to ask—

"I know that sounds like I'm just mad because he got caught up with the team or the rink or something, but I would literally watch his car pull in to the driveway. He'd wait until my mom rushed to open the door, and then he'd just stare at her a moment before driving away."

"Fuck," Blane muttered.

The Roger Shallows he and the rest of the world knew was a charismatic and gifted player. He'd color commented many a game after his career-ending injury, had always come off as upbeat and fun to be around.

Hell, there hadn't even been a rumor of being difficult floating around locker rooms.

Everyone loved the guy.

"I know," Mandy said. "And then later it would be because she wasn't wearing the exact outfit he asked for or that he left because I didn't get straight A's or eat my food right or—"

She broke off. "It was never enough. No matter how good my mom and I were, it was never enough."

He tilted her face up. "And after?"

Her expression tightened. "Worse than before. He wasn't playing but would disappear for days at a time, blow off doctor's appointments he demanded my mom set up. And he drank"—her laugh was brittle—"fuck, I'm surprised he wasn't a pickle for as much as he drank."

"Shit, Mandy," he said. "I had no idea."

She swallowed. "No one does. I mean, the only good thing really is that he never brought us around the team, so a lot of people don't know that I'm his daughter, and I don't have to pretend much."

Her fingers traced a button on his shirt as he asked, "Is your mom better now that he's—?"

"Gone?" she asked. "No. Of course not, because she was as bad as he was in a lot of ways. She'd be furious with me when he left, yell at me, hit me, and tell me it was my fault, that I wasn't perfect enough, pretty enough, whatever." A shake of her head. "I tried for a long time to live up to those expectations, but who could? No matter what I did, there was *always* something I was doing wrong."

He touched her cheek. "I understand now why you didn't want to date me."

"Well," she said, her words quiet. "*That*, and it was a convenient excuse in a lot of ways. You're pretty scary."

"No," he said fiercely, understanding fully now what Brit had been trying to tell him on the bus.

Mandy was maybe the toughest woman he knew, and he knew a lot of strong women—his mother and best friend included. But Mandy had not just endured and carried on and succeeded in a world that was typically male-dominated. That alone would have garnered his respect.

Knowing her past just made that admiration for her grow so much more than he thought possible.

She was the woman he loved, but also an incredible woman in her own right.

"No," he said again when she opened her mouth. "I mean, I get the scary, yes. I know it's frightening to put yourself out there." He brought her hand to his heart. "But *this* beats for you. I know I'm just a normal guy who had two parents who loved each other, who was picked on at school occasionally, who may have had his heart stomped on a few times. I know I've been so, so lucky, sweetheart. I haven't had to endure what—" His throat tightened and fuck, his eyes stung. "I'm so sorry you had to go through that. But I also feel so incredibly lucky to have you in my life."

"Blane . . ."

"And I hate that—"

She kissed him gently. "Thank you. For being angry, for caring that I was hurt." Her eyes went serious. "But I need you to understand that what happened tonight can *never* happen again. I can't be someone's afterthought, can't wait around wondering if you might turn up. It might be completely unreasonable, but I just can't be in a relationship with someone who doesn't consider me a priority." Her lips pressed flat. "Logically, I understand that it has nothing to do with mind games with you, but I'm messed up, Blane, and tonight my mind started going to this really dark place, and I just—"

"I get it," he said. "And it's not unreasonable or unfair. Forgetting about you was unforgivable, even without knowing what happened to you."

Her gaze dropped to where her palm still rested on his chest. "I'm sorry."

He gripped her face in his palms. "Tell me again why in the fuck you're apologizing? You were upset, shared why it hurt you so badly, and are asking for what you need. Isn't that called adult communication?"

She bit her lip. "I don't like it. I don't *want* to be an adult. I want to binge on *Harry Potter* and sleep in way too late."

Blane chuckled at her petulant tone. "Next day off and we are so doing that."

She laughed and he relaxed, tugging her close so he could hug her tightly.

Eventually, she pulled back. "Thank you for understanding." A pause, her lips curving as she held up her phone and showed him Brit's text message. "You're also apparently an idiot, though not one on purpose."

He snorted. "There's my best friend, always standing up for me." With that, he helped Mandy to her feet. "Should we go back to the hotel?"

"Only if you're sharing your bed," she said.

"As if that was in question." He touched a fingertip to her nose, wanting to tell her how he felt, almost desperate with the need to declare his love for her. But this wasn't the right time, and he didn't want what they were building to be tainted by the past. "Anything of mine is already yours, sweetheart."

She stared at him for a moment, her expression soft, then turned to grab her bag, glaring when he took it from her and slung it over his shoulder.

But instead of protesting, she just sighed, laced her fingers through his, and squeezed.

Three times.

"I need a bath," she said.

He leered at her, waggled his brows. "Seeing you naked? Now *that* can be arranged."

Her giggle made him feel ten feet tall.

TWENTY-FIVE

Mandy

"OKAY, I LIED," Mandy said, rolling over in her bed and handing Blane the remote. "I want to binge watch that flat earth documentary on Netflix. Brit said it's insane."

Blane, one arm behind his head, shirtless, and yummy chest on display, took the remote with a smile. "Blasphemy! You promised me magic and really evil wizards. What the hell?"

She climbed on top of his chest, heart full, happier than she'd ever been.

These last two weeks with Blane had been incredible. Also, insane with the extended road trip followed by two games at home. Then there had been a dinner for the Gold Institute—the charity the team supported that funded local sports and education, and *then* that night was Sara's gallery opening.

But for now, she was enjoying a PJ Sunday with Blane and bad TV.

His hands dropped onto her hips, the controller pressing into her side.

She snagged it back from him and flopped onto the mattress. "Fine." Mandy gave her best impression of evil villain laughter. "I take back control of the television then."

He tickled her side in response then drifted his fingers lower, making her alternatively squeal then groan in pleasure. "How about we watch the documentary later and instead"—a brush of his thumb between her thighs—"we make some magical sparks in the here and now?"

Mandy froze and stared at him, one brow raised.

"It wasn't that bad," he protested.

"It was bad," she replied, smirking at him. "Really, *really* bad. Cheese ball bad, so awkward it was totally cringe-worthy bad."

"I—" His objection cut off when she grabbed his free hand—meaning the one that was not currently between her thighs—and brought it to her breast.

"And while it might have been absolutely terrible," she said. "I'm still willing to make some *sparks*."

He snorted then grumbled, "Who's the cheese ball now?"

Her hand snaked down to his erection, which was doing an admirable job of bursting free of his boxer briefs.

"I want you inside me." A squeeze to punctuate her statement. "Is that better?"

Blane rolled on top of her, dropping his mouth to hers, kissing her so intensely that Mandy felt as though her heart would beat out of her chest. Her skin went tight, her thighs clenched, and her nipples tingled, aching for him.

God, but could the man kiss, she thought as they broke away for air.

Every time, every *single* time he pressed his mouth to hers, she was transported, taken away to a place where it was just the two of them in the universe, where the rest of the world couldn't intrude. Every kiss was special and different and meant something.

There was only one explanation for the way he made her feel.

She loved the man.

Only, how to tell him? How to take that leap when all of her love had always been tied up with the fucked-up shit from her past?

What if she could *never* say it?

A finger tapped the middle of her forehead lightly. "What's going on in that big juicy brain of yours?"

She winced. "That I'm screwed up?"

His brows drew down and he rolled to his side. "Sweetheart."

"No"—she grabbed at his shoulders to tug him back over her —"come back. It's not like that and *plus*, you asked what thoughts were in my mind. They're not always going to be, *Blane's so amazing!*"

His expression turned affronted.

"No," she hurried to say. "Ah geez. I *do* think you're amazing. I was—That is—dammit, Blane, I was thinking that I loved you so much and that I had no clue how I was ever going to tell you because I'm so messed up, and—"

He stilled, half on top of her.

Mandy realized what she'd said. "I know it's too soon, and I—"

His lips pressed to hers, giving her one of those kisses that made her forget all of the bad thoughts swirling through her head and focus on the way he made her feel—cherished, precious . . . loved.

He was smiling when he pulled back. "Had to outdo me, huh?" Blane tucked a strand of hair behind her ear. "I've been trying to find a way to tell you that I love you for weeks. But I thought it was too soon and didn't want to scare you off."

She wrinkled her nose. "I think, based on the facts, you should be scared off by me."

His eyes rolled heavenward. "Should we just both admit that we're scary?"

Taking a moment to consider that, she nodded. "Yes. Yes, we should."

"Okay. We're scary," he said. "Also, I love you."

Yikes. But also, holy shit did that feel incredible. He loved her. Blane Hart loved Mandy Shallows.

And she hadn't been struck down by lightning or anything.

A smile split her face. "Also, I love you, too."

"There you go again," he teased. "Outdoing me in the declaration department."

Her brows drew together in a frown. "Because I said I love you, *too*?"

"No," he said. "Because when you say those words, you make me feel like the most important man in the world. You make me feel like I could climb Mt. Fucking Everest, just because you asked. You make all of those holes in my heart, the missing pieces, the jagged edges disappear." He brought her hand to rest above his heart. "You make me feel *more*. With just those three words, I become somebody."

"You're somebody, Blane," she said, feeling his heart pounding beneath her palm. "You've always been somebody."

"Maybe." His fingers tangled with hers. "But you've made me somebody who's finally living instead of waiting on the sidelines, watching everyone else find their slice of happiness."

"Yes," she whispered. "I understand."

Because that was exactly what Blane did for her in return.

TWENTY-SIX

Blane

BLANE WAS WEARING A SUIT, and it wasn't even a game day.

He smiled over at Mandy, who was dressed in a gorgeous dress Monique had brought over that afternoon.

Having been kicked out of the apartment, Stefan, Mike, Spence, and Blane had found themselves at loose ends. They'd ended up getting a beer and watching some basketball on TV at a local bar while the girls had taken over Mandy's apartment for their own personal version of *Say Yes to the Dress*.

Yes, he was now intimately familiar with the show.

No, that didn't make him pussy-whipped.

Or maybe it did, and he just didn't give a damn.

Either way, he was propped against a wall, a beer in one hand, his eyes locked on his woman, when he felt a tap on his shoulder.

He turned, expecting a fan and was shocked to see his mother.

"Mom?" he said stupidly. He hurried to hug her. "*Hi*. I didn't know you were coming into town."

"Brit invited me." Eyes similar to his own narrowed. "*She* invites me to things."

Blane shook his head. "Nice try with the guilt, Mom. But I believe I extended an open invitation even before the season started, and you told me work was crazy."

His mom worked for the FBI in a very classified and highly demanding position.

Her lips twitched. "Maybe."

"I'm glad you're here," he said, dropping an arm over her shoulders. "And I like your dress."

She patted her hips. "This old thing?" But she smiled anyway.

It was odd now, thinking about how hard his mom had worked when he'd been a kid—hell, she *still* worked insane hours—but he'd never felt resentful of the time she'd been away. She had always tried to come to everything important, to be home for dinner, for games, and school plays, even if she had to return to work afterward.

Why had Mandy's dad not done the same?

Was it because *his* dad, whose job was significantly less demanding, had been accepting of the time his mom had spent at work while Mandy's mom had made it a huge battle with Mandy forced to play a pawn?

They both had similar stories in a way—one parent gone a lot with a demanding career, while the other picked up the slack at home.

Why had his childhood been great when *she'd* been dealt a shitty hand?

"I can hear the wheels turning, baby," his mom said, startling him out of his thoughts. "Everything okay?"

"I'm fine. Just thinking about when I was a kid."

"Is it because of Mandy?" she asked.

His eyes flew to hers. "How do you always know?"

"I work for a very powerful government organization."

He fixed her with a look. "You mean Brit told you."

A shrug. "Sources are an important part of intelligence."

"Unbelievable."

Brit glanced over then and gave an awkward wave. He sent her a glare in return. "Yes, it's because of Mandy. I love her."

His mom tucked her arm in his. "Come outside for a minute. I want to talk to you."

They walked through the exhibit and out onto a patio. The air had a bite to it. When his mom shivered, Blane slipped out of his coat and placed it on her shoulders. God, but the city was beautiful sometimes, or maybe that was seeing it through the lens of Sara's artwork. She had a way of capturing the buildings and lights and traffic and transforming it into something beautiful.

"Sara's very talented," his mom said.

"Yes." He nudged her arm. "But that's not why you dragged me out here and stole my coat."

"You're a good boy, Blane," she said. "Always have been, and I'm proud of you."

Uh-oh.

"Why does that sound like the other shoe is about to drop?"

"Well"—she winced—"kind of because it is."

"And this is about Mandy?"

His mom nodded. "I ran her."

"You background checked my *girlfriend?* What the fuck, Mom?"

She put her hands up. "I background check all of the girls you date . . ."

Which had been pathetically few, but still. "Mom!"

"You never know what some of those women might want. You're a wealthy man, an athlete. I'm trying to protect you."

"Protect me?" He scoffed. "And you're telling me that Brit put you up to this?"

"No. I mean—*yes*. Yes, she told me you were dating someone and that I should come out and meet Mandy because she was great and things looked serious, but I did the background check all on my own. That wasn't Brit's idea." She lifted her chin, touching his arm. "You're *my* baby, Blane. I—"

"Invaded my privacy," he said, furious. "You did this behind my back."

"Well—"

"That's *not* okay, Mom. I love you. *Shit.*" He pulled away. "But you don't get to do that."

He hadn't really ever been mad at his parents. Sure, there was the usual teenage strife, pissy about not being able to go to a party or being allowed to spend time alone with a girl. But he'd been too busy and focused on hockey to care all that much.

Especially since they'd let him play hockey as much as he had ever wanted.

So not much room for conflict there.

But *this* was different.

His mom had delved into Mandy's life, something that was so painful and vulnerable that his forgetting to meet up with her had dredged it all up again and driven her to tears just a few weeks before.

"Look, Mom," he said. "Mandy and I have talked about her past, about *my* past, as boring as that is. I already know everything she's wanted to share." He shook his head. "If there's anything else, then she'll tell me on her own terms and we'll get through it. Together. But you can't do this—you can't cross that boundary and expect that I'll be okay with it."

"Don't you want to know what I found?"

"*No.*" He made a noise of disgust and strode over to the railing, clenching it tightly enough that he was half-surprised it didn't shatter under his grip. "*I don't.*"

"I do."

Mandy's voice made him panic. *Shit.* How much had she heard?

TWENTY-SEVEN

Mandy

SHE HADN'T MEANT to overhear. Really.

But when she'd asked where Blane was and had been told the patio, she hadn't expected to find he'd gone off with another woman.

She'd thought he needed fresh air, a break from the stuffy room.

And she'd wanted to surprise him.

Imagine her surprise at coming up to the door, Blane's arm laced with the gorgeous blonde.

She didn't look old enough to be Blane's mom, but the conversation had quickly transmuted the slice of betrayal she'd been trying to stifle into admiration for her man spending quality time with his mom into shock and horror and . . . so much more admiration.

He'd stood up for her.

Stood by her.

"I do," she said again from the doorway. "I'd like to know what you found out that was so important it warranted a trip across the country."

Part of her was furious. How dare his mom do that? Part of her was hurt. Would her parents' screwed-up relationship never just stay in the past? And part of her was curious. Growing up, nothing had ever been transparent—it was all mind games and hidden meanings and—

Well, she'd rather know all of it. Now.

Both of them had frozen when she'd spoken, Blane turning in almost slow motion, a look of horror on his face.

She crossed to him, grabbed his hand, and squeezed. Three times.

Rising on tiptoe, she whispered. "You know that means I love you, right?"

His lips curved. "Outdoing me again?"

A shrug. "It's a gift."

His fingers brushed her wrist. "I'm sorry. I—"

She just squeezed his hand three more times, heart pulsing when he did the same in return.

God, she loved this man.

Then she blew out a breath and turned to face off with his mother.

"Hi, Mrs. Hart," she said. "I'm Mandy, though I guess you already know that."

Blane's mom extended a hand for Mandy to shake. "Allison." Her tone was, rightfully so, chagrined. "It's lovely to finally meet you."

"Yes," Mandy agreed. "Though maybe we can skip the formalities just this once, and you can tell me what it was that brought you out here."

Allison sighed. "Okay. But I do want you both to know that I really did come because I wanted to meet you. I had a conference in the city that lined up with Blane's schedule, so I wanted to watch him play and meet the woman that Brit has been raving about."

"But?" Mandy asked.

"But then the background check came in."

She pressed her lips together. "Yeah."

"You know your father—"

"Was an alcoholic abuser? That my mom wasn't—*isn't*—a peach? Yeah. I lived through that touching story the first time."

Allison's eyes softened. "Oh, sweetie. I'm sorry you went through that. I"—she sighed—"it wasn't right for them to treat you like that. You deserved better."

Mandy sniffed. "Don't do that."

"Do what?"

"Be nice and genuine. I'm trying to stay mad at you for invading my privacy."

Allison laughed softly. "I really *am* sorry. I know that I shouldn't have done it, but I am glad I did. And not just because I thought I was protecting Blane, but because I found out something that you really should know."

Mandy glanced up at Blane. He shrugged. "It's up to you."

Her chin dropped to her chest, and she inhaled deeply. Should she ask?

Did she really have a choice *not* to?

Dammit.

Because no.

Blane had told her his mom worked pretty high up in the government. If Allison was here saying what she'd found out was important, then it was.

"Tell me." Mandy straightened and waited for the blow.

"You have a sister."

She blinked, the statement about as far from anything she could have ever imagined. "Uhh, what?"

"Your dad—"

Mandy put her hand up. "Oh, my God. Sorry, just give me a second."

Holy fuck, she'd expected money laundering or something, not *Jerry Springer* type shit.

Blane cupped her cheek. "Are you—?"

She nodded, breathing out carefully. "Okay, freak out semi-averted. How old is she?"

"Twenty-seven."

Gut punched. Hard enough to stall her lungs.

Two years younger than her. Two *fucking* years.

"Sweetheart," Blane said, crouching down in front of her. Somehow, she'd ended up bent at the waist and fervently thanking the fact that the tight dress was made of stretchy material and she hadn't just ripped an ass seam in front of Blane's mom.

Ass seam?

Fuck.

She began laughing. This was completely unbelievable and yet not at all surprising.

Of course, her dad had another kid.

Of course.

She blinked hard and straightened. "And did he do the same stuff to her—"

Allison nodded. "I'm afraid so. He was just smart enough to have them both sign NDAs before he passed. No post-mortem scandals."

Mandy pressed her fingers to her temples. "Did my mother know?"

"There is no indication of that one way or the other."

"And is this girl—is my sister okay?"

"Yes," Allison said. "She seems to be doing exceptionally well. She works for RoboTech."

"Here?"

Allison inclined her head. "At the San Francisco office, yes."

"Oh, sweet baby Harry." Allison's brows pulled together. "Sorry, it's a movie reference. I just—" Mandy shrugged helplessly. "I'm just a really big nerd."

Allison's mouth twitched before straightening out. "Are you okay?"

"Oh God, I don't know," she said. "I *think* so. I mean, I guess it doesn't *surprise* me, exactly, because my dad was . . . well, my dad. But I just can't believe I didn't know until now."

"I'm sorry I was the one to have to tell you"—Allison raised both palms—"Look, I *know* I shouldn't have pried. But consider this me making penance for me prying." She reached into her purse and pulled out a piece of paper. "Her email and cell if you want to contact her."

Mandy took the slip.

Angelica Shallows

555-555-1234

ashallows@robotech.com

She had his last name.

Un-fucking-believable.

Allison lifted her arms. "Can I hug you now?"

"Mom. *No*," Blane said.

Mandy snorted but patted his arm reassuringly. "Come here." And she embraced Blane's mother.

Because drama brought people together?

No. Because Allison had cared enough to come here and make sure Mandy knew the truth. That was enough for a hug . . . and maybe more. Maybe they could build something that she'd never had with her own mother? Maybe they could have something truthful and real and—

"Thank you for telling me," she said and pulled back. "But I'm going to need a promise from you that you won't do any more prying."

Allison made a face but nodded. "I promise." A pause. "But I reserve the right to check up on any boyfriends or girlfriends my future grandchildren may have."

Mandy felt her chin drop.

Blane muttered a curse and said, "Christ, Mom. You're not helping my case any. I want her to stay, not run for the hills."

Mandy smiled and shook her head. Somehow, the thought of little Blanes running around didn't scare her as much as it probably should. She touched Allison's arm. "Future baby background checks are up for discussion at a later point."

Allison grinned and clapped her hands together. "Grandbabies!"

"Now you've done it," Blane grumbled to her, before adding, "She said later, Mom. As in at a *much later* point."

Allison ignored him and grabbed Mandy's arm. "Let's get back to the show before we miss anything exciting. And then I think I owe you and Blane dinner for all the trouble I caused."

Mandy turned, glancing back over her shoulder at the man she loved.

"For the record, I didn't say *much* later," she said, half because it was the truth and half because she wanted to see his response to the words.

His jaw dropped, but then he grinned and hurried to catch up to them. Allison shrugged off Blane's coat as they entered the exhibit, shoving it at him so she could rush over to Brit, no doubt to share the gossip.

Blane took the jacket but didn't put it on. "Not much later?" he asked, brow raised.

"How about semi later?"

He brushed a thumb over her cheek. "That sounds perfect."

TWENTY-EIGHT

Blane

"ARE YOU OKAY?" Blane asked a few hours later.

Their bellies were full of good food and drink, their minds full of Sara's amazing art, but he was worried about Mandy.

His mother.

Fuck.

First, he couldn't believe that she'd run a background check on the woman he loved and second, he couldn't believe what she'd found out.

Mandy had a sister. One who was only two years younger than her.

Her father was even more of an asshole than she'd known.

And yet Mandy was lying next to him in bed with a smile on her face.

"I'm fine," she said, snuggling closer. "I mean, I think I'm okay. Like I said, it's . . . not surprising, I guess."

Considering her dad had been an absentee, cheating father, that was true.

"I just"—she began tracing circles on his chest—"do you think she might want to know me at all?"

Blane slid down until they were face to face. "She'd be a fool not to."

One half of her mouth turned up. "You're too sweet."

He scoffed. "I'm exactly the right amount of sweet, thank you very much." A brush of his thumb across her lips. "But I think if you want to contact your sister, then you should. Worst case, she's not interested in getting to know you. Best case, she is and is someone you want in in your life."

Mandy nodded. "You're right, of course, but I don't think I'm ready yet."

"Your terms, sweetheart," he said. "You get to decide if and when you're ready to reach out. And that can also be never. We've got a good group of people around us. Hell, my mom wants to take you shopping before she goes home."

A snort. "Only because Brit refuses."

"Maybe." He chucked her chin. "But also because she knows you're a good person."

"Ugh." Mandy sniffed. "Why do you do this to me?"

He slid his hand to her ass. "Grope you?"

"Be so fucking perfect. You're everything I ever hoped for." She sucked in a breath, dashed a tear away, then shot him a mock-glare. "But all these emotions you make me feel. Also," she said, shooting him a grin after he'd wiped her tears away with his free hand. "Let it be noted that I like the groping."

He squeezed, tugging her closer to his side. "I'm good with groping."

"Also, I love you," she said. "Even despite your mom being kind of cuckoo for Cocoa Puffs."

"I'm still so furious that she did that. I swear, if she ever crosses that line again I—"

Her lips found his. "No," she ordered when they broke apart.

"She did it because she loves and worries about you. I'm *glad* you have someone who cares about you that way."

He rolled his eyes. "Just wait until you meet my dad."

"I'm looking forward to it." Her hand snaked down. "But let's discuss your parents later."

Blane's eyes rolled into the back of his head. "Yes." He groaned when she slid down and her mouth teamed up with her hand. "Later."

———

THE SEASON FLEW BY, and before they knew it three months had passed.

And that only meant one thing: playoff time.

AKA, he was living and breathing hockey.

Of course, Mandy had been breathing it alongside him, pulling longer days with the team as the brutality of the eighty-two-game season took its toll and injuries became prevalent. The team was in fairly good shape overall, but even the healthiest player couldn't go out on the ice night after night for months on end without experiencing at least a minimal amount of bruises and strained muscles.

Blane was no exception, having taken a puck high up on his chest just the night before.

But he had his personal physical therapist.

"You're all black and blue," she said and *tsked*. "Did you even put ice on this?"

Blane raised a brow.

"Okay, fine," she muttered, smoothing some cream on his skin before buttoning up his shirt. "Of course, you put ice on it. But, babe, you're lucky you didn't break a collarbone."

"That's what Doc said." Blane rolled his shoulders and bit back a wince. "But you've trained me well, sweetheart. I'm fine. It's not broken, and I can deal with a bruise."

"*We* can deal with a bruise," she reminded him.

"We," he agreed. "We'd better go before we run late for the bus."

They had stayed at Mandy's apartment the night before since it was closer to the arena—where the bus would pick them up and take them to the airport.

"Yes. Let's hit it," she said, shrugging into a sweatshirt. Blane grinned, making the innocuous statement into a euphemism and she shook her head. "Sicko."

A tug of her ponytail. "You like my sick tendencies." He smirked. "You also like when I *hit* it."

"Oh, my God. You are *such* a dork."

"It's one of my best characteristics."

She laughed and even though it was zero dark thirty—okay, so it was only sixty-thirty in the morning—his heart still felt so fucking full.

Mandy did that. She just filled him with so much love and joy—

"I love you," she murmured.

"My line," he said and leaned down to kiss her.

Her eyes filled with tears before she shook her head and closed the door behind them. "Don't make me cry, Blane. You know I get emotional during playoff season."

He snorted. "And they say I'm the dork."

"I say. *I* say that." She locked the apartment and started down the hall. "I am a little emotional, I guess, though," she said as they hit the stairs. "I've been feeling all out of sorts."

Blane froze mid-step. "Holy shit, are you pregnant?"

"What?" Her jaw dropped open. "*No.* I mean, I don't think so. We haven't—I'm on birth control."

If he was honest, her not being pregnant gave him the slightest pang of disappointment. "Oh, okay."

She frowned, glancing at her stomach as they continued their way down the stairs.

"What is it?" he finally asked.

"Have I put on weight or something?" She tugged at the hem of her sweatshirt.

Shit. "No, baby." He scrambled, trying to unfuck his words. Impossible, considering what he'd said. "It's just that you said you were feeling off and emotional and—"

They pushed through the door into the garage. "And what?" she asked.

"And"—he winced—"we have a lot of sex."

Mandy stopped. Then smacked him on the chest.

Right on the bruise.

He hissed and she frowned, probably because she hadn't hit him that hard.

"Oh shit," she said, tugging at the collar of his shirt. "I didn't mean—"

It only took him a second to trap her hands and haul her close. "Sweetheart, I'm fine. Big, tough hockey player, remember?"

She snorted but didn't fight his hold.

"And you're as beautiful as ever. We've been together for a bit now, and . . . I guess I wouldn't be opposed to it."

"What you're saying is that it's semi-later?"

He brushed back her hair. "Yes. *That.*"

"And that your parents want grandbabies?"

"God, yes." He groaned, thinking of the sheer amount of times his mother had inferred that marriage should be happening soon and babies coming shortly thereafter. Or babies first.

She wasn't picky.

"We should wait until the end of the season."

His heart skipped a beat. Because this was very adult and mature and *fuck*, he so wanted Mandy to have his babies.

"You'll have to marry me first," he said.

She stiffened, and Blane cursed mentally. He'd pushed too hard. *Ha.* What was new?

"Or not," he said. "I just want to be with you, baby. *Only* you."

She slipped out of his arms, started walking for the car. "We need to get moving. And for the record," she added. "I'm not opposed to marrying you, so that better not have been your fucking marriage proposal."

His stomach unclenched.

"It's not." He opened her door, helped her in.

"Good." She smiled up at him. "Because, with you, I want it all."

Blame it on the early hour or the pregnancy misunderstanding, or maybe the almost botched marriage proposal, but they were already driving to catch the bus by the time he remembered to ask her to clarify why she had been feeling out of sorts.

"I emailed my sister." She wrinkled her nose. "I know it's not a big deal and I shouldn't expect an immediate response when I had several months to get used to the idea of her, but . . ."

"You kind of expected an immediate response?"

Mandy shrugged. "Yeah. I shouldn't have, but yeah, I did."

"And," he said, turning into the arena and parking. "So you've discovered you're normal."

"Charmer." She punched him on the shoulder. "But, yes, you're right. I get it. But enough serious stuff," she said and turned to grab her bag from the back seat.

As usual, he beat her to it, throwing it over his shoulder.

"Men," she muttered and got out of the car.

He met her at the front of the hood. "We take care of each other. Get used to it."

Her lips twitched. "I *am* used to it. Doesn't mean I'm going to skip a chance at grumbling this early in the morning, especially when I'm cranky."

"I like you cranky." He took her hand as they walked for the bus.

Once aboard they went their separate ways for the drive to the airport. He sat in the back with the players and Mandy used the short drive to discuss any outstanding issues with Gabe.

The plane was a different story.

Mandy was his good luck charm—he was coming off a regular season with the most points ever—so she would sit by him.

"Blane," she said as he turned to take a seat in the back.

He stopped.

"For the record, I will *so* marry you."

The bus was silent, as was typical this early in the morning, so every single member of the Gold—player and staff alike—heard Mandy's declaration.

As she'd known they would.

Someone whistled, there were catcalls, and no small amount of hoots, but then she kissed him and the world faded away.

At least until Max poked him in the ribs. Hard.

Blane broke away, panting.

"Get a room," Max growled, shoving past them.

Mandy raised her brows, but Blane just shrugged. Max had been surly for the last few months. It would pass.

Mike called, "You buy him a ring yet, Mandy?"

"I heard he likes princess cut diamonds," Blue added.

The chirps continued, and he bopped her on the nose. "So much trouble for that."

She grinned. "For the record, I like princess cut, too."

One more kiss before he strolled to the back of the bus, knowing that so long as he had this woman in his life, he would be okay.

Brit raised her brows.

He waved her away. "Long story. I haven't proposed, but I'm going to."

"Yes!" She fist-pumped then grinned and said, "You better get some pointers from Mike, because he set the proposal bar really high."

Blane punched Stefan on the shoulder. "That what you did?"

His captain only smiled, revealing nothing.

Mike, on the other hand, leaned in and nodded. "That's a yes. The key is to know what's most important to your woman and run with that." He pretended to pat himself on the back. "I know. I am the proposal guru."

Blane rolled his eyes. "Well, proposal guru, here's what I was thinking . . ."

TWENTY-NINE

Mandy

MANDY SMELLED A RAT.

Or rather, a proposal.

But considering it was July and the season had been over for two months—the Gold making it to the Western Conference finals but no further—she'd smelled a proposal at every dinner date and gathering of their friends, so she knew she was being silly.

Still, Blane had called, asking her to meet him at their favorite restaurant—a burger joint on the Peninsula that was super campy in its décor but had, hands down, the best hamburgers in town.

She was almost there when her phone rang.

Frowning when she saw it was Gabe calling, she quickly accepted the call on her Bluetooth. "Gabe?" she asked. "Is everything okay?"

"I need you to come to the arena, there's an issue."

Her heart sank. They were supposed to be completing the construction of the new PT suite that week. A major issue meant delays, and they couldn't have delays.

"What's wrong?"

His voice sobered. "It's better if you come see."

Shit.

"Okay. I'll be there in ten. I'm actually pretty close," she said and hung up. "This had better not be my proposal being ruined by a leaky pipe or something," she muttered.

Sighing, she dialed Blane's number and quickly explained the situation.

His ready agreement at her putting off their date told her that no proposal was planned that evening. She tried to tell herself that she wasn't disappointed, but that was a lie.

They'd already pulled the goalie—meaning she'd stopped her birth control and they'd ditched the condoms—and so she might already be pregnant.

She didn't really care about being married . . . except it was Blane and she wanted *all* the things with Blane.

A wedding and a white dress. Little hockey players running around their house.

Plus, he'd said—

"It doesn't matter," she reminded herself and turned into the arena parking lot.

The lot was full, but she managed to snag a spot right in front. Rushing, she grabbed her purse and hauled ass down to the PT suite, which—

Was finished?

Her breath caught as she walked in and she blinked back tears. The room was so pretty and full of so many tools.

Gabe stood to one side, his cell in his hand, a smirk on his face.

She crossed to him. "You jerk. I was panicked."

"Don't blame me," he said. "Blame him."

And then he pointed behind him.

Blane strolled out of the newly expanded weight room, along with every current Gold player and some of the former. Even both Rebeccas, Monique, and Sara were there.

"What—?"

They crowded into the room, each holding a rose, huge grins on their faces.

Blane was wearing a suit, a huge bouquet in one hand, a ring box in the other. He walked over to her.

Mandy was crying already. She could feel the tears streaming down her cheeks.

"I'm sorry it took so long, but I wanted to wait until everyone could get back together. I wanted all of your family here with you."

Her family. Yes, these people meant more to her than her own family ever had.

"Oh my God. *Blane.*"

He handed her the flowers and, robotically, she took them, but could hardly spare the bouquet a glance. Her eyes were on Blane.

Who had kneeled before her and opened the box.

It held a huge princess cut diamond ring.

"Mandy," he said. "When I open my eyes in the morning and see you there next to me, I think I'm the luckiest guy in the world. You are so fucking smart and beautiful, and I can't imagine a world that doesn't have you in it." He took her hand, pressed it to his chest. "*This* beats for you. Only you. Will—"

"Yes!" she cried and launched herself into his arms.

Everyone crowded around, cheering and chirping in equal parts.

"You didn't let me finish the question," Blane teased, wiping the tears from her cheeks after he'd slipped the ring on her finger. "What if I had been asking for extra ketchup?"

She squeezed him tight. "No matter the question," she said, "the answer would have always been yes."

The team let them hold each for approximately one more second before they tugged her and Blane apart, and congratulatory hugs and back slaps were shared all around.

Which was just the way it should be.

The Gold was her family.

It was as simple as that.

EPILOGUE

Max

MAX STOOD on the perimeter of the crowd, edging toward the door.

Yes, he was an asshole to escape in this moment, but Blane and Mandy wouldn't miss him.

Plus, he'd been here for the big moment, after all.

No one would even know he'd gone.

He cracked the door and slipped out into the hall.

Then nearly mowed down a tiny little fairy.

Okay, not a fairy, but a woman with pale amber hair and a curvy little body. Some players were about the statuesque model type, but not Max. *He* liked them curvy, and he certainly didn't mind them small.

That meant he could more easily lift them up and they could wrap their legs around his hips while he—

Fuck. It had been a long time since he'd been with a woman.

And this tiny, voluptuous angel was trying to make a quick getaway.

"Hey," he said, snagging her arm when she would have slunk down the hall. "You lost, sweetheart?"

Shoulders straightened and she ripped out of his grip. "Don't touch me," she snapped, keeping her back to him, and *fuck*, even her voice made his cock twitch.

"Okay. No problem." He slid around to her front. "But this area is off limits."

Her gaze stayed on the floor, her jaw clenched tight. "I was invited."

"Oh?" Max crossed his arms, leaned back against the wall. Sexy voice, banging body—he was desperate now to see her eyes, the shape of her nose, her lips. Please let her be as pretty as she sounded. "By who?"

Finally, she looked up.

Max sucked in a breath as though he'd been gut-punched.

Those eyes. They were—

"Mandy Shallows," the woman said. "I'm . . ." She hesitated then lifted her chin and said, "I'm her sister."

Mandy had a sister? Holy shit.

But something was off. Max took a step closer to her, noted that the tip of her nose was slightly rosy, her lids reddened and puffy. "Why don't I think those are happy tears for her engagement?"

The woman pushed around him, striding down the hall before stopping and hanging her head again. "I didn't mean to intrude," she said. "I—" Her voice caught. "She said anytime, but I should have called first. This wasn't mine to witness." A sigh. "If she saw, if she's upset, tell her I'm sorry."

She started walking again, this time faster.

"Wait," he said and caught her arm again. "I'm sure Mandy will be happy—"

"No." She yanked out of his grip, her purse slipping down her arm and falling to the floor. The contents went every which way.

"Shit," he muttered. "I'm sorry." He knelt to help her, but she batted his hands away.

"Just go, dammit! Just leave me the fuck alone."

"Okay—" he began but didn't get the chance to leave.

Because she'd snatched up her things and was gone.

Sighing, he turned back toward the PT Suite. He should probably face the music. Congratulate the couple, break the news of Mandy's sister running off.

He took a step and the crinkle made him freeze.

Max bent, picked up the paper that must have fallen out of the woman's purse. It was an email addressed to . . . Angelica Shallows.

Fuck, if that wasn't the perfect name for the beautiful *fleeing* angel he'd just met.

BENCHED

Benched, book four of the Gold Hockey series,
is now available
(www.books2read.com/Benched)

EMPTY NET

A GOLD HOCKEY NOVELLA

ONE

Shannon

SHANNON SNIFFED AND PROMPTLY GROANED.

So. Much. Regret.

Why had she thought baking a cake was a good idea?

Tentatively, she opened the oven door.

And promptly slammed it shut—which didn't make one lick of difference. A cloud of black smoke had already poured into the room, filling the air with the pungent scent of burnt sugar and flour.

"Fucking hell." She raced across the kitchen and flung open the back door.

Then, without thinking, she rushed back to the oven and reached for the smoldering brick that was supposed to be a cake for her best friend and business partner. She'd tried out a new recipe, hoping to impress Molly enough that her friend might actually allow her to take a bigger part in the baking portion of their bakery business. They'd recently expanded with a stand in the Gold Mine, the home arena of the San Francisco Gold, the NHL's newest expansion team.

Things weren't going to plan.

Shannon realized she was reaching into the oven without donning a mitt a moment too late. Before she could stop herself, her fingers grazed the hot pan.

She jumped back with a very unladylike curse word passing her lips.

Which was the exact moment the smoke detector went off.

Turned out, she knew even naughtier words.

Ignoring her singed fingers, she snagged a towel from the counter, pulled out the pan, and dumped it into the sink. Then she turned on the water full blast and opened the kitchen window.

The peals of the alarm hurt her ears and head, and she was momentarily grateful the other half of her duplex was empty. Especially since it was nearly midnight.

She yanked a chair into the hall and clambered up on it. There were two buttons on the front of the smoke detector, and she pressed them both. When that didn't work, she proceeded to wave her towel like a madwoman, or perhaps a really terrible color-guard girl, in a futile attempt to get the damn thing to shut up.

For the record, it didn't.

"Need some help?"

The masculine voice made her shriek. She whirled around, forgetting her precarious position on the chair.

Arms floundering and already knowing the fall was going to hurt like hell, she prepared for impact.

It didn't come.

"I've got you." The words—confident with a touch of humor— were spoken as warm hands steadied her hips. It was sexy, that voice, smooth as silk, and a tendril of heat curled through her stomach, slid down her spine.

"Thanks," she said, shrugging off the zing of pleasure. So what if she'd been on a bit of a dating hiatus? That was the smart thing to do when one possessed her track record of exes.

See?

Logical.

That was her middle name.

Yeah, it could definitely be considered logical to bake in the dead of the night when she burned everything, *including* cookware, on a regular basis.

"Want me to turn it off?"

She jumped then realized she'd been standing there like an idiot, thinking about her variety of baking fails and not addressing the fact that a stranger was in her house or that her smoke detector was still blaring.

"Here," he said and before she could figure out what he meant, the man lifted her down from the chair and took her place.

Irritation crept through Shannon, dousing the heat from a moment before. She'd tried that already. "It won't shut—"

The sound cut off.

"Off," she finished.

The man smiled down at her, and without the incessant blaring, she noticed everything she'd missed from her brief perusal before he'd climbed up on to the chair.

Namely, that he was hot.

Short brown hair framed blue eyes that twinkled in amusement. When he stepped down carefully to the floor, she realized he wasn't that tall, probably not quite six feet. But since she was short—hardly over the five-foot mark herself—that didn't bother her. Not when she could see muscles rippling through the thin cotton of his T-shirt, and how well he filled out a pair of jeans.

"Late night excitement?" he asked.

She blinked. "What?"

The strong spice of his scent momentarily distracted Shannon as he squeezed past her to turn off the kitchen faucet. She watched him, totally discombobulated, as he glanced into the sink and frowned.

"Do this often?" he asked instead of answering her question, then turning back and sauntering over.

Forcing herself to concentrate on the fact that a strange man was in her house and not that she really liked the way his butt looked in those well-worn jeans, she countered with, "How did you get into my house?"

Those blue eyes went wary. "The back door was open."

Oh, yeah. There was that.

A sliver of fear prickled down her spine. "Why were you in the back yard?"

"I knocked," he said, as though that were supposed to make a difference. "Before I came in, I knocked."

"Great," she replied. "But why were you in *my* back yard?"

"Our." His eyes narrowed slightly. "*Our* back yard."

Dread knotted her gut. "No, that's not possible. Molly was supposed to let me know if she rented the place out . . . " She trailed off. After her friend had married Jackson, she'd kept her half of the duplex with the intention of making a little money by renting it.

But she'd promised Shannon the final veto power for tenants. She'd *promised*—

"You're Shannon, right? Molly is supposed to give me the key tomorrow," the man said. "I'd only popped by to check it out when I heard the noise."

"At midnight?"

He shrugged. "I just got into town."

She narrowed her eyes. "Go outside."

Blue eyes went wide. "Wait, what?"

"Wait. Outside," she repeated, shooing him toward the door then closing and locking it behind him. "I'm going to call Molly."

And maybe strangle her friend through the airwaves.

Because she had an idea of why a very sexy stranger had suddenly shown up next door . . . and it certainly wasn't to evaluate her baking ability.

TWO

Shannon

SHE DIDN'T STOP to think about how late it was when she called Molly. Her friend picked up on the third ring. Her "Hello" rasped out, obviously woken from a dead sleep since they had to get up in—she mentally checked her watch—*four* hours to open the bakery.

Sleep, apparently, wouldn't be happening tonight.

"What the hell were you thinking?" Shannon blurted out.

"Shan?" Molly asked, alarm flooding into her tone. "What's the matter?"

"Want to tell me why a certain brown-haired, blue-eyed man is currently standing on my back porch?"

"Hang on." There was some rustling and the soft rumble of a man's tone. "It's Shannon," Molly murmured, presumably to Jackson. Then her voice came back on the line. "That's Evan. He's Jackson's friend."

"But why is he *here*?"

"You know *he* can hear you, right?" Evan interjected from the back porch.

"Hush," Shannon said and reached over the sink to close the window that looked out over the wooden deck. "Why is he here?" she hissed. "You promised you'd check with me before."

"It's just for a little while," her friend said, her words rushed and touched with guilt. "And I couldn't tell you. You just got back from vacation, remember? Plus, Evan just got out of the army. He doesn't have a place to stay, and Jackson offered. I was going to tell you tomorrow—"

"*That's* why you wanted to meet?"

"Yes," Molly said. "He wasn't supposed to get here until tomorrow." A beat of quiet. "What'd you think I wanted to talk about?"

Not sexy-as-hell, ex-military men, that was for sure. No, she had imagined the meeting was to discuss their burgeoning success, how all the Gold hockey players would suddenly want them to bake all their birthday cakes, or maybe that Molly would say they were finally established enough that Shannon could have some creative purpose in the business. Recipes, advertising, *something*.

She was tired of just balancing the books, doing the taxes, and making budgets. She wanted to get her hands dirty.

Yes, Shannon might be a former accountant, but she wanted the chance to do something completely different.

Her gaze trailed to the blackened mess in the sink, and her heart sank.

Maybe she *wanted* to have a different role, but that didn't mean she should.

"Shan? What is it?" Molly asked.

"I—uh . . . *nothing*." She shook her head, brown hair escaping from her haphazard ponytail to get stuck across her face, and stifled a sigh. It might be midnight and she might not be looking forward to a new tenant, but it was bound to happen at some point. Better she got over it sooner rather than later, especially since Evan needed a place to stay. She knew a little bit about what it was like to have that uncertainty and wouldn't wish it on anyone else.

Plus, the other side was empty.

More logic.

Ugh.

Albeit this was a more reasonable variety, giving shelter to someone who'd served their country. "I'll let him into the other side," she said then hardened her voice. "But you *have* to promise me that I'll get to meet any new tenants in the future."

"Of course!"

There was something else in Molly's tone that raised the hairs on Shannon's neck. Her friend was up to no good.

"*Promise*-promise?" she asked.

"Shan! I said yes."

"Promise on your favorite Bundt pan?"

Silence.

"*Molly*."

"Fine," Molly said. "I don't like you making me risk that precious tin of gloriousness, but I promise to check with you for future tenants."

There. That was done. Shannon nodded, not that her friend could see it, then said her goodbyes and hung up. She could see Evan through the window. He was leaning against one of the porch columns, one knee bent so that his foot rested against the wood, his head tilted up toward the sky. As she opened the back door and crossed to him, he glanced down at her.

"What's the verdict?" he asked. His demeanor had shifted, grown quiet and still. Focused. And when those intense blue eyes turned in her direction, Shannon's heart skipped a beat.

No good would come from this.

"The verdict is that you're in. Come on." She indicated the back door to the other half of the duplex with a tilt of her head and went down the three stairs that led to the garden.

He followed her silently across the grass.

"Molly said you just got out of the army."

Silence.

Tense silence.

Shit. Her and her big mouth. "I'm sorry, I didn't mean to pry."

"Okay."

Um.

Okay, then.

Deciding to let the silence stand, Shannon led him across the small expanse of grass between their separate porches and walked up the stairs that led to Molly's side—or former side anyway.

"Need some help bringing in your stuff?" she asked.

"Nope."

Another one-word answer.

Cool.

She glanced back, saw that Evan's face was blank, the dim lights of the deck highlighting the tense lines of his expression. Apparently the charming, joking guy from five minutes ago had gone, disappearing as quickly as her chances of baking something edible. *This* man was taciturn, stone, unnervingly closed up tight.

"Well, okay then." At the back door she hesitated, jingled the keys in her hand. "I think I have a spare key. I'll dig it out for you so you can have it in the morning."

"Okay."

One word. Again.

She unlocked the door.

"Thanks."

She nodded.

He stared at her. She stared at him, *staring* at her. God, this was ridiculous. She needed her bed and to forget this night happened and—

Biting back a sigh, she turned to leave. "Good night—"

"You're very pretty."

Shannon blinked. "Um . . . okaaay?"

First, it was the middle of the night, second, Evan was an unexpected and temporary interloper into her life, and third, she was average, maybe slightly better, but had never considered herself particularly pretty. Cute, maybe. Huggable, sure. She had plenty of extra padding to make her cuddly. But *pretty?* That wasn't something she usually heard.

"Um . . . *thanks?*"

His lips twitched and the last dredges of his tense expression faded. "Don't sound so thrilled." He took a step toward the door, paused. "So tell me, do you always burn things at midnight?" he asked, a full smile escaping. "Just so I can be prepared with the fire extinguisher."

Her mind scrambled for something to say. He'd gone from charming to quiet. Sexy to aloof. And now back to charming. It was disconcerting enough to give her whiplash.

"Not generally," she said, nibbling at her bottom lip. "I was trying out a new recipe and got distracted."

No need to mention that her testing out the smoke detectors happened every time she baked or that the reason for her distraction that night had been one very large bowl of popcorn and one very heartwarming rendition of *Pride and Prejudice.* Mr. Darcy. *Sigh.* He got her into trouble every time.

His eyes shone with that twinkle again, the same one that had made her belly clench in her kitchen.

Danger, her mind shouted.

And yet . . . so long since an orgasm that hadn't been courtesy of her vibrator, so long since her body had seen a danger it really wanted to investigate.

Okay, time to go.

She opened her mouth to say good night.

"So, are you going to let me stay?" He leaned back against the wall, winced, then shifted his weight so one ankle was crossed over the other.

She tilted her head, studying him and the too-casual way he held himself. The entire thing—the flirting, the relaxed pose—seemed forced, as though he were trying to cram himself into a too-tight pair of jeans. No matter how much he wriggled and squirmed, they just didn't fit.

She knew the feeling well. It had chased her through her years as an accountant, *still* chased her in the bakery.

The only thing about Evan that seemed genuine was the quiet moment on the porch after she'd called Molly, the steady way his blue eyes had studied her. He'd seemed at peace then.

This—the tension masked by false nonchalance—wasn't natural. This was chomping at the bit, struggling to maintain the façade that everything was all right, even when it wasn't.

Shannon was very familiar with that particular notion.

And so, she said the only thing she could. "You can stay."

Then she called out a good night and fled.

THREE

Evan

HE WALKED INTO THE HOUSE, trying to ignore the burn between his shoulder blades, telling him to turn around and watch Shannon leave.

She was pretty.

Exactly the kind of girl he would have gone for in the past.

Now?

He laughed, but nothing about the situation was funny. His career in the military was over, he was struggling to find a job with his current skill set and physical limitations, and . . . nothing felt right.

Not work. Not his life. Not this place.

Though, the first bit of right he'd felt was smiling down at the pretty woman, watching her eyes soften when he cottoned onto saying the right thing.

At least until he'd remembered.

That nothing would ever be the same.

"Fuck," he muttered, shutting and locking the door behind him.

No, nothing would be the same, but that was life. He was alive, others weren't, and so he just had to buckle down and move on.

Right.

Stifling a sigh, Evan went out the front door and grabbed his duffle. He'd been planning on crashing at the motel he'd seen just off the freeway, but this was easier.

Thankfully, Jackson's girl's place was furnished.

He just had to throw some sheets on the bed, grab a few blankets, and he was as settled as he'd been in the last months.

See? Easy.

Moving on was easy.

He snorted. Yeah, sure it was.

That was why he still had the dreams, why he'd always have the permanent reminder of everything that went down. Kind of hard to move forward when he only had to glance down to be reminded of the past.

"Enough," he muttered.

It was the middle of the night, and there was something about this time that made it difficult to keep the memories at bay.

But he had to.

California was a fresh start.

He had a couple of interviews set up, a place to live, a pretty girl next door. That had to be enough for the moment.

Even if it didn't feel that way.

Sighing, Evan got settled under the blankets and deliberately shut his eyes.

Thankfully, his body was trained enough to take the chance to sleep when it came around. His mind stopped spinning with memories, his body stopped aching, and blackness swept up, taking him under.

Sleep.

That was the first step.

As to the second . . . well, only time would tell.

FOUR

Shannon

THE BAKERY WAS BUSY, a line out the door, every single table full, when Evan walked in the door.

Fuck, he was even prettier in the daylight.

All lean and rugged with a bit of dark stubble on his jaw.

Her thighs clenched and she nearly dropped the change she was making.

He stopped, his gaze flicking from side to side before he took a step backward. Shannon had the distinct thought that he was about to run out of there.

"Hey! Evan!" she called from her place behind the cash register.

He turned and blinked, as though he hadn't expected to see her there. But after a brief hesitation, he gave a little wave and picked his way across the crowded floor.

"Thanks for the key," he said.

"No problem." She'd left it under his mat that morning. "You here to see Molly?" she asked, handing the customer her change.

He nodded then glanced around. Again, Shannon had the feeling that he was uncomfortable. Maybe it was the crowd. "Molly's in the kitchen," she said and pointed to the swinging door. "Go on back."

His relief was a palpable force. "Thanks," he said and hesitated, that twinkle in his eyes—the one that turned her insides to mush—making an appearance. "*You* work in a bakery?"

She swallowed the little burst of pain his words brought and plastered a smile on her face. It felt as fake as it probably looked, but she did manage to keep her tone light. "Oh, hush. I don't bake here. I just run the money side."

He grinned, mimed wiping the sweat off his forehead. "That's a relief."

More fighting to keep that smile in place. "Sure is."

"Hey." He reached over as though he were going to touch her shoulder but halted the movement midway. "I didn't mean—"

"No harm done," she said and returned her attention to the customer. "Go on back."

"Shannon—"

"How can I help you today?" she asked the customer, ignoring him.

But she couldn't ignore him completely as he walked around the counter and into the back. He was limping. Huh. Was that—

"Can I have a cranberry scone?" a woman asked.

Successfully pulled back on task, Shannon hurried to help the customer and then the next and the *next*. By the time there was a lull, more than an hour had passed and the cases were nearly empty.

She poked her head into the kitchen to tell Molly what pastries they needed to replace, half-hoping that Evan was still there and he hadn't slipped out the back.

Stupid. But there was something intriguing about him.

Yeah. That he was tall, dark, and gorgeous with smoldering eyes and squeeze-able muscles. *That* sure as hell made him intriguing. She snorted, knowing that even though he *was* pretty, that wasn't why she was looking into the kitchen. Evan had almost seemed lost, and that was a familiar feeling in her life, something that tied them together in common understanding.

Another snort, Shannon straightening her ponytail and smoothing down her apron. What could *she* and a sexy military man possibly have in common?

Nothing.

Yeah, *that*.

And yet, her eyes whipped around the kitchen searching—in vain, it seemed—for Evan.

He wasn't there.

She swallowed her disappointment. Yeah, that was about right. Plus, better that she knock down any fantasy of a connection between her and Evan straight away.

After relaying the items to Molly, Shannon crammed a croissant into her mouth and slurped down a coffee. They'd have maybe thirty minutes to recover from the breakfast rush before the lunch rush began. And true to form, they'd just managed to finish their snack, restock the bakery cases, and check the change in the register when their first lunch customer walked in.

And then it was a blur of sandwiches and salads and soups, of running items to tables and ringing up, and sore as hell feet.

A little after three o'clock, Molly called her goodbye.

"What about our meeting?" Shannon asked. Regardless of her partner's original intentions in scheduling the time, she still wanted to talk about taking a bigger part in the bakery's creative side.

"Can we talk tomorrow?" Molly said. "Jackson's waiting for me, and I lost track of time." Before Shannon could respond, Molly waved her fingers and skipped out the door.

"Yes," Shannon murmured. "I guess we can."

Since her shift at the bakery was over, their smaller dinner shift crew starting to roll in, she began her end of day tasks, tallying their inventory, taking note of what was selling the best. Molly came in early, did all the baking, made copious lists of supplies, but she wasn't always focused on the little details. That was fine because those little details were Shannon's specialty.

Then she packed up the leftover pastries from breakfast, snagging a couple of cinnamon muffins for herself. Everything else was divided between two boxes: one large, one small. Shannon made her escape out the back door, locking it behind her.

Roger was waiting in his usual spot, half-hidden in the doorway to the vacant suite at the end of their cluster of businesses.

Shannon hurried over to him. "Hey, Rog," she said and set the small box on the ground at his feet. If she tried to give him something, he wouldn't accept it. But if she *forgot* a box of food, he would eat it, so it didn't "go bad."

He looked away, not meeting her eyes, but when she set a bottle of water next to the box, he murmured a soft, "Thank you."

"See you tomorrow," she told him and circled the building to her car.

"Why did you do that?"

She jumped, letting out a little shriek when the male voice came out of nowhere and almost upended the large box of pastries in her arms.

"Sorry," Evan said, pushing off the building, and she realized he'd been leaning against the brick not far from her car.

"Stop *doing* that," she muttered, hand resting over her pounding heart.

"Sorry," he said again, moving to stand next to her. "I . . . being quiet is sometimes just second nature to me."

"Oh," she said, not able to think of anything better when he suddenly sounded so forlorn. Silence fell, uncomfortable. Tense. And she couldn't help wondering what was going through his brain to make his face look like that. "Do what?" she asked, adding when he merely blinked and glanced back at her, "Why did I do what?"

He was just close enough for her to smell his scent, but not within arms' reach. Which was probably a good thing, given her earlier thought that his pecs were particularly squeeze-able.

She hardly knew the man. There would be no squeezing.

Plus, it seemed a little insensitive to think about pecs and squeezing when he looked so sad.

But then the sadness disappeared, curiosity taking its place.

"Why did you give that guy food?"

Oh.

It was so ingrained, that little exchange of leftovers, that it didn't even occur to her that it might seem unusual to someone else. She shrugged. "He's hungry, and we have extra."

Evan's face was a study in disbelief. "*That's* it?"

Another shrug. "That's it. We'd have to throw it away, so . . ." she trailed off on a shrug and changed the subject, wanting the focus off her. "Why do you care?"

"I was following you and—" He broke off, probably realizing he'd moved into creeper territory.

"You're following me?"

Red spread over his cheekbones. "No." She lifted a brow. "Okay, *yes*. I was waiting for you, and when I saw you come out the back door, I—" She raised her other brow. "It's not what you think," he quickly added, both hands lifting, palms out in surrender.

"Um," she said. "I guess you'd better tell me *what* I should be thinking."

His gaze dropped to the pavement then lifted to meet hers. "I just wanted to apologize for earlier," he said. "For hurting your feelings."

"You didn't—"

"I did. And I'm sorry."

Shannon hefted the box, turned back for her car. "It was nothing."

"It was something to me," he said, catching her arm. His tone laced with a fierceness that surprised her. "I don't hurt women."

He sounded so genuine that she felt herself fall for Evan a little bit right then.

Fuck.

She bit her lip, tugged her arm away. "I don't know what to say."

He placed a hand on the roof of her car, partially blocking her in, and instead of making her nervous—which she knew was incredibly stupid considering she didn't know this man from John Smith and he'd just admitted to following her—she found herself leaning closer.

"I also wanted to apologize for kind of freaking out."

Her brows drew down, trying to figure out what he was talking about.

"Earlier, in the bakery," he said. "I—uh—sometimes it's hard for me to be in crowded places now. You . . . helped me remember where I was."

Her heart convulsed, both because he was struggling and also because he'd thought his slightly anxious expression and hesitation when he'd first come into the bakery was freaking out. How strong did this man think he had to be?

"I'm glad I could help." She wavered for a moment then just said the first thing that came to mind. "I'm sure it's hard to adjust to civilian life after being deployed. That many people." I shivered. "I mean, it's a little overwhelming for *me*, and I work there."

"It's not that." He sighed, glanced down at his toes. "Okay, it's *that* a little bit. I'm not used to navigating such a crowded space. I panicked."

She frowned. "So, it wasn't the crowd? Or it was?"

Evan pushed a hand through his hair and muttered a curse. "Sorry," he said. "I'm not used to explaining this."

She started to shake her head. "You don't have—"

"It's not exactly a secret. I—" He lifted one pant leg.

Shannon bit back a gasp.

Because it wasn't a leg beneath his jeans . . . or at least not a typical one. The silver and black of the prosthesis glittered in the afternoon light.

"I'm still getting used to it," he said. "Turning, shifting away from people in a crowded space is a challenge. The whole thing feels strange, unnatural . . . "

"I'm sorry," she said into the silence. "I had no idea."

"I know." He smiled, though it was a little sad. "Jumping onto that chair in your kitchen and turning off the fire alarm was the first natural thing I've done in months."

Shannon went for a joke, hating the morose tinge to his expression and wanting to erase it. "Me burning things is natural to you?"

Evan laughed. "I guess maybe it is." He raised a brow. "You plan on doing it often?"

She played along. "I think I can arrange to do it every night."

They both chuckled, and she hefted the box again. It was starting to make her arms ache.

"You want to get dinner?" he blurted.

"Oh." She did, she really did. But . . . "I can't," she said. Disappointment slid across his face before it went carefully blank and she hurried to add, "Or at least not for an hour or so. I've got to make a quick stop. Can we meet later?"

At that, he smiled, and it curled around her heart, squeezed tight.

There was something about him—his sweetness, his sexiness, the way her body and mind responded—that made her want to step closer instead of farther.

Which was unusual for her.

Indifference tended to be her modus operandi with men.

But Evan wasn't like the men she'd met—he was vulnerable in a way she identified with and yet still incredibly masculine. It was an odd juxtaposition, but one she wanted to investigate further.

"About seven?" she asked. "You want to go out?"

His face told her he'd rather not.

"Or maybe we can stay in?" she asked. "I can order a mean pizza. We've both had firsthand experience with how well I *can't* cook—"

"I'll make something," he said.

"You will?"

He laughed. It was ridiculously sexy. "I will, and I promise it'll be edible."

"O-okay." She took a breath to steady herself. That laugh had skated down her spine, sliding directly between her thighs and reminding her exactly how long it had been. "So, I'll just come over when I get home?"

He gave her a smile that made her pulse race. "I'll count on it."

FIVE

Evan

HE WATCHED SHANNON DRIVE AWAY, feeling equal parts excited and freaked the fuck out.

What had he been thinking, inviting her over?

She was Jackson's girl's best friend. And Molly was the most important person in his friend's life. Jackson definitely wouldn't appreciate Evan fucking over Molly's friend and business partner. Plus, Shannon was his neighbor, and she was—

Sweet and beautiful and hadn't looked at him like he was broken, even after she'd seen his leg.

And he wanted sweet and beautiful.

But now he had to cook for sweet and beautiful, and he didn't think that Shannon would consider boxed macaroni and cheese or instant noodle gourmet fair.

"Fuck," he muttered, getting into his own car.

Now he had to go to the grocery store. He'd already hit up the big box place, restocking his toiletries and picking up some towels that weren't bright pink and edged with lace that he was afraid he'd ruin.

But now that he'd promised to cook for Shannon, he needed real food.

His leg was aching, still getting used to the exertion of living with the prosthesis and the physical and mental exhaustion that came from having to think through every move he made.

But it was better than being stuck in a fucking hospital bed.

He knew that for a fact, after spending too many days in one.

So, it wasn't the worst thing in the world to be mentally groaning about having to do something as mundane as going food shopping.

"Steaks," he muttered, turning on the car and navigating it out of the lot. He could barbeque up a piece of meat with the best of them and he could buy a salad, throw a few potatoes into the oven to round out the meal.

Really, all he had to do was not turn everything to ash and he'd consider it a win, especially after seeing what had come out of Shannon's oven the previous night.

His lips twitched.

She'd torched whatever had once been food in that pan to ash.

"Well," he said, navigating the streets and taking the exit that led to the grocery store, "if you're going to do something, might as well do it right."

Taking his own advice, Evan shoved his ass out of the car and grabbed a cart.

He was going to cook for sweet and beautiful.

And it was going to be fucking incredible.

SIX

Shannon

"THANKS AGAIN," Brit called, taking a giant bite of Molly's double chocolate chip cookie into her mouth. "These are totally worth breaking Nutritionist Rebecca's diet plan!"

Shannon smiled as Mike Steward hurried past her. "Hi, Shannon," he said. "That had better not be the last cookie. I was helping . . ."

Biting her lip and knowing the box was probably nearly empty, considering the players and veterans tended to descend upon Molly's baked goods like a hoard, Shannon slipped back into the hall.

She might need to consider upping their usual box of pastries to two at the VA Hospital, where several of the Gold hockey players had begun volunteering a few months before. While she and Molly had been bringing goodies here for as long as she could remember, six months ago Shannon's path had crossed with Brit's, and it turned out the first female hockey player in the NHL had been obsessed with Molly's baked goods since moving to San Francisco.

Then Brit had ordered some cookies and pastries for the team's holiday party, the right people had tasted Molly's delicious offerings, and a space had opened up for rent at the Gold Mine.

Kismet.

But then again, her life seemed to have a knack for bringing the right people into it at just the right times.

First Molly, when they'd both been alone and single in the city.

Then Brit, when they were looking to expand the business.

Now . . . Evan.

And *now* that was dangerous thinking. Sighing and yet unable to stifle her excitement about her dinner with Evan, Shannon got in her car and drove home through the usual stop-and-go rush hour traffic.

Once she made it inside—*finally*—she stripped off her work uniform then hopped in the shower. Five minutes under the hot spray went a long way to making her feel—and smell—like a normal human being again, though she was never quite able to get rid of the smell of cinnamon and sugar from her skin.

Perks of working in a bakery.

People paid lots of money for those scents.

Smiling, she stepped out, dried off, and walked into the bedroom, opening the doors and staring at the contents.

Sigh. Her closet was hopeless.

This was a date. Kind of. Or at least she *thought* it was. She supposed Evan could just be acting neighborly. But neighbors didn't readily tell neighbors they were really pretty.

So, it was decided. This was a date.

And she didn't have any date clothes.

She hadn't been out with a guy in a long time. Not since Ryan, her ex-fiancé, and they'd broken up more than two years ago. He hadn't supported her quitting her job to go into business with Molly, and she couldn't support being with someone who didn't *support* her.

They'd parted ways, fairly amicably. *Fairly.*

"Get it together," she muttered, pulling out the nicest pair of jeans she owned—which also happened to be the ones that made her butt look fucking fantastic—and was buttoning a floral blouse that made the golden streaks in her eyes stand out, when she heard it.

Her head cocked to the side, brows drawing together.

Noise was blaring from next door. A repetitive blare of the . . . fire alarm?

She shoved her feet into her sneakers and ran downstairs. Then out the back door, across the shared lawn, the sound only getting louder. She banged on the back door. Waited.

Then waited some more.

When there was no answer, Shannon tried the handle and since it was unlocked, she pushed through . . . and was immediately assaulted by black smoke and the ear-piercing shriek of the fire alarm.

"Evan!" she shouted.

He was standing on a chair, a towel in hand, curses pouring from his mouth.

"Evan!" she yelled again.

In an abrupt movement, he turned toward her and almost fell. She ran toward him, but he'd already caught himself. He reached up, pressed something on the alarm, and the noise cut off.

They stared at each other in the resultant silence.

"Um . . . " She bit her lip. "I thought you said you knew how to cook," she said carefully.

With a groan and a careful movement, Evan stepped down from the chair. "I do," he muttered, grabbing the smoking pan and putting it in the sink before dousing it with water. "I got distracted."

She frowned. "Distracted by what?"

"I'm guessing it was the same thing you got distracted by last night."

Historical romances didn't seem high on his list of things to do. Maybe he'd been, *well* . . .

"Porn?"

Evan whirled and stared at her, mouth agape. "You were watching *porn* last night?"

"No," Shannon said, her cheeks flaring hot. "I was watching *Pride and Prejudice*. But I can't imagine you were watching that."

"No." He grinned, wide and slow and sexy. Her stomach fluttered. "I wasn't watching *Pride and Prejudice*. I was—" The smile fell away, and he winced. "Um . . . was watching something else."

"Not porn?"

He shook his head. "No, not porn." In an abrupt movement, he grabbed the pan out of the sink and dumped the entire thing in the trash.

Shannon waited for him to explain. He didn't.

So she asked, "Then . . . *what?*"

There was that wince again. It was actually cute. It made Evan seem younger and without the burdens that had turned him so quiet and tense the previous night. "I'd rather not say."

"But if it's not porn—"

"Can we stop talking about porn?" he asked with an exasperated sigh. "I was watching you."

"*Me?*"

He gestured toward the window.

She followed his gaze, felt her stomach clench. She'd been living alone in the duplex for so long that she'd forgotten that the two units formed a U-shape, facing toward the back yard. Which meant that if she looked out her kitchen window, she could see into Molly's kitchen. But she'd also forgotten that if you were at the wrong angle . . . or maybe the *right* one depending on how much of a creeper a person was, if they glanced up and at an angle, they could see directly into the opposite side's bedroom window.

Which meant . . . Evan had seen—

She gasped, took a step back. "You watched me *change?*"

Okay, first he was following her, now he was a Peeping Tom. She took a step toward the door.

"I couldn't help it." Evan's cheeks were flushed, adorably so, and she felt her inner creeper-detector stop blaring at his reaction. Especially when he said, "Okay, I guess I *could* have helped it. But I was making the sauce for our steaks and saw you through the window, and . . . and I got distracted."

Her face went red-hot as she recalled standing naked in her bedroom, staring at her closet. For a long time.

"It was a good distraction." Evan's voice was soft. "A *really* good distraction."

She huffed out a laugh and dropped her head into her hands. "Oh, my God. How embarrassing."

He peeled her fingers away. "I'm the one who should be embarrassed, staring at you like some stalker."

Her eyes locked with his, and a sliver of amusement crept through her.

"In my defense," he said. "It's been a really long time since I've seen a naked woman."

"Yeah?"

He nodded and his eyes were molten. They undid her, made her heart pound, her thighs tremble, and her mouth blurt out the most inane things.

"It's been a long time for me, too. For a man, I mean. Not a woman. I've seen myself naked, obviously. I was just never into other girls. Well, there was that one time, but"—*Oh my fucking God. Stop talking*—"it was college, and I found out it wasn't for me and . . ."

She. Had. To. Just. Stop. Talking.

"Tell me more about that one time."

"*What?*" she gasped.

His lips quirked, but his gaze was hot. He took a step toward her. "Tell me about that time in college." His voice was husky, and a shiver skated down her spine.

Shannon's mouth took over again. "Why don't you tell me about your Peeping Tom tendencies?"

He laughed and it filled the space between them, warmed her heart. He pushed a lock of hair behind her ear. "That I saw your gorgeous luscious body and got hard?"

Her breath caught.

"You're beautiful, Shannon."

Her pulse picked up its pace, her skin flushed. "I don't do this— I — Not on a first date—" She sucked in a breath, more turned on from Evan coming close, from the heat of his body, from the smell of him, his voice, and blurted, "I just fill the void with Mr. Darcy."

He'd stepped back while she'd stumbled through her words, reading correctly that she was overwhelmed, but at her blurt, he laughed again, the husky chuckle skating over her skin.

Heat.

Desire.

Moisture pooling between her thighs.

Fuck, she wanted him.

Shannon took a step closer.

His eyes widened, dropped to her mouth.

There was the slightest hesitation, a moment where they were both frozen in indecision. Then she rose on tiptoe the same time he bent down to slant his lips against hers. Fire flooded through her, heady and intoxicating, filling her limbs, making them heavy and shaky, and when she wobbled under the onslaught, Evan pulled her into his arms.

His chest was broad and strong and overwhelming. She wanted it pressing her down into bed, bare against her breasts—

Just as she'd processed that mind-blowing need, her brain caught up. Evan's seemed to be on the same wavelength, because he cupped her cheek gently and stepped back.

"I guess I should order pizza?" he asked, his voice soft and slightly raspy.

SEVEN

Shannon

THE NEXT WEEK proceeded along the same fashion—minus the shrieking of their respective fire alarms. She and Evan had dinner almost every night, either at his place or hers.

He'd proved to be an excellent cook, and after a particularly bad attempt on her part at spaghetti two days in, he'd begun making all their meals.

But although they were spending lots of time together, Shannon was confused. After the kiss—the hot, sexy, soul-encompassing kiss—there had been nothing. No contact. No make-out sessions.

Nothing.

They'd been getting along so well that she would have made the first move, would have stepped closer and eliminated the distance between them, if not for Evan.

Every time she got near, he backed up.

If her shoulder brushed his at the fridge, he stiffened and stepped away. If their fingers tangled over the pepper shaker, he pulled back like he'd been burned.

She would have thought he didn't like her. Except . . . he kept inviting her back for dinner.

Eventually, Shannon accepted that she'd been firmly friend-zoned and decided to just go with it. Evan was funny and sexy and a good cook to boot. She'd just enjoy it and move on.

Still, it was hard to move on when she found herself drawn to him more by the day. But it was either press forward as friends or strip naked and throw herself at him. Since that wasn't really an option—she'd already done that once, well, the naked part anyway. But he'd seen the goods, had the chance to make a move, so regardless of how tempting her body found the notion of Evan, it seemed he wasn't interested.

And she had *some* pride, dammit.

So, she'd ignored her growing infatuation with him.

A knock at the door startled her out of her thoughts.

"It's me, Shan," Evan called through the panel.

"It's unlocked," she called back, tugging a T-shirt over her head and hurrying down the stairs.

It was Thursday night, the start of her weekend, and normally on the eve of two full days off, she would be slipping into sweats and heating up a frozen meal.

Tonight was different.

"Hey," she said to Evan as she walked into the kitchen. He was unloading bags of delicious smelling food—garlic, tomato sauce, warm bread, and cheese, she couldn't forget the cheese.

She was drooling already.

"Decided not to cook," he said, handing her a container of pasta. "Alfredo okay?"

"Any combo of carbs and sauce is fine with me," she said and took the plastic container.

"I knew I liked you for a reason," he said, lips curved as he grabbed his own container.

She snagged two forks and some napkins and smiled up at Evan. "How much do I owe you for this?"

He waved away her question. "You can get next time."

"Okay."

They sat at the kitchen table and dug in.

"Mmm," she moaned at the first bite. "Oh my God, this is great." And then proceeded to devour the entire thing. She would never be a size two, mostly because aside from hating to work out, she also loved eating too much and was not shy about professing her love for all that was carby deliciousness.

It was when she was nearing the bottom of her container that Shannon realized the air had gone still. She glanced up and found Evan staring at her, an intensity in his blue eyes that raised the hairs her nape.

"Are you okay?" she asked tentatively, setting her fork down before she resorted to scraping every last bit of sauce out of the dish.

"Fine." It was a clipped down word, fierce blue eyes on hers for a moment before they dropped down onto his food. He hadn't eaten much.

She sucked in a breath, let it out slowly, suddenly unsure.

But then he looked up, face calm, tone light. "So, it's your weekend, huh? What would you normally do?"

She was quiet for a long moment, still unsure, maybe even more so because of the rapid mood change. She'd hadn't seen Evan do that over the last week, and now she was feeling like it was her fault.

Shit.

Just ask him what is wrong.

But then it might ruin things and . . . Shannon sighed. She couldn't just ask him. Maybe it was pathetic, but she really liked him and felt like if she pushed then she'd lose having him as a friend.

And so, she stifled the urge to ask him to tell her why he wasn't eating or why she'd upset him and instead kept things superficial, starting with her reply. "You suuure you want to know? It's tip-top-secret girl information."

Yes, she knew it wasn't feasible to keep doing this with a relationship, that they couldn't build a foundation on something that wasn't real and solid and truthful, but . . . what right did she have to press him for more?

"Tip-top-secret *girl*—"

Evan had such a panicked look on his face that she forgot about foundations and ferreting out truths, and she had to laugh.

"I don't know where your mind just went, but unless you're freaking out about bingeing on some chick flicks and popcorn, your mind has gone to the wrong place."

"Oh."

She flashed him a smirk. "We're not talking about porn again. I promise. More like Elizabeth Bennett and Mr. Darcy and murder documentaries. *That's* how I spend my days off."

"Oh," he said again.

She lifted a brow. Maybe she wasn't going to press him on what was bothering him, but she also wasn't going to change the subject. Especially when his cheeks were red enough to pique her curiosity.

"I just . . . " He fiddled with his fork, picking it up, placing it back down again. "I just thought you might have a date or something."

That was such a ludicrous idea that she laughed.

"What?" He frowned.

She scoffed. "I mean, come on. Are you being serious right now?" He'd friend-zoned her and now seemed surprised she didn't have a date.

Evan frowned. "What are you talking about?"

"Look at me," she said, gesturing between them. "And look at you. At *us*."

His brows drew down. "You're a beautiful woman. Why wouldn't you have a date?"

"If I'm so beautiful, then why did you friend-zone me? You kissed me then set me away from you and haven't touched me since. If I'm so beautiful, then—"

She clenched her jaw shut, teeth clinking together, words cutting off.

"Shannon."

Know what?

Fuck it.

"Did I do something wrong or hurt you or—"

"*No.*"

"Or maybe"—her gut twisted—"I . . . was I *that* horrible of a kiss-
er?" Eyes burning, she popped up from her chair, moving across her
kitchen to toss the container in the trash.

"I have no idea what you're talking about," he said and though
the words were innocent, the expression on his face wasn't.

Her heart sank. She'd been right, all of those swirling doubts
she'd tucked down, the tentative hope that he'd just slowed down
because they barely knew each, but that he did actually want her,
withered and died. "Was it really *that* bad?" she asked.

"Yes."

Well. Ouch. The most spectacular kiss of her lifetime and . . .
that.

She shook her head, turned for the stairs.

"Wait."

Shannon didn't. She bolted.

"Shan." Evan snagged her arm and she jerked in his grasp,
pulling free "Hey. *Hey,*" he said, slowly reeling her in. "Look at me,
baby."

When she didn't, he grabbed her shoulders again and exerted
steady pressure until, finally, with a sigh, she rotated to face him.

"I like you."

She rolled her eyes. "As a friend."

"*Yes.*"

She flinched.

"But that's not all," he said, jostling her lightly. "I enjoy spending
time with you. You're funny and chill and sexy as hell."

"So why—?"

If she was so sexy, why—?

He shook his head. "Shan, I'm a mess. I'm still getting used to my
leg, to being back. I don't even have a job. I want you. A whole

fucking lot, but when I kissed you, when I felt how good it was between us . . ."

"What?" she asked when he trailed off.

"I realized that as much as I might want you, I'm not a good bet." He shoved a hand through his hair. "You should be with someone who's whole. Or at least someone who can get a job and provide and—"

That was when things began to make more sense. Evan had been keeping his distance because he thought . . . what? That he wasn't good enough? How typically male. How utterly ridiculous.

"Shut up," she said.

"What?"

"Just. Shut. Up."

She launched herself into his arms and kissed him. His lips were soft, the heat of his mouth even more intense than she remembered.

"You think *you're* a mess?" she asked. "*I'm* a mess. I've been working with Molly for two years and still harbor a ridiculous desire to help her bake, to be partners with her in *every* sense." She shook her head. "And, the thing is, I *can't* bake. So, I keep punishing myself by trying, pretending that one day it might be something *I* made in the case at the Gold Mine, *my* recipe that people are clamoring for, instead of accepting that it's just not going to happen."

Evan's arms tightened around her. "You have made something," he said. "What you and Molly have built—"

"*She* built it," Shannon said.

He cupped her cheek. "Maybe she built it, but you're integral to its function now. Jackson told me it was *you* that got the contract with the Gold. Not Molly."

She shook her head. "That was just dumb luck," she said. "I came into the business when it was already established. So, you may talk about being a mess. I, on the other hand, am a wreck and just . . . white noise."

Evan froze for one long moment before growling low in his chest. "That's bullshit."

"I—"

He dropped his head, slanting his mouth across hers. A beat later, his tongue thrust past her lips to tangle with hers in a wild, maddening rhythm. It was . . . *good*. So good she was ready to tear her clothes off and sacrifice the leftover garlic bread if it meant that he would just fuck her on the kitchen table.

But Evan didn't move.

Just held her tight and kissed her, lips trailing down her neck, nibbling, licking, sucking. She moaned, arching against him.

But to her frustration, he slowed to a stop, hot breath puffing against her throat, but mouth halting on her skin. He pressed one more kiss to her throat before releasing her and backing away. Her chest rose and fell, her breath coming in short, rapid gasps, and if her eyes looked remotely like his—hot, lion-stalking-the-zebra predatory— then they were definitely not *just* friends.

"I'm a mess, too," she said when she could speak normally again. "I've got a successful business that I want to fiddle with because I'm not feeling *creatively challenged*, I have no dating life to speak of, and I live vicariously through Elizabeth Bennett." She chewed on the corner of her lip and pushed on. "But . . . who's to say we can't try being messes together?"

Evan stared at her for a long moment.

But then he grinned, and her heart leaped. "No one." She released a breath, the tension leaving her. "So . . . will you kiss me *every* time we argue?"

And just that quickly, the tension was back. Partly because she liked the sound of *every time*, but also just the thought of how it felt to be in his arms, how his mouth felt against hers . . . yeah, it wasn't a hardship to kiss this man. "Yup. Probably."

"Good." He took a slightly hitching step forward and ran his fingers down her cheek. "So, we're going to try this?"

"Dating?"

He nodded.

She put her hand over his. "I hope so. But, did I hurt you when

I"—she gestured between the two of them, to the leg that had hitched stepping toward her just then but had been moving smoothly before —"threw myself at you?"

"No." He gave a little grimace and shifted his weight. "Well, maybe my prosthesis needs a tweak, but no. I liked it. A lot."

A thread of guilt wove through her. "I'm so—"

He put a finger over her lips. "Did you not hear the part where I said I liked it?"

She nodded, spoke against the digit. "I heard it."

"Good." He pushed back a tendril of her hair before taking her hand and leading her to the other room. "Now, show me this Mr. Darcy you're so fond of."

She grinned. "You sure? My ex used to tell me that his balls shriveled up whenever he caught a glimpse."

"I think I can handle it."

Yeah, she thought that maybe he could, too.

EIGHT

Shannon

EVAN WAS asleep before the movie was halfway over.

Not that it was a surprise that period dramas weren't his thing.

So maybe not ball-shriveling, but perhaps sleep-inducing.

She watched him sleep, face peaceful. He looked younger, and the pain was gone from the corner of his eyes. Awake he had the happy-go-lucky thing down—was charming and funny and pretended that things didn't bother him. But every once in a while, she caught a glimpse of the discomfort he was hiding.

It was physical—in the occasional limp, in the wince when he couldn't do something that must have once been easy.

And . . . it was mental, when a loud noise startled him, when he told her about struggling for the last few months to find work. The previous day, he'd calmly told her that the job he'd lined up had fallen through and while he'd made a valiant effort in making it seem like it wasn't a big deal, it was.

He was disappointed. He'd served the country, sacrificed so much and—

He'd spent the previous four months looking for work.

Hopefully California would bring him better luck.

Because the quiet disappointment, the stoic resolve in the face of things going wrong wasn't something she wanted to see in his face. And still, it was familiar to her. She'd seen it often in the patients she brought baked goods to at the VA Hospital. Time and again, she had seen their bodies—cobbled back together—and minds—strained from combat—struggle to cope.

In the week she'd known him, Evan seemed to be doing a better job than most. But that didn't mean it was easy. She wondered who he was able to talk with, who he could vent to. Because though they discussed lots of topics, his experience at war and his injury weren't on the table.

A few days before, Shannon had broached the question again but had been firmly shut down.

Which was fine.

She wasn't Evan's mother or his wife. But they were kind of exploring the possibility of a relationship. Well, maybe even more than kind of, after the scene in the kitchen.

So, if he didn't confide in her, what did she do? Ignore it?

That wasn't hard. She hardly noticed that he was missing a limb —aside from the occasional grimace or faltering step.

Yet she couldn't help but wonder if the pain he was so good at pretending didn't exist was going to eat him alive.

And so, she wondered if she *could* ignore it. If they were going to date or be exclusive or whatever category they ended up with, could she be satisfied with a man who buried his problems?

No. No, she couldn't.

But . . . it also wasn't something she needed to deal with now. They'd gone from friends to dating.

Tonight, that was enough.

And maybe . . . maybe she *could* find a job for him, one that got him to open up, one that gave him an avenue to vent. Maybe it would work, just maybe. But it was a possibility, and so she was going to take an extra box of goodies to the hospital on Sunday to find out.

She smiled down at Evan snoring softly on the couch next to her before cuddling into him, heart filling with hope when his arms tightened instinctively around her.

Then she turned her eyes back to the TV and got lost in Mr. Darcy.

SHANNON WOKE UP SWELTERING. She was pressed tight to Evan's chest, the steady *thump-thump* of his heart in her ear.

The room was dark, the home screen of her TV the only illumination. Her arm was asleep, but she wasn't ready to move yet, to break the spell of peacefulness. So, despite the fact that Evan was roasting her like a stuffed pig, she snuggled into the broad expanse of muscles.

"Hey," he whispered, stroking back the hair from her face. "We should probably move. It's late."

"I don't want to," she pouted.

Evan huffed out a laugh but didn't move other than to tighten his hold on her.

They stayed like that for a long while. Finally, when the TV turned itself off, transitioning into power-saving mode, she sat up. "I'll turn something else on." She inclined her head toward the TV. "Something that won't put you to sleep."

She reached over him and grabbed the remote off the side table, turning on the screen and choosing some random comedy flick about professional thieves, before stretching across him again to put it back.

The remote didn't make it.

As the movie blared to life, Evan's hands settled on her hips, tugging her against his chest again, his lips finding hers as the sound of the thieves planning their heist filled the room.

Her fingers tangled in his hair.

The remote ended up . . . somewhere.

His tongue swept across the seam of her lips, and she opened, quickly lost in a flurry of heat and teeth, of dueling mouths and trailing caresses. He pulled her closer, and she climbed into his lap, straddling his hips, grinding against the hard length of his cock.

They both groaned in pleasure, but he pulled back.

"We should stop," he murmured.

"No," she said, leaning up to press her mouth to his again. Then she broke away, panting. His lips just tasted so damned good. "No," she gasped between ragged breaths. "We really shouldn't."

"Shan."

She bent and nipped his neck. He hissed out a breath, brought his hands up to the back of her head and held her to him.

"I don't want to rush you—"

"I want this," she said, her fingers trailing down his chest, lifting his shirt. Her mouth watered—actually watered—at the sight of those flat abs, the light sprinkling of hair leading beneath his jeans. She needed to taste.

She was leaning down to do so when Evan stopped her.

"I haven't done this yet."

Shannon frowned as she tried to decipher the statement. Evan was thirty. Surely, he'd had sex before. But then—

Focus.

"Since your injury?" she asked gently.

He swallowed, nodded.

"Okay." Her teeth found her lip and bit down. "Do you want to wait a while longer, to give yourself more time?"

"No. I do." He sighed, thrust a hand through his hair. "I just don't know what I'm doing. I don't want to hurt you or—"

"Come on." She slid off his lap, held out a hand.

"What?"

Her fingers wiggled, an impatient gesture to get him to stop talking and hurry up. She wanted him out of his own head and focusing on them, on how good it was between them.

He hesitated one more brief moment before standing and following her. His leg hitched for a step, but then he was very close behind her, his chest rubbing her spine as he trailed her up the stairs.

Into the bedroom. Onto the bed.

The moment her back hit the mattress, it was as though Evan forgot all about his leg, forgot about his worries, forgot about everything except the heat exploding between the two of them. His mouth descended, his fingers working deftly to tug off her shirt and jeans. His own clothes and the prosthesis hit the floor moments later.

She didn't have a second to think, to wonder whether her pressing in this moment was the right thing to do. Because in a heartbeat, she was naked, Evan sucking one nipple into his mouth, even as his fingers traced paths across her abdomen, between her thighs, through the damp heat of her pussy.

And, for once, a man didn't need a road map.

He found her clit, circling it with his thumb before pressing down firmly. She cried out, arching against his palm, moaning when he slipped a finger inside.

"Evan," she groaned. "Condoms in my nightstand—"

"Shh," he told her and knelt between her thighs.

Oh, thank you, God.

Because his tongue. Holy *fucking* shit, his tongue.

"Oh God. Yes. Like that," she panted. Her body was on fire, the desire within her intense and overwhelming and . . . "Inside," she groaned. "I need you inside."

He laughed, the jerk, and redoubled his efforts.

But she couldn't even be irritated because his tongue was against her, pleasure was spiraling, and it felt like flames were shooting through her fingertips.

Or maybe that was just her flying over the edge.

When she descended back into reality, he was leaning over her, gently stroking her cheek. He smiled. "You were saying something about condoms?"

In response, she flung an arm behind her and rifled through her nightstand. The familiar square packets were buried beneath a slew of magazines, a box of tissues, and what felt like fourteen remotes.

"Take your time," Evan murmured, brushing his fingers across her stomach.

Her eyes flew to his, a scathing remark already on her tongue. She was looking, *dammit*. But though he was smiling, he wasn't making fun of her. Or not really.

His eyes were glued to her breasts.

Apparently, it was a good view because when they bounced, he groaned and brought one hand up to massage them.

"Not helping," she gritted out. A sigh escaped her when he brought his mouth back down to her nipple.

Then she had it!

Tearing the wrapper with her teeth, she shoved her hands between them and rolled it on. "Hurry," she muttered, grabbing his hips, trying to get him inside her.

He laughed, peeling her hands away and pinning them above her head. "In my experience, these things go better when people take their time."

"Lies." But he cut off further protests when he slid inside her in one, long sure stroke. His mouth came down to hers, his hips slid in and out, slowly at first, but then the pace steadily increasing. He ground against her, ramping her desire up and up and . . . *up* until she fell off the cliff again, Evan joining her a few strokes later with a soft groan against her throat.

Yes, things were better when people took their time.

Or rather, when Evan took his time with her.

She closed her eyes, limp with pleasure, sleep drifting closer, when he kissed her forehead. "I'll go take care of the condom."

"Okay," she said lazily.

He rolled away.

Her eyes stayed closed.

At least until she heard the *thunk*.

Heart lurching, she sat up. "Are you okay?"

Evan's shoulders were shaking, and her gut clenched. She jumped off the bed, reached for him. Oh God, what if he'd hurt himself?

He met her eyes and all the tension inside her faded. Because . . . he was laughing. Crouching next to him, she asked, "What happened?"

"Nothing," he said, nuzzling at her throat. "Except, I reached for my leg and misjudged because you pleasured me blind."

Her lips twitched, all her fears *poofed* out of existence. "I thought that happened from masturbating."

"Maybe I've been busy." He shrugged. "Or maybe . . ."

Her lips twitched. "Or maybe my vagina is magical?"

"Or poisonous."

She made an affronted noise. He kissed the sound from her lips . . . and then kissed her some more for good measure. Eventually though, they broke apart, and he grabbed his leg, spending a few moments putting it on correctly.

"Couldn't expect the entire thing to be perfect, could we?" he asked.

Shannon brushed his hair back from his forehead. "It wasn't anything less than perfect." She leaned in and kissed him once more before he rose and went to the bathroom to get cleaned up.

When he came back into the room, crawled into bed, and wrapped her in his arms, she reveled in the moment that was perfect in its imperfectness.

NINE

Evan

"FUCK," he muttered, hanging up the phone and leaning back onto his couch. He'd been in California for almost three weeks and all the job prospects he'd headed out to this coast to explore had come to . . . absolutely fucking nothing.

This latest one, hired security for local tech company events, had said their insurance wouldn't cover employees with pre-existing conditions.

The third time he'd heard the same thing.

Apparently, losing a leg from a fucking IED was pre-existing. Well, it was pre . . . and post and *still* not a fucking thing he could do about it.

What the hell was Evan supposed to do? Grow it back?

He didn't like that he'd lost his leg, felt that gaping hole from missing out on being able to do many of the things he loved—from his work and just hopping out of bed to take a fucking piss—but he couldn't change what his body was like now.

"Shit," he said, dropping his head into his hands.

He needed to pivot here, to rethink what he was doing. Maybe go more on the consulting side? Then he wouldn't need to rely on another company and their insurance.

Now, that was an idea.

"Hey."

He turned, saw that Shannon was leaning against the doorframe leading into his living room.

At least things were going smooth on the sweet and beautiful side.

Shannon was the coolest chick he'd ever hung with. Smart as a whip, funny as hell, and he didn't think he'd ever get enough of hanging out with her. Luckily, she seemed to like him, too.

"Hey," he said, pushing up from the couch and moving over to kiss her.

Fuck, it was cool that he got to kiss this woman any time he wanted.

She slipped her arms around his neck and kissed him back, breasts brushing his chest in a way that had his cock twitching and heat snaking down his spine.

"Do you want to go upstairs?" she asked against his lips several minutes later.

"I thought we were going to a movie?"

There was a new chick flick she wanted to see and after seeing how she reacted to that particular genre of films here at the house— laughing and crying, turning to him with warm eyes and a soft smile when the couple got together at the end, and then attacking him once the credits rolled, giving him the single hottest sexual experience of his life—then Evan hadn't complained about going.

If chick flicks got his Shannon to do all of *that*, then he'd watch a hundred of them.

She smiled, though there was a trace of something in her eyes.

Was it sadness?

But then it was gone, and her hand was sliding down toward the button on his jeans.

"It'll hold."

"Shan—"

She flicked the button open, reached inside.

"Come upstairs, baby," she murmured, brushing her lips against his, body pressed to his, and Evan stopped fighting it.

He just took her hand and led her upstairs.

It was only later that he learned what had brought that flash of sadness to her gaze.

And it destroyed everything.

TEN

"WHAT THE HELL IS THIS?" Evan's voice was almost unrecognizable in its fury. Shannon slanted her eyes away from him, at the rage barely contained, to the customers packed into the bakery. After a heartbeat of consideration, she called for Molly to take over the counter.

When she reached for his hand to lead him toward the back, he recoiled. She swallowed, shoved her hands into the pocket of her apron, and shuffled into the kitchen.

Evan followed, his anger smothering.

"What's the matter?" she asked once the door was shut and she was sure they were alone.

"What's the—?" he spat. "Are you *kidding* me?" He thrust a paper into her hands.

Unbidden, her fingers took it.

But she'd already seen the seal, already knew what had made him so angry.

A month ago, she'd overheard one of the doctors at the VA saying they needed a new person to lead their group discussions and so after hers and Evan's first time together, she'd asked if the position was still open.

It was.

A group therapy leader—one where professional experience wasn't needed, but only a willingness to share and preferably common ground to relate to those in treatment. The doctor who she'd asked for specifics from had explained that the hospital would provide any required training.

And so, after watching Evan's disappointment when several more job opportunities had fallen through, she applied for him two weeks before.

She hadn't been sure of Evan's "willingness to share," but she *knew* he had common ground, and if the job encouraged him to discuss the memories that made his eyes take on that occasional haunted glaze . . .

Well, she'd thought the solution was perfect.

He'd get help. The other veterans would get the support they needed.

So, she'd filled out an application.

And now . . . he'd gotten the job.

Looking into the fury in Evan's blue eyes, she realized that she'd overstepped. "I— uh—" Her mouth snapped closed, excuses were on the tip of her tongue before she realized there was no talking her way out of this.

She'd screwed up. Big time.

His curse startled her out of her thoughts.

"Why did you do it, Shan?" he asked, hurt in his eyes, his words. "I thought you saw me as *me*. Not some broken thing that needs repair."

"No!" she said, stretching her hand out. Her fingers clenched into a fist when he stepped back, out of reach. "It's not that. I just thought that since you didn't want to talk to *me* about it, that you could maybe —I don't know—take a chance with them."

"Take a chance?" The question was ice, a biting lash across her skin.

"It's perfect," she said, her words rushing together as she desperately tried to explain herself. "You can help them, and they can help *you—*"

Oh, fuck.

All at once, her mistake hit home.

Help him. Like she saw him as damaged goods.

Her stomach tied itself into knots. "I— Baby— I—"

"Help me," he repeated, so quiet she had to strain to hear.

"Evan, I made a mistake." She swallowed when icy eyes met hers, and then jumped when he snatched the paper from her hands and crumpled it into a ball. "I'm sorry," she said, words coming fast, desperate to explain, to make him see that she didn't think he needed fixing. "I just know you didn't want to talk to me about it. I thought if you had someone you could discuss it with then you'd—"

"I'd magically be okay?"

His words were bullets to her heart, razor-sharp and red-hot. "I didn't want to talk about it because the past is the past. I wanted to move forward and be who I am now." He sucked in a breath. "I didn't want to sully what we were building with darkness, with fucking nightmares."

"But I want to know every part of you," she said, desperately, reaching for him again, heart throbbing when he retreated again. "Evan."

He shook his head.

"I don't want there to be pieces you just shove away," she said. "I want to know everything about you, light *and* dark. I worry . . . that it's not healthy for you to bottle it all up. Don't you think it would be better if you had people you could confide in?"

"No," he growled. "*You* think that. *I've* had therapy, have talked myself blue about my injuries during those sessions. I lost my leg from an IED, but I lived. Two of my friends didn't. I'm lucky to be alive, and I live that way."

"But you never—"

He always redirected the conversation if she tried to bring it up.

"I didn't think I *had* to." His voice was frigid. "Or rather, I thought if it was a huge issue, you would have talked to *me* about it. Not go behind my back and—" He broke off with a curse.

Oh no.

Oh God.

She *should* have talked to him. She should have—

"Baby."

He took a step toward the back door. "No."

"But—"

"Just"—he sighed—"*no*." Cold blue eyes met hers, lush lips she'd kissed just that morning compressed into a firm line. "You talk about taking chances, about discussing issues, but you're the biggest hypocrite of them all. You moan about having nothing to do with the bakery besides cleaning and balancing the books, but you don't talk to Molly, don't demand what you want."

He was right. So. Painfully. Right.

"I don't care about the bakery. I just want you."

At least she could make that much clear.

"It's too late for that."

"I'm sorry," she said, tears pouring down her face, heart breaking into a million pieces. She'd ruined everything.

For the first time since he'd set foot in the bakery that afternoon, Evan's face softened. "I know you are."

Hope grabbed onto her heart, made it buoyant, and—

"And I wish it were enough."

Pop. Hope disappeared like a balloon meeting a sharp pin.

"I need to go," he said.

She nodded, but he was already gone, already pushing through the door, the metal panel slammed closed behind him.

Molly came into the kitchen a heartbeat later.

Tears were clogging Shannon's throat, but she stammered out a question about the register.

"Matilda's got it," Molly said. "What's going on? I saw Evan—"

That only made her sob harder. Shannon tried to explain, to tell Molly how much she'd messed up, but her words came out garbled and incoherent.

Finally, she wiped her eyes with her apron, took a deep, shoring breath, and glanced up at her friend.

"We broke up."

"*What?* Why?"

Tears threatened again, and Shannon definitely was *not* going there. Not now. Not until . . . her heart no longer felt like it had been thrown in a garbage disposal.

"It's complicated."

"Comp—"

"I don't want to talk about it, okay?"

Molly studied her for a long moment. "Okay."

Shannon nodded then thought, after all Evan had said, after all she'd done to screw up her life, why stop now?

Her heart was shredded, the man she loved gone.

If not *now,* then when would she ever have the courage to say what was on her mind? Because maybe if she had with Evan, things would be different.

"I need to talk to you about something else," she said, and then she and Molly talked. Shannon told her everything she'd dreamed of doing with the business over the last years—marketing and social media, changing the hours and different ways to expand.

"Why didn't you tell me sooner?" Molly asked when she'd finished.

"Because I'm a mess." And Shannon's eyes filled with tears again. "And I'm so screwed up that I don't talk to people when I should an —and—"

Evan.

Her.

Finished.

"Oh, honey," Molly said, pulling her in for a hug, holding her tight as she cried. "It'll be okay," she murmured.

"I know I can't bake," she wailed.

"We both know that," Molly murmured. "But you still have other ideas, and I promise you that I'll be more open to hearing them."

Eventually, Molly bundled Shannon into her jacket and led her out to the parking lot, insisting on driving her home.

She hadn't realized she'd been holding onto hope that Evan would understand, that he would be in the parking lot, ready to invite her to dinner the same as any other day until it was empty, until he didn't appear when she gave Roger his box.

But of course, Evan didn't.

Maybe after he calmed down, she could go over to his side of the duplex and explain, tell him she'd talked to Molly. Maybe he would see that she was trying to be different, that she wouldn't make the same mistake twice.

He had to understand that was huge, that she was trying and had only made a mistake.

That they were different together. They *meant* something.

The moment she got home, she would do her best to convince him of that.

But it turned out that her resolve didn't matter.

When Shannon unlocked her front door and wandered over to his, she found the back door unlocked, Evan's side of the duplex was cleared out, her spare key smack dab in the middle of the kitchen table.

He was gone.

ELEVEN

Shannon

HOURS LATER, Shannon had just fallen asleep, her eyes crusted with tears, her heart heavy, her soul weighed down with boulders of despair, when a sharp, piercing noise penetrated her consciousness.

She bolted upright in bed, cursed loud and long, then staggered downstairs.

The kitchen light flicked on before she could reach for it.

Next to the switch, his hands on the back of a chair, stood Evan.

Her gasp was audible even over the fire alarm.

He held out a hand and she crossed to him, sucking in a breath when he lifted her into the chair then followed her up so that their chests were only a hairsbreadth apart.

"See the button there?" he bent down and spoke directly in her ear, loud enough to be heard over the alarm. He pointed to a small red knob she'd never noticed before that was tucked away on the edge of the device.

She nodded.

"Push it."

Shannon did. The noise abruptly cut off.

And they stood there, precariously perched on the chair, staring at each other.

There was so much she wanted to say, to apologize for, but seeing the softness in his eyes made her tongue stick to the roof of her mouth.

Evan smiled and smoothed a hand over her head. "I love your bedhead."

"I'm sorry—"

"Hush." He stepped down then lifted her off the chair.

When her feet were on the ground, she tried again. "I'm sorry I—"

"Shut up."

She blinked, would have been offended if not for Evan's smile and the warmth in his expression.

"I was halfway to who knows where when I realized it."

"Realized what?" she asked carefully.

He crouched slightly so he was level with her eyes. "Realized that I'm in love with you."

Her heart leaped into her throat and, unbidden, her head shook.

"Yes, I am." He chuckled, brushed his knuckles along her cheek. "I was driving, feeling all betrayed and hurt, when I realized that you were trying to help me." She sucked in a breath. "Because you cared." Evan hesitated, eyes on hers, and she nodded in agreement. "That you'd tried to ask me about my experiences, and I'd shut you down."

"It wasn't your fault."

"No," he agreed, fingers brushing gently across her cheek. "It was both of our faults. I should have talked. You should have told me what you needed."

Bubbles of hope were welling within her blood, lifting her heart, filling her soul with tentative optimism.

"I hurt you," she said. "I'm so sorry."

Evan tugged her into his arms. "And I didn't do the same to you?"

"No." She shook her head, wanting to deny it, but he tilted her chin up, brushed a finger beneath her each of her eyes, which were sore from crying.

"Nice try, but I don't think so." He pressed his mouth to hers, a fleeting brush of lips. "I love you, Shan. I'm sorry I ran off." He brushed her hair back. "Think we can promise each other to not screw up again?"

"No." She laughed. "But how about I promise to ask before I do anything crazy with regards to your job, and you promise me you won't run away without talking it over again?"

He smiled. "I think it's a deal."

Their lips met in a kiss that was as sweet and tender as it was burning hot. She wanted him desperately, not just with her body, but with her mind, her heart, her soul.

When they broke away panting, Evan asked, "So how do you feel about a roommate?"

"Will this roommate watch *Pride and Prejudice* with me?"

"Every Thursday night."

They laughed and then they were kissing again, their mouths and limbs moving in tandem. Evan's hand was just sliding up to cup her breast when—

The fire alarm went off.

He cursed and said over the noise, "I'm going to rip that thing out of the ceiling."

"I'll love you forever if you do."

GOLD HOCKEY SERIES

GOLD HOCKEY

Did you miss any of the Gold Hockey books?
Find information about the full series here.
Or keep reading for a sneak peek into each of the books below!

Benched
Gold Hockey Book #4
Get your copy at books2read.com/Benched

Max

HE STARTED UP THE CAR, listening and chiming in at the right places as Brayden talked all things video game.

But his mind was unfortunately stuck on the fact that women were not to be trusted.

He snorted. Brit—the Gold's goalie and the first female in the NHL—and Mandy—the team's head trainer—would smack him around for that sentiment, so he silently amended it to: *most* women were not to be trusted.

There. Better, see?

Somehow, he didn't think they'd see.

He parked in the school's lot, walked Brayden in, and received the appropriate amount of scorn from the secretary for being thirty minutes late to school, then bent to hug Brayden.

"I'll pick you up today," he said.

Brayden smiled and hugged him tightly. Then he whispered something in his ear that hit Max harder than a two-by-four to the temple.

"If you got me a new mom, we wouldn't be late for school."

"Wh-what?" Max stammered.

"Please, Dad? Can you?"

And with that mind fuck of an ask, Brayden gave him one more squeeze and pushed through the door to the playground, calling, "Love you!" over his shoulder.

Then he was gone, and Max was standing in the office of his son's school struggling to comprehend if he had actually just heard what he'd heard.

A new mom?

Fuck his life.

—Benched, books2read.com/Benched

Breakaway
Gold Hockey Book #5
Get your copy at books2read.com/BreakawayGold

Blue

"Thanks for the ride."

"Try not to go out and get a fresh bimbo to ride tonight. I hear STIs on are the rise in the city."

Blue sighed, turned back to face her. "Really?"

She shrugged, smirk teasing the edges of her mouth, drawing his focus to the lushness of her lips. "Just watching out for Max's teammate."

He rolled his eyes. "Not hardly."

"Okay, how about I'm trying to prevent you from spreading STIs to the female populace."

"I'm clean, and I'm smart," he told her. "Condoms all the way."

"Ew."

Except there was something about the way she said it that made Blue stiffen and take notice. Because . . . he stared into her eyes, watched as the pale blue darkened to royal, saw her lips part, and her suck in a breath.

Holy shit.

"You're attracted to me."

Her jaw dropped. "No fucking way," she said, too quickly, pink dancing on the edges of her cheekbones. "You're delusional."

Blue got close.

Real close.

Anna licked her lips.

And fuck it all, he kissed that luscious mouth.

—Breakaway, www.books2read.com/BreakawayGold

Breakout
Gold Hockey Book #6
Get your copy at books2read.com/Breakout

PR-Rebecca

"You should go have your turn."

"I'll get mine," he said with another shrug.

She frowned, honestly confused. "You don't want—"

Suddenly he was in front of her on the bench, towering over her even though she was wearing her four-inch power heels. "You know what I want?"

Rebecca couldn't speak. Her breath had whooshed out of her in the presence of all that sweaty, hockey god-ness. Fuck he was pretty and gorgeous and . . . so fucking masculine that her thighs actually clenched together.

She wanted to climb him like a stripper pole.

"Do you?" he asked again when her words wouldn't come. "Want to know what I want?"

She nodded.

He bent, lips to her ear. "You, babe," he whispered. "I. Want. You."

Then he straightened and jumped back onto the ice, leaving her gaping after him like she had less than two brain cells in her skull.

The worst part?

She wanted him, too.

Had wanted him since the moment she'd laid eyes on the sexy as sin hockey god.

"Trouble," she murmured. "I'm in *so* much fucking trouble."

—Breakout, www.books2read.com/Breakout

Checked

Gold Hockey Book #7

Get your copy at books2read.com/Checked

Nutritionist Rebecca

She'd been trying to slip by the happy couple without ruining the romantic moment Kevin had planned for Bex. But they were right by the front door and they'd see her if she moved forward.

And the guys were behind her, along with the girls.

All of whom were perfectly lovely people.

But she'd reached her limit on socializing for the day.

Thus her pinned-in position in the hall. She was desperate to be out of here, more than desperate to get back to her empty and quiet house, slip into her pajamas, and watch Hallmark movies through the night.

God, life was so much simpler in Hallmark movies.

Kevin jumped up and kissed Bex, and when it seemed as though they were fully distracted, Rebecca made her move, slipping past them on quiet feet and opening the front door.

She'd just begun to close it quietly when a hand shot out and prevented it from shutting. Rebecca didn't scream because Kev and Bex were still only feet away, but she also didn't scream because her body already knew who it was. Her traitorous body, that was.

Gabe pushed through the opening and quietly closed the door behind him.

"You're leaving," he said.

Nope. Not doing this.

Ignoring him, Rebecca turned and started for her car. She'd purposely parked it so she wouldn't be blocked in.

Girl scout, she was. Always planning ahead.

"Rebecca."

She kept walking.

She might work with Gabe, but she sure as heck wasn't on speaking terms with him. He'd dismissed her work, ignored her contribution to the team. He'd made her feel small and unimportant and—

She kept walking.

"*Rebecca.*"

Not happening. Her car was in sight, thank fuck. She beeped the locks, reached for the handle.

He caught her arm.

"Baby—"

"I am *not* your baby, and you don't get to touch me." She ripped herself free, started muttering as she reached for the handle of her car again. "You don't even like me."

He stepped close, real close. Not touching her, not pushing the boundary she'd set, and yet he still got really freaking close. Her breath caught, her chin lifted, her pulse picked up. "That. Is. Where. You're. Wrong."

She froze.

"What?"

His mouth dropped to her ear, still not touching, but near enough that she could feel his hot breath.

"I like you, Rebecca. Too fucking much."

Then he turned and strode away.

—Checked, www.books2read.com/Checked

ALSO BY ELISE FABER

Billionaire's Club (all stand alone)

Bad Night Stand

Bad Breakup

Bad Husband

Bad Hookup

Bad Divorce

Bad Fiancé

Bad Boyfriend

Bad Blind Date

Bad Wedding (July 19th, 2020)

Bad Engagement (October 12th, 2020)

Love, Action, Camera (all stand alone)

Dotted Line

Action Shot

Close-Up

End Scene

Love After Midnight (all stand alone)

Rum and Notes

Virgin Daiquiri (June 29th, 2020)

Gold Hockey (all stand alone)

Blocked

Backhand

Boarding

Benched

Breakaway

Breakout

Checked

Coasting

Centered

Life Sucks Series (all stand alone)

Train Wreck

Hot Mess (coming soon)

Roosevelt Ranch Series (all stand alone, series complete)

Disaster at Roosevelt Ranch

Heartbreak at Roosevelt Ranch

Collision at Roosevelt Ranch

Regret at Roosevelt Ranch

Desire at Roosevelt Ranch

Phoenix Series (read in order)

Phoenix Rising

Dark Phoenix

Phoenix Freed

Phoenix: LexTal Chronicles (rereleasing soon, stand alone, Phoenix world)

From Ashes

In Flames